Joy Chambers was born in Ipswich, Queensland, Australia. She began acting at an early age and has had a successful career in Australia, winning awards and appearing in numerous shows. Joy currently appears as Rosemary Daniels in the international television series 'Neighbours', and views her writing as a natural extension of her self-expression. She is a businesswoman and is chairman of a group of companies owned along with her husband. Joy thoroughly enjoys the extensive historical research she does for each of her stories and is the author of two previous novels, MAYFIELD and MY ZULU, MYSELF.

Acclaim for Joy Chambers's previous novels:

'Joy Chambers has written a real blockbuster here' *Best*
'A saga brimming with drama and intrigue' *Publishing News*
'Written with an ease of style and sophistication' *Liverpool Echo*

VALE VALHALLA

Joy Chambers

HEADLINE

First published in 1999 by
HEADLINE BOOK PUBLISHING

First published in paperback in 2000 by
HEADLINE BOOK PUBLISHING

10 9 8 7 6 5 4

ISBN 0 7472 6088 5

Typeset by Palimpsest Book Production Limited,
Polmont, Stirlingshire
Printed and bound in Great Britain by
Mackays of Chatham plc, Chatham, Kent

HEADLINE BOOK PUBLISHING
A division of the Hodder Headline Group
338 Euston Road
London NW1 3BH

www.headline.co.uk
www.hodderheadline.com

Acknowledgements

Thanks are due as they always are to my darling husband, Reg Grundy, OBE, who provides me with truly inspirational editorial help. Reg has grown almost as close to Matthew, John Conrad and Caro as I have over the years of writing.

Thanks to my wonderful brother, Dr Jack Chambers, who also read every word.

Thanks to the rest of my marvellous family and friends who take an interest in all I do.

And thanks to those people who helped me with certain detail: Bill Connell of the Glenbrook Museum, who set me on the right course with the court martial scene, and to our office folk who have helped in various ways: Di, Robbie, Maggie, Eva, Neil, Elaine and Alex.

And heartfelt thanks posthumously to my darling aunt, 'Millie' Millicent Mary Gedge, my father's elder sister, who left me notes and details of family life before the First World War.

Dedication

As the new millennium in 2001 is upon us; soon the last of the men who fought in the 'Great War' – World War I – will have completely faded away.

This book is dedicated to:

My Uncle Jack, Bombardier John Harrison Chambers, who fought on every front in Belgium and Northern France in the four years and fifty-two days he served in the Royal Field Artillery, and was one of only two survivors of his original battalion of over 1,000 men.

My father, Alan Chambers 63645, who joined the British army when he was an under-age soldier of sixteen. He trained in Wales and Ireland, and was sent with the 16th Lancashire Fusiliers of the 32nd Division to the front line trenches in the Valley of the Somme. He was gassed in Montdidier in the final allied offensive of 1918 and invalided home to England, where he lay blind in Portsmouth Hospital for six weeks.

And to all those boys, from Australia, Belgium, Canada, England, France, India, Ireland, New Zealand, Scotland, South Africa, USA, Wales and the reaches of the Empire like Bermuda and the West Indies, who fought for the Allies in the trenches of Belgium and France between August 1914 and November 1918, and who died in their millions for reasons few of them understood.

ENGLISH CHANNEL

● Ostend

● Dunkirk

Ypres
✕ Passchendaele
Messines Ridge

BELGIUM

● St-Pol

✕ Loos

Arras

● Doullens   Beaucourt
St Pierre Divion
Beaumont Hamel ✕
Y Ravine   ✕ Grandcourt
Rest Camp   ✕ Bapaume
Ancre R.   ✕ Thiepval
● Albert   Péronne
Somme R.
● Amiens
✕ St Quentin
● Villers
Bretonneux

● Montdidier

FRANCE

Oise River

Verdun off Map
→

Seine River

End of 1916: Front Line in Flanders and the Somme ——————
BATTLEFIELDS ✕
TOWNS ●
Border between Belgium and France ― ― ―

PARIS

THE PEACE

Chapter One

The young man rode as fast as was possible in the ugly weather, his horse, as sure-footed as any in the colony, taking him through the mud, wind and lashing rain.

Lightning ripped coldly through the storm, showing the unsealed road ahead as it stretched like a taut black wire across the landscape. Thunder resounded as the horse and rider charged along towards the makeshift Victoria Bridge across the river: the original had been washed away in the Great Flood of the previous February.

The unseasonal winter storm reflected the one breeding upon itself in the youth's mind, fed with thoughts of Emma, his precious younger sister who had died in his arms this very night. Fury pushed him on, one idea dominant: to kill Matthew Craken, the man who had murdered her.

As the rider sped past the wharves at the end of Stanley Street, he hardly noticed that he was now soaked to the skin, his whole being concentrated on urging his horse expeditiously to the river and on into Brisbane to Jamie Russell's tavern.

It was common knowledge that Matthew Craken's habitual Friday night occupation was to drink and play cards at Russell's Tavern in Upper Edward Street. The place had a dubious reputation and a rowdy, drunken, fast group they were who gathered there. In recent years, particularly during the Great Strike of '90, when many shearers had descended on Brisbane from the west country, Russell's Tavern had been their mecca. The depression did not seem to affect the public houses: in May, when eight of Queensland's eleven banks had closed, record business had been done in beer sales.

As the stallion's hooves thudded across the swiftly built,

3

rickety bridge, the young man saw visions of Emma dancing, her best blue silk dress swirling high in the air; and as he held his horse steady to swing down George Street she was singing carols in the summer heat of Christmas Eve, and when he splashed round the corner into Adelaide Street, where the storm-water spilled over the new but inadequate drains, the sunny sounds of Emma's laughter filled his ears. But by the time he rode up the Edward Street hill and dismounted under the awning to smash open Russell's Tavern door, Emma had ceased to dance and sing and laugh.

He stood for a few seconds in the tired light, his rain-drenched coat dripping water. He did not notice that he shivered.

It was close to two o'clock in the morning yet some die-hards remained at a table with cards between them. A few others lounged at the bar and billiard table. Gaslamps burned low, throwing long shadows and emphasising that enervated mood which descends on rooms once revellers have dispersed. Those left, to a man, turned to the open door. After the intitial surprise of his intrusion, the youth held their gazes, for there was something restless, even worrisome about him, like that sort of subdued tension found in big cats. The youth spoke very loudly. 'Matthew Craken! Where is he?'

The card players leaned back in their chairs. This was a diverting interlude: it amused them.

Now his voice was more insistent. 'I said, where's bloody Craken?' He strode over to an individual who wore an apron and had been drinking with the loungers at the bar. He took hold of the man's shoulder. 'Don't trifle with me. You belong to this house. Tell me where Craken is or you'll be sorry.'

The man evidently believed what he heard for he answered quickly, 'I ain't seen him . . . not for a while I ain't. Think he went upstairs . . . with someone.'

The young man turned away and as he lifted his eyes to the balcony above, he saw, in the insipid glow, a figure he recognised.

Matthew Craken's pale fingers rested lightly on the wooden railing as his languid gaze focused on the wet, bedraggled intruder, and he sniffed through his aquiline nose as if he smelt something unpleasant. 'So, John Conrad Fleet, you noisily

4

repeat my name! What do you want?' He came forward and began to descend the staircase.

'You bastard!' John Conrad shouted, running across the room and up the steps to meet Craken.

'What the devil . . . ?' cried the man as John Conrad came leaping up to him and took him by the throat. 'Fleet! Have you gone mad?' He lifted his hands in protest.

'My sister's dead.'

Craken's eyes lost their lethargy and opened wide. 'No . . . never, how can she be?'

But John Conrad was not there to talk. His hands tightened around Craken's throat and the man lashed out, striking his attacker in the face.

John Conrad fell back on to the rail but rallied immediately, returning in one leap to his quarry so that the two men grappled on the staircase.

'My sister's dead!' he shouted again as he struck Matthew Craken's jaw with a blow that sent the man staggering backwards.

As he straightened, he lifted his hand in a halting gesture again, and shouted, 'Are you mad, Fleet?' He backed up a step, turned and began to run up the stairs, but John Conrad threw himself upwards, lashing out, grabbing his legs and bringing him down. In one move he seized the man by the back of the neck, and smashed his face down on the steps. Matthew Craken gave a loud groan of pain but managed to pull his body to a half-standing position where he tried to throw his assailant off. 'Leave me alone, Fleet, for Christ's sake. I've no quarrel with you. Listen to me . . .'

But this only served to further enrage John Conrad, and he held on to his quarry and pushed him with all his force against the railing. As Craken attempted to preserve his balance he half turned back to his assailant and received another closed fist to the side of his face.

Matthew Craken had no idea what had befallen Emma. All he could see was that her brother was blaming him and acting like a madman. He had to counter the assault; it was obvious to him that if he did not he would be killed. 'Fleet, you're insane!' He jerked full round to face his opponent as his right hand went down in a swift movement to snatch out the dagger he wore on his belt. 'Now stay back, Fleet. I don't want to hurt you.' He menaced his attacker with the blade, which served to halt the onslaught briefly, and in those seconds Matthew took the advantage to spin round and leap away up the stairs again, but John Conrad was reckless now, and he scrambled up after him, grabbing hold of the skirt of his coat and ripping it as he pulled the man back towards him.

Now the two were interlocked, beads of perspiration on each man's temples. John Conrad captured his adversary's wrist and the blade swung violently between them, its razor-sharp edge cutting an arc through the air as fierce grunting sounds of hatred filled the tavern. Down came the knife and slashed across John Conrad's left shoulder. Blood sprang from the wound, but the bleeding youth did not feel the pain, though he knew he had been cut, and in an instant he brought up his other fist to strike his foe hard on the face. It sent him reeling even though he still held on to the dagger.

Matthew Craken fought to hold his footing on the stairs but he stepped into air, pulling his wrist from John Conrad's grasp, the knife hurtling over the handrail as he toppled and spun around, tumbling backwards and breaking the banisters with his boots, his impetus such that he continued careering headfirst down the steps, bumping, thudding and smashing his way to the bottom . . . to lie still.

By now, the whole of the tavern was animated: shouts and yells, whistles and catcalls filling the tired night. One enterprising drinker had even mobilised enough to take wagers on the fight.

John Conrad was deaf to the uproar. He strode down the long staircase and stood above Craken before lifting his damp, muddy boot to nudge him in the side.

The man rolled over groaning.

'I see you're not dead, more's the pity. But Emma is, you bastard.'

Matthew Craken's bloodshot eyes opened but he could not focus on the man towering over him. He thought his legs must be broken for there was agony in both of them. He felt that his face was broken too for he could not speak. The pain was as if all his childhood nightmares rose up in one flood of anguish in his mind. He could not think. He groaned again.

John Conrad knelt down on one knee, bringing his head to a level so that only his foe could hear. 'Listen well, you bastard. Tonight my sister took arsenic because she carried your child, and you'd denied her. I know the whole bloody sickening truth. I've let you off too lightly; I should've killed you.'

Matthew Craken was suffering so much that he did not understand everything that was said, but he did realise that Emma Fleet was dead. He was shocked. He had hoped to see her tomorrow. He liked Em, with her pretty eyes and laughing mouth. Yes, she had told him she carried his baby, but he had not believed her. A girl had tried that on him a year ago. His father was a store owner and rich. Women wanted to trap him . . . trap him . . . trap him . . .

He tried hard to see, but the man above him was a blur. Then he attempted again to speak, for it seemed impossible that Emma was truly dead, but all he did was cough up blood.

John Conrad rose and looked contemptuously down, the blood from the wound in his shoulder dropping indifferently into the widening pool of Matthew Craken's blood upon the floor; blending as if in perverse prophecy.

He noticed this anomaly: it seemed bizarre that his blood mingled with Craken's. He shook his head, turned, and strode away.

The following day the sun hid, a bitter wind blew and a little rain drizzled on and off. As the light behind broken clouds snaked up the Brisbane River to the West End it found John Conrad a few hundred yards away from Brewery House, as they called the Fleet home, and his father's brewery, standing at the water's edge, looking east into the meagre morning light.

When he had arrived home the previous night he had found both his father and his Aunt Leigh distraught over Emma's death. Bart, his sixteen-year-old brother, who knew the truth, had maintained Emma took the arsenic accidentally, and when John Conrad endorsed this stance, the older couple finally accepted it. And while they continued to harangue him about his wound and where he had been, he parried their questions, and at last they had let him retire. Aunt Leigh, between tears, had dressed his gash and bandaged it.

Now, as the youth watched the overcast sky, his clean-shaven face was grave and the gentle lines at the corners of his eyes had turned to creases of concentration. He remained that way, down by the river, until an hour later, he answered Bart's call to his father's study.

He found three men there: Arthur Craken, Matthew Craken's father, the Chief Inspector of Police, and his own father, Barrington Fleet.

Barrington Fleet had standing in the community. Even though his father had been a convict, transported to New South Wales in 1831, the family had left that behind them, as many Australian families had: the unspoken rule to avoid discussion of origins; and all his own children had been born into relatively easy circumstances. His sons had attended Bowen House as children and then the Boys' Grammar School, two prestigious institutions. The brewery was situated in the West End, a working-class suburb, but Barrington Fleet could have lived anywhere, though he chose to live right next to his brewery in the finest house on this side of the city. He had made his mark and was counted among the leading businessmen of Brisbane; was a member of the best clubs and the Royal Society. The news of his eldest son's actions of the night before had come from his friend, the Chief Inspector of Police. Fleet was a law-abiding man, and to have his son before him in this manner profoundly disturbed him.

'Sit down, John Conrad.'

The youth sat.

'You know the inspector and Mr Craken.'

John Conrad nodded to them.

'We're all aware of what happened last night. Matthew Craken has suffered very badly: his nose is broken, he has cuts and abrasions on his face and there are fractures in his ribs, and both legs.'

John Conrad maintained a silence as his father dropped his eyes to the floor and the inspector took up the dialogue in his heavy Scottish brogue. 'It's been mooted that there's a connection between the death of your sister, Emma, and the fight between you two. Is that so, laddie?'

The youth did not meet the gazes of any of the three men. 'I'm sorry I cannot say.' He looked across the room to the window.

The police inspector turned to Barrington Fleet and then to Arthur Craken. 'Interesting, is it not, that both these boys can't tell us anything about the fight or the death of Emma? Yet the witnesses say they heard John Conrad charge Matthew with Emma's death. Seems to me there's much to know here.' Then he turned back to John Conrad. 'As you and Matthew wish to hold silence on these issues, there's not too much I can do about that, young fellow, but I can tell you that had charges been brought against you, Matthew Craken's injuries are such that you could have been sentenced to five, even ten, years in gaol, do you understand that?'

John Conrad remained silent.

'I'll assume that you do, so think yourself a very lucky young man.'

Now Barrington Fleet spoke, occasionally his voice breaking just slightly with emotion. 'Son, that you didn't kill Matthew Craken is mere luck. This is a law-abiding town in a law-abiding colony and if you had, you might have found yourself at the end of a rope. As it is, and the inspector has said, no charges have been laid, a fact about which you should be eternally grateful. But one thing's clear to Mr Craken, the Chief Inspector and myself: you and Matthew Craken cannot live in the one town. It may be years before Matthew can walk again – if ever, I'm very sorry to hear. And as eyewitnesses say you were the attacker, it is *you* we have decided to remove. Through the Chief Inspector and Mr Samuel Griffith, the Chief Justice, we have this morning spoken to Colonel French of the Defence Forces and he will arrange for you to join the army, one of the New South Wales contingents. Since the depression has had such a marked effect on our forces they can do with recruits. You'll leave for Sydney immediately after your sister's funeral. Your future's to be as a professional soldier.' He breathed a quite audible sigh. 'While I had always thought for you to follow in my footsteps here at the brewery, it must be your brother, Bartholomew, who will fill that position now.'

John Conrad's eyes widened. His shoulder ached, his forehead was bruised and sore, he felt hurt and frustrated, and he spoke quickly. 'Father, my future surely is my own. I must decide it. It's my right.'

Barrington Fleet shook his head as the policeman answered,

fingering his wide moustache, 'You have no rights, lad. By your actions last night you have foregone them.'

A voice in John Conrad's head said, 'He killed my sister! He got less than he deserved,' but he did not give it rein. Instead he bristled at the suggestion of the army. 'I will not have it. I must decide my own future.' He strode to the window. Below he could see the brewers taking their early morning tea across the yard under the brewery awning. The sun was coming through at last, and they sat around in groups near pools of water that had formed in the yard overnight. They were laughing and calling to each other and the sight was so normal, so peaceful, that the deeds of the last twenty-four hours seemed absurd.

He did not turn round as his father spoke. 'You're not yet twenty-one, my boy. You've not yet achieved man's estate, and I can legally make decisions for you whether you like it or not.' His voice quivered as he added, 'Hasn't enough damage been done, damn it? Our darling Emma is gone, and you, in your stupidity, have sustained a wound and half-killed a poor man who—'

'Who deserved it . . . deserved it and more.' John Conrad spat out the words as he rounded from the window.

Arthur Craken made a noise of affront and stood up. 'It's my son you speak of, young man. I've been more than tolerant up till now, knowing my lad is a bit of a rogue, but this goes too far. I can't stand for it.'

John Conrad met Arthur Craken's gaze. He said no more but the expression in his face showed his contempt for the man's son.

Barrington Fleet rose from his chair. He was fifty-six years of age and in his prime. While he was heart-broken over his daughter's death, he was still in charge, head of this family and father to the boy who stood before him. John Conrad drew his eyes from Arthur Craken's to meet his parent's. A few seconds passed. If only father and son had realised it, their expressions were identical as they faced each other. Barrington's grey eyes glinted and his thick brows drew together as he lifted his hand towards his son, index finger raised. 'You are in my charge, You *will* be a soldier. If you refuse I'll bring the courts to bear. That's the end of the matter.'

And it was.

Emma's funeral passed off, as funerals do: full of over-whelming sadness. It rained again and the dark, wet mourners made dark, wet sounds of solicitude. John Conrad watched his father's stiff face; his aunt's sagging shoulders; the grim line of Bart's mouth.

Death had come into his young life for the second time; his mother five years ago and now Emma.

It was cold as they left the graveyard, and John Conrad looked back only once to where men threw shovels of mud into the gaping hole in the ground.

Chapter Two

Getting through the wake was not as bad as John Conrad had foreseen. It was the funeral that had been hard: drained him, numbed him.

He listened to the talk going on in the big kitchen. Funny how the people of Brisbane gathered in the kitchen. Most were seated around the great oak table that had been brought out from the old country by his mother's family – the oak table where the little blue bottle had stood on Friday night. This was the fourth wake he had been to in his life. They always disconcerted him: the chatter, the food and drink, and the occasional laughter; seemed wrong when mourning filled the air.

He had listened while Captain Jack Dere, a seaman and family friend, had made a remarkable speech about the passing of youthful and beautiful things. It had not been sentimental, just appropriate, and when the man had finished John Conrad moved outside on to the wide verandah. The sun had gone down almost an hour since, early as always in the great southern lands. Rows of black umbrellas hung like massive bats along the wall. Much of the talk inside was fear of another flood. Queensland was like that: long stretches without any rain at all and then entire days of rain, and solid round drops they were! Not like the gentle misty rain of England and Ireland that his mother had told him about.

For the first time since the events of last Friday John Conrad Fleet smiled, thinking of his mother, Constance Baldwin Fleet. She had been born in Ireland and spent her first ten years there before going to England, the daughter of a volatile mixed marriage, her own mother, a Roman Catholic, and her father, a Protestant. Perhaps that was why she had been fair, tolerant, caring; certainly he believed it was one reason. Her conversation had been dotted with words like conciliation, compromise and tolerance; her bequest to the world, philanthropy and kind deeds. She had been his guiding light . . . well all the family's, not just his. He was sure if she had lived Emma would not have been involved with Craken. They had all lost direction once she had gone, and his father had become a different man: grey-faced, aloof.

There was one photograph of his mother taken when John Conrad was small. He thought she had been most beautiful, like a passing angel, with her bonny round face and dark curls falling gently over her forehead; but then perhaps all sons thought of their mothers this way. He recalled her honest brown eyes and strongly marked eyebrows, as if drawn with pencil on her smooth forehead. How badly he missed her patient sweetness. She had died of typhoid fever. The world had been somehow purer with her resident in it. And now Emma too had gone into that void humans did not understand. He closed his eyes and bent forward, holding on to the verandah railing.

'John Conrad.' The voice sounded quietly behind him. He turned to face a girl. She stood a few feet from him in the beam of light thrown from the lantern dangling from the verandah ceiling.

'Hello, Caroline.' He had known Caroline Dere, Captain Jack Dere's daughter, all her life, but for the first time he noticed her eyes were a burnished brown like his mother's had been . . . unusual. Caroline was a nice kid, and, through her mother, some distant relative of Aunt Leigh. She looked quite grown-up today. Maybe it was the severe black lace she wore.

Caroline felt very sorry for John Conrad. His sister had died last week in what people were calling 'a scandal', although she didn't know why. And today her mother had told her John Conrad was going away to be a soldier. She had never thought of John Conrad as a soldier, and it seemed odd. They would all miss him. He had such a hearty laugh and always gave her – well, everybody – a good feeling. 'Popular' was the word her mother used for him. Somehow she liked him better even than her own big brother, Paul, though she would never admit it to anyone.

She had watched John Conrad at the funeral today. She could never recall his looking sad before. Everybody knew how he had doted on Emma, and they all said that he had gone almost mad when he found her dying. Caroline's brother, Paul, had been in love with Emma, but then so had many of the boys of the district. Caroline had almost envied Emma in a way, and now Emma was not even alive. She felt so sorry for Emma . . . and for John Conrad.

Aunt Leigh had told Caroline's mother that John Conrad had beaten a man half to death the very same night Emma died. Now, Caroline found that really hard to believe.

'So how are you, Caro?'

Caroline's fine freckled nose crinkled with emotion. 'Well, I'm sorry for you, is how I am, John Conrad. It's terrible about Emma and all.'

'Yes, lass, that it is.'

She liked the way he called her lass, and she didn't mind that he called her 'Caro' either, though oddly enough she didn't like it much when others used it. 'My mother says you're going away to become a soldier.'

'Yes, I am.'

And now she could feel her heart beating. 'Will you ever come back?'

'Of course I will. This is my home.'

'Do . . . you want to go?'

For some seconds he eyed her as if deciding how to answer, then he asked, 'How old are you, Caro?'

'I'll be fifteen next birthday.'

'When's your birthday?'

'The twenty-sixth of May.'

John Conrad gave a wan smile. 'Caro, then you're hardly fourteen, let alone fifteen.'

She gave a small embarrassed laugh. 'Yes . . . I suppose so.'

'In answer to your question, no, lass, I don't want to go. I'm damned if I do.'

'They say you're leaving tomorrow, on the morning train.'

He nodded and her heart sank.

At that moment the door on to the verandah opened and John Conrad's brother Bartholomew came out and claimed him. Caroline watched them move away.

Later, when she left the wake with her parents, her father

shook John Conrad's hand and said comforting things. Her father always knew the right sorts of things to say. He had made a wonderful speech earlier tonight about Emma.

As Caroline passed him she smiled sympathetically and John Conrad gave her a brotherly pat on the shoulder.

That night the rain stopped and Caroline Dere slept fitfully. She dreamt of a funeral where the minister asked how old she was and John Conrad Fleet kept saying she was hardly fourteen.

She woke to the streaming sunlight, great lengths of brilliance shooting across the rain-drenched land, and soon the relentless Queensland sun, effective even in winter, was drying out all that had been waterlogged.

The same sunlight found John Conrad packing the last of his belongings before heading to the Central Railway station in Brisbane; in his pocket, the letter of introduction to Major General Hutton written by Colonel French. He hugged each of his family in turn. His Aunt Leigh was still crying; it seemed as if she had been crying constantly since last Friday night. He too felt like crying. She managed to whisper, 'Parting is such sweet sorrow, as the Bard said.' His Aunt seemed to have a quote for every occasion.

The hardest to leave was his nine-year-old brother, David. The child did not understand. All he knew was that his big sister was gone and now his big brother was leaving.

His father took his hand and shook it, and John Conrad looked into Barrington Fleet's cool eyes. When his mother had been alive Barrington Fleet used to laugh, there had been a kindness about him; nowadays he was more remote, more unapproachable. *I'm leaving, Father . . . going away . . . hug me Father, please . . .* but the wish was not answered and Barrington Fleet dropped his son's hand.

'Do well, son. Make me proud.'

Bartholomew drove him to the station in the dray: along the dirt roads, past the sterile grounds of the West End State School and by the butcher shop into Cradder's Lane where the local push – as a gang of youths was called – hung out; through the short cut to Melbourne Street. Some of the people who were abroad knew him and called greetings: 'Goodbye, John Conrad.' 'The Volunteers'll make a man o' ye!' 'Farewell lad.'

He was not surprised they knew he was leaving; rumours passed swiftly around the West End.

As they rolled across the substitute Victoria Bridge he looked down at the muddy water, reliving the last time he had traversed it, in fury and despair. He made a bitter sound in his throat as his brother looked sideways at him. As they trundled along Anne Street to the railway station they even passed the corner of Edward Street where John Conrad could see the front of Russell's Tavern. Finally, when they alighted in front of Central Station, there, under the wide corrugated iron awning, stood Hargy Lightfoot.

Hargy Lightfoot was John Conrad's friend. They had been boyhood companions from the day Hargy's mother had arrived to help in Constance Fleet's kitchen. The two little boys had responded to each other from that first moment. They had learned to swim in the Brisbane River together, fished and played and dreamed together. Hargy had always lived in Spring Hollow, an overcrowded tenement. But since his mother had died – not six months after Constance Fleet – Hargy had been less reliable and often would not turn up for his job at the brewery. Actually there were very few Aborigines in Brisbane now; most lived out of the towns in the bush areas. It was natural for them to go on 'walkabout'; they were semi-nomads by nature.

John Conrad leapt down from the dray and approached his friend. 'Hargy, old pal, I went up to see you yesterday but your sister said you were away on walkabout, didn't know when you were coming back.'

Hargy moved from one foot to the other. He took off his cap as his dark eyes clouded. 'Got back this mornin'. Me sister said Emma dead. I'm real sorry.'

John Conrad nodded. 'Yes, pal. It's not a pretty story.' He looked in his friend's eyes. 'I know you knew about her and Matthew Craken.'

Hargy sighed. 'Yeah. Craken not a good bloke. Plenty of girls.'

John Conrad too took a deep breath. 'He got her into trouble. Then denied her. Em killed herself.'

The other youth's dark eyes widened briefly. 'Him bloody bad bugger. Me sister said there's talk around that you bashed him up real good.'

16

John Conrad gave a grim smile. 'Yes, it'll be a while before he destroys another girl's life.'

'Anyhow, I'm real sorry. She was a good girl, Emma, and I feel plum bad.' Hargy extended his strong dark hand and his friend took it. Then they clasped each other close for a second or two.

'When you come back?'

John Conrad looked skywards. 'Don't know, pal, but you be careful. Not too many fights at the Colosseum, please.'

Hargy was a natural pugilist. He picked up a little money by taking part in bouts down at a rambling old tin shed satirically called the Colosseum in a back street in Fortitude Valley.

'Fightin's easy.'

By this time Bart had unloaded the trunk from the dray and he came to stand beside his brother.

'And, pal, you make sure you go back to the brewery and your job. Bart here will see to it everything's all right.'

Bart smiled. 'That I will.'

The two friends shook hands once more and the brothers walked away under the small arch into the railway station.

Hargy watched, standing perfectly still in the cool breeze for a few seconds, and then as he turned to walk away, he saw Caroline Dere come hurrying down towards him.

Across the road Caroline caught sight of Hargy at the same time. She had always liked Hargy. He was much older than she was, like John Conrad, but he did odd jobs at the brewery and she always spoke to him when she was over there. They said he was a really good boxer and he looked it – sort of stringy and hard like wire. She avoided a milk cart as she crossed the road to join him.

She asked, 'Did you see him?'

They both knew whom she meant.

Hargy closed his dark eyes briefly. 'Yes. He's gone inside now.'

Caroline tried to smile but her chin wobbled uncertainly. 'I had hoped to catch him . . . well . . . to say goodbye.'

The youth nodded. It was plum obvious to him that Caroline Dere sure seemed sad. 'Don't worry. John Conrad come back again. Won't stay gone for ever.'

Caroline took a deep breath and nodded.

'Yeah. Goin' away meself again soon.'

She tried to sound interested. 'Walkabout?'

'Yeah. See me brother and me uncle over past Beaudesert for a start.'

'Look after yourself then, Hargy.'

'Yeah, you too, Miss Caroline.'

They gave each other a kindly smile and Hargy left her standing there.

By the time John Conrad had purchased his ticket to Sydney and walked on to the wooden platform which squeaked under his boots, he had decided life was insane. Emma was dead. Craken was alive. And he was off to join the army. At least Hargy had turned up to say goodbye.

Bart pointed to a wooden seat and they sat silently, John Conrad with his portmanteau between his legs, a trunk at his side.

Bart turned to him. 'Won't be the same at the brewery without you.'

'Just make sure you finish all your schooling and go on to Sydney or Melbourne University, no matter what the old man says.'

Bart nodded.

As the train backed into the station, chugging and spewing steam in great clouds, they stood up and collected John Conrad's luggage.

'All aboard the Sydney Mail via Ipswich, Toowoomba, Warwick, Stanthorpe to Wallangarra! Change trains at Wallangarra for the onward journey to Sydney. All aboard!'

When his trunk and portmanteau were stowed in the baggage compartment, John Conrad took his brother in his arms. 'Look after David and Aunt Leigh. And make sure Hargy's job is always there for him. He's a great bloke.'

'Yes, he is. Good luck.'

The guard called, 'All aboard!' John Conrad mounted the Sydney train and under the canopy of blue Queensland sky extending from horizon to horizon, Bart waved until the train disappeared from view.

When Bartholomew came out into the street he was surprised

to see Caroline Dere standing there under a wide-brimmed straw hat.

'Caroline?'

She stepped aside as if to let him pass. 'I just saw Hargy Lightfoot.' She glanced across the railway sheds where the track led away. She seemed fidgety and looked down at her feet. 'He's gone, hasn't he?'

'John Conrad?'

'Yes.'

Bart nodded.

'He said he'd come back.'

'He usually does what he says.'

Her eyes returned to Bart's. 'Yes.' She forced a smile and moved on.

Bart watched her walk away. Caroline was a funny kid. He shook his head and mounted the dray.

In the train gathering speed to the south John Conrad stood in the corridor gazing sightlessly at the landscape as it sped by. Last Friday night he had found his sister on the floor in the darkened kitchen; her pretty young face had been distorted, perspiration ran in rivulets over her white cheeks and she had felt like fire to his touch. Between gulps of air she had told him enough for him to guess the rest. He had wiped the vomit from the side of her mouth and when he had carried her out into the storm to get her to a hospital she had died in his arms. He would never forgive Matthew Craken, never, not as long as he lived.

As he continued staring at the passing countryside he became peripherally aware of movement at his side.

'Mister,' a small voice said.

He looked down at a girl of about five or six years. It was the startling colour of her hair he noticed: it was a bright sienna red.

He smiled perfunctorily and turned back to gazing out the window. Some time later he felt his coattail tugged. He looked down again. The little girl had not moved. He felt mildly irritated, he really did not want to be pestered by a small person.

'Where's your mother?' he asked automatically.

19

'In heaven,' came the definite reply.

He was slightly taken aback by this unfortunate revelation, and now he looked more closely at the child. Her mouth was pursed and she seemed to be studying him. Her nose was covered in freckles and two plaits of her red hair trailed across her shoulders, one with a ribbon at the end, the other without. 'Oh, I'm sorry,' he said.

She appeared to ignore the sympathy; instead she smiled, showing a missing front tooth. 'We're going to meet Uncle Hewitt,' she stated in her grown-up fashion.

The child's gaze was so unequivocal. John Conrad felt almost uncomfortable. 'That's nice,' he answered. 'Now run along.' He turned deliberately back to the passing countryside.

'Mister,' the insistent voice repeated at his side.

He sighed. This really was not how he wanted to spend his train journey to Sydney. 'What now?' he asked.

'We're going on a ship, to England.'

He was in this conversation whether he wished to be, or not. 'Are you now?'

She was holding a dainty blue silk purse on strings, and he watched as she loosened the strings and put her tiny hand inside. She brought out a small holy card with a saint's picture on the front. She handed it to him in a definite gesture. 'This is for you,' she said. 'What's your name?'

Now his irritation gave way to amusement. With her adult style and her serious face, she certainly was an eccentric little creature. And while he did not want the proffered card, he took it. 'Thank you,' he said, and in reply to her question answered, 'My name's John Conrad Fleet.' And merely to be polite he added, 'What's yours?'

Before the child could answer a woman's high-pitched voice called, 'Emma, there you are! I've been looking for you everywhere. I thought I'd lost you. Naughty Emma!' And the hulk of a buxom woman bore down on the child and, swiftly taking up her hand, pulled her away. John Conrad stood holding the card and watching the pale silk of the child's dress shimmering and fading along the narrow corridor.

Emma. The woman had called the child *Emma*. John Conrad could hardly believe it.

Mechanically he turned the holy card over to the other

side. He actually started as he read the neatly printed words: *Emma Louise Blackstone*. This was more than coincidence . . . That the child's first name was Emma, the same as his dead sister, was enough, but that her second name was Louise dumbfounded him, for Louise was his dead sister's middle name too.

The train was gathering speed now, and the breeze came strongly in through the open window. When the child had handed him the card, his first thought had been to throw it away.

He remained for a long time watching the swiftly changing countyside, feeling the strong air movement across his face, eyeing mechanically the vast open spaces dotted with gum trees. Turning from the window at last, he shook his head, placed the holy card in his top pocket and moved along the swinging carriage, randomly choosing a compartment. He could feel the train slowing as it passed the wooden houses with their rectangular backyards on the outskirts of the town of Ipswich, twenty-three miles south-west of Brisbane. His journey would take him through other lonely towns, out over the Darling Downs, to Wallangarra where he would change trains to the wider gauge of the New South Wales railway.

As he opened the compartment door, two young women looked up from where they sat and eyed him appreciatively. He was used to second glances. John Conrad's demeanour, overlayed with his appearance, gave him a presence not often seen in the youth of Queensland: his skin was sun-browned and smooth, his nose was straight and his bone structure regular. He appeared to wear expensive and fashionable clothes, but it was his size and his proportions that prompted this illusion.

He sat down, much to the pleasure of the girls who smiled a welcome at him . . . but his head was too filled with his recent encounter to return their greeting. Somehow meeting the odd little adult-child had comforted him.

He leaned back into the corner as the train chugged to a halt. The opening and slamming of doors ricocheted along the carriages and he focused on the words *Ipswich Station* painted in green and black on each of the wooden seats along the platform. It was a pleasant town; one of Aunt Leigh's relatives ran a mine here somewhere.

Feeling the train's staccato action as it took up its journey John Conrad automatically lifted his hand and tapped his top pocket where the holy card lay, before he moved his fingers to rest momentarily on his wounded shoulder. He was going to be a soldier and only heaven knew where that would take him, but he would always remember his darling sister . . . yes, and the small, yet strangely adult Emma Louise of today.

There was much to reflect upon during this journey into his future. He closed his eyes and settled back more comfortably against the cushioned seat, and within a few minutes, the constant rhythmic vibration of the moving train assisted his meditations.

Chapter Three

Brisbane, five years later: 17 June 1898

The sun of the southern hemisphere came up over the rooftops of the city. From the élite heights of Hamilton the morning light broke over the river where the government steamer *Lucinda*, a replica of Queen Victoria's yacht, was making an early morning sweep down past the workers' cottages on the river flats of the suburb of Newstead. The sunlight, in its eternal efficiency, snaked across the city proper to the tenements of Spring Hill and on into the windows of the imperious double-storied doctors' houses facing Wickham Terrace to cross the river once more and awaken the districts of South Brisbane and the West End.

The all-enveloping morning light revealed new building going on in the streets of South Brisbane, a substantial sign that the city was slowly making its recovery from the great depressions of the decade.

Gradually the occupants of the homes of Brisbane awoke and the women of the colony made breakfast for their men. In the early years of Australia the ratio of men to women had been greatly disproportionate, owing to the dominance of males among convicts and immigrants, but now the female proportion of the population had increased. The percentage of women was larger in the capital cities than elsewhere, for women tended to settle more in the civilised areas than in the country, and those country towns had been substantially deserted by men in the great strikes of the early nineties.

On this clear, pre-winter morn, as Brisbane yawned and awoke, one young woman had long been working.

Caroline slid the wide tray of apple pies inside the oven, closed the door and brushed the flour from her apron. Her hair fell in tiny ringlets across her forehead. She really wished her hair grew differently, so that she could pull it backwards in a swathe like the ladies did who strolled down Queen Street after church on Sunday mornings. But, no, she must accept herself as she was. She pushed her hair back from her eyes as she lifted her gaze to the window in the early morning light. The chill westerly wind moved the small branches of the trees outside, and it looked as if it might rain, but she had a smile on her face because it was Friday. She loved Fridays, for once she had helped to complete the day's baking she took the rest of the day off and had luncheon with Aunt Leigh Fleet over at Brewery House.

The door opened behind her and her brother, Paul, came in. 'Morning, Sis. It's warm in here; pretty cold out there, though. There's been a frost.'

'Really? I'm just off for my walk. Then I'll go over to see Aunt Leigh.'

'Don't know why you bother with long walks. Especially on chilly days like this.'

'I like to, I think it does me good.'

Her brother shrugged as she hurried away through the brick corridor which led from the bakery to their wooden house with its verandah on all sides and nestling into a high stone bank on the west. The verandah was surrounded by ferns and box wood and jacaranda trees. It was June and beginning to get cold but even in the summer, in the worst of the Queensland heat, the plantings gave the suggestion of coolness. The jacarandas were almost stark now, their wide branches becoming daily more bare, but in the spring and summer the wonderful lavender-blue blossoms fell on to the verandah. Somehow, for Caroline, the flowers had become synonymous with her father. He loved these trees, had planted every one himself, and had built this house virtually single-handed when home from his long sea voyages, working nights with a hurricane lantern swinging over his head as he hammered the great lengthy nails into the weatherboard. It amazed her that he knew how to build a house. 'My father was a master builder back in the old country, some of it must have rubbed off,' he would say. Many nights Caroline had sat beside her father, watching him labour. That was before the Great Flood of '93 but the house had stood up

24

to the flood waters even though it had gone under right up to the top of the verandah. She was so proud to have him for a father, and she missed him when he went away, often six or eight months at a time. Yet she understood that was his life, just as her mother always had.

Since she had been a tiny child he had spoken to her of Shakespeare and Greek philosophy. Many of the words he used she did not know, but patiently he would explain them. She had learnt so very much from him. Once, when she asked him where he had been taught the magical things he knew, he had simply said, 'Self-taught my darling, self-taught. In my youth there was not money enough for a formal education, but I managed.' Then he had trained his pale, oh so pale, blue eyes on her and said, 'But you are different. I've worked hard to make sure you have an education. You and your brother. You'll be as well-educated as any girl in Queensland. Trouble with your brother is, he likes to handle food and to bake – strange to me, for I reckon that's women's work – but I've told him, if he still feels the same when he's finished his schooling, then I'll try to set him up in a bakery, I will.'

He had been as good as his word, of course. Her brother now ran Dere's Family Bakery along with Caroline and their mother. And Caroline herself was educated well enough to have worked six months as a clerk in the office of the publishers Gordon and Gotch, and only left when Paul asked her to help him. She also did his book-keeping and paid the bakery bills.

Her father was away on a trip to China but if she concentrated she could hear his voice in her head, a good solid voice with a cloudy, almost thick timbre to it. He spoke with perfect diction, and all his stories had messages, but one remained with her more vividly than all the others; touched her, moved her: the tale of three thousand years ago relating love and beauty in the incongruity of war. The Greeks were camped in their tents around Troy, the walled city. They had been in siege for eight years and as night fell, Crathe, a young Greek soldier-poet who talked philosophy – a gentle and learned man – studied in his tent, while his friend, Natham, prepared himself to scale the Trojan wall and dispose of an enemy sentry. Crathe recited, 'My father's meadows are full of song and dreams pervade the air.' Natham laughed, and bade him farewell.

Natham passed silently through the encampment and out into the black night. He slid across the open ground and scaled the wall, stabbed a lonely Trojan guard to death and returned the way he had come. As he entered his tent he called to his companion, 'Crathe, my friend, come drink a glass of wine with me. My task is completed.' Then he halted in horror. His friend, the gentle poet, Crathe, lay dead on his bed, his throat cut. A Trojan had crept down into the Greek camp and done just exactly as Natham had done: killed one of the enemy . . . This tale affected and impressed Caroline. Beautiful lives eclipsed in a moment in the futility of war. It said so much to her about the human condition, not just about war and soldiers.

And yet, there was John Conrad Fleet, a soldier; and that was the oddest thing too: sent away against his wishes, and now, five years later, a full lieutenant.

He had not come home for the first two years of his soldiering, but he had taken leave here every twelve months since. Last year he had told her that the army suited him. She had given him a side-long look and reminded him, 'I recall the very words you said four years ago. "I don't want to go," you said. "I'm damned if I want to."'

John Conrad had looked serious. 'Ah Caro,' he answered, 'your memory's too good. People change, you know. There's more to army life than I ever could have imagined.'

Over the years since Emma's death, Caroline had become closer to Aunt Leigh Fleet. Caroline supposed the older woman had sought her company to fill the gap created by the loss of Emma. Even her own mother laughed good-naturedly and said she really didn't know what house Caroline lived in. Caroline liked Aunt Leigh; the woman was straight to the point and enjoyed a laugh. She was big and, as she laughed, would shake all over. She read John Conrad's occasional letters out aloud and they would discuss the things he said. These confidences helped Caroline feel as if she knew the soldier well.

A year ago, at the annual church dance when he had been home on leave, he asked her for the last dance and then walked home with her and Aunt Leigh and her mother. Life had been so different that month John Conrad was back. When he was around there seemed so much to do, more activity, and amazingly, people seemed to smile more often.

26

The night before he returned to Sydney, Uncle Barrington had given a party. The soldier was in uniform. When he walked into the room Caroline thought that John Conrad in uniform was like catching sight of Apollo in his golden chariot. Everyone had such a happy time. He had smiled his special smile; it was hard to explain, for it was hardly a smile really, he parted his lips just slightly and his blue eyes seemed to haze over for a second. Caroline noticed these things. Again he had danced with her and this time she fancied it was more than with anyone else. At the height of the revelry he had put his arm around her and said, 'Caro, lass, you're the prettiest girl in the room.' She relived that moment frequently.

She had not told anyone, but a few months after he returned to Sydney she had taken his address from one of his letters to his aunt and written to him. That was many months ago and he had never replied. That did not concern her, for even Aunt Leigh had not had a letter for months. She knew soldiers were busy people; especially lieutenants.

Caroline leapt up the stairs, hurried across the verandah into the kitchen and took off her apron, hanging it behind the door. She passed into the hall and paused to look in the mirror on the stand. She had turned nineteen a few weeks ago and the girlish freckles that had seemed so pronounced on her nose a year or two since had virtually disappeared. She was pleased about that for she thought freckles were not very sophisticated. She brushed her curls off her face but insistently they fell back over her forehead. She smiled as she placed her straw hat firmly on her head: a hat made her look older, she was sure.

Caroline walked spiritedly along the street. Cows grazed on the footpath at the side of the dirt road, and chickens wandered hither and thither, and there, standing outside Mr Pace's blacksmith's shop was her friend Lucy Emmet, John Conrad's second cousin. She had a basket of groceries on her arm and a smile of greeting on her mouth.

'Good morning, Lucy.'

Lucy shivered in the wind. 'Hello, love.'

'How're things?'

A month ago, Lucy had become engaged to a fellow called George Goodward, a young coal miner, and up-and-coming leader in the labour union movement. He was known as a bit of a hot-head and seemed very sure of himself, but he was good to Lucy and her two young sisters, and that's what mattered to Caroline.

Lucy smiled. 'Great.' Then she took her friend's arm. 'George's got the day off. He's taking me to a display, an exhibition, in town this afternoon. Would you like to come with us?'

'What sort of an exhibition?'

'Photographs of the horseless carriage. They're calling it a *something* car, I think. I forget. Anyway, the photographs have come all the way from London. George says horseless carriages will be everywhere. They're all the rage in the big world cities. He reckons there's a time coming, I suppose a long way off, when there'll be no horses in towns at all.'

Caroline looked sceptical, her mouth pursed in thought. 'Really? George says that does he? Well, he's up-to-date on most things, I'll hand you that.' Then she broke into a smile. 'Yes, I'd like to come.'

'Oh, good. We'll come by after luncheon then, about two o'clock.'

'Pick me up at Brewery House, will you?'

And the two girls kissed and parted.

At ten past two o'clock that afternoon, Aunt Leigh waved off George and the two young women, who walked down to Vulture Street and caught the brand-new mode of transport, the electric tramcar, introduced less than a year ago and brightly painted with its number on the side above the words, 'Brisbane Tramways'. Caroline liked to travel this way. During the summer months she had preferred sitting in the open seats at the back or the front to feel the gentle breeze, but today they sat inside the compartment. Soon they were across the new Victoria Bridge, with its multiple arches, and into Queen Street, the main street, and then down to Fortitude Valley, the part of the city where seven hundred British migrants had first opened up the area in 1849.

George helped the girls down from the vehicle on the corner of Brunswick Street and they strolled up the unsealed road past T. C. Beirne's, one of the main stores in what was simply called 'The Valley'. Here they halted while Caroline and Lucy oohed and aahed at the bolts of colourful materials stacked on the footpath.

Caroline turned to George. 'So where's the exhibition?'

The young man pointed with his hat and they crossed the road and entered one of the many auction rooms in that part of the city.

The sign at the entrance read: *The Motor Car, a Horseless Carriage – Leading us into the New Century*. Caroline had seen drawings of these amazing contraptions in newspapers, but the photographs were very much more impressive.

George turned to his companions. 'You know that safety bike that Tubby Evans fitted with a motor? Well, I saw it last week. He was riding it across the Victoria Bridge.' He pointed back to one of the photographs 'This is the step forward from that, you know.'

Lucy nodded her head vigorously. 'Would you ride it, George?'

'Of course I would, dearest. We must keep step with the new age.' He whispered something in Lucy's ear and the young woman giggled and took his arm. They moved forward into the auditorium ahead of Caroline.

Caroline hung back to peruse a picture of a motor man all dressed up in leather overcoat, goggles, gloves and a vast leather cap which came down over his ears. He stood beside his vehicle in a such a peculiar stance, one leg up on his carriage's engine, looking so in charge that it made Caroline laugh quietly to herself.

As she bent into the photograph, a voice behind her said, 'You're the prettiest girl in the room.' She straightened up immediately. Her first thought was that somehow John Conrad Fleet had been miraculously transported home. These were the very words she heard him say so often in her head. She turned round with an expectant look in her eyes, but the speaker was a man she had never seen before.

A slanted half-smile showed a chip missing from one of his eyeteeth. The smile made her feel a touch uncomfortable and his eyes above it were dark and unfathomable. A scar ran from the side of his temple down across his cheek to his slightly crooked nose. Yet, the sum total of his features was singularly striking; as if all these flaws made a perfect whole, bestowing upon him the appearance of a dashing vagabond. His hair was longer than most men's, and it brushed his modish collar. He had the most arresting appearance she had ever seen . . . well, other than John Conrad Fleet in uniform.

Briefly she felt self-conscious, but then her good sense took over and she replied, 'Do you always accost girls in this manner?'

He laughed. 'Only when I'm captivated by them.'

Caroline shook her head. 'Where on earth are you from?'

'This part of the earth actually, but I've been away for a while. Went off to the tropic heat a few years ago – for my health, you might say. Been in all sorts of places in the South Seas as far as Tahiti and then up to Singapore, The Straits, Rangoon, fascinating places . . . fascinating women . . . different from you . . . with your lovely pale skin, fair hair, and eyes that pierce a man's heart. You're what I call a cool beauty.'

'And you're what I call very *rude*.' Caroline had attempted to sound severe, but she knew it made no difference to the man in front of her: his eyes were laughing at her.

And he was appraising her. 'I'd like to sketch you some time.'

Caroline was amazed. 'Sketch me? What do you mean?'

'Caroline?' The call came from Lucy as she and George crossed the room to her. The stranger immediately bowed from his shoulders and said, 'But I must not keep you from your companions. Until we meet again.' And he nodded to George and Lucy and walked away, leaning on a most remarkable cane which appeared to be made of ivory. Caroline had never seen such an object before.

George watched his departing back. 'Who on earth was he?'

Caroline shook her head. 'I've positively no idea.'

Lucy's voice sounded oddly sharp and strident – even to her own ears. 'Well I have. Didn't know he was home, heard he went away to the Orient.'

'Well, don't keep us in suspense. What's his name?' asked Caroline.

'Matthew Craken, that's his name.'

Caroline's sharp intake of breath was quite audible. 'The . . . man . . . John Conrad nearly killed?'

'The very one.'

George shook his head and placed his arm around his fiancée. 'So that's Craken. There're hundreds of stories about him – and every one warranted by all accounts. What the devil did he want with you, Caroline?'

'I'm sure I've no idea.'

Lucy looked searchingly at Caroline for a second or two. 'He's got a cheek, he has. Come on, love, stick by us now. We mustn't get separated any more.'

They moved on to the rest of the photographs but Caroline's mind danced between the exhibition and Matthew Craken. It seemed unbelievable that the man John Conrad blamed for Emma's death would come up and speak to her that way – and right out of the blue. What a hide he had, and then he hadn't even introduced himself. Thank the Lord John Conrad wasn't here.

When Lucy and George left Caroline at her front gate, they talked about the rugby match the following day. Caroline smiled. 'I wouldn't miss it. Paul's playing and he says it'll be a great game. It's the old boys of BGS playing the old boys of Nudgee.'

This was the Brisbane Grammar School pitted against the Catholic College and was one of *the* events of the old boys' calendar.

'I'm more of a soccer man, myself,' George informed them, 'but I'll go if Lucy wants to.'

Lucy was enthusiastic. 'Yes, George, let's.'

As Caroline entered the house, she called out a greeting but there was no reply, and then her eyes caught the envelope leaning against the mirror on the hall stand. She recognised the handwriting immediately. As she took it her fingers trembled slightly and when she opened it she read that John Conrad was coming home. He had written to tell her! He had over a month's leave and was coming home next Tuesday.

She ran through to the kitchen where her mother turned from the hob, kettle in hand, and smiled. 'Oh hello, darling.'

Caroline could not help herself. 'John Conrad's coming home,' she declared excitedly.

'Really? Is that whom the letter is from?'

'Yes.'

31

'I didn't know you corresponded.'

'I . . . we don't. This is the first letter I've ever received.'

Her mother looked squarely at her. 'And have you ever written to him?'

Caroline sighed. 'Once.'

Elizabeth Dere smiled gently. Her daughter was holding the letter as if it were a missive from the Lord Himself. Caroline was a good girl, a sensible and competent girl, but inexperienced in the ways of life. 'Don't make too much of his letter then, love. He probably writes to a lot of people.'

Her daughter looked disappointed.

Elizabeth patted Caroline's hand, looking compassionately at her child. 'Darling, John Conrad's a soldier. They're not the best people to have as . . . friends. They might be off to war at any minute.'

'But there aren't any wars, are there?'

'Well, yes, my dear, there are, but let's say there aren't any I know that our colonies are involved in; but I'm afraid that doesn't mean there won't be, my girl, and then . . . well, a professional soldier is a professional soldier, and they're the first to go to fight.'

'But that doesn't stop them from having friends.'

Elizabeth gave the suggestion of a smile. It appeared her daughter was sweet on John Conrad Fleet. That concerned her. The young man was so good-looking he made even her fifty-four-year-old heart quicken when he smiled at her, and she had a theory that handsome men made bad husbands – especially handsome, professional soldiers.

She turned away as she answered, 'Yes, they do have friends, and as a rule, many. Don't fall for a uniform and a good-looking face, Caroline. There's more to a real friendship than that.'

Caroline fell silent as the kitchen door swung open and Paul walked in. 'It's cold out there. Is tea ready, Mum?'

Elizabeth nodded, placing a china cup and saucer down in front of him.

'Real good day at the bakery today – sold the lot, only a couple of loaves of white left.' He leaned over and took a cake from the plate in the middle of the table as he went on, 'My mate Kenny Neverson just came into the shop. Guess what? He's just had the telephone connected today. Can you believe it?'

His mother's eyes widened. 'My goodness, the Neversons with a telephone. What for?'

'Well, Mum, it's for his building business. He thinks in time all businesses will have them.'

'Does he now?'

Caroline shook her head. 'What's his number? Don't you have to give a number to the switchboard lady when you use a telephone?'

Her brother nodded. 'Yeah. His number's eight three O.'

'What does that mean? Eight three O?' his mother asked.

Paul regarded his poor mother as if she were the child and he the parent. 'It means his is the eight hundred and thirtieth telephone to be connected in Brisbane. When you turn the handle and ring up the switchboard you ask for eight three O and the woman working there switches you through to Kenny's telephone and it rings in his shop.'

'Well I never,' responded his mother. 'Who'd believe there are eight hundred and thirty of those contraptions in Brisbane.'

'Oh, Kenny told me something else too,' Paul went on as the bringer of the day's tidings.

His mother poured his tea. 'What's that?'

'John Conrad Fleet's home. Kenny saw him. So spiffing he thinks he is and all, in his lieutenant's uniform, no less.' He gave a short laugh, 'That'll get the girls all agog! Reckon he thinks he's the ant's pants, I do—'

And now his sister broke in. 'John Conrad's home? But he said he wasn't coming until Tuesday.' Spontaneously she touched the letter on the table in front of her.

Paul's expression was disapproving. 'What? He's writing to *you* now. Good heavens, don't tell me you're as silly as all the rest of them? Falling for a uniform! Thought you had more sense, Caro.'

Caroline looked affronted. 'Mind your own business. And don't call me Caro.' She turned to her mother. 'Oh, Mummy, he's home.'

'Yes, darling, it seems he is.'

Caroline rose from the table.

Her mother gestured to the teapot. 'Don't you want your tea?'

'Oh no, Mum, no thanks, don't feel like tea.'

The grandfather clock struck five as she passed out into the hall and hurried along to her bedroom. Out of her wardrobe she took her newest dress, a pale pink flowered cotton with lace insets in the bodice. She spent the next hour thoroughly scrubbing herself, brushing her hair and tying it back in a red bow at the nape of her neck, putting on her dress and prettiest shawl, and her best shoes, then finally pinching her cheeks to bring a little pink to the surface.

The sun was setting as she went to sit on the front verandah.

She was still there when her mother came and called in vain for her to come to the evening meal; and she waited on after that, in the chill of the settling night, sitting alone on the verandah in the old wicker chair with the fallen leaves of the jacaranda around her feet, and the moon throwing solemn beams of light across the wooden planking.

Even her brother had enough sensitivity not to speak to her as he left the house on his way to join his mates for a Friday night drink at the Lion's Mane public house.

At a few minutes to nine Elizabeth Dere opened her front door and came to join her daughter. She sat gravely opposite her child, wrapped in a warm cape. 'Darling, I don't like this. It's too cold to be sitting out here. It's John Conrad's first night at home. Remember he's come back days earlier than expected. He'll be with his family tonight, surely you realise. That's only to be expected. Now, you come on in and we'll play a game of chess together. Remember how Daddy loves a game?' She leant forward, took Caroline's icy hand and brought her to her feet. 'Come on now.'

Caroline could not speak. The inside of her chest felt full as if her bones pressed against her skin, and even in the cool air her throat was so very hot. She nodded. Of course her mother was right. She had been very foolish to even consider that John Conrad would come here. It was his first night home in almost a whole year. Naturally he was bound to spend it with his family.

Her mother smiled sympathetically and moved away, the heels of her shoes making clicking sounds on the wooden boards.

Caroline took a deep breath; it seemed to wander around in her chest for a few seconds before it tremored out into the night.

A sudden breeze came up and lifted two of the last of the jacaranda leaves from the tree which overhung the verandah; they floated down into Caroline's curls. She did not realise it, and with another deep breath she moved off to follow her mother back along the verandah in the chill of the night, with the melancholy leaves resting lightly in her long curling hair.

Across the streets of South Brisbane John Conrad sat beside Bart in one of the many pubs near the wharves. They were drinking Fleet Ale from seven-ounce glasses.

The night wind had risen now and the streets were cold, but the bar of the Southern Cross was warm and buzzing. People passed back and forth and an enterprising pianist attempted to be heard over the convivial noisy chatter.

Bart took a swig of his beer before he half turned on his bar stool. 'It's great to have you home, John Conrad.'

'Great to be home.'

'Big game tomorrow. We play the Nudgee blokes at Musgrave Park. Will you come?'

His big brother grinned. 'Wouldn't miss it. I suppose Aunt Leigh has her usual seat.'

Bart smiled self-consciously. 'Never misses a game.'

They were silent for a few seconds as each took a mouthful of beer.

'So what's it really like being a lieutenant?'

John Conrad did not answer immediately. When he did his expression was earnest. 'I'm happy enough, Bart – in fact, more than that. The army's given me meaning. I like the discipline and the accountability I'm beginning to shoulder. I'm what they call a sapper. You know, an engineer. That's what I've been studying these past few years: how to build and construct all manner of fortifications, magazines, bridges and things.'

'I thought you were in a mounted regiment?'

'I am. The New South Wales Mounted Rifles, but we have a unit of engineers. Most of the boys in our field companies are what we call "partially paid" because they're not permanent. I'm one of a small group of permanents who lead them. Just been down in Port Kembla, south of Sydney, building a fort. Enjoyed that, but I'm back at Victoria Barracks in Sydney now.'

'But what if a war comes?'

'That's one way of rising quickly through the ranks, young brother, of becoming someone of importance. Most people live mundane lives, and I've decided I'm not going to do that.'

Bart took another drink. 'You've changed.'

John Conrad slapped his brother on the back. 'Now, how do you mean *changed*?'

'Well, back five years ago you were against the militia; you hated being sent away to join the Volunteers.'

John Conrad didn't answer.

'Even for the first few years you were in the army, you didn't seem so, well, caught up in it, but now. Gosh . . .'

John Conrad trained his steady gaze on his younger brother. 'Lad, I'd be a strange man if the years hadn't altered me. Look at you. You've altered too, been away to university. Know a lot more now, don't you?

'The army has become a force, a real and lasting standard for all the colonies, and a soldier can have something to be proud of. Fifteen years ago in New South Wales the number of troops were an infinitesimal three hundred and nineteen permanent and one thousand eight hundred militia, hardly the numbers for anything, let alone an army. Today there are over twenty thousand troops in the Australian colonies. Did you know that?'

Bart looked thoughtful. 'No, I didn't.'

'My lad, last year we raised a National Guard, and an artillery band made up of regulars, and as it seems that federation will come, it's a great career for the future. You're correct, I did not see it that way five years ago, but then I was a boy. Now I'm an officer in the 2nd New South Wales regiment. I get to ride horses, which I very much like, and to fire at targets, which I'm very good at hitting, and to build things – which gratifies me. Remember I had to sign years of my life away when first I joined. I'd have been a damn fool to have kept on fighting the system.'

'Yes . . . I suppose so.'

John Conrad gazed around at the noisy pub and, over Bart's shoulder, through the window, he perceived vaguely in the gaslight outside the profile of a ship berthed at the wharves.

He wore a most odd expression as he added, 'A good life is shaped, not given, lad.'

'How do you mean?'

The soldier met his brother's eyes. 'We each make of our lives what we can; it's up to us. I believe a man makes his own destiny. Anyone who waits around expecting fate to look after him is a fool.'

As he finished speaking a hand landed on his shoulder and he turned round on the bar stool to a wide smile from Chris Buckle, an old school friend. 'Hey, John Conrad, I thought it was you . . . I like your fancy dress!'

As John Conrad burst into laughter the gaslight played about him, gleaming on his fair hair and the light bronze of his forehead, glinting in his eyes, and shining on the back of his hand as he lifted it in greeting to the new arrival. Bart couldn't help thinking his big brother was just too damn good-looking for words.

Chapter Four

John Conrad Fleet opened his eyes and looked at the ceiling. He was home in Brisbane, in his own room. He smiled. Tiny particles danced and shimmered in the generous beam of light thrown from the window across to the counterpane draped on the end of his bed. The sun was well up; it must be late.

Yesterday he had surprised his family by walking in on them: everyone in his unit had received an early leave. He had arrived at Brewery House as his father and Bart came in for luncheon. Aunt Leigh's eyes had shone with happy tears and the family had taken the afternoon off and gone into the city. After refreshments at the Inca Tea Rooms they spent an hour at the new art gallery in the upper floor of the Town Hall in Queen Street; it had been opened three years before by the Governor, and the good people of Brisbane were proud that, at last, there were semblances of culture.

The railway had linked Queensland's capital with Sydney since 1887 and now, over a decade later, urban and suburban railways ran in all directions. It was fair to say that the town was beginning to come out of its rough, pioneer stage, for here and there could be seen such substantial examples of progress as the tarred metal roads of the inner city, where dignified constructions like the Treasury Building, Parliament House, the Queensland Club, and the museum in William Street stood. There were premier schools for Brisbane's sons and daughters to attend, and fine churches dotted all over the city.

John Conrad noticed for the first time that there were no cows grazing near the Victoria Bridge. In the past that had really made the place look ramshackle. And while Brisbane was not the energetic or elegant city that Sydney, and Melbourne, were, it perhaps at last approached, with its 100,000 plus inhabitants, what could be classified as a city.

They had gone to meet David as he came out of school, and

the entire family took a walk in the Botanical Gardens and, in spite of a cool wind blowing, they stood and watched for a time some men playing lawn tennis.

When they had returned home Aunt Leigh made John Conrad's favourite meal: chicken and dumplings, followed by apricot pie. Afterwards he and Bart wandered along to a few pubs in Melbourne Street; had a really good chat in one by the wharves, and ended up at the Lion's Mane Hotel, in Stanley Street, a small establishment which still survived even though many businesses had left that part of South Brisbane since the Great Flood of five years before. There, he caught up with a lot of his old mates and enjoyed the energetic music made by two accordion players. Around eleven o'clock he ran into his cousin Lucy, who introduced him to her fiancé.

George Goodward had taken his hand in a firm grasp. 'How do you do, John Conrad?'

He did not know what to make of George Goodward. The man had gone proudly on to inform him that he was a cousin of William Lane, the journalist fellow, who, a few years ago, took a group of Australian socialists, disillusioned after the Great Strike, to found a new Utopia in Paraguay. It sounded like a damned impractical idea to John Conrad, but then, people did very odd things! Still, he had been polite for Lucy's sake.

John Conrad smiled, remembering how he had danced the night away in the ladies' lounge with a number of pretty girls. He nodded to himself as he climbed out of bed and walked to the window. Yes, his first night home had been most enjoyable.

He was thirsty and there was a little bit of a tight feeling in his temples this morning . . . must have been that last rum. He closed his eyes. He had a vague memory of meeting Paul Dere on the footpath after he and Bart had left the Lion's Mane . . . Must have been pretty late then.

Dere had seemed belligerent. What was it that he said? Something about his sister? Even from being a small boy, Paul Dere had been a disagreeable sort of bloke. Dere was referring to Caro, obviously. But John Conrad could not really recall exactly what had been said. He smiled to himself. Caro was a sweet kid. Those lovely eyes . . . and a sensible sort of kid too. She would make some fellow very happy.

Down below him two brewery workers crossed the yard. One looked up and saw him, waved and passed on. John Conrad responded in kind, calling out to the man by name. He looked past the brewery, down the lane to the stables, and immediately it was five years before and he held his sweet Emma again in his arms. She had died right there by the entry gate. He made a sad sound and turned back into his room.

Strange about life. Given his own way five years ago he would not have been in the army; not that there was any regret now, but it was because of Emma's death he had taken this path. Yes, Em's death and bloody Matthew Craken.

Last time he had been home on leave he had heard Craken was up in the Straits Settlements: Singapore, Penang and Malacca. Good enough! He had not seen Craken since the night of the fight. If he never laid eyes on the man again it would suit John Conrad.

He took a long drink of water and then bathed and dressed. In the big homely kitchen a fire still burned in the grate and a note lay on the table.

Darling,
    Didn't want to wake you. Gone to my garden club. Your father is in the brewery, Bart's gone to rugby practice – big game this afternoon. David is at band practice – fresh bread in the safe and bacon warm on the hob.
    Love, Aunt Leigh

John Conrad made a swipe at a few flies, that even in winter buzzed around the big metal safe in which they kept food away from the insects. He took out the bread and made himself a hearty breakfast which soon dissipated the tightness in his temples.

He decided to stroll down to the river. It was a good place to think; ever since being a child he had gone there when he wanted to be alone with his thoughts.

He wore mufti as soldiers often did on leave. He was glad to be out of uniform – there was a tiring sameness to it when one wore it day after day. He wandered by the tall native gums and the bottlebrush shrubs and scribbly gums, down the path towards the Brisbane River where he sat down on a flat stone near the bank and clasped his hands around his knees. It was warm in the sun and he remained that way for a long time as if mesmerised by the water.

It was such a pretty spot, this reach of the river where the long grass grew to the water's edge and the pink boles of the gum trees lay exposed by the peeling grey bark. In summer small white wild flowers grew in the river bank and brown ducks glided by. It was a tiny oasis of respite when so much of Brisbane was barren and ugly – street after street of dirt which turned to mud during rain, and suburb upon suburb of sterile small square wooden houses, many of them with just four rooms and a corrugated iron water tank attached to the side. And then the multitude of back yards with the ubiquitous lonely structure that held the dirt box and had its waste removed once a week.

He knew he had been very lucky to grow up in Brewery House which was two storied and surrounded by trees, and was recognised as a grand building by the standard of most homes on this side of the city.

He recalled the laughter of his childhood days and his eyes rested on the old weeping willow sixty yards upriver, past a single native fig tree with parakeets in its branches, where he and Emma and Hargy Lightfoot used to climb when they were children. He had learned to swim right here, and he and Hargy had fished this spot more times than he could count. He recalled the day when they were in their teens and Emma fell in the water fully clothed and he and Hargy had jumped in with her. They had all frolicked like small children: how they had laughed.

For a few minutes Hargy filled John Conrad's thoughts. Each time he came back he went up to Hargy's sister's little wooden house in Spring Hill. Lena and her children were always there, but never Hargy. He missed Hargy; apparently he did return to Brisbane occasionally and Bart always held his job open at the brewery for him.

John Conrad's eyes glazed over and he sat staring into the water, enjoying the sun on his face and hands. Life had a way of separating the adults when the children had been so close. He would like to see Hargy again, he really would. He turned to look upriver and suddenly he felt the presence of someone near him, and a shadow fell across his feet. He turned and, shading his eyes, looked up into the face of his old friend.

He leapt to his feet in delight. 'Hargy, this is amazing! I was just daydreaming about you.' He held out his hand and Hargy took it in his broad firm palm before he clasped John Conrad close to his heart.

Hargy's eyes were clouded with emotion and so too were his companion's. John Conrad blinked. 'Pal, how are you?' He fell naturally back into his youthful, affectionate form of address.

Hargy smiled and his teeth gleamed. 'It good to see you, Johnny Conrad. Long time you gone from Brisbane.'

'No . . . you're the one who's been gone a long time. Where have you been?'

'I bin lots of places. Seen a bit too. Goin' back I reckon. Too many people here. Brisbane's too big now. Just stay to make a bit . . . you know, fight and take me earnin's . . . and do a bit a work for your old man.' Then he pointed to his companion with his thick index finger. 'Jimmy Briggs, he told me you back home. Reckoned you'd be here.'

John Conrad eyed his friend. Hargy had not altered much in the five years they had not seen each other, except that he was now physically mature. They both were: two fine physical specimens, John Conrad being an inch or two taller than his friend.

'Five years is a long time, Hargy, but you haven't altered.' John Conrad mock punched a fist to Hargy's chin. 'So you're still fighting?'

Hargy grinned as he closed one eye against the sun and pretended to take a fall from the blow. He rolled over on the grass and they both laughed. 'Yeah . . . now and then. When I'm here. Helps me sister's kids a bit.'

His friend nodded thoughtfully.

'What about you? You like the army?'

'It suits me, Hargy.' Automatically he sat down, and Hargy lifted himself to sit cross-legged beside him.

They remained together for a few comfortable hours and they fell into their roles of long ago, reminiscing and reliving their childhood together: skimming stones across the water; pulling long sheafs of paspalum grass and chewing the soft inside; making ships out of the wide flat leaves of the native lily plants and setting them to drift upon the water. At one point a wide happy smile broke across John Conrad's mouth and he turned to his companion. 'Perhaps men are always boys.'

Hargy looked questioningly.

'Well, think about it, we're playing. I mean we're both almost twenty-six years old and we're playing games!'

And Hargy in his disarming fashion replied, '*You* are almost twenty-six. We don't know how old I am!'

This made them burst into laughter: the clear, bold, uncompromising laughter of youth . . . for it was true. Hargy had been born at the foot of the McPherson Range where his people still lived in the tribal way, and did not know the date of birth.

Later, they talked about Emma.

John Conrad's eyes softened momentarily as Hargy waved his hand in the air. 'She fine girl. Hair shiny like sunlight . . . always nice to me too, not like some.' Then he brought his hand heavily down into his other palm, making a slapping sound. 'But you give it to that Craken, good. Smashed him up oright. All the fellas know he have lotsa girls.'

John Conrad made a grim sound between his teeth. 'Yes.'

'He back in Brisbane too.'

John Conrad's expression hardened. Surprise registered. 'Are you sure about this? Thought he went away overseas.'

'He did. Away long time, but back now. Me mate told me he's lotsa weeks in Brisbane already.'

John Conrad knew Craken had been to a number of ports in the Pacific and the Orient. He had gone away about a year after their fight. So he was back? Well, Brisbane was a big place now, and he was only home himself for a month. Unlikely their paths would cross.

Hargy thumped his fist in his hand once more. 'We find him and break his legs again.'

John Conrad could not help but grin. 'Mm . . . not a bad idea.'

Some time later the two friends stood outside the Musgrave Park rugby field. They had walked over to the ground together. Soccer and Union were played at Musgrave Park: it would be ten years before League came in.

John Conrad attempted to talk his friend into coming in with

43

him to find his Aunt Leigh in the grandstand but Hargy shook his head. 'They don't want black fellas in there. Off you go.'

His companion's lips tightened and he shook his head. It was true, he would cause an outcry if he tried to take Hargy into the area near the grandstand; even though *grandstand* was most definitely an overly exalted description of the twenty bare wooden tiers that raised themselves above the bar and changing room.

John Conrad put his arm around Hargy's shoulders. 'Well, pal, if they don't want you in there, I'm not going in. Yet we must see the game. Bart's playing. He'll score for certain. We'll go around to the Hill.'

The Hill was a slightly raised part of the ground to the side of one of the goal posts where during the matches the more disreputable gathered, like the members of the local push and the ne'er-do-wells. Hargy grinned. 'That's it.'

They found a spot to sit on the dry grass. There was no one else around here today. When the teams left the field at half-time, Bartholomew had lived up to his brother's prediction and scored a try and converted. The two friends lay back on the uneven ground. After a few minutes John Conrad asked, 'Want a drink, Hargy? We'll pop over to the bar and get a lemonade.'

Hargy raised his hand. 'You go, I wait here in the sunshine,' and John Conrad jumped to his feet. It was against the law for Aboriginal people to drink alcohol, though in the past the two friends had drunk their share together, away from prying eyes.

The bar was round beyond the grandstand, and soon John Conrad had purchased the lemonades and was returning under the gum trees to Hargy lying on the ground in the distance, when he saw two young women strolling towards him. He recognised Lucy and Caro Dere, and took off his hat as he crossed over to them. 'Ladies, good afternoon.'

His cousin Lucy kissed him in greeting and Caro Dere gave him a strange smile and said, 'It's been a long time, John Conrad . . . Thank you for your letter.'

He took Caro's hand. She really was such a pretty kid. 'It's good to see you Caro. Glad you received it.'

Lucy pointed to the goal post where Bart had scored. 'Bart's playing well.'

'So's Paul,' added Caro loyally.

Lucy laughed, then taking her cousin's arm, asked, 'Are you coming with us to the picnic? It's three weeks tomorrow.'

'Where to?'

'Sandgate. It's the West End Club's annual picnic.'

The West End Club was a working man's club notorious for the gambling which took place on the premises.

John Conrad frowned. 'Why? Who the devil do you know who's a member of that thing?'

Lucy's eyebrows rose. 'John Conrad, you can be so uppity sometimes. My fiancé, of course.'

Naturally, George would be a member, John Conrad realised.

Lucy went on, 'There's some man down in Sandgate who's going to take us out on the bay in his boat. Some of the boys are hoping to go fishing. So you'll come?'

'I don't think so.' Then he looked at Caro. 'Are you going?'

Before she had a chance to answer Lucy replied, 'Of course she is.'

He shrugged his shoulders. 'In that case I'll come.'

Caro knew her cheeks were going pink; she spoke quickly to take her mind from the feeling. 'Where're you sitting?'

'On the Hill with Hargy?'

Lucy looked round. 'The black fellow?'

John Conrad took a deep breath. '*My friend*, Lucy dear, my friend.'

His cousin shrugged. 'Then there's no point in asking you to join us. We're with George and a mate of his, down near the fence. Aunt Leigh's up in the grandstand.'

Caro half raised her hand and then dropped it to her side. 'I haven't seen Hargy for a long time. Didn't know he was home. Please tell him I asked after him, will you? Tell him I'd like to see him.'

John Conrad put his hat back on and glanced towards the Hill. 'Yes, I will.' He smiled at the two young women, before looking directly at Caroline. 'See you at the picnic then, Caro. If not earlier.'

She felt a little quiver in the chest where she suspected her heart was, and as he walked away she eyed his steady movements. She had cried while she waited for him last night. That had been foolish of her, she knew, and now she could not help but concentrate on the way he had looked right at her . . . not at Lucy . . . and his last words had been, 'See you at the picnic . . . if not earlier.' *If not earlier . . . if not earlier* – surely that was a message?

She came back to reality as she heard her friend say at her side, 'I thought you didn't like being called Caro.'

'Well, as a rule I don't.'

Suddenly Lucy rounded on her friend; her eyes narrowed and she had a knowing expression. 'You're sweet on him, aren't you? Never realised it before, but you are.' Lucy was thinking about last night and how all the girls in sight had flocked around John Conrad. If she weren't his cousin, she thought she would be half in love with him too.

Caro did not answer.

Lucy thought it was time to give her friend some advice. 'Well, love, I can understand how you might take a shine to him. I mean, most girls do, don't they? He's so good-looking and all. But I honestly doubt if he has thought seriously about being with just one girl.'

This was not what Caroline Dere wanted to hear. She wished her father were home from China. Things seemed easier when he was around.

Lucy picked up her friend's hand and tucked it through her arm. 'Come on, love, let's get back to George.'

They wandered back through the lacy shadows of the gums while a flock of seagulls seemingly looking for the ocean of miles away, swept screeching overhead.

As the girls found their seats the players re-emerged from the side of the changing shed. Caroline decided to concentrate on the game, but she could not help the way her eyes wandered over to the Hill and the man that sat on the grass holding his knees and watching the play.

From behind, a few rows back, she too was watched – not in quite the same way as she gazed at John Conrad, but not impassively either. The moody eyes of Matthew Craken roamed across Caroline's back. He was in company with his best mate, Knobby Clark, and he had asked Knobby who she was. He knew her name now, Caroline Dere. Oh, he had seen

46

her in conversation with Fleet, all right, but he had made sure they had not seen him.

So, the enemy was home on leave. Well, that was of immense interest. He had dreamed for years about getting even with Fleet one day, somehow, somewhere. Opportunities presented themselves if one waited long enough, he had been taught. During his years in the East he had become aware of many things; he had discovered, memorised and embraced a great deal. One of many of the valuable attitudes he had learned was patience.

By the time the match was over, Matthew Craken had spent much of the afternoon with his eyes upon Caro, who had spent much of the afternoon with her eyes upon John Conrad.

Matthew had followed the many turnings of her head and he was aware of the object of her gaze, sitting over there on the Hill with the Aborigine. This fractionally bothered him, but he would not let it matter much.

He made certain that as the crowd milled towards the exit he moved in right behind the girl, who intrigued him. He remained close to her as they all passed by the grandstand. He enjoyed the fact that she did not realise it was his arm that her back touched as the people behind crowded forward. Outside the gate, on the footpath, as the crowd began to disperse, he leant forward and whispered, 'How lovely to see you, Caroline.'

The young woman turned sharply, and gave a surprised gasp as she recognised the back of the man, who, even now, was disappearing swiftly away through the dispersing crowd.

Matthew Craken! Again. And talking in her ear just like yesterday! Whatever was the man up to? A little ripple ran through her: she was uncertain whether it was a thrill or a shiver. He was by far the strangest person she had ever met. To think he was here at the rugby, and John Conrad had been at the same match! This turned her thoughts to the soldier, and as she and Lucy said goodbye to George and his friend and headed towards the tram, she was hoping quite vehemently that she would see him – as he had actually suggested – earlier than the picnic to Sandgate.

Chapter Five

Caroline did see John Conrad sooner than the day of the picnic: a couple of times. The first was the following Friday night at Lucy's house in Wooloongabba, where they all played cards and sang round the old stand-up piano. Lucy lived there with her mother and two little sisters, and they had all agreed when she married George that the newlyweds would remain until they saved enough for their own home. John Conrad and Caroline came separately with their brothers, but they spent a lot of time talking to each other. It was that night Caroline decided she liked the name *Caro* after all. John Conrad said it in such a way that it had a flattering sound and when midnight came and they said their good nights she was sure he held her hand a trifle longer than was necessary.

The following week she saw him again at the Wednesday night market in Melbourne Street near the railway terminus, and while he stopped and chatted to her for quite a time he did not suggest they walk out together or meet again. Throughout the next seven days she lived in hopes that he would visit, and by the time she 'accidentally' ran into him again at the Wednesday night market she was beginning to think any feelings of affection were all one-sided . . . her side. But her hopes were revived when he bent forward to her in the ebbing and flowing crowd to say, 'I'm really looking forward to seeing you at the picnic on Sunday.' She went home with a spring in her step.

On the Friday of that same week she arrived as usual to spend time with Aunt Leigh in the big kitchen at Brewery House. Caro watched as the older woman baked scones, the homely cooking smell filling the air. Aunt Leigh talked away while Caroline listened – well, listened to some of what was said, but missed some too. Her eyes were constantly turning to the door in the hopes that John Conrad would arrive. Each Friday she waited for him to appear but she had only seen him twice at Brewery House, both times in the distance in the stable yard. To Caro it seemed he never came inside!

The sound of steps on the verandah came just around one o'clock, and the young woman looked up expectantly. It was Uncle Barrington and Bart coming in from the brewery for their lunch.

Time passed, but no one else arrived. During the meal Barrington Fleet asked, 'Where's John Conrad?'

Aunt Leigh looked up from her soup. 'Well, I thought he was actually coming in for this fine lunch today. But his heart won't grieve what his eye hasn't seen. He's been fishing every morning by the river with Hargy so I expect that's where he is.'

The patriach nodded. 'Those two always had a hankering for each other. I thought the lad would have outgrown Hargy, but there's no accounting for a man's likes and dislikes, I suppose.'

Bart nodded. 'He brought Hargy to the game last Saturday; typical of John Conrad. Caused a bit of comment in the dressing room.'

This interchange had told Caro what she needed to know, and as soon as lunch was over and she had washed and wiped the dishes, as she did every Friday, she removed her cotton apron and took leave of Aunt Leigh.

The older woman looked around from the hob where she was cleaning the grate. 'You're leaving early, love.'

'Yes, I've a few jobs to do this afternoon. And I have to iron my dress for the concert at St Paul's Hall tonight and I must wash my hair.'

'Yes, m'dear, you'll be beautiful . . . and "Beauty is the Gift of God". Aristotle. Off you go.'

She kissed Aunt Leigh and left. It was not coincidence that she headed towards the river.

Half a mile away, on the river bank, Hargy turned to John Conrad. Between them lay four good-sized bream, which Hargy continued to flick with a piece of red rag to keep away the flies.

'You must take these to Lena, pal. She'll cook them for you.

You need a good meal before you fight for the championship tonight.'

Hargy nodded. 'Yeah, me sister's a good cook, all right.' Then his wide mouth stretched in a grin. 'To think, at last, I'm goin' to be Brisbane Champion tonight. Hey, you can write, Johnny. You can make a big placard for me with writin' on it sayin' "*Brisbane Champion*".'

His friend smiled. 'I'll do that, pal. I reckon you could be a lot of other things, but you sure like to fight.'

'Always have.' Then he leant back and put his hands behind his head. 'It's real good havin' you home, Johnny . . . Remember just before me first fight at the Colosseum when you and me, we went walkabout?'

They had been about sixteen, and the two of them had gone over south of Beaudesert to where most of Hargy's family and cousins lived in the old way at the foot of the mountains.

'I do.'

'We sure had fun. You weren't bad at livin' out either . . .' he looked over at his companion and winked, 'that is, for a white fella.'

They both laughed and Hargy pulled a paspalum grass and chewed the end before he went on, 'And when you get outa the army, you and me, we'll sort of go walkabout again, only we'll make real good money. We'll – what's that word? . . . *tour*, that's it – around towns and I'll fight . . . you know local blokes. You can take wagers. We can make drayloads.'

This brought a wide smile to John Conrad's mouth. 'No, pal, we'll think of something else. I don't want you fighting the rest of your life.'

Hargy rolled over and eyed his friend speculatively. 'I reckon you mean that.'

'I do. I want you to stay at the brewery and work. You like it there. Bart's a good man and he'll make sure you always have a job. Then one day, yes, you and I will go touring, but just that, seeing the whole country . . . Australia. No fighting, just us travelling.'

This definitely appealed to the nomad in Hargy's soul for his eyes gleamed with the thought of it. 'I'd like that . . . the whole country eh?' He looked serious. 'Dunno if they'd let me.'

'Who?'

'The Government. There was some sorta protection act passed last year . . . for Abos: lots of us. They're gone onta reserves, though our one tribe down on the range is still there.' He sniffed philosophically. 'Then I suppose they don't care that much about us fellas in the towns, eh? 'Cause we don't add up to much.'

John Conrad shook his head. 'I don't know a lot about it Hargy, though I did read something. It annoyed me because it sounded more like they were separating your people from white settlements rather than *protecting* you. That's the trouble with bloody law-makers. They make sweeping decisions up in their ivory towers and don't really know what's going on with the people at all.'

'Yeah,' replied Hargy in a matter-of-fact voice, 'they're mad.'

This amused them and they burst into laughter. When they calmed and settled, Hargy wagged his finger at his companion. 'You're my best friend, Johnny. I sure miss you.'

John Conrad met his comrade's eyes. 'I miss you, too; there's no one in the army like you.'

'Of course not . . . them buggers wouldn't have a black fella!' Hargy laughed hard at this, and John Conrad leant over and cuffed him affectionately on the shoulder. The laughter was again infectious and they both lay back as the river bank reverberated with their boyish mirth. Finally Hargy sat up and pulled them both more paspalum grass to chew. As he handed the pale yellow stalk to his friend, suddenly, without warning, he dropped his head and brought his hand to his temple, making a small groan.

His companion started. 'Hargy, what's wrong?'

'Nothin' . . . happens sometimes. It'll pass.'

But John Conrad was insistent. 'What is it? A sharp pain?'

His friend shook his head. 'Just a headache.'

'How often do you get them?'

Hargy was reluctant to answer.

'Tell me.'

'Oh, I dunno. Now and then.' He held his head in his hands and leant forward.

'How long do the headaches last?'

'Not long.'

John Conrad fell silent; he was reminded of the fight last year between Casey and Johnson, two young lieutenants in his corps. Casey had complained of a headache before the bout and had been knocked unconscious during the fight. He had lain that way for over a week afterwards and had never seemed quite normal since.

'Don't fight tonight, pal.'

'Gotta fight. It's the championship, Brisbane Champion, remember? I'm goin' up against Tommy Kelly. Reckon I'll beat him too. Easy.'

A furrow lodged between John Conrad's eyes. 'Is the championship that important?'

His companion continued to answer without looking up. 'Yeah. Anyway . . . need the money. I get some of what's wagered on me. I'll beat that bugger. He can't fight.'

John Conrad's voice was resigned. 'Hell, pal, you're a hard man to convince. I hate these endurance fights where you go on like gladiators until one corner throws in the towel. They have rounds in other places, you know. After three minutes you get a rest before you begin again; a darn sight more civilised.'

Now Hargy lifted his head. 'They wouldn't like that at the Colosseum, matey. Too tame. Anyway, they're all comin' to see me.'

'So, what time's the bout? You know I'll be there.'

'Ah it'll be the last fight. Around half-past eleven, I reckon.'

John Conrad nodded. 'Then promise me something?'

His friend looked questioningly.

'Take the fish, go home now and sleep for a few hours. Just rest. Do nothing else at all. This is a big fight.'

Hargy leaned over and patted his comrade's shoulder. 'You don't worry about me, Johnny. I'll win.'

'I know that. Still, I want you to promise me you'll rest this afternoon.'

Hargy's black eyes narrowed and now he grinned. 'Yeah, I will.' Slowly he rose to his feet. 'You sound bossy like your father . . . but he's not a bad bloke.' He picked up the fish and put them in his bag.

As Caro came to the river path she saw Hargy carrying a bag and disappearing through the gums in the opposite direction. She called out and waved but he did not see her, so she continued on under the pale trees and round the clumps of scrubby bushes, all the while looking around.

Several minutes later she saw him. She halted. He was sitting alone upon a flat rock in the sunlight close to a weeping willow tree. He was concentrating on something small he held in his hands. From where she stood it appeared to be a card and she watched as he held it up to his brow and leaned forward. He remained that way for a few seconds before he put it in his top pocket. Every move he made seemed graceful in Caro's eyes.

Suddenly she wished she had not come; she felt shy and made a move to turn round. He called out without looking at her. 'Good afternoon, Caro.'

So he had seen her coming after all; though he had not turned in her direction. She answered haltingly. 'Good afternoon, John Conrad.'

Now he lifted his head to look over at her. 'What brings you down here? Or should I say, what brought you and then altered your mind? For you were going to leave without speaking, weren't you?'

'I suppose I was, yes.'

He beckoned her and as she came forward she felt awkward and then found herself saying, 'I thought Hargy was here with you.'

His eyes were laughing at her as he said, 'So, it was Hargy you came to see?'

'Yes . . . No . . .' She sighed. This was very uncomfortable. 'It's just that people might think I shouldn't be here alone with you.'

He stood up. 'Most people are hypocrites, Caro, I don't believe it matters what they think. Come and talk to me.'

The girl edged forward and he moved nearer to her.

'Hargy *was* with me, actually. He's just left to take our catch home to his sister.'

There were a few seconds of silence and she dropped her eyes to the back of his hands where the sun rested on the fine fair hairs as he brought his palms together and interlaced his fingers. His pink oval-shaped nails contrasted with the sun brown of his skin and she could clearly see the half-moons at the base of his thumbnails. She shivered and he noticed. 'Are you cold, Caro?'

'No.'

He looked out across the river. 'Why did you come to find me?'

His presence alone like this was quite overpowering. She did not know how to answer him, but she found some strength somewhere. 'The truth is, I think I wanted to be sure you were coming on the picnic on Sunday.'

He half turned to where she stood at his side. He looked thoughtful and appeared to be weighing her. 'Is it important to you?'

She could feel the beginning of a flush creeping up her neck. 'Yes, I suppose it is.'

He smiled. 'Then I'll be there.'

She looked down to where the wind blew a frond of the willow tree around his leg, and now she surprised herself. 'There's a concert tonight in St Paul's Hall. It starts at seven o'clock. We're all going. I . . . that is . . . Lucy, George and me.'

It was a few seconds before he said anything. He looked down into her bold brown eyes. 'I'd like to accompany you to that concert, Caro.'

Her pulse quickened. 'Oh . . . and I'd be pleased if you did, John Conrad.'

'But I'd have to leave you at the intermission I'm afraid. Hargy fights tonight and I must be there.'

The only thing that mattered to Caroline was that John Conrad had said he would go. It didn't matter that he had to leave halfway through; that he would be there, by her side, was everything. 'Yes, of course you must go to the fight. I won't mind. And the first half of the concert should be good.'

The expression in his blue eyes warmed her soul even in the chill of the winter wind, which had risen and was sailing over the river. 'I'll see you tonight then, Caro. I'll be by at half-past six.'

And so it was that Caroline Dere, wearing a becoming soft pink silk outfit with lace insets in the skirt and jacket, a warm velvet cape round her shoulders, walked on John Conrad Fleet's arm into St Paul's Hall, her hand resting lightly on his forearm. They found their seats in the seventh row.

'Lucy and George should be here soon,' Caro said as they sat down.

John Conrad nodded.

As they sat waiting Caro ventured, 'John Conrad?'

He turned his head to look at her.

'I . . . believe Matthew Craken is home in Brisbane.'

A singular expression rose in his eyes. 'I know, Caro. Why are you telling me?'

'I suppose I wanted to warn you . . . in case you didn't know.'

'Well, thanks but I do know.' He was silent for a time then he said, 'And, Caro?'

'Yes?'

'I would prefer it if you don't mention him to me ever again. He's not someone you should associate yourself with in any way whatever. He's scum.'

Caro was saved from any continuation of this topic when she heard her name called and they looked round to see Lucy waving to them. Shortly afterwards, Lucy and George were seated beside them.

The opening act was Jimmy Delfort, an American, whom, it was said, had appeared on the stage in New York with a famous actress named Sarah Bernhardt. He gave a marvellous rendition of Coleridge's poem *Kubla Khan*, and the audience applauded unselfconsciously.

Through the ten acts of the first half Caro sat glowing with pride. She knew that every single girl had looked with envy as she came into the hall with John Conrad.

The last act before interval was a singsong with the audience participating. St Paul's church warden was the master of ceremonies and he leant out from the stage, his long arms raised in conductorial fashion as the church quartet played behind him. The final tune was a local folk song which everyone knew, and Caro, so conscious of the man at her side, actually imagined she could feel the breath going in and out of his body. This image was so evocative to her that she began to tremble slightly and even her fingers tingled with excitement as those gathered lifted their voices in unison to sing:

'One Sunday morning as I was walking
By Brisbane waters I chanced to stray,
I heard a convict his fate bewailing
As on the sunny river bank he lay:
I am a native of Erin's island
Transported now from my native shore
They tore me from my aged parents
and from the maiden I do adore.'

The audience had rendered this oftentimes from childhood, and they sang zestfully in contradiction to the lyrics, which told of the terrible fate dealt to the wretched convicts of Moreton Bay where Brisbane now stood.

As the curtain fell, just avoiding the warden, who moved smartly to the side of the stage, people began to talk.

'Let's go and get something to drink,' Lucy suggested, and John Conrad turned to Caro.

She was very aware of the arm he lifted to rest on the back of her chair as he asked, 'Well, Caro, shall we accompany Lucy and George for some refreshment?'

When they walked on to the verandah of the hall the Ladies' Guild were selling soft drinks, tea and cakes. The men drank lemonades and the girls creaming sodas.

A few minutes later, John Conrad shook George by the hand, kissed his cousin on the cheek and, taking Caro's hand and pressing it to his lips, asked, 'Will you walk me to the corner?'

The corner was only about fifty yards away and illuminated by a gaslight. Caro's laugh tinkled from her lips.

'Go on, love, we can all see you from here,' prompted Lucy.

'Then of course I will.'

They passed down the wooden steps together, John Conrad supporting his companion's arm and watched by most people on the verandah.

It was close to nine o'clock and the street was empty. A lone brush box tree near the corner threw dark shadows across the footpath. As they entered the few yards of gloom John Conrad stopped and the girl at his side turned to him.

'Thanks for your company this evening, even though it was short,' he said.

56

Caro knew she was blushing and was pleased to be in the darkness. 'Yes. I've enjoyed it so very much.'

She was unsure of how the next thing happened. He turned his head and she registered the gaslamp yards away behind his profile, and then he moved and his head blocked out the streetlight, and he was kissing her gently and briefly on the mouth. He did not take her in his arms, in fact he hardly touched her with his body, it was only his lips that rested on hers. She stood perfectly still as he lifted his mouth away. 'I'm a man and you're lovely. Good night.'

She did not speak as he moved away from her into the glow of the corner lamp where he paused and stood watching her. His voice seemed to echo around in the chill breeze, 'Caro, you'd better return to your friends, before I do it again.'

And now she smiled widely. 'Would you?'

'I would.'

'Then yes, I'd better go.' She turned and hurried away.

She was twenty yards from the tree when he called out, 'Caro?'

She turned back.

'Will you let me actually take you to the picnic on Sunday?'

And now she laughed, 'Oh yes,' and the whole of her glowed warm in the cold of the night.

When Caroline left Lucy and George at her front gate it was after ten o'clock. She pulled her shawl more tightly as she walked along the path, a pale figure in the insipid winter moonlight. She was just about to put her foot on the first of the steps leading up to her verandah when she heard a rustling sound behind her. She turned and saw a form near the trunk of the jacaranda tree.

'Is that you, Paul?'

The man did not answer but stepped forward. Then she saw the cane. Her sharp intake of breath was clearly heard on the night air. 'You,' she said.

'Yes, Caroline Dere, me.'

'What are you doing here?'

'I wanted to see you.'

He walked forward, leaning slightly on his cane. His motion was like a mariner, a gentle rhythmic swaying as he moved.

Automatically she stepped back and felt the post at the bottom of the steps in the small of her back. He came to within three feet of where she stood.

She was not frightened, but she felt her swift heartbeat. 'You always seem to appear out of nowhere. It's a trifle disconcerting.'

He smiled and his teeth gleamed. She smelt a pleasing aroma. It was a similar smell to the one she'd noticed in Mr Wang's Chinese Silk and Lace shop in Woolloongabba. She thought it must be coming from something he wore.

'I'm glad I disconcert you, for that certainly is what you do to me. I have waited here an extended time hoping to see you.'

The moonlight was making strange shapes in the garden and as it rested on him it highlighted his angular face and the scar beneath his eye. She thought he looked like some mountain brigand of old, or a Caribbean pirate.

'I think you know I was at the rugby match the other week? I walked behind you out the gate and you had no idea.'

'Yes, I didn't realise you were there until you whispered in my ear.'

'I saw you last Wednesday night too.'

Now she was surprised. 'Where?' she asked.

'At the street market, Caroline. I was there.'

She was feeling rather heady. This whole night had been amazing. John Conrad Fleet had kissed her and now she was being confronted by Matthew Craken. Why was it this man always managed to make her feel flattered, yet uncomfortable?

He smiled again. It was slightly crooked, somehow bewitching and so different from John Conrad's smile. 'You've never called me by my name. Why don't you say it? I reckon you know it well.'

'Why should I say it?'

'Because I'd like you to. Go on, say *Matthew*.'

She shook her head. 'No, this is silly.'

'And do you think this is silly?' he asked.

She looked enquiringly at him. 'What?'

And in the next second he stepped forward and took her in his arms and kissed her full on the mouth. Her cape fell to the ground as she stiffened and he released her.

Her voice shook slightly. 'That wasn't very gentlemanly.'

'I'm not a gentleman.'

Caro knew this was moving her quickly out of her depth. She turned on her heel and hurried up the stairs.

He stood there leaning on his embossed silver cane that shimmered nebulously in the cool darkness. 'You're a lovely girl, Caroline Dere.'

She did not answer as she passed across the verandah and opened her front door.

'Is that you, Caroline?' her mother's voice sounded from the kitchen.

She took a very deep breath. 'Yes, Mother.'

'Come in here. Paul and I are just taking supper.'

Caro closed the door behind her and stood perfectly still for a few seconds. It was astounding. She had only been kissed once before, at a church fête, and that had been years ago, and now she had been kissed by John Conrad and Matthew Craken in the same night. It did not seem possible. John Conrad would be so angry if he knew about Matthew. She could never tell him. Not after what he had said about the man tonight . . . Matthew Craken was not someone to bring up to John Conrad. The oddest thing was that there was something devil-may-care about them both and it so appealed to her. Yet with John Conrad she felt safe and wonderful, whereas with Matthew Craken it was like standing too close to something that might explode. Yes, she admitted it; she was in love with John Conrad Fleet . . . deeply and for ever. She must not ever let Matthew Craken kiss her again. Knowing how John Conrad felt she really should never even speak to him again.

She sighed and moved slowly along the corridor to the lamplight and her mother's voice in the kitchen.

Outside in the westerly wind Matthew picked up her cape on the end of his cane and brought it up to his nostrils and held it there.

After a time he moved to the low front fence where, leaning on his stick, he used his hand to lift his right leg over the wooden palings, in just the same manner as he had to enter the garden over thirty minutes previously. His legs were so much better now. He was sure his four years in the intense heat of the tropics had mended them as well as anything could.

His left leg was normal; it was his right that troubled him; was always a touch stiff and still ached badly from time to time. He continued to need canes for operations like this. Years of use had made the stick a friend, as if it were another limb; he knew for a fact that some women found his use of it quite alluring, giving him a sort of dash and distinction that other men did not have. Yet he would gladly give up such a distinction to be able to run and dance.

His eyes clouded in the black night as he watched the lighted windows of Caroline's home, remembering how grotesque his legs had looked when first they came out of the splints. But he had never given in and had worked every day, the pain at times approaching torment, and when he found Long Chi, the cleverest of all Penang's bonesetters – as they called men who used unorthodox methods to help weak limbs and broken bones – the Oriental's strange skills had transformed his left leg, bringing it back to strength and health. It was his right that did not respond so well for it had been broken in two places: bad breaks and one a compound fracture. How pure and unadulterated was his hatred for the man who had done this to him. His face contorted with emotion as he lifted his cane and brought it heavily down on a bush, scattering leaves all around in the moonlight.

He moved to his horse, tethered to the low branch of a wattle tree as a supercilious expression settled across his face and he almost smiled. Yes, he had known women who adored him. He had always been able to attract them. They stretched across his memory: a ribbon of lips and eyes, smooth skin and shining hair. He thought briefly of Luella in Tahiti . . . her bewitching chocolate eyes, smooth warm skin and hard dark nipples. Now why the devil would he think of Luella? He decided that perhaps because her looks were the very antithesis of those of the girl who had just left him.

He turned back from his horse to lift his eyes past the surrounding trees to a lighted window in the house behind him just as the form of Caroline Dere passed across it. The disdain living in his eyes almost softened for a moment. He would be thirty-six years old soon; perhaps it was time he settled for just one girl.

Then he threw Caroline's shawl up over his horse's back

60

before carefully mounting, all the while protecting his right leg. He took out his fob watch. It was close to half-past ten.

He drew his scarf more tightly round his neck. The last fight at the Colosseum did not start for an hour. He would just make it in time to place a wager. It was the Brisbane Championship tonight, not that it mattered: he would gamble on whatever the bout was.

The west wind made a sudden dart at his black stallion and lifted the hair of his mane high in the air as Caro's cape fluttered out from the hands that held it. In a swift move Matthew Craken brought the flapping material down and, setting his cane in the holder specially made in the cantle, he took a final look at the Dere house before he spurred away.

Chapter Six

'I'll take evens on the Abo,' shouted a large-bellied man who
lifted a gold sovereign between thick fingers in the swirling
shadows milling and intertwining in the gaslight. There was
no electricity in the Colosseum, though the new way of lighting
the world had found its way to certain parts of Brisbane as early
as a decade before.

At twenty minutes after eleven, while men jostled one
another and yelled and called out, the hoarse voice of Harry
Miller, the so-called manager of this overgrown tin shed,
made itself heard above the hubbub. 'Last wagers for the
Lightfoot-Kelly fight for the Brisbane Championship!'

A few rows of seats extended away from the pit, a twenty-
four-foot-square ring with two sets of ropes around it, all
correct according to the London Prize Ring Rules, but most
of the men stood, preferring to elbow one another and barrack
for their favourite.

Though the Marquess of Queensberry Rules were widely
followed, and gloves were now worn by combatants, so far
this option had not been greeted with much enthusiasm by the
habitués of the Colosseum.

Harry Miller ran a 'straight establishment', as he was often
wont to remind those who attended; and kicking, biting, butting
and gouging had always been ruled illegal. Indeed, he was
proud to remind his patrons that he had already adopted some
of the Queensberry Rules and while there was talk from time
to time of bringing in three-minute rounds, those congregated
at the Colosseum still preferred to see the two boxers fight until
one corner threw in the towel.

In a tiny back room where one window looked out on to
a row of dilapidated houses, Hargy sat, leaning forward, his
elbows on his knees. He was watched by John Conrad, who
stood across from him near the window.

'How are you, pal?'

'Great. I'm goin' to win. I'll knock Kelly out, real easy.' Hargy wore his customary red handkerchief around his waist and was bare-chested, his deep brown skin, covered with oil, gleamed in the gaslight. He grinned showing his perfect white teeth. 'You know what?'

'What?'

'I reckon I'll end up with five or six quid tonight. I'm gettin' some of the wager money.'

'That's a lot of money, Hargy.'

Hargy's grin widened. 'Yeah.' He lifted his hands above his head and clasped them, displaying his shining biceps which protruded rock-hard from his upper arms.

A loud rapping sounded on the closed door and two men came in, carrying buckets and towels into the insufficient light of the single gas lamp. One was Jimmy Heno, an old mate of Hargy and one of the few Aboriginal males still living in Brisbane. The other was Bill Whitley – a sixty-three-year-old butcher from Highgate Hill, a suburb on the south side – who was always in Hargy's corner.

John Conrad watched as Bill slammed the door behind him and, moving the few feet across to slap the fighter on his back, said, 'We'll make some loot tonight, kid. There's a lotta money gone on both of ya.' His big frame leaned over the fighter's wiry one as he ended with, 'Howdya feel, kid?'

Hargy looked up at his second. 'I feel great.'

'Hey kid, that's the spirit, a winnin' statement.'

'Yeah, I know.'

The butcher straightened up and punched the air. 'Now remember, don't get caught on the ropes.'

And now Jimmy spoke for the first time. 'Harg don't need to worry about that. Ya'll keep 'im off with ya straight left, won't ya, Harg?'

'Maybe, maybe,' responded the big man for his fighter, 'but Kelly'll try ta crowd ya. These endurance bouts can go on for a bloody long time and while Kelly'll try ta tire ya out . . .' He turned to Jimmy. 'How heavy is he?'

'Ah, fourteen stone three pounds, they reckon.'

The butcher made a growling sound. 'Yeah, well, he's more'n two stone heavier than ya, Harg, but you have the

63

advantage with your height and your reach, so remember that, kid.'

Hargy nodded at these warnings and looked over at John Conrad, who winked at him and said, 'We'll go fishing tomorrow, pal,' and Hargy nodded in agreement as another banging on the door began. 'Kelly's ready! You ready, Lightfoot?'

'Yeah, we're ready,' called the butcher, turning and picking up his bucket and towel.

As the fighter and his seconds made their way out the door, John Conrad moved from the window and touched Hargy on the arm. 'Good luck, pal. I'll be cheering for you.'

'See you after the fight, Johnny.' He winked. 'We might have a drink.'

John Conrad lifted his fist. 'Sure will.'

The noise outside the door made speaking futile; shouting and sign language were the only forms of communication. The butcher gestured for John Conrad to follow, which he did right along to the apron of the ring, where he found himself a position immediately behind Bill and Jimmy, as Hargy and Kelly bent under the ropes and stood eyeing each other. Tom Kelly was younger than Hargy, stocky, and iron-hard. Hargy's silhouette was more classical, but both were exceptional fighters and the crowd waited expectantly.

John Conrad's nostrils twitched in disapproval of the stale, smoke-filled air, and he gave a quick glance around at his comrades of the night. When Hargy had first started fighting, he had often accompanied him here. Harry Miller's patrons had not altered in the five years he had been absent from Brisbane; they were still, in the main, a seedy lot: many of them out of work, and those in work hoping to double their week's wages. There were a number of wide boys from various pushes, and finally those members of that particular echelon who deemed themselves above the others: the sons of wealthy fathers, here to have a bit of Friday night knockabout fun.

In amongst the shadows coalescing about the roped-in ring, one man's moody eyes settled upon John Conrad as he came in behind Hargy Lightfoot's seconds, and a grim expression hardened on his face as the corner of his mouth lifted in a sneer. He leant more heavily on his cane as he became aware of a dull ache growing in his right leg. He felt a hand on his shoulder as Knobby Clark asked, 'Who're you on, Matt?'

He was slow to answer; when he did he spoke abruptly. 'Kelly,' he replied, his eyes never leaving John Conrad on the far side of the ring.

'Me too,' replied Clark, slipping in beside him. 'He's a good counterpuncher, he is.'

Matthew Craken sniffed the smoke-filled air, then added to it by lighting a cheroot. 'Though the Aborigine can fight right enough. He's tough. I reckoned it'd be mighty close, so in the end I tossed a coin.'

The man on the other side of Matthew Craken leant in. 'Tossed a coin, eh, Matt? It'll be that close, ya reckon?'

The malevolence remained in Matthew's gaze as he kept his eyes on John Conrad and exhaled a long funnel of smoke, 'Yes, cousin, I do.'

A bell was rung and abruptly Harry Miller's voice lifted above the general noise. 'Listen up! Fight's startin'. This is the annual contest for the Brisbane Championship. The title holder, Billy Statham, is unable to defend his title owin' to the fact that he's doin' five years' hard labour.' He turned to the gladiators still eyeing each other in the ring. 'Instead we have the two finest contestants the colony can offer: Tommy Kelly and Hargy Lightfoot!'

General cheering, yelling, hooting and booing descended over the ring as Bill leaned in to Hargy's ear, his lips touching the lobe. 'Remember, kid, he's a square-on, walk-up fighter with trouble in both of them bloody big mitts. Keep movin' and don't let 'im get ya against the ropes.'

Harry Miller struggled to be heard. 'You two ready?'

'Ready,' said Kelly.

'Ready,' said Hargy.

The manager of the Colosseum lifted his large arms in the air, then in his customary way he dropped them and shouted, 'Then let the Brisbane Heavyweight Championship begin!'

Kelly was slow to come out of his corner and Hargy moved in towards him as he rose.

They circled cautiously around each other for a time, before Kelly threw a right and a left to his opponent's head but true to his name Lightfoot, Hargy ducked them. Then Hargy followed up swiftly with a left and right rip to the other man's ribs and stomach. Kelly kept coming and Hargy felt the sting of his punches as he dodged and weaved, though most of the blows landed harmlessly on his shoulders. None of this did any real damage but was the beginning of the way the fight would progress and by the end of the first five minutes both men had landed good punches.

These gladiatorial contests only ended when one man was knocked out or his seconds threw in the towel – a heartless procedure but one that continued to bring crowds to the Colosseum.

John Conrad's eyes had not shifted from his friend in the ring since the fight began and now, in the seventh minute, as Hargy moved quickly inside Kelly's round-arm right the Aborigine's hand went to his temple and for a second or two he appeared disoriented, but he rallied immediately and was soon swapping punches as the big man waded in again.

For a full half-minute the two fearless warriors stood toe to toe and exchanged blows. Both men were obviously tiring and sweat flowed freely across their faces and bodies.

In the twelfth minute Kelly landed a few good right crosses but Hargy always came back with sniping blows to Kelly's midsection. Over and over Hargy landed what he threw.

In the fourteenth minute Kelly was tucking his arms and elbows into his body to protect his midsection and Hargy saw his chance. With his opponent's hands held low he stepped in with a left hook and a right uppercut to the jaw that snapped Kelly's head back. The big man stumbled, lunging and reaching out. As he tumbled forward the top of his head collided with Hargy's eyebrow bringing blood spurting from the cut. But it was all over, Kelly fell panting to the ground and his seconds threw in the towel.

'The winner is Lightfoot! Hargy Lightfoot, Brisbane Champion!' cried out Harry Miller, entering the ring and holding Hargy's right hand in the air in the midst of the screaming hooting din.

The place was in uproar and Bill Whitley bent under the rope to jump forward and lift Hargy in the air in a bear hug. 'You did it, kid! You're the champine!'

Kelly's seconds dragged their fighter under the ropes and

away along the aisle which opened up in the bustling yell-ing crowd.

Hargy turned around and lifted his triumphant hands high in the air to great acclaim from his admirers and shouts of disdain from Kelly supporters. The place was now in general uproar and John Conrad climbed under the ropes to take Hargy from the butcher's grasp.

Hargy's eyes were cloudy and the wound on his eyebrow was still bleeding but his smile was wide with delight. His hand went to his temple and he rubbed the side of his head as he said, 'What did I tell you, Johnny?'

'You were great, pal.' He took Hargy in his arms in the middle of the ring amidst all the noise and smoke and hugged his wet, sweat-covered body tightly. 'You were just great!'

And Hargy whispered in his ear, 'We'll go fishin' tomorra.'

John Conrad was elated for his friend, 'Yes, yes, we will.'

'You're my best friend Johnny.' The fighter was exhilarated as they embraced.

Men were yelling congratulations over the thunderous noise and the rafters of the tin shed resounded with hooting, whis-tling, booing, excitement and uproar.

And then, suddenly, Hargy gave a peculiar sigh and John Conrad felt his body sag. Jimmy Heno saw Hargy's legs buckle and he leaped forward to help John Conrad ease him to the floor. 'He's collapsed!' shouted Jimmy to the encroaching throng. Now people were under the ropes and shouting advice and congregating around.

'Lightfoot's out to it.'

'Give the champine air!' yelled the butcher wildly. 'Get some water!'

John Conrad kneeled down, and took up Hargy's wrist to feel for the pulse, which was not there. He called Hargy's name and felt his face and forehead, but the fighter did not respond. Panic ran through him as he raised his eyes, seeking some sort of help from the sea of faces all pressing in upon him.

In the incessant din he heard Bill's voice in his ear. 'He ain't . . . ? I mean . . . he ain't . . . ?'

John Conrad could not speak. The back of his throat was burning. He looked at the butcher in a dazed way before he closed his eyes and bent his head.

He remained there kneeling, holding Hargy's wrist, as the noise around him grew ever louder and men speculated on many things. Distantly he heard Harry Miller shouting and moving men aside and telling them to 'Bugger off now. Clear out. It's all over.'

It seemed an age before the Colosseum was quiet and only Harry Miller and the butcher and Jimmy remained with him.

'God-awful thing,' Miller said.

John Conrad was mortified. 'I shouldn't have let him fight . . . for God's sake. I should have realised . . . He had a bad headache today.'

The butcher sighed. 'Aw, ya can't blame yerself, kid. But we'll have to take him somewhere.' The words echoed in the expanse of the empty tin shed.

'I'll take him,' John Conrad replied, his eyes on the crimson handkerchief around Hargy's waist. 'I'll take him . . . to his sister's place.'

Jimmy spoke for the first time. 'Yeah, that's best. He'd want that.'

'I'll come with ya,' the butcher said.

Jimmy stood and moved away. 'I'll get the horses.'

To John Conrad the procedure had the unreal quality of a bad dream as they carried Hargy's body through the silence and the hundred weird phantom shadows of the Colosseum, out through the doorway and into the street. Once they had placed him across John Conrad's stallion and strapped him there, Harry Miller put his hand in his pocket and held out seven pound notes. 'He fought well . . . was a darn good bloke. Never gave no trouble. Give this to his sister, Lena.'

John Conrad took the money and nodded. They stood looking impotently at each other for some seconds before Harry sighed, slapped John Conrad solicitously on the shoulder and retreated back into the black interior of the tin shed.

Bill and John Conrad were about to mount up when they heard the clanging sound of horses' hooves coming from round the corner of the Colosseum.

Both men turned to watch two horsemen approach, their silhouettes delineated against the paleness of the moonlight. The animals snorted in the chill cold as the glow in the sky revealed enough of the gothic looks of the man on the leading horse for John Conrad to flinch. He had not seen this face for five years and yet he knew it well. 'What the devil do you want?' he asked.

Matthew Craken's voice was as ice-cold as the air around them. 'Good evening, Fleet.' He spat out the name. 'It seems appropriate to offer condolences, though while I've got nothing against him, your poor departed *friend* cost me five bloody sovereigns tonight! My pal Knobby and I weren't pleased about that.'

'Yeah,' agreed the black form of Knobby. 'Bloody unfair. Kelly's as good a fighter any day. Your friends sure know how to make enemies.'

Matthew Craken turned slightly in his saddle. 'Now now, Knob, old son, that's as may be, but you're right: any friend of Fleet's is an enemy of ours, not that it has any relevance in the current case as the poor fellow's beyond caring.'

John Conrad's jaw tightened, but he held himself in check. 'Yes, my friend's dead. Isn't that enough? It'd be best if you left us alone with him.'

'Bugger off, Craken,' growled the butcher.

Matthew Craken ignored Bill Whitley and leaned forward to rest on his horse's neck. In a strange aberration the moonlight intensified momentarily and highlighted the scar upon his cheek. It gleamed ominously as his sleepy eyes found John Conrad's in the night light. 'Now, Fleet, if your friend was so sick, why the hell was he fighting?' He sat up and slapped his hands together. 'Ah! Of course, I should have realised . . . No doubt it's my fault. Needless to say the whole world should be aware it's because I backed Kelly that poor old Lightfoot here has kicked the bucket. Yes, indeed it's common knowledge that anyone who dies suddenly around *you* has *me* to blame!'

John Conrad held himself back. 'Listen, you bastard, just leave us alone.'

'Now, now, Fleet, your temper's always getting the better of you. Knobby here and I are merely pointing this out to you. We're being forthright . . . so you know how we feel. We're all conscious of the fact that you blame me when people up and depart the earth, but can't you see it's clear that the reaper hangs around *you*? It's you who walk the silent halls of death; you who're the common link, Fleety old boy.'

The oblique references to Emma, as well as Hargy, were too much for John Conrad. He sprang forward, raising his hand to grab Matthew's horse's reins to pull him down. But Matthew was ready. Spurring his horse forward and lifting the reins high in the air, he pushed his good, left knee out to thud into his attacker's ribs. His horse reacted instantly, leaping forward and helping to bring John Conrad heavily to the ground as Matthew continued to charge along the street with Knobby in close pursuit.

Bill Whitley shouted after them, but the riders did not stop, and they were soon gone into the black silence of the night.

As John Conrad rolled over, Bill bent down to him. 'You all right, kid?'

He lay on his back, getting his wind for a moment before answering, 'Yes, I'm all right.'

He became aware of Hargy's dark form stretched over his horse's saddle, his dead hands hanging limply down like a puppet's. He felt sick.

Bill helped him to a sitting position. 'You sure you ain't hurt?'

'Yes.'

He stood up as Bill patted him on the back. 'Craken sure hates you. He's only been back in Brisbane a month or two and already he's causin' mayhem. Bad bugger!'

John Conrad's stomach was aching, the side of his head hurt and he was sore in a number of places. In fact, he had rarely felt worse. He was having trouble holding back the tears of anger, resentment and pain. 'Let's get Hargy over to Lena. She'll be devastated, poor kid.'

And she was. In the early hours of the morning, when they came to the little shack lying between the boot factory and the joiner's shed in Spring Hill and woke Hargy's sister, she was heart-broken. She kept repeating, 'Shouldn'ta fought. His head was hurtin'.'

Bluey, the man she lived with, was a decent enough fellow, and when John Conrad and Bill were leaving them an hour later, he was holding Lena's youngest child in one arm and Lena in the other.

John Conrad tucked the money her brother had won in Lena's hand and attempted a smile of support. 'He was a true champion, and my good friend. I'll be back tomorrow.'

They crossed the river and twenty minutes later, he and Bill left each other in the bitter westerly wind. Clouds were chasing each other across a watery-looking moon as they shook hands at the corner of Vulture and Boundary streets and rode their separate ways.

Chapter Seven

Caroline Dere rolled over and blinked. What had woken her?

Moonlight shone through her window and fell in a shimmer of silver across the blankets to illuminate the small ormolu clock on the mantelshelf. It was just after three in the morning.

Something rattled on the verandah outside. She was the only one who slept at the front of the house and usually noises did not disturb her, but these sounds were very close. She was a little fearful as she raised herself on to her elbows to listen.

Her mother's collie, Litmus, obviously had not heard anything or she would be barking, though it would have to be a very loud noise here at the front to wake the animal sleeping in Elizabeth's room at the back.

A scraping movement sounded; a shadow fell over the window and the moonbeam disappeared. Someone was on the verandah.

Caro sat bolt upright.

The dark form outside moved into the window and tapped gently on it. 'Caro, can you hear me?'

She tried to calm herself, recognising the voice of John Conrad. She slipped out of bed and, dragging the blanket up around her shoulders, moved swiftly across the room. She unlocked the window and as she raised it she felt a gust of cold air. She shivered.

'John Conrad. What's wrong?'

'Everything.'

She could see his face now. He looked weary and his fair hair was dishevelled. He lifted his hand to a dark patch, like a bruise, on his temple. His hand was shaking slightly, and she took it in her own.

'Oh, John Conrad, you're freezing,' she said, and spontaneously she pulled him to her. 'Come . . . come inside, please. You're so cold, you feel like ice.'

He stepped over the sill and into her room. She pulled the window down behind him. He seemed to be dazed as she gently pushed him to sit upon her bed.

'Whatever has happened?'

He turned his eyes up to her as she stood in front of him. His sun-browned skin looked ashen in the moonlight.

'Hargy's dead,' he managed to say at last. 'I didn't know what to do . . . where to go.' And now he was rambling. 'He won his fight, Caro . . . won . . . not three minutes later he was dead . . . in my arms . . . Hargy dead. Didn't know where to go who to tell . . . oh hell, poor Lena.' And now, finally, after hours of tension and holding his emotion back, the tears welled in his eyes and slipped over his lids.

Caro was devastated for him. 'Oh no, my . . . darling. Please don't,' she whispered as she sat beside him and cradled him in her arms.

She was kissing his eyes and the bruise on his forehead and his face, before she even thought about it. He was so cold. Of all the people in the world he had come to her, no one else. Oh, how she loved him.

She felt tears fill her own eyes. 'I'm so sorry. Poor Hargy. He knew how you cared for him. Hargy, of all people, wouldn't want you to be like this. Please . . . please.'

And she continued to whisper sympathetic, gentle, loving words and as she did she caressed him, until at last, she felt him respond and he turned to her in the cold, yet beautiful moonlight.

'Caro, lovely Caro,' he whispered, and his arms came firmly round her as he kissed her deeply on the mouth.

And now he was moving her down, back upon the bed. 'Oh Caro.' She did not restrain him, why would she? She loved him and he needed her. She wanted to restore him, repair his soul . . . take away his grief . . . And so she offered herself unrestrainedly to him as his urgent mouth revived itself upon hers; and his cold body sustained itself upon the warmth of her bare breasts and belly, and his virile need for her fulfilled itself in the generous yielding of all she had to give.

The pain was fleeting: it was as nothing in her overwhelming boundless love for him. He was all she had ever wanted. She felt as if her very spirit expanded to encompass him. Never would she love anyone the way she loved John Conrad Fleet. Her lips roved across the scar upon his shoulder, her breath came in short gasps as she experienced the joy which lay in the knowledge that he had left of himself, inside herself.

And as he groaned she continued greedily to kiss his lips. 'John Conrad, how I love you.'

And he stroked her face and whispered, 'Caro, lovely Caro. I think I love you too.' He was aware of a place in his heart that had been soothed and he spontaneously murmured, 'Thank you.'

Her hair tumbled over him as she moved to lie in his arms. He wound a curl around his finger and caressed the waves that flowed across his chest. They lay together in silence, she did not feel shy: being in his arms was intrinsically right; she was meant to be here.

After a time he rose and brushed his lips across hers. 'I will come to you tomorrow, my lovely Caro.' He stood and picked up his clothes, and she watched him. His body was faultless, the only asymmetry the mark of the scar upon his shoulder, and she vaguely wondered about that. To her eyes, even his movements flowed with a perfect harmony. It was wonderful to watch him dressing in the moonlight.

She found herself looking longingly at his sun-browned body as it disappeared beneath his clothing. He was bronzed to his waist and she thought that soldiers must often expose themselves to sunlight. He bent to the floor and picked up his shirt and as he did, his wallet tumbled from the pocket and a card fell out.

'What's that?' she asked, rolling over on her tummy to look down from the bed.

'My wallet,' he said as he retrieved the items and came back to the bed to her.

'No, I mean the card.'

He smiled in the moonlight. 'It's a holy card given to me by the oddest little child I've ever met. Sometimes I just look at it. It's nothing, really.'

And then she remembered something. 'Is that what you were looking at when I found you on the river bank?'

He nodded and smiled, leaning over to kiss her lingeringly one last time. Then he touched her hair and patted her face

74

before he crossed the room, lifted the window and climbed through to the verandah.

'Tomorrow,' she said.

'Tomorrow,' he replied.

When John Conrad awoke, the sun was mounted high in the sky streaming its brilliant light over all of southern Queensland. He immediately remembered Hargy and the iron tightness returned to his stomach. There had been a closeness with Hargy that was hard to explain and he would miss him more than anyone would know. And then he thought of Caro and her arms around him and her body under his, and he felt calmer. He had made love to one or two girls in Sydney. Perhaps it was the uniform, but soldiers were often sought after by the young women of the city, yet none had made him feel like Caro had. He smiled tenderly at the memory of her. And then finally he thought of Craken. The man had goaded him to make him lose his temper. And he had succeeded. John Conrad wished he had not taken the bait so easily. No doubt his reaction had been exactly what Craken had desired. The tight feeling in his stomach returned and a sick sensation wafted over him just as he heard Bartholomew's voice outside his door.

'You awake, John Conrad? It's after eleven.'

John Conrad sat up. 'Yes, come in, lad.'

Bart entered. 'We've let you sleep because we all heard you come in close to sunrise. Father's been bleating about it.' He noticed the bruise on his brother's forehead. 'What happened? Where were you?'

John Conrad took a long deep breath and, holding his arms around his knees, related the happenings of the night to Bart; all about the fight, and Hargy's headaches and the Brisbane Championship and the horrible culmination. He went on to recount Craken's arrival outside the Colosseum and his provocation, and his own reaction and then how he and Bill had taken Hargy home to Lena. 'So you see, lad, it's no wonder I was late. It was one of the worst nights of my life.'

While Bartholomew listened, his expression had grown ever more serious. 'I'm so sorry. It's rotten about Hargy. He was such a good bloke. Damn good fighter. Guess you feel real bad.'

'I do. If only the bloody championship hadn't meant so much to him.'

'Well, it did. And he won. He wanted to win. You know how he always used to hang around the Colosseum, even when he was just a kid, before he started fighting there.'

John Conrad nodded. 'It's such a bloody waste. I'll miss him.'

They were both silent for a time and Bart sat down on the bed. 'And to think Craken was waiting for you like that. But then I imagine he hates you. It would be natural if he did.'

His older brother nodded. 'Yes, Matthew Craken hates me and that suits me.' Then he moved out of bed. 'Anyway, I'd better get over to Lena. She was in a terrible state, poor kid.'

Bart stood up. 'I'll come with you.'

John Conrad hesitated momentarily, his back to his brother, before he said, 'I'll meet you there, lad. There's something I have to do first. I'll be at Lena's by one o'clock.'

John Conrad gulped down only part of his breakfast, much to Aunt Leigh's disappointment. And her words followed him to the door. '"He that will not when he may, When he would he shall have nay." Heywood.'

Her nephew called, 'I'll have the rest tomorrow,' as he leapt down the stairs and ran across to the stables to saddle his stallion speedily. He thought his aunt was wonderful and so quaint the way she was always quoting proverbs and adages and pieces of poetry. He knew she was very well-educated for a woman. She had been married to his father's brother and she had come to take care of them after their mother had died. They were lucky to have her.

Ten minutes later he was hitching his horse to Caro's front fence. Hurdling the gate he ran up the steps, only to be told by her mother that Caro was next door in the bakery.

Elizabeth Dere's eyes narrowed slightly. She was aware that Caroline had been in the soldier's company at the concert the previous night. 'Is it something special you wish to see my daughter about?'

John Conrad doffed his hat. 'Ah, yes and no, Mrs Dere. I'll just go in to the shop and see her, if I may?'

Elizabeth did not answer. She simply gestured to the side door of the bakery with her hand.

'Don't you approve of me, Mrs Dere?'

Elizabeth was taken aback by this forthrightness, but she collected herself quickly. 'It's not you in particular, John Conrad, it is soldiers in general that perhaps I don't approve of.'

'May I ask why?'

She pursed her lips and then looked him straight in the eye. 'My Caroline is, well, very young . . . impressionable. You're a professional soldier. I have a theory about soldiers, especially good-looking ones, and you, John Conrad are too good-looking for any mother's liking.' She sighed. 'There, I've said it now.'

'Well, you've said something, but not all. You didn't tell me what your theory is.'

He was not letting her get away with anything and she admired him for it. She had known him all his life. He had always been able to impress. 'All right. My theory is that soldiers are not reliable. They can be off to war at any minute. They love girls . . . and leave them.'

John Conrad nodded. 'I understand. Thank you for telling me how you feel, Mrs Dere.' He returned his hat to his head. 'I shall go through to see Caro now.'

Elizabeth watched him as he strode across the yard, opened the bakery door and entered. At the counter, Caro turned towards the sound and a smile of delight mounted her mouth. There were no customers so she went quickly to the front door and faced the 'Closed' sign to the street.

She returned across the stone floor to him. 'John Conrad, I wondered when you'd come.'

He took her in his arms and held her briefly, smelling the freshness of her, then he pushed her to arm's length. 'Caro, I'm sorry about last night.'

A bewildered expression rose in her eyes. 'Why? Why ever would you be sorry?'

'Caro, Caro . . . there are some who'd say I took advantage of you.'

And now she surprised him. 'Did you?'

He looked within himself as his deep blue eyes met her mild brown ones. 'I don't think so.' And now it was his turn to surprise her. 'Perhaps the truth is, you took advantage of me.'

Her smile was wondrous. 'Perhaps I did. It matters not. We

were together and I can never regret it.' She moved in to him again and he opened his arms to receive her.

'I don't regret it either,' he whispered into the tumble of curls on her forehead. And as he held her he told her he must go to Lena and see what was to be done about Hargy. When he moved her tenderly away he said, 'I don't know what Lena will want to do, but I must go and find out. I fear I won't be taking you to the picnic tomorrow after all.'

She gave a wan smile. 'Doesn't matter. I won't go without you.'

'I'll come back here to you the first minute I can. Wait for me.'

She nodded. 'Poor dear Hargy. I liked him so much.' She felt she was going to cry. 'There'll have to be a funeral, I suppose.'

But a conventional funeral there was not.

When John Conrad arrived at Lena's little shack, Bart was already there. They were sitting in rickety chairs on the tiny four-feet-wide verandah.

Lena's big black eyes were bloodshot in her thin face. She was not more than about twenty-three but she looked much older today. She lifted her hand to John Conrad as he came up the wooden stairs. 'Gotta take 'im to the ranges. To the tribe. Must . . . yeah must.'

Her de facto husband, the big man called Bluey – for in the Australian tradition men with red hair are inexplicably dubbed Bluey – sat beside her holding the baby. He touched her limp hair. 'Yeah, it's what Lena wants.'

John Conrad agreed. 'Right, then that's what we'll do.'

Bart asked, 'But how will you get him there?'

Lena shook her head. 'Dunno.'

But John Conrad knew. 'Don't worry. We'll manage. Bart and I'll get a dray from the brewery.'

And so they made their strange pilgrimage to the old tribe in the endless bush in the foothills of the McPherson Range. They went in one of the brewery drays used in the delivery of the casks: John Conrad and Bart up front, and in the back, Lena in a floral dress with a threadbare cape around her small shoulders alongside Bluey, still holding the baby, with Hargy on the floor under blankets and his two little nieces sitting beside him with wide smiles on their faces, for they did not understand the predicament and it was an enchanting dream for them to be riding along the highway.

It was late at night when they arrived on the bush track leading into the encampment. They were greeted with much solemnity and afterwards went to sleep under the stars. The next day there was a special tribal ceremony which John Conrad and Bart could not attend but they waited politely and met the elders afterwards. In a clearing in the middle of the broken-down huts and shanties, a short corroboree took place in their honour as Hargy's friends, which only the male members of the tribe attended. Later, they all took Hargy to a creek and left him in the branches of a tree on the bank.

John Conrad stood looking up at Hargy – native son of this land returned to it under the open sky – and thought this a fitting end for his friend, for he knew how he, like all his race, needed to roam in the free wilds of the bush, and his spirit could do that now.

The two brothers watched Lena's children running with innocent abandon alongside their tiny unrestricted cousins of the bush and it did not surprise them when Lena and Bluey resolved to stay with the tribe for a time. Life with the tribe would be hard, especially for Lena, as Aboriginal women did all the heavy work, but with her European man at her side she was somewhat of a celebrity and that would count for something.

There was a moment beside the creek, in the golden glow of the Queensland twilight, when Lena's eyes met John Conrad's and he believed he saw great sadness there . . . not just over Hargy's death, but countless griefs that only an Aboriginal woman could know. Impetuously he made her a gift of the two horses and the dray. He told her it was from all the Fleet family, deciding he would face his father later. Lena, who had lived in Brisbane for many years, knew the value of the gift and briefly her melancholy lifted from her soul and her eyes lit up. She promised to take care of the horses and use the dray wisely. She stretched out her thin hand to pat John Conrad many times upon the arm. 'You very good man . . . and Hargy's very good friend.'

Bluey thanked them sincerely. The dray and horses would make a difference to their lives. He asked the brothers to come and visit them in Spring Hill any time. 'We'll be back there in a few weeks. Lena and me, well . . . we do like to live in town.'

John Conrad took the big man's proffered hand. 'I might have returned to my unit, but Bart here will stay in touch with you.'

They made their goodbyes not long after sunrise the following morning, and the whole tribe gathered to bid them farewell. In a strangely moving formality, with the long shadows of morning snaking across the land, all the elders, surrounded by the tribal members, stood under tall stately silver gums, and the children sat quietly, for a change, wrapped in skins and blankets, all in lines near a clump of casuarinas that pushed their olive-green branches to the sky.

The two brothers set off to walk the fifteen miles into Beaudesert where they would catch a coach to Brisbane. At the crest of a hill they turned and waved to the survivors of the ancient race standing still, like carven black statues, exuding concord and harmony with the ancient landscape.

'Well, we put Hargy to rest,' Bart said softly.

'We did,' his brother replied.

By the time they reached the little settlement of Beaudesert, it was late morning and they were in good time for the noon coach.

It was on the way to Brisbane on the potholed bumpy road that John Conrad mentioned his feelings for Caro. 'Bart, I've felt for weeks she was special, and well, Friday night after Hargy died, I went to her.'

Bart turned to him. 'Really . . . ? What, to her house?'

'Yes. I reckon I'm in love with her.'

His entire life Bart had been hearing things from John Conrad that surprised him, so he took this latest piece of news sedately enough. 'She in love with you?'

'I'm sure of it.'

When they alighted in Melbourne Street, South Brisbane at half-past five in the afternoon it was dark and cold. And when they arrived at Brewery House, Aunt Leigh stood up from where she had been knitting before the range in the big kitchen. 'Well, here you are at last. I thought you said you two would be home yesterday. Your father and I have been half distracted!'

'Sorry, Aunt Leigh, we were detained.'

'Detained, is it? Well, thank the Lord you're both safe. Did you bury poor Hargy?'

John Conrad gave a wan smile. 'Sort of. They did it in their way, which is definitely as good as any.'

Aunt Leigh nodded sympathetically. 'He was too young for death. Always had a smile for me, he did. The way he'd go awandering for a few weeks and then turn up for work hale and hearty as you like.' She sighed. 'Ah me, "Bright youth passes swiftly as a thought." Theognis.'

As her two nephews walked by her into the hall of the house, she called, 'John Conrad, I almost forgot. This came for you today.' She held out the yellow envelope of a telegraphed message.

He took it and turned it over in his hands. Aunt Leigh passed him a knife and he opened it.

'What is it?' Bartholomew asked from the doorway.

John Conrad looked at his brother and then his aunt. 'They want me back. I'm to report for duty on Wednesday at fifteen hundred.'

Aunt Leigh sat down with a thud upon the chair near the grate. 'Oh no, my heaven. You've been here no time . . . "Like angels' visits short and bright." John Norris.' She looked as if she were about to cry. 'I've hardly seen you.'

He bent over and kissed her forehead. 'I'm sorry.'

Bart was disappointed and he sounded it. 'But that means you'll have to leave on tomorrow night's Sydney train.'

'I'm afraid so,' answered his brother, folding the message and putting it in his pocket.

At that moment Barrington Fleet came in from the brewery. He took off his boots at the door and lifted a tired solemn face, but when he saw his two sons, a brief expression of relief showed. 'So, you two are back. Thought you were supposed to help me today, Bartholomew? I had the Queensland Club order to get out, and you were missing. All your aunt and I knew was you'd gone off somewhere with poor Hargy Lightfoot's body.'

Bart stepped forward. 'Sorry, Father. We took Hargy to his tribe. It's what his sister wanted. We'd intended to be back yesterday, but we were delayed longer than we thought.'

The older man's expression remained grave. 'Bad business. Damn pugilism . . . dangerous and foolish . . . and Hargy so young.' He sat down at the end of the table, and his sister-in-law put a beer in front of him. He drank a mouthful and lifted his eyes to his sons. 'Where's the dray and the two horses I lent you?'

John Conrad coughed, hesitated and then enlightened him. 'I gave them to Lena, Father, Hargy's sister.'

Barrington Fleet choked on his beer and the mug thudded to the table. 'You what?' His eyes were flashing as he stood. His voice rose in a formidable tone. 'What the hell do you mean? Those horses alone are worth thirty pounds. What the devil were you thinking?'

John Conrad moved close to his father. 'Sir, I *gave* them to Hargy's sister from you . . . from all of us . . . the family.'

'You had no right, none at all.'

'Please hear me, Father. Hargy worked for you. We know he went walkabout, but that was in his soul, and he always came back and when he did he worked hard.'

Barrington Fleet could not deny this.

'Lena lives in pretty desperate circumstances and has three little children . . . mere babies. God knows what sort of life's ahead of them. And with Hargy gone, she seemed so . . . so without hope. We have no conception of how she feels.' He looked deeply into his father's eyes. 'I gave them to her because I believed had you been there, in my place, you would have done exactly as I did.'

Like dew in sunshine, the anger dissipated in Barrington Fleet's eyes. He stepped back and sat down. He did not speak for many seconds, then he lifted his face to his son's and nodded his shaggy head. 'You did right, lad, you did right.'

John Conrad took a deep breath. 'Thank you, Father. Your approval's very important to me.'

There was silence for a time, and Barrington Fleet sat eyeing his eldest son while the crackling sounds of the fire seemed loud to their ears.

Bart spoke first. 'John Conrad's been called back from leave. He must depart here tomorrow night.'

Aunt Leigh dabbed her eyes with the edge of her apron. 'It's such a shame and all. "Time lost may never recovered be." Chaucer.'

Her brother-in-law appeared to take the news dispassionately. 'Why have you been called back?'

'I don't know, sir.'

'Ah, that's the army. Reasons are not in its ken.' He lifted his mug in a salute to his eldest son. 'But as I was instrumental in turning you into a soldier, it's not for me to complain when the army takes you back from us.'

John Conrad smiled. It was a warm smile, and he felt quite gratified when his father responded in like fashion.

As Aunt Leigh looked on she cried a little more, for it had been a long, long time since she had seen such a tender moment between her brother-in-law and his eldest son.

John Conrad cleared his throat. 'And now, please excuse me . . . I must go out for a time.' He noticed his aunt's disappointed expression. 'But I'll try not to be too long.'

Barrington Fleet amazed him by saying, 'Be as long as you like, my boy, but try to give your family a little of your time tomorrow, if you're to leave us on the night train.'

His son turned at the door. 'I will do that with pleasure, Father.'

Chapter Eight

Caroline sat on the front verandah of her house wrapped in a woollen cape Aunt Leigh had knitted for her; it served her well against the winter night. She knew she had dropped her best velvet cape near the stairs on Friday when Matthew Craken had kissed her, and when she searched for it the following morning she realised he must have taken it. That upset her and brought the frown to lodge on her smooth forehead where it had sat on and off ever since.

How was she going to retrieve it? She looked up to where the moon sat behind a bank of cloud defining the puffy grey mass with a luminous edge. There had been rain over the weekend but the air was dry now, and crisp.

Her fine forehead puckered even more as she remembered what John Conrad had said to her on Saturday afternoon when he was off to bury Hargy. His very words had been, 'I will come back here to you when I can. Wait for me.' And yet she had heard nothing since. She had even gone over on a pretext to Brewery House today, but Aunt Leigh didn't know where he was. And now it was Monday night and still no word. She knew that John Conrad could take care of himself; it wasn't that she was worried about him, she just badly wanted to see him, that was all.

And now as she toyed with the tassle on the front of her cape she thought about Friday night and his body on hers and the love between them. Her conception of the world had altered. She felt different: freer and more capable, in harmony with life. Her girlish dreams had been replaced by grown-up desires; she knew what she had done and why. She had taken a step into the future, a step beyond, and the only other girl she knew who had taken it too, was Lucy.

Lucy had told her lots of things and one was that if you made love to a man during the week prior to, or the week after, the monthly change in a woman's body, there was no fear of a pregnancy. She said she and George did it that way all the time. Caro smiled to herself, for Friday night had fallen within the week before for her, and there was something magical about having been loved by John Conrad Fleet. It was her secret and she smiled confidentially at last, dispatching the frown from her youthful face.

'Caroline!' Her mother's voice sounded along the verandah, and the girl turned. 'There you are, sitting out here in this winter wind. You'll catch your death of cold. Come on inside this minute. Lucy and George have just come by with Paul. It looks rude if you're out here.'

'I'm all right, Mum, I was just sitting thinking.'

'Thinking about what? What has a nineteen-year-old girl got to think about all alone in the dark at night?'

'Oh Mummy, please. I like to be alone sometimes.'

'Well, your brother and I agree that you've been out here long enough. Come on inside.'

Caro rose reluctantly to her feet and moved spiritlessly along behind her mother. They turned the verandah corner in tandem and as they came to the kitchen door, Elizabeth halted and faced back to her child. 'Caroline, please don't become too enamoured of John Conrad Fleet. He's not for you.'

Hurt flooded up inside the young woman. 'How can you possibly say that?'

'Because I'm your mother and I know.' She took Caro's cold fingers in her own. 'Darling, please. He's a soldier with a soldier's ways.'

Caro removed her hand and tucked it inside her cape, eyeing her mother indignantly, and with a sigh Elizabeth opened the wire fly screen on the kitchen door.

Dragging her feet, Caro followed.

As mother and daughter entered the kitchen, Lucy rose from where she sat and kissed Caro on the cheek. 'Good evenin', love, you look cold.'

'I'm not really.' She gave a weak smile to George. 'Hello, George.'

He half stood and then sat again.

Paul grunted a greeting and looked up from the kitchen table where he sat reading the day's *Brisbane Courier*. 'Hey listen to

85

this,' he said as he folded the newspaper to see it more easily. 'It seems that General Kitchener is still pushing his desert railway across the Sudan. It says here that he'll have the railhead to that Atbara place by the middle of this month. That's where he won the battle in April, isn't it? Sounds like he's got those Dervish blokes on the run.'

George scowled. 'Can't imagine fighting battles in that desert heat.'

Paul laughed. 'Be just like fighting one in Brisbane, hey, mate?'

'Soldiers cannot pick and choose,' interrupted Elizabeth, taking the advantage to push home her beliefs to her daughter. 'If there's a battle they must go; there's no picking and choosing.'

Paul nodded. 'And if men have got to fight, Mum, then they need someone like Kitchener leading them, I reckon.' On that note his head went back into the newspaper while Elizabeth looked meaningfully at Caro.

'Personally,' stated George, looking over Paul's shoulder at the newspaper, 'I'm more interested in that.' He pointed to an article. 'Read that out, Paul.'

Paul obliged. '"The Queensland Federation League was formed yesterday under the Presidency of the Chief Justice, Sir Samuel Griffith. There are fifty-three on the League's Committee, and a Pro-Federation campaign will be run from their headquarters. Premier Byrnes has promised a 'one man one vote' prospect if a referendum for Federation is passed."'

Lucy looked puzzled. 'Federation of what?'

George's eyebrows rose as he leaned back in his chair, looking askance at Lucy. 'Now, my girl, I've told you all about it before. The *Federation* of the colonies. They're proposin' that all of us – Queensland, New South Wales, Victoria, Tasmania, South and Western Australia and even New Zealand – federate as a commonwealth, under one federal government, with a capital city for the whole of the nation. Now do you remember?'

Lucy smiled at him in wonder. 'Oh yes, George, I think I do. Is that a good thing, George?'

George opened his mouth to pontificate but Elizabeth spoke quickly, leaning across the table. 'There are those for and against. Don't you read the newspapers, dear?'

And before poor Lucy could acquit herself Paul interrupted. 'My mate, Kenny Neverson says it'll make us a real nation . . . Drop the apron strings of the old country and be upstanding alongside them as a sister nation for ever. I agree. Must say I like the sound of The Commonwealth of Australia, myself. It has style.'

And now George was determined to have his say. He rapped briefly on the table. 'That's all very well, but I was readin' yesterday, in the *Telegraph*, and I agree, that there are real dangers in federation and that means to our employment – workers, I'm talkin' about. I was at a meetin' at the railway workshops on Saturday and the speaker was sayin' that all sorts of Queensland industries will suffer: timber mills, flour and furniture mills, not to mention other manufacturers like boot and shoe makers and factories for biscuits and jam. Them large southern factories would consume us, they would. The tariff barriers'll go. None of that's any good. There'd be reduced wages, if not worse.'

While Caro's thoughts were mostly elsewhere, this prospect caught her attention. She moved closer to the warmth of the fire as she asked over her shoulder, 'What do you mean, George, *worse*?'

'Well, Caroline, outright closure . . . depression again . . . poverty. We wage-earners have a lot to worry about in Federation, I can assure you of that.'

Caro winked at her brother. 'Seems to me you're the one doing the worrying for all of us, George.'

George sniffed and a slight colour rose to his cheeks. 'It's no joking matter, Caroline. Federation for Queensland's a mistake, I'm tellin' you.'

Elizabeth Dere gave George an inscrutable look. 'Now, George, I thought you and your friends in the labour movement were always espousing how patriotic you are – going on about nationalism all the time, and now you're being anti-federation. That seems to me to be the opposite of what you all say.'

George held his ground. 'Not at all, not at all, Mrs Dere. We oppose *commercial* federation, we don't oppose *political* federation.'

Paul laughed. 'Ah George, old boy, that's double-talk. I reckon you'd make a perfect politician!'

'No matter what,' Caro now added her opinion, 'it's a big step for all the colonies and no doubt we'll hear a lot more bleating about it yet.'

Her mother nodded. 'True and we'll be sick of hearing about it, I'll be bound. There's something comfortable about being a colony of Great Britain. It's always been the mother country to me.' She stood up and moved to put the kettle on the hob. 'And yet, Mr Parkes was all for federating and he was a real statesman, if you ask me. Anyway, there's going to be a referendum, they say.'

George was persisting with his argument. 'There's no doubt we should all be aware—'

At that point there was a loud knocking on the front door. 'I'll go,' said Caro, jumping to her feet and hurrying out.

On the verandah stood the man she had been wanting to see. Her face broke into a welcoming smile. 'You've come at last. I've been . . . worried about you.'

He moved in to her. 'Bart and I stayed longer with Hargy's people than we thought we would. I'm sorry if I worried you.'

'Who is it, Caroline?' called her mother from the kitchen.

'It's me, Mrs Dere, John Conrad.'

'Ooh . . .' the portentous sound rang along the hall.

Caro took her visitor's arm. 'Won't you come in?'

He shook his head. 'I need to speak with you . . . alone. Can you come out with me for a while?'

'Are you coming back, Caroline, or are you remaining at the door?' Elizabeth's insistent voice called.

Caro looked at John Conrad in despair. He stepped past her and walked down the hall to the kitchen. There he was greeted enthusiastically by his cousin Lucy, and less warmly by Elizabeth, George and Paul.

After the formalities, the newcomer directed his words to Elizabeth. 'Mrs Dere, I have something of a personal nature to tell your daughter. I hope you will allow me to take her from you for an hour or two.'

'Why? Where are you going?'

'I have my father's phaeton outside. I'd like to take her over to my place.'

At the word *phaeton* George's eyebrows rose and Paul pursed his lips. Phaetons were only for the wealthy.

'Mother, it's only nine o'clock,' Caro said.

'It's a work day tomorrow,' objected Elizabeth. 'Besides, you should have a chaperone.'

Paul looked John Conrad up and down. His sister was obviously very taken by the soldier, and while he thought John Conrad was too uppity and sure of himself, he wanted her to be happy. 'She's nineteen, Mother, and they're only going over to his place. There's no harm in that.'

Caro bestowed an almost beatific smile upon her brother while her mother frowned, responding stiffly, 'All right, but please remember what I said, it's a work day tomorrow, and I'm sure you'll be mindful of that John Conrad.'

'Yes, Mrs Dere.'

The two said good night and left by the front door. Outside in the cold night air John Conrad helped Caro up into the phaeton and wrapped a blanket around her legs. Then he mounted beside her and took the horses up to a jog as they sped down the street and around the corner.

Her spirits were lifted by the very presence of the man beside her. 'It's wonderful to be with you again,' she laughed. 'Must we go to Brewery House? Can't we be alone?'

He pulled back on the reins to slow the horse. 'I . . . But I told your mother . . .'

She touched him earnestly on the arm. 'Forget my mother. I want to be alone with you.' She almost whispered the next sentence. 'Don't you want to be with me?'

'You know I do.'

'Well then? We could go down by the river where the park ends.'

He hesitated and then pulled the horses to a halt. 'Down by the river?'

'Yes.'

And with the ease of this victory she smiled and leant to kiss his cheek as he turned the horses and vehicle in a circle to head the other way.

When they came to the river's edge and he reined in, she watched the shape of his dark form come across the seat to hold her close. He spoke softly. 'Caro, I'm sorry but I've been summoned back to camp. I must leave on tomorrow night's Sydney train.'

She felt as if the bottom had fallen out of the carriage, so hard did her stomach seem to drop. 'How long will you be gone?'

He took her hands in his and kissed them. 'Please understand. I don't know. I don't even know why I've been recalled. But one thing I do know is that I'll hate to leave you, Caro.'

She was thinking about what her mother would say – not that she would gloat, she wasn't like that. But she would believe that what she had been saying about soldiers and unreliability had now been proved. Caro shivered and John Conrad pulled the blanket up around her.

'I'm so terribly sorry.'

She nodded as she felt the tears spring to her eyes. She must try not to cry.

He took a long breath. 'There's so much to say and yet I don't know how to begin.'

She was looking straight ahead, still fighting her tears, so she just nodded in the darkness.

'Ah, Caro. I suppose the army's like this.'

They said nothing for a time and then she controlled herself enough to ask, 'Do you like the army?'

It was such a simple question and yet he recognised all the implications it carried. He did not want to lie to Caro, he had come to think too much of her for that; but he knew he must couch his reply in terms which would not dismay her. He thought of what his brother had said to him on his first night home on leave . . . 'You've changed.'

Well, time altered people, and they learned to live with situations they once might have denounced. He remembered his first weeks in the barracks, rising before dawn and making the long marches. They had all been worked hard that first year; but then in time he had come almost to welcome the routine. During the marches you looked forward to the hearty breakfast to follow; during the parades you finally admitted you enjoyed appearing smart and reacting instantly. And the comradeship and the hearty laughter of the boys in the mess made you feel part of something pretty special. It all kept a man fit, agile and healthy. He admitted that in the beginning he had only tolerated it, but he had signed away seven years of his life and somewhere during the last five years, a change had occurred and he had started to feel fulfilled and conscientious.

He moved his body on the seat to face round to where she sat staring ahead. 'Caro, I've achieved a lot in the army, and will achieve more. If I keep going as I've started, I might end up . . . who knows, a colonel, even – dare I say it? – a general.'

'So you *do* like the army?' she returned doggedly to her question.

'I do, yes.'

Her voice sounded thin. 'What if a war comes?'

'I suppose I'd have to go. Professional soldiers have no choice. It goes with the occupation.'

She felt his fingers on her chin as he turned her face towards his, meeting her lips with his own, and moving his mouth upon hers in such a way that she felt her body's warm response to his touch. He whispered, 'But, Caro, lovely Caro, I'll come back. I'll always come back . . . to you.'

And she believed him.

His fingers slid down across her body to the small of her back, pulling her into him as she lifted her hands to caress his shoulders and the blanket fell to the phaeton floor.

Caro made a decision. 'Love me again, John Conrad, please love me again.'

He brought his head back a few inches to look in her eyes. 'Caro . . . I don't think we . . . Are you sure?'

She leant forward and caressed his lips with hers. 'Yes, I'm sure. You leave tomorrow.' Her voice was husky with emotion. 'I'll miss you so. I want you to love me again, now.'

'Ah, Caro.' The words caught in his throat as he took her hand and in silence helped her down from the vehicle. Taking up the blanket from the carriage floor and the rug from the seat, he led her through the long grass and underneath the fronds of a large weeping willow.

'Are you cold?' he whispered and she murmured, 'No,' as he eased his body down upon hers.

The feel of her was magical; the taste of her was magical.

Caro blocked the thought of his leaving from her senses. Tonight was all they had: here concealed beneath the trees in this secluded little universe. The cold air tasted almost sweet as it drifted across her tongue, as if it were so refined that it had never been breathed by anyone before. She moved beneath him as he slid between her legs and she opened her eyes to look at him in the vague light.

'I'll always love you,' she whispered as their bodies melded to become one.

Later, she lay in his arms and watched the arc of the moon between the branches over their heads. 'When will you come back?'

And he meant his answer from the depths of his soul. 'As soon as I can.'

Caro, acknowledging that tonight was the last time they would be together, turned to him and eased her body on to his to feel the hardness of him inside the softness of his skin. She wanted it moulded into her memory, a perfect imprint of tonight in the heart of her.

When they left the spot under the weeping willow to return to the phaeton, Caro looked back: she wanted to retain all that had created this night. She suddenly started.

'What is it?' John Conrad whispered in her ear.

She looked again at the trees and their indistinct outline in the murky cloud-filtered light. No, she was mistaken. She thought she had seen movement but all was still. 'Nothing, my love,' she answered as she held his hand more tightly.

They were silent on the drive back; she lay against him, her head on his shoulder.

At her front gate John Conrad brought the horses to a halt. He jumped down and came to her to lift her from the vehicle. She was conscious of his fingers, strong and firm round her waist.

'It's after midnight,' he whispered. 'I'm afraid your mother will be awkward in the morning.'

'Don't worry, my love, for I won't.'

'I hate to leave you, Caro.'

'Come and see me tomorrow, before you catch the train.'

'I will.'

He walked with her through the gate and up the steps to the verandah.

Caro knew in her heart that she wanted a promise from him, but she did not know how to ask for it.

They stood together at the front door, their hands loath to part and themselves reluctant to leave.

He leant down and kissed her lingeringly upon her mouth. It was a lover's kiss.

'I will see you tomorrow, darling,' he whispered, opening her door.

She entered only to turn back and respond, 'You know . . . I've been in love with you since I was twelve years old. You didn't realise it but I was heartbroken when you left here five years ago. I didn't want you to go away. I . . . even came to Central Station to say goodbye, but I missed you. You'd gone.'

'Oh, Caro, no, I didn't know.' He grinned. 'Just goes to prove how you've always had good taste.'

Her hand went up as she stifled a giggle.

And now he became more serious and he lifted his hand to touch her on the mouth, his fingers tarrying on her lips. 'Good night, darling.' He smiled in that glorious way – his lips just slightly parted.

'Until tomorrow,' she answered, wanting so badly for him to stay.

He turned from her and bounded down the wooden steps while she remained watching as he jumped with ease up into the phaeton and drove the horses down the street. She stood looking until he was illuminated by the gaslamp as he passed around the corner, and then she sighed and closed the door behind her.

Across the street a cat padded softly along the stark leafless branch of a poinciana tree. It leapt to a lower limb and slid down the sleek bark of the trunk to land close to the motionless gleaming boots of the man who had stood silently and observed the two lovers part from each other. The cat scuttled away as the boots moved and the man lifted his jade-handled cane to tap it restlessly against his knee.

His right leg was aching tonight, and blast that devil's eyes for being able to leap so easily up into the carriage.

Matthew moved cautiously back to his horse, standing in the shadows of a row of trees growing across two empty allotments. He lifted the velvet cape that lay across his horse's saddle and brought it to his face to smell the aroma of *her*.

Then steadily and with care he mounted and edged his animal forward into the street as he placed his cane in its holder.

Chapter Nine

John Conrad sat reflecting, half-hearing the rhythmic clatter of the swaying train in the background of his thoughts. It was an hour since he had left Brisbane. In his mind's eye he saw Caro's face and the tears she tried unsuccessfully to halt as she lifted her lively eyes to his. He pictured the small red stone brooch she wore on her white lace collar and the little pearl-shaped buttons running down to the waist of her chemise.

She had been in the bakery when he arrived at five o'clock. They had gone for a short walk down the street and round the corner and then returned to her front garden and stood holding hands under the leafless branches of the jacaranda near the verandah. A few minutes later they had gone inside into the front parlour where Elizabeth Dere waited.

John Conrad took her offered hand. 'Goodbye, Mrs Dere. I'm uncertain why I've been recalled from leave. So I don't know how long it will be before I return to Brisbane.' He looked sideways at Caro. 'But I *will* return and I hope you will do me the honour of allowing me to court Caro.'

Elizabeth sniffed. 'It would seem to me that in recent days you've already been doing that.'

John Conrad smiled in his most charming manner and for a moment Elizabeth forgot that she did not approve of him.

'Mrs Dere, you miss nothing. I see why your daughter's so astute. Then perhaps my request should have been to *continue* to court Caro.'

The woman met his eyes. 'Whatever is Caroline's wish.'

Caro beamed at her mother and they took their leave. In the front hall John Conrad pulled Caro tenderly into his arms and kissed her goodbye, lovingly, passionately.

Two big tears welled over her lids as they moved to the front door. She took a deep breath. 'You know I miss my father so much when he's away and now I'll have the two of you to worry about.'

'When are you expecting him home?'

'Mother says by October.'

He smiled. 'That's not long. Then you'll only have me to think about.'

Her last words as he crossed the verandah had been, 'Don't forget me.'

He had jumped down the stairs and turned at the bottom to face her. 'Never.'

He loved Caro, he was sure of that now. He would ask for a long leave next year, and they would get engaged. Heck, no, maybe they should get engaged soon, and get *married* next year.

With that satisfying and comfortable thought in his mind, he leant back in the corner of the train compartment and closed his eyes.

Forty-odd miles behind him, in the city he had just left, the sun had gone down, a golden moon and the southern cross were hidden in the night sky by cloud cover and the west wind was making another foray along the river.

In a small hall in South Brisbane the Women's Auxiliary of the Society for the Prevention of Cruelty was assembled for its monthly meeting. The Auxiliary of the SPC always had a good turn-out and tonight there were sixty-three women present, from all walks of life. In the fourth row Caro sat between her mother and Aunt Leigh. It was half-past eight, business had ended, and the guest speaker was about to address them before supper was served. The winter wind charged at the windows and rattled the loosest of them as Mrs Finney, the president, looked over her glasses at the assembly.

She stood. 'You will all recall that the guest speaker tonight was to have been Mrs Leighton-Brown, who was to lead us through a talk on the subcontinent of India where she lived for a decade. Sadly she has taken ill, but at short notice we found a fine replacement and we're very proud to introduce her. She's well known in Brisbane and is on numerous charity committees, and tonight will speak about her experiences during her two-month visit to that jewel of the Orient in the Colony of the Straits Settlements – the island of

95

Singapore. I will now ask Mrs Josephine Craken to join me on the podium.' Aunt Leigh's intake of breath was audible to both Caro and Elizabeth as a very small slender woman in black silk rose from the front row and glided forward to join the president as she continued speaking. 'As some of you may be aware, Mrs Craken is the widow of Mr Arthur Craken, who was the owner-manager of the well-known Adelaide Street department store, Lewis and Craken.'

Caro looked round to her mother, who gave her one of those expressions which said 'Say nothing' in no uncertain terms.

The small woman placed her notes on the lectern and looked at her audience. She was close to sixty years of age and at her throat was a large jade brooch, and small jade triangles hung from her ear lobes. 'I'm not used to public speaking . . .' Her voice was thin, like the rest of her, '. . . but I was persuaded to come here tonight because I admire the work you do with animals and I was impressed to hear you've extended your good works to include children as well. For that I applaud you all.' She seemed to have gathered some sort of strength from this statement, for her voice became more powerful and energetic as she went on. 'I'm here to tell you of my eight weeks in Singapore. My husband had just passed on and I was visiting my son, who was living there at the time for his health's sake. He's home now and well, I'm delighted to inform you.' Here she gave a smile which only a mother can manufacture when mentioning her one and only son. 'Singapore is Malay for . . . City of the Lion, and what I found there was unlike anything I'd experienced before.'

Caro was in an odd state of suspense. This was Matthew Craken's mother speaking. It was amazing. All during the talk she found herself thinking of John Conrad and then looking sideways at Aunt Leigh, whose lips were pursed and whose arms were stiffly crossed over her rotund body.

Actually Caro had to admit she found Mrs Craken very entertaining and she was intrigued to learn about Singapore and the way in which Sir Stamford Raffles had turned the wholly uninhabited island into a thriving commercial centre.

When Mrs Craken informed them the highest shade temperature for the year 1895 was 93 degrees and the humidity reading was often close to a hundred per cent Caro thought that it must be like living in hot water: Brisbane was bad enough!

The little woman spoke for almost three-quarters of an hour and finished with the statement, 'My very dear son saw me on to the cargo vessel *Francis Drake*, which carried six passengers including myself via Java and the Sunda Islands home to Queensland. And that, ladies, ended my experiences in the City of the Lion.'

The sixty-three listeners acclaimed her. Most of the applause was long. Aunt Leigh's was very brief. Mrs Finney's praise was extreme. 'Wonderful, wonderful . . . you have left us all with a penchant to see the City of the Lion. Please do promise to return to us again.'

Mrs Craken closed her small eyes and bowed her head briefly in gratitude as Mrs Finney broke into a wide smile, showing gum above her longish teeth. 'Thank you. Thank you, dear lady. We'll break now for refreshments, but first the National Anthem.'

They sang praise to their Queen with gusto before they rose as one, to move to the back of the hall where tea, cakes and scones were served. Women fussed about and thanked the speaker, and Elizabeth and Caro came over to Aunt Leigh, who stood aside sipping her tea. After a few minutes Aunt Leigh said in a definite tone, '"Talking and eloquence are not the same . . ." Jonson.'

'Now dear,' replied Elizabeth. 'Don't upset yourself. She had a nice turn of phrase and was quite good in parts.'

'Mm,' replied the other woman as she put her teacup and saucer on a windowsill. 'But I was put out when she mentioned that son of hers . . . and our Emma gone for ever. There's no doubt in my mind she carried his child, the poor darling.' She took out her handkerchief and patted the corner of her eyes. 'Preferred to kill herself than shame us.'

Elizabeth touched her tenderly on the arm. 'Now now, dear, please don't trouble yourself. Thoughts like that are too painful. Come on, it's time we all went home, anyway. We've an early start tomorrow.' And with that she ushered Aunt Leigh and Caro forward to the president, said good night, and moved them out on to the verandah of the hall where they kissed good night and ventured out into rain to their vehicles.

On the ride home, the west wind chased Elizabeth and Caro, and even though they had the top up and a blanket round their knees, by the time they arrived home they were chilled. Caro kept thinking how peculiar it was to have Matthew Craken's mother stand in for the guest speaker on the very day John Conrad had left Brisbane.

Entering through the wide stable door Caro leapt down to light a lamp. As they released the gig from Fancy, their three-year-old mare, Caro said, 'I'll rub Fancy down a little, Mummy. She must be cold too. You go inside.'

'All right, darling. Thank you.'

As her mother moved to the doorway, Caro pointed to a stallion in one of the stalls. 'Look, there's a strange horse here. One of Paul's friends must be visiting.'

'Probably, darling, I'll see you inside.' And with that her mother disappeared along under the overhang from the stable roof and ran to the front steps of the house.

When Caro entered her home some minutes later she stopped at the hall stand to take off her damp cloak and could hear her mother's voice in the parlour. Suddenly Paul appeared in the hall. 'Sis, there's someone here to see you. He's been waiting an hour since.'

Without thinking, Caro came forward in strange eerie expectation. Had John Conrad somehow returned to Brisbane? She hurried to the parlour door and as she looked in she drew in her breath in surprise.

Matthew stood up from where he had been sitting. He was dressed in a suit of black with a brilliant red cravat at his throat and his scarred olive skin, dark eyes and imposing bearing made him somehow startling, almost overwhelming. With his suit he wore black riding boots polished to a brilliant shine, which on another could have looked incongruous, but on him, did not at all. Caro noticed the slender ebony cane which he passed from his right hand to his left before he took Caro's velvet cape from over his left arm and extended it to her in his long fingers.

'This, I believe is yours. I've spent a most gratifying time in your brother's company awaiting your homecoming and now I've met your charming mother.' Fleetingly Caro thought she saw a mocking expression in his eyes, belying the agreeable smile on his face as he stepped forward and handed over her cape.

'Thank you,' Caro managed to say.

Elizabeth looked up from where she sat. She had been astounded to find the infamous Matthew Craken in her parlour and had looked daggers at her son for letting the man in, but what was done was done, and now she would try to move him out of her house as quickly as possible. Her voice sounded strained. 'Well, Caro, aren't you lucky *Mr Craken* found your cape after the concert was over? Did you know you'd left it behind?'

'Concert?' Caro said.

'The St Paul's concert last Friday night,' Matthew replied.

Elizabeth stood up and moved towards the door in the hopes that her visitor would take the direction. 'Apparently *Mr Craken* was one of the organisers and he found it after you'd gone.' She turned to him. 'Now thank you, Mr Craken, but I feel we've delayed you long enough.'

Paul, who still stood by the door, asked, 'How is it you knew it was my sister's cape?'

His mother looked sharply at him; what was wrong with Paul? Didn't he realise she did not want this man in her house. If Leigh ever found out she would not know what to do.

And Caro stood as if mesmerised as Matthew replied, 'Ah . . .' and smiled a smile that worried Caro greatly. She believed this man who acted in such cavalier fashion might tell her brother anything.

'Mr Dere, your sister was the most beautiful girl in the room. She caught my attention immediately, and the fact that she was on the arm of an *old enemy* of mine made her even more a cynosure for me.' The way he said the words 'old enemy' brought a shiver to Caro's frame. Then he gazed directly into Caro's eyes. 'It was a cold night; I thought it odd that you would forget your warm cape. You must have felt quite hot for one reason . . . or another.'

Caro did not answer. She hoped she did not look as flushed as she felt.

Much to Elizabeth's chagrin Paul asked another question. 'Did you feel hot, Caroline?'

As Caro opened her mouth to reply, over her mother's

shoulder Matthew winked at her. Caro managed to say, 'Yes . . . I must have,' as she met Matthew's insolent grin.

And now Matthew became the perfect gentleman. He stepped forward and bowed his head momentarily to Elizabeth. 'Such foul weather we've been having tonight, and I expected you to be home here warm and comfortable when I called, but no, your son informed me you were off at an SPC meeting. I've nothing but admiration for you, Mrs Dere. There's such cruelty and neglect applied to poor vulnerable animals who cannot speak for themselves . . . have no way of fighting back. And what you and your admirable society do deserves great respect. And to think you take your duty so seriously that you'd go out in a night like this to continue to perform charitable deeds. Well . . . it's remarkable.'

Elizabeth eyed him speculatively. 'Why, thank you.' And then she could not help but add, 'We now try to help neglected children as well.'

'Do you?' Matthew answered, shaking his head as if he had never heard of such benevolence before. 'You all must have such genuine and loving hearts. I'm in awe of you.'

Elizabeth acknowledged this exceptional praise with a nod. 'Your mother was our guest speaker tonight. She spoke about her time in Singapore.'

Caro thought she was the only one who noticed the momentary surprise in Matthew's eyes which he covered immediately with a wide smile. 'Ah yes, that's right, dear Mama. She does seem to enjoy elucidating upon the City of the Lion. She found the east converse to Brisbane. It had a strange effect on her.' And now he smiled warmly into Elizabeth's eyes. 'You've been more than gracious to a stranger, and have made me most welcome. I've been delighted to meet you, and your family. I've done what I came here for, to deliver Miss Dere her missing robe.' He bowed again from the neck in a formal, cordial manner. 'So do excuse me, please, dear lady.'

Caro could hardly believe it when Matthew extended his hand and her mother actually took it. Elizabeth hesitated and then, withdrawing her fingers from his grasp, said, 'I knew your father a long, long time ago, you know.'

Matthew's eyebrows rose. 'Did you really? But surely you are too young to have been a contemporary of his?'

And now Elizabeth almost smiled. 'Oh, he was a little older than I.'

'I'm sure he was,' observed Matthew, who proceeded on: '*Poor* old father. Typhoid fever removed him to the next world while I was away in the Orient.'

'Yes, I'm sorry.'

'Don't be. He was a sick man for years before he caught it. I deem it was for the best.' He smiled. 'And now sadly I must leave you.'

He shook hands with Paul, turned to Caro and addressed her at last. 'Good night, Miss Dere.'

No one else could see his face, and as Caro replied, 'Good night and . . . thank you,' he winked again at her before he turned back to her mother and brother and crossed the room to the front hall.

Paul accompanied him out on to the verandah and Caro stood silently listening to their voices as the two men passed towards the stable. She heard Matthew say, 'Good night, cousin,' and her brother answer before her mother's voice sounded behind her. 'My goodness. I was quite put out with your brother when I found Matthew Craken here. I was under the impression from Aunt Leigh that he was a barbarian.' She was silent for a second or two. 'But he acted like a perfect gentleman. So different from most Queensland men.'

Caro turned round and looked straight into her mother's face. It was astonishing that today John Conrad had left, she had listened to a talk by Mrs Craken and then had found Matthew Craken sitting in the parlour of her own home. She sighed. It was all very peculiar and she was missing John Conrad dreadfully already.

Elizabeth frowned thoughtfully. 'You know, he reminds me of Lord Byron, all moody and poetic. Yet we know how heartless he must have been to poor Emma. I don't know what to think.'

'I don't know either,' Caro said, and walked past her down the hall.

Small craft bobbed up and down over the white caps on the water of Sydney Harbour. The wind churning the harbour swirled on its way over Circular Quay along the length of Pitt Street to Oxford Street, chilling the pedestrians all the way to Paddington Hill and the obdurate stone walls of the Victoria Barracks, standing sentry to the south-eastern side of the city since 1845. The barracks had seen a number of British regiments come and go, and now was home to John Conrad and a nerve-centre of the armed forces of New South Wales.

The wind flurried lifting the tail of Major Henry Driver's greatcoat as he strode through the great arched entry by the smart sentries who stood guard on either side near two large leafless acacia trees. He crossed the cricket pitch and parade ground, and passed along the colonnaded verandah of the main building and round the corner to the door leading into his staff office. There he found Lieutenant John Conrad Fleet.

'Fleet, good, thanks for coming. Damn cold out there.'

John Conrad stood up and saluted. 'Good afternoon, sir. I was asked to come here on my arrival.'

The major nodded and moved round his desk to be seated. 'That's right. Sit down.'

John Conrad sat.

'Sorry to get you back from leave, but Colonel Ayres had been asking for you.' Major Driver took a quick look at the pile of papers in front of him and then lifted his face to his visitor. 'He wants you to accompany him on a trip to London . . . on his personal staff. You must have a made an impression on him, Fleet.'

John Conrad was surprised. 'London, sir? When?'

'I believe in four or five weeks. That's why we had to recall you. He wants to know you better, and for you to know exactly what's required of you before you go. He's asked that you report to his office tomorrow morning at O eight hundred sharp.'

'Yes, sir.'

Henry Driver was respected through the ranks. He was a firm but fair officer, and he leant back in his chair as he surveyed the young man in front of him. 'You've learnt a lot since you came here, Fleet, and MacPhee did a good job with you over at Hyde Park Barracks before that. This sort of assignment usually goes to a captain, so I wouldn't be surprised if you get a promotion before the end of the year.'

John Conrad grinned. 'Do you know anything about what we'll be doing, sir?'

'I know the colonel is taking his aide, Major Neil Smith, and two or three others aside from yourself. He's been chosen to lead the delegation by General Holmes himself. I'm sure he'll tell you all you need to know.' He held out his hand and John Conrad took it.

'You can help me this afternoon, if you like.'

'Yes of course, sir.'

'I need a list of every telephone number in the barracks. Seems like there was one but it can't be found and my master sergeant is on sick leave.'

So for the next couple of hours John Conrad walked every building in Victoria Barracks, including the military prison, checking all telephone numbers, positions and departments. By evening he had earned the major's gratitude.

But by the time John Conrad left Henry Driver and made his way back across the open parade ground he was having mixed feelings. He was excited to be chosen for this honour to accompany the colonel, and going overseas was something he had always dreamed about; but what niggled at his stomach and took the edge off his satisfaction was how he felt about Caro. London was a long way from her. How long would he be there? After all, he was a professional soldier and a posting was a posting. If only he could see her one more time before he went away . . .

He hurried up the hill in the driving wind to the officers' quarters with thoughts of Caro's smooth skin and warm brown eyes swirling in his head. Yes, he had fallen in love with that girl. But for now he must concentrate on what the army wanted of him even though he knew Caro was a certainty in his future. Tomorrow, when he learned more about the coming trip, he must write to her and tell her about it. She would not like it, he was sure, but she would wait. He knew Caro was that sort of girl.

He spent the night in the fire-warmed mess with his friend Donald Greve and Major Driver, and retired early, dreamed of

Caro and presented himself outside the colonel's office door at one minute to eight.

Colonel Ayres looked up as the young lieutenant was ushered in. 'Fleet. Good morning.'

John Conrad smiled and saluted.

The colonel had a wide moustache and a kindly smile, which lit up his face now as he introduced his aide, Major Neil Smith, and gestured for John Conrad to follow him into his innner sanctum, a large office decorated in warm dark leather.

He held out his hand, which John Conrad took as he said, 'Well, Fleet, I suppose Major Driver mentioned to you that I'm off on a trip to London?'

'Yes, sir.'

'Sit down.'

John Conrad sat and the colonel walked round and took his seat behind the desk. Above him on the wall a likeness of Queen Victoria looked benevolently down. 'You seem a good man, Fleet. I first noticed you during the week of the conference at Government House six months ago. You were efficient and effective and I like that. I've watched you since; Major Driver speaks highly of you and you're young and seem willing to learn. I want you to continue your work as a member of my personal staff.'

'I'll be honoured to try, sir.'

'Don't try, lad, just do it.'

'Yes, sir.'

'That's it. Major Smith will introduce you to our other travelling companions in due course. And, now, here's what's in store. We're following up on meetings held at the Colonial Conference in London last year. We'll sail in a month or so on HMS *Invincible* to Melbourne where we'll join HMS *Cornwall* for the rest of the journey through the Suez on to Marseilles. There we'll disembark and cross France to England. If federation becomes a *fait accompli*, new decisions on the military will need to be made here. I'm meeting with the Colonial Defence Committee in London and will be presenting the New South Wales point of view. You'll be accompanying me and there'll be reports and studies to be made. In the meantime, work with Driver; he's a good soldier and knows my ways.'

That night John Conrad wrote to Caro. It was a long letter in which he assured her of many things. He told her of his forthcoming journey and what an honour it was to be chosen. 'Why, our colonel says we might even stop in the Sudan and Egypt on the voyage. That's where Major General Kitchener leads the Egyptian army. He's the most famous soldier in the world and has built a railway stretching hundreds of miles across the desert sands!' In the last paragraph he poured out his feelings:

> For I will return to you, my own darling Caro, and we will have a wonderful life together. I believe that now. This posting overseas has made me think and I know now how precious you are to me. I will always love you and I'll write to you whenever I can.
>
> Wait for me, Caro.
>
> Yours lovingly, John Conrad

It was nine o'clock the same night, Thursday, 14 July, while John Conrad sat penning his love letter to her, that Caro, some five hundred miles to the north in Brisbane, stood looking into her bedroom mirror and brushing her curls that lay in shining layers across her slender shoulders.

John Conrad had only been gone for two days and she felt bereft. He filled her thoughts during the day and her dreams at night. He had promised to come back to her and she knew in her heart he did not make promises lightly. He was too strong-minded and moral for that . . . but the two days had seemed like an eternity, what if he could not come home for another year?

Her mother was out at the choral society and Paul had gone to see a friend. Lucy had asked her to come over and spend the evening playing cards but Caro had declined. From Monday to Friday she and her mother took it in turns to rise at half-past four and help Paul to bake, and tomorrow was her early start. She had best make a cup of tea and go to bed.

In the kitchen Caro put the kettle on the hob and was bending to sit at the smooth wooden table when a shadow fell across the open top of the stable door which led from the kitchen to the verandah.

'Is that you, Paul?' she asked.

'No.'

She knew that voice now.

She watched as he pushed open the half-door and stood leaning on another cane – silkwood with a gold handle this time. He always gave her the feeling of being observed rather than merely looked at. 'Well, good evening, Caro old girl. How are you?'

Caro found her voice. 'Please . . . don't call me Caro, and what are you doing here?'

He smiled and Caro experienced that weird exciting discomfort she felt with him.

'Now one thing at a time. Don't call you Caro? Why would that be? Does someone else call you Caro?'

'Mr Craken, what are you doing here?'

He came further into the room. 'Who is *Mr Craken*? Please call me Matthew. I'm here because you are here. I like to be where you are. I saw your mother and your brother depart . . . and, well, I waited. I'm good at that – waiting. I learned infinite patience from an old friend of mine in Penang.' He eyed her for a time and the only sound in the room was from the kettle on the hob. Then he moved over and leaned against the wall near the meat safe which hung from the roof on a long metal chain. 'Talking of learning, I learned something from my friend Knobby Clark today that pleased me. No . . . in fact, elated me – brought me almost to a state of euphoria.'

Caro did not ask what that was, but he was intent on enlightening her. 'My old acquaintance, well, let's call him what he is, *my enemy* – a certain soldier of the realm – has left Brisbane. The abnormality is I thought I saw this soldier kissing you, Caro, only a few nights ago; Monday to be exact, right outside your front door.'

'What? Where were you?'

'I was *waiting* for you, Caro. Could I hazard a guess at where you'd been?'

Anger flickered in Caro's eyes. 'How dare you? It's no business of yours where I was.'

He moved over to a chair and sat down, placing his cane on the table top. 'Ah, but I take an interest in what you do. I'd like to make it my business.'

'I didn't ask you to sit down.'

He met her eyes. 'True, you did not.'

'Then please get up and leave.' She gestured to the door.

'Caro, Caro, why do you resist me when I find you so alluring?'

It was out of her mouth before she could help herself: 'As alluring as you found Emma Fleet?'

He did not speak for many seconds. He sat there staring straight into her eyes until she blinked and looked away. Then he gazed slowly around the room before he finally answered, 'Ah now, Emma Fleet. So . . . which particular tale about poor Em and me is it you know? For there are numerous.'

'I know the only one that matters.'

He nodded his head thoughtfully and leant back, closing his eyes. 'And enlighten me; which one is that?'

Caro did not want to be drawn into this, but against her better judgement found herself answering, 'I know that poor Emma was with your child . . . that you denied her and she killed herself rather than shame her family.'

He opened his eyes and met Caro's with a succession of expressions, the final one being resignation. 'Not quite the right story, old girl, but it'll do for tonight. Let's forget about Em.'

Caro brought her hand up sharply to point her forefinger straight at him. 'How can you dismiss Emma like that? As if she didn't matter. I think you're disgusting.'

He did not look at her as his long fingers went out and touched the cane lying on the table. Caro started and, dropping her hand, moved back a pace from him, fearing he might strike her with the stick, but he merely caressed the gold handle while he exhaled, and finally spoke. 'All right, Caro. I'll elucidate here tonight upon something which I've told no other.'

He spoke quietly, but there was a note of exasperation in his tone, as if he disliked having to explain himself to anyone. 'Emma was carrying my child. Correct. She killed herself. Correct. I denied her. Incorrect. She killed herself rather than shame her family. Incorrect. Now as the first two statements were true, I will deal only with the others.' He stopped fingering the handle of his cane and brought his gaze up to Caro.

The kettle was boiling now and singing so loudly that she moved to it and took it off the range. When she turned round he was still looking up at her. He motioned to a chair. 'Now why don't you sit down?'

'I prefer to stand.'

He accepted this calmly and took up his explanation. 'Firstly, I told Em that if she could prove to me she was with child I'd marry her. Secondly, she did not kill herself rather than shame her family, she took the poison rather than shame herself.'

'What do you mean?'

He looked past Caro, his gaze fixed on seeming infinity, a tense, strained edge to his voice.

'I informed Emma the only way I would believe her was when I saw her belly expanding, and if that occurred, then, at that time I would indeed marry her.' He lifted his hand to draw his fingers across the scar on his cheek which gleamed in the gas light. 'Perhaps she did not believe me. Emma liked to laugh, to enjoy the thrills of life, to make love with me, but she was very aware of her place in society and terrified of what mere mortals thought. And while I did not love her, I certainly liked her, and if she had proved her pregnant state as I asked her to do, then, you see, I *would* have married her. Em just didn't have the strength of character to grow large before she caught a husband.'

He took a deep breath and hesitated for a few seconds while his fingers tapped in drumming movement on the table top. Caro was extremely uncomfortable. How could it be that she was standing in her own kitchen listening to Matthew Craken explain his actions in relation to Emma Fleet?

His voice rose. 'A year before, a girl by name of Sarah had acquainted me of the very same information, that she carried my child. She demanded that I marry her. You're probably aware I have an inheritance – my departed parent was a wealthy fellow – and I actually became betrothed to her. But something rankled in the back of my mind and I decided to let some time pass to see if she expanded. Six months passed and she was still one of the slenderest women in Brisbane. I broke off the engagement.' He lifted his hands palm upwards in the air, his expression sombre, intent, even sad. 'So you see, I believed the same of Em. I was wrong . . . and she is dead. I do not dismiss her as you charged me earlier, for she does matter. I was . . . not happy . . . when I knew she was dead. I have learned many things since that night; imponderables. Had I known them then, Emma Fleet would be alive today, as my wife.'

Caro did not speak. The completely astounding thing was that she believed him. She stood looking at him as his serious expression melted away to reveal the supercilious Matthew Craken she had come to know.

In the silence he winked at her and she felt relieved. She was more comfortable with his arrogance.

Again he drummed his fingers on the table. 'But then I would have been related to the bastard soldier as my brother-in-law, and that would never have done. Tell me, why on earth would you desire him when you can have me?'

Caro's eyes widened. 'How dare you say that? Matthew Craken, you are the . . . the . . . most profane, immoral man I've ever met. It'd be best if you left immediately.'

To her surprise he nodded and stood up. 'You might be right about that.' He came a step closer to her. 'At last you've finally uttered my name, even if in anger and in its entirety. One of these days you'll actually manage to simply call me, Matthew.'

'Don't be so sure,' she retorted.

'I'm never sure of that which I don't know to be true,' he replied enigmatically.

He spun round on his good leg, picked up his cane and her gaze followed him as he moved over to the kitchen door where he halted and, turning back, tapped his cane against his knee-high boot. And then he amazed her. 'Caro, you are one of the most spirited girls I've ever met . . . and I've met a lot. Remember this will you? If ever you want to get married, come and see me first.'

Caro had actually opened her mouth to reply, 'Never,' but something halted her, and, meeting his penetrating stare with her own uncompromising one she said deliberately, 'Good night.'

'Until we meet again, Caro,' he answered, and pushing open the half-door, swung nimbly across the verandah on his cane and departed down the side steps.

She stood silently for a few moments, staring at the space where he had been. Again he had appeared out of nowhere, and managed to irritate and trouble her. He was everything she disliked. He was reckless, intemperate, outrageous and probably even amoral. He was an enigma.

What on earth would John Conrad think if he knew?

She shook her head to herself, walked over and locked the two halves of the kitchen Dutch door before returning, deep in thought, to the kettle on the range.

Chapter Ten

A week later Caro received John Conrad's letter. She read it multiple times each day, poring over it and concentrating on every word. A second letter arrived seven days after the first, telling her of his expected departure date to Melbourne, the first stage of his journey.

It was two weeks after the second letter had arrived, Thursday, 11 August, around three in the afternoon, when Caro sat warming herself in the winter sun; at her feet the collie, Litmus, watched the world through her alert brown eyes. They sat near the clump of fiddlewood trees her father had planted when she was a little girl and which now towered above them. In her hand was John Conrad's first letter and she was reading the end of it aloud to herself: '"This posting overseas has made me think and I know now how precious you are to me. I will always love you and I'll write to you whenever I can. Wait for me, Caro. Yours lovingly, John Conrad."'

She trembled, even though she was not cold.

She thought of the first time she really knew she loved him: when he had gone away to be a soldier after poor Em's funeral. She lifted the letter to her lips and kissed the handwriting as she closed her eyes and imagined him. He was the handsomest man in the whole of Australia, she was certain.

'Hello, Sis.'

She opened her eyes and hurriedly folded the letter as Litmus sat up and greeted Paul.

'You weren't *kissing* that, were you?' her brother asked, bending down to stroke Litmus.

'Of course not.'

'Looked mighty like it to me.'

She ignored this. 'What do you want, Paul?'

'Well, your tea break must be almost over.' He smiled pleadingly. 'Are you coming back to the shop? Fact is, I've got to get in supplies and Mum's going out and she wants to take Litmus. Do you mind coming back to look after the shop right now?'

She stood up. 'All right. I'm coming.'

'Come on, Litmus,' Paul called as the collie jumped up and followed him. Over his shoulder he shouted, 'Thanks, Caroline.'

A minute later she passed through the side door of the shop into a wooden room with two oak counter tops and a window on to the street, with a painted glass entry door beside it. Behind was the small stone-walled bakehouse. Dere's Family Bakery sold bread and buns, scones, pies and cakes. The shop opened at eight o'clock in the morning and closed at four in the afternoon. They traded well enough for Paul to pay Caro a reasonable wage and to put some money aside for himself. Elizabeth helped out of the goodness of a mother's heart.

It was quiet in the shop in the afternoons, and Caro sat on the tall stool behind the counter to knit and pass the time looking through the window at the occasional passing horse, dray, dog cart and sulky. It was so warm and peaceful in the shop with the wonderful aroma of freshly baked food floating in the air that Caro became quite drowsy. She had slept fitfully last night. Slowly her eyes glazed over and her head bent as the needles slipped from her hand.

Suddenly her head dropped sharply forward and she shook herself and woke up. 'Oh no!' she said as she focused on the man who stood leaning in the doorway.

He lifted his cane in greeting. She noticed this one was of red-wood. 'Haven't seen you up close for a few weeks, Caro. I was at the National Association's exhibition this morning. By the way, some of the exhibits there I'm sure you'd enjoy, there's a miniature federal city of the year two thousand which is most intriguing. Makes one consider what life might be like then, a hundred and two years from now! And there's a side-show you really should see, a lady boxer who fights a bear . . . quite a laugh that one. Sure you wouldn't like to close the shop right now and go there with me?'

Caro's expression was uncompromising. 'No, thanks.'

He shrugged his shoulders. 'Anyway, there I was watching the grand parade when suddenly I thought of you, so I left

112

Knobby Clark and came posthaste here. Thought I'd drop by and offer my condolences.'

She frowned and stood up. 'What does that mean?'

'Whatever you like.'

'Stop talking in riddles. What are you doing here, anyway?'

'Why do you always ask me that? The reason I seek your company, Caro, is to look at you. Now tell me you've missed me.'

'Why would I, when I haven't?'

He came forward into the shop and smiled at her. As always his expression carried a sinister overlay to her. Caro was pleased the counter was between them.

'You're a spirited girl . . . or should I again say *woman*? Are you a woman now, Caro?'

She did not like the turn this conversation was taking. If only a customer would arrive; but no one answered her wish. 'I . . . don't know what you mean.'

He nodded. 'Perhaps you don't.' He came forward to lean on the counter. His eyes were strangely cold. 'And then again perhaps you do.'

He took a small pad out of his inside pocket and, resting his cane, lifted a lead pencil from his top pocket and began to draw her.

'What are you doing?'

'I thought it'd be obvious.'

She put her hand up in front of her face. 'Don't.'

He continued. 'Come on, Caro, put your hand down. Be grown up.'

This infuriated her, but she dropped her arm. 'Why are you like this?'

'I don't know what you mean. I'm being perfectly amenable, sketching a lovely face.'

She looked away and, noticing her knitting had fallen on the floor, bent to retrieve it. When she stood up he had come round to her side of the counter top. Her pulse quickened as he put down his sketching pad.

'You shouldn't be around here. Customers aren't allowed—'

'I'm not a customer, Caro.'

'Why do you do this to me?'

'What?'

113

'Make me feel uncomfortable all the time.'

He seemed to be laughing at her, but no sound came from his mouth.

'Please . . . you shouldn't be around here. What if my mother or my brother come in?'

'What if they do?'

She was getting nowhere, and then a thought came to her. She locked eyes with him. 'This really isn't right. If a customer comes in, it looks . . . well, it looks improper. You should not be around this side of the counter. I'd be grateful if you would go back around the other side, please . . . Matthew.'

He smiled widely and she noticed again the chip from his missing eyetooth.

'There you are . . . at last! You've used my Christian name and it didn't hurt a bit, and in a very pretty speech. How could I not relent to such sweet imploration?' Slowly he moved back to the customer side of the counter.

'Thank you,' she said.

'Thank you . . . who?' he asked.

And to keep him where he was, she placated him. 'Thank you, *Matthew*.'

At that moment a customer did appear: Mrs Manders, the wife of one of the leading journalists on the *Brisbane Evening Observer*. She bought two white loaves and looked Matthew up and down as he leaned on the counter and responded in exactly the same way to her. Caroline thought it could have been quite amusing if only Matthew were not such a threat.

As she placed the bread in her basket Mrs Manders asked, 'So your dear mother is speaking at the meeting tonight?'

Caro nodded. 'That's right.'

Mrs Manders went on, 'Yes, it's a most important vote and we must get as many members there as we can. I think we've got the message out to most of the auxiliary.'

Caro gave a strained smile. 'Thank you, Mrs Manders.'

The woman shot Matthew another look before she turned back to Caro. 'See you tonight then.'

'Yes, thank you.'

As she passed through the door Matthew looked after her and then turned with equanimity to Caro and, placing his hands palm down on the counter, asked in a droll manner,

'Now, what meeting is that you'll be attending tonight, my dear Caro?'

Caro looked at the clock on the wall. It was ten minutes to four. She decided to close early. 'It's closing time. So you'll have to go now.' She walked round the counter to go to the door. As she passed him he grabbed her arm and she turned to him, alarm in her eyes. He asked again, 'What meeting are you going to tonight?'

'It's none of your business. But if you must know, the SPC meeting.'

He still held her and pulling her closer, stared into her eyes. 'Ah again, the wonderful women of the Auxiliary for the Prevention of Cruelty. You should practise what you preach, Caro.'

'I don't know what that means. And let go my arm.'

'It means you should be kind to animals and children.' With his usual impudent style he winked at her. 'Think of me as one or the other.'

'Yes, the animals.'

His grip tightened on her as he brought her even closer to him. She resisted but his arms were powerfully strong. He leaned in as if to kiss her but she pulled her head back from him. Abruptly he let her go. She thudded forcefully back against the counter and would have fallen to the floor except being young and agile, she rallied and kept her balance.

She flung her arm up and pointed to the door. 'Get out.'

'Certainly, appealing *woman*. Your wish is granted. I depart.'

She stood still, her heart racing as he made his way to the door to pause and impudently turn the 'Closed' sign around to face the street before he passed out on to the dirt footpath.

She watched as he carefully mounted his stallion and then turned in the saddle to salute ceremoniously to the window through which she gazed, before he rode away.

With deliberate steps she walked over and bolted the door.

An hour passed while she thoroughly cleaned the shop and as she was locking the side door her mother drove the gig into the front yard. 'There you are, darling,' she called as Litmus barked a greeting. 'We must have an early meal and then get on our way to the hall. I've worked out my speech. It'll be a big night.'

Caro came slowly forward as her mother climbed down from the vehicle. The young woman's face was troubled. 'Mother, do you mind if I don't come tonight? I didn't—'

'But you must come,' Elizabeth broke in. 'It's very important. I'll need your vote, darling. You know that.'

Caro sighed. 'Yes, yes, of course you will. Don't worry, I'll come.'

Her mother smiled. 'Good. Now we must rub down Fancy and then get inside for tea.'

Later, dressed warmly to go out, Caro sat on the edge of her bed. She reached out and automatically stroked the counterpane as her memory took her back to that one night of wondrous love, here in this very bed. 'John Conrad,' she whispered, and a large tear rolled down her cheek. She looked across to where his letter lay folded in its envelope upon the glass tray on her dressing table. 'Oh dear,' she said as she moved over to stand in front of the mirror.

She peered into her face. Did she look any different? No. Then why was it that she felt so different? Her whole body felt strange, especially the odd drawing sensation she experienced from time to time in her pelvic area. She had tried not to think of it, but she knew that at last she had to admit she was almost four weeks overdue for the monthly change in her body.

Her brown eyes stared back at her from the mirror. She could see the apprehension living there deep within them. She wondered if anyone else could. Matthew Craken flashed to her mind. She had the worrying feeling that he knew more about her than she could imagine. But he couldn't know anything like this . . . it was impossible.

She heard again his clipped, sarcastic tones in her head. *You're a spirited girl . . . or should I say woman? Are you a woman now, Caro?* She turned from the mirror as her mother's voice sounded outside her door, 'Are you ready, darling?'

In the hall Elizabeth handed Caro an envelope. 'Paul found this in the letter box. It's addressed to you.'

Caro took it. It read: Miss Caroline Dere. That was all, no address.

'Must have been hand-delivered,' Elizabeth said looking questioningly to her daughter as Caro slipped it in her purse-bag.

'Well, aren't you going to read it?'

Caro shook her head. 'Later.'

There was a gleam in Elizabeth's eyes as she said, 'In that case I'll be most interested to hear who it's from . . . later.'

Her daughter said nothing and Elizabeth eyed her thoughtfully as they left the house and climbed up into the gig. She looked sideways at Caro a few times on the ride to the hall where the Ladies' Auxiliary of the Society for the Prevention of Cruelty gathered but she was soon distracted by the dozens of women arriving for the specially called meeting. By half-past eight, after some brief general business had been attended to, there were seventy-nine women from all walks of life ready for the coming debate. In their usual seats in the fourth row, sat Caro, her mother and Aunt Leigh.

The loosest of the windows rattled in the winter wind as it always did in this hall, as Mrs Finney rose and brought the room to order. Looking along her extensive nose she lifted her voice to summarise the matter before them.

'We of the auxiliary of the SPC fight cruelty to animals whenever we can and as you're aware we have extended this fight to cover poor neglected children.' Polite applause broke out at this statement. 'Society does not accept babies born out of wedlock. A scandal's a scandal and a woman never lives down the shame of giving birth to an illegitimate child. Nor will society let the child forget that it's illegitimate. We in the SPC have worked without success recently to prevent the *baby farming* of illegitimate new borns. Sadly it still goes on but we do have care for unmarried mothers. The Salvation Army and the Brisbane Female Refuge have helped for many years and, as you know, latterly the Catholic Magdalen Asylum and the Anglican St Mary's Home have opened.

'We don't know how many illegitimate children are born each year, but we do know that in Queensland's orphanages there are well over two thousand children whose parents are deceased.'

Miss Fain, the secretary, looked up and noted, 'Two thousand five hundred and sixteen to be exact, Madam President.'

Mrs Finney repeated the number and proceeded, 'As you all know, some of these children are out in foster care and the SPC supported the move by the Government to pay foster parents a

117

weekly amount: eight shillings a week for children under two years and six shillings a week for older children. Now we have been asked to support a private bill to be brought before the Government. The issue, which you'll tonight vote upon, is whether we, as a Queensland-wide body, will give our support to the suggestion that the Government offer six shillings a week for the last twenty weeks of an unmarried mother's pregnancy. So that when she finally leaves whatever home she's in, she'll have a small cache to support herself while trying to find a position.'

At this point Mrs Finney picked up a glass of water, took a sip, cleared her throat and added, 'We have two speakers tonight – one for and one against – our support for the bill. First we'll hear from Mrs Elizabeth Dere who takes up the case *for* the bill.'

Elizabeth stood up and the assembly applauded briefly as she walked to the front of the hall, her back straight. She had auburn hair streaked with silver and it shone in the gas light as she pointed to the nearest window where the high wind rattled the glass. 'Ladies, think of yourselves out there in this cold winter night, all alone and destitute with the knowledge that you carry a child. For as surely as I stand before you there are women in that exact desperate situation this very minute. We, in this room, have so much – good homes, good husbands, good families. The Government has a duty to all citizens and that includes unmarried mothers. These women are, more often than not, abandoned by the men who got them into trouble, abandoned by their families, living in asylums until their children are born, with little hope of ever relinquishing their shame. These sad souls have a right to some chance of starting again, and a mere six pounds each, which is what the subsidy will amount to, is not much to ask of Queensland.'

It was obvious Elizabeth spoke from the heart. When she came to the end she implored the gathering, 'Look into your hearts and recognise that none of us is perfect. But for the grace of God, there go I. Please, vote yes and help some desperate women who cannot help themselves.'

Caro had sat stiffly through the speech, with her eyes straight ahead. Tiny beads of perspiration had formed on her temples and as the audience applauded she wiped them

118

away. She thought her mother had spoken very well and she was proud of her.

The second speaker was Mrs Alice Blackwell. She was the wife of one of the aldermen of the city council and she was on many committees throughout Brisbane.

She was a fine-looking woman in her late thirties, and she opened with the words, 'The book of Matthew says, "Wide is the gate, and broad is the way, which leadeth to destruction." We've heard Mrs Dere and her *noble-minded* cant, for that's what it is. She's told us to think of ourselves out there on this winter night, all alone and destitute with the knowledge that we carry a child. But I say to you it is impossible for us to think of ourselves in that position. We of the SPC do not encourage indecency, nor do we condone sexual licence, but that's what Mrs Dere is asking us to do, not only condone it but *pay money* for it. There are many truly needy cases in our society: the blind, the deaf and dumb, who through no fault of their own are suffering, and the aged and infirm who are so often forgotten. These are the ones who should enjoy any excess monies from the state.' She had a powerful voice and she enunciated clearly, and as she proceeded with her reasoning she looked around the room and met the eyes of her audience. Her final statement was, 'We need to make moves that will help to stop illegitimacy, not to *reward* women for it. Vote no tonight.'

At that point her two sisters in the very front row called out, 'Hear, hear,' and Mrs Blackwell smiled widely at the applause as she moved back to her seat in the body of the hall.

In habitual manner the president looked along her nose at the assembly, 'You have ten minutes to discuss it amongst yourselves.' Which all the women did, all at once, all except Caro, who listened rather than talked. After the stated time Mrs Finney and Miss Fain crossed to a large blackboard and standing in front of it Mrs Finney asked, 'All those in favour of support to the bill please raise your right hand.'

Hands rose and were counted. The wind increased and howled as she then called for a show of hands against the bill. Four women abstained from voting. Miss Fain picked up the chalk and wrote in large print on the board: '35 FOR 40 AGAINST'.

Caro's eyes closed momentarily then she turned to her mother and hugged her. 'Oh, Mummy, I'm so sorry.'

Immediately all the women gave their opinions and Mrs Finney called loudly for order. 'Ladies, we will *not* support the private bill.'

The vote was the last item on the agenda and the meeting closed as usual with the women standing to sing. As their voices rose in 'God save our gracious Queen', Caro's throat was dry and she felt hot and flushed.

When the anthem ended she moved over to one of the windows where she could place her hand on the chill of the cold glass. She thought of John Conrad. Lifting her eyes she saw her face reflected in the windowpane – big frightened round eyes gazing back at her, into the core of her. Then it hit her, hard like a slap in the face. John Conrad was going away to England. He might as well be going to the moon. And here she was in Brisbane . . . all alone.

At eleven o'clock, after her mother had gone to bed and the house was still, Caro sat up in bed and took out the letter from her purse-bag. She opened it and read:

Caro,

I know you were annoyed with me today. I forgive you. You are young and as yet you do not know the world.

Come a week on Saturday – 20th August at ten o'clock in the morning to the Raven Rooms at 105 Queen Street, where it will be the final day of an exhibition of a large number of my paintings. I will be very pleased to see you.

I believe you will find a deal of interest in some of the subjects I choose to paint.

Matthew

Although he had sketched her, she had not been aware that Matthew Craken was a painter. The fact was that until now she had not been aware of a lot of things. She had been oblivious.

Deep in the penetralia of her mind stirred a memory, and she heard the words John Conrad had used about Matthew Craken on the night of the concert: 'He's not someone you should associate yourself with in any way whatever. He's scum.'

She was at her wits' end and he was going half a world away when she needed him most. What would she do?

Why had she been such a fool? *Why* had she listened to Lucy's obviously flawed reasoning about lovemaking? Lucy always seemed so grown up and so knowledgeable, that was why Caro had taken as truth everything her friend had told her. Now she knew the girl was fallible. She had heard there were people who terminated babies. Her single informant, Lucy, had told her about that too. Even if it were true, how could anyone find these people? And then, would God forgive her? She hung her head forward in despair. Was there a God at all?

All her dreams, so real a few weeks past, extinguished in crude reality; all her hopes, thwarted. Her head ached and her temples felt tight.

Two tear drops fell and landed on the letter she held, blurring the word *Matthew*. She continued staring at the note for a very long time until tears entirely obscured her vision.

When finally she lifted her eyes from the page, folded it and blew out the candles at her bedside, there was an alien tightness to the girlish softness of her mouth and she was conscious of her heart pulsating, beat after beat in her chest.

Chapter Eleven

In the pale electric light of the barracks John Conrad looked around at his trunks ready for his forthcoming journey. Over the course of the day a number of messages of good luck had come in from army comrades while his batman had done most of the packing. Now as the sun sank, his friend, Lieutenant Donald Greve, had arrived and sat on the bunk recounting the day's play of the barracks' first cricket eleven. They had won the single-innings game which had taken place against the New South Wales Artillery side on the pitch in front of the eastern end of the main barracks.

'So we were all out for a hundred and ninety-one. Dan Williams made a hundred and two; it was wonderful; he was hitting fours all over the place.'

'Yes, Dan's a great batsman. Pity I wasn't there.'

Donald laughed. 'Well, we can't all be crawlers and be taken to far-off lands by the colonel, now can we?'

John Conrad leaned over and cuffed him on the shoulder. 'Jealousy doesn't pay, my friend.'

Donald laughed, slipping off the bunk. 'True. Now can I do anything for you?'

'You can take that drawer over there and dump everything in it in the rubbish. This leaving has its advantages: one gets to clean out years of mess.'

Donald picked up the drawer and walked across to a bin that was near to full with discarded items. He emptied it. 'Anything else?'

'All that stuff on my chest of drawers can go as well.'

Donald moved over to the bits and pieces and started sliding them off the top of the cabinet and into a box.

Suddenly John Conrad called, 'Just a moment,' and he reached over and retrieved a small card.

'What's that?' his friend asked.

John Conrad did not answer for a moment. He thought it probably was foolish keeping this little holy card given to him in the train years ago by that strange child Emma Louise, and he stood turning it over in his hand as his friend waited. Then he shrugged, 'It's something and nothing, I suppose. But, as I've kept it this long I won't throw it away.' He tucked it into his pocket and turned back to his bags on the bed.

An hour later the two of them sat drinking with a couple of their friends in the officers' mess under the ever-present gold-framed likeness of Lieutenant Colonel George Barney, Royal Engineers, the revered soldier who, amongst other significant achievements, had planned and constructed the Victoria Barracks. There was a lot of talk about the cricket match, but shortly the conversation turned to John Conrad's departure.

'So what time do you leave tomorrow?' asked Lieutenant Andrew Freestone.

'At seven hundred hours from the barracks, eight hundred from the Quay.'

'Lucky bugger,' opined Donald.

'May as well drink champagne tonight then,' said Derek Thomas, motioning to the steward. 'Bring us champagne, Lenny, and put it on Lieutenant Fleet's account.'

This brought objections from John Conrad and laughter and loud agreement from the others.

'You won't be here to pay it anyway old boy,' shouted Donald over the mirth.

They drank and told stories and joked for another hour or so, and when the clock behind the bar chimed eleven, John Conrad stood up. 'Don't want a hangover in the morning, chaps, so that's it for me, I'm afraid.'

Donald Greve stood up beside him and called for quiet. There were a couple of billiard tables being used and about a dozen young officers lounging at various places around the bar.

Donald slapped John Conrad on the back as his words rang clearly around the mess. 'Tomorrow this lucky bloke's off to the Old Dart with the colonel. Let's all raise our glasses, and wish him the best of luck. May he work as hard as us and not enjoy himself too damn much!' He lifted his glass high in the air. 'To Fleet!'

There was a general shout of 'To Fleet!'

John Conrad grinned. 'Thanks a lot. Look after Sydney for me.'

Derek Thomas shouted. 'Anyone in particular to look after for you, old chap?'

All manner of suggestions followed this, some verging on very bad taste, and finally John Conrad moved to the door and laughingly protested above the noise, 'Thanks for your consideration everyone. Good night, and I know you'll miss me!'

Catcalls and howls of protestation met this, and Donald hurried him outside, where they met the chill winter night and hastened across to their quarters. As they came to John Conrad's door they halted and Donald turned to his friend in the weak light thrown through the windows of the buildings. 'I'll miss you, old boy.'

'I'll miss you too.'

'Shame you couldn't get home to Brisbane to see that girl you told me about. What's her name again?'

John Conrad nodded and pulled his coat more tightly around him. 'Caroline. I call her Caro. Pity of it is I could be away a long time.'

'Will she wait?'

'Definitely. She's that sort of girl.'

'That's good then. Have you written to her?'

'Mmm. More than once.'

'Well, keep it up. That way she can't forget you.'

John Conrad smiled. 'I know you'll look after Cromwell for me.' Cromwell was his hardy stockhorse, bought from a breeder in Parramatta, west of Sydney, two years before. At the time he had been reading the life of Oliver Cromwell and for some reason it had just seemed the right name.

Donald was enthusiastic, 'Absolutely. He's in good hands.' Then he shook his head. 'Won't be able to see you off tomorrow. I'm on duty at six hundred hours.' He held out his hand and his companion took it. 'Good luck, John Conrad.'

'Thanks, Don, and good luck to you too.'

They parted and Donald moved on as John Conrad waved once before he closed the door. Inside a fire glowed, warming the cosy room, and he took a deep breath. Tomorrow he was on his way to England. He liked the idea, but there was misgiving at having to leave Caro over here. He supposed in time he would get used to it and then he could simply look forward to seeing her again and making her his wife. To think he was in love with little Caroline Dere, the girl he had known all her life. It was somehow fitting and comfortable that she was the one.

At noon the following day Caro stood in the long gloomy corridor outside the Raven Rooms. Her hand shook as she put it out to take hold of the doorknob. She had spent a sleepless night just as she had every night for the past week, for she now lived with the constant dread of what she knew to be true. With a sick feeling she remembered the words her mother had said to her a few weeks earlier: *Caroline, don't become too enamoured of John Conrad Fleet. He's not for you . . . He's a soldier with a soldier's ways.'*

She had been angry with her mother at the time, but how fatally true those words had swiftly proven to be. Yes, she loved John Conrad Fleet, probably always would, but now she was paying the price for it. He had gone away across the world and she was left here alone to face the consequences. And she was now absolutely sure of what the consequences were.

Just as her fingers touched the brass handle the door opened and she stepped back as three people came out.

Their words echoed in the hallway.

'I don't understand them really. Except that one of the angry woman in black, that was clear.'

'No, I don't think she was angry, more like sad or that she'd seen something which frightened her.' The man laughed. 'Probably him. He's got such a reputation with the women, you know.'

And as they moved on down the corridor the third commented, 'I think a lot of what Craken does is called *impressionism*. Been reading a bit about it.'

Caro faced squarely to the door and watched her hand as she held it out, clutched the brass handle and after a moment, turned it.

The first thing she saw was herself. Her mouth formed a silent O as she halted, stock-still, her hand on the doorknob. There was no doubt of it, it was herself opposite in a great

golden frame, and yet while she recognised that it was undeniably her, it confounded her for it was a self she was hardly
aware existed. Matthew had painted her with her body side-on
and head turned full face to the onlooker: her unruly curls were
pulled smoothly back, the way she dreamed they could be, and
she appeared to be dressed in mourning. In her gloved hand she
held a tiny white shoe, like a baby's bootie. She shivered. And
yet it was the eyes looking out of the canvas that truly startled
her: they were anguished and hurt.

She remained there some seconds transfixed, just staring at
the revelation that was herself. Suddenly realising what she
was doing, she looked quickly around where three or four
people milled close by. Embarrassed and overwhelmed by the
thought that they would recognise her if they looked her way,
she turned and left the salon, closing the door behind her.

She hurried quickly towards the stairs to take her to the
street. How could Matthew Craken have painted her like that?
What did he know? How could he know?

She had taken hold of the rail at the top of the staircase
and begun the descent before she heard his voice behind
her.

'Why are you leaving?'

She rounded to meet Matthew's probing gaze. 'Where the
devil are you going?' he asked, coming forward swiftly on
his cane.

She did not know how to answer. She stalled a moment then
replied, 'I . . . I didn't know you had painted me.'

He shook his head. 'What sort of an answer is that? I *know*
you didn't realise I'd painted you. What I asked was, where
you're going? I expected you earlier, anyway.'

How dare he speak in such a proprietorial way? Angry, she
retorted, 'Matthew, how could you have painted that?'

As ever, he disconcerted her by smiling widely. 'Wonderful
. . . you've used my name again.'

Caro sighed. 'You are the . . . most annoying man.'

'Thank you.'

She hesitated a moment then stepped back up towards him.
'I was leaving because I saw that painting. I didn't wish people
to see me . . . to know that it was of me.'

He managed to look hurt. 'Didn't you like it?'

For some seconds she angrily met his eyes, and then without answering she turned away and began to descend the stairs.

'That's not fair,' he called. 'Don't go. Wait for me.' He began to follow her as quickly as it was possible for him. 'Caro, wait.'

At the bottom of the staircase she halted and turned back. With one hand on the banister rail and the other on his cane he swung down the last three steps and landed on his good foot.

She eyed him. 'Isn't that an incautious thing to do?'

'Of course it is but I thought you mightn't wait.' He gestured with his cane to the arched front door of the building. 'Come outside with me. There's a tea room round the corner. We can talk there.'

He took her arm and she allowed him to move her out into the street. Two minutes later they were seated in a red plush booth inside the Haddon Hall Tea Room.

He spoke first. 'Don't you like it?'

'How could I? It's terrible. You've painted it, me, with a . . . haunted expression.'

'Really?' He leaned back into the corner of the booth. 'Personally I think I captured you absolutely beautifully.'

'It's not beautiful. That expression is full of . . . fear.' She noticed how the light from the window played on his face and made the jagged scar running below his eye shine.

He was silent for a long time during which he stretched his arm out and tapped his fingers on the table top before he uttered, 'Yes, that's true.'

'What is?'

'That your face is full of fear. I see with a painter's eye, Caro. A Frenchman I once knew told me how to look – to *really* see. Taught me a great deal about colour and replicating people's expressions, on an island called Tahiti. When I began to paint you two months ago, you were merely lovely. But for some weeks now you have been quite . . . terrified of something.' He gave a strange sound, not quite a laugh – it started and died somewhere in his throat. 'Made you so bloody interesting, actually. Gave you a quality I had to work hard on to capture and show . . . had to alter the eyes a lot to depict you as you are now.'

She remained silent, aware of a hard lump sitting under her

127

diaphragm. At that moment the waiter arrived. 'What'll you be having?'

Matthew leaned forward. 'Come on, Caro, have a cup of tea.'

In reply she simply nodded.

'Anythin' to eat?' the man continued.

Caro shook her head.

'No thanks, cousin,' Matthew answered, 'just tea for two.' Then he took Caro's arm. She did not move it away even though she wanted to. He gave one of his supercilious slanted smiles. 'Talk to me about yourself sometime, Caro . . . when you're ready. I'll surprise you and listen.' His tone became almost kind. 'Really I will.' Then he took his hand from her arm. 'Look, my exhibition closes at five o'clock. The fact is that exhibitions of art are somewhat new to Brisbane – culture's hard to push down the throats of the locals – so actually it might close at four, though today being the final day, there seem to have been more people through. To my surprise I've sold some, I'm pleased to say. Anyway, Caro, I'm sure you'll like my work when you take time and look at it all. I paint the world as I see it, whether people like it or not, and perhaps if I keep working on my style, people will take me seriously.' He shook his head. 'That's pretty hard for an Australian painter I can tell you.' Quite suddenly there was an uncharacteristic gleam of light in his eyes; gone was the sardonic expression and he became almost animated. 'I want you to come back later. Will you? I'll be there alone then. I'd like to show you all of my paintings. Say around six o'clock?'

She did not reply and he went on, 'Caro, come on. Stop being difficult. I want you to see my work.'

When she still did not reply he cajoled her. 'We could go to the National Hotel for a nice dinner afterwards. They do a marvellous roast lamb. We'll have a fine time. Come on, Caro, say yes.' He took a deep breath, then he grinned. 'You might actually enjoy yourself.'

He had such a peculiar look on his face that she succumbed. 'All right, I'll be back at six.'

He squeezed her arm.

When six o'clock arrived Matthew sat waiting in the Raven

Rooms. And twenty minutes later he stood up and moved to the door. His bad leg ached slightly.

He was not going to admit he was disappointed that she had not come back. Damned if he would. Ah well, instead of dinner at the National Hotel he would go and seek out Knobby. There would be a game of cards going somewhere. That would fill in his Saturday night instead of Miss Caroline Dere. His mouth was tight as he put out his fingers to turn the key and lock the door, when abruptly it opened and there she stood in front of him.

He eyed her for several seconds before he said, 'You're late.'

'I know.'

'Why?'

She gave a tiny smile. 'It doesn't matter. I'm here now.'

He nodded. 'Yes, you are.' He moved back from the door. 'So enter.' He waved with his hand and she passed by him.

The paintings were illuminated by gas light and the portrait still stared down from the far side of the room. It was disconcerting for Caro to admit that Matthew Craken could see into her well enough to replicate her innermost self, but now she looked beyond that single picture and saw the remainder of his work.

'You see,' he was saying, the light of enthusiasm again gleaming in his face as he pointed to a colourful image of a Chinese fisherman in a seascape, 'this one I did in Singapore. It was the view I had from a little place I lived in. That fisherman was there every day, weekends and weekdays all the same to him.' He moved her along. 'And these two are Singapore at night.'

In the first one she could make out dark huts in a gloomy street with figures sitting in circles around small fires. She liked it. It gave the idea of the situation without the detail, but it was quite powerful because Matthew's sweeping brush strokes were large and vital. She had never seen anything quite like it. The second one was an interior. 'It's in a Chinese doss house,' he told her. The figures were sleeping in a long dormitory with beams of light hitting them: it made her feel the mood of the place; the hopeless despair of the inmates.

She knew she was not educated about painting, but suddenly

she felt quite sure that Matthew Craken painted well. 'I like these,' she said, 'but why do you do it this way?'

'What way?'

'Well, it's not detailed like the great painters. You seem to sweep your subjects along. Knowing you now, I think it's natural for you to break away from the old traditional painting.' She paused then added haltingly, 'Yet while I'm not too sure, I think they're . . . good.'

He actually laughed quite loudly and it seemed wrong, unfitting for his persona. 'Well done, Caro, old girl,' he said. He seemed delighted with her. 'Let me explain. I'm trying to express what's happening in a way that the human eye would receive the scene when glancing across it, as if one did not remain in continued scrutiny. I'm trying to give an impression, yet attempting to portray more than a sketch.'

'Then you do it well,' she replied.

'I know I do,' he answered, and she felt quite comfortable with his arrogance. This was definitely the Matthew Craken she had come to know. He *was* this way.

He took her arm and steered her through his exhibition and to her surprise she actually enjoyed it; enjoyed it all. There was no doubt this self-assured, arrogant, obnoxious individual knew how to use the brush and cover a canvas.

A few of the works had little red cards tucked into the sides of the frames and when she asked why he explained these were the ones he had sold. The majority of them had been done on islands in the Pacific Ocean. He pointed out things to her and talked of Pago Pago and Hawaii and Tahiti and the Cook Islands. 'I spent a delightful six months there with a . . .' He hesitated, then giving a crooked enigmatic smile, added, 'but you wouldn't want to hear about that.'

She felt sure he was right. No doubt he had been there with some woman. Common sense told her he had always been a womaniser. She thought of Em and looked sideways at him, his stark profile and the mark on his cheek seemed to radiate veiled cryptic messages about his life. She trembled briefly in that way that people said was *someone walking over your grave*.

The last painting he showed her was vastly different to the others, a contrasting style, almost two dimensional and of vibrant overpowering blues, greens and yellows. It was of a woman on a horse coming down a hillside riverbed.

'I'm never sure about this,' he said in his perfunctory manner. 'In this I tried to paint for the first time like Paul, the Frenchman I met in Tahiti in early '96. I did a few others like it, but didn't have the belief in primitivism that he did. Though I loved what he did; Paul was a master of it as no one else could be, though he apparently was inspired by a fellow called Ingres, or so he said. In the main I simply attempt to fill the canvas by impression.'

'It's very powerful all the same. Who was she?'

He lifted his finger and ran it along the frame of the painting and up to the girl's foot hanging at the horse's side. It was the strangest gesture – a possessive sort of action – and Caro felt uncomfortable for asking.

He answered, 'She was the daughter of a Tahitian king. I suppose you'd say a princess of a kind. I think I perceived her as a type of primitive Artemis.' His last sentence sounded condescending, as if he believed it beyond Caro's understanding.

She felt annoyed and asked sharply. 'And so, did you have a liaison with this primitive Greek Goddess?'

He rounded on her with a laugh. 'Well done, Caro. So you have studied the classics.'

She did not return his mirth. 'A little. Enough to know of the *virgin* goddess of the hunt.' Her face was stiff and formal. 'You haven't answered my question.'

'Is it important to you?'

This query had a tangible effect on the girl at his side and his painter's eye noticed how she stiffened, her discomfort obvious. He suspected she searched herself to find the answer.

He was right. Inside Caro multiple tormenting feelings collided: was his conduct important to her? Did she care about Matthew Craken? And what of her love for John Conrad? That truly tormented her. She loved him with all her soul. What in God's name was she doing here with this eccentric arrogant individual?

The answer came patently to her, sharp like a bee sting and as unequivocal as the sun breaking through clouds after rain. It was purely a question of remembering some words he had said to her weeks before. *If ever you want to get married, come and*

131

see me first. They were vivid in her mind. Yes, she admitted, that was exactly what it was.

She actually surprised him with the flow of words that rushed from her, and she completely amazed herself at how very easily she lied. 'Yes it's important to me,' she replied. 'I've never met a man like you before. I know you've had many girls. People say things about you. You're enigmatic and perhaps you toy with me. But what you do is important to me . . . yes it is.' She was looking straight in his eyes.

He bent down and kissed her mouth. She had never been kissed this way before. It was a shock. John Conrad's kisses had been wonderful, sensual, but loving. This kiss was a thrilling assault. She hated that she found his mouth hot and delicious. She hated that she could feel her heart thudding in her chest as his tongue explored and then withdrew between her lips.

The gas light from the wall lamps danced in his eyes. 'Well, we have a common bond, my sweet Caro. For what you do is important to me too. Why the devil you haven't realised that before today is beyond me.'

She did not speak, and he thought her silence charming. He leant down and kissed her forehead. 'Come, come with me. We'll go to the National Hotel and have that meal together. You can tell me things, Caroline, that you have told no other, and perhaps,' he lifted his hand and touched her cheek, 'I'll tell you some things too.'

He took her arm and guided her around the room to turn off the gaslamp. When they passed into the corridor and he locked the door he said softly, 'I'm glad you liked my work, Caro. Now that was of immense importance to me.'

They walked to the hotel for it was not far past the Customs' House along Queen Street. His gait was swift for one hampered as he was and the way he was greeted by the gentleman who ran the dining room impressed Caro. This hotel was one of Brisbane's finest, built about ten years before; it had a regular and wealthy clientele.

'Good evening, Mr Craken, sir. Wonderful to have you with us again so soon.'

Caro had only eaten dinner at a commercial establishment twice before in her whole life. Both times had been in the dining room of Mayberry's Hotel. Once when her father had turned fifty years of age and the other when her mother's cousin was visiting from Wales.

She could not help feeling quite special on Matthew's arm as they were shown to a corner table with white tablecloth and small vase of red geraniums in the centre. They ate roasted lamb and she joined him in a bottle of wine. Matthew drank sparingly for him: four glasses to Caro's one.

Caro's head was positively spinning as she listened to Matthew. He spoke of his painting and his travels. She even managed to ask questions which obviously pleased him, but in the silences her heart left her and drifted into the arms of a boy in uniform with his honest blue eyes and open smile. She reminded herself many times that her head was in charge of this expedition and she at last gave her full attention to the man at her side. She peered into his cold appraising eyes and told herself that he was her only hope. His conversation was as himself: a plethora of extravagance, witty and filled with intriguing detail. But he altered when he spoke of painting: he became almost solemn, so earnest was he about it. He talked about other Australian painters and how he had met men in Sydney and Melbourne whom he admired. Even Caro had heard of the one called Arthur Streeton. 'Streeton's in London now,' he informed her. 'He exhibited here for the QAS in '93. I would have particularly enjoyed seeing that . . .' he looked past her and his voice hardened, 'but I couldn't walk at the time. Later when I could I sailed the South Seas.'

He spoke of others, like Tom Roberts whom he had met in Sydney, and Fred McCubbin; names she did not know. And said he liked the work of two women, Jane Sutherland and Clara Southern. He had met them one weekend in Melbourne. 'Jane's probably the better of the two. She can hold her own with the fellows who're calling themselves the "Heidelberg School". Does impressive clear work.'

At times he spoke almost poignantly with his revelations about his subjects and what he saw that moved him to describe them on canvas. She could not help but wonder how many he had charmed in this very fashion.

The meal had ended and the single minstrel had departed when Matthew leant across and took Caro's hand. 'It's close to ten o'clock. Do you wish to catch the last tramcar across the bridge? Or, I left my gig in Vanter's Stables. I can take you home in that.'

She answered quickly. 'Let's go in the gig.'

The ride across the bridge was invigorating in the cool night air. A goodly breeze was coming up the Brisbane River and her hair lifted from her neck. She liked the feeling in the dark of the air on her face as the vehicle took them along, it gave her some comfort in a peculiar way. But then she was swift to tell herself there was no comfort for Caroline Dere, not until she had security and peace of mind, and she knew the only man in the world who might give it to her was the one at her side.

Matthew turned off Melbourne Street and after a few minutes rounded the corner into Vulture Street. In a troubled voice Caro asked, 'Where are we going?'

'Along to Riverside Park. You must know it – it's not far from your home.'

The blood flow accelerated in Caro's veins. 'Why . . . why are we going there?'

'To talk. That *is* what you want to do with me, isn't it, Caro? Talk to me? In the quiet with only the two of us to hear.'

In a very small voice she replied, 'Yes, I do.'

When he reined in just off the road she was sick at heart. It was almost the same spot where John Conrad had halted in the phaeton on that wonderful and perfect night she would never ever forget. How could it be that Matthew would bring her here to the very same place?

His voice broke her thoughts. 'Do you want to get down and walk over there?' He pointed into the darkness. 'There are some weeping willows by the water. It's a lovely place.'

This was uncanny. 'No, I'd rather stay here, in the gig.'

'Are you cold, Caro? I have a blanket.'

'No.'

His arm went up behind her and he leant close to her face. She could feel his warm breath on her cheek as he spoke. 'Caro, what is it you want to tell me, for there is something you want to say. I know.' He touched her ear with his lips, his full sensuous lips. He kissed the lobe. 'Go on, what is it? I know you well, even though you refuse to admit I do. Tell me, or should I say . . . *ask me*?'

She recoiled. He knew. He knew.

134

His left arm was along the leather at the back of the seat and he put out his right hand and drew her back to him. 'Don't be afraid. Go on.'

She experienced again the ambivalent emotions that made up her feelings for Matthew Craken. She knew she did not know him at all. He was an enigma. Yet he was her only hope in this whole frightening world.

She began to speak and she listened as if the sounds issued from someone else. 'I . . . some weeks ago in the kitchen of my home you said to me, I was one of the most spirited girls you'd ever met. Your words were . . . you said, *If ever you want to get married, come and see me first.* I remember them particularly for—' She faltered and stopped.

His right hand slipped down to cover her own cold one. 'Yes, Caro, you remember them particularly for . . . what?'

She felt tears spring to her eyes. 'For . . . for . . .'

There was a perverse part of him that wanted her to suffer, to have to go on with this, to make her say it. But surprisingly he quelled it. 'Are you asking if I still mean my words?'

'Yes . . . I am.'

'Are you saying you want me to marry you, Caro Dere?'

Oh, sweet Lord in heaven, am I saying that? She thought her heart had stopped beating. She felt as if her blood stopped flowing in her veins. Her head seemed vacant of her mind. She could not feel her hands or her feet or any part of her body. 'Yes, Matthew, I am saying that.'

He almost laughed out loud. The damnable joy of it was so exquisitely extreme, so on the edge of reality. But he used his strength and contained himself. 'Why?' he asked in a voice he had to subdue in case he spoke too excitedly.

He was not surprised when she came right out with it. He knew that Caroline Dere was a match for any woman he had ever met.

'I cannot lie to you, Matthew. What would be the point? You will either marry me or you will not. I'm with child. I'm six weeks into a pregnancy, and there's no hope of marrying anyone but you. You're my child's only chance. You're *my* only chance . . . if you'll have me.' She knew the tears were falling from her eyes. It was the only thing she really *did* know.

Didn't she realise that there was no question whether he would marry her? She did not understand it but he would marry her, child or not; Caro Dere had captured him as no other had. And into the bargain she carried his deadly enemy's child! It was the most excruciatingly delicious revenge in the whole universe. He could think of nothing but the pure ecstasy of being a father to his enemy's seed. To have the child grow, hold him, kiss him, confide in him, think of him, Matthew Craken, as its parent. Oh, sweet, sweet revenge. He could hardly hold back his sheer joy. He wanted to scream it, shout it, but he did not. And yet his voice was not quite calm as he said the words Caro thought she needed to hear more than any others. 'Yes, Caro, I'll marry you. We'll be husband and wife, and damn them all.'

She was aware he kissed her again in that same way he had earlier in the day. He must have tasted her tears, but he said nothing of that. In a weird world of dream she felt him draw her to the side of the gig and help her down to the ground. She felt him take her in his arms and whirl her around, and as they revolved he hummed a tune, a merry tune, there in the cold winter night.

For the first time in five years Matthew danced and for the first time in five years he felt no pain in his right leg as he did so. There was always shooting pain with heightened activity . . . but there was none at all tonight. In the impassive moonlight he twisted the girl in his arms in twirling arabesques. Along they swirled and gambolled across the grass, round and round until they found themselves tangled in the draping fronds of the weeping willows.

Now Matthew's tune transformed into a gleeful extended peal of laughter as he actually lifted the girl up and swung her off the ground there under those same prophetic trees that had sheltered Caro and watched impartially in the black of night six short weeks before.

Chapter Twelve

Caro stood in the bakery, waiting for her mother to come in. It had been raining all night and as the dawn broke the skies continued their dreary deluge. She shivered as she watched raindrops trickling down the window pane, the heat of the ovens causing the inside of the glass to fog.

The aroma of the baking bread, usually delicious to her, went unnoticed and the nervous tapping of her foot revealed her inner disquiet. She was thinking of a month earlier when she had tentatively informed her mother that the reason John Conrad had been recalled to his unit was that he was going overseas. Elizabeth had made a clucking knowledgeable-sound between her teeth and had eyed her daughter squarely. 'There you see. What did I tell you?' she had answered. 'Soldiers. You can set no store at all by them. Now go about your business and forget him. Find a good man here in Brisbane. That's my advice.'

Caro had retaliated strongly. 'How can you say that when you're married to a seaman? We only see dada a few months of the year. I don't understand you.'

Her mother had slowly nodded her head as she stretched out her right hand to take Caro's left. She paused a long time before she said, 'What you say is true to a certain extent, Caro. But your father's in the merchant navy, not the service arm. At least I don't have to worry about losing him if a war starts.'

Caro's small frame shook with a sigh as the door opened and Elizabeth came in along with a stream of rain. 'It's horrible out there,' she said as she closed the door behind her. 'There's been so much rain this year, it makes you worry about another flood like in '93, especially when it's lashing down this way. And we've got that order for the convent to finish before eight o'clock.'

As her mother put down her wet umbrella Caro took the initiative. 'Mummy, there's something I want to tell you.'

Elizabeth brushed the rain spots off her skirt. 'Yes, love, what is it?'

'I'm not sure you'll understand but please try.'

Her mother straightened up and faced her. 'Yes?'

'You know Matthew Craken . . . ?'

'Yes, I do. What about him?'

'With your permission, he and I . . . well, we . . . would like to be married a week on Saturday.'

Elizabeth's astonishment forced her to sit on the nearest thing, which in this case was a large sack of flour leaning against the bakery wall. Her hands took hold of her knees as if to steady herself while a stream of consciousness came tumbling from her. 'Whatever do you mean? Matthew Craken? You don't even like him. Married? But you're not yet twenty. Why are you upsetting me like this? Caroline, this is ridiculous, you can't be serious.'

Her daughter took a deep breath. 'I am, though . . . very. So please say yes.'

Elizabeth shook her head as she looked up at her daughter. 'But I know you don't love him.'

There was an odd detached look in Caro's eyes which belied the fiery intense words that came from her lips. 'Please, Mummy, I know what I'm doing. I must have your permission to marry him. I *must*!'

'Why do you want to do this? John Conrad Fleet was the be-all and end-all for you just a few weeks ago. You were besotted. Caro, talk to me.'

The girl turned her eyes away from her mother's gaze. 'Mother, please, I've grown very fond of Matthew of late. Don't refuse me permission to marry. You'll be sorry if you do.' She walked to the window and stood looking at the rivulets on the pane. 'In fact you'll be ashamed.'

Elizabeth regained her senses a little and stood up. She moved across to her daughter and putting out her hands turned the girl to face her. There was immense sadness in her voice as she asked, 'Caroline, am I to understand that you *must* get married?'

Caro did not answer. She stood silently looking at Elizabeth until suddenly her face crumpled, the strange coldness in her eyes died, and tears welled in its place, her sobs in competition with the pummelling rain on the roof.

Elizabeth gulped, taking in air as if she were drowning. 'Oh, Caroline. I'm astounded. You . . . and Matthew Craken?'

And between her sobs Caro answered, 'Yes, Mama, that's right. I'm tr-truly fond of him, you know.'

Elizabeth was in confusion. 'I can't believe it . . . you of all girls?' She hesitated, then the probability dawned. 'Then you were *with* Matthew Craken at the same time you were going out with John Conrad Fleet?'

The question hung in the air. The rain intensified while both women stood silently staring at each other. When Caro finally answered, her words were almost lost in the thudding on the corrugated iron roof above them, but her mother heard them as clearly as if they had been screamed at her. 'Yes. I was.'

Elizabeth was in disbelief. She had brought this child into the world and yet it seemed she did not know her at all. All the advice, all the care, all the nurturing, had come to this! Her own daughter was a stranger. Caro was in the family way to Matthew Craken!

'Whatever will your father think? There's no way of telling him and he won't be here until October.' She stood there shaking her head, watching the tears streaming down Caro's face until she could stand it no longer. With a step forward she wrapped her daughter in her arms and hugged her to her heart. 'Don't cry, please. It's just that I'm in shock.'

Her daughter continued to weep. 'I know, Mummy, I'm so sorry.'

They clutched each other for a long time, both in a chill downpour of disbelief there in the tiny bakery, until at last Elizabeth pushed her daughter gently away to where she could look right into her eyes. Her voice was almost lost in the noise of the continuing rain. 'Is this what you truly want, Caroline? To marry Matthew Craken?'

Oh Lord, forgive me. 'Yes, Mama, it truly is.'

'All right. All right.'

The silk of Josephine Craken's skirt made a swishing sound as she crossed the paved garden-walk to stand at the edge of her property under the wide bare arms of the poinciana tree and look down from Hamilton Heights back towards the city. It had been a glorious day after twenty-four hours of heavy rain, and she breathed deeply as she brought her gaze down to the toe of her black leather shoe where it touched a gerbera plant growing at her feet. She always thought what a marvellous plant it was to bloom all year round. Gerberas gave her 'a show', as she put it to friends. And now she bent to break off a brilliant crimson flower.

The sun was low in the sky, its last rays still attempting to illuminate the world as she straightened up and noticed her shadow stretching across the garden wall. This brought a smile to her mouth for she was such a tiny person and it quite delighted her that her shadow was so long.

Josephine always felt lonely at the end of the day. Even as a child the approaching dusk had affected her like that. And since Arthur had passed away, well, it was even worse.

She tucked the gerbera in one of her bodice buttonholes as a voice sounded her name and she rounded to see Matilda, her companion of twenty years, approaching across the lawn towards her. Matilda had actually begun in service to the Crakens as their housekeeper, but over the two decades she had become a friend, and since Arthur Craken had died, Josephine had treated her as an equal.

'What is it, Matilda?'

'Your son's here, dearie.'

Josephine's birdlike features lit up. 'Matthew here? Really? How wonderful. I'll come in immediately.' She hurried off the paved walk and across the lawn to the tall French windows that dwarfed her small frame as she passed through them.

In the drawing room directly under the chandelier stood Matthew Craken, dressed in leather from head to toe. His clothes were quite ostentatious for Brisbane, which was old-fashioned in the scheme of things Australian; and positively a backwater in the world of style. No doubt most who knew him thought of him as an extreme dandy, but not Josephine; she thought he was simply perfectly elegant and fashionable. She glided up to him and he bent and kissed her clinically on the forehead. 'Good evening, dear.'

'How darling to have a visit from you, Matthew. It's been weeks.'

His right eyebrow rose. 'Weeks? Is that so? Doesn't seem more than a few days to me.'

She gave him a side-long glance as if there were no point in pursuing the matter and he turned from her and moved across to the cedar-panelled door which lay ajar, and pushing it open with his cane he called, 'Matilda, I'm thirsty. A brandy, please. Can you hear me?'

Matilda's voice answered from down the hall, 'Of course I can, no need to shout. I'm coming Mr Matthew.'

Now Matthew trained his proud eyes on his small parent. 'Will you join me in a drink?'

She shook her head. 'Not before half-past six o'clock, darling. You know Matilda and I never imbibe before then.'

He took this with equanimity. 'What have you been up to, then, mothering one?'

'The usual things. You know my charities take up most of my time since your dear father left us.'

Matthew's lip curled. 'Now Mother, let's not use euphemisms. Father did not *leave* us, he died. Heart stopped and he died.'

Josephine Craken shook her head. 'Matthew why are you so hard? So brittle? I see no reason why I should say your father died, when I prefer to say he left us. It's kinder, it's nicer.'

'Ah, Mama, and you are all for kind and nice. Spending your life with dozens of charities. People falling over themselves to be taken care of by my dear little mama.'

The door opened and Matilda came in. 'Your brandy.' She held out a silver tray and upon it was a crystal glass.

'Matilda, you're a gem!'

The woman sighed, she was 'a wake-up' to Mr Matthew, he did not fool her with his pretty words; he could be a true devil when he pleased. She answered dryly, 'I know I am,' and, before she left, crossed to the gaslamps and lit them.

Matthew gave a brief laugh and swallowed a mouthful of his drink before he sat down, stretching his legs and crossing them at the ankle. He waited until Matilda had departed before he spoke. 'So, dear girl, I'm thinking of selling my house.'

141

His mother reacted with interest. 'Are you now? And where will you live?'

'I'm considering spending some time up at the farm, might be easier to paint up there . . . more room for a studio. Presently the whole house is a studio. I need more space.'

She looked surprised. 'I didn't think the farm interested you. Anyway you've plenty of money, you could build a new house here, near me.'

This had zero appeal to her son and he asked immediately, 'Did you go to my exhibition?'

'Don't tease me. You know I did, you were there with me once. Matilda and I both went four times.' Her tone became confidential. 'How many did you sell?'

A flicker of real interest flowered in his eyes and he gave an almost genuine smile. 'Five. Five out of thirty. For only my second showing I suppose that's good. The French painter I was friendly with in Tahiti said he didn't sell a blasted thing for ages!'

His mother nodded. 'Don't swear, dear.'

He went on as if he had not heard her. 'I've brought my latest two works for you to see.'

He did not move so she asked, 'Where are they?'

He remained still for a few seconds and then taking his weight on his good left leg rose and moved out into the hall. He returned with two three-by-four canvases under his right arm.

She crossed swiftly to him. 'Oh, here, darling, let me help you.'

'No.' He carried them by her to a round walnut table and, bending down, rested them against it, facing away.

Josephine stood waiting expectantly. 'Come on, show me, even though I often don't understand them.'

He turned the first one around.

She studied it briefly. 'I think that it's meant to be a field with children playing . . . well, at least I think they're children playing.' She pointed to a large dark area of the painting. 'What's that?'

'That, my dear Mama, is the storm brewing.'

'In a way it seems to encompass the children.'

He gave the glimmer of a smile. 'You're coming along,

Mother; as Paul would say, light is dawning. Yes, the storm is waiting, waiting . . . as storms do.' He hesitated then added, 'To alter things.'

His mother seemed to miss this philosophical reference for she replied brightly, 'Storms pass, dear.'

He blinked and looked skywards, but after a second or two bent and turned the second picture.

She pointed to the face in the painting. 'Ah, the girl you made the centre of your exhibition. She looks different in this one . . . happy. This *is* meant to be the same girl, isn't it?'

He nodded.

'Who is she, Matthew?'

He gave his parent an extended look. 'I'll inform you when I think you should know. Anyway, do you like it?'

'Yes, I think I do. The other one of her was well . . . unsettling somehow. She looked so sad . . . full of woe, but this one's lovely. I suppose it means you're a good painter, my son, if you have the ability to show such nuances of mood.'

'Mmm. I'd like to think so.' He walked a few paces to the nearest window and stood looking out to the garden before he spoke again. 'Mother, painting's my life now, you must realise that. I've always known you regard it in the same way Father did – very Bohemian.' He tapped his cane on the edge of a chair as he went on, 'But then, mothering one, I *am* a Bohemian by taste and circumstance. There was a time when I know my father wanted me to follow him, learn to manage the store, settle down to be an upstanding citizen and a businessman.'

'You had good reasons not to,' his selfless ever-understanding mother replied. 'If it hadn't been for the accident . . .'

'There you go again – euphemisms. It was not *an accident*. It was perpetrated with *intent* by my accursed enemy. And, dear woman, while I appreciate your loyalty, please don't continue to make excuses for me. I was thirty-one years old when my enemy attacked me and I had shown no interest in the department store business up to that point.' He stopped tapping with his cane on the chair and finished off his drink with a flourish of the wrist. 'But that's as may be. Today is today and I think perhaps it's time to go in and see old Lewis. He seems to run the store well since the death of my father, as my monthly cheques verify. Thought I should show a bit of interest in where the money comes from. Damn decent of Father to make that arrangement.' He looked back over his shoulder. 'Or was that you, my dear thoughtful little mother, applying pressure to ensure I inherited my share of the profits without working for it, eh? I'm beholden to whichever one of you it was.'

'You're outrageous, you know.'

He gave a sharp laugh. 'I've been thinking perhaps that I'll go into the store next Monday. What time does Lewis and Craken open?'

His mother's face grew solemn. She came across the room and stood in front of him, the silk of her dress rustling as she did so. 'My son, if you're serious about this intent of yours – to show a modicum of interest in the store – then you don't arrive when the store opens. You arrive early, even before the office opens and that's at half-past eight.'

Matthew took a long breath. He looked out the window at the descending dusk and then brought his gaze round to her. 'You mean I'd need to be there before that?'

'I do. If you truly intend meeting with Mr Lewis, then I suggest I send a message to him. But don't waltz in at any old time. You'll impress him if you're there before the office opens.'

'In that case I'll think about it over the weekend.'

He noticed her disappointment and did not care. He moved across to the sofa again and sat, his bad leg stretched straight out, his good one bent. Closing his eyes he leant back. With his lids remaining closed he asked, 'What if I got married?'

The sound of her gasp was so loud he opened his eyes to look at her. She hurried back across the deep pile of the Axminster carpet to stand in front of him again. 'Matthew, do you trifle with me?'

He met her fixed look. 'I do not.'

A look of hope sprang to Josephine Craken's eyes. 'Oh, darling, really? And you'll stop the bad habits – all the wagering and drinking and going—'

'Now, now, Mother dear, let's not get carried away. I didn't say that.'

'But, Matthew, marriage is a very serious step.'

'I know, that's why I've never taken it.'

144

A small smile began to hover optimistically around her mouth. 'You . . . married . . . oh goodness . . . I'd given up hope.'

He laughed, a truly hearty sound, such as she had not heard from him in many years. It delighted her and she smiled happily, her birdlike eyes positively wide with interest. 'Matthew, come on, I'm dying of curiosity. Who could possibly have influenced you enough to think of marriage?'

He pointed with his cane to the painting lying adjacent. 'That's who.'

'For heaven's sake,' his mother exclaimed, 'so she *is* real!'

'Yes, she's real all right.'

'Oh, Matthew, thank the Good Lord, at last you've fallen in love.'

He looked away. 'Oh, come along, mothering one . . . what's love?'

Confusion flowed across his poor parent's face. 'But . . . if . . . Matthew? Surely you aren't thinking of marrying someone you don't love.'

'Now, now, don't start that line of conversation. It's complicated. I'm certainly enchanted with her, but love – well, I don't know much about love. Who the hell does?'

His mother was about to remonstrate, but she thought better of it and instead declared, 'But marriage is a life-time commitment. How could you not love the person you intend to share your life with?'

He shrugged. 'Let's not confuse the matter by discussing the principles underlying my conduct. There's little hope for a logical analysis of that, my dear Mama.'

Her hopeful expression died. 'You shouldn't talk of marriage in this flippant way. It's not proper.'

'Sit down, Mother, don't get offended. I'm not being flippant. First please understand that I *am* going to get married. I've decided. Secondly, I'm as fond of her as I'll ever be of anyone. I don't like the overuse of the word *love*. Most people who bandy it about have no conception and even less perception of the sentiment.' He turned to where his mother had dutifully sat. 'That, my dear little mother, is the beginning and end of it all.'

She blinked. She would never understand her son as long as

she lived, but she had doted on him from the minute the nurse had placed him in her arms thirty-six years ago. 'Matthew, I want to help you. I'm your mother. No one loves you as I do so please listen to me this time. I have your interests at heart always. Don't marry thinking you can live the same way afterwards. It won't happen like that.'

She was never to know whether he had registered what she said or not for he lifted his long index finger towards her and simply stated, 'So, Mama, I'll bring her here to meet you tomorrow.'

'Who is she?'

'Her name is Caroline Dere.'

'Dere . . . Dere . . . isn't there a mariner, a sea captain of that name?'

'Her father, I think.'

'Where did you meet?'

'I first saw her at an exhibition, and then at a rugby match.'

Josephine Craken had very little time for contact sports. 'Oh really? Where did she go to school?'

'I have no idea. It doesn't matter.'

His mother thought it mattered very much and she wanted to know more. 'What religion is she?'

He shook his head. 'Again I've no idea and if you're going to keep firing these questions at me, I'll leave.'

'But, darling,' she protested, 'people's backgrounds do matter.' Then, giving up, she sighed. She hoped with all her heart he was not making a mistake, and yet there was a part of her that was still pleased. This could actually turn out to be wonderful news. He might settle down, and even start a family. She knew he was dedicated to his painting but what sort of a life was it to go on doing that? With a wife at his side he might see that instead of just going in to pass the time of day with Mr Lewis, he should take a real and active interest in the firm. Yes, she would be positive. This could be the making of Matthew. *Fond* was the word he had used about his future wife and knowing him as she did, she had to suppose that the description was as good as anyone else saying he couldn't live without the girl.

She knew it would make no difference how she felt when she met this Caroline Dere. Matthew would do exactly as he pleased. So she decided to be happy about it and broke into a smile. 'Well, at least you can tell me when you're becoming engaged so I can be ready for that. There'll have to be a party, of course.'

He crossed his legs again and leaned back, hands behind his head and appearing to focus on the stuffed parrot on the mantel. 'Well, dear mothering one, that's why I'm here actually. There won't be an engagement. We'll forgo that. We're getting married soon.'

'Soon?'

'Next Saturday week.'

His mother did not speak; she could not speak. If she had only known, her reaction mirrored exactly that of Elizabeth Dere's the day before. She sat down on the nearest piece of furniture, which happend to be upon the keyboard of a small ornate spinet. Her face had become grey as her hand went to her forehead.

'Well now,' Matthew went on. 'Obviously I want you there. I've spoken to Knobby Clark's uncle, who's a minister over at St Luke's in South Brisbane. He's going to read the bans rather hurriedly.' He made a mirthful sound. 'Gracious of him, though I had to cross his palm so to speak . . . Anyway, we'll do the deed there in his Methodist church.'

His mother tilted forward as she whispered in shock. 'Methodist! Oh, no . . .'

And as Matthew rose to his feet she sank to the floor, where she lay unmoving amongst the stylised woven flowers on the carpet.

Matthew rolled his eyes. It was no more than he had expected. His mother took everything so bloody seriously. Lifting his cane he crossed to the door, pushed it open and called out, 'Matilda, are you there? Mama has fainted again!'

Matilda's voice sounded loudly and moments later she came bustling down the hall, smelling salts in hand. She was not afraid of Mr Matthew, never had been, but he did give his poor mother such a time of it. Always horrifying her one way or another. What had he done now? As she passed him and moved to the prostrate woman she spoke severely: 'What on earth did you say to her this time?'

'None of your damn business, you inquisitive old blood-hound.'

'Cheek!' Matilda replied as she knelt down and lifted his mother in her arms. She gave him a fierce look as she waved a bottle of smelling salts under her patient's nose and Josephine emitted small moans of returning consciousness.

Matilda was all concern. 'There, dearie, how do you feel? Come on now, sit up if you can. Whatever it is don't take it so hard.'

A few seconds later Josephine opened her eyes and registering her son seated on the end of the sofa, groaned the word, 'Meth . . . o . . . dist.'

Matthew took a long breath. 'Mothering one, you will just have to become used to it.'

'Methodist what?' asked Matilda.

Josephine did not answer.

'Methodist what?' she repeated.

Matthew looked at Matilda. 'Methodist church. And you're not invited.'

The kneeling woman patted Josephine on the cheek. 'What on earth is he talking about, dearie? Not invited to what?'

And as Matilda remained holding Josephine Craken in her arms Matthew leant forward and swiftly kissed his half-conscious mother on her forehead. He moved to the door where he halted and brought his gaze back to the pietà-like image of the two women on the Axminster. 'Mama, do get to bed early and look after yourself. I'll bring Caro over for tea tomorrow. And, Matilda, if you insist on being here, keep your opinions to yourself and please both try to behave sensibly, will you?'

They listened to the tapping of his cane as he passed along the hall, followed by the front door slamming, then Matilda helped her friend to a chair. 'What on earth was all that about? Who's Caro?'

Josephine had returned to her senses. 'He's getting married. In a *Methodist* church . . . to a girl I've never met . . . Saturday week.'

Matilda said nothing for a few seconds. Then she cleared her throat, gently moved her friend out of her arms and stood up.

She took a moment to smooth her ruffled apron. 'I see. Best thing we can do is have a sherry. I'll be darned if we'll wait until half-past six tonight.'

Caro held her stomach in the age-old fashion of the woman with child. She was only just into the seventh week of her pregnancy but oddly there was comfort in this action. She turned her head as she heard the movement on the verandah and a shadow fell across the open door.

Matthew.

He filled the doorframe and stood leaning on the jamb, his carved ivory cane tapping in habitual movement on his boot. He smiled in that odd way that left her in doubt whether it was a greeting or not.

'Caro, I've come to see you about something important.'

'And what's that?'

He glanced back to the front verandah as if to be sure he were alone. 'Are you here by yourself?'

'Yes, my mother and brother are both away.'

'Good.' He moved inside and closed the front door behind him. And now he did not look in Caro's direction as he said, 'I suppose you've wondered how I knew.'

She frowned. 'Knew what?'

'Oh, Caro, don't pretend. You're to be my wife.'

Yes, she was to be his wife and the world was for ever altered.

'You know very well what I mean – how I knew you were carrying my enemy's child.'

Caro sighed from the heart. So . . . he had finally brought it up – the thing that could have lain dead between them for ever, but no, he would not do that. She was beginning to understand that Matthew Craken could not let things lie, that the painter's soul in him had to dig in and open all wounds, expose everything to the acid light: the good, the bad, and the sacred. She watched his aquiline profile. 'Yes, it's true I wondered, but then I decided I knew.'

Now he turned to her. 'Oh?'

'Why have you brought this up? We're to be married, isn't that enough?'

'No.'

'All right, I decided you'd followed me . . . us. That you'd . . . seen things.'

He began to laugh.

'Oh God, how can you laugh?'

The sound echoed around the room and seemed to hang muffled in the long drapes over the windows. As he laughed Caro realised he would remain an enigma to her; she understood nothing about him, nor did she believe she wished to. Silently she watched him laugh.

When he ceased, he sat on the nearest sofa and leant back in the seat, turning his face up to hers. 'You're right, Caro, old girl. I *had* seen things . . . and oh what things they were. Things that angered me, Caro . . . and made me unhappy . . . *things* that will never be happening again.' He winked at her. 'That is, unless they're happening with me.'

She closed her eyes in disgust. 'Must you do this, Matthew?'

He smiled. 'Yes, I must. For there's something I want you to understand, now and for ever.'

She did not speak, but her eyes asked the question.

'You're to become my wife Saturday week. Correct?'

She nodded.

'The child who will be born is my child. Correct?'

She remained standing looking down at him. 'What do you want me to say, Matthew?'

'I want you to swear to me here on this bright Brisbane day that you will die with the truth never passing your lips.'

'I've no reason to believe I'll ever wish to speak the truth.'

'That's not good enough, Caro. I'm asking you to swear.'

She moved across the room. He was overpowering her so much she opened the door and stood looking out into the street, remaining silent.

He regained his feet and, leaning on his cane, followed her swiftly. Taking hold of her chin he pulled her head around to him.

'Stop it, you're hurting me.' She tried to move out of his grasp but he only increased the pressure of his fingers, holding her head round to face him as he moved her back inside the room. He pushed the door closed with his cane.

His fingers were digging into her flesh and he brought his face close to hers. 'Caro, I'm sorry I'm hurting you. But

150

you see you must swear it now, here, today, that's all there is to it.'

She relaxed the taut muscles of her neck and stopped pulling away and in turn the pressure of his fingers loosened and he released her. She truly wondered why she were resisting this. She had bonded herself to him for propriety's sake; to do the very thing he was asking her to swear to; to save anyone from ever knowing the truth, so why should she not agree to his wish? It was she who should be asking *him* to swear. That appealed to her. 'And if I do not swear it?' she asked, staring at him.

He shook his head. 'Caro, you must know the answer to that.'

She thought of all the consequences. And now she actually managed a bitter smile as she relented: as he knew she must; as she knew she must. But she was strong, for all her weaknesses. She might never understand him, but she was learning to understand herself. 'You swear it too,' she said softly.

And now he broke into laughter again, and this time there was true mirth in the sound. 'Caro, Caro, you don't disappoint me. But no, old girl, that's not the bargain. Only you must swear.'

She thought of John Conrad and felt sick, he seemed pure and wonderful and uncomplicated by comparison with this man. She brushed by him and crossed the room to enter the hall. He followed her and she turned back to him. 'All right, all right, I swear.'

He stepped forward and kissed her lightly on the mouth. Then he lifted his index finger towards her, shook it good-naturedly and said, 'Excellent. And be ready at four o'clock tomorrow afternoon. I'm taking you to meet your inevitable mother-in-law.'

She remained where she was as he swung round on his cane. She heard him cross the room and open and close the front door. For some minutes she stood as if mesmerised, staring at the square of afternoon sunlight on the carpet runner, then she heard the front door open again. Slowly she moved down to the parlour door in expectation of his return, but it was not Matthew, it was her brother, a heavy frown creasing his brow.

'Mum tells me you're marrying Craken, and as if that's not enough she implied you're going to have a baby.'

Caro said nothing but the look on her face told him he was right.

'Bloody hell, Caroline, what the devil did you want to go and get into trouble with him for? Only a few weeks back you were all google-eyed about that blasted stuck-up Fleet and now this. I'm flabbergasted.'

'Don't, Paul, please.'

'Don't, Paul, please,' he mimicked her. 'I've got every right. With Father away I'm the man of this house and you go and shame us like this. I'm disgusted with you.'

She sighed. 'Yes, as you well may be. But please understand one thing.' Her ardent brown eyes widened momentarily with the intensity of her feeling. 'I'm marrying . . . Matthew, to ensure that I *don't* shame you, so please stop going on about it. Get used to it. The world can believe it's a seven-month baby.'

He made an angry scoffing sound. 'You'll be bloody lucky if you get away with that one. I thought Craken avoided marrying the girls he got up the duff. How come you're the flaming lucky one?'

Caro swallowed the bitter taste that rose in her mouth and she turned quickly and left the room. As she made her way down the hall she called over her shoulder, 'Keep out of my affairs. It's none of your business.'

And her brother retorted, following her, 'Well, it damn well is my business. Are you still going to help me in the bakery or what? You're a bloody floozy, that's what you are!' He reached Caro as she opened her bedroom door. She slammed it in his face and locked it as he shouted loudly, 'I suppose it was his flaming money that got you in!'

Caro did not reply. She was lying on the bed face down as tears wet the counterpane beneath her. She wept for a long time, mumbling John Conrad's name rosary-like over and over to herself until she could cry no more.

When her mother called her for the evening meal she would not leave her room, and when Elizabeth came again an hour later to plead with her to come out, she still refused.

She lay on her back staring at the wooden fretwork around the cornice of the room, feeling as if she were not a participant in her own life, but being swept along and manipulated by events that were out of control.

Chapter Thirteen

In the small private bar at the back of the Chevron Club where the windows faced across the river and into the dying day, Matthew gulped down the last of his rum and looked across at Knobby Clark sitting opposite. The sun was low to the horizon and its final rays angled through the glass illuminating Matthew's face and giving his scar the impression that it had been polished to gleaming. He crossed his arms and lounged in his chair, eyeing his large companion.

'I should paint you, Knobby. You have developed an unusual head.'

'What the devil does that mean?'

'It means you don't have a run-of-the-mill face, old son, that you have character, lines, angles, things like that.'

Knobby chuckled at this. 'God, Matt, you're a card and no mistake. I missed you all those years you were away. And you haven't really altered, you know. You could always goddamn make me laugh.'

His companion gave an odd smile. 'True.' Then he lifted his finger in the air and wagged it at his friend. 'But I *have* altered, Knobby. Learnt how to hold a grudge. Important stuff, old man, how to hold a grudge properly, sufficently and irreparably; exceedingly important. As a teacher of mine in Penang used to say, "When you come to know what's important, it's like a great awakening out of a dream of errors."'

Knobby took this rationalisation serenely enough and, lifting his glass, quaffed the rest of his beer.

Matthew bent slightly forward. 'Why don't you come over to my studio tomorrow? Not early – around noon – and I'll make a start on a portrait of you.'

His comrade groaned disbelievingly. 'Why, all of a sudden when you've known me most of your life have you decided you must paint me?'

'It's taken you over thirty years to begin to look interesting.'

This made Knobby break into peals of laughter and even Matthew appeared amused. When some composure had returned Matt took out his sketchbook from his inside pocket and, eyeing his friend, made a quick impression. A minute or so later he put down his pencil and gave a sound of satisfaction, 'Mm,' before returning to regarding his friend thoughtfully. 'Weren't you sued for breach of promise years ago around the time I went away?'

Knobby's big eyes rolled. Then he grinned. 'Ah Matt, you're always ready to embarrass a man.'

'Tell me. How did it come about?'

Knobby hesitated, and shook his head. 'Na.'

'Come on, I'm sure it's one of the world's great anecdotes.'

Knobby inhaled on his cheroot, and finally stated, 'Happens a lot here. Women suing for breach of promise. Poor men.'

'Mm, they're without pride, if you ask me.' Then he prompted, 'Come on. Tell me about it. The plea against you was dismissed, wasn't it? You were vindicated?'

Knobby nodded. 'Yes, of course I was. I was always a fair-minded bloke, though I was young and silly at the time. She was . . .' He made a gesture out from his chest, 'you know . . . well-endowed, you might say. We went out for seven months.' He grinned. 'I wanted more than just kisses.'

Matthew nodded and replied with a mock-serious expression. 'Every man deserves more than kisses after seven whole months of waiting. You were a saint, my dear Knobby, a veritable saint.'

This statement induced more laughter from Knobby while Matthew allowed himself to smile.

'Go on,' Matthew urged.

His companion gave way. 'Well, she wouldn't er . . . how shall I say? *succumb* until I became engaged to her so I bought her a diamond ring, and we got together much more meaningfully. But she had a right old tongue – was always picking about this and that. Drove me to distraction and about a year later she implied that I was seeing other women and she would not have it and she demanded we marry immediately. I

154

told her I failed to understand why this would be necessary. That I needed more time.'

Matthew lit his pipe and grinned.

'She didn't like that at all, and well, putting it bluntly, she called me all sorts, got real nasty and . . . sued me for breach of promise.' Here he took a deep noisy breath and now Matthew actually began laughing and, lifting his cane, rapped it merrily on his boot.

'And then?' Matthew asked.

Knobby was flattered. Hearing genuine mirth from Matthew Craken was a great rarity and Knobby believed that he was perhaps the only person honoured in this significant way. He sat up proudly in his chair as he screwed up his face and tried to look serious in an effort to continue to entertain. 'And then . . . Fact is she lost the suit.'

'Yes, yes,' said Matthew, 'and why was that?'

'You know damn well why, old friend. Because it had never been in the engagement columns of the newspaper and therefore my dear fellow, the judge agreed I'd never committed to her publicly.' He smiled widely, 'A wonderfully intelligent understanding man's man was Judge Joshua Amhurst.'

Matthew nodded approvingly, an amused expression still hovering in place of his usually saturnine one. 'Love it. Love it, a most satisfactory ending.' Then he reclined and crossed his legs at the ankle, his bad leg over his good. 'Of all the women in Brisbane you had to pick one of those who wouldn't go quietly.'

The big man nodded. 'Just don't have your luck with women, Matt.'

His friend sniffed, 'Luck with women is like luck with cards, one's never quite sure what one's getting next, old son.' He lifted his hand to the man behind the bar. 'Another rum, please, cousin.' He turned to Knobby. 'Another beer?'

Knobby nodded.

There was silence until the drinks were brought and after he had swallowed a mouthful Matthew informed his friend of his current thoughts. 'Talking about women and such deep and meaningful matters as that type of connection, I'm thinking of going to the altar with one.'

Knobby choked loudly on his beer and some ran from the

corner of his mouth as he spluttered, coughed and finally managed to ask, 'What? You don't mean married, as in churches and stuff? Like I was sued over.'

'I do, my dear Knobby, I do.'

Handkerchief to mouth the big man's eyes widened. 'I don't believe it. I know you're joking. You aren't the marrying kind.'

'I'm not?'

Knobby slapped his comrade's arm, 'For one thing you enjoy my company too much.'

This was obviously the funniest thing Knobby had heard himself say for weeks because it brought him to near hysteria this time. The other drinkers in the bar turned to look at him as Matthew eyed him indulgently, and when he had dried his eyes and a modicum of quiet descended, Knobby asked confidentially, 'You were joking, I take it?'

Matthew shook his head. 'No, my dear, I was not. And I'll need you at my right hand. I want you to be my best man – see me through the trouble, so to speak.'

Knobby was unable to communicate for some time. He sat shaking his head until he finally became articulate. 'This is hard to believe. Who the devil is she?'

'Caroline Dere.'

'Dere? Pretty, curly hair, the girl I pointed out to you at the rugger?'

'Mm.'

'Didn't even know you knew her.'

'It may surprise you to know I don't tell you everything, my dear.'

'You don't?'

This they found decidedly amusing and Knobby burst into laughter again while Matthew's mouth curled with gentle mirth. It was some minutes before Knobby returned to normal; when he did he tapped Matthew's knee conspiratorially, 'All right, I'll pretend you're serious. So when's the wedding?'

'Next Saturday week.'

This apparently was also truly hilarious, because once more Knobby could not control himself and while he took his time to settle, Matthew leant back in his chair and watched him. 'Glad you think it's funny, my dear Knobby. I do so like to

and enduring dervishes just north of where the Blue and White Nile rivers join at a desolate desert city called Omdurman. That day, Horatio Herbert Kitchener and his British and Egyptian armies broke the power of the memory of the Mahdi – *God's Prophet* in the Sudan – and laid waste his successor's army, while John Conrad Fleet leant back in the railway carriage in Australia and thought of Caro Dere.

The Battle of Omdurman was an event that John Conrad would read about with fascination and hear about with interest, but it was the iron-man victor of the battle who waited on the life-path of the young Australian soldier when he jumped down from the train in Brisbane forty-nine hours after he left Melbourne – a fast journey for the times.

He was tired for he had been unable to acquire a sleeping compartment on either leg of his journey, from Melbourne through Albury to Sydney, nor from Sydney to Wallangarra and on to Brisbane. But that did not matter, now he was here, home in Brisbane, where Caro was the adrenalin that pumped him up, and on the two long train trips, he had decided on his plans.

He carried his dress uniform in his small portmanteau. He hoped Caro would wear his mother's wedding veil. It had been saved in the thoughts that Emma would wear it one day. His face hardened as he thought of Em and her demise, but he did not dwell long on his sister for he was too happy to hold mournful thoughts.

His father's second cousin, the Reverend Hamish Harimore, was the resident minister at St John's. He would go and see him this very afternoon. If he would not marry them quickly they would marry civilly and have a big church wedding next year when he returned from England. And they could have a wedding breakfast at one of Brisbane's finest hotels, perhaps the National; that seemed to be the place these days.

He smiled widely and slapped his palm enthusiastically on his thigh; he could hardly wait to see Caro's reaction when he confronted her today.

When he arrived at Brewery House the place was empty. It was a beautiful sunny afternoon, not cold at all, and the whole western verandah was illuminated in gold. He guessed his family were all attending to their particular Saturday pastimes.

161

He did not unpack, but bathed swiftly and put on clean clothing, and was soon in the stables saddling Geena, a good-natured grey mare. He made fast time to the Dere house, tethered Geena, bounded the fence and in two great strides was upon the verandah and across to the door. He rapped on it, called out and waited. When no one appeared he checked the rest of the house and the bakery and then the neighbouring houses and in another few minutes he stood looking at the vacant blocks of land directly opposite. The whole area was still.

On Saturdays Caro's brother, Paul, sometimes played rugby and as there were a couple of grounds within a few miles he decided to ride by them and see if he could find him.

He mounted Geena and, taking the mare off at a trot, was soon in Boundary Street where the Crown Hotel, one of the South side's busiest pubs, stood. As he passed the hitching rails he saw Bluey come out through the swing doors. The man raised his eyes and, recognising the rider, lifted his hand to halt him. 'Hey, John Conrad, great ta see ya. Come in and 'ave a pint wiv me.'

John Conrad reined Geena in and took Bluey's raised hand. 'Thought you'd still be out with the tribe.'

'Yeah, we were until yesterday.' He gave a little laugh. 'Lena wanted to come back, she likes town. Guess I do too.'

'Sorry I can't join you for a drink, Bluey. I don't have the time.'

Bluey's smile faded. He had been hoping John Conrad would buy the drinks. 'Aw, it's good ta see ya, John Conrad. Come on matey, just one, eh?'

John Conrad shook his head. 'I'd like to, Bluey, but really, I can't.'

The man nodded, a downcast expression covering his face. 'I understand. Guess drinkin' wiv the likes of me here in open daylight is too much to ask.'

At this remark, John Conrad jumped down out of the saddle. 'I'd really like one drink, Bluey, but it's all I have time for.'

The man brightened quite noticeably. 'Hey, thanks. Great, matey.'

As they entered the pub, John Conrad slapped Bluey on the back. 'I'll try to come and see Lena in a day or two. Sorry about only having one drink but I'm on my way to see my girl.'

Bluey raised his eyebrows. 'A girl, huh? Good on ya, matey.'

John Conrad paid for the pints and they leaned on the bar. Bluey had been a wharf labourer and he knew the comings and goings of ships, which they talked briefly about. Then Bluey asked, 'What're ya doin' back home anyway?'

For a moment the young soldier looked sheepish, then he smiled and admitted, 'Well, fact is I'm home to get married before I leave Australia and go on a military trip to England.'

Both these ideas struck Bluey as fantastic. 'England gosh, imagine that, and married eh?' He swallowed a great mouthful of beer. 'Yeah, Lena'd really like that too.'

'Then perhaps you should take the step and just marry her. She's a good woman.'

Bluey nodded his shaggy head. 'The best. But I can't do it. No, sir.'

'Why not?'

'Already married, matey.'

That ended that. And now Bluey frowned for he was reminded of something he had heard recently. He put down his glass and turned his head sideways to his companion. 'Talkin' of weddin's. Know what I heard this mornin'?'

'What?'

'That bloody Craken is gettin' married today. Ran into one of the wide boys who work down at the Colosseum. 'Ee told me. Said Craken was there last night lordin' it over everyone as usual and bettin' real wild with his cronies. Told me informant that 'ee was gettin' married this very mornin', today.'

John Conrad's lip curled in distaste. 'Poor girl. What a fool. Whoever she is, she has my deepest sympathy.'

'Yeah,' rejoined Bluey, 'mine too. Man's a fair bugger.'

John Conrad then delighted Bluey by buying him another drink. 'Though I can't stay with you, Bluey. Got to go, but you remain, finish your ale. Tell Lena I send my very best. I'll try to get up and see her before I go back.'

The young man left the bar to Bluey's big hand lifted in a wave, and he was soon riding away.

It was one of those Brisbane afternoons in early spring when the summer's oppressive heat has not yet emerged and a gentle wind from Moreton Bay wafts across the city in a comforting caress. He rode along at a trot, breathing in the clear air and stimulated by the brightness of the afternoon, the dust of the unsealed streets kicking up behind his horse's hooves. He sat straight-backed in the saddle as he turned into Brighton Road and took the dirt track which led diagonally across a small open park-like area between Hampstead and Gladstone Roads.

He admitted he had fallen for Caro pretty fast, but that didn't matter because his love was real. And Caro had told him that she had been in love with him for years . . . just imagine that.

His blue eyes reflected the unadulterated colour of the sky above as a broad smile pulled up the corners of his mouth and thoughts of Mrs Dere crossed his mind. He must conquer that woman somehow; perhaps he needed to try some charm. He glanced sideways through the trees to his left and suddenly his thoughts seemed to manifest into reality as he fancied he saw Mrs Dere herself. The familiar-looking woman, wearing a large blue hat, was amongst a small group of people who issued out the front door of a grey stone church in the distance.

A brougham was parked at the kerb and a few gigs and horses tethered at the side of the building. Obviously there was a wedding in progress; always were a lot of weddings in spring. He decided the woman was not Mrs Dere and turned his attention to a group of children playing with hoops in the dust at the side of the road. Now his lips turned up in a sneer as he was reminded of what Bluey had told him: that bloody Craken had been married this very morning. So even Craken finally took the step. Now that really was a stupid mistake for some poor unsuspecting female.

He looked back through the gumtrees over to the church again and saw the guests now milling around what must be the bride and groom. It did not appear to be a large wedding as so many Queensland weddings were; there were perhaps only twenty or so people around the couple. As the entourage flowed down the wide brick steps towards the footpath, a small woman threw confetti. People did that more and more at weddings these days so Aunt Leigh had told him.

John Conrad smiled to himself, projecting thoughts of his own marriage so very soon, while he watched the wedding party arrive on the footpath about fifty yards away.

A slight crease formed between his brows. Now he noticed there was something familiar too about a tall man who shouted out to the driver of the brougham waiting in the gutter. Automatically he reined Geena in to a standstill as he took more of an interest in the celebration through the trees.

At that moment the guests parted to each side of the married couple to allow them passage to their vehicle. The bride was hidden but he could see the groom. It was then John Conrad saw the dark cane that the groom lifted high in the air.

It can't be! Craken?

It was. Matthew Craken.

John Conrad brought his horse entirely round in the road to watch.

Bluey had said the bastard was married this morning. Obviously Bluey was a few hours out. John Conrad was fascinated. He edged Geena up on to the dirt footpath and into the shadow of a gum. This was amazing to think he was witnessing bloody Craken's wedding.

Suddenly he recognised that the big man who had shouted was Knobby Clark. Then he saw Paul Dere gesturing to the brougham driver as he moved the carriage forward. Now he realised it was Mrs Dere after all in the blue hat and it was his cousin Lucy who appeared round the horse's head into the street at the side of the carriage. And finally Craken turned and helped his bride up into the vehicle. He recognised the bride!

Caro!

John Conrad had to steady himself in the saddle. How could this be?

Caro stepped forward towards the carriage and Craken followed, then the guests flooded in around them and hid the couple from John Conrad's sight. He sat riveted in the saddle.

A minute later as the brougham moved away from the kerb it was Caro's face that looked out through the window and it was Caro's gloved hand that waved through it.

John Conrad remained like a statue, his hands motionless on the reins, his face a mask, stiff and pale, his body taut, his eyes fixed on the disappearing carriage. He had seen what could not be! It could not be that Caro – *his Caro* – had married his sworn enemy. But the scene that continued through the trees – wedding guests now dispersing and entering their own vehicles to follow the brougham – persisted to give truth to what was for him a monstrous lie.

The breeze lifted his hair at the back of his neck and Geena stamped her feet and snorted but her rider was transfixed. It was not until the last gig drew away from the side of the church to follow the others that he urged Geena forward out of the shadows of the trees to follow. John Conrad rode as if mesmerised, following at a distance behind the last vehicle, which happened to carry Lucy and George. Along Melbourne Street by the shop fronts and box-like houses, across the new Victoria Bridge and right into William Street, he followed in a trance, the clanging of the tramcars and general noise of the people and the street vendors all lost on John Conrad Fleet.

Along past the museum and the government printing office the small retinue of vehicles and horses meandered finally to come to a standstill outside a stately stone building with long white verandahs emulating the prestigious Queensland Club. This building housed the recently formed Chevron Club: an amalgamation of three of the suburban polo clubs. It too had a charming wooden motif verandah and it was upon that pretty portico that the wedding guests soon arrived.

John Conrad halted Geena a little way up the sealed street and sat staring at Mrs Dere's back as she passed across the verandah and into the darkness of the entrance. He was at a loss to know what next to do. His beloved Caro, the girl he was going to marry, the woman he had committed his heart to, was in there . . . inside with *him*. No . . . not just inside with him, . . . *married* to him! How on God's earth could she have done this?

His stomach turned, but fighting the sensation and regaining his equilibrium, he straightened up.

He watched as the big form of Knobby Clark disappeared after Mrs Dere and moments later the verandah was empty. Automatically he dismounted, threw Geena's reins around a hitching rail and stood in the shadow of the awning of a boot and shoe seller, staring at the edifice that was the Chevron Club.

Inside the building that John Conrad watched Matthew Craken swallowed a mouthful of neat Scotch as his bride moved away to talk to her mother. He was dressed in a white silken shirt, his necktie open, and he had abandoned his deep blue velvet jacket which his dutiful mother had taken. He raised his exquisite silver, filigree-covered cane and turned to Knobby Clark, Jack Renton, Grahame Magnus, David Webster and Walter Pine. All five had been celebrating with him the night before at the Colosseum.

'Didn't think I'd do it did you?'

Knobby guffawed, his big mouth almost showing his tonsils. 'No, sirree, you always manage to surprise me, and that's definite, Matt.'

Walter grinned. 'There I was thinkin' you'd up and scoot right until the minute you said "I will"; then I had to believe it. What an amazing day!'

They all laughed and Grahame Magnus put his arm affectionately around the groom's shoulders as he turned to the waiter nearest him, holding up his empty glass. 'No one has signed the pledge here, cousin. A refill please, this isn't a Band of Hope meeting.'

From where she stood Caro watched him, surrounded as he was by his cohorts who admired him and deferred to him. She was living in a half-world, had been since the night he had said he would marry her. Since then life had taken on a surreal quality. And her wedding today had been the climax. She could not recall a single word of the ceremony.

Matthew was prepossessing she supposed: if she tried to be impartial she admitted he had flair and elegance. He certainly was the centre of attention and while he was cynical, abrasive and indolent – except for his painting – she knew somehow she must find other sides to his character. Over the past two weeks she had constantly reminded herself of the night in the kitchen of her home when he had told her unequivocally about Emma, and she had not only believed him but felt real sympathy for him. She needed to keep finding that emotion.

She saw him smile, his mouth creased up into a slant as he put his arm around Knobby. Matthew certainly cared for his friend, that showed he must have a heart . . . surely.

Caro turned her eyes to her mother and, excusing herself, crossed the room to stand by the window which looked out over the wide verandah onto William Street. She felt odd –

that did not surprise her, she had been feeling peculiar for weeks – but something had drawn her to the window. It was beginning to grow dark; a few riders passed by. She thought of John Conrad, refined, gregarious, debonair – she wondered if he would ever forgive her? Did it matter? Yes, it mattered, for she would love him all her life. She must stop thinking about him or she would go mad. All that he meant was over for her now. Far in the distance up the street she saw the silhouette of a man climb upon a horse and ride away. She shivered. Then she heard her name called and she turned to look into the face of her new husband, the scar on his cheek glowing with the intake of his third Scotch.

'Caro, come, it's time to sit down.' He held out his hand and she watched his long fingers come towards her as she lifted her own to place her palm in his. They crossed the room together, the foot-long train of Caro's cream lace dress fanning out behind her as the guests applauded politely.

As Matthew helped her into her chair, Caro looked across the table at the sharp features of Mrs Craken, and as she did the woman's face melted into a smile. As their guests sat Caro turned her eyes upward to her husband who stood beside her. She could only guess at what was to come, but she had taken the single course she knew possible to save her pride, her family's pride and to give her child a name. Matthew had married her for his own aberrant reasons; she had married him for hers. In that particular eccentricity they made a match.

John Conrad stood looking at the Chevron Club, feeling dazed, as if his eyes had played some degenerate trick upon him, but the brougham and the horses, gigs and sulkies outside the building substantiated what he could not believe. She whom he had seen as truth and honour had contaminated all that he believed in. She had cheated and deceived him, and the final decay was the treachery of marriage with his enemy.

He remembered the night in St Paul's hall. She had said in soft innocent tones, *I believe Matthew Craken is home in Brisbane*, as if she did not know the man. He thought of her and how she had been the night under the trees in the park by the river and he felt the taste of bile in his mouth. How could she have loved him like that and betray him like this?

Then the unholy thought pierced his mind. She must have been seeing Craken at the very same time. He could hardly bare to think it, but it must be true . . . if she had been with him like that, then she had been the same way with Craken.

With this last sickening thought in his mind he remounted Geena and, taking one final look at the windows of the Chevron Club, fancied he saw a female figure with the light behind it. He shook his head and rode at speed back down William Street in the now gathering dusk, turned across Victoria Bridge and kept the pace all the way over the river.

It was dark by the time he reached Brewery House again and as he was dismounting in the dim light thrown from the windows of the house his father called from the wide verandah across the cobbled stable-yard, 'John Conrad, lad, fancy seeing you home,' and he hurried down the stairs and over to his son. 'We found your portmanteau; how is it you're here?'

Even in the wan night light Barrington Fleet could see the look on his son's face and it shocked him. 'What is it, lad? What the devil's wrong?'

'Did you know that Caroline Dere was married today?'

Lines formed in his father's forehead. 'Now, son, yes, Leigh did mention that.'

At that moment Aunt Leigh appeared on the verandah, followed by Bart and David. The child shouted excitedly, 'It's John Conrad! Aunt Leigh, look, it's John Conrad!' And the boy ran past his aunt leaping down the steps two at a time to run to his brother.

John Conrad hugged his little brother but avoided his aunt's embrace as she came over to him exclaiming, 'Darling!'

Holding David in his arms he asked over the boy's head, 'Did you know that Caro Dere was married today?'

Aunt Leigh halted and with eyes downcast replied, 'We did. "Hades is relentless and unyielding."'

John Conrad ignored the quote. 'How could this be?'

Bart stepped forward, gently extricated David from his brother's arms and moved the child across to Aunt Leigh. 'It'd be best if you took the boy inside for a few minutes.' He looked down at David. 'We won't be long, kiddo.'

He turned to John Conrad and took his wrist. 'Come with me.' And he began to move his brother on, glancing back to

169

say, 'Excuse us please, Father and Aunt Leigh. I can best handle this.'

The two older people ushered David up the steps to the verandah while Bart led his brother around the side of Brewery House under the trees. When they were well away Bart turned to John Conrad. 'We only heard about it earlier this week. Caro's mother came here and told Aunt Leigh. Seems it was decided in an almighty hurry. There's a hell of a lot of speculation. Needless to say the rumour about is it's a shot-gun wedding.'

As pale as John Conrad's face was, it now became ashen. 'What?'

Bart nodded. 'Yeah well, it's usually the way when a wedding goes ahead this fast, isn't it? Aunt Leigh took it pretty badly, what with her thinking so much of Caro. She sees it as a real betrayal: Craken being a dirty word in this family.' He sighed and took hold of his brother's shoulder. 'And my knowing how you felt about her . . . well, it really shook me. I wrote to you, sent it to the barracks in Sydney, thinking you'd left the country, reckoned it'd take months to get to you, but I thought you ought to know.'

John Conrad was in turmoil. *Shot-gun wedding*. Yes, of course it had to be. This afternoon he had thought her wanton and treacherous, but she was even worse. He had to know the truth. He shook his head and then met his brother's eyes in the beam of light thrown from the kitchen window. 'I saw them come out of the bloody church together.'

'Oh no. God, I'm sorry.'

John Conrad nodded. 'Me too.' He swallowed before he added, 'What a stupid bloody fool I was.' And now a contemptuous smile formed on his mouth. 'I'd come home to marry the damn girl before I left for England.'

The impact of this statement was too much for Bart. He simply stood there repeating almost inarticulately, 'Oh no . . . Oh no . . .' until his brother broke in, 'Bart I need your help. There're things I must know once and for all. Can you possibly find out if they're going on a honeymoon, and if so . . . where?'

'What are you going to do?'

170

'I must see her, Bart, one final time, have the plain truth from her. Will you help me?'

'Are you *sure* you want to do this?'

'Yes.'

'Then I'll do what I can.'

John Conrad held out his hand and his younger brother took it. 'Thanks, lad. Now I truly think I'd like to get very drunk.'

'I can understand that,' Bart responded.

Chapter Fourteen

Bart was as good as his word. Even though he had a slight headache from attending to his brother's need for alcohol the night before, the following morning found him seeking out Paul Dere. He knew it was Dere's habit to go over to his friend Al Baker's house on Sunday mornings and thus Bart waited en route.

When Paul's horse advanced towards him, Bart urged his alongside. ''Morning, Paul.'

Paul reined in. They were approximately the same age and often played football together, though Caro's marriage to Craken had led Paul to believe he would see a lot less of Bartholomew Fleet. His surprise showed on his face. 'Hallo there, Bart, nice morning.'

'Isn't it? Ah . . . how did the wedding go?'

It surprised Paul even more that Bart would bother to ask. 'Went all right. Caro looked nice. Plenty of grog at the reception.'

'Where was it?'

'The reception?'

'Mm.'

'Chevron Club in town.'

'Are they going on a honeymoon?'

Paul hesitated. 'Look, I don't mind talking about it, but I really thought you'd be one bloke who wasn't interested.'

Bart grinned widely, which completely disarmed Paul. 'So . . . are they going on a honeymoon?'

'Yeah, in a couple of days. Leaving on a schooner. Going up the Queensland coast. Apparently *he* likes that sort of thing.'

Now Bart knew they were on common ground. 'Don't take to your new brother-in-law, eh?'

'Who would? He dresses like a bloody dandy, paints flamin' pictures, uses words that you only find in the dictionary and sounds like he's straight from the pages of that Debrett's Peerage thing.' He grimaced. 'I'll say one thing for him though, he can certainly drink.'

'Are they staying with you then, until they go away?'

'No, spent last night at the Belleview Hotel in town; today they're going over to his mother's, big palatial place in Hamilton Heights, more room, though actually Caro's coming home to us tonight. He's off playing cards somewhere. Said it was a grudge match he couldn't miss.'

'Funny thing to do on your second night of marriage.'

Paul agreed. 'Bloody funny.'

Bart had the information he required so he leant over and slapped Paul on the shoulder. 'Well, as long as you harbour ill feelings towards Craken, you remain a friend of mine.'

They both laughed and Bart rode on by.

The wedding night had seen Caro and her husband arrive in their suite at the hotel just before eleven o'clock. Matthew had taken a lot of liquor and she, a little, but he was as clear-minded as if he had imbibed as meagrely as she. This frightened Caro: normal men got drunk.

She was surprised by the beautiful flowers in their rooms: bowls of white roses, almost impossible to find this time of year, and when she asked where they had come from, he turned to her with one of his inexplicable expressions. 'I know a man who grows them.'

She felt oddly touched and very shy. 'Why, thank you.'

He waved his cane around the room and it made great leaping shadows in the lamplight. 'White roses,' he said, 'images of you Caro . . . innocent. But you'll alter. All things are ephemeral.'

Then he took her in his arms and kissed her in that deep and sensuous way that disturbed her, and his hands ran down her body and felt her hips and the tops of her legs through her wedding dress. He whispered in her ear, 'You're my wife now, Caro, make the best of it.' And as he undressed her and took her to bed, she did exactly that. She told herself a hundred times that now she was sanctified by marriage, that before it had been wrong and now it was right.

Her body did not respond; how could it? She did not

173

love Matthew Craken and believed she never would; but one aspect of her character was now clear to her: she was stoical and determined and would do whatever had to be done. Her rationale that to have Matthew as a husband was better than the alternative, had motivated her to this point and would continue to do so.

And when finally he murmured and shuddered and rolled his tongue down the side of her throat, she felt something akin to a sick sad pride as he said, 'You're not bad at all, Caro.'

Before he went to sleep he said something she thought untypical. He turned to her and whispered in her ear, 'You looked truly lovely today.'

She went to sleep beside him, trying not to think of the previous times she had made love, when she had given of her true self with ultimate abandon, and for a brief moment she allowed herself the indulgence of the memory of the feel of him, the one she would always love, and the hot flush of emotion rose to colour her throat. And before she slept, as a single tear rolled across her cheek to fall in her hair she whispered in her head, *Forgive me John Conrad, please forgive me.*

The morning saw Matthew up and washed before she woke. He stood leaning on the door jamb of the annex where a blue porcelain jug and dish sat waiting for her to begin her ablutions. His expression was again unfathomable to her. Would he always be this mystery? Did she care?

'Good morning,' he smiled down at her in the bed. 'Wear the white woollen dress, with the matching jacket; I prefer that, it suits you,' and so she had, and they breakfasted at a table with white starched cloth in the great dining room on the ground floor before they paid their bill and departed in the brougham.

There was a breeze blowing as they drove along Queen Street and down through Fortitude Valley, where they were passed by two electric tramcars. Brisbane was fast accepting this form of travel and tramlines now ran almost the entire route the newlyweds would cover out to the suburb of Hamilton. When they arrived at the wooden bridge over Breakfast Creek, named in 1823 when John Oxley, the explorer, halted there for breakfast, Matthew reined in the horse.

Great grey and white seagulls swooped in formation down

across the river where the water gleamed mirror-still. Further along Hamilton Reach there was activity in tiny boats, and on the bank close to them a group of children played with hoops under the steady inspection of their mothers.

He turned to her. 'A new life for you, Caro.'

'Yes.'

'And for me.'

'Yes.'

'Make the best of it, old girl.'

She did not answer and he sat eyeing her for a time, then in his customary baffling style he abruptly changed the subject. 'I'm thinking we might go out to the property after we come back from our honeymoon.'

This statement received Caro's full attention. 'What property? Where?'

'That's right, you don't know much about me and the family, do you? Well, tons of time for you to learn, old girl. There's a farm we own out past Ipswich near Gatton. It's called Cedar Grove. Anyway, they've let it run down in recent years though it has a certain beauty and it's large. Just one fellow and his wife manage it – the Bradys – a few crops, some pigs, cattle and horses. I used to go there as a child. Great place to paint, I'm thinking.' He looked away across the river. 'That is, er, for a while. We could live there, say, until after the . . . baby is born.'

When he said the word *baby* it sounded like an aberration. The coming existence of the child had been almost unspoken between them. And yet it was the reason for all this; the reason they sat side by side in this carriage in absurd unity.

Caro pulled her jacket more closely around her as she shifted on the seat. 'Do you mean to leave Brisbane?'

He drew his eyes back to her. 'Caro, Caro, don't ask the obvious. It's implicit in my suggestion that we leave Brisbane. I didn't think you'd mind actually.'

The sharp cries of gulls overhead coincided with her reply. 'Well, I'm not sure. I hadn't thought to leave my family. Won't I be lonely? And what about friends, neighbours in the country? There won't be any for miles, I suppose.'

'My dear woman, that's the part I thought would appeal to you. *No one* up there will know you. No prying hypocritical little Brisbanite eyes to see that you don't go full term. Thought you'd like that.'

Caro fell silent and considered what he had said. It was a great deal to take in all at once: leaving her mother and Paul, all her friends, going away to a farm with this man she hardly knew, even though she was inextricably joined to him. 'Must I answer this now, Matthew? It's a lot to decide just like this.'

He patted her arm. 'That's right, it is. But I think it's the right thing for us, Caro. Right thing for *you* for a year or so. Mary Brady up at Cedar Grove's a good sort of girl. She'll take care of you. Nothing to worry about, old girl. You'll see.' Then he lifted the whip and cracked it over the horse's head and they rolled on across the Breakfast Creek Bridge.

When they arrived in Hamilton Heights Josephine and Matilda were waiting for them on the verandah and after unpacking they took luncheon on the terrace. They talked small talk; that is, Caro and her mother-in-law did, Matthew did not – he made it plain that chat bored him – but he drank three brandys while the sun slowly encroached upon them from behind the large house, bringing an agreeable warmth to the afternoon. When Matilda brought dessert, Matthew smiled amicably at his relatives as if in fact he had been communicating throughout the meal, and stood from the table and brought out his easel and paints.

When Josephine left the table, Caro joined Matthew. 'Do you mind if I watch?'

'Not at all, though be warned: I don't talk.'

She was becoming used to that. 'I don't mind.'

It was the first time she had seen him at work, and it was an initiation. She became aware that he was quite oblivious to outside forces when he painted. His absorption was such that she knew she was superfluous, yet she was quite enthralled to watch how he translated the neat garden and what appeared in it to brush strokes upon his canvas. She sat watching him and then she slipped into meditation, using the time to dedicate herself to her own world as he so clearly was to his.

Two hours passed before the mood was broken by the arrival of afternoon tea, brought to them by Matilda, whom Caro had liked on sight at first meeting her the week before, and around four o'clock, when the spring shadows were lengthening, Josephine appeared from her room and asked her daughter-in-law to join her in the garden.

Matthew continued to paint, and on and off he gazed through languid eyes down over the flowerbeds and plants, to the two women.

They spent almost an hour under the trees in the lovely established garden together, and talked about charities and flowers and Caro's family – and for a first attempt alone at mother-in-law, daughter-in-law relations, it had gone well enough.

As they stood to make their way back across the neat garden towards Matthew, Josephine gave a small cough, and busily smoothed the grey silk of her dress with both hands before she looked up at Caro. 'My dear, this is perhaps an embarrassing moment, but I feel I've a right to know. My son isn't one who acquaints me with the intricate elements of his life: he's not forthcoming, you see, so it leaves me to guess; mothers like to know particulars. And in your case, that is, in the case of this hasty marriage you have both entered into, well, I'm assuming you are . . . that you are . . .'

Caro returned Josephine's gaze. She did not dislike this birdlike little woman who looked up at her so earnestly; in fact, she liked her, and in a fashion felt sorry for her. It could not have been much fun being Matthew's mother. She inclined her head. 'If you mean, Mrs Craken, am I carrying a child? Yes I am. And yes, you do have a right to know.'

And now Josephine astounded her new daughter-in-law. Continuing her ardent perusal of Caro, she asked, 'Do you love my son?'

The look on Caro's face revealed her amazement. Difficult seconds passed in silence . . . long silence.

'I see I've caught you unawares. Never mind. It's perhaps not a matter we need to press.' Josephine took a step forward out of the shadow of the tree into the fading afternoon sunlight before she inclined her head to add over her shoulder, 'But I hope for your sake, you do; it will be difficult living with him, if you do not.' Then she almost skipped forward across the grass. 'Come along, my dear.'

Caro followed a pace behind her new relative as they moved over the lawn to Matthew at his easel. There was more to Josephine Craken than one would at first observe: her mother-in-law was no fool. She might dote on her son, but she was no fool.

Matthew was looking at his watch as they arrived at his side. 'Caro, if I'm to take you to your mother's, before I go to Knobby's, we'd best be leaving.'

Caro nodded and his mother asked, 'What time will you be home tonight, darling?'

He pursed his lips. 'Ah, mothering one, there's the rub. We might not be home here tonight at all.' Before his surprised mother could open her mouth he moved across to Caro and placed his arm around her shoulders. 'Caro, I might have to leave you at your mother's tonight.'

The quizzical look on his new wife's face brought even Matthew to continue with some explanation. 'Well, the fact is, these grudge matches often go all night. Don't want your waiting up indefinitely. Best you stay there and I'll pick you up in the morning.'

And Matilda, who had come out on to the terrace in time to hear what had been said, spoke up. 'As if playing cards and betting money on the Lord's good Sunday isn't bad enough, but no! You have to stay out all night.'

He half turned his head to her. 'Mind your own business, you disagreeable old busybody, and stop eavesdropping.' Then he returned his attention to Caro. 'So be ready in fifteen minutes, will you?' and he patted her on the bottom as his mother pretended not to see, before he moved away to pack up his easel and paints.

Caro said nothing. It suited her to be home in her own bed, in her own environment with her own family tonight. For many weeks she had been in a half-world between life and mere existence. Sometimes she had thought to kill herself as poor Emma had done; but then she would be damned if the two of them would die because of what sanctimonious people said was right and wrong. And even if she could have done the deed and killed herself she could not bring herself to kill John Conrad's child as well. No, she had to live, had to face whatever it was the years would bring. To see the miracle that would be John Conrad's child come into this world, give life to a part of him and nurture it, even though he would never know.

It was just after seven and pitch dark when the newlyweds, side by side in the brougham, pulled up outside the house that had been Caro's home until yesterday. She had been married exactly twenty-seven hours and already she knew a little more of the world than she had the day before.

She could hardly accept that this peculiar individual who alighted gingerly from the seat beside her, was her husband. And as he helped her down and delivered her to the door where Elizabeth met them, she shivered as he bent forward to kiss her on the forehead.

'I'll see you in the morning,' he said as he turned to look his mother-in-law in the eye, 'Good night, Mrs Dere.'

As swiftly as he could he returned to the brougham and drove it away. The two women stood watching and Caroline felt the tension in her mother. 'Please, Mummy, don't judge him. It was a game he had set up weeks ago. It's important to him.'

Elizabeth sighed quite audibly. 'At least it allows me to have your company for the night. Come.' And she ushered her daughter into the house.

As the door closed behind Caro and Elizabeth two forms moved in the vacant lot across the street. One spoke. 'What're we going to do now?'

John Conrad thought before replying. There was a part of him that believed he should have been on the evening train to Sydney – accept all that he had found here and leave it to reconcile itself, but his overriding desire was to know the answers to the questions that burned in his mind. 'We wait. She has a habit of spending time alone on the verandah. I'm counting on the fact she does it tonight.'

His brother's reply was an extended sigh.

Sunday nights in Brisbane were as quiet as the tomb. The street was devoid of activity and the two young men went unseen. They had come on foot the last four hundred yards; had left their horses in another vacant yard on Tribune Street. Fortunately Bart had thought to bring a blanket, for as time passed they tired of standing.

At one point Litmus began to bark and they saw someone they assumed was Paul, cross from the house to the bakery with the dog at his side. Half an hour later the man and the dog returned to the house.

Three hours went by, during which time John Conrad anguished: perhaps he should walk right up to the door and demand to see her; have it out with her there and then in front of her family; or should he write a letter, make a tryst with her, but what if she did not turn up at the meeting place? Should he wait until the early hours of the morning and rap on her bedroom window like he had once before? That thought only enraged him.

In his short life he had lost so many he had loved: his beautiful mother, Emma, Hargy and now Caro: yes, after tonight he would have to think of her as dead. That way he would stop from going mad.

As ten o'clock passed the moon was a brilliant ball in a clear night sky and the whole of the West End and Highgate Hill were asleep, along with Bart, who snored gently on the blanket beside him.

John Conrad held his knees and watched the lights go out in most of the Dere house, leaving a single glow at the side from the kitchen. It reflected on the wall of the bakery, so he assumed someone was still awake. A few minutes later his wait was rewarded when the moonlight showed him the figure which appeared around the kitchen corner to pass along the verandah towards the jacaranda trees. It was her! He waited a few minutes. Yes, she was definitely alone. She moved slowly along towards the jacarandas and then halted, appearing to stand holding the railing and looking out on the street.

He silently woke Bart, whispering, 'She's on the verandah. I'm going over. Go back and get the horses, bring them here and wait for me.'

Bart stood up beside him and as John Conrad crossed the street, he moved silently off in the opposite direction.

Caro saw the man crossing the dirt street quite clearly in the moonlight. He appeared from the vacant lots across the way and leapt the gutter, heading straight on towards her. She was about to shout out to Paul when she recognised the way in which he bounded over the fence.

Oh, Lord God in heaven . . . it could not be! This could not be happening.

But it was. He came straight up the wooden steps and on to the verandah. She stiffened in shock, standing as if petrified.

He strode right to her, took her hand and dragged her back along the verandah and down the stairs, across the garden and in amongst the trees, the green shoots of early spring starting life in the branches above their heads. To Caro it was some morbid miracle to have him manifest in front of her this way. He could not be a ghost for his hand was real and rock hard inside her palm. Under the branches he dropped her fingers like a brand and rounded on her.

There was enough light to see the countless emotions that crossed her face. She was in disbelief and yet her heart thudded against her chest with the thrill of seeing him. It was incredible that he was here. She still could not find the voice to speak.

But he, who was more prepared, could find his. 'How could you?'

She said nothing. Still she could not accept his presence.

'I turn my back and you marry . . . ah, but not *just marry*, that perhaps I could have simply hated you for, but no! You marry he whom I loathe.'

Caro tried to speak but nothing came.

'Why did you let me believe you loved me? Why did you trifle with me that way?'

And still no sound came from Caro's throat.

'The talk is that you carry a child. Do you? It's true, isn't it? Whose is it? Or are you so vile that you don't know? His or mine?' He laughed. It was such an unstable sound it terrified her. Then he wiped his hand across his mouth. 'Or were there others as well?'

These words broke her heart and cauterised her soul, but they drove her to speech. 'I'm not like you . . .'

He laughed again, the bitterest sound she had ever heard in her short life. 'Ah ha, how very true. *I* would have loved *you* to the grave.'

Caro's eyes were wild. 'All right, I'm weak. I thought you'd gone away, God knows where . . . for God knows how long. I was alone and afraid.'

He stepped forward and took her wrists in his hands, the pain making her wince as he dragged her out from the shadows of the trees into the chaste moonlight. 'I want to see your face. Now tell me. So I'd gone . . . and that was good enough for you. Whoever is around will do. Is that it?'

181

'No . . . please, it wasn't that way.'

'Wasn't it? Damn you, tell me . . . are you with child?'

She did not answer and his voice rose on the night air. 'Tell me, blast you!'

They were both imprudent now, both reckless. He still held her wrists but she did not feel the pain in them as he twisted her savagely around. 'Are you pregnant, damn you?'

She met his eyes in the wan moonglow and for the space of a single second he thought he saw a wavering light appear in Caro Dere's eyes before she replied, 'I am.'

Back on the verandah Elizabeth Dere's voice sounded, but they did not heed it. 'Caro, Caro,' her mother called. 'What's happening? Who's there with you?' But the two heard nothing except the ringing sounds of outrage, fury and hurt ricocheting in their heads.

He pulled her wrists high in the air, bringing her body closer to him. 'Whose is it? Is it mine?'

Her body was shuddering and the tears flowed from her eyes.

'Tell me, is it mine?'

Now Elizabeth realised her daughter was in some sort of struggle in the darkness and she shouted loudly for her son. Across the street Bartholomew arrived with the horses to hear the raised voices beyond the jacaranda trees. He rode forward and called to his brother.

But the two locked in the struggle heard nothing as John Conrad threw away Caro's wrists and swung his arms down her back to pull her close to him so that his face was a mere inch from hers. His anguish was like a living thing between them, and she could feel his intemperate breath coming in rushes across her face. 'Tell me, for Christ's sake. Is the child you carry his or mine?'

The misery and torment in his voice drove her to distraction, but in all the madness in her head she kept one sane thought: *I am married to his enemy, if I tell him the truth it will shatter him completely. I've betrayed him; I must do no more evil. A lie is kinder now. It will allow him to nurture plain clear hatred of me.*

'It's not yours. It's his! It's his!' she cried at last, feeling to her bones the violent quake that ran right through him.

182

Bart yelled loudly for them to ride away as Paul came running out of the house shouting, with Litmus barking unchecked at his heels and Elizabeth calling and gesturing wildly to the trees.

John Conrad still held Caro so tightly she could feel his body trembling. It was as if the whole galaxy were out of control around her as his mouth collided with hers in raping flight across her face, his teeth ripping into her lips in a grotesque kiss that covered their faces in blood. Then he flung her away and she stumbled backwards to fall at the base of the jacaranda tree.

'I loved you, how I loved you, curse you!' His face was waxen in the moonlight, and tears clouded his vision. 'And all the time you were deceiving me.'

Paul leaped down the verandah steps and ran to his sister, where, suddenly, he recognised the intruder and he lifted his voice above the din of Litmus's barking. 'You . . . what the hell's happening here?' He made a move towards John Conrad but the misery in Caro's shrill voice halted him. 'No, Paul! Don't! Leave him alone. Let him go.'

With dead eyes John Conrad backed away across the garden to the fence, gazing all the while at the silver-white dress that was Caro Dere in moonlight.

Paul looked from the man who moved away, back to his sister, and saw the dark smudges of blood on her ashen face. 'Oh no . . . What the hell has he done to you?'

She did not answer and as the man she adored reached the fence and left her life, she heard his words, cold-blooded, inflexible. They were to fill her nightmares for years to come. 'May God forgive you, Caro, for I never will.'

Chapter Fifteen

The sun made a yellow corridor across the dark water. The man who stood at the bulwark had been on deck since dawn. He liked to do this, it had become a habit on the long voyage, and he was comfortable with the early rising and the communing with whatever was out here on the sea.

Indeed it *had* been a long voyage. Not that John Conrad had minded the weeks at sea; he had needed time to adjust, and thanked whatever gods may be for it. The events in Brisbane would not fade – sometimes they were still as real as the night they happened – but that was during his waking hours; they had less intensity now in his dreams. He regarded Caro Dere as dead; gone out of his life for ever, but not leaving the sweet sentimental aura that he nursed for those others he had loved and buried; no, Caro Dere was simply *dead*.

He turned his eyes to a row of hills that appeared crimson in the distance and noticed, as he looked across to the calm murky seas on the port side, great red streaks on the water's surface, dirt blown from the ruddy desert which ran down to the shore. Perhaps the reason for the Red Sea being so named was the dominance of crimson in this landscape.

He put his hand in his pocket and took out his wallet. He used to carry a small likeness of Caro inside until the ghastly night in Brisbane, but he still kept the holy card given to him by the strange little girl on the train five years ago. He drew it out, turned it over and fingered the name *Emma Louise Blackstone*. Somehow it comforted him. Then he smiled ruefully and replaced it in between the folds of leather and returned the wallet to his pocket.

He heard his own name called and turned to see Bernard Houston. They left the deck together to go below for breakfast.

Four days later they landed in Port Said.

The talk of the whole city was of Herbert Kitchener, the Sirdar, the commander-in-chief of the Egyptian army and his victory at the Battle of Omdurman. It was on everyone's lips from the British officials down to the merchants and the street sellers of the alleys. The battle had been the culmination of years of work by the Sirdar. He had been dedicated to relieving the Sudan of the bloody rule of the Khalifa, the understudy of the Mahdi, who had claimed divinity and banded together the dervishes in a holy war over a decade before to 'purify' the Sudan.

The Mahdi's followers had assassinated General 'Chinese' Gordon at Khartoum in 1884 and Kitchener was determined to avenge the death of the great man who had been his hero and his mentor. Overcoming one difficulty after another Kitchener built a railway south across the desert to Atbara. From there he had taken his British and Egyptian troops up the Nile to the desert city, where he fought and won the bloody battle with the dervishes. Afterwards the victors had finally entered Khartoum.

At last, on Sunday the 4 September 1898, fourteen years after Gordon's assassination, a funeral service was held for him in his original palace garden and led by Herbert Kitchener, who, as a young major, had risked his life to ride dressed as an Arab, through hostile and dangerous country to collect news of Gordon besieged in Khartoum.

It was many weeks after Omdurman when John Conrad heard the story in Port Said but the whole of Egypt still seemed to be celebrating the event, and a few days later in Alexandria in the officers' mess at the East City Barracks, John Conrad and Bernard learnt the detail from an officer of the 21st Lancers, who had been with the Sirdar's Egyptian army for four years. His hair was bleached white from years in the African sun and his face and hands were the ruddy colour of one born in the heart of the desert rather than Birmingham, which was the fact.

The lancer was thrilled to have new ears for his tale and his eyes shone with the light of thrilling memory as he related his tale to his Australian listeners. 'Wonderful it was. We'd been training those Egyptians for years . . . made bloody good soldiers of them, out of nothing really. We showed the whirling dervishes, all right. Although they are fighters to the death, I can tell you. They keep coming even when they're filled with lead. Pretty frightening to look at too and that's a fact. But our boys were more than a match for them, especially the lancers!' He grinned with satisfaction. 'One British soldier is worth six Arabs any day.' Then he took a swig of his beer. 'The Sirdar's gone back to the Old Dart, where I believe they're making him a Lord . . . and only proper it is too, Lord Kitchener . . .' The man's face filled with pride. 'And to think I fought with him.'

The entire mess drank a toast to Kitchener of Khartoum, as he was now being called and the next day John Conrad and his companions left Egypt for London. Colonel Ayres was keen to arrive in England as he had a meeting set up with the Colonial Defence Committee on 31 October, so in the event they followed the same route that Kitchener took: disembarking at Marseilles, catching the express to Paris and then crossing the English Channel to Dover.

They arrived in Dover on the 28 October 1898.

The talk of the whole waterfront town was of the previous day when Kitchener had arrived from Egypt. He had been met by the Mayor, Sir William Crundell, a number of Generals, Mr Winston Churchill and even the American naval and military attachés. The Seaforths had made a guard of honour on the pier after which the hero had lunched at the Lord Warden Hotel where they still flew the Union Jack and the Egyptian flag over the house. Later Kitchener had spoken briefly to the huge crowds of well-wishers before taking the seven o'clock train to London.

'Seems like wherever we are, sir, K has been there shortly before,' John Conrad commented to Colonel Ayres as they stood together on the Dover dock, watching their trunks being unloaded.

The senior officer smiled. 'Yes, it does. Interesting, isn't it, how all we military types call Kitchener simply *K* with such affection? I don't think there's an army in the world that hasn't been following his exploits for years in the deserts of the Sudan.'

'Yes, sir, I think he's every soldier's hero. Especially now.'

'Indeed. It would be marvellous actually to meet him.

There's no better man in all the world to advise Australia on how to run our proposed federal army. Though I very much doubt an audience with him will be in the offing.'

That afternoon the Australian contingent travelled to the British Barracks in Canterbury and on Monday the 31 October went on to London where the colonel had his first meetings with the Colonial Defence Committee at the War Office in Pall Mall.

The newspapers were full of articles on Kitchener and his quest to raise a hundred thousand pounds for his proposed, 'Gordon College'. It was to be the first of its kind in Khartoum to educate the children of the Sudan. Articles in *The Times* quoted K's enthusiasm to care for the neglected of the Sudan and carried his statement, 'Those who have conquered are called upon to civilise.'

For the Australians the following weeks passed in accompanying Colonel Ayres on visits to the Royal Military Academies of Sandhurst and Woolwich, sitting in on lectures and learning how these establishments were organised and administrated. From the castellated building on the Woolwich Common they went on to the Royal Engineers at Chatham where they did the same. Colonel Ayres was one of many of Australia's senior officers who believed that after federation must come demands for better trained officers which only an Australian Military Academy could supply. And while the need for such an institution was indeed warranted, it was to be over twelve years later before the Australian equivalent, Duntroon, eventuated under the guidance of Lord Kitchener himself.

It was the fourth week of November, and the Australians were back in London when John Conrad, Bernard and Alex Grew, at twenty-four the youngest of the Australian officers, visited Chelsea Barracks and went on in the evening to the Criterion Theatre at Piccadilly Circus to see *The Castaways*, one of those new musical renditions with comedy, singing and dancing.

When the curtain fell at ten thirty Bernard and Alex were all for heading into Soho to visit the Trocadero and perhaps a late-night tavern, but John Conrad was not keen and said good night to his friends at Piccadilly Circus. He had found London to be a great city for walking and, as the Australian officers were billeted in Hyde Park Cavalry Barracks in Knightsbridge, approximately a mile and a half away directly along Piccadilly, he set off on foot for home. He made his way along the wide thoroughfare by St James's Church and Prince's Hall where, through the windows, late-night revellers laughed in the golden glow of the new phenomenon, electric light.

He stopped briefly to look in the window of Hatchards booksellers where only a day before he had purchased the recently published, melancholy and moving 'The Ballad of Reading Gaol' by Oscar Wilde, the writer who had provided a great scandal in London a few years earlier and been gaoled in 1895.

A few minutes later he strode across Duke Street and passed the leafless trees of Green Park as he pulled the collar of his greatcoat up around his face. Ahead of him the wind lifted a discarded newspaper and wafted it along in the direction of Hyde Park Corner.

The few pedestrians who passed him were now all swathed in overcoats and scarves. It was close to eleven at night and a chill had descended over London as he arrived opposite Apsley House, the Iron Duke's London home, called in his lifetime, 'No. 1 London', and which still stood, forty-seven years after his death, stately and regal in the night light. The young man halted a few moments looking at it before he walked on towards the construction that glorified the Duke: Wellington Monument.

Here, alone in what was usually one of the busiest parts of London, he stopped across from the entrance to Constitution Hill. He thought he must have picked up a stone in his boot for his heel was definitely hurting and he bent to untie his lace. As he did so he saw a movement in the corner of his eye and, looking round, espied a man on the single bench to the side of the footpath.

The man sat gently illuminated by a gaslamp, which showed him to be between forty and fifty. He had a strong wide jaw and even in the wan glow his face appeared sun-coloured and brown. John Conrad nodded and the man replied in kind. It was then he noticed the stranger's eyes; they were of the palest ice blue and the gaze was fixed, almost staring as he met John Conrad's look. Under his perfectly straight nose he wore a large, quite splendid moustache and as he bent forward to rest his elbows on his knees, the shape under his heavy outer coat appeared long and lithe.

'Good evening,' the stranger said.

John Conrad smiled. 'Good evening.'

'Am I correct that you wear an Australian army uniform?'

'Why yes, I do. How did you know it?'

The man straightened and smiled, yet the expression was without real mirth. 'How is it that you're here in London?'

As John Conrad emptied his boot he answered, 'I'm with a contingent from Sydney.'

'And why would that be?'

John Conrad met the formal countenance. 'I'm afraid I'm not at liberty to say.'

'Good man,' the stranger answered, and then he went on, 'I'm only visiting here myself.' He gave an odd-sounding cough and fell silent.

John Conrad retied his boot-lace as he asked, 'Do you live abroad now?'

The man gave another wry smile, hesitating momentarily. 'Well, yes, I suppose I do. I'm staying nearby. I've come here once or twice late at night, just to sit . . . and think.' He paused again and then asked, 'Are you at liberty to say how long you'll be in England?'

John Conrad grinned. 'Yes, that's not a state secret. We head for home on Friday, this week.' He regained his feet. 'I've enjoyed being here, learned a lot, though I suppose I'll never come back.'

For a few moments the stranger appeared to reflect on the soldier's words, then as if making a decision, he moved along the bench and gestured for John Conrad to sit. For some inexplicable reason John Conrad felt he should comply.

'I see you're a captain. I suppose a soldier's life is a good one,' the man added confidentially.

And John Conrad, thinking of recent months, said, 'Sometimes.'

'That sounds as if you're disillusioned.'

He answered quickly, 'No, not at all with the army . . . ah . . .' He hesitated and said no more.

The older man turned on the seat. There was an expression

of interest in his eyes, as if he had taken an instant liking to the young Australian. 'We all can be disillusioned at times but it seems to me that one so young as you shouldn't have experienced that most draining of emotions quite yet.' He was obviously wanting to talk and this attention made the young man feel oddly flattered.

John Conrad was surprised when he heard himself reply, 'Truth is, I was disillusioned by a girl.'

The other man did not say anything and in the night silence they heard a dog barking somewhere in the distance. When the stranger did finally speak it was quietly. 'A girl. I see. Is she in Australia?'

'Yes.' As he said this, John Conrad looked round into the light brittle eyes to hear the man ask, 'What happened?'

Before he knew he had said it; it was out: 'She broke my heart.'

There was another silence, then the man asked, 'And how did she do that?'

The young soldier recognised an instant when he thought he should politely say good night, stand, and leave immediately, but the moment had no real influence and he found himself actually talking about Caro Dere . . . about how he had felt about her and what had happened, about Matthew Craken and the marriage and all the aftermath.

The wind increased in the cool faded glow of the London night during the many minutes that the young Australian related his tale. He was not aware of the air movement or the drop in temperature as he opened his heart. The cold London night became the backdrop to the dramatic cameo of the young soldier emoting to the stranger who listened in silence, never interrupting, as the minutes passed.

John Conrad had not thought to reveal his heart to anyone in the world, but the dark of night and the presence of the stranger had somehow achieved it. His final words seemed to echo around the dark parkland when he came to the completion of his account. 'And now she is dead to me, for ever and entirely.'

For some time the stranger did not speak; it appeared to be a habit of his to consider things before replying. He rubbed the side of his neck in an automatic action and John Conrad's sharp youthful eyes noticed what appeared to be a scar which ran there above his collar and beneath his fingers. It looked like an old wound. In the silence John Conrad felt perhaps he had been rash to reveal himself as he had. He leaned forward hesitatingly, 'I . . . excuse me, perhaps it was wrong to take up your time this way; to speak so forthrightly. I'm . . .'

The other man raised his hand, 'No, don't say that. You spoke from your heart and told me things that were obviously immensely painful to you. That in itself has given us a sort of intimacy not usual at first meeting. Your tale of the girl called Caro's an unhappy one and you couldn't have done other than you did. Though I would tender the opinion that things are sometimes not as they appear, it does appear to follow that in your case you *were* betrayed. There seems no other explanation.'

Again he fell into silence and John Conrad felt that the conversation was at an end, but then abruptly the stranger continued: 'So from what you tell me you became a soldier, but not out of choice?'

'Yes, it was used on me as a discipline after I had injured the man in the fight. I was only twenty and didn't want to leave Brisbane. I was angry and resisted the army for a time, but it's funny how fate alters people. One day I realised I was actually enjoying the routine and the vigorous life and I was lucky enough to serve under a Scottish major who taught me much, attended to many of my failings and really, I suppose, made a soldier of me. We don't have any Sandhursts in Australia but my three years with Major MacPhee, I believe were the equivalent of such an institution. By the time I became a lieutenant, I knew the army suited me. I like the life. I like the routine. I understand fully now what being a professional soldier means and the responsibility that we carry, even though I've never seen any action. I suppose I feel as prepared as a man can be. I'm even more dedicated to my career now, because of what I've told you . . . because of her.'

The older man nodded to himself. 'Yes. I understand that.' He remained quiet while he moved his long legs and leant forward to rest his elbows on his knees for a few seconds as if contemplating the lights of St George's Hospital across the wide thoroughfare. Then he brought himself straight upright and asked without looking in John Conrad's direction, 'You leave England this coming Friday, you say?'

'Yes, that's right. We sail from Plymouth, I believe.'

The man turned his head and studied John Conrad. He hesitated momentarily as if torn by indecision and then, looking straight ahead at some very distant star, he began speaking in a deliberate way, each word coming as if forced from a definite place within him.

'I . . . once had . . . a girl I loved very deeply too, yes, once, in the past. Though she's as dead as your Caro is. More so, for she is literally gone out of this world. Her name was Hermione. It was a long time ago – fifteen years. To think she'd be thirty-odd now. She was eighteen and beautiful when she died of . . . typhoid.' He said the word with vitriol as if it were blasphemy. 'Damned disease killed her mother too.' Then he inhaled deeply and made a sad sound between his teeth. 'Her father was a good friend. He had had his troubles too. To think he lost his daughter and his wife within a month of each other . . . what bitter blows, to us both.'

He wiped his long fingers across his brow. 'I can see her in my mind playing croquet.' He spoke quietly. 'We'd have been married a long time by now.' His eyes remained fixed on the place he watched in the distant sky. 'Never felt the need for any woman since.' He gave a short staccato laugh. 'Some people say I avoid them,' he shook his head, 'though that isn't essentially so.'

And now his voice dropped almost as if he spoke to himself and John Conrad actually bent closer to listen. 'When Hermione died I was not there. That's the part which remains to trouble me even after all these years. That . . . I . . . was . . . not . . . there.'

As John Conrad watched the other man's rigid profile, he felt sure he had never told any of this to a soul before, and he knew with a certainty that the revelations of this night would remain with the two of them. The muscles in the stranger's jaw tightened as he turned to face John Conrad. 'What's your name, soldier?' The voice was quite normal again.

'John Conrad Fleet.'

As he said this the man stood up and offered his hand. John

Conrad gained his feet and, facing him, took the proffered palm in his.

'I'm pleased to have met you.'

'Thank you.' And as John Conrad in turn was about to ask the older man his name, the stranger shot the question, 'Who's your commanding officer?'

'I'm here with a colonel: I don't think I should say.'

The stranger smiled. This time it was a warm expression and the severe lines of his face melted momentarily. 'Perhaps you shouldn't. And I imagine Australia and the Empire can be proud of you. I must leave you now, goodbye.'

The man turned on his heel and walked off to cross Wellington Place in the direction of Grosvenor Crescent. John Conrad eyed the tall departing form for some time, admitting the peculiarity that he wished the man had not gone. There had been a sense of liberation in revealing his feelings about all that had happened in Brisbane and he felt restored by it. And the compliment the stranger had paid him in relating his own tale John Conrad felt was somehow of immeasurable importance.

He stood a little while breathing the cold air in his lungs and tasting the silence of the night around him. When he too brought himself to depart the spot under the streetlamp, he remained immersed in thoughts of the chance meeting.

Long after he had gone to bed, John Conrad lay awake, hands behind his head, listening to the unremitting wind as the fire in his bedchamber projected a parade of shadows on his walls. The stranger had left a marked impression on him and he regretted he had not learnt his name. When finally slumber stole upon him, delicately fusing his conscious thoughts with that moment of delicious disassociation of mind and body, the encounter metamorphosed to a dream.

The following morning John Conrad and Bernard rose early. It was quite dark when they took the horses out of the stables and crossed to Rotten Row where they rode for over half an hour before they witnessed the new day come up over the water of the Serpentine reflecting little golden arrows of light that skipped in quick succession across the ripples made by the wind. To their gratification and that of London the dawn was a prelude to a sunny late autumn day, most of which they spent working on reports. In the evening they dined with the colonel.

The next day the colonel called his officers to his quarters. He stood side by side with Major Smith, who directed the men to sit around the long table which took up a deal of Colonel Ayres' quarters.

The Old Man stood now and smiled behind his beard and bushy moustache. He was a capable soldier and a competent leader, and his men respected him. They had seen him since his arrival here conduct himself with dignity and efficiency and when, on occasion, it had appeared that he may have at first been seen as 'a mere colonial soldier' those who had regarded him as such had not been long in reassessing him.

'Gentlemen, we have been over five weeks in Great Britain and I feel we've accomplished a great deal. My meetings with the Colonial Defence Committee have been rewarding and we have all learned much.'

There were nods and murmurs of agreement.

'We were to depart London on Friday, as I think you're all aware, but we've been invited to an important event on Saturday afternoon. Major General Gatacre has asked us all to witness a most interesting test on a range near Southampton, at the edge of the New Forest and I've accepted.

'While you'll all be aware of the hand grenade from your military history, you'll also know that the armies of this century have not employed it in battle. Though such weapons were used as early as the sixteenth century they've become obsolete in our time. Well, now an explosives expert in Cardiff has been experimenting and he has constructed a new hand grenade which is meant to be efficient and powerful. We're to be honoured by being amongst the first to witness its demonstration.'

Colonel Ayres glanced round at the major and smiled knowingly before he turned back to his staff. 'And I've learned that someone else will be there, someone I think you'll all be greatly interested to see.'

The men looked at each other.

The colonel continued, 'We are very honoured . . . to be attending the new weapon's performance in the presence of a great hero: I'm speaking of Lord Kitchener, the Sirdar.'

There was a murmur of surprise from them all as the senior officer lifted his hand. 'K is returning to Egypt soon, I'm told, so we're in great luck.' Then he added, 'Wear your woollens underneath; it'll be cold on the range.'

And it was. They arrived at the range at the edge of the New Forest at one in the afternoon and stood waiting under a sulky sky where the wind chased menacing rain clouds.

A captain, a sergeant and two privates were at ease on a gentle rise. At forty-five degrees from the four soldiers and forty yards distant stood a small wooden building, and at ninety degrees and fifty yards away a slightly larger stone construction in the shape of a blockhouse.

Colonel Ayres and the general were in conversation, and John Conrad and the other Australians stood amongst the group of officers and politicians gathered to view the display.

Suddenly there was a ripple of movement among those gathered and men began turning around and whispering.

'Here he comes.'

'It's K.'

'Look.'

'Attention.' It was the sergeant speaking to his men, but the entire group gathered itself and the officers stood alert while the politicians lengthened into a replica of a line.

Across the field a small herd of rough-coated ponies cantered by in the middle distance, past a row of bare oak trees, and from behind them rumbled an entourage of men, one, in the middle of the oncoming retinue, taller than all the others.

Colonel Ayres moved away from the general and over to his men, taking up a position beside Major Smith. Next to the major stood John Conrad and beside him Bernard Houston.

The newcomers came straight into the waiting assembly and up to General Gatacre. The tall man stepped forward from the middle of the party and took the general by the hand.

John Conrad's murmur of surprise was so loud that even though there was a rumble of thunder in the distance, both Major Smith and Bernard, standing on either side of him, turned towards him.

John Conrad was in disbelief. He was looking at a man he knew. He was perhaps six feet two or three, his skin kissed bronze by the desert sun, his brittle blue eyes set above a straight nose and a wide moustache. John Conrad had revealed his innermost secrets to this man near Wellington Monument in the chill wind of a London night. It left him a little unsteady on his feet to realise he had exchanged confidences with none other than Lord Kitchener of Khartoum!

Lord Kitchener turned from the general and briefly greeted the politicians. Then he moved back to General Gatacre, who introduced him to Colonel Ayres.

'Lord Kitchener, may I introduce Colonel James Ayres from New South Wales, Australia. He's visiting here with his staff.'

'New South Wales,' K replied smiling. 'A place I want to visit some day.'

The colonel smiled back. 'You'd be more than welcome, sir.' Then he turned to his six officers who stood at attention beside him. 'Sir, these are my officers.'

The six Australians saluted as one and K returned the formality, then he began to turn away, and even as he did, his eyes met those of the man standing two from Colonel Ayres. No one but John Conrad noticed the flicker of instant recognition from Kitchener. K nodded almost imperceptibly as John Conrad stood fixed at attention. Then the Sirdar faced back to the colonel. His voice was formal, but polite. 'Have you met with the War Office?'

'Yes Lord Kitchener, and the Colonial Defence Committee.'

And then the Australian senior officer smiled quite delightedly as K turned to his aide. 'See if I can find an hour to meet with Colonel Ayres before I leave. There could be things we can discuss.' With that he moved over to General Gatacre. 'Now, General, where's this potent new small weapon I've heard so much about?'

'This way, m'lord.'

The sky was darkening and a storm was appearing inevitable as General Gatacre gestured for K to take a position behind a stone partition about five feet tall and about thirty feet long to the side of the rise where the sergeant and the privates stood. K moved behind the wall at the nearest end to the soldiers, and the rest of the company, including the politicians, filtered to his side along the length of the wall. Some began to fiddle with umbrellas though as yet no rain had fallen.

General Gatacre's voice rose above the chatter of the assembly. 'Now Captain Drake will explain the procedure.'

As thunder rolled above, the captain stepped up to the mound. He pointed. 'Please look carefully at the wooden structure forty yards away. Then, sirs, please use the seats behind the wall until the explosion occurs. We believe the new hand grenade, which we are calling the Disdale bomb, after its creator, will completely annihilate the wooden structure. Privates Boyle and MacMillan will demonstrate the weapon to us. Take over, Sergeant.'

The sergeant saluted and moved briskly the few paces to his men. He picked up a cylindrical metal object about five inches in length from a stack of the same. Holding the weapon in the air he used his parade voice. 'This hand grenade has a fuse inside which will burn for five seconds once it's ignited. At the end of that time it will explode.' He pointed to two pin-like protrusions at the top of the object. 'Once a soldier removes these nails the lever they sit in can be held down by the fingers indefinitely, but once the lever is released, as in when it's thrown, then a spring inside drives a hammer upon a cap and that ignites the fuse.'

He turned to his men. 'Boyle!' he shouted.

Another loud clap of thunder sounded and a few spots of rain fell as Boyle stepped smartly forward and took up a grenade. He brandished the metal object in the air with his right hand, and with his left pulled out one nail, then the other. He said the words, 'One and two,' before he pitched the object with all his might in the direction of the wooden hut. Swiftly he jumped down behind another wall where the captain, sergeant and MacMillan knelt.

Seconds later the hut exploded with a mighty bang.

K and the entire company stood and peered over the wall. Where there had been the wooden construction was instead an indentation in the ground and smoke and debris all around. 'Excellent,' opined the Sirdar, at which his companions, taking this as permission to verbalise their own judgements, all began to speak at once.

The captain's voice rose in explanation. 'That, distinguished guests, is how the Disdale bomb works on wood. Now we will demonstrate it against brick and stone.' He nodded to the sergeant who called, 'MacMillan!'

This soldier stood and took up a grenade. Just as Boyle had done, he raised the object in his left hand and removed one of the nails with his right. At that very moment a flash of lightning hit a tree on MacMillan's right about thirty feet distant and most of the assembly cried loudly out in shock. MacMillan started and swung round on his heels, looking in horror as he dropped the Disdale bomb. He stood petrified as it hit the ground and rolled directly towards Lord Kitchener, coming to rest at his feet. The men clustered around him hurled themselves from their chairs. Umbrellas leapt in the air, and decorum disappeared.

The sergeant and Boyle seemed turned to stone and it was only the captain who remained calm and attempted control crying, 'Don't worry, only one nail's been removed!'

In the empty space left around K only John Conrad stood. He bounded forward, took up the hand grenade and hurled it in the air, then he threw himself at K and knocked him to the ground even as the Disdale bomb exploded in the air, spitting pieces of death in all directions. The captain, who had begun once more to shout that there was no need to panic, died with the words of assurance on his lips and metal fragments in his head.

John Conrad felt a searing heat across the back of his left leg and then all was silent.

The two men on the ground did not move for some moments. John Conrad could actually feel K's heart beating beneath his own. Then the young Australian rolled away from the Sirdar. Blood ran from the wound in his leg and was staining the ground.

Kitchener sat up and saw the injured leg of his saviour. He looked around to see General Gatacre running towards him and other men drifting back. It was then that K realised who had saved his life. Their eyes met.

'You . . .' K said softly. 'I should have known it would be you. And I thought you were to leave England yesterday.'

'I'm only glad you're all right, sir.'

General Gatacre dropped to his knees beside K and others moved over to the dead captain.

Kitchener raised his hand. 'I'm all right. Though sadly I

see the captain was not as fortunate. Please see to him first.' He began to rise and waved away the general's offer of help. When he was upright, he gestured to John Conrad. 'This officer saved my life and has wounded himself in the process.' He smiled across at John Conrad. 'I'm eternally indebted to you, Captain Fleet.'

When K used John Conrad's name only Colonel Ayres frowned. No one else noticed that John Conrad had not been introduced to the Sirdar. The Old Man's lips pursed in thought and he looked speculatively from K to his young officer.

Lord Kitchener had insisted John Conrad be taken to Southampton Military Hospital, even though it had been established that it was only a flesh wound. There his leg was dressed and he was allowed to leave that same afternoon. The Australians caught the five o'clock express from Southampton and were at Victoria Station in London by half-past seven.

The Disdale bomb was never heard of again. It was on this single occasion that it was demonstrated. The powers that be obviously believed that if some new weapon had almost killed the United Kingdom and Empire's greatest living hero, it was not only bad luck but badly devised, and from that day the Disdale bomb, the two-pin hand grenade, accelerated into oblivion.

John Conrad was the hero of the mess that night. Everybody insisted on the event being retold as each new officer entered. He sat on a lounge with his wounded leg up on a stool and drank gin and tonic bitters from a long glass. Sturdy fires crackled in three fireplaces around the long room, and the cosy air was only disturbed by short bolts of cold that shot through the door when it opened to shouts of 'Hurry up! Close the bloody door and listen to this!'

By half-past ten the evening was getting rowdy. 'Here's to our very own bloody hero,' shouted Bernard, lifting his glass in John Conrad's direction. The other Australians lifted their drinks in unison. 'To our own bloody hero,' sounded the chorus of voices.

John Conrad laughed as Lieutenant Bill Ashman came and sat beside him to observe, 'You know, people say Kitchener likes all his officers to be single men. Doesn't have one married man on his personal staff.'

Bernard looked up from his glass of whisky and responded, 'Yes, they say that way he gets their full attention. They're not mooning about with their minds on a woman instead of their work.'

Bill Ashman continued with his point of view. 'I've heard he's a woman hater.'

One of the cavalry officers agreed, 'Yes, I heard that when I was at Sandhurst.'

'What's the word for that?' asked a captain at the bar, swallowing his Scotch and drawing deeply on a cheroot.

'Misogynist,' replied John Conrad from where he sat listening, 'but he's not, you know. It isn't true.'

Ashman turned round to raise his eyebrow and face his companion on the lounge beside him. 'Oh, how interesting. And how in hell would you know that, Fleet?'

John Conrad met the other man's gaze. 'Let's just say I do.'

Ashman shook his head. 'Today didn't only make you a hero, mate, but it turned you into a bloody mind-reader.'

Those within earshot began to laugh and the lieutenant was warming to his subject. 'Fleet, m'boy, you *don't* know. Admit it, you don't know.'

'Yeah,' shouted Alex Grew over the general noise. 'Bet the great Sirdar's never been in love in his life. Unlike you, Ashman who've been through . . . how many fiancées is it?'

Laughter and catcalls followed this exchange, and Bill Ashman rose unsteadily to his feet. He lifted his rum in a general salute. 'I speak in defence . . . of my position. My dear comrade in arms here, wounded as he is, suggests, because he saved K's life, that . . . he *knows* how he feels. Bloody thought transference if ever I've seen it! Amazing!'

John Conrad lifted his arm and pulled Bill down beside him with a thud. 'Look, the world speculates on K. Let's just agree to disagree.'

'Absolutely,' shouted Bernard from across the room where he had gone to take up a billiard cue. 'If we all agreed there'd be no more wars then K, and all of us here united, would be out of our jobs!'

This was obviously the consensus because the whole mess

began to talk, and in the noise and hilarity that followed, the discussion on K's sensibilities died.

Two days later the Old Man sent for John Conrad. As the young captain came through the door and saluted, the colonel looked up from the papers on his desk and pointed to a chair.

'So, Fleet, how're you feeling?'

'Well, sir, quite normal.'

'Wound not giving you any trouble?'

'No, sir, none at all.'

'Good.'

Then the colonel leaned back in his chair and tugged gently on his goatee beard as he looked penetratingly at his visitor. 'You know our new departure is the day after tomorrow.'

'Yes, sir.'

You're a good soldier, Fleet.'

'Thank you, sir.'

'I'll be sorry to lose you.'

John Conrad's eyes widened. 'Excuse me . . . Lose me, sir?'

'Fact is, I've agreed in principle, providing that you do too.'

'I'm not following you, sir.'

The Old Man hesitated and then smiled. 'You're being offered the chance of a lifetime. It'll have a momentous effect on your military career. Lord Kitchener has asked for you to transfer to his personal staff, the move to take effect immediately. If you agree, instead of leaving with us on Wednesday . . . you'll leave with him, from Dover, en route for Egypt.'

John Conrad did not answer. He could hardly believe he was being offered a position on the Sirdar's staff, and the colonel sat on the other side of his desk smiling at him and waiting for a reply. When one was not forthcoming the Old Man said, 'Nothing like this has ever happened to an officer in the Australian army to my knowledge. You've been with me for only four and a half months but I've learnt much about you in that time, Fleet. I cannot stand in your way. This is too important. It's a unique privilege and a great honour, and I'm certain you're up to it. What do you say?'

And now John Conrad gave his reply. 'Thank you, sir. I'd very much like to take up the position with Lord Kitchener.'

Colonel Ayres stood and walked round the table, holding out his hand to his young officer who jumped to his feet, forgetting his wounded leg. The Old Man looked straight into John Conrad's eyes and revealed something to him that surprised him almost as much as what had just occurred. While the colonel continued to grasp his hand he said, 'The Sirdar's perceptive. I'm sure he's not only motivated by what you did for him two days ago, though doubtless he's extremely grateful indeed. No, Captain Fleet, there's more to K's request than that. I noticed something that I believe no other did on the day you saved his life. He called you by name and yet you hadn't been introduced to him.' The Old Man continued to stare into John Conrad's eyes as if he might read the answer there and when he did not, he finished, 'You'd met him previously somewhere, hadn't you?'

'Yes, Colonel, I had.'

'Would you enlarge upon that?'

The eyes of the two men were locked and in absurd counterpoint John Conrad was acutely aware of the noise of a pigeon outside tapping with his beak on the window.

'I'm afraid I cannot, sir. It'd be breaking a serious confidence.'

The Old Man nodded very slowly. His was a generous spirit. 'I understand. No wonder K wants you.' He squeezed John Conrad's hand, then released it to pat him on the back. 'I'll watch your career from afar. Make me and Australia proud of you.'

'Thank you, sir. I'll do my very best.'

Chapter Sixteen

November 1901

Caro threw the last handful of the golden grain out in a long arc from her body and watched it fall like tiny points of light in front of the squabbling bronze-feathered chickens. It was still officially spring but the moulten ball in the sky above her head was already presenting Southern Queensland with intense temperatures and offering a sample of the steady inflexible bonfire of summer heat in store.

She had grown used to the country life in the three years she had spent here at Cedar Grove. Odd how she did not miss the city now, except for certain amenities like gas light and running water, though she did miss her mother and father terribly – it was a shame her mother would not come to the country – and she missed Aunt Leigh. Along with the continuing pain of her loss of John Conrad was the loss of Aunt Leigh. The woman had been a second mother figure to her all the formative years of her life and she still had not come to terms with the fact that Aunt Leigh despised her.

She had only seen the woman once since her marriage and it had been a disastrous meeting. They had all been so close before her liaison with Matthew, and Caro knew her mother had visited Brewery House in those fearful days just prior to her wedding but Elizabeth had never revealed what had been said.

When Caro and Matt returned from their steamer honeymoon voyage north to Mackay he had convinced her to leave Brisbane for Cedar Grove and it was then she made up her mind to go and face Aunt Leigh. Perhaps to say goodbye; perhaps just to see the woman again. Later, she supposed she had been naïve, dreaming of Aunt Leigh's forgiving her; of continuing some sort of intimacy; all in youthful, even childish hope . . .

Caro arrived at the kitchen door of Brewery House as she had hundreds of times before, and she entered to the wonderful smell of Aunt Leigh's apple pie sitting on the hob. A minute later when the woman came in from the hall she found Caro standing in her old familiar spot near the high stool by the airing cupboard. Aunt Leigh showed no real surprise, though if Caro had not been so preoccupied with her own concerns she would have seen the muscles in Leigh's jaw tighten and her hands turn into fists at her sides.

'What are you doing here?' she asked.

'I just wanted . . . to see you.'

The older woman made a scoffing sound. '"You who are falser than vows made in wine," here to see me. Really? Why?'

'Aunt Leigh. Please. You've been like a second mother to me. I wanted you to know. I didn't wish to hurt you . . . or anyone.'

'If that were true you would not have.'

Caro sighed. 'It isn't simple like that. I know it's hard and I don't expect you to understand, but I—'

The woman cut her off. 'Good, I'm glad of that for I don't and never will. How you could have betrayed this family, as you surely have; how you could have broken John Conrad's heart, as you surely have, will remain a mystery to me for ever. You, whose mother is my second cousin; you whom I thought I knew, now allied in the most intimate fashion with the man who ruined this family . . . killed my little Emma.' Leigh's voice broke but she controlled herself and now her eyes narrowed in distaste. 'Barrington will never forgive you and nor will I. How could you do this to us?'

Caro did not answer but her hand came up to finger the still tender scar that ran across her bottom lip. It was fortunately faint and not very large and had needed only three sutures. Matthew had seen to it that the wound had been attended to by Brisbane's best doctor, and he was often known to remind her that they had 'both been scarred by the *enemy Fleet*'.

Aunt Leigh continued to eye Caro fiercely. 'How could you?' she repeated.

204

When Caro still did not reply she said, '"Secret guilt by silence is betrayed."' She pointed to the door. 'Begone and never come back.'

Caro stepped forward, lifting her hand towards her aunt. 'Please. I truly did not ever think it would come to this.'

The woman knocked the girl's hand aside. 'You didn't think at all. You're a Craken now. No one who bears the name Craken is ever welcome here. Get out!'

Caro's cheeks were flushed, her pulse had accelerated and she could feel the sting of tears beginning but she managed her final statement. 'All right, I'll go. But I want you to know that I too have been hurt beyond all measure, even though you don't believe me. You're suffering and for that I'm truly sorry. And though you never will heed me, I've had no choice but to do as I have done.' She took a step backwards. 'And whether you like it or not, I will continue . . . to . . . love this family.'

'Such love as yours we can do without,' Aunt Leigh retorted as she shook her head in disbelief and threw her hand out once more to point fixedly at the door.

Caro said no more, and turned round and left the room where she had spent so many happy hours. Hurrying down the steps she could no longer contain her tears and they ran from her eyes as she passed by the stables.

'Is that you, Caro?'

She inclined her head to see Bart coming through the stable doorway. He hurried over to her. 'What brings you here?' He saw the tears on her cheeks. 'Oh. Are you all right?'

She kept walking on as she nodded and wiped her face with the back of her hand. 'Yes. It doesn't matter.' She passed the stables where a couple of mares watched, big soft round eyes upon her, and then she ran out the gate and across the footpath.

Bart had kept pace with her all the way and now he stayed her with his hand and brought her to a halt. 'It's such a strange thing you've done, Caroline. You can't expect anyone here to understand it, you know.'

She nodded.

'Did you go to see Aunt Leigh?'

She nodded again.

'It's useless. She won't forgive you.'

Caro found her voice. 'I know.'

'Well, it's best you don't come back.'

'I won't.' She went to walk on by.

'Caro?'

Her eyes met his.

'Why?' he asked very quietly.

They stood facing each other on the street, standing on the grassy dirt footpath a few feet apart. It seemed a long time to Bart before she answered.

'I can't tell you.'

'John Conrad was in love with you, you know.'

'I do.'

'Makes you seem hard and callous, Caro.'

'I'm not.'

'Then I'm lost to comprehend. Gosh, Caro, you were like, well, a part of this family, here all the time and one of us. Now you've made a choice that broke my brother's heart . . . hurt us all pretty badly as well. The man you've married to our way of thinking's a rotter. And everyone knows the reason you've married him. They're all saying you must be—' He broke off.

'Having his baby,' she finished for him.

'Yes.' He looked up into the blue cloudless sky and hesitated momentarily before he brought his gaze back down to hers. 'I'm not one to go on about things but it doesn't make you a good woman, Caro. I mean, to be with *him* when John Conrad thought you were his alone. He was stung to the core the night – the night he came to you at your place.'

Caro could feel more tears welling up. She took a deep breath as her hand automatically rose to finger her lip once more. 'Bart, I know that and I have to live with it all my life. I can't explain. I can only say I didn't mean to hurt anyone . . . least of all your brother. I may not see you again for a long time. Perhaps one day you'll understand. Goodbye.' And with that she hurried across the street.

He stood watching her until she disappeared around the corner. 'Goodbye,' he said softly.

Caro knew she had offended the Fleet family beyond redemption and while Bart had been the fairest of them all, even he couldn't understand. How could she blame him for that? She could not blame any of them for how they felt. She hardly understood the machinations of that strangest of times herself. The only one she ever felt anger towards was John Conrad. Oh, she loved him still – the years had not altered that – but now in her quiet moments she sometimes imagined he should have known better; should not have so easily accepted that she was capable of all he had believed.

Yet when she felt this way she recalled the night in her mother's garden, his pallid face and his devastation in the knowledge that she was married to Matthew. He had not been capable of rational thinking and she had lied to him . . . to somehow save them both from further agony. When she thought this way she would forgive him, her anger would dissipate and she would cry a little for all that could have been.

'Ma-ma!'

She turned sharply at the sound and the chickens closest to her fluttered a few paces away.

'My darling.' She bent down, placed the empty corn dish on the ground and held out her sun-browned arms as Harry broke from Knobby Clark's hand and ran forward unsteadily into his mother's embrace. She lifted him up, kissed his pink cheek and stood waiting as the big man strode over.

Knobby tipped his hat. 'He's had a good time riding in front of me on the new mare; I think he'll be able to ride alone soon.'

Caro laughed. 'Whoever heard of a baby not even three years old being able to ride alone.'

Knobby leant forward and tickled the little boy under his chin. 'Well, I just reckon this one might.' He swung his own chin up to look at the sky. 'No rain up there, wish there were, we need it.' Then he returned his hat to his head. 'I'm going into the store now for some tools I've had on order. Jacob's coming with me. I'll pick up the mail too and a newspaper if there's one – Matthew'll want that and so will Jacob. There's always news of our boys over in South Africa.'

'Yes, with his young brother over there it's understandable Jacob takes a personal interest in the war.'

Knobby agreed. 'Aye, and with old Lord Kitchener in charge now and his system of fencing in areas with this blockhouse business it seems like we've got those Boers on the run.'

Caro's response was a sigh and a nod of her head. Whenever Kitchener was mentioned she wondered if John Conrad Fleet were still with the great man. It had been through her mother that she had first learned that John Conrad had been chosen to be on Kitchener of Khartoum's staff. She often wondered how it had happened. Apparently Aunt Leigh was so proud and boasted to all and sundry about her nephew's success.

How clearly she still saw in her mind his special smile; hardly a movement of his lips really, and the way at the same time his blue eyes seemed to haze over for a second.

Abruptly she realised Knobby was speaking.

'. . . and so, we'll see you all this afternoon then.' He patted Harry affectionately on the head. 'Bye, little fellow,'

Caro contrived a smile. 'Say bye-bye to Uncle Knobby, darling.'

The child did so, waving his tiny fat hand in the air.

Caro watched Knobby take great strides across the yard and over to the stables. She gave a sharp little shake of her head. Knobby had become her right hand; she never would have believed it, but he had. The Bradys, Jacob and Mary, relied heavily on him too. Lately he had taken more and more responsibility here and was turning into a type of manager of their small establishment at Cedar Grove. For the first time ever this year Jacob said they had made a profit from the sales of their stock and vegetables, and they were almost self-sufficient now. And the oddest occurrence of all was that Caro had come to like him: while he was outspoken and sometimes, with Matthew, rowdy and a little undignified, he was also honest and dependable. He had a girl over in Forest Hill nearby, a smart, sensible girl – Jane Kruger, daughter of another farmer.

When they had first come to live at the property Matt brought Knobby for companionship much to Caro's disapproval, but her husband had been adamant that Knobby must be part of the entourage and so that was that. He was a journalist by trade though he did not seem to miss city life and wrote a few articles for publications now and then. He and Matthew continued much as they always had: most nights they drank and played cards. They had soon found a few like compatriots in the district, though Matt covered his step down in class by reminding them, 'when one's in rustic surroundings one must accept rustic companions.' And while Matt praised the air and the light of the country and for a time became so enthusiastic about his painting that he even began to go to bed before midnight, his ardour for early rising waned as his passion for nightly card-playing regained its conviction.

While she stood now nursing Harry in her arms and watching Knobby leap a low fence and cross to the stables, for the first time she wondered about his age. She realised she did not know when his birthday was. He must be in his late thirties – her husband had not long turned thirty-nine. She puckered her lips to kiss Harry's cheek again. 'It's time your uncle married Jane,' she said softly. 'I've just realised how old he must be.'

Harry laughed as babies do, showing the little white pegs of teeth in his lower gums, and Caro kissed him again in adoration. The first time she had laid eyes on him she gloried in him and from the moment she had realised she carried him she had been so aware of him growing inside her, forming, becoming a person. She used to talk to her stomach every day, soft tender compassionate loving words she had for no one else. And when they had moved here, in the early mornings while Matthew slept and there was a dew on the grass and the air carried the pleasant coolness of post-dawn she had taken to walking great distances across the fields and gullies, and along the stretch of dirt road that led to the outside world, singing songs of her childhood to her growing stomach.

She had first felt Harry move within her when she had been carrying him fifteen weeks and three days. She had been knitting a baby blanket, sitting under the gumtrees near the side verandah of the big old wooden house of Cedar Grove. She had stood up and cried out with joy, waved her hands in the air and laughed in the ecstasy of the revelation.

By the sixth month of Caro's pregnancy, when her belly extended like a little ball in front of her and she had taken to enjoying her baby's movements – the kicking, the wiggling, the rolling – she was quite used to her life here in the country.

She had felt satisfied that Matthew had been away in Brisbane on the first of February when the little person inside her persisted on and off all day with continuous movement. She had been busy that day and it almost seemed as if his activity were to constantly encourage her. It had suited her to be alone with that part of John Conrad she carried, without Matthew to spoil it.

Matthew had moved to the country only in a sense: his perception of moving was not quite like his wife's. He had remained the first four weeks in situ and then had returned to Brisbane for the same amount of time. But he had come back, much to her surprise, and so a pattern had developed: Matthew's arriving and Matthew's leaving. In the beginning, Knobby had joined him and gone back to Brisbane every time but now occasionally he remained when Matt left; not that they weren't still just like brothers, they were. She knew Knobby adored Matt, and she also knew, while he might never admit it, that her husband was pretty fond of this friend.

Yet when she would have desired him away, Matt was not. For Harry's birth, he had been home. That had not pleased Caro. She had wished to be united with the child, just the two of them. Funny how wishes did not come true; so many dreams foiled. Harry had been due on the Saturday, but no, he had been a week late and by then Matthew had returned to the farm.

Even two and a half years later, with her feet planted firmly apart on the rich brown earth beneath her, a tiny tremble ran down Caro's spine as she recalled Mrs Brent, the midwife, leaning over her and saying joyfully, 'Your son's father is here.' Caro had lifted her head in some absurd expectation that John Conrad had manifested at her bedside but no, it was Matthew, standing at the foot of her bed in the lamplight. He had smiled crookedly; if she had not known him so well she could have mistaken it for tenderly. Then he leaned over her and touched the baby, the scar on his cheek glistening as if it were a statement of the evidence of their unnatural confederacy made to give a name to the child she held in her arms.

Matthew had been the one to suggest calling him Harry and Caro had not objected. As she could not call him John Conrad, Harry suited her well enough.

'Hey! Caro, old girl, where's Knobby?'

She started, coming out of her reverie, and rounded to see him leaning against the verandah railing twenty yards away, tapping his ebony, silver-handled cane on the floor, his two Great Danes, Rubens and Hogarth, at his side. He wore a white shirt with an edging of lace on the collar and black pants and boots, as ever his boots polished to a high shine. Matthew always dressed totally unsuitably for his environment and yet Caro had to admit, somehow, amazingly it looked appropriate on him.

'Dada!' called Harry, wriggling in her arms to be freed. She let him down to the ground and he toddled unsteadily towards the steps of the house, making his baby noises.

Matthew swung along the wide verandah on his cane and with his bad leg straight eased himself down on the steps. He commanded the dogs to stay as he urged the toddler forward. 'Come on, my bonny boy. You can make it.' And he opened his arms wide as the infant staggered the last few steps and fell into his embrace. 'Well done,' Matthew cried, lifting the child high in the air as Harry's pure baby delight echoed around the yard: 'Dada, dada!'

Matthew watched Caro pick up the empty corn dish and dawdle towards him. 'So where's Knobby?'

'Gone with Jacob into Gatton to the store. Getting the newspaper and mail for you too.'

Her husband winked at her. 'And detouring to see Jane Kruger, I'll be bound.'

'Yes, I'd say so.'

'So,' said Matthew to the baby in his arms, 'I'm thinking I'll spend the time painting until your Uncle Knobby comes home.' Harry ran his tiny finger down the indentation on Matthew's cheek and the man took hold of the little hand and kissed the fingertips, then he placed the child on the ground before he looked up at Caro standing in front of him. 'Hot, isn't it?'

'Yes, Matt. That's Queensland for you.'

'What time did I go to bed last night?'

Caro shook her head. 'Don't know. I went at midnight and you were still enjoying your rum then. I didn't hear you come in so it was probably a lot later than that.'

He stood up and regarded her through half-closed eyes. 'Lucky you didn't wake then, eh? Or I might have kept you cognizant of your surroundings for quite a while.'

'Not the state you were in you wouldn't have.'

He gave one of his rakish half-grins and bent down to ruffle the hair of the baby who was sitting on the ground. 'Listen to

211

your mother, Harry, going on at me.' He laughed. 'Take it from me, don't get involved with women, lad.'

'Dada,' was Harry's response as he tapped on Matthew's boot with his tiny fist.

'Good boy,' he said before he called the dogs to heel and propelled himself off across the yard towards his studio, one of the outhouses, formerly a barn. At the door he called back over his shoulder, 'I'll paint until Knobby returns.'

'What about your luncheon?'

'I'll have it at the easel.'

Caro picked up her child and with him in one arm and the corn dish in the other, mounted the steps. The enticing smell of fresh bread met her at the doorway and she tracked it to the big homely kitchen where Mary Brady looked up from her baking dish. She was a warm-hearted, unaffected country woman of forty years; her attractive round face bronzed from the sun, and her deep auburn hair, traced through with gentle strands of white, pulled back in a bun.

'Fed the chickens, love?'

Caro placed the baby on the floor where he immediately began to crawl towards the door, which his mother walked over to and closed, as she answered the question. 'Yes, and saw Matt. He's off to paint. What time is it?'

'After ten. Want a cuppa?'

Caro smiled. 'I'd love one.'

So Mary put the kettle on the iron stove to boil and the two women spent a pleasant half-hour together until Caro left to go outside to meet Hannah, the Bradys' eighteen-year-old daughter, where she waited near the water tank ready to light a fire under the metal boiler in which the teenager would boil the household's sheets, pillowcases and any other linen that needed washing. Hannah was leaving the farm soon; she had found work in the North Star Hotel in Ipswich.

At lunchtime the females brought the midday meal to a shed over past the stables for the three farm hands who helped Jacob and Knobby work the place. Then the women fed the baby and Matthew and the dogs, and finally themselves, and by three o'clock when Harry had gone down for his nap and Hannah was washing up the dishes and a mountain of ironing claimed the attention of Caro and

Mary, they heard the sounds of the dray returning from Gatton.

The three women graced the verandah as the two men climbed down from the dray.

'Pretty hot in town,' Jacob informed them, taking off his wide-brimmed hat and wiping the sweat from his brow.

At that moment Matthew's studio door opened and he came out into the glaring sunshine sixty yards from the arrivals. 'Halloa to the returning providers. Where's my newspaper, Knobby, and did they have a *Bulletin*?' This was a national publication whose pages often offered the elucidations of the literary élite, such as Henry Lawson, Banjo Paterson, et al. Much to his delight Knobby had had essays published in the *Bulletin* in the past.

Knobby waved the said entity high in the air. 'Yes, Matt, got one and have your mail here as well: a whole bunch of letters.'

'Any for me?' called Caro, and Knobby grinned, 'Yes, two.'

Jacob and Knobby soon had the dray emptied and the residents of Cedar Grove returned to their various occupations, some in the fiery open air and others indoors, where, depending on the job, it could be done in a modicum of comfort.

But there was no such comfort if labouring at the kitchen table over Matthew's white shirts with a heavy iron heated on the hob, and that was how, about half an hour later, Matthew found Caro.

He entered languidly and in usual mode leaned against the big cheese safe by the door. He eyed his wife: her slender bronzed arms and stately carriage and unruly curls adorning her damp forehead even with her hair pulled back. 'You're perspiring, old girl. Should you be lifting that heavy iron in your condition?'

'Matthew, I'm not an invalid.'

'Certainly you're not but you're carrying my baby and I don't want any mishaps.'

'Starting a dynasty, are you?'

He gave a rumble of a laugh in his throat but there was the cutting edge of sarcasm in his voice. 'Now, now, old girl, the dynasty began when *our Harry* was born. Right?'

213

Caro did not reply.

'Hey? I said *right*?'

She looked directly into his eyes for a few seconds before she replied very slowly. 'Right.'

He grinned. 'That's the way. Must have accord and unification in the family.' And he crossed to her and patted her on the bottom and kissed her cheek.

'Don't do that, Matt.'

'What? The kiss or the pat?'

'You know.'

'Affection, old girl, all affection, stemming from the one great source of my passion.' He grinned. 'Well, now there was news in my missives that I must act upon. Have to return to Brisbane posthaste.'

This was not noteworthy to Caro. After Matt had been at the farm five or six weeks there was always something to take him back to Brisbane for a few weeks.

But on this day she surprised him. She turned a grim expression to him. 'And there was news in mine which moves me to do the same.'

His right eyebrow rose. 'Oh?'

Caro put down the heavy iron on the hob behind her. 'Matthew, I've had a letter from Mummy. I'm worried. Daddy's ill . . . seems he was in a small fishing boat in the bay which capsized. Strange to think, he, a man of the sea, would be affected, but he has been. His shoulder took a bad blow and he's been unwell ever since. The doctor thinks it's now pneumonia. Mummy says he's worsening and that she believes if he sees me he'll feel better, that I should come home . . . soon.'

Matthew shook his head. 'Of course, then you must.'

'Good, I will. I hate to think of my darling father ill. Please God it's not as serious as it sounds.' Her chin puckered with emotion. 'So then, what's your news?'

He hesitated. 'Ah, not of such importance now.'

'What? Tell me.'

He moved over to the window and sat on the sill before he responded. 'Just that there's going to be a get-together. You know, old friends.'

She remained looking steadily at him.

214

'Caro, old girl, let's say it's an evening that I'd like to attend.'

Caro continued eyeing him, a supercilious expression appearing on her face, equal to any he could affect. 'So . . . a party. I can see why you had to return to Brisbane posthaste. Ah yes, all very important.'

He smiled enigmatically at her; she was unsure whether it was in approval or scorn. Then, as if he had an illuminating idea, he added, 'Actually you could accompany me, now that you'll be down there in Brisbane.'

Caro spoke as she turned round to pick up the iron from the hob. 'Why on earth would I want to accompany you to one of your dos? They're not the sort of functions I like to attend.'

The silence was so extended she had time to pick up the iron, turn back to the table, put it down on the tin plate she kept to the side of the pressing and look up at him in expectation.

He was still sitting on the windowsill. He leant his cane on the wall at hand and folded his arms. 'As a rule, Caro, I think you're indubitably correct, but in this case I think not. I've a feeling you'd be happy, even gratified, to dignify this fine social gathering with your presence.'

'And why would that be?'

'Because there are going to be *soldiers* in attendance. And we all know you have an undeniably lasting affection for . . . uniforms!'

Caro said nothing but she bit the edge of her lip as she picked up the iron and began to press the shirt in front of her.

'It so happens that my good friend Grahame Magnus has a cousin who went off a year ago with the 4th Queensland Imperial Bushmen to the South African war. And while some of those stalwart and loyal fellows lie buried six feet under on the veldt in a foreign clime, young Clement Magnus has survived to come home with the majority of his contingent. Arrived last month. There's going to be a big function to commend them; a welcome home party, all official and proper, being held at the City Hall on Saturday night in the presence of the Governor: orchestra, food, singing and dancing, and I . . . er *we* . . . are invited.'

Caro kept her head down, her gaze on the shirt in front of her. Her heart was racing and she was praying he would notice

215

nothing. She knew from Lucy that Bartholomew Fleet had volunteered and gone to the South Arican War last year, and she knew too that his contingent had been the 4th Queensland Imperial Bushmen. This party now took on proportions of immense importance to her for she had the opportunity to see Bart, even speak to him, learn something, *anything*, about his elder brother.

She spoke as calmly as her accelerated pulse allowed her. 'But today's Wednesday. You don't mean this coming Saturday?'

'Yes I do, the sixteenth. We can leave here tomorrow. Knobby'll drive us into Ipswich and we'll catch the train into Brisbane. And if Knobby prefers to come back to the city too then we'll ask Jacob to do the honours. It'll do you good to see your father too, Caro.'

'Matthew, how can going to see my darling father in dire straits possibly *do me good*? You say the strangest things.'

'Now, old girl, don't misconstrue deliberately. You know I was merely indicating that the visit will set your mind at rest about his condition. You've only seen him two or three times in three years that I can recall.'

'Four,' Caro corrected. 'I was down for the whole month of June this year when Daddy left the sea. That was the fourth time.'

Matthew inhaled. 'All right. Four.' He fell silent briefly then said, 'We'll leave Harry here, eh? Be easier travelling without the little fellow. And being around a sickroom is no place for a child. Mary will take excellent care of him.'

'No, Matthew, I won't leave him. His place is with me. I've always taken him when I've gone before.'

He gave a half-laugh, dripping with sarcasm. 'So you have and let's not suggest any change to an obviously ingrained habit.'

She glanced up angrily and he confused her by winking before he bent down to take hold of his cane and pass across to the verandah door. 'I'm going back to the studio. Bring me a gin and tonic bitters, will you, old girl?'

'Matthew, it's not even four o'clock.'

He pivoted round in the doorway to face her, the afternoon sun shining behind him and establishing him only as a back-lit ebony figure with an ebony cane. 'My dear Caro. When has the time of day ever been an issue in the commencement of my alcoholic intake?'

She made an impatient sound between her teeth. 'All right. I'll bring you the drink.'

'That's it, old girl, much obliged.' And the ebony-black figure swiftly disappeared across the verandah down the steps into the afternoon blaze of light.

Chapter Seventeen

To her left the jacaranda blooms were as a purple-blue painting framed by the window. To her right lay her father in the big four-poster bed, carried in pieces from the old country a generation before and put together with loving care in the new land. The matchless jacarandas and her daddy; one always led her to think about the other.

Jack Dere lifted his fingers towards Caro and she shivered as she took his palm. The dark veins on the back of his hand stood out markedly against the paleness of his skin. She turned his hand in hers and gently rubbed the cushion pad of his thumb. It had always intrigued her, from being a tiny child; she used to call it 'squishy' for it was pliant and yielded under the pressure of her touch much more than the pads on any of his other fingers. It made her recall the carefree times, when life was uncomplicated and he was the authority on all things. She leant into him and kissed his forehead.

'Daddy, I'm so sorry, darling.'

He smiled and his blue eyes showed something of their natural sparkle. 'Don't be, my joy, my Caroline. Just seeing you is a tonic in itself. I'll be up in a few days and better in a week, you see. Can't die in the same year as our good Queen now, can I? Don't want to be that fashionable.'

Elizabeth shook her head and gave a wan smile. 'You will have your joke, my love.' She met Caro's eyes across the top of his head.

Caro patted her father's hand. 'Oh darling, we just want you well. That's why I'm here.'

'So you'll stay?' Jack Dere asked of his daughter hopefully.

'I will.'

Her father beamed.

'And I have someone here to see you. Your grandson. I'll just go and get him.'

Jack Dere seemed to take heart from this interchange and he actually pulled himself up a little on the pillows as Caro moved by the end of the bed and Litmus stood up from where she lay to lick Caro's hand. Caro took hold of her elegant, long, tapered head and stroked her abundant coat, and Litmus followed her dutifully out along the hall to the sitting room to find Lucy, who was looking after Harry and her own one-year-old, Jake.

When Caro and Litmus returned with little Harry, Jack Dere kissed the proffered child, who reached out and touched his grandfather's moustache.

'See, he likes that,' Elizabeth approved.

Jack nodded. 'He's a great little laddie. Time we had him here for a bit, Caro.'

'I know, Daddy, you're right. But until you left the sea in May you weren't here to see him anyway.'

'Am now, though, lass,' he replied with unassailable logic.

'Yes,' opined Elizabeth, 'it seems to me that if Matthew can find time to spend six months of the year in Brisbane so could you. It's not as if he didn't keep his house here in New Farm – he did.'

This was a running argument with Caro and her mother, though now that her father was home Caro was more inclined to come to Brisbane regularly. Her mother hated the land, always had. She had been brought up on a property outside Gladstone, hundreds of miles north of Brisbane, and had never forgotten the hard work, the intolerable heat, the flies, the smell of the animals and all that went with farming. When Caro had invited her to come and stay at Cedar Grove, her mother's reply had been, 'You know how I detest the country, darling. I'm a city lover and you're over thirty years younger than me. Now there's a dear, you come to me.'

Caro sighed. 'All right, Mummy, not now, please. Let's just help Daddy to get well.'

'I'm all for that,' responded Elizabeth, sharply.

Soon when her father dropped off to sleep, Caro, Harry and his grandmother left the sickroom with Litmus in tow and returned to Lucy, whom they found feeding her little one with a bottle.

Lucy smiled at the arrivals. 'Is Mr Dere feeling better?'

'Yes, I think he is,' responded Elizabeth. 'He seems to have

219

picked up a little bit, seeing Caroline and his grandson, thank the Lord.'

As Caro sat down next to her, Lucy turned to face her friend. 'I hear you're going to the welcome home for the Imperial Bushmen tomorrow night, lucky you. Everyone wants an invitation to that. The Governor's going and all the toffs'll be there, the Liedertafel male choir will sing; that's unusual these days.'

'It's Matthew who's invited, actually.'

'But you're going, surely?'

Caro appeared to think for a moment, looking over at Harry, who stood at her mother's knee, playing with a doll. 'Oh yes, I'll be going all right. Perhaps it's time Matt's compatriots were reminded that he's married.'

Elizabeth lifted her head quickly to meet her daughter's eyes. 'I should think so. He has responsibilities now.' Then she picked up Harry and stood. 'I think it's time our little darling had something to eat. I'll take him through to the kitchen.'

Caro nodded. 'Thanks, Mum.'

When the older woman was gone Lucy smiled enthusiastically at her friend. 'The party's the talk of the town. I wish I could go.' She hesitated, and then spoke in matter-of-fact fashion. 'George has been against the war. Well, naturally, he would be with his views on things, but I feel we shouldn't lose sight of the way the war has brought us all together. There's been a feeling of unity, especially now in our first year of nationhood.'

Caro regarded her friend with surprise for a few seconds. 'Goodness, Lucy, I never thought I'd hear you disagree with George.'

'Well, I don't usually but I do have opinions of my own, you know.'

'Well done. I agree, men think they know everything.'

They looked at each other and then both laughed.

Caro leant over and stroked Jake's fuzzy fair hair as Lucy took up the conversation. 'What on earth will you wear? Do you have a new dress?'

Caro patted her friend on the arm, 'No, but I've got something I think will do. It's got a jacket to hide things for me.'

The following night, Caro walked into the Exhibition Concert Hall on the city's northern side wearing the 'something'. It was the pretty soft pink silk outfit she had not worn for years – well, not since the concert she had attended with John Conrad at St Paul's Hall in '98, which all seemed an eternity ago. It had a scooped low neckline but the jacket hung down to hip height so it hid the gentle bulge that was already forming in Caro's girth, and as it was a warm spring evening, she needed no cover-up.

While the élite of Brisbane were regarded as socially subordinate to the richer and more influential of their southern counterparts in Sydney and Melbourne, there had evolved in Brisbane a quite distinct social and cultural life, the most interesting phenomenon being events which engaged most of the social classes, and no occasion was more typical of this particular Queensland ethos than the welcome home party for the returning soldiers. It was a purely Queensland mixture of the formal and informal, so ably expressing the values of the society as a whole.

When Matthew and Caro arrived at the Concert Hall door there was the formality of ceremonious announcement: 'Mr and Mrs Matthew Craken, of Lewis and Craken Department Store.'

After each family had been announced they were ushered officially past the Governor and his good lady standing obligingly at his side, then on by the political leader of the state, the Premier Philip Robert. As there were over three hundred of the returning soldiers, plus the odd friend such as the Crakens, individual introductions to Governor and Lady Lamington would have been far too time-consuming.

The guests passed by the Governor, who nodded to each in turn. This official prelude was followed inside the hall by the more informal mingling of the returning soldiers and their officers and families. The ranks covered all social classes and the people touching shoulders at this pre-eminent event covered almost the entire strata of social division in Brisbane. It was a more carefree and less pompous affair than would have been attempted in the southern capitals.

A huge sign hung down from the ceiling reading: 'WEL-COME HOME TO OUR BOYS: THE 4TH QUEENSLAND

IMPERIAL BUSHMEN'. The 2,800 seats had been removed and replaced by alcoves side-by-side covering the walls and looking on to the dance floor in the centre of the huge room. At the far end stood six grand buffet tables upon which the gala dinner would be served. The orchestra sat above them in the balcony surrounded by a number of makeshift bars.

The returning contingent of Queensland heroes were seated with family, wives and girlfriends in special alcoves of their own, over which the new and exciting red, white and blue Commonwealth of Australia flag with its Union Jack and Southern Cross aptly united, was draped beside all manner of colourful floating decoration.

There were about seventeen hundred people in the hall but immediately Caro optimistically looked for Bartholomew. She could see scores of uniforms, and as Matthew seated her by Grahame Magnus's girlfriend, Eva, Caro gave perfunctory greetings, but her eyes wandered around the room. Matthew sat down beside her for a minute or so, patted her arm and then promptly stood and pulled Grahame to his feet.

Turning to Caro he gave an imitation of a smile, 'What will you have, old girl?'

'I'll have a very small glass of red wine.'

In a flourishing gesture Matt picked up her hand and brought it to his lips. 'Yes, it's a special occasion, but as the health of the coming addition to the Craken family is paramount we'll allow you but one glass, my dear.'

'I only want one, Matt.'

When the two men crossed the dance floor to go upstairs where the drinks were served, Caro was aware that many eyes were on Matthew. There were various reasons why: he was notorious in Brisbane circles and the stories about him were legend. Every other man in the room was either in uniform or in regular evening dress but not Matt: with his Gothic looks and somewhat dandyish garb he always appeared as if he had stepped out of a catalogue from London or Paris. Tonight was no different: he wore a brown velvet suit with gleaming brown patent leather shoes and the spotted bow at his throat had taken twenty minutes to tie to convey the illusion of casual elegance. The cane he used was polished red cedar with a marble handle.

Caro knew now what others could only guess: Matt had thirty-nine canes. She had counted them. Two dozen he had carried back in a special trunk with him from the Orient and the others were made by Won Won, a Chinese artisan who lived above a cooper's shop in Wooloongabba. He was, incidentally, the same man who tailored Matt's clothes and sporadically supplied him with a little opium to smoke. Matt affectionately called him 'Won Won the Wonder One'.

As she watched her husband smoothly crossing the floor, using the cane as if it were another leg, most of the eyes in the room upon him, Caro shook her head to herself. That was Matt, enjoying being the cynosure of eyes. They broke the mould when they made him. She thought it impossible that little whippet-like Josephine Craken had brought Matthew into the world, but it appeared she had. That always brought her to speculate on what Arthur Craken, Matt's father, had been like. Her own mother, who knew Arthur as a young man, could only tell her that he had been a real gentleman and dressed well and had played cricket and polo. That was not really a character analysis. Perhaps she would ask her mother-in-law to tell her more sometime.

When she realised the woman at her side had spoken to her, Caro had no idea what had been said. 'Oh, I'm sorry, what was that, Eva?'

The girl's pretty, slightly freckled face came round to hers. 'I asked how far gone you are? The coming baby?'

'Oh, just on five months.'

'Ah, so it'll be . . . what? A March or April addition then?'

'Yes that's right, March.' It was at that moment, when Caro lifted her eyes that she felt a tremor of tension run through her; she had just seen Bart Fleet with Aunt Leigh on his arm, moving through the crowd halfway across the dance floor.

Suddenly the voice of the master of ceremonies, Ron Archibald, one of the city aldermen, brought silence to the room. 'Ladies and gentlemen, the dancing is about to begin. We'll have an hour of dancing followed by our gala buffet dinner: the largest dinner I might say, ever to have been attempted in Queensland, and no men more worthy than our own 4th Imperial Bushmen.'

Spontaneous applause broke out all around the room. When it died down he went on, 'After dinner we'll be entertained by the Queensland Exhibition Orchestra and we will have the delight of hearing the famous Liedertafel male choir sing: a night to remember. But first we have a treat for you. Six of our boys from the 4th Queensland Imperial Bushmen have a song to sing which one of them learned in Winton in 1895. It's catching on and becoming a popular tune now in parts of Queensland. It's been set to the tune of the English song, "Soldier of Marlborough" and so here . . . give them a big welcome!'

He turned with a flourish of his hand and brought on to the stage five privates and a corporal who ranged around him as the orchestra struck the first chord and their voices lifted in the rousing melody:

'Once a jolly swagman camped by a billabong
Under the shade of a coolibah tree,
And he sang as he watched and waited
  till his billy boiled,
"Who'll come a-waltzing Matilda with me.

"Waltzing Matilda, waltzing Matilda,
Who'll come a-waltzing Matilda with me."
And he sang as he watched and waited
  till his billy boiled,
"Who'll come a-waltzing Matilda with me."'

Some of the boys in the body of the hall knew the words and joined in, and soon the room rang to what was to become 'the song of Australia'.

'"Waltzing Matilda, waltzing Matilda,
Who'll come a-waltzing Matilda with me."
And he sang as he watched and waited
  till his billy boiled,
"Who'll come a-waltzing Matilda with me."'

Eva and Caro applauded loudly with everybody else. 'Well, I've never heard that before,' Eva said. 'Catchy, isn't it?'

'Definitely. I liked it.'

The master of ceremonies waved his arms again. 'Thank you, Privates Finimore, Lees, Cornish, Cox, Baker and Corporal Muller. So now, please take your partners for the first dance, "The Pride of Erin".'

Caro turned to Eva. 'Excuse me, please, I need to go outside for a minute.'

Eva frowned. 'Oh Caroline, are you unwell?'

'No, dear, just need some fresh air. When you're in my condition you'll understand, you see.'

The girl put down her gloves and went to stand. 'I'll come with you.'

Caro shook her head. 'No, don't be silly. When our boys return with the drinks someone should be here. Just tell Matt I needed a little fresh air.'

Eva looked uncertain as her companion stood and walked off across the floor around the moving couples. Caro knew Bart had gone in the direction of the returned soldiers' alcoves and that was where she headed. She must not worry about Aunt Leigh, just get Bart's attention and speak to him. He was a good man, he would tell her news of John Conrad she was sure.

Caro pushed and shoved her way through the celebrations and merriment until finally she saw Bart some twenty feet away through the throng. He was laughing, as a soldier should returned from war; and the tilt of his head and the way he lifted his hand to brush a strand of his hair back from his forehead reminded Caro too well of his elder brother. She shivered. Then took a deep breath to build up her nerve to advance upon him.

'Caro, old girl, what the devil are you doing?'

She jumped in fright. 'Oh heavens, Matt, you startled me.'

'I can see that.'

Matthew stood with a glass of rum in one hand and the small red wine she had requested in the other while Grahame Magnus smiled over his shoulder with two bottles of beer and three glasses in his hands.

'Come on, let's go back and sit down.' Matt urged her round in the other direction. 'Where the devil were you heading, old girl?'

Trying hard not to sound despondent Caro informed him, 'I'd been out for some air, just got lost on my way back.'

When they were all seated and the men were drinking steadily, Caro sipped her wine throughtfully. It was just like Matt to come back promptly when he was not wanted. If she had asked him to return swiftly, he would have been away an hour!

And so the dancing went on. Grahame and Eva proved their prowess in the barn dance and the waltz but Matt remained drinking steadily. When Clement Magnus, Grahame's cousin and one of the returning soldiers, asked Caro to dance, Matt gave his consent readily. 'Go on, old girl, you like dancing and you know it isn't a favourite pastime of mine.' He returned to the bar for more alcohol while Caro danced, and when Clement brought her back to her seat to chat to the other ladies, Caro did not dare to leave and search for Bart again.

Just after half-past nine, when Matt had returned with his third rum and another drink for Grahame, the drummer up in the balcony hit the cymbals for attention. The dance floor was filled with couples who remained standing and turned to the meagre stage set in one corner of the room where the master of ceremonies appeared again.

'Ladies and gentlemen, you all know why we're gathered here tonight.'

There was the sound of polite applause.

'There's no better man to welcome home the heroes of the 4th Queensland Imperial Bushmen than our own popular Governor, Lord Lamington.'

There was the punctuation of more acclamation.

Governor Lamington appeared and took his notes from his pocket and placed his pince-nez on the bridge of his nose.

Matt leaned into Caro's ear and whispered, 'I know him from the Polo Club. He has an eye for the ladies.'

'Who hasn't around here?' asked Caro, and Matt whispered, 'Touché, old girl.'

Lord Lamington had a strong voice and was used to public speaking. 'Thank you, Alderman Archibald. Yes, we are here to welcome home our boys who've risked their lives fighting for Australia, in the hard uncompromising land of Southern Africa against the Boer aggressors. We must remember those who did not return; those who paid the ultimate price for what they believed in.' He fell quiet momentarily and there was silence throughout the hall.

He coughed and continued, 'The 4th Imperial Bushmen, to whom this country owes great gratitude, were fighting to help Great Britain and for our new nation: the Federation of Australian States, which began as such on the first day of January this year: the first day of the new century. We have taken great care to form a constitution which will guarantee that every Australian citizen, for hundreds of years to come, will have a life better than any republic could ever offer. Our boys here in this room with us tonight have helped create that feeling of real nationhood.'

Shouts of 'Hear! Hear!' greeted this statement.

'They have come home, not to a loose union of six colonies but to the Commonwealth of Australia, an equal of Great Britain or any country on the world stage, and which is today, exactly three hundred and twenty *days* old. May the days turn into years and may we last as a commonwealth for three hundred and twenty *years* and then three hundred and twenty *years* after that!'

This brought thunderous applause and more shouts of 'Hear! Hear!' ricocheted round the hall.

The Governor bowed from the shoulders. 'Thank you. God bless our returning soldiers and now before I return you to Alderman Archibald I have two very important men here tonight to introduce to you briefly. Men of whom we are proud and to whom we owe great praise.' The Governor looked pointedly down in the direction of the alcoves where the servicemen were seated. 'I wish to introduce you to a soldier who has been decorated with the Victoria Cross, our highest honour, for his bravery on the field of battle when he ignored heavy Boer gunfire to save three unhorsed and wounded comrades. A round of applause please for our own Brisbane-born Sergeant Simon Herlwyn.'

And those of the seventeen hundred people not already standing rose to their feet and loudly acclaimed their own Queensland hero.

Simon Herlwyn came swiftly forward, jumped up the two stairs to the stage and stood beside the Governor, who shook his hand and patted him warmly on the back. The sergeant was a slight man but wiry and hard, with a fixed look under a shock of sun-lightened hair. One could imagine that he would not give in even under extreme circumstances. He cleared his throat as the hall fell silent. 'Thank you one and all. I was proud to do my duty for my country and for the Empire.' He bowed and walked off to more thunderous applause.

Matt leant into Caro's ear again and whispered, 'I know his brother, Henry, fine bloke, plays one hell of a hand of loo.'

The Governor raised his hands and silence fell. 'The next brave man I wish to commend here is also from Brisbane and a son of one of our finest families. He too has been in more than one skirmish on South African soil and though he was not part of the 4th Queensland Imperial Bushmen contingent, he did join the same ship which returned them to us. He's here to take a short leave in his home town. He's done this city great honour for he's on the personal staff of the world's greatest soldier, the man who is turning the war in South Africa in our favour . . .'

Caro stiffened, and Matthew, with his arm touching her along the back of her chair, inclined his head to observe her.

'. . . Yes, I'm talking about one of the right-hand men to the great Kitchener of Khartoum.'

There were murmurs of surprise.

'Welcome home, Captain John Conrad Fleet.' The Governor again held out his arm to the crowd below him and as people parted to make way for John Conrad, he too came forward from the hundreds of people present and mounted the steps to stand beside the Governor to prolonged applause.

Even in the noise and tumult Caro was well aware of her husband's whistle and the removal of his arm from the back of her chair as he lifted his cane to place it across his knee. His voice was icy. 'Well, well, well, the enemy . . . How extremely diverting.'

John Conrad stood tall and dignified in his uniform, his ruddy brown boots gleaming, his battle sword gleaming, the bandolier across his shoulder gleaming, the buttons on his jacket the same: the epitome of every child's soldier hero, even of every grown-up's soldier hero.

Caro's baby kicked her and she felt suddenly ill. She took a deep breath as the voice she loved rang out across the room, clear and pleasing and yet the most haunting sound, reminding her of sunny days when her love was innocent and crisp winter winds unfolded her flawless and abiding dreams.

'Thank you, Lord Lamington. It's a special honour for me to be here in Brisbane tonight. The men of our own contingent of Imperial Bushmen have done justice to our new country. I can tell you that the Australian soldier is the *only* military man who can shoot as well and ride as well as the Boer who is born to the saddle. In fact we came as a real shock to the Boers and have outdone them in many a fight.'

Loud clapping began and John Conrad raised his hand to hold it back.

'I'm proud to share the stage with Simon Herlwyn, who's a true hero, and for all you others down there,' he waved in the direction of the soldiers who shouted tributes to him from the floor of the hall, 'my companions of a long voyage and all gallant men. My own brother Bartholomew is one of you. I'm immensely proud of you, Kitchener is proud of you and the Commonwealth of Australia is proud of you.'

The applause was deafening.

'Fancy that, our little soldier-boy has turned into a bloody politician.' Matthew now faced Caro, whose cheeks carried a high colour. 'My goodness, you're a brighter shade than your outfit, Caro. Now why on earth would that be?'

'Don't, Matt. Can we go? I'm feeling unwell.'

'Go? Caro, Caro. Wanting to spoil my fun? The dinner hasn't been served, there're hours of good drinking time ahead, and now we're appraised of the fact that there are a fleet of bloody Fleets in the room, I would have thought you'd prefer to lose your right arm than leave.' He turned his back on her; his bad leg had begun to ache, damn it.

The cymbals clashed again and Alderman Archibald lifted his voice to shout from the stage. 'The buffet dinner is now ready on the tables and we ask that you allow our returned boys to partake first and then the rest of us should follow. Tonight the rule is, soldiers first!'

This brought a rumble of laughter and as the official ushers moved in to sweep the military men down to the tables the orchestra began to play Mozart's *Eine Kleine Nachtmusik*.

Grahame Magnus turned to Matthew. 'So that bastard's back.'

'Apparently.'

'Pity the Boers didn't do for him.'

'Isn't it?'

Caro stood. 'Excuse me, Matt, I need to find the ladies' toilets.'

Matt stood. 'Of course, my dear.'

As Caro moved off he called, 'Remember the way back, old girl, won't you?'

Caro was near to tears. It had been too much. Yes, she had played false to Matthew to come here in the hopes of speaking to Bart. She had hidden from her husband the fact that Bart was one of the returned soldiers. But never could she have dreamed that John Conrad would be here too. Matthew was too clever for his own good; he had already gathered she had been searching for someone earlier, though whether he believed she knew John Conrad was to be here was another matter. But he would be putting two and two together and making more than their natural addition.

The toilets were outside along a short path, and men and women passed back and forwards. Caro swallowed the refreshing air in great gulps. She really did feel sick and hoped she would not retch. She moved off the path some yards in the vague night light to stand under a poinciana tree and lean against the trunk where she placed her palms on the honest impartial wood. She watched the soldiers and guests laughing and chatting as they walked back to the hall. A few minutes later, after the people became fewer, she felt slightly better and took from her little purse-bag the small fan she always carried.

As time passed a gentle breeze came up and Caro folded up her fan. She decided she must go back and face Matthew: prevail upon him to leave and get away from here. There was nobody outside now and she realised the dinner would be in full swing and all the people would be partaking. She looked up through the branches and saw the moon, golden and full, and again her baby moved within her. She felt guilty: this child she did not talk to, did not count the movements of and had no songs for. She touched her stomach; 'I'm sorry, little one,' she said aloud. 'It's not your fault. I will start to sing to you tomorrow.'

She had just stepped forward when she saw the silhouettes of two soldiers coming down the path; that was the last thing she did see, for at that second the black ground came up to meet her as she fainted into it.

'Did you see that?' Bartholomew said to John Conrad, touching his arm.

'What?'

'A woman, over there, alone, she just fell to the ground. Quickly, you go and see to her and I'll find the army doctor.'

'Right,' his brother answered and hurried over to the female form lying prone under the tree. He was within a few yards when he suddenly knew. *Oh Lord in heaven no! This can't be happening.* He had prepared himself to see her in the street, ignore her at a church gathering or a football match, pretend she was not in the world. But not this. This was not right!

He looked wildly around, but there was no one. He drew the cool air across his teeth in one extensive swallow. Then he knelt down beside her. Abruptly he stood up again and faltered. What if she were dead? He had regarded her as dead for years. Once more he knelt and this time took up her wrist and found her pulse. It was beating. She looked as if she might be having another child. Trust Craken to be populating the earth!

Her face was the same, as lovely as he remembered except for the smudge of the scar on the bottom lip of her mouth. He did not feel good about that. And as he remained there on the ground beside her, she groaned and he bent forward.

Caro returned to the living world to see the beloved face of John Conrad above her. She knew then she must be still unconscious; this could only be a dream; a wonderful incautious dream.

'Stand up, you bastard, and move away from my wife!'

John Conrad, still on his knees, straightened up and rounded to see the flaring hatred of Matthew Craken looming above him in the night light.

'Listen, Craken, she had fainted. I—'

And to John Conrad's amazement and Caro's terror Matthew raised his red cedar cane and a long rapier-like knife shot out of the end to fly by the side of John Conrad's neck where it

231

met the flesh and brought blood pouring out across his collar. The soldier dropped sideways and Matthew smiled, a grim and ruthless thing to see.

Caro thought she screamed as she blacked out again.

'I said, bastard, move away from my wife.'

John Conrad's hand shot to his neck. 'You're the bastard, Craken.'

'What's happening?' It was Bart, returning with the doctor and another soldier. They could only see the figures in the dark but as they arrived the doctor immediately saw John Conrad was wounded and stepped in to help him, but he shook his head. 'No, I'm all right, attend to the woman. She fainted.'

'God, Craken, what have you done?' Bart exclaimed as John Conrad rose to his feet, blood seeping between his fingers.

'Forget it, Bart.' John Conrad touched his brother's shoulder as the other soldier looked on in amazement. 'I'm all right. It's a flesh wound. Come on. Let's leave the Crakens to themselves.'

Matthew lifted his hand to stay Bart as the moon came out from behind a cloud and momentarily brightened, illuminating and defining the little group of players. 'You ask what I've done. I'll answer your question. What I've done is to become intemperate, exactly mirroring your brother eight years ago. To act without asking questions first. To injure without hearing any defence. Though he's bloody lucky, for his injury tonight is nothing.' He switched from Bart to meet John Conrad's eyes. 'You see, soldier-boy, when you come back here you step into our little universe of hatred and it's a place of retribution. So be warned. Be careful in the extreme about returning to it again, won't you?'

'Please, John Conrad, come on. You don't know what he's capable of. We should get the police.' Bart took his brother's arm in an effort to pull him away.

John Conrad shook off his brother's hold and faced the soldier who had accompanied Bart and the doctor. 'Forget completely what you saw here, Jenkins.'

The man saluted. 'Yes, sir.'

Then the two enemies looked at each other once more, neither having the faintest notion, nor the faintest interest, in the needs of the other.

Abruptly John Conrad moved off across the grass and Bart followed as Matthew regarded their departure and touched the catch which shot the knife back into the hollow of the cane.

Then he knelt down on his good knee beside the doctor. 'How is she?'

'I'm sure she'll be all right, sir. She's fainted but all her vital signs are normal.'

'She's carrying a child.' Now his voice possessed the edge of worry. 'They *will* both be all right, won't they?'

'I should think so, sir. But best get her home.' He looked at Matthew. 'What the devil happened out here?'

'Don't concern yourself. It's what you call a continuing vendetta.' He drew his long fingers across his eyes. 'Makes for a fascinating life.'

At that point soldier Jenkins could not contain himself any longer. 'I never did see one o' those before. It's amazin', really.' He pointed at Matthew's walking stick.

'Then best you pretend you never saw this one either, cousin.'

Later that night, after John Conrad's flesh wound had been treated and bandaged, and the four adults of the Fleet family had returned to Brewery House, he and Bart sat alone in the big kitchen. Both young men had thought it best if their father and Aunt Leigh were not apprised of the truth so they had placated the older folk's concern by telling a story of an accident with a ceremonial sword as it was being lifted behind the stage. It had spoiled their night, of course, and they had insisted on returning home all together.

Aunt Leigh had fussed and been compassionate and made tea and toast for her men-folk. Then finally she and Barrington retired and left the two brothers alone.

'Wake me if you need me now,' the good woman had said from the kitchen door. 'What a night. "Let's contend no more, Love, Strive nor weep: All be as before, Love, – Only sleep!" Browning!' she stated as she wandered off down the hall.

John Conrad glanced after her. 'Dear Aunt Leigh. What a character, but wonderful . . . and loyal to this family. I remember when Mum died and she came straight away to fill her place and to care for us. She's been a second mother to us all, especially David. I don't know what we'd have done without her.'

'Yes, I can tell you I missed her hearty breakfasts on many a cold morning on the veldt.'

'Bet you did. Me too.'

They fell silent momentarily and then Bart looked admiringly at his elder brother. 'She's so proud of you she's almost bursting with it. Actually we all are, you know, being with Kitchener and everything. What's he really like? In South Africa we often wondered that. Some of our blokes used to say he was ruthless.'

John Conrad nodded. 'Ruthless, eh? Well, if getting the job done makes him that, then in that sense he probably is. K's countless things, my brother, probably as all great men are. But, Bart, you've been a soldier and you know, he's a general with a war to win; he can't be fussy.'

'No, I realise that.' He made a move to stand up. 'Your neck must be hurting. You'd better get to bed.'

John Conrad raised his hand to halt his brother. 'It's not actually, though it's a bit tender. It's hardly a wound like some of the poor blokes, on both sides, have suffered over there.' He looked over at the range where Aunt Leigh had left the kettle. 'I wouldn't mind another cup of tea.'

Bart leaped up and put the kettle on as John Conrad continued his philosophies. 'This is a damned strange war, as you and I know. K analyses his enemy, that's how he's learned to surprise the Boer. They were a loose army of deadly raiding parties appearing from anywhere at any time and he saw that, much more than Roberts ever did. Once K was in charge he changed tactics.'

'Yes,' agreed his brother. 'There's nothing about this war that's normal. There's no "there you are and here we are; let's fight it out." As you said, they used to pop up; out of a donga or a river bed, from behind a hill, and then disappear back the way they came. Bloody good shots though, aren't they?'

'They sure are; can hit a moving target at four hundred yards. Yes indeed, they're a worthy enemy. We've had to lay waste to the land to beat them and that means farms have been destroyed and so the old folk, women and children have been interned. That's been something I've been involved in and I can tell you those families aren't harmed. God! Some of my men have given them their own food at times; though I know the odd extreme thing has happened. It always damn well does and then the newspaper correspondents make a meal of it. And those Boer women are a fierce lot, worse than their husbands, many times.

'To win against the commando tactics of the Boers K saw the need to line the country with blockhouses. They're but a few hundred yards apart now and he's winning; playing the Boers at their own game. He's isolating them and it's working.

'I'll tell you what, Kitchener's indefatigable and you have to be to work for him. He understands his army, but I doubt he understands the individual common soldier much. Occasionally he says, "I have enemies – some I have made myself."'

Bart leaned across the table, his mid-brown curly hair shining in the lamplight. 'Remember when we ran into each other? Oh boy, did I have to live that down. You . . . my brother on K's staff. Took me bloody months before the boys forgot that.'

John Conrad smiled. 'Oh really? Common buggers.'

This made them laugh and both men silently recalled the incident.

It was the only time they had seen each other during the fourteen months that Bart had been in South Africa. Bart's contingent was in the Transvaal near Middelburg on the Delagoa Bay railway line, which ran straight east from Pretoria. K and four of his personal staff including John Conrad had been there briefly. The brothers had been able to take an afternoon's ride together across the wide open veldt where a comforting breeze moved the long yellow savannah grass gently beneath the horses' bellies. They had seen a herd of buffalo and a family of baboons around a series of kopjes and on their return ride they had come across flocks of white storks and geese, and even two of the idiosyncratic secretary birds striding in eccentric fashion along a donga. It had been a special few hours for the brothers and in the evening, when they returned to the encampment, K had said a few words of encouragement to the Bushmen.

Bart placed a cup in front of John Conrad and poured the tea before he broke the silence of their thoughts. 'When K spoke to us that evening on the veldt as the sun set, I must say it did cheer up the boys. Gave us a sense of what we were there for, I suppose. Though he sure has a fixed and steely look in his eyes. How do you put up with that?'

'I don't notice it except for the odd times when he does seem to look through me; slightly mesmeric, I suppose. He won't admit it, but his eyes aren't really good any more. They were badly damaged nearly twenty years ago on a two-hundred-mile-long camel ride through violent desert storms.'

Bart was enjoying this talk with his big brother. 'When we left the Eastern Transvaal those Australians had just been arrested – they were Bushveldt Carbineers, I think. There was talk of a court martial. Supposed to have slaughtered a lot of Boers and a missionary.'

John Conrad swallowed a mouthful of his tea. 'Yes, apparently. There's a whole group of them in custody, including some English irregulars. Seems they murdered a batch of prisoners. One of the English is called Picton, and I think some of the Australians were Witton, Handcock and . . . Morant.'

'Morant, that's right,' Bart said, 'a lieutenant; he was a tough bugger, met him a couple of times. Now he *was* ruthless.'

'Yes and I'm afraid he'll get the firing squad for being so.'

'Heck!' exclaimed Bart.

The clock in the hall chimed one and John Conrad filled his cup from the teapot. 'I've been with K three years and this is the first real holiday I've had away from him . . . and he told me to hurry back! Mind you, we've had another ADC with us since last December, a fellow called Frank Maxwell whom K has really taken to, so that's good. K's very thorough, some say *driven* and he doesn't favour patricians at all. Perhaps that's why he chose me, for my simple beginnings. But I wouldn't want to answer to any other general on earth now, except him.'

Bart grimaced. 'Oh Lord you should hear yourself,' he said good naturedly: '*Wouldn't want to answer to any other general*, eh? My, my, big brother, you do sound high and mighty.'

John Conrad broke into laughter and the action reminded him he had a sore neck. He put his hand up to the wound. 'I suppose you're right. Actually K's still a major general but he'll be a lieutenant general in no time and a general shortly after that I'd say.'

'And you, no doubt, will be a major before long.'

John Conrad gave his brother a hard look. 'We know I've wanted to make a career of this army business and it seems like I'm doing just that. But I'm one thing, you're another, and I was damned annoyed when I read from Aunt Leigh that you'd volunteered and were on your way to South Africa.'

Bart grinned. 'Hell, Captain Fleet, what seemed good enough for you seemed good enough for me.'

Now John Conrad became serious and his eyes narrowed as he surveyed his sibling. 'Well, you've seen that war isn't fun and you're home now safe and sound. I'm a professional soldier and cognisant of the risks. It's part of what I bargained for, but I don't like to think of you in danger. Please forget about armies and fighting and get back to running the brewery. It's a very good business. Dad told me you've opened another up in Bundaberg. I'm pleased about that.'

'Yes, you're right, they've already got a rum distillery up there. Thought we'd bring a bit of competition.' He grinned. 'No, fact is the labour's good and pretty cheap; far less expensive to live there than here in the south. The new brewery's a solid business. I'll admit I'm happy to be home. I really joined up for a bit of adventure, you know, like a lot of blokes, though I'm glad I went and did my bit for the Commonwealth like the Governor said tonight. Makes a man feel good. But war sure isn't like you think it'll be. There's no glamour.' He paused looking searchingly at his brother. 'Will you have to go back there?'

John Conrad smiled, still holding the bandage at his throat. 'Yes I will, and K won't believe that I sustained this in the safe harbour of Brisbane. It's funny, you know, he was shot in the lower jaw at Handub in the Sudan many years ago. He has a fine scar right about where mine'll be.'

'Heck, that's amazing.' Bart swallowed the last mouthful of his tea and patting his big brother gently on the shoulder, recalled the events of the night. 'Fancy Craken acting that way. He's a bad bugger right enough.' He gazed candidly into his brother's eyes. 'What did he mean when he said about his actions tonight mirroring yours eight years ago?'

John Conrad hesitated. He looked across to where a 'billy' beetle fluttered its wings and then buzzed around the meat safe

237

to land on the wall. He took a long deep breath. 'Look, this is all pretty complicated. We'll both leave the planet hating each other, I suppose, that's the only certainty. But he was referring to the way I attacked him the night little Em died. The bastard's just trying to make out I was irrational and in the wrong when the fact is I should have killed him then and there. I really should have.'

Bartholomew nodded slowly as he sat back in his chair. It appeared his brother had learnt about distributing death. After a second or two, Bart stood. 'I don't suppose you want to say anything about Caro?'

'You're right. I don't,' his brother responded.

In the Dere house, where Matthew and Caro were spending the night, Caro lay in the bed.

Matthew sat in a chair against the wall sipping a brandy, his bad leg stretched out straight, his good bent at the knee. 'Sure you're all right now, old girl?'

She nodded.

'Won't ask you any questions tonight, but you'd best tell me the whole story in the morning.'

Caro shook her head, eyes closed. 'There's no story to tell.'

'Never mind. I want to know the "no story" as well. But, I reiterate, we'll leave it until daylight.'

Caro sighed.

'Now how about another cup of tea? Your mother's out there fussing around still.'

'No. Please tell her to go to bed. I'll sleep myself now.'

He rose to his feet, came over and kissed her forehead. 'I'll be back in a little while.' He looked down upon her. 'Might be best if you go back to Cedar Grove. Don't want you here where you might *accidentally* run into the enemy again.'

'Please, Matthew, don't talk like that. I want to stay here for Daddy's sake. He seemed to rally today just seeing me and little Harry.'

She watched him turn down the lamp and move across the room. Before he closed the door he said, 'Caro, old girl, we'll talk about it tomorrow.'

Caro was still in disbelief. To think John Conrad had been

there bending over her. All Matthew had told her on the way home after she insisted on knowing was that 'the bastard's alive so you don't need to worry'.

Now Matthew wanted to leave Brisbane. Or perhaps he didn't. Hadn't he said he wanted her alone to go to Cedar Grove? What if he intended to harm John Conrad again? No, surely not. Matt wouldn't be that reckless?

Her head ached. She sipped a little water from the glass at her bedside.

When she lay back she rested her hands flat on her stomach, fingertips touching across her navel and the words came quietly out of her mouth, almost a whisper. 'Perhaps in time I will love you but I do not love your father.' Then she moved her hands to her sides and inclined her head to where she could see the outline of Harry fast asleep in his cot in the corner. 'But I do love and adore you,' she whispered across the room. 'And I do love and adore your father.'

Chapter Eighteen

Dum Dum, north of Calcutta, India: February 1908

The bold Indian sun beat down upon the white-clothed players and as the umpire lifted his hands high in the air and called for a halt to play, K, who was not an interested sportsman, turned to John Conrad sitting beside him. 'So, Johnny, now they've halted for drinks do you think we could leave without offending any one?'

John Conrad smiled. The decade with K had seen him mature: his boyish smile still hung on his mouth but the eyes that looked out above it were harder, less enthusiastic perhaps, and more pensive, as if they had seen unhappy things and noted them all. He had not succumbed to his leader's penchant for a moustache but remained clean-shaven, the only one of K's six personal staff who had, and the muscles of his cheeks still held firm, his profile remained classic and the sun-kissed skin of his face continued smooth and virtually line-free except for those few at the corners of his eyes, his concession to the enduring Indian sunshine.

'Well, sir, perhaps we really shouldn't depart until they take tea. But as there are pressing matters for us back at Fort William I suppose we could, if you like.'

K nodded. 'I do like, as it happens. Cricket lasts too damn long, if you ask me. All these hours and still no result.'

On the other side of K sat Captain Oswald Fitzgerald, his military secretary and, along with John Conrad, his personal favourite. 'Fitz' as the commander-in-chief was wont to call him, had joined K's team in 1906 and he looked across to John Conrad. 'And the truth is, with your departure on leave tomorrow, Major, there are, in fact, a hundred things to do at the fort.'

K stood. 'Right, we'll make our goodbyes to Colonel Dunne.'

The three men took the three stairs in one stride and inside the long dark room made their way by the punkah-wallah, who pulled hard on the rope attached to the great ceiling fan to make the air current ventilating the room. There, surrounded by the players, stood the colonel. He saw K and turned from the cricketers, a knowing look on his face. 'You're leaving, m'lord?' He knew it had not been a particularly brilliant game but was aware, as all the men under K's command were, that their commander-in-chief was more interested in the cost to the army of the cricket equipment than in the matches themselves. It was, in fact, a battalion joke that K spoke of cricket as if it were 'a medicine to be taken by the troops twice weekly in summer'. Nevertheless it had been an honour to have their leader witness even some of the match.

K nodded formally and John Conrad explained. 'Lord Kitchener has pressing matters to attend to this evening back at Fort William; I hope you'll forgive us, but as it's a long ride from Dum Dum into Calcutta, we must extend our goodbyes.'

Colonel Dunne's expression was enigmatic. 'Yes, of course, well, thanks for coming. It's been an honour and of great importance to the men.'

K smiled. 'We know, Dunne, that's why we came. Thanks and goodbye.'

The colonel saluted K, the players all did the same, and John Conrad and Fitz returned the gesture to Colonel Dunne before the three men strode to the exit and out along the arched stone verandah to the wide front stairs detailed in colourful mosaic design. The Sikh on duty bowed his proudly turbaned head as the soldiers descended the marble-pillared staircase and moved across the open yard to Sergeant Major Mahadevan and the two privates, who had waited with the horses, and who now urged their charges forward.

They made their way back towards the thriving city, along the banks of the Hooghly River on the narrow dirt road. Past the villages, dotted in their similar thousands across the whole of India, they rode two by two: the privates in the rear, K and Fitz in the middle and John Conrad and Ashok Mahadevan in

241

front. John Conrad very much liked the Tamil: he was a good man, a fine soldier, the same age as John Conrad, and had a sparkling sense of humour which the Australian had responded to at their very first meeting four years before.

At a turn in the dusty road an ascetic, ash-covered and painted, seeking spiritual truth, wandered along in thought, as his counterparts had for centuries, past the herds of goats and camels and cattle that straggled at the stony roadside. There were graceful women in colourful robes with earthen jars on their heads, moving down the slope to the river bank to draw water for the coming night, accompanied by others with children at their heels and wide-eyed infants on their hips. The walking children called and waved at the passing soldiers.

At various points along the way, tribes of monkeys dripped from tree limbs. Occasionally these bold fellows destroyed crops and so had become unpopular with the farmers but they were a fascinating sight, and the soldiers never tired of such spectacle.

As the afternoon waned and the party of riders came closer to the city proper, they heard the barking of a lone pariah in the distance and, glancing to their right, witnessed elephants bathing in the river after their day's work, their great hulks bending at the knee, as their personal mahouts washed their massive backs. Later, when dusk began to fall, the acrid but not unpleasant smell of cooking fires, and the dust of returning cows and bullocks, swirled in the purplish haze of the fading light.

As the soldiers passed by a grove of ancient banyan trees a tinkle of a temple bell wafted to their ears across the flowering lotus at the road's edge and a group of happy children ran across in front of them, laughing and shouting.

It was these very simple yet fascinating Indian details that had kept John Conrad intrigued by this country the five years he had spent here. He glanced round at Ashok, whose intelligent dark eyes flashed as he smiled across at him.

The light was quickly fading when they came to the north-east corner of the Maidan, the huge park in the centre of Calcutta, and advanced upon Fort William by the marble hall memorial to Queen Victoria, opened two years earlier with great pomp by the Prince of Wales. During the day the ever-present artisans spent their time here, most now gone, and the few remaining folding and packing away their implements. Each morning brought weavers fabricating their rugs, and temple sculptors chipping away at granite, sitting back on their haunches day after day refining the statues of the various gods and goddesses for the temples and the homes of Bengal. Generation after generation the skills were ingrained in each and handed down from father to son; the same eternal labour of fashioning their articles.

A great flock of parrots, colourful wings glistening, lifted from a flowering tamarind and sailed into the setting sun. John Conrad looked around. 'India is a paradox,' he commented.

'Yes,' replied Ashok, 'there are many contradictions here. It's a puzzle at times.'

John Conrad nodded. 'I think of it as a believe-it-or-not country.'

'I like that,' the sergeant major answered. 'Yes, a believe-it-or-not country. And perhaps often, it is *not* to believe.' He pointed across to a sadhu. 'Look at that, sir.' The holy man, his body smeared with yellow ochre, was attracting a crowd for the final time this dying day, as he lay on his bed of thorns.

'I thought you could do that, Sergeant Major,' John Conrad teased.

'I gave it up when I found holes in my back.'

They both laughed and they heard the strong tones of K behind them. 'If the joke's that good then kindly share it with us.'

John Conrad turned in the saddle, the last rays of the golden light of evening catching in his fair hair and illuminating his eyes to a vivid blue. 'We were just speculating on the sergeant major's capabilities of being a sadhu, sir.'

'I think the army needs him more,' K replied light-heartedly.

Later that night, after an hour's work had been followed by a fine dinner prepared by the Indian chef who had been with K now for three years, the commander-in-chief and his aides sat on one of the stone balconies of Fort William facing out in the direction of the racecourse. The fort, completed in 1773, had undergone various alterations in the hundred and thirty-five years since and was the Bengal headquarters of the commander-in-chief. He looked now to the silver orb dominating the night sky above them and then glanced round at those gathered. They were all comfortable together; in fact K was often heard to call them 'my boys'. They remained absolutely dedicated to him and he demanded high standards from all, but after a hard day's work they often enjoyed social evenings together.

K sat with two baby tigers in a box at his feet. The little cats, only a few weeks old, had been found starving by a brigade of troops as they crossed the Ganges near Katwa to the north. The mother had been killed by poachers. K had called them Brandy and Port Wine and had been hand-feeding them for weeks and they were gaining weight at last. Every now and then he bent down and patted the little fellows as one would with house cats. K's poodle regarded the newcomers with suspicion but so far they had all tolerated one another. John Conrad and the others wondered what they were going to do with the babies when they grew.

K rotated his long body to look at John Conrad who sat beside him. 'I would've liked you to have spent your last night out at Treasury Gate. That way it would've been a more gracious farewell.'

Treasury Gate was K's residence just outside the city, where he had undertaken a deal of restoration just as he had in his two residences at Simla in the hills, turning them into quite beautiful and comfortable homes.

John Conrad shook his head, 'We've had far too much work to do here this week, sir. And this is as pleasant a gathering as I could have wished for.'

'You always make light of things, it's a fine trait.' K bent forward to stroke Brandy and the little fellow made a sound quite similar to a purr. 'I wonder how large they'll grow?'

'Too large for comfort. I've heard there's a maharajah up near Jaipur who keeps three or four. I think you'll have to give Brandy and Port Wine to him in the end.'

K smiled wistfully. 'Yes, I suppose you're right. Remember Ashford in Natal?'

Ashford had been a baby baboon for some reason abandoned on the edge of one of the army camps and K had doted on it, until one morning it had disappeared.

'Yes,' John Conrad responded, 'I sometimes wonder what happened to him.'

'Have to assume he returned to some troop of monkeys in the bushveldt. At least I hope so.'

On the far side of the balcony Major Nigel Livingstone-Learmonth leant back smoking a cigar and blowing great circles in the air above their heads. He looked across at John Conrad and then at K before he spoke. 'I think, with your permission, sir,' he inclined his head to K, 'I'd like to propose a toast.'

K nodded approval.

The major raised his long spare body slowly from his chair and stubbed out his cigar before lifting his fingers to draw down on his moustache in habitual fashion as he began speaking. 'We are gathered this evening to say *au revoir* to one of our small but élite circle. As you all know, Fleet here has decided to leave us for a period of some months.' His lean features turned skywards in mock horror. 'How he'll manage without our daily supervision is beyond me.'

One of the younger aides, Captain 'Wally' Basset, smiled widely to show his row of white even teeth as he leaned forward and slapped John Conrad on the back while the others all laughed and gave their opinions at once.

'You'll be like a babe in the woods without us.'

'Yes, poor Fleet out in the big world all alone.'

'Take me with you, John Conrad.'

Learmonth raised his hands and called for silence. He was the one who often chaffed John Conrad for being Australian. 'Nevertheless, we hope Fleet remembers everything we've taught him as we send him off in the morning to Australia, that largest of islands and smallest of continents which he, poor fellow, calls home.' He lifted his brandy balloon towards John Conrad, 'Enjoy yourself, but don't have too much fun without us.' Then he looked serious. 'Joking aside, old man, we all do hope you have a well-earned rest.'

A chorus of 'Hear, hear' greeted this and all present drank a toast.

'To John Conrad.'

And as the others drank, K raised his glass in John Conrad's direction, 'To my longest serving companion.'

John Conrad breathed deeply, rose to his feet and bowed

from the shoulders to K. 'My leader,' he began, then glanced around the upturned faces, 'and my good companions. I'd like to assure dear Learmonth that as odd as it may seem, I shall be able to manage perfectly well without your supervision.'

This caused a rumble of mock disbelief.

'I'm looking forward to seeing my family again, whom I've not visited for seven years. But four months isn't so long, it'll fly by and then I shall be back to rectify all the mistakes you'll undoubtedly have made during my absence. Thank you.' He raised his glass to them all, then drank to catcalls and Learmonth's shouting, 'Touché!'

The following morning John Conrad rose at dawn. The river gleamed and the capital of British India shone with the pristine light of day as the complex rituals of Indian living began again in the overcrowded city.

The ship was leaving at nine, and John Conrad's trunks had gone aboard the previous night. K had requested breakfast for the two of them at seven. They talked mainly about military concerns and certain matters that were to be attended to in John Conrad's absence. When they had finished eating and K's tea was poured, John Conrad lifted one of the papers he had in a pile at his side. 'As one last thing, if you don't mind I'd like to make a point about your latest memorandum to the troops.'

'Which one?'

'Excuse me for bringing this up at the breakfast table, but the one on avoiding VD.'

K peered over his great moustache. 'Mm, what about it?'

'Well, K, there's a sentence here where you say, and I quote, "Avoid temptation, it is your duty to keep yourself clear of excesses. Remember the better influences in your life. What would your mother, your sisters and your good friends at home, think of you if they saw you overcome and degraded by this disease?"'

K nodded. 'Yes, what's wrong with that?'

'It's just that the home life of the average soldier may not be what you imagine. Certainly I'm sure some of them have caring relatives, mothers, sisters, et cetera, but a lot of them come from pretty awful backgrounds; some of them are in the army as an alternative to a prison sentence. And I'm sorry to have to tell you that there are the odd regiments who take some grotesque pride in having the highest VD statistics in the army.'

K did not speak for a time, then cleared his throat. 'Then what is it you would have me say?'

'I think it would be better if you simply dropped the "remember the better influences" and the bit about mothers and sisters and that it read: "Avoid temptation, it is your duty to keep yourself clear of excesses, venereal disease is not glamorous, it's painful and it kills."'

K grunted. 'Alter it before you leave. I'll meet you in the quadrangle at eight.'

The motor vehicle was waiting when K met John Conrad on the steps. 'Ready?'

John Conrad nodded.

K was unsmiling and he asked in brusque tones, 'Have you seen Orders this morning?'

He was referring to the posting of the Routine Orders of the Day, which appeared on the board in the fort's main hall. They were usually full of such items as times of church parades, numbers required to mount various guard duties, disciplinary offences, etc., and most soldiers avoided reading them.

Taken aback, the younger man hesitated. 'Actually no, sir. I didn't look, as I'm leaving today.'

K's features did not soften. 'Then I suggest you turn around and go back and do so.'

'Sir.' John Conrad did as he was bidden and smartly returned inside along the stone corridor, across the small interior courtyard and along the overhang to the main hall. He wondered if he had upset K by his reference to the VD message, but he was sure that K in his gruff way had appreciated it. Crossing to the board he read the items. There was nothing unusual, just the type of things he had expected. Then as his eyes ran down the lists he exclaimed out loud and a wide smile broke across his mouth. There it was, in the day's orders; his promotion to brevet lieutenant colonel. How like K not to tell him, to have him find out like this.

Swiftly he returned, actually running across the interior

courtyard to the raised eyebrows of the sentry on duty. K stood waiting on the steps.

'I assume you recommended me for the promotion I've just read in orders, sir.'

And at last K's face broke into gentler lines. 'Mmm, I suppose I must have.'

'What a marvellous way to go on leave. I'm absolutely delighted. Thank you so very much for your continuing belief in me.'

And K, who was always somewhat uncomfortable with expressions of gratitude, smiled but said nothing and immediately gestured for John Conrad to get in the car. 'We should go.'

Both men climbed into the back seat for the drive south of the city to the docks at Kidderpur. The car was a four-cylinder Rolls-Royce limousine and the hood was folded down concertina-like behind them, allowing them to enjoy the morning air.

In front beside the driver sat Sergeant Major Mahadevan. John Conrad had said he would go to the ship alone, but K had insisted on accompanying him. Another smaller vehicle with a sergeant and a private led the way out of the fort through the streets and along the south road, to the delight of many of the inhabitants, who watched and waved unselfconsciously at the small motorcade. The docks covered many miles of the river and finally they came to the entrance that took them down to where the 404 feet cargo vessel *Commonwealth*, gross tonnage 5590 tons, lay ready to take John Conrad and its cargo of tea across the seas via Madras, Singapore, Batavia, Fremantle and on to Sydney, Australia.

One soldier remained with the car, and Ashok and the second soldier accompanied K and John Conrad along the wharf where the workers and frequenters of the docks made way for K, many recognising the commander-in-chief.

'Slow down, Johnny,' K said at his side.

John Conrad slowed immediately. He was very aware that K's leg sometimes bothered him. It was an injury from five years earlier when he had broken both bones below the knee in his left leg in a fall from his horse. John Conrad recalled those convalescent days well. K had not been a good patient.

'I wrote to Lady Cranborne yesterday. She's always on about taking more exercise for my leg, but she doesn't have the blasted thing attached to her, I do.'

Lady Cranborne, the Marchioness of Salisbury, had been his letter writing confidante for many years and since Lord Salisbury had died in 1903, K seemed to write even more often to her. Not that there was a hint of anything other than a platonic friendship.

John Conrad sympathised. 'Yes, I'm sorry it still troubles you, but the heat here's probably good for it.'

K was not about to agree readily to this. 'Perhaps and perhaps not. I often think it seems better when I'm up at Simla.'

At the ship's side John Conrad turned to Ashok. The Indian's black eyes radiated friendship as he came to attention in front of John Conrad.

'I shan't be gone long, Ashok. Look after yourself.'

'And you too, sir.' He saluted and John Conrad held out his palm. 'I prefer to say goodbye this way, Ashok.'

Pleased, the man smiled and grasped the proffered hand. 'Thank you. I will miss you.' Then Ashok looked to K and saluted.

When Ashok and the other soldier had retreated to a respectful distance, John Conrad met his leader's eyes. Yes, he had been many years with K, growing from earnest youth to discerning and experienced man. He knew Horatio Herbert Kitchener, the most celebrated hero in the entire world, possibly better than any human being. Some people said K was an opportunist – cold, abrupt and even rude – but John Conrad knew that this was often just the man's shyness, and that his soul was completely devoid of intrigue. There was no doubt that he did not tolerate well frivolous people or silly chatter and this was sometimes misconstrued, though in agreeable company he could be less inclined to introspection.

Over the years John Conrad had heard officers call K grim and unsympathetic but he knew a different man who was kind and friendly even to humble strangers. K was actually turning his head and smiling now at a small boy who passed along the wharf on the back of a donkey.

But when K brought his gaze round again to John Conrad his eyes were ever penetrating and seemingly grave, though the unique truth was that the younger man's own eyes were very much the same. For John Conrad's eyes were, remarkably, the same pale ice colour as his leader's and they possessed an equally autocratic expression and analytical stare.

'What's the name of the ship you return upon?' K asked.

'The steamship *Boadicea*. I can even embark upon her in Brisbane, which of course suits me perfectly. She heads to Singapore and then on to Madras. I've given Fitz the departure and arrival dates. She apparently comes here at the same time each year for a cargo of jute.'

'It's strange for me to be losing you, though I do recall you had a very long leave once before. Six months, wasn't it? At least this is not quite so lengthy.'

John Conrad smiled ruefully. 'That was hardly a leave, K.' He used 'K' in the familiar way which he always did when they were alone. 'That was when I went to staff college in England, merely to be more qualified for you.'

K was uncompromising. 'I counted it as a leave.'

John Conrad gave a throaty laugh and shook his head. 'Yes, I suppose you did.'

'Anyway, we've only eighteen months more here, and while in many ways I'm loath to leave the continuing restructuring of the whole Indian army, my hopes are for the Constantinople appointment, as you know.'

'I do, and you deserve it. You deserve all you get and more. You must know what we thought when they awarded you the Order of the Grand Commanders of the Indian Empire last December?'

K shook his head.

'We all thought they should have made you a field marshal. It's long overdue. They'll just have to make you one when you leave here.'

K's eyes actually widened. 'Heavens, Johnny, you make me sound like India's saviour. I think you're a touch partisan, m'boy.'

The younger man shook his head. 'No, I'm merely reminding you of the facts. The Indian army actually works properly now. It was you and your resolve that made it all happen. I, of all people know.' He looked searchingly at the commander-in-chief. 'Always remember I saw what went on with Lord

Curzon when he was here and how difficult he was; wanting to retain control of everything.'

'Ah, Johnny, that's water under the bridge.'

'Yes I know, but you had to make it a fight to keep the military in your power. Thank goodness Lord Minto succeeded Curzon and the council have been more favourable to our ideas. It was tough but you won.'

K smiled. 'Ah Johnny, if the world saw me as you do . . .'

John Conrad looked hard at his leader. 'Most of the world does.'

'I don't know about any of that. Still, sometimes I feel like a prisoner in India.' He sighed. 'You must go. I'll miss you, Johnny.'

At that moment the *Commonwealth*'s captain and first mate arrived down the gangplank. A fuss was made over K, who took it a touch self-consciously. K introduced John Conrad to the captain. 'This is your passenger, Lieutenant Colonel Fleet, take good care of him. He's important to me.'

Captain Peel had already assumed that John Conrad was significant to Lord Kitchener as he could guess that the commander-in-chief did not come to the wharf to see off every soldier who went on leave. 'We'll take care of him especially. Your Lordship need have no disquieting thoughts on that matter.' Then he nodded to John Conrad's shoulder. 'You should alter your insignia, sir. It appears you're still only a major.'

K smiled and John Conrad replied, 'I will. My promotion's been rather recent, to say the least.'

The captain then had the good sense to say, 'I shall leave you now. We sail in fifteen minutes.' He nodded to John Conrad. 'Sir, please be good enough to be aboard then.' With that, he turned and strode up the gangplank.

'Goodbye, K. I'm sure you'll be well looked after by Fitz, and the others.'

K exhaled audibly. 'True, Fitz is turning out to be a marvel. But I prefer it when I have two marvels.'

They both laughed and John Conrad was pleased, for K's dignified and sober face did not soften in laughter very often. And then K lifted his hands and placed them on both the younger man's shoulders so that he was looking directly in his eyes. 'You've said kind words this morning, and now it's my turn. You've turned into my strong right hand.' He hesitated. 'It must be nearly ten years now . . . is it?'

As John Conrad answered the noises of the wharf labourers, the sounds of ships straining against their ropes and the buzz of activity all orbited around them. 'Yes it is, on the sixth of December this year, exactly. I left England for the Sudan with you on the seventh, ten years ago.'

'I know you're ambitious and that suits me. I was the same at your age. Ambition breeds performance of a distinctly primary class.' He affectionately squeezed John Conrad's shoulders, then offered him his right hand. 'Have a good rest in Australia and enjoy being home with your family.'

They held gazes briefly and the younger man's lips parted in a warm smile. 'The promotion's marvellous. I hope I'll continue to prove your belief in me.' He turned smartly away and hurried up the gangplank. From the deck he turned and waved, and the commander-in-chief and Sergeant Major Mahadevan lifted their hands, then walked away.

John Conrad watched as K and the sergeant major disappeared through the throng, then his eyes lifted across the wharf to the river plains of Bengal where the water from the slopes of the Himalayas poured down to this river and the sea. He gave a thoughtful smile as a voice sounded at his side.

'Sir?'

He turned to see the first mate. 'This way, sir. Though we be merely a trading vessel we have seven berths on the starboard side upper, made available for passengers.'

'How many passengers do you have this voyage?'

'You're the first to join and all, sir. There'll be three other gentlemen, two ladies and a married couple embarking in Madras. We lose all the gentlemen between here and Australia, excepting yourself, though the ladies sail the whole way with us and all.'

As the mate led him through the gangways, Captain Peel gave his orders on the bridge and the *Commonwealth* slipped from the wharf and into the river delta.

The following day they tied up in Madras. It was after seven at night and dinner with the captain was at eight. John Conrad stood at the bulwark amidships, listening to the noises of India and looking out on the busy port where the same bright orb sat in the sky above as it had in Calcutta two nights before.

He turned from the evocative smells and sounds of the wharves and sat for a time on a hatch, thinking of all he had left behind and of what he would find at home in Brisbane. All the years of his army life Aunt Leigh had written regularly though the Indian post was such that he usually received great piles of letters all together even though they had been written, sometimes months apart. Bart was his other reliable communicator, though it pleased him to note that his father did put pen to paper once or twice a year. It was his youngest brother, David, whom he did not hear from, other than a very occasional line at the bottom of a missive from Bart. He was not close to David – how could he be? He had been away from home for fifteen years in all and David had been a small boy of nine when he left. They really did not know each other.

Momentarily a picture of Caro Dere came to his mind. He had not thought of her for a very long time. On his leave seven years before he had seen no more of her after the fatal night at the welcome home party for the South African Campaign soldiers. Briefly he wondered about her second child. He had heard her first was a boy. He shook his head. Knowing Craken she could have had one or two more since then. His features hardened at the thought of Matthew Craken and he moved slightly sideways as if he were uncomfortable sitting on the hatch.

He had learned so much in the years with K. He supposed, he had learned abstinence too . . . well, to a certain extent, for there was a girl called Nadia in Calcutta who tempted him back to her side now and then. Though as John Conrad sat looking out at Madras harbour with the smells of India assailing his thoughts he recalled the one woman of recent years whom K had felt deeply for: in England after the South African Campaign. They were lodging in Belgrave Square with K's friend Pandeli Ralli, whom he had first met in Cyprus in the early 1880s. John Conrad remembered the last night that K had ever seen the woman.

K had returned home much earlier than expected and gone immediately to bed. They had left England shortly afterwards and only once more had K ever referred to 'the lady'. It was on the ship out to India and they were walking on the deck under the stars one night when K had halted at the rail.

'You know that night a week or two ago? When I came home early from that, er, certain lady's company?'

'Yes K.'

'I asked her to marry me. She refused.'

'Yes K, I suspected that.'

He had looked around like a schoolboy full of wonder in the clear night to find his companion's eyes. 'You had?' he asked in amazement.

There had been no woman to interest K since and John Conrad thought perhaps now there never would be. K would turn fifty-eight in June and was in reality every inch a man's man.

John Conrad took a deep breath and looked up to the sky. He felt odd being here alone without K or Fitz or one of the others of their select group. Just for a minute a picture of them all playing tennis at Wildflower Hall, K's summer house near Simla, came into his mind; comfortable happy days in between the hard work. He placed his arms straight out behind him and leaned back on them looking skywards and deeply breathing as the last light of twilight disappeared and the night began. With the arrival of the darkness the worst of the heat had disappeared. There was a fresh sea wind blowing and he smelt the salt and the ozone-laden air. The atmosphere was somehow so clean and beautiful he was reminded of the Hindu belief that man was reborn and reborn until perfection was reached and he blended with the divine. On such a night it could be possible to believe such a thing.

But then in swift heartless contrast, the markings upon the moon gave credence to the view that it was a face laughing, as if the man in the moon were there all right, for ever a universal witness amused by the machinations of the poor human puppets below. The idea of blending with the divine slipped away into the blackness of the night.

He brought his eyes down to the deck. As he did so, thirty feet away, around the section of the forward hatches two females appeared and moved across to the far bulwark. The hanging lanterns showed the women were in very different decades of their lives. The youngest appeared in her twenties, straight-backed she glided along with a shock of striking auburn curls plummeting in rows to dance upon her shoulders. The hair was such a radiant colour even in the weak lantern light, that, as her head turned, the side of the girl's face took on a creamy pink luminosity as if reflected from the startling hair. She was holding the arm of a woman who was probably in her late fifties.

They halted in conversation. After a few minutes they moved away out of sight and John Conrad checked his fob watch to find it was almost eight o'clock.

Two minutes later he entered Captain Peel's quarters and the commander of the vessel introduced him to some of the companions of his voyage: two tea planters on their way to Malaya, and a merchant returning to Singapore. They made small talk for a few minutes and then the captain exclaimed, 'Ah, some more of the passengers.'

The men looked round to see the first mate enter with a couple who were introduced as Mr and Mrs Lewis Henderson, an archaeologist and his wife on their way to China. Then the door opened again and the third officer came in with the two ladies John Conrad had seen not ten minutes since.

'I'd like you to meet Mrs Jerome-Frith and Colonel Hewitt Harvey's ward, Miss Emma Blackstone.' As the captain spoke the young woman gave a small smile to the Hendersons and then looked past them, making eye contact with John Conrad, who stood behind them. She again gave the glimmer of a smile before averting her eyes. John Conrad was peering at the girl and a crease settled between his brows as he stood frowning in contemplation.

By the time she had been introduced to him, and they all sat at the captain's long dinner table, John Conrad was still frowning. This young woman was the right age; and there was something whimsical about her that reminded him of the child of so long ago. It could be that she was one and the same, it really could . . .

And as the dinner advanced he attended the girlish turning of her head and the bouncing red curls and the pert pink mouth as she answered questions in forthright breezy manner. He became more sure of her as the hours passed. By the time dessert was eaten she had caught his eye on more than one occasion. With the arrival of port, the ladies retired to the long room. As she reached the door John Conrad nodded to her open smile of good night. Now he felt certain.

Half an hour later the soldier left the other men still enjoying their nightcaps and made his way along to his cabin, his footfalls ringing purposefully on the wooden deck.

Inside his quarters, the wall lamp illuminated the gleaming woodwork and he stood momentarily looking in the oval mirror above the washstand. Mechanically he lifted the folded white towel that lay awaiting, before he turned away, and, throwing it on the bunk, knelt to open the trunk positioned between the stand and the door. For some minutes he rifled through his possessions; then he found the old wallet tucked in a small compartment in the lid. He was half surprised that it was still here, and that in fact, he had brought it; but then it had gone everywhere with him over all the years.

He opened the tired leather leaves and there it was. He took it out and held it. A saint smiled up at him with serene otherworldly aspect. He turned it over and observed the name in precise copybook writing on the back of the holy card: Emma Louise Blackstone.

He would prove it tomorrow even though there was no need; he knew it was his little Emma of fifteen years before; the same strange sweet adult-child who had given him this card on the train between Brisbane and Ipswich. Yes, he was sure Emma Louise Blackstone was in a berth with her aunt not a dozen yards away.

Chapter Nineteen

When John Conrad approached Emma Louise the following day, the ship was heading fast south-east, pushing its majestic way through the dark blue swell of the Bay of Bengal.

It was mid-morning when he sighted her. He had been up early, dined with the first mate and walked on the deck where he had run into the tea planters and talked with them for a time.

He was sitting in his deckchair when he saw her. She emerged up the companionway from the lower deck amidships. He knew she had spied him immediately but she threw her radiant hair back over her shoulder with a toss of her head and gave no indication of being aware of him. She turned and walked away, disappearing round a forward hatch towards the forecastle.

He rose and followed her, to find her standing at the bulwark looking out to sea.

'Excuse me, Miss Blackstone.'

She turned her pretty eyes, pretending surprise. 'Oh, you startled me.'

'I did not mean to.'

She smiled and her nose wrinkled. Somehow it reminded him of the child he had only seen once, but recalled well. 'My name's John Conrad Fleet.'

'I know, I remember from last night.'

He felt flattered. 'I have something to show you.'

'Really? What?'

He placed his hand in his inner pocket and withdrew the small holy card. He handed it to her as she regarded him quizzically.

She shook her hair back again as she looked up at him.

'Turn it over,' he said.

She did so and now a little furrow of confusion lodged on her silken brow. 'But this is my name.'

'Yes, you gave it to me, a long time ago.'

She laughed. 'I never did.'

'You were in Queensland, Australia at the time, and I suppose you were just five or six.'

She laughed again. It was a childlike, delightful laugh, infectious, and he laughed too. 'It's true,' he added, 'it was 1893, and we were on a train, between two towns, Brisbane and Ipswich. I think you were travelling with a lady.'

'How simply amazing.'

'Yes, isn't it?'

Her eyes sparkled with the fun of it all and she waved the card in the air. 'I remember I used to save them, holy cards. I had dozens.' She fixed him with a severe expression. 'Did I *really* give it to you?'

'Yes.'

'And you've kept it all these years?'

'Yes. Don't you remember anything about it?'

She hesitated, bringing the card up to rest it on her chin. He noted the oval nail of her index finger. A mischievous half-smile edged her lips apart. 'Well . . . perhaps I do. Yes . . . I think so.' Now that he had reminded her she recalled a nice man in a dark part of a train with windows up above her head, and she fancied she remembered the incident. She knew she had been in Australia for four years when she was a child and did remember that long train journey. 'Was it in a corridor or something?'

'Yes.'

'I think I remember it.'

'A woman came and called you away.'

She stared hard at him. 'My goodness. But why did you keep it?'

For a moment he paused, unsure of what to tell her, and as he did so, a gust of wind came up from the bows of the ship and lifted the card from Emma's pale fingers. It blew along the deck.

'Oh, you must save it!' she called as he ran after it.

Skipping and bouncing away, it fluttered, leading him across ropes and by cleats and past the forward derrick. He caught it up against the port bulwark.

As he stood upright she arrived at his side laughing. 'Oh,

my goodness, what a to-do. At least you caught it. It would've been a real shame to lose it, wouldn't it?'

'Yes,' he said as he put it in his inside pocket.

They stood silently looking at each other. Emma Louise found this whole business so diverting. This military Adonis had carried a card from her for teens of years. It was truly amazing and somehow quite poetic. She was so flattered. It was a testimony to marvellous, magical spiritual coincidences and reminded her of works by Byron and Scott and stories of strange unrequited loves, of epic poems and romance. She smiled widely up at him and stared into his eyes.

Abruptly he asked, 'Would you like to take morning tea with me? They serve it in the saloon at eleven.'

Her eyes twinkled. 'I'd very much like to.'

He gave her his arm as a cough sounded behind them.

They turned around to find Emma's aunt standing a yard away.

'Oh, Aunt Gertrude, I wondered when you would come. This gentleman, Lieutenant Colonel Fleet, has been so kind as to invite me into morning tea.'

'Has he now?' Gertrude eyed John Conrad. 'In that case I'm sure the offer extends to me as well.'

'Of course, madam. Do come along.'

The three of them spent the next hour together. Gertrude used the time to find out all she could about the soldier, and with the rate she asked questions her knowledge could have become extensive except that John Conrad, after years involved in the diplomacy which surrounded K, was expert at parrying questions. He avoided many of her queries with questions of his own. Gertrude already knew from the previous night's conversations that he was on Lord Kitchener's staff in Calcutta: she had questioned the captain for that information. This had deeply impressed Gertrude and she had looked kindly on the handsome soldier ever since. Her one mission was to see Emma Louise walk down the aisle with a man of standing, reputable and proper – not the likes of that working-class sergeant at arms in Madras; that had been a nightmare. The girl would be twenty-one next month, and most girls were engaged or married by such an age. She herself had walked down the aisle at eighteen. It really was time that Emma Louise was betrothed.

She had asked the first mate more about the soldier this morning and had learned he had just received his lieutenant colonel's brevet. This impressed her too. After all, her brother, Hewitt, was yet a colonel, and he was about to retire. John Conrad Fleet was only a young man. No doubt he was going places. It pleased her to see Emma Louise in such elevated company.

And in fact, Emma Louise was delighting in the *elevated company*. She thought John Conrad Fleet positively the most handsome man she had ever seen. Indeed, maturity had only enhanced his looks. He still turned heads wherever he went. Those of the officers' wives who had their grown daughters with them in India had all set their caps at him without success. He was talked about in ladies' circles as 'Fleet by name and fleet by nature'. No girl could catch him.

Gertrude did not know any of this so it did not deter her, though she knew of Kitchener's rule that his personal staff should remain single. All India knew that. She was very taken by Lieutenant Colonel Fleet.

She and her brother, Hewitt, Emma Louise's guardian, had removed the child from Madras for a reason: the influence of one Sergeant Hector Flynn of the Lancers, a man definitely not for Emma Louise. It had been a traumatic upset to find the child had been seeing the soldier. It had been a most unwelcome association. Emma Louise's Hindu maid had assisted her in the subterfuge and the whole episode had almost given Gertrude a breakdown. She had been terrified of a scandal, but thank the good Lord in heaven it had not come to that. No one had found out.

It was Hewitt who had thought to remove the girl to Australia, away from Hector Flynn. Gertrude and Hewitt had a cousin in Queensland, and since Hewitt's stint there in the early nineties as a liaison officer, it had always been his intention to retire to the new country. Thus the idea of Gertrude taking Emma Louise there early had materialised.

And though Emma Louise had cried her eyes out and taken tantrums and been difficult about it, they had prevailed, and here she was on the *Commonwealth* on her way to Australia. The astonishing consequence was that her good spirits had returned immediately the ship had set sail from Madras. It had been like a miracle. Gertrude had prayed nonstop for months and finally felt she had been heard. She had the suspicion that the change in the child was to do with Lieutenant Colonel Fleet; he was a positive Apollo. Anyway, whatever the reason she was gratified and eternally grateful to see her niece behaving normally again.

John Conrad had left the ladies with a promise to join them in a cocktail before dinner. Twenty minutes before the appointed hour he arrived in the saloon which served as a bar and adjoined the captain's quarters, to find Emma Louise already there. The only other person was a steward. The young woman stood on the far side of the room, her fingers playing with the tassel on a curtain tie, and she looked around to him, her eyes gleaming a welcome in the lamplight.

'I hoped you would be early,' she said, gliding across to him.

He raised a quizzical eyebrow.

'I wanted to see you alone for a while.'

He smiled. Her directness appealed to him. He was not used to it in the women he socialised with: they were much more worldly and artful. It was quite delightful to find this candour. For some reason when he looked at Emma Louise he seemed to see the tiny child of the train. 'Did you now?'

'Yes. I need to be alone sometimes. Aunt Gertrude's from the old school.'

'Oh, and what school is that?'

'You know . . . chaperones and good behaviour. Young women should do this and young women should do that. Positively medieval.'

Amused, he shook his head.

'What's Kitchener of Khartoum like?'

The question had come from nowhere. He was to note this more and more as he came to know her better. She would alter course right in the middle of a conversation; never rudely interrupting others, but interrupting herself; altering direction on her own train of thought.

At that point the steward did his own interrupting and they ordered drinks: a gin and bitters for John Conrad and a sherry for the girl.

As the steward departed she flung her brilliant hair back

over her shoulders, sat down on a long sofa and eyed her companion. 'So come on, tell me, you know him well, what's the great man like?'

He met her gaze for a few seconds and, easing down opposite her on to an upholstered bench, answered, 'He's remarkable.'

She burst into laughter and John Conrad, taken aback, asked, 'What's funny?'

'You, you're so serious. Of course he's remarkable – the world knows that! He's famous.' She lifted her hands high in the air and twirled them around for emphasis. 'Obliterating the whirling dervishes and thumping the boring Boers. No, I mean what's *he* like? The one the world doesn't see. The one *you* see.' She was smiling widely and the child was peering through at him asking the question.

And when he replied it was as if to a child. 'He's many things. He's complicated, as you would expect him to be. And brave and forthright. I've learnt a great deal from him.'

'How long have you been with him?'

'Almost a decade.'

'Is your father still alive?'

It was another of those odd, out-of-the-spirit-of-the-conversation questions.

'Yes, why?'

'I thought perhaps Kitchener was a father-figure for you. You know, a surrogate, like Uncle Hewitt is for me. He's my father-figure.'

John Conrad was glad of the change in subject. He took advantage of it. 'I see. What happened to your real father?'

'He died when I was five. Killed in Egypt. And my mother was never well afterwards. She was . . . "delicate" is the word Aunt Gertrude uses. Anyway, she died in the same year . . . broken heart, everybody says. Uncle Hewitt and Aunt Gertrude have looked after me ever since.' She stopped speaking as the drinks were placed on the small table in front of them.

She took a mouthful of the sherry and made a wry face, looking more like a child than ever. 'Funny taste this, not like the sherry we had in Madras.' She looked over his shoulder to the door. 'Oh pooh, here comes Aunt Gertrude.'

The woman was in company with the two tea planters, so

conversation became more general and the night progressed much as the one before had done.

John Conrad left the other men smoking at around half-past ten and made his way along the deck. As he approached his cabin he halted and stood a minute at the bulwark, feeling the strong sea breeze in his face. He bit the edge of his lip as he thought of Emma Louise Blackstone; imagined her tilting her head and throwing her hair back over her shoulder. It was most perplexing running into her like this and he carried ambivalent feelings about it. She was a strange adult-child in his eyes; appealing and quaint and very entertaining. He wondered what K would think; but then he thought he knew. He could hear K saying it: *Yes, she's an amusing child.*

He missed K. He stepped forward, deep in thought, and held the capping rail of the bulwark. The commander-in-chief would be going soon to Simla in the hills, returning to the cooler mountain climate, to his other home up there, to Wildflower Hall. They all liked going there, especially the Sunday afternoon tennis matches. K had decorated the interior walls with the coats of arms of the great Indian Princes. He often just sat there contemplating them.

How many times John Conrad had ridden with his leader in the cool woods of Elysium and gazed upon the outer ridges of the Himalayas reaching beyond the clouds, with the little roads like pencil marks upon them winding up the tree-covered slopes.

He looked into the darkness, sniffing the ozone appreciatively and mentally comparing it with the air of Simla. He had now been on a number of sea voyages and he noticed the wind had picked up a little; perhaps the seas would be bigger tomorrow.

His guess was correct, and for the next three days the seas did become rougher and most people spent the majority of their time in their cabins. In fact the only people who continued to take their regular meals were John Conrad, Emma Louise and Mr Henderson. Emma Louise cheered them with her chatter. On the third night the seas abated somewhat as the *Commonwealth* maintained her course into the Strait of Malacca and south to Singapore. Still, the only passengers who appeared for dinner – sandwiches and cake, because of the difficulty of serving – were the usual three. The captain and the mate took their meal on the bridge.

But Emma Louise's high spirits did not fail. When Mr Henderson left she turned with a smile to John Conrad. 'I don't mind rough seas. It's exciting.'

'You're lucky you don't feel it like your aunt does. Shouldn't you go and see to her?'

'Yes, I will soon. She was sleeping when I left. The seas are much better than yesterday though, aren't they?'

'Yes, and the captain believes they will abate entirely by morning. We've entered the strait and, all being well, we'll be in Singapore in forty-eight hours.'

'Oh pooh,' she retorted.

'Now why do you say that?'

The mischievous twinkle that regularly danced in her eyes appeared. 'Ah, the truth is . . . apart from Mr Henderson, I've had you to myself . . . sort of, that is. And it's been very nice.'

'That's a very forward thing to say.'

'I know.' She tossed her hair back over her shoulder and he smiled.

'Where do you live in Brisbane? What part?' she asked quickly.

'My family have a brewery in the West End.'

'Oh, is that a nice place?'

'No, quite ordinary really: much of Brisbane is. It's a sprawling place, though there are parts of the city that are pleasant enough. But it's hot, a lot like India.'

Her lips curled in distaste. 'Oh dear, and I'm tired of the heat. We were going to a place called Jimboomba. I never could believe there was a place called that, it's just the oddest name. But there is. Anyway Aunt Nevis, Aunt Gertrude's cousin, the one we're going to live with, has moved . . . to somewhere called Southport. Now that's a sensible name. So we're going there. Uncle Slattery breeds horses and they run a guesthouse or something. How far away's that from Brisbane?'

John Conrad thought. 'I think it's fifty or so miles; a small seaside township to the south. There are long golden beaches. Good swimming.'

Her nose crinkled. 'Ladies don't go swimming, or so Aunt Gertrude says.'

'I wouldn't have thought you'd worry about that.'

She laughed spontaneously and then gave him a stern look, appearing most childlike again to her listener.

The ship jolted and she slipped slightly along the sofa.

'Shouldn't you go and see your aunt?'

She nodded and rose.

A steward jumped forward. 'I'll take you to your cabin, miss.'

John Conrad lifted his hand. 'It's all right thank you. I'll escort Miss Blackstone. Give me your arm.' She held it out and he took it firmly in his grasp. They passed along the companionway to the deck.

He steered her safely to her cabin door. On the way they were hit by a little spray, which made Emma Louise laugh heartily.

At the door he patted her shoulder. 'Good night, sleep well.'

'I will.'

'Shall we have breakfast at eight again?'

'If you like, Lieutenant Colonel Fleet.'

John Conrad smiled. 'And, Miss Blackstone, please call me John Conrad. As I would prefer to call you Emma Louise, if you don't mind. *Miss Blackstone* sounds like the name of a very serious restrained elderly lady, none of which has the remotest resemblance to you.'

She giggled. 'Oh yes, of course. Thank you, John Conrad. Good night.'

She opened the door and disappeared inside, where she stood watching his dark form disappear into the wind of the night. She took a deep breath and closed the door, leaning her back against it and feeling the rigidity of the wood along her spine. John Conrad Fleet; she even liked his name, and he was just too good-looking for words. She had not believed she would meet anyone more handsome than Hector Flynn, but she had. Hector seemed so far away now, and John Conrad Fleet was so close. To think he had carried a holy card of hers for a positive age . . . goodness, since she was six or something. What could be more surprising? He was sort of old, but so refined and cultured, and his eyes were wonderful. She knew he thought her forward and high-spirited, but he did not seem to mind that at all; in truth she felt he quite liked the way she was. She smiled to herself as Gertrude's voice sounded from the bunk.

'Is that you, darling? I'm feeling a little better.'

'Guess what?'

'What?'

'He asked me to call him John Conrad. We're on a first-name basis now.'

Gertrude smiled in the darkness. 'How very satisfactory.'

Outside, along the deck, John Conrad opened the door of his own cabin and went inside. He sat on his bunk and rubbed the dampness of the spray from his hair with his towel. He thought of Emma laughing when the spray hit them. She was a delightful child, she truly was, there was no doubt about it.

The next day the seas had abated and all the passengers reappeared. By the time they entered the safe harbour of Singapore spirits were high.

They said their goodbyes to the tea planters and wished them well, and then Emma Louise asked John Conrad to accompany her and her aunt into the markets of Singapore. 'For they say the silks here are wonderful and I do wish to buy some. Aunt Nevis in Southport is a marvellous seamstress, so Aunt Gertrude tells me.' Her eyes glowed with thoughts of much finery. 'She can make me some special new dresses.'

John Conrad smiled and agreed to escort the ladies as requested. It seemed natural to indulge Emma Louise. He did not take her seriously; it was interesting, even astonishing, that he would run into his fairy-dream child like this.

He thought of India and how they all dined and socialised with various wives and daughters of the military, but they did not consider women in their own private lives. Except for Learmonth: he had a lady friend back in Wales who had been 'almost a fiancée' for six or seven years. Everyone said he would marry her eventually.

They spent two days in Singapore while the ship took on water and some provisions, and John Conrad and Gertrude watched Emma Louise enjoy herself. The girl laughed in the Chinese street markets where she found her beautiful silks; she laughed in Raffles Tiffin Room; she laughed in the botanical gardens and in the Hindu temples and at the cricket ground on the esplanade where they went on the second afternoon to see a match. Singapore seemed to delight her and the two people with her could not help but be delighted too.

And so it followed that Emma Louise laughed her way through the entire voyage to Sydney. Each port saw some of the passengers disembark until finally there were only John Conrad, Emma Louise and Gertrude left.

Nearing the last stage of their sea journey, they rounded the peninsula of Wilson's Promontory in the state of Victoria in unusually calm evening seas and headed north towards Sydney. The peaceful waters were conducive to writing, and Gertrude sat at the small desk in their cabin bringing her diary up to date. Emma Louise was brushing her radiant hair in the lamplight and as she caught the eye of her aunt in the mirror, she said, 'John Conrad's really very good-looking, isn't he?'

Gertrude sighed. 'Almost insufferably so.'

'How old do you think he is?'

'Thirty-four or -five, perhaps thirty-six.'

'Oh dear, that old?'

Gertrude smiled 'That's not old, angel. It's really very young.'

'It's old to me.'

'Yes, sweetheart, but you're twenty. As the years pass you'll realise that one is a mere child until around forty-five, then a modicum of sensibility and intellect takes hold.'

'I can't imagine being so ancient as that.'

'No one can, dear, until they are. Then one sees age in a wholly different manner. Anyway, wait until you're my age.'

Emma Louise made an amused sound in her throat. 'Well, I can only guess at what that is, as you never tell anyone.'

Gertrude took off her pince-nez, a sombre expression drawing her chin down. 'Really, Emma Louise, why do say these irritating things?'

The girl knew she was touching a tender spot and swiftly altered course. 'How is it that he's not married?' she asked quickly.

'Who?'

'John Conrad, of course.'

'Well, for one thing he works for Kitchener of Khartoum, who's not very fond of women, so they say, and makes a rule that his personal staff be single men.'

'I know, and at first I thought that was so very silly, but now I don't at all. You know, if a man's married then perhaps he doesn't give one hundred per cent of himself. His mind might be on his wife instead of his work, especially in a dangerous situation. Single men might be more reliable.'

The age business forgotten, Gertrude nodded. 'A very perspicacious thing to say, my dear. If ever you meet Kitchener you must tell him.'

Emma Louise put down her brush and burst into laughter.

Gertrude turned her eyes back to her diary. 'Well, who knows. John Conrad Fleet's very close to him and you know him.'

The girl stood. 'Guess what?'

'What?' asked her aunt, without looking up.

She put down her brush and turned round. 'He carries a holy card. I gave it to him.'

Gertrude stopped writing and gave her full attention to her niece. 'Whatever do you mean by that?'

'What I say. For many years he's kept in his possession a holy card, with a saint on it. He insists that I gave it to him. And the funny thing is it has my name on the back of it, in your handwriting.'

Gertrude frowned. 'Really? And when does he say you gave it him?'

'In Australia, in . . . 1893, I think he said. In a train between two towns. One was Brisbane. I forget the name of—'

Her aunt cut her off, 'Ipswich. It was Ipswich. Oh, my goodness. Don't tell me. How very odd. How very, very odd.'

'Do you remember it? I sort of think I do.'

'Yes. We were on our way to Sydney to meet Uncle Hewitt. You went off on a wander as you sometimes did. I found you two carriages away talking to a young man. You said at the time you'd given him . . . Saint Theresa, I think it was. You collected them, you'll remember that. I used to write your name on the back of each one. What a remarkable occurrence.'

Emma Louise smiled widely. 'Yes, isn't it?'

Now Gertrude's frown deepened. 'But why on earth would a young man keep it all these years: it must be . . .' she calculated, 'fifteen.'

The girl nodded. 'Mm, you're right. I asked him that once, but I don't think he answered me. I'll ask him again for it's strange all right.'

The woman watched the girl closely. 'Is he Catholic?'

'I haven't any idea.'

'It would be better if he is . . . but no matter. These past weeks you appear to have become very fond of him. That's true, isn't it?'

A tiny flush of pink rose in Emma Louise's cheeks. 'Yes, I suppose it is.'

'From my observation it certainly is. And he's the sort of man for you, angel. Well bred, an officer and a gentleman. He's the right class.'

The oblique reference to Sergeant Hector Flynn was not lost on the girl.

'I know, I know. And I suppose I agree . . . now.' She pivoted back to the mirror and peered into it. 'I think he likes me, I hope he does, even if he is old. And he knows so much . . . about everything. Don't you think his eyes are just the most beautiful colour you've ever seen?'

'Beautiful is not an adjective we use about men, dear.'

This revelation was as nothing to Emma Louise. 'Well, I do, and they're beautiful.'

Gertrude stood up. 'So you'd best be off to meet him. Seven o'clock for drinks, wasn't it?' She handed Emma Louise her dainty silver purse-bag.

The girl took it and stood up. 'You'll be along shortly then?'

As the door closed behind the young woman, Gertrude's smile was of gratification. She returned to the desk and took out her rosary beads.

As she knelt beside the bunk her voice sounded in prayer.

> 'Hail Mary full of grace
> The Lord is with you
> Blessed are you among women
> And blessed is the fruit of your womb,

269

'Holy Mary mother of God
Pray for us
Send us a sign
To show if John Conrad Fleet
Is the chosen one for Emma Louise.'

Three hours later she left Emma Louise and John Conrad playing whist with the Hendersons in the long room and retired to her cabin.

It seemed a very long time before the cabin door opened and she heard John Conrad's footsteps retreating away across the deck. In the beam of the single lantern she had left alight, she saw her niece close the door.

'It must be late, angel,' Gertrude said.

'I suppose it is,' her niece replied. 'Oh, but do listen to this.'

Gertrude sat up in expectation, her tied curls popping out from under her night bonnet. 'What?' the word had a barely disguised excitement in it.

'Remember I said I'd ask him about why he had kept my St Theresa card?'

'Yes, yes, go on.'

'Well, he kept it because *Emma Louise* was the name of his sister. Can you believe it? The exact same name? She had only died a few days before I gave it to him. He says it's been a comfort to keep the card with his sister's name on it. That's why he never threw it away. He saw it as a sign.'

'Oh, my goodness,' Gertrude's hand went to her heart.

'What is it?'

'Nothing, just a surprise that's all.'

'Yes, isn't it?' Unconsciously Emma Louise twisted one of her long strands of hair around her finger as she sat on the edge of the bunk. Her voice took on a dreamy quality. 'It's so romantic really. Like . . . it's as if I were meant to meet him. Do you know what I mean?'

Her aunt definitely did know but all she could do was nod.

Then the girl bent forward to look gravely at the woman in the bunk. 'Aunt Gertrude, I know I *thought* I was in love . . . before. But now it's different. I think I know what love really is.'

Gertrude was in quite a state. She knew about girls on the

'rebound'; but this was exactly what she had hoped for. The soldier was truthfully perfect for her niece. All they needed now was to get John Conrad to love Emma Louise. He did seem so awfully taken by her. Surely that meant he was falling in love . . . surely. And then the sign . . . yes, the sign was the same name. His dead sister had been called Emma Louise! She had asked for a sign and one had been bestowed.

She took her niece's hand. 'All I ever want, all your Uncle and I ever want, is your happiness, angel.' It was the truth and the words came from her with unequivocal love. She had never been able to have children of her own and when her darling husband had died in a fall from a horse she had made her bachelor brother and the motherless and fatherless Emma Louise her life's work.

Emma Louise kissed her aunt and continued to talk about John Conrad well into the morning hours. And when at last she lay across from the older woman in the other bunk, Gertrude prayed silently. 'Holy Mary, Mother of God, in your eternal wisdom, I thank you. For answering my prayer with the swiftness of your almighty judgement. I understand the sign. John Conrad Fleet is the one.'

A few days later John Conrad and Emma Louise stood together at the port side bulwark of the *Commonwealth* as it sailed through the imposing, towering heads of rock to north and south at the entrance to Sydney Harbour. Gertrude was below. Since her revelation that John Conrad was the man for Emma Louise she had affected to give them more time alone.

The azure seas were calm and there was the gentlest breeze. It was a glorious Antipodean morning and Emma Louise's hair shone a scintillating red in the bold sunlight as the soldier pointed to the simple, graceful white lighthouse on south head.

'That was designed by a convict called Francis Greenway, transported for forgery; he became the colony's official architect. In fact I think it was this lighthouse that earned him his pardon.'

Emma Louise's rose-pink lips parted in a happy smile. 'You know so much.' She was delighting in the brilliant day and the gentle movement of the air in her hair and being at the soldier's side. She put up her hand to shade her eyes from the brilliance of the sun as a flock of pristine-white seagulls made wide swoops overhead. 'How long did you say you'll be in Queensland?' she asked.

'Just over two months. I return to India on a ship in the first week of June. I'll be back for K's birthday, I hope. We've only eighteen months more in India. K's hope is for the appointment in Constantinople after that. He's restructured the whole Indian army, reorganised and reformed it to where it's well set up for the twentieth century. We've done our best there. Time to move on.'

Emma Louise did not want to hear of John Conrad going back to India, let alone going to Constantinople. She sniffed. 'You sound as if you'll be with Lord Kitchener for ever.'

He gave a cheerful nod of his head. 'I haven't really thought of it, but it's not such a bad idea. It's a great life and there are so many sides to him and he's interested in so much.' A smile broke across his mouth. 'He'll be in Simla now, in his wonderful garden. He'll be enjoying that.'

Emma Louise sounded wistful. 'You talk as though you miss him a lot.'

'Well, I do. We've shared so much: the Boer War for one, and India's been difficult too. We've had a hard time there all right. When we arrived we found ourselves in a most ridiculous system of Dual Control. K was appointed as commander-in-chief, and yet all we were responsible for was the training of the army and Lord Curzon held responsibility for all other military affairs. The system was absolutely unworkable and the intrigue was unbelievable. But finally K exposed it and retrieved control of the army and military matters for all commanders-in-chief who come after him.'

He was not looking at her and his eyes were on the shore. 'We've achieved a great deal: thwarted any Russian ambitions in Afghanistan now and even extended the railways to ensure rapid troop transference to the North-West Frontier. There's a lot for India to thank K for.'

Emma Louise's bottom lip was trembling. She felt quite odd. Suddenly she had been given an insight into the man who stood beside her, and she did not like it. It was a shock to a twenty-year-old who had thought that she was making this soldier fall in love with her. She had truly believed she was succeeding until this rude awakening.

She turned her head away.

John Conrad touched her shoulder. 'What is it? Are you all right, child?'

This was too much. That he called her *child* as well. After the shock of the discovery, to be called *child* was the last straw. Two big tears rolled down her cheeks.

He took her shoulders and turned her round. He was astounded. 'What on earth is it? Emma Louise, what's wrong?'

She looked up into his eyes and another tear rolled down her cheek. She had difficulty speaking. 'I . . . oh dear . . . I hoped that I would see you again. I was . . . hoping we would be . . . *friends*. But all this talk of India and Constantinople and Kitchener. Now I know I won't see you again ever.'

He did not like to see her crying. It distressed him. To him she represented laughter, and good times and the happy carefreeness of youth. He had thoroughly enjoyed her company during the weeks of the voyage. He did not understand the complexities in Emma Louise's tears, but he did realise that she was very fond of him.

'Now, now, wipe your eyes and come over here.' He took her hand firmly and drew her across to a hatch and they sat down upon it. He still held her palm in his. She was very aware of his hand resting on hers; the coolness of his skin; it was exquisitely moving and she trembled slightly.

He smiled at her but she looked away. 'You called me *child.*'

Tenderly he turned her face to his. 'Emma Louise, I'm sorry. Please listen to me. We *are* friends and will remain so. Your aunt's told me you stay a week in Sydney and then you travel to Queensland to Southport. Is that right?'

She nodded.

She looked so very young and so very sad that he could not help himself. He took her in his arms and hugged her. 'I shall come and see you.'

Comforted she whispered into his chest, 'Will you really?'

'Yes, I really will.'

He pushed her gently away to arm's length. At that moment

she prayed that soon he would kiss her. She knew she was so in love with him; if only he would love her.

'Now, come on. Please, my dear Emma Louise, here, dry your eyes.' He gave her his handerchief. 'There's so much to see. Now, look through these.' He took his binoculars from where they were attached to his belt. 'You can see the city of Sydney over there in the distance on the left.' He pointed and she brightened up and, taking the glasses from him, looked up into his eyes. 'You will truly come and visit me?'

'I have said I will.'

Suddenly she brightened with a happy thought. 'Will you come for my birthday?'

'And when's that?'

'On the tenth of April. It's special. I'm turning twenty-one.'

He could not disappoint her. 'Yes, all right, the tenth of April.'

Her smile was radiant. She was discerning enough to realise that she had not won John Conrad Fleet's devotion but she was young enough to be lacking in those doubts that come with maturity; thus he had given her hope . . . and for Emma Louise Blackstone hope was enough for now.

When the *Commonwealth* had been brought in and tied with thick ropes to the bollards along Circular Quay, at the city's heartbeat, the holds were opened and the unloading of the ship began.

Emma Louise reluctantly left her companion and went below to find her aunt, and John Conrad returned to his cabin to make ready for disembarkation.

A few minutes later there was a tapping on his door. He opened it to find Gertrude standing there.

She held our her gloved palm to him. As he took it she said, 'I wanted to say goodbye. I do believe we'll have your company on Emma Louise's birthday next month. I'm delighted. And as it's almost the end of March now we won't have to wait long before we see you again. I must say, we . . . Emma Louise and I, are both . . . very fond of you.' Her faded eyes met his brilliant ones. 'And for Emma Louise, well, she's come alive in your company. She's such a dear, sweet unaffected girl. I must say thank you for giving her a wonderful voyage.'

She still held on to his hand. 'I've enjoyed your company too, Mrs Jerome-Frith.' He extricated his hand.

'Dear boy, please do call me Gertrude.' She took a breath and momentarily closed her eyes. 'After all, a sea voyage of our duration surely gives us licence to be a little more familiar.'

John Conrad cleared his throat. 'Certainly, as you wish . . . Gertrude.'

She beamed at him. 'I know that Emma Louise particularly wants to say goodbye to you. We're actually ready to depart now, and she's waiting for me near the top of the gangway . . . alone.' She patted his arm. 'Do you mind?' she added.

'Of course not. I intended to see her before I disembarked. Excuse me.'

He found the girl as her aunt had indicated, standing amongst her boxes and trunks on the holystoned deck.

She saw him coming and her pulse quickened.

As he walked over to her, she looked very young and girlish to him. He came to within two feet of her, noticing the freckles on her nose. Her head was tilted to one side and she looked up at him from under her flower and lace bonnet, her hair tumbling in a sheen of waves to her shoulders. She broke into a tentative smile. 'So we are off. Our friends are on the wharf; Aunt Gertrude has already waved to them.'

'Yes, my dear. I hope you enjoy your stay in Sydney. There's much to see. Do go to the Australian Museum in William Street and the Domain and the botanical gardens and the art gallery. You'll enjoy them all.'

'I will.'

He took both her hands in his. 'I shall see you soon . . . on the tenth.'

'Would you kiss me goodbye?' she asked in that ever frank fashion of hers.

She could see immediately that she had caught him off guard. She thought she felt his hands contract upon hers in the tiniest movement of surprise. For what seemed like an age to the girl he examined her, and she returned his gaze unblinking.

A gentle breeze wafted the strings of her bonnet forward to touch his coat, as if beckoning him and yet he still did not move. She waited as he continued to hold both her hands, then he stepped closer, leant down and rested his lips upon

275

her parted ones. He tasted the wetness of her mouth as his lay upon hers for a second or two. Then in deliberate manner he dropped her fingers and stepped back.

A rush of excitement pulsated through Emma Louise.

John Conrad gave the glimmer of a smile. 'I will see you on the tenth.' Then he turned and walked away, to be met by Captain Peel coming down from the bridge to say his farewell to his last three passengers.

Twenty minutes later John Conrad entered a hansom cab in Pitt Street to head to the Redfern Railway Station. As he rumbled by the first block from the quay, past the pubs and wine shops and ships' purveyors, he cast his gaze across the seamen with their rolling walks but his mind was on the woman-child, Emma Louise Blackstone and the kiss she had requested. In the ten years with K, females had won no place in his life. Caro Dere had cured him of the desire for a permanent liaison. There were only a few women who had been able to allure him even for a single night. As he glanced through the window at the Stock Exchange, and a boy on a bicycle came pedalling swiftly by, he thought of the only two women whom he had felt anything for since Caro Dere: the first was the storekeeper's daughter in Ladysmith in South Africa, with her sun-kissed skin and her bushveldt vitality, the other was right now back in Calcutta, Nadia, the French girl, widow of a Hindu merchant, with eyes of bronze and flowing black hair reaching down her smooth back. But he had never cared for any woman enough for it to matter; no, never enough.

But this morning, kissing his odd little dream-child to a woman grown had been significant, and it disconcerted him. Her full young lips beneath his had given him sensations that had been buried along with the dreams he dreamt with Caro Dere. He did not like it: it bothered him greatly.

He reclined on the cushioned seat and stared out at the passing hoi polloi of the Sydney streets, the statue of Queen Victoria, regally holding her place, and the trees and greenery of Hyde Park.

He deliberately passed from troubling reflections of Emma Louise to thoughts of his family and how good it would be to see them all again. His father was still able and strong, so the last letter from Bart had informed him. Strange to think back fifteen years to how he had joined the army, at his father's exigency. What a true favour his parent had done him after all. He smiled. Then his meditations fused and his father turned into K and he found himself picturing the commander-in-chief on a morning ride in the hills of the Himalayas.

By the time he arrived at the railway station he was thinking of his family again and looking forward to being home in Brisbane.

Chapter Twenty

The homecoming was an emotional affair.

Aunt Leigh cried and fussed over him, repeating, '"The time to be happy is now, The place to be happy is here."' Bartholomew grinned with delight and patted his big brother's shoulder with obvious pride. When David came in John Conrad did not recognise him: he had not seen his youngest brother since 1901. The spare lean boy of seventeen he remembered stood in front of him a muscular man almost twenty-four with a shock of fair hair and sun-browned limbs and a face that many of the girls of the West End dreamt about.

David appraised the stranger-called-brother and held out his hand somewhat warily. John Conrad took it enthusiastically. 'David, you look marvellous. You're a man!'

'Yes, it does happen,' his youngest brother replied.

But when Barrington Fleet came through the parlour door he halted, standing silently and studying the arrival. An almost wistful look settled on his heavy-browed face as he stepped sharply forward and took his eldest son in his arms. It was the first time John Conrad could recall his father's hugging him since he was a small boy, and he revelled in it.

'My boy is home,' Barrington Fleet whispered, 'at last.'

When the excitement had died down and Aunt Leigh had poured tea for the third time, Bart made a suggestion.

'So let's help you unpack and then you can come and take a look at the brewery. We've made big changes and it's a pretty good operation now. In fact I'm off to Bundaberg next week to see how things are going. As I think I told you in my last letter, we're expanding up there.'

Aunt Leigh coughed discreetly, hoping the new arrival would be home for dinner. 'About the evening meal?'

'Anything you cook will be wonderful,' John Conrad

responded, putting his arm around her shoulder and kissing her cheek.

Barrington laughed. 'That's true. She's still the best cook in Brisbane.'

John Conrad agreed, pointing along the hall towards the big kitchen. 'But let's eat at the kitchen table, Aunt Leigh. I want to feel really at home.'

Aunt Leigh began to protest that the dining room was more suitable but Bart took his brother's side. 'No, we must do as John Conrad wishes, but make an apricot pie, dearest, you know how John Conrad likes that.' Then he turned round to his big brother. 'After dinner I'll take you to a few of the old pubs,' he laughed, 'though only those who serve Fleet lager and ale! Gosh we haven't done that in a decade.' Then he slapped his brother on the back. 'Oh, and there's the pony and galloway races on tonight at the Gabba.' This was an affectionate reference to the Wooloongabba Cricket Ground. 'Reckon we could go there first tonight, if you like. Hotels don't close till eleven.'

'Sounds good to me,' John Conrad responded, accompanying him into the hall.

When the two older brothers had gone Aunt Leigh turned to David. 'Isn't it just a treat to have your brother home? "Home is the sailor home from the sea, And the hunter home from the hill."'

'And where do soldiers come from then?' David responded dryly. 'As to having him home, Aunt Leigh, I don't really know the bloke so I don't know if it's good to have him home or not. He dresses like a bit of a toff, if you ask me.'

Leigh's eyes went to the ceiling. 'Good heavens, David, he's simply *well* dressed, that's what he is. Always was. Always looked like he was dressed by a London tailor. You should be so proud of him, what he's achieved and all. Personal aide to Kitchener of Khartoum; he's dignified this family, that's for certain. We can hold our heads up in any company, any company at all. And that's because of your big brother. Not that we couldn't before, but now it's different.' Then she reached out and tugged her nephew's ear. 'And don't use the word *bloke* about him, it's common.'

David moved out of her grasp, across to the airing cabinet. 'Think I'll have an orange,' was his impassive response.

A few hours later the family sat together in the convivial atmosphere of the big agreeable kitchen with not a single portion of Aunt Leigh's tasty pie remaining in front of them. The worst of the summer heat had passed and with the falling of night, a mild breeze blew benignly in the back door, caressing the well-fed group.

Bart pushed back his chair and sighed with an air of satisfaction. 'Delicious, Aunt Leigh, delicious. Now John Conrad and I are off. Do you want to come, lad?' he asked David.

The young man shook his head. 'No, I'm seeing Chas Griffin for a bit.'

The two eldest brothers kissed their aunt and said good night to their father.

'We won't be late,' John Conrad told his family.

'I'll be up,' Barrington called, watching his sons cross the verandah and descend the stairs into the brewery yard.

Twenty minutes later the two brothers stepped down from an electric tram in East Street at the five-way junction with Logan Road in the suburb of Wooloongabba.

Bart placed his arms round his brother's shoulders as they crossed the intersection. 'It's so good to be with you again. Why don't you come to Bundaberg with me next week? See the brewery up there . . . ?'

'How long will you stay?'

'A week or two. Got a good manager, bloke called Grant, hard worker. Brewery's in a great spot right on the river.' He smiled, thinking about it. 'You know there's the most amazing kid up there. Comes down to the open space by the brewery most afternoons, builds gliders and is besotted with the idea of flying. He was up in a glider the last time I was there and he flew it like a flaming bird right along the river. Amazing . . . Hinkler's his name and I reckon he's going places.'

John Conrad sounded interested. 'Flying eh? Yes, it's hard to believe. Those American brothers have gone pretty quiet, haven't they? Was their name Wright? Haven't heard anything of them for years.'

'True. Anyway, you think about coming along with me,' Bart responded as his arm came off his brother's shoulder and he pointed to the bright beams of light over the cricket ground where they were heading. 'It's a wonderful time to be alive, eh? The age of electricity too.' His eyes brightened as if with the energy he mentioned as he went on, 'Isn't it great? I haven't told you, but I've been working on electrifying the brewery. There're such machines now, they're using them in Sydney already. It'll take a bit of capital but we're doing well with the business in Bundaberg and I think we've enough money to bring in the new machines here. There's talk the West End isn't far away from being connected so I've gone ahead and ordered from the Sydney manufacturer: a new malt mill and grist hopper and a mashing machine.' He nodded vigorously to himself. 'And the boiling, cooling and fermenting can all be done with electricity; even the cleaning and grading of the malt eventually . . . the whole brewery will be *electrified*. We have to stay ahead of the competition and this way, though it's a big initial expenditure, we'll save a lot on labour in the long run. I assume you know that Guinness in the United Kingdom are the largest brewers in the world?'

His brother smiled. 'I do.'

'Well, they brewed upwards of two million barrels in 1905. Read it in the *Courier*. Think of that.' He shook his head. 'I know we've no chance to ever be that enormous, but it spurs me on, if you like. Gives me incentive just to think of brewing over two million barrels.'

His brother laughed and Bart looked hurt. 'Why are you laughing?'

'Not at you, brother-mine. I'm only laughing because it's great to see you so intense about it. Damned if I could have ever worked up any excitement over barrels of beer. It's marvellous that the business fell upon your competent shoulders, that it went to you, who so obviously love it, rather than me.'

At that point they arrived at the entrance gate, paid and went in.

It was the fourth race on a ten-race card.

'Now, Bart, do you know anything about these ponies and their form?'

'No, only come here now and then for a bit of fun. We'll have to choose names we like.'

Bart put a shilling on Random Chance and John Conrad did

the same on Empire and, as it was fifteen minutes to the start of the next race, Bart decided, 'Let's have a beer first.'

In the bar John Conrad received a lot of second glances; possibly because of his impeccably cut suit, tailor-made in the heart of world fashion in Jermyn Street, London, or perhaps because he simply drew attention with his looks. His brother who was proud of him beyond measure could not help but feel a tiny passing touch of envy looking at John Conrad, with blue eyes gleaming and his sun-bronzed skin and fair hair; a picture of health and vitality. Even the way he rested on the bar was out of the ordinary, somehow elegant and yet still manly and masculine. It all added up to make him the best-looking individual most of the drinkers that night at the Gabba had ever seen.

A few men who knew Bart greeted him and he introduced his elder brother.

'Didn't know you had an elder brother,' Jimmy Costain who played rugger with the old boys of GPS, said. 'Where the devil you been hidin' him?'

'He hides in India actually . . . with the British army.'

'A soldier eh?' Jimmy imitated a salute to John Conrad. 'By the looks of you, you could be a bloody general.'

John Conrad smiled. 'I'm doing my best.'

That brought a bout of laughter round the bar and the two brothers took the moment to leave to watch the race. The winner was a hackney pony, but to their amazement and delight Empire came second and Random Chance came third, and having made place bets they were both winners.

Bart slapped his brother's back, 'Trust you to best me even when we both get a place.'

As Bartholomew moved away to collect their winnings, John Conrad noted his surroundings. Most of the crowd were men hoping to win a 'few bob', though some had women hanging on their arms. He wandered along under the thick branches of a jacaranda tree where a small counter had been set up and the good smell of roasting sausages pervaded the surrounding air. A sign read: '2 FOR 3d.'

There were not many people about near this spot and he thought perhaps he would help sales by buying a couple for himself and Bart, when he noticed a small child over by the long fence separating the grandstand from the betting enclosure. He was a boy no more than eight or nine, with a shock of blond curls, and he was crying. As he watched the child sank to the ground and hid his head in his hands.

John Conrad walked over and crouched down beside him. 'Now then, young man, what is it? What seems to be the matter?'

The tear-stained face turned up into John Conrad's. The eyes were a brilliant blue, quite astonishing, and a small frown of unhappiness lay between them. 'Can't find Daddy.' He began to cry again, and a large teardrop ran down his face to drop off his chin.

John Conrad took out his handkerchief and dabbed the tears away, then ruffled the child's fair hair affectionately and handed him the handkerchief to use. 'It's all right, lad, we'll find him, don't you worry. I'm good at finding lost daddies. Don't you worry about that.'

The little boy stopped sobbing and brightened slightly at the words of encouragement. John Conrad could see the child was well dressed and well fed so he was obviously not an abandoned waif. No doubt he had simply become separated from his father somehow, but it did seem odd to have a boy of such tender years at a night race meeting.

'Now you take my hand,' he said to the child, and as the boy did so, he asked, 'What's your name, lad?'

'Harry. My name's Harry.'

'All right, Harry, come along and we'll find your daddy as soon as we can,' and he lifted the child to his feet as the little one looked up and gave a tentative smile.

They had taken two steps hand-in-hand when a shout from behind them rent the night air.

'What in bloody Hades goes on here?'

The words were like gunshots, and even before John Conrad turned to look into the face he hated he recognised the voice. With resignation he whispered the name, 'Craken.'

Matthew's eyes were cold with contempt, but his face was stiff and calm, belying the rage in his voice. The scar cleaving his cheek gleamed in the brittle electric light.

'How in the devil's name can this be?' He lifted his silver cane and pointed it at the man who held Harry's hand. John

Conrad flinched, recalling the last cane Craken had pointed at him, and the dagger that had shot out. 'I only lay eyes upon you twice in a decade and both blasted times you're molesting members of my family: first my wife and now my son.' His lip curled in distaste. 'Why is it that you have this unerring desire to harass my near relatives?'

Before John Conrad could speak Harry dropped his hand and ran to Matthew, clutching the man around his legs. 'Dada,' the child shouted in delight.

'Yes, yes,' Matthew answered, patting the child briefly on the head. 'Well you're a damn foolish boy to detach yourself from me. Don't you know better?' He continued to point his cane at John Conrad. 'See this man. Look at him, Harry, look carefully and remember him all the days of your life. He's our enemy! And you? You made the vital mistake of holding his hand.'

Harry looked in horror at John Conrad, who so recently had been his friend and now was his foe.

John Conrad was disgusted. 'Craken, don't. The child doesn't understand. It's not right.'

'Not right?' Matthew lowered the cane and leant on it. The child still clung to him, eyes wide, looking at the enemy. 'So . . . you'd have a say in what I tell *my son*, would you? You want to dictate how I should bring up *my son*, eh? Ah no, soldier-boy, it's not for you to say. That particular right belongs to me, not you.'

At that moment Knobby came up behind Matthew. 'There you are, Matt. Thank God you've found him.' Then he saw John Conrad. 'What? You! What're you doing here?'

Matthew made a sneering sound. 'Very question I was about to ask, Knobby, dear heart, very question.' Then he took a step closer to John Conrad. 'What the bloody hell were you doing with my son, you bastard?'

By now a few people had gathered. This was a most entertaining sideshow to the races.

'Come here, kiddo,' Knobby said, taking the boy from Matthew. 'Let's go, Matt. We've found Harry, that's all that matters.'

But Matthew was enjoying himself. His voice became quieter, sedate and controlled. 'No, Knobby. I want to let this cur know that he's not to interfere with my family. Not now, not tomorrow, not ever!'

'Hell, Craken, you're hopeless, I didn't interfere with the boy. He was alone and crying – lost, for heaven's sake. Have some sense. I'd no idea he was your son.'

'Ah, and what if you had? Would you have left him alone to cry?'

'Of course not. He's only a child. He's nothing to do with us, or the feeling between us.'

'Is that so? Well I say he is. He's *everything* to do with our . . . feud. Let's call it what it is. You don't know what I mean, do you?' Matthew gave a short sharp mirthless laugh.

'Come on, Matt, let's go,' Knobby interrupted.

'Knobby dear, leave me alone. I'm enjoying myself.'

John Conrad stepped away. 'I've had enough of this.'

A sudden shout resounded from near the sausage seller's stand and Bart came running over. 'At last! There you are!' He quickly took in the situation and the players. 'Oh no, what the hell's happened?'

'How exquisite,' Matthew spoke loudly now and lifted his silver stick to point at Bart. 'It's as if we have a dear little reunion every few years . . . the enemy and his brother and me . . . and someone . . . that is *anyone* providing the fourth of the incongruous team is a relative of mine. This time it's Harry.' He half turned to Knobby, bringing his stick higher in the air. 'You should be honoured, Knobby. This time you're included as the fifth participant.'

'Damn it, Craken,' Bartholomew's voice rose in anger, 'we don't want anything to do with you. Come on, John Conrad.' He took his brother's arm and pulled him away.

The few people assembled had now become a few dozen. Some of them recognised Matthew, and all were intrigued by the look of the man who was the object of his anger.

As Bart led his brother away Matthew's voice became high and hatred-filled. 'And, Fleet! I notice the small scar on your neck. If ever I see you with my wife or my child again, it will be my pleasure to enlarge that scar . . . to cut your bloody throat! Understand? You yellow-livered bastard?'

This was too much for John Conrad. He wheeled round even though Bart still held him in his grasp. 'To buggery with you and yours, Craken. If ever we find ourselves alone we'll see who cuts whose throat!' He strode back in anger towards his enemy, dragging his brother along.

But Knobby had seen sense and was pulling Matthew away while holding the child in his other hand; they were soon enveloped in the throng of watchers and John Conrad halted in frustration.

'Suits me,' shouted Matthew over his shoulder, then abruptly he shook free of Knobby's hand. 'So, that little play's over. Pleasant reunions, aren't they?' He bent down and ran his fingers through Harry's curls. 'Don't think about the enemy any more, Harry, but remember his face.' Then he took the child's free hand 'Come on, my dears. I've a sure winner in the next race. Then we must pop by and see Won Won the Wonder One. He's got a parcel for me.'

Little Harry liked Won Won. His rooms smelt good and he always made sweet Chinese tea and gave them quaint little biscuits to eat. 'Yes, Daddy, let's.'

Knobby hesitated, then he sighed and spoke quickly. 'No, Matt, we shouldn't; not tonight. I promised Caro we'd have the boy home and in bed by half-past nine and it's well gone nine already.'

Matthew looked skywards, his voice resigned. 'Knobby old son, you should have been in the police force.'

The two brothers left the Gabba forthwith and caught a tram back to the West End. They had two beers in the Lion's Mane in Stanley Street for old times' sake, and were home at Brewery House by twenty minutes after ten o'clock.

In the moon glow they came by the stables and into the brewery yard, where under the mango tree they saw a figure move on the wooden seat. 'Well, Father, here we are,' Bart said.

'So you're home. Thought you two would be later. Young David's not back yet.'

John Conrad sat down beside his father. 'I must spend some time with him, get to know him. He's turning into a man, and I remember him only as a boy.'

His father chuckled. 'Well, let's say David *believes* he's a man, but Bartholomew and I'd say there was still a mighty lot of boy in him, eh, Bart?'

His second son gave a gentle laugh of agreement. 'You're right about that Dad, you really are.'

'So how was your night?' Barrington asked his sons, and Bart moved on by touching his father affectionately on the arm and replying, 'I'll let John Conrad tell you. I'm off to bed. Good night to you both.'

'Good night.'

Barrington took out his pipe and filled it. 'Only smoke once a day now. Out here around this time. Nice time of the night, all still and only the owls and me to share the tranquillity. Do you smoke, son?'

'I did for a few years when I first joined the army, Dad. But it has no real appeal to me, so I haven't since, though most of the fellows I work with do.'

'What about Kitchener?'

'A cigar now and then.'

Barrington lit his pipe and puffed with gratification.

They both sat quietly for a time side-by-side until Barrington broke the silence, 'So, how *was* your night then?'

John Conrad took a noisy breath. 'I ran into Matthew Craken.'

Barrington's throat filled with a rumbling sound of misgiving. 'On your first night back. That's bad luck. Have either of you enough sense these days to forget the past?'

'No, Father, we haven't. Some pretty harsh words were spoken.'

'As long as it was only words.'

'If he hadn't had his young son with him, it might have been otherwise.'

'And where was this?'

'At the pony and galloway races at the Gabba.'

'What? He takes a child there? That boy can't be more than eight or nine at the most. What's Caro thinking of to allow it?'

John Conrad's tone was one of disgust. 'I don't know and I don't care. Craken's so damn dissolute, shouldn't be allowed to have a child.'

'Mm, more than one now you know. Little girl as well.'

'So they say.'

The moon passed behind a cloud and it became darker under the leaves of the mango tree.

'Father?'

'Yes, son.'

'I don't want you to mention this to anyone, but that boy, Matthew Craken's son . . . well . . .' He paused and fell silent.

'Yes, what?'

'He's . . .' Abruptly John Conrad stood and moved further into the darkness under the tree to lean upon the bole. 'Oh hell, Father, I don't know. Nothing, it's not important. Shouldn't be taking up our precious time talking about Craken and his bloody offspring. He's a bastard and the kid'll grow up to be one too, no doubt of that. Let's talk about important things . . . Brewery looks good and the new wing for storing the barrels is marvellous. Bart was telling me tonight about his ideas for the electric machinery. Almost have a mind to go up to Bundaberg with him next week to see the operation there.'

Barrington liked this idea. 'Now, why don't you? It'll be worth seeing.'

His son came back and sat down again. 'No, Bart intends to spend about two weeks there and I don't want to lose that much time with you . . . and actually, fact is, Dad, I've an arrangement that I must keep on the tenth of April. I promised to attend a birthday party in Southport. Some friends I met on the ship coming out.'

The golden morning light of the following day fell across the terrace outside the big studio house by the river in New Farm to find Knobby and Harry breakfasting together.

Harry stirred his porridge and looked over at his father's confidant. 'Did you carry me in last night, Uncle Knobby?'

'I did indeed, lad. You're no weight.'

'I will be when I grow up?'

His uncle smiled. 'You surely will. Won't be able to carry you then.'

'When did I fall asleep?'

'On the way home. Mr Winken, Blinken and Nod visited you and off you dropped.'

The child took a spoonful of his breakfast. 'Who was that man?'

'What man is that, my boy?'

288

'The enemy.'

Knobby sighed and lifted his knife to butter a piece of toast. He thought before he answered and the child watched him with big interested eyes. 'He's a man your father had a fight with a very long time ago. Long before you were born. They don't see each other very often.'

'But what's his name?'

'It's Fleet.'

'We hate the enemy, don't we?'

'It's not for children to hate anything. Forget about him.' Then Knobby quickly lifted his hand and made an arc over his head towards the sky and the bright day. 'Isn't it a great morning? Now Mummy should be back today, won't that be good?'

The child giggled. 'Yes. She's bringing me a present.'

Knobby pointed to the bowl of porridge. 'Come on, finish your breakfast and then I'll take you to school . . . and when I pick you up and bring you home, Mummy and little Katy will be here.'

It was three in the afternoon when Caro drove a gig through the gate in the hedge at the front of the studio house and, lifting her daughter down in one arm and her portmanteau in the other, she headed towards the door. Before she reached it, Knobby came out, striding across the lawn to meet her.

'Good day, Caro. Welcome back. How's Lucy?'

'Ah, Knobby, nice to see you. She's on the mend, a really bad cold. I took the children over to George's mother's place, washed the dishes, cleaned the house and made George's dinner for tonight. She's got a good doctor in Bill Leeman, should be back on her feet in a day or two.' And as Knobby took her bag she asked, 'Where's Matt?'

'He's in the studio. Asked for you to come and see him when you arrived. He's lost something and also wants to talk to you about which works to put in the exhibition.'

Caro smiled widely. 'Really? As if he needs anyone else's opinion.'

Knobby chuckled. 'True. He'll put what he wants in it anyway.'

When they were inside Knobby relieved Caro of Katy, who kissed his sizeable cheek. 'Thank you, precious,' he said, kissing her in return. 'Aren't you the lucky one, missing two days of school like this?'

Katy clapped her hands which seemed to symbolise concurrence.

When Caro entered the studio Matthew's back was to her. 'Is that you, Caro? About time you were home. I can't find a letter I received from Norman Lindsay. The one where he talks about starting a publication for artists in Australia. Came about two weeks ago.'

Caro halted, hands on hips. 'Well, thanks for the welcome home greeting, Matt. Only need me to find a letter do you? Typical.'

He turned from his canvas, holding his brush. He had two bright blue patches of paint on his forehead and she could not help but smile as he came forward, limping slightly without his cane, and pointing his brush at her. 'God woman, there are many things I need you for. Come here.' He took her arm and pulled it from the akimbo position, bringing her in to him. He kissed her nose. 'Welcome home, old girl. Now please find the letter.'

Caro sighed. 'Aren't you interested in how Lucy is?'

Matthew's right eyebrow rose. He released her and sniffed with disdain. 'No, I'm not. For your sake I hope she's not seriously ill, but I've no interest in her wellbeing as such. Don't look surprised! You know that her husband is possibly the most boring individual I've ever had to tolerate, simply because he's married to her. Serves the damn girl right being ill when she's tied to such a tiresome human being. Actually, it's a pity he isn't the one who's sick, and the longer the better . . . it would at least relieve me of the odd occasion when I have to endure his inanities.'

Caro shook her head. 'Thank you, Matthew. How enlightening. I'll go and see if I can find Norman's letter.'

'Thanks, old girl.' He patted her on the bottom as she made a pseudo-offended sound and hurried out.

She was back in ten minutes, holding the letter out to him. His lips parted in pleasure. 'Well done; knew you'd find it.'

'It was under the bed. You must have been reading it there and dropped it.'

They heard a noise and both turned to the door as their two

290

children burst in, shouting greetings. Both parents hugged and lifted the child they had not seen for two days.

Caro kissed her son and returned him to the floor. 'Were you a good boy for Daddy and Uncle Knobby?'

'Oh yes, and we went to the pony races.'

'Thanks, Harry, you don't waste any time in letting the cat out of the bag,' his father observed dryly, then kissed his daughter and placed her upon the floor beside the boy.

Caro looked sternly at Matthew. 'The pony races. All right, we'll talk about that later.'

But Harry was intent on telling his mother more. 'And we met the enemy. He was nice at first but then he was the enemy. I must remember his face.'

Caro twitched as a shot of adrenalin rushed through her. Her head came sharply round to Matthew, who stood behind her. 'What? What does the child mean?'

Matthew paused but Harry was keen to enlighten her. 'I asked Uncle Knobby and his name's Fleet, Mummy, and he's the enemy.'

Caro shuddered. She scooped up a hand of each of her children and led them from the room. Matthew watched this display with an enigmatic expression and then turned to his easel, picked up his oil brush and palette and continued with his painting.

It was not long before the door burst open and Caro came in. Her voice was high and there was a distracted sound in it. 'What's been going on, Matthew? How could you allow the child to talk in that way? *Enemy!* It's not proper for him to say that. What have you told him?'

Matthew did not turn round nor did he stop painting. Caro fell silent, her eyes upon his back as the vivid Brisbane afternoon sun blazed in streams through the windows and the skylight and appeared somehow mysteriously to include him in the large canvas before him. His form seemed to scintillate upon it like a living part of what he was creating.

She put her hands up to her eyes and shook her head to clear her vision. 'Matthew? Answer me. What the devil has gone on in my absence?'

He put down his brush. She waited, holding her breath as slowly, so very slowly, he faced round to her. His eyes were cool and distant and he bent over and took up his ebony and gold cane from the windowsill and moved across to come within a foot of her. 'Caro, dear Caro, why is it that you're so distraught? So you believe it is not right for *my* son to call *my* enemy by a just and suitable title . . . *enemy* . . . Well, old girl, that's where we differ, and differ dramatically. I think it's perfectly appropriate that the hatreds of the fathers be visited upon the sons.'

'Matthew, how can you say this? I'm not hearing you right, am I?'

He swung round on his stick, moved across to a rattan chair and sat. His leg was painful today and he was not in any mood for Caro's odd sensitivities. Even so, his voice remained languid and detached.

'I will enlighten you of what occurred, old girl, as obviously you are going to bloody well harass me until I do. Fact is, dear Knobby and I went to the races . . . took Harry as we had no option. *You* were not here to take care of him. The devil only knows how, but while we were in the betting ring Harry disappeared. Knobby went off in one direction to find him, I in the other. And lo and behold! Like some quasi-repetition of seven years ago when I found Fleet bending over you, I found the bastard *holding Harry's hand*. There's no need to point out to you of all people that I was marginally incensed by this. As usual he too was delighted to see me. We had our customary blissful reunion, delicate loving words were spoken, felicitations exchanged, and then we parted.' He held up his hand to stop her from speaking. 'Before you ask, no, I do not know anything about why he's here. Unless Kitchener of Khartoum has finally come to his senses and sacked the bastard. But then, that's not *really* what we want, is it, old girl? *We* might keep running into him if he came back here to live and that would never do, would it?'

Caro came forward to stand in front of her husband. Her eyes were pleading, her voice was strained. 'Matt, couldn't you just once have let things be? Why couldn't you have taken Harry from John Conrad and left without getting into all the past?'

Matthew waved his cane at Caro. 'If you're going to hover over me like a vulture deciding on its prey I'm leaving. Either sit down or move a few feet distant.'

She moved back as requested, looking at him with an immeasurably sad expression. She forced herself to hold her ground. 'It's terrible and you're wrong. To think Harry heard you use the word *enemy*, and now in his childish fashion he mimics you.'

For the first time Matthew's voice had an edge to it. 'Leave it, Caro. I'm not in the mood for your proclivities of language. The only two people in the world who know why such a thing afflicts you with melancholy are in this room.' He gave a cold laugh. 'Though I must say there was a time when I considered telling Knobby . . .'

Caro was horrified. 'You wouldn't, Matt, you wouldn't!'

'No, I wouldn't, not now. That particular inclination left me years ago when I saw how fond he became of you. That he's fond of you is quite sufficient, that he could feel sorry for you we, under no circumstances, can allow.'

Caro closed her eyes to stop the tears from springing to them. She turned away and walked impotently to the door.

Matthew watched her go and as she put her fingers on the handle, he called, 'Old girl?'

A small sigh quivered out with her words. 'Yes, what is it?'

His leg was hurting badly. It had been thobbing most of the day, and he lifted it to rest it on a foot stool. 'Bring me a drink, would you? Bit of an ache in my leg today. Must be the reaction of my bones to the delight of having Fleet in the vicinity.'

She opened the door and he called out once more. 'And bring yourself one. Sit with me a while, would you? I'd like that. Oh, and thanks for finding the letter. It *really* is good to have you home, old girl.'

Chapter Twenty-one

On the morning of Friday, 10 April, John Conrad caught the train from Brisbane. He changed trains at Beenleigh, a tiny settlement where the only industry occurred in a big corrugated iron shed which served as a rum factory. He smiled, recalling Bart and his forward-thinking ideas for the brewery. They could do with him here.

He was in Southport by noon. He carried the address on a piece of paper written in Gertrude's copybook hand. As he passed by a number of nondescript wooden cottages, he thought of the vast contrasts between this country and India. In all the entire train journey of over fifty miles he had seen only tiny Beenleigh, all the rest had been endless gumtrees. In India the same distance would have housed village after village; inhabited by tens of thousands of people. Australia was immense, but almost an immense wilderness.

It was strange but he had thought a lot about Hargy on the train. Perhaps it was the never-ending bush that had reminded John Conrad of when he and Bart and Lena took Hargy's body back to the tribe. He missed Hargy, the companion of his youth; but that was life. He had been a boy with Hargy, a time when they could be carefree; when they had spoken truths and dreams. They had been soulmates. He liked to think that sometime somewhere in the universe he would meet with Hargy again and they would go swimming and fishing and chew paspalum grass. It made him smile just to think of it.

Now, his days were taken up with running the Indian army, diplomacy and the needs of K. To think, Hargy had been gone a decade already. He shivered. He must go and visit Lena when he returned to Brisbane. See how she was these days, and in any case he wanted to see the children. When he had been home in 1901 he had visited Lena and Bluey and made arrangements to pay for a woman called Sarah Howard to teach the children in her home three days a week. Lena had seen the sense in such a circumstance immediately. She wanted with all her being to give her children 'a chance', as she called it. Miss Howard was a spinster who once had run a school in Sydney, but she had retired and come to Queensland for her health.

John Conrad wandered slowly along the main street of Southport, Nerang Street, and turned a corner where there were a few substantial houses. He walked on for about an eighth of a mile of open ground before he arrived in front of a two-storied wooden house with delightful white iron lace surrounding the verandah and three gables on the upper story. It was set in a large well-tended garden with a row of casuarina trees running along one side.

There was no fence at the front, though he could see a shallow trench had been dug in readiness. He stepped towards the narrow opening in the ground and heard his name called.

'John Conrad!'

He spun round to see three women on horseback riding towards him. One rode side-saddle, and as they came closer he realised this was Gertrude, the other two rode astride. He recognised Emma Louise, who continued to shout his name as they drew closer.

'Oh, we were so hoping you'd come and here you are.' The girl spoke with high-pitched excitement as she arrived beside him and dismounted. 'Have you ever seen anywhere so different to India?' and she stepped forward. She did not throw herself at him but she certainly opened her arms to be hugged. 'Welcome to Southport.'

When she released John Conrad he helped Gertrude down. She thanked him, shook his hand and gestured to their companion, a small-boned, sweet-faced girl of about Emma Louise's age. 'This is Sophie, my cousin's daughter.'

Emma Louise was so excited. She had dreamt two or three times about John Conrad and here at last, he was. He had kept his promise and she was both gratified and flattered. 'The party's all arranged for tonight,' she informed him. 'Aunt Nevis's friends are coming as we know nobody much yet. The local priest is coming too – Father Michael. We met him last Sunday when we arrived.'

'Yes, it'll be a nice affair,' Gertrude added, beaming upon John Conrad.

And a nice affair it was. Emma Louise was radiant in pure white silk with soft green and pink scrolls upon it, bought in Singapore, and apparently made in haste, but made well, during the course of the week by Aunt Nevis. It exposed her smooth round shoulders and classic long neck, and the girl's resplendent curls were held up with two ivory combs covered in silver filigree. Upon her feet she wore brilliant magenta slippers brought from Madras.

Nevis and her friends had been baking for weeks in preparation for the 'spread', as the supper was called in this part of the world. The mouth-watering treats covered a long table and in the centre stood the three-tiered cake iced in pink, green and white to match the guest of honour's dress. Upon it were written the words 'Enjoy Your 21st Birthday Emma Louise'. At ten o'clock the food began to disappear quite swiftly and the entire company drank to Emma Louise's long life and health. Father Michael gave a short entertaining speech and the girl responded well, and everyone applauded vigorously.

A trio of piano, violin and guitar played at one end of the wide verandah in the mild warm autumn night, and the guests danced and laughed and were merry until the wee hours of Saturday.

John Conrad was the talk of the gathering – well, he and Emma Louise – for they did indeed look spectacular together. He wore a brown gaberdine suit, cut so well it showed off his marvellous physique, and when the word passed round that he was one of Kitchener of Khartoum's personal aides home on leave from India, the house positively buzzed with excitement.

'The handsomest couple I've ever seen, anywhere,' Gertrude declared, swallowing her third cream puff, 'and I've travelled the world in my time.'

'He's something to look at, that's for sure,' stated Nevis in her straight Queensland fashion as the couple in question danced by. 'She's pretty, with that radiant hair and he's a real dish.'

The night was a marvellous success. At around one in the morning a furious waltz was in progress and Emma Louise was dancing with one of the young men of Southport though her eyes kept wandering to find her soldier's whereabouts. He was standing on the lawn under the lanterns that hung in the branches of the acacia, gum, frangipani and casuarina trees, chatting with Sophie and a lady guest and hearing about her teaching position at a prestigious girls' school called St Hilda's, when two young men claimed the women for the dance.

John Conrad wandered away along the row of trees towards the back garden, sniffing the clean smell of the encroaching bush and the eucalyptus that mixed with the ozone pervading the air. They were only about a quarter of a mile from the sea in a straight line. It was good to be home in Queensland again, good to be outdoors in the clean night air.

He was passing the kitchen window when he halted because he heard his name spoken. There were women inside doing the washing-up.

'He's the one I'm sure.' The voice came clearly to him and hung in the night air. 'His name was Fleet, of that I'm certain, and John Conrad sounds right.'

'But that was a scandal. He doesn't look like the type who'd have been involved in a scandal.'

'And what would that type be?' spoke up another.

They all laughed at that and then the first voice began again. 'I lived in Kangaroo Point at the time and it was all over Brisbane. He had a sister who was going out with Matthew Craken – he's now a well-known painter, I believe.'

'Yes,' replied another, 'I know him.'

'Well, Fleet's sister, she committed suicide. Next thing there was a terrible fight, ending up with Craken going to hospital for almost a year and Fleet being sent away to the army.'

'That hasn't done him any harm,' commented another woman.

'He's sooo handsome.'

The first voice broke in again. 'It gets juicier. My friend Harriet told me that some years later, Fleet came home and was walking out with Caro Dere – you remember her? Father was the sea captain . . . word is they were very close, if you know what I mean – well, the next thing Fleet returns to the army and within no time, I'm talking about only a few weeks, Caro Dere marries Craken. She was in the family way. My friend Harriet, who used to live near the Deres, said there was a terrible screaming match between Caro Dere and Fleet the very next night after the wedding.'

'What?'

'Seems Fleet had come back from the army and went to see her. It was a free-for-all, both of them in the street screaming at each other. Her brother broke it up. Harriet said the rumour was that he didn't know she had married Craken and had returned to marry her himself, would you believe it?'

'And it's him what's here tonight,' added another. 'How romantic.'

'Yes, isn't it?' said the first voice again. 'He carries his chequered past with aplomb, don't you reckon?'

John Conrad had heard enough. He stepped forward to move away when another voice from inside halted him again. 'So whose baby was it?'

The first voice became very confidential in tone. 'My friend Harriet says the kid's got fair hair and brilliant blue eyes . . . remind you of anyone you've seen tonight?'

John Conrad turned back.

A few of the women giggled and one said, 'Wouldn't mind having his baby myself.'

'But you don't know that!' spoke up another voice. 'From what I hear Craken's not the sort to marry a woman unless it's his baby. Anyway, has anyone told Emma Louise all this?'

John Conrad tensed for the reply.

'Yes, she knows all about it. Doesn't bother her a bit. She's pretty sure of herself for a youngster, you know. Sophie said she thinks it *enhances his attractiveness*.'

The women burst into laughter and at that moment someone called from an inner room 'Are you all coming out to dance or are you going to talk in there all night?'

The women fell quiet.

Unwittingly John Conrad lifted his hand to rub the side of his neck where the small scar lay; the reminder of the night seven years before. He felt very odd. Caro was fair and so was her mother, and he reckoned Jack Dere's eyes were blue. That could account for the child's blue eyes. Craken's eyes were black like coals. But he had heard tell it was the father who dominated the colour of a child's eyes.

He took off his coat and loosened his tie. Then he forced himself to recall the night he did not wish ever to recall: under the tree in her front garden by the light of the cold impartial moon.

He had pulled her wrists high in the air, bringing her body close to his. 'Whose is it? Is it mine?' he had shouted at her. He could almost feel her body shuddering against him now in the humid Southport night, nigh on ten years later. He could see the tears flowing from her eyes.

He had shouted again, 'Tell me, is it mine? For Christ's sake.' And pulled her face to within a finger's width of his own.

And she had looked straight in his eyes and cried, 'It's not yours. It's his! It's his!'

John Conrad took a deep vibrating breath and moved across under the branches of one of the acacia trees. He leant his hot forehead on the coolness of the living wood of the trunk and closed his eyes. 'God in heaven, surely you didn't lie to me that night, Caro?' he murmured.

He recalled the pony races at the Gabba and the little tear-stained face of Craken's child. He shivered though he was burning hot. After a time he turned round and rested his back on the trunk, looking at the flickering light of the lantern and the lamps along the verandah in the distance, and through the windows at the back of the house. He had to stop thinking like this. It was all water under the bridge and Caro Dere was Caro Craken and the child with the tear-stained face was Craken's. Of course he was. Hadn't Caro Dere bloody well sworn it to him? *The bitch was with us both but she knew who the father was all right.*

He heard a male voice call on the verandah in the distance, 'Take your partners for the last dance!' and the music began again and the rumbling mirth of the party continued.

John Conrad hated thinking about Caro Dere. She was nothing to him, damn her, and her child was nothing to him as well. Bloody Crakens, they were all blights on the world! He wanted to think about things that made him happy, that gave him peace and made him feel good.

'John Conrad, where are you?' came the bright voice of his fairy creature and he saw the dainty white figure of her come gliding along under the trees towards him. 'Are you here? John Conrad?'

'Yes, here I am.'

'I looked all over for you. It's the last dance. Oh, and I must have it with you.' She came running right up to him into the obscurity under the tree.

Before either of them had time to analyse it he had enveloped her in his arms and kissed her mouth with all the pent-up emotion brought on by the angry thoughts of Caro Dere.

When his lips left hers she made a small sweet sound of pleasure and he placed his hands on her bare shoulders and ran them across the skin to her neck and up to grasp the sides of her young face. 'Come,' he said, 'of course we must have the last dance. It's your birthday. It's imperative.'

He put his jacket back on as his arm went round her waist and he steered her back over the lawn to the steps of the verandah. As she put her dainty magenta slipper on the first step to join the other dancers he pulled her back. 'No, Emma Louise, we'll dance here,' and he took her in his arms and twirled her across the lawn, around and around they swirled. Some of the guests turned to watch them and some of the dancers stopped to do the same, as John Conrad and the girl he thought of as his woman-child flowed and swayed to the rhythm of the music between the rows of pale flowers of the night.

That was the start of the soldier's weekly visits to Southport. From then on he came every Friday and remained until Monday morning, when he caught the train home to spend the weekdays with his family.

It was Sunday afternoon in the middle of May on his seventh visit when he and Emma Louise went with the rest of her relatives – Gertrude, Sophie, Nevis and Uncle Slattery – to enjoy some hours on the golden white sands that actually stretched for twenty miles and more along this coast of unsullied Queensland beaches.

They took a picnic and the day smiled upon them. The sea glistened like a massive sparkling aquamarine and the sand glowed like yellow gold. Emma Louise and Sophie ran in exhilaration along the beach and then paddled while the men swam and the two older women watched from the haven of a blanket placed in the shade under the trees that grew along the foreshore. After lunch Emma Louise and John Conrad strolled away hand in hand towards a cluster of rocks that loomed along the beach about half a mile away.

The girl was in good spirits as she always seemed to be, and she laughed at a flock of seagulls that flew close overhead to land along the water's edge, and pointed with delight when a wallaby appeared about a hundred yards in front of them and leapt along the sand for a minute or so.

'It's amazing to me,' John Conrad said, sweeping his arm out in a wide arc. 'Look at all this. And no one here but us to enjoy the beauty of it.'

They looked up the beach and it was true the only signs of life were the screeching sea birds and their own companions in the distance. 'One day,' he went on, 'it wouldn't surprise me if this became a spot where people flocked to: the long days of sun, the wonderful sandy beaches, the climate.'

'Well, Southport is almost a proper little town, you might say,' the girl replied.

'No, I mean all of it.' And he pointed into the distance. 'All the way to the border with New South Wales. There, where there's nothing today, I predict homes and hotels and guesthouses. People frolicking in the sea: picnics and frivolity. This is a wonderful spot.'

'You're probably right. For you seem to be right about so much. And Uncle Slattery says the climate is pleasant all year round. They just get some strong winds in winter and occasional summer storms.' Then she altered the course of her conversation as was her habit. 'Shall we play whist tonight? I know Aunt Gertrude and Sophie want to play.'

'Of course, if you would like to.'

She dropped his hand, ran forward and climbed up a few feet off the ground on a single cluster of small rocks gracing the long white sands. She stood above him, peering down, the gleaming brightness of her hair billowed out in the wind, her dress caught the wind and lifted to her knees and she waved her hands above her head in sheer high spirits.

John Conrad shook his head and smiled indulgently up at her.

Suddenly she said, 'Catch me,' and she dropped forward like a felled tree towards him. He caught her, of course, but she had startled him and as he swung her round in his arms and brought her down to the sand where he landed lightly on top of her she laughed up at him. He bent forward and kissed her.

'You surprised me,' he said as he took his mouth from hers.

'Ah, but you're a soldier and your reactions were perfect. What sort of a shot are you, anyway?'

'Good, so don't misbehave.'

This made her laugh again. And as her glee subsided she looked up from under half-closed lids to meet his gaze. 'Are we more than friends?' she asked.

His expression became serious and he smoothed her hair with his hand. 'Yes, my dear, I expect we are.'

'Good,' she answered, and he smiled at her directness.

She continued to lie on the sand looking up at him and he gave a small cough. 'Emma Louise, I've something very important to say to you.'

'Yes?'

'You know I'm attached to Kitchener. I mean in both senses of the word. Emotionally attached – he's been my leader and my friend for a long time – and also that I work for him.'

She nodded.

'When I return to India we must remain there until next year. Then I don't know where we'll go.'

She did not speak and he went on, 'K does not like his personal staff to have any strong emotional attachments, but some do, of course, and then they leave him and marry. Now, Learmonth, who's an aide to K and works with me – sort of friend of mine, I suppose – has been engaged to a girl in England for . . .' he paused, 'for a long time. No doubt they'll marry in the end.' He paused again and stroked the side of her face. 'The point is . . . what I'm trying to say is . . . do you feel enough for me to . . . I'm asking you to wait for me.'

She lay silently watching him, before she prompted him, 'And what is it exactly that you're asking me to wait for?'

He took a loud deep breath. 'Emma Louise Blackstone, I'm telling you I must return to India and remain there until the end of our term, but I'm asking you if you'll be my wife when I come back to Queensland . . . and if you'll become engaged to me now, before I leave?'

A lot of thoughts had gone through Emma Louise's head in the last weeks. She knew Aunt Gertrude had made up her mind that John Conrad was the right man for her. The woman had told her often enough about being sent a sign from God. The girl was not really sure about that one, but she knew her aunt believed it. Emma Louise definitely waited impatiently for each Friday when he would come again and she knew he was the best-looking man she had ever seen, and that he was extraordinary. He was so learned and so important and he had taught her much she knew nothing about. Everybody who met him was impressed with him. Sometimes her whole body tingled when their fingers met or he touched her arm. And, his kisses made her feel weak and spongy in the knees. Sophie said that this was definite proof. And Emma Louise had decided some time ago that all this meant love. When she had been in Madras she had believed she loved Hector Flynn, but she recognised that as mere infatuation. She was twenty-one now and an adult; it was time she was engaged and married. People expected it. Aunt Nevis and her friends all said John Conrad was 'a most fantastic catch'.

She lifted her head and kissed his lips. 'Yes, I will,' she said against his mouth.

He kissed her deeply for a long time and she made gentle noises of satisfaction in her throat. When he took his mouth from hers he was smiling. 'Great, wonderful. You must meet my family, my darling. There's no time to lose. Aunt Leigh and Father and Bart and David will all love you, I know they will.'

As he said this, a snap of thunder sounded above them and a flash autumn shower erupted.

They jumped to their feet and ran back down the beach towards the others. The shower was not heavy but it was enough to wet them through by the time they reached their companions, who were sheltering beneath the trees under two umbrellas that Nevis had the foresight to bring. But the rain did not dampen the glee of the girl who had accepted John Conrad.

'I can't wait, I must tell you,' she informed them all between her bouts of merry laughter. 'John Conrad and I are engaged to be married. Isn't it wonderful?'

303

Gertrude looked skywards as if in thanks, and everyone spoke at once and laughed and forgot about the rain. By the time they reached the house the sun was out from behind the clouds and bestowing its warmth of approval on the happy couple.

That night they did play whist and John Conrad and Emma Louise won. During the supper that Aunt Nevis prepared later, a discussion began on when the engagement party would take place. Everyone was aware that John Conrad's departure for India was imminent on 10 June.

After a little prompting by Gertrude, Nevis smiled, turned her powdered cheeks to John Conrad and patted his hand, which lay on the bright cotton tablecloth. 'John Conrad, we've made arrangements to go up to my sister Freda's place in Ipswich this coming week. Her husband's the deputy mayor and there's an important dinner for him being held which we're all supposed to attend. They're particularly wanting to meet Emma Louise. So would it suit you, dear boy, if we went there on Tuesday as planned, attended the dinner on Thursday and then on Friday our darling engaged girl could come to Brisbane to you and you could keep her there to meet all your family? Then on the following Saturday, which would be the er . . .'

Slattery helped her out: 'The sixth, love.'

'Yes, the sixth. With your agreement we could have the engagement party that night . . . at a venue of your choice. We'd come into Brisbane for it, of course.'

John Conrad patted Nevis's hand in turn. 'While I don't want to lose a minute with Emma Louise, I understand, and it all sounds admirably workable.'

'Oh wonderful,' sighed Gertrude.

'And then we'll see you off, darling, on that nasty ship that's taking you away,' Emma Louise said dispiritedly. She picked up a pencil and looked round their faces, swiftly changing her mood to brightness again. 'Now we must make a list of who to invite.' Then she grinned up at her fiancé. 'Where will we have the party, sweetheart?'

John Conrad shook his head. 'On such short notice I don't know, but Aunt Leigh will, darling.'

Harry dawdled along the platform, carrying his hoop and following the swirling movements of his mother's long dark blue travelling skirt which reached down to the top of her buttoned-up shoes. She held his little sister, Katy's, hand and he watched as she turned her head to him. 'Come on, Harry darling, the train goes in a minute. Do hurry.'

He loved the train, the noise it made and the speed of it. He liked to kneel on the seat and look out the window as he sped through the countryside. His mother would not allow him to stand on the seat. 'Not proper' was her phrase for that. But she allowed him to kneel so that's what he did to watch the sights as they passed by outside the window.

He turned his head to look back along the platform. People were climbing aboard and carriage doors were slamming.

Ahead of him his mother opened one of the heavy wooden doors and lifted his sister to deposit her inside. At that moment his hand loosened on the hoop he carried and it fell from his hands to roll a few yards along the concrete flooring. His mother called to him in exasperation as his toy ran up against a lady who raised it up high in her hands. Harry ran over to her and she smiled down at him.

'Your hoop,' she said, handing it to him and he smiled his thanks up at her. She was very pretty, like his mother, and as he stood there she turned and kissed two old ladies goodbye. He could hear his mother behind him calling out to him, and suddenly the pretty lady bent down to him and ushered him towards his mother with the words. 'Now come along, for I think we both need to catch this train.'

They moved across the platform to where his mother held the door open. She greeted the other lady with a smile. 'Thank you. I'm sorry my son was careless enough to hit you with that.'

'Don't concern yourself. There was no speed in it, didn't hurt a bit.' The newcomer followed his mother along the corridor and entered the same compartment. 'Do you mind if I travel with you?' she asked, and his mother gave her a wide smile. 'Of course not.'

The lady took off her hat, placed it up in the rack and sat down opposite them. 'Going all the way?' she asked.

Harry's mother took his hoop and put it overhead too, answering at the same time, 'Yes almost. Into Roma Street Station.'

'Me too,' answered the other lady, smoothing her skirt and

305

crossing her knees. Then she turned to her handbag and took out the *Queensland Times* newspaper and unfolded it. She looked over it to catch Harry's eye as he climbed up on the seat near the window. 'Do you like the train?' she asked.

Harry nodded and his mother said, 'He loves it. They both do.'

As Harry knelt and let the window down a porter looked into the carriage and called to the lady with the newspaper, 'Your portmanteau will be taken off for you at Roma Street, miss.'

She thanked him and waved to the two old ladies as the train lurched forward and Harry's mother asked her, 'Do you mind if Harry leaves the window open? If any soot comes in I shall make him close it.'

Their travelling companion shook her head. 'I like fresh air and if the soot troubles us we'll worry about it then.'

So with this agreeable atmosphere pervading the compartment the journey from Ipswich into Brisbane began. For some time while the lady read the newspaper Harry leant out the window, enjoying the wind, and the speed of the train as it rattled along and swayed and sped through the miles of gum trees under the dependable blue Queensland sky. The engine wheezed and snorted, stopping at stations at Dinmore, Wacol, Corinda and Indooroopilly where more passengers boarded, but none entered their compartment.

It was a little time later that the lady offered his mother the newspaper. She smiled and shook her head. 'No thanks. Read it early this morning.'

The pretty lady folded it and put it away.

It was then that Harry tired of leaning out the window and he sat back, snuggled in against his mother's body, and a few minutes later as his eyelids drooped, he heard her tell Katy to read the book that Uncle Knobby had bought her, then he fell asleep.

When he awoke his mother and the lady were talking. For a time they chatted about the wonders of train travel and the reliable weather of Southern Queensland.

'Do you live in Ipswich?' the lady asked Caro.

'No, we have a property up country from there.'

'And a house in Brisbane,' Harry added, sitting up and looking out the window again. 'Where Daddy lives.'

The lady was not sure what to make of this but she took the information calmly enough.

'We live at Cedar Grove,' little Katy revealed.

The lady smiled warmly. 'Now that sounds like a nice place.'

'It is,' the child informed her. 'We live with Uncle Knobby, Uncle Jacob and Aunt Mary and when Uncle Knobby marries Jane she'll come and live with us too.'

It sounded like a complete menagerie to the listener but she smiled all the same.

'Where are you from?' Caro asked.

'I was born in England, actually, though I've lived in a few places. I was here in Queensland as a small child as a matter of fact and my aunt and I have only recently returned. We've been to visit the deputy mayor of Ipswich. He's a relative.' Then she surprised Caro by changing the subject completely. 'Do you know a good store in Brisbane where I could buy dresses and hats?'

'Why yes, there's John Evans, and Lewis and Craken, and T.C. Beirne down in the Valley; they all have good ladies' wear.'

The train slowed and Caro looked out the window. 'We'll be coming into Roma Street Station soon. Anyone meeting you?'

The lady stood, reached up to her hat in the rack above, and placed it over her brilliant red hair answering brightly, 'Yes, my fiancé. I'm dying to see him.'

'Of course you would be,' Caro said understandingly.

'Anyone meeting you?' the lady responded, and when Caro told her there was not, she added 'Do you need any help to get off the train?'

'Oh no, I can manage. You go along to the door if you like.'

And as the train slowed even more, the companion of their travels looked to left and right. 'I will I think. Do you know what side we'll get out?'

'Yes,' Caro answered, 'this one,' pointing to the left, and the lady with the vibrant shining hair bent down to Harry and Katy and farewelled them. As she straightened up she smiled at Caro. 'Goodbye. So nice to have travelled with you. Fact is, I'm rather excited. Going to be a big engagement party for us tomorrow week.'

'How wonderful,' Caro replied, waving goodbye as the lady moved out of the compartment into the corridor and disappeared along it. She turned to her children and readied them for departure from the train, getting Harry's hoop down from above and handing it to him. 'And don't drop it this time,' she cautioned, looking almost severely at him as the train decelerated.

At that precise second she looked up and out through the corridor windows to the platform of the Roma Street Station. Her heart leaped and an involuntary sound of shock escaped from her as she saw through the windows, standing on the platform, John Conrad Fleet.

She felt dizzy and her hand went to her temple. His face was before her, filling her head; his special smile with hardly a movement of his lips and the way at the same time his blue eyes seemed to haze over. She stepped back in an attempt to steady herself and she thumped down hard on the seat.

Katy and Harry reacted together. 'What's wrong, Mummy?'

She held her head in her hands to recover. 'Nothing. I'll be all right in a second or two.'

The train was creaking to a halt. She managed to stand. 'Come.' She hustled the children to the floor and took up her handbag. 'Come this way, quickly.'

In the corridor she watched as the train finally halted and she saw the girl with the red hair open the door and jump down on to the platform and run along it. By the time she had the children to the door and she descended to the platform, she could see through the few people who milled about that the girl and John Conrad, about forty yards away, were in each other's arms. She felt ill.

The guard called out as he walked along slamming open doors. 'All aboard for Central . . . All aboard.'

'Help me down, Mummy! Help me down!'

Caro stood motionless until Harry, who had jumped down to the platform on his own, pulled sharply on her hand. 'Mummy! Katy's still on the train.'

Caro came to life and turned to her daughter, who had begun

to cry. 'Oh, sweetheart, don't cry. Here.' She lifted Katy out of the train as it began to move.

She dabbed her daughter's eyes with her handkerchief but her concentration was on the couple along the platform. They moved off hand in hand.

'What's wrong, Mummy?' asked Harry, looking up at her with his blue, blue eyes . . . with his father's eyes. But Caro did not answer. She was silent, still, watching through the moving people the two who walked away. She saw the porter bring the portmanteau on a trolley to them and then abruptly they halted and the girl said something and pointed to the sign: 'Ladies' Lavatory'. She kissed John Conrad's cheek and she parted from him while he and the porter remained by the portmanteau.

Caro's mind sped. She had perhaps three or four minutes while the girl was inside attending to her needs. She turned to her children and took up their hands, almost pulling them in her haste to remove them to the waiting room. She sat them on a leather seat, pulled the two storybooks out of her bag, and handed them to the children. 'Now wait here. Do not move. There's something Mummy must do.' She kissed Harry and patted Katy's head and tried hard to sound light and happy. 'Stay right here. I won't be long. We'll all have a lovely ice cream when I come back.'

With that she left them and hurried out the door.

As she drew close to him his back was towards her. 'John Conrad.' She said it quietly but he heard it. At the sound of her voice down through the endless corridors of his mind floated a gentle smile. He was turning towards her when the reality hit and his face hardened. 'What are you doing here?'

She wore a dark blue travelling suit and a white lace collar sat high around her throat. Her eyes were imploring and as she opened her full rosy lips to speak he noticed the smudge of the scar on her mouth and an uncomfortable sensation rose in his chest.

'I . . . I travelled in the train from Ipswich. With the girl . . . the girl you met. She said you were her fiancé.'

He swallowed. 'Yes.'

Caro's pulse raced and there was pain in her temples. 'I wanted to speak to you. To say . . .' she faltered and fell quiet, standing looking up at him.

The thoughts that ran through John Conrad's head only served to confuse him. He never wanted to see this woman. Every part of him said he hated her. She was nothing to him. She was married to Craken. Slept with Craken. Gave herself to Craken . . . She disgusted him and yet there were fleeting traces of happy times attempting to emerge from his memories. Were they tears he saw in her eyes?

She found her voice again, strained though it was. 'I wanted to say . . . I'm so deeply sorry for all that happened. Life goes on. But the pain is always there, like an immortal thing that won't die.'

He thought it an odd statement for her to make, but agreed with her absolutely so he nodded his head.

It was exquisite torment to look at him, to be within touching distance of him. This was enough. She thanked God for it. These precious moments would last her the rest of her life. She held back the tears that were bent on coming. 'Though I did not realise it,' she continued, 'I've just spent an hour in the company of the girl who's to share your life. A coincidence, wasn't it?'

His voice came from a long way off. 'Very definitely. But life's full of them. I ran into your husband again a few weeks ago.' He paused and met her gaze. 'And your son . . . Harry.'

In that moment his eyes asked again the question of the dark black night of misery and suffering ten years before, but Caro knew the truth was a wretched ugly thing waiting to destroy him. She would forever protect him from it. She looked away. 'I know. I heard. I'm truly sorry about what happened.'

'Don't be. It seems to be the unavoidable pattern of our meetings.'

Then she looked back at him 'What's the name of your fiancée?'

'Emma Louise Blackstone.'

Caro shook her head with surprise. 'Emma Louise, how strange?'

'Yes it is. Another coincidence.'

They both fell silent and a void of emptiness hung in the space between them as the clock above them began to chime three.

Caro gave something akin to a smile and wiped her eyes with the back of her hand. 'I'd better go, she'll be back soon.'

'Yes, I suppose you'd better.'

Caro's heart was aching, along with her head. She held out her hand. 'Goodbye, John Conrad.'

He delayed briefly before he took her hand. It was the oddest sensation, as if in a dream. The touch of her again. His nerve ends twinged with pain. It was a poignant thing. A few seconds passed.

She pulled free of him, turned, and hurried away.

He watched her slender back distancing itself, and a myriad of memories hung at the edge of his awareness, begging to be noticed, to be given form again. As she approached the waiting room he saw a boy standing outside who said something to her and pointed in John Conrad's direction. It was her son and an uneasy troubled feeling washed over John Conrad again.

'Here I am, darling.' Emma Louise's voice was bright and cheerful at his side. He flinched slightly as his head came round to her. 'You look strange, darling,' she said, taking his arm.

'Do I? Don't know why.' He took a deep resigned breath. 'Now, let's be on our way.'

They moved off, and the porter, who had heard the peculiar conversation with the woman in blue, followed them, wheeling along Emma Louise's portmanteau and shaking his head. He knew people were bloody odd, they proved it all the time.

Behind them in the waiting room, Harry berated his mother. He had gone searching for her. He did not like that she had left them . . . and he had seen the enemy.

'It was the enemy, I know it was. I saw him. And you were speaking to him. I'm going to tell Daddy.'

Katy began, 'But I want to see the enemy. Show me the enemy. Where is he? Show me.'

This was too much for Caro. She could not bear it. The tears sprung from her eyes. 'Stop!' she shouted, and her two children, who, unaccustomed to this behaviour from their mother, fell quiet, eyes wide with surprise.

She wiped her face with her handkerchief and bent down to her son. 'Now, listen to me. Harry sweetheart, you're wrong. Firstly we do not use the word *enemy* even if Daddy does. It's not . . . nice. And secondly you mustn't talk this way because that man was not who you think he was.' She met his eyes. 'Always remember, Harry, to have compassion for those who suffer. Compassion is the major difference between humans and animals.'

Harry had no idea what compassion was, nor what it was doing in the conversation, but he left it there.

'Now I've had enough, I've got a terrible headache.' His mother stood up. 'Come on, let's go.'

'What about our ice cream?' Katy reminded her.

'All right. All right. We'll have an ice cream, but you must promise to behave.'

It was the following day that Harry came into the studio to show his father the drawing he had done. Drawing and painting were the only things Matthew ever encouraged the children to do and, though both had a reasonable aptitude for it, Harry showed more interest.

Matthew stopped his own work and placed his brush between his teeth, which made Harry laugh.

For some seconds he studied the drawing. 'So what is it?' he asked.

Harry looked hurt, he thought it was quite obvious to any viewer what the subject was. 'It's a railway train in the bush.'

'Ah . . . of course it is. Not bad, my son.' He took the brush from between his teeth and pointed to the engine. 'Perhaps a bit more emphasis on the shape here would have been helpful. But it's quite good, now that I know what it is. Where's Uncle Knobby?'

'He's writing in the drawing room.'

'Go and tell him I want to see him, will you?'

The boy turned to leave, then he hesitated and looked back at his father. 'I saw the enemy, Daddy.'

Matthew cocked his head to one side, affecting sudden interest. He came over to his son and drew the boy to him. 'Where and when?'

'Yesterday at the railway station.'

'What? In Ipswich?'

'No here. Mummy said it wasn't the enemy, but it was. I saw her talking to him. I remember him because you said I must.'

312

'So I did my boy, so I did, and you're a stickler for instruction, pertinaciously following the commands of your father, I'm gratified to note.' He kissed him on the forehead. 'Excellent child.' Then he moved Harry over to the sofa and they sat together.

'Now, my boy, am I to understand that the enemy was on the train itself?'

'I don't know, Daddy. I didn't see him on the train.'

'So it was here in Brisbane at Roma Street Station that you saw him?'

'Yes. Mummy left Katy and me in . . . on a seat inside . . . and she went out. I followed to look where she had gone . . .'

'And?'

'She was talking to the enemy.'

'On the platform?'

'Yes. She said we could have an ice cream, but then she forgot and so Katy told her to—'

'No, sweet boy, let's not get side-tracked with edibles. Back to the point. So . . . Mummy left you somewhere on a seat and went to talk to him.'

'Yes.'

'Was Mummy a long time?'

'No, not very long.'

'And so you went out to see what was happening and you saw Mummy with the enemy?'

'Yes.'

'Did you hear what they said?'

Harry shook his head. 'They were too far away.'

'Did you see anything else?'

'No.'

'Are you sure?'

'They shook hands.'

Matthew closed his eyes. His right leg had begun to ache and he forced himself to say, 'Anything else?'

'Mummy was crying.'

Matt's mouth twisted with emotion but he managed to contrive a wide smile. 'You're a very good boy. Now pop off and find Uncle Knobby, then we'll all go out for a pleasant ride somewhere and Knobby and I can indulge in

313

what pleases us and you can enjoy an ice cream. How would you like that?'

'You'll indulge in a drink,' the wise child stated.

Matthew gave the imitation of a laugh and chucked Harry under the chin. 'Perspicacious of you. Now, my dear, go and ask Uncle Knobby to come here.'

When the boy had gone he rubbed his leg. It was throbbing now. As he applied the pressure to ease it that he had learned in Penang fourteen years before, he considered what Harry had told him. So damn it, Caro had spoken with the bastard yesterday. She had been cold to him last night, which was unusual for her as she mostly went along with his desires. She had told him her temples were aching and perhaps they were, but now he knew why. The woman's mind had been on her old lover.

Matthew's face tightened with emotion. How he detested Fleet. He would like to see Fleet's head on a plate. 'How biblical,' he said aloud as he stopped manipulating his leg and stood up, leaning on his gleaming white cane. Then a thought came to his mind and he added aloud, 'And how magnificently bizarre,' as he moved across to his desk and, picking up a charcoal, did a quick sketch.

At that moment Knobby and Harry came in and he covered the sketch with another piece of paper before he picked up his cane and hastened across the room towards them. 'Ah good, my dears, let's be off then.'

Knobby held up his hand. 'Shouldn't you be working on finishing for the exhibition? It's next Saturday, you know . . . only a week to the opening.'

Matthew made a scoffing sound. 'Knobby, don't be the voice of reason. I loved you when you were as unreliable as me; since you've become dependable under the tutelage of Caro and Jane Kruger you can be positively relentless . . . *not* a charming attribute in my eyes, I assure you. The exhibition will open on time. Don't become a worrier, I could not abide it in you of all people. Now, I know I've a busy week of painting ahead, so before that happens I have things to meditate upon and I'll do that better in Green's Hotel than I will here.'

'Well, we can't go into the bar with the boy.'

Matthew made a sound of exasperation. 'I know that, Knob,

my dear. He's been in Green's Lounge before, haven't you, son? The lounge there's eminently comfortable. Don't know it from your mother's drawing room, do you, Harry?'

The boy grinned.

As Matt ushered Harry from the studio, Knobby sighed and followed them.

are that. He always wanted it and I knew it before David I was. That he would always mention it to me strange to me is if you want money ... when you don't need it they ...
He ... to himself.
At the same again I slept long, she walked. Deeply perfect and odourous ...

Chapter Twenty-two

Emma Louise closed the solid wooden door to her room and entered the hall; a smile bordering on smugness hovering on her pretty mouth. Tonight was her engagement party. Aunt Gertrude and Aunt Nevis and Uncle Slattery and the Ipswich relatives were all staying at Uncle Slattery's club somewhere in the city, and everything was prepared. It was going to be at the Bellevue Hotel, which was *the* place, apparently. Aunt Leigh had organised it. One of her friends at the RSPCA was married to the manager of the hotel.

The small blue velvet box on her dressing table came into Emma Louise's mind. Inside was a ring with three large sparkling diamonds in a row along the band of gold. She was used to seeing precious stones; the Indian princes and their wives wore garments and turbans of glittering gems and outsized colourful jewels but she had never seen anything more elegant and classical than her engagement ring. It had taken Aunt Gertrude's breath away, and Aunt Leigh had said she could not believe anyone in Brisbane had made such a tastefully beautiful thing.

Suddenly a voice sounded behind her in the hallway and she swung round.

'Good morning.'

David was leaning on the door jamb of his bedroom a few yards away. She gave a tiny shiver. 'Goodness, you startled me.'

He walked towards her. He was shorter than John Conrad by some inches but his physique was quite perfect and he moved with a certain smooth fluid motion; it was the single feature about him which reminded her of his eldest brother. He was quite dissimilar in looks from either John Conrad or Bart: his hair was dark and his eyes were chocolate brown with long lashes that were quite startling on a man. His features were poised in the blandness of the years between boy and man, before lines gave character; and his smooth skin was highlighted by strong cheekbones and a round chin modified only by a small cleft. He oozed self-confidence, and as he halted a few feet from her, he smiled widely. His teeth glowed in the semi-darkness of the hall.

She knew he watched her and she noticed how he found excuses to spend time in her company.

He cocked his head on one side and regarded her. 'John Conrad's gone out.'

'Oh, where?'

'To see a friend. Seems there's an Abo woman he goes and visits.'

Emma Louise had been in Australia long enough to know what 'an Abo' was.

'Do you mean an Aboriginal woman?' she asked.

'Yes, seems she's a friend of his. He's been going to see her each week since he's been back.'

This was something Emma Louise knew nothing of and she made a mental note to ask her fiancé about it.

'He's got some funny friends.'

'Don't you like your brother?' Emma retaliated, and now it was David's turn to be surprised. He could not help but be impressed with the way she was so straightforward about things.

'He's my brother. I'm stuck with him no matter how I feel. Don't really know him, anyway. He left home when I was nine and he's only been back now and then.' He leaned forward and she took a step backwards as he said, 'Anyway, *you* must like him.'

'Of course I do. I'm in love with him.'

'Ah yes.' He put out his hand and rested it on her waist as he moved past her, so close that his shoulder brushed hers. 'He's too old for you,' he whispered, and then he jumped down the stairs three at a time and disappeared.

John Conrad held out his hand and took the cup of tea from Jenny. She was a pretty child of fourteen. There had been one addition to the family in recent years – Danny, a little boy of three. Bluey had remained with Lena and they had used well

317

the horse and cart that John Conrad had given them. They were in the second-hand business and the back yard of the little house here in Spring Hill boasted a shed full of all manner of oddments that spilled out and over the small lawn. Still, it was enough to keep them, to clothe the children, put food on the table and buy beer and cigarettes.

John Conrad was happy to notice Lena smiled more these days than she used to in years gone by. She was still spare and her shoulder bones showed through her dress, but she was a tough woman trying to make a life for her children. And though there were very few Aboriginal people in Brisbane, for they mostly lived in country areas, and the family was often the butt of cruel jokes, she insisted on remaining in the city, believing the children would have a better life than hers.

John Conrad took a sip of the tea. 'Thanks, Jenny, it's very good. Even better than they make in India and that's where tea leaves come from.'

The child preened and Lena laughed as Tess, Jenny's younger sister by a year, handed across a plate of biscuits. 'Try these.'

The back door opened and Dave, the eldest boy, a bright ten-year-old, who constantly reminded John Conrad of Hargy, and who had been the baby in Lena's arms when Hargy died, came in. He halted in surprise as he noticed a brand-new set of leather reins and bridle on the side table. 'What's this, then?'

Lena supplied the answer. 'John Conrad brought 'em for us. We need 'em.'

'I know,' Dave replied sliding his hand across them and feeling the quality.

'What did you learn from Miss Howard this week?' John Conrad asked the children in general, and they all answered at once.

'One at a time,' John Conrad counselled as Tess came snuggling into his side.

Tess spoke up. 'I'm goin' to learn about the world and all the countries this week. *Geography* she called it.'

Her elder sister gave her a superior look. 'Miss Howard taught me that years ago.' Then she came over and sat by John Conrad. 'I can write, and Miss Howard said perhaps next year she'll teach me a way to write fast . . . called Pitman's shorthand. It was invented by an Englishman, Isaac Pitman, a long time ago.'

John Conrad was surprised. 'That's wonderful, Jenny.'

'Yes, Miss Howard thinks I might get a job in a few years.'

As her daughter spoke, Lena's whole face glowed with pride at the thought of a job for her daughter. It had been unheard of for any Aborigine even to think of having a proper occupation. 'Miss Howard say she try to help Jenny.'

Jenny shook her head. 'No, Mum, you mean "Miss Howard said she will try . . ."'

As her daughter corrected her, Lena's expression fluctuated between pride and delight.

When the time came for John Conrad to leave, Lena came out with him on to the little front verandah, closing the door behind them. Her eyes always looked too big for her thin face, but today they were large with pride. 'Thanks for what ya're doin' for me family, John Conrad. It's big thing, 'cause Hargy was ya friend not Lena.'

'Oh, Lena, you too are my friend.'

She gave a small smile. 'Yeah, but payin' for Miss Howard teachin' the kids readin' and writin' is real kind.' She sighed and her small frame shook. '*Half-castes* can't go ta real school. Miss Howard a real good woman teachin' them an' all. Hope me kids don' wanta go walkabout.' Then she laughed. 'Lena never did but . . . Lena always like the city.'

Affectionately John Conrad took hold of the woman's shoulders. 'Lena, how's it going with Bluey? I've only seen him twice since I've been home.'

Lena made an affirmative sound. 'Bluey's all right.'

John Conrad's expression was sceptical and she hurried on. 'Look, Bluey don't hit me or nothin'. Never has. Yeah, Bluey drinks a bit, but he ain't a real bad bloke. True. Bluey works hard tryin' ta sell stuff. Man's out in South Brisbane now.'

'He's lived with you a long time, Lena. Had children with you. What about his long-term commitment to you?'

Lena looked questioningly.

'What I mean is . . . I know he has a wife so he can't—'

'No he don't.' She brought her dark eyes up to his. 'Not now. His wife die back a bit. Bluey wants ta marry me all 'proper like.' She shook her head. 'Thirteen years Lena bin with Bluey . . . Jenny – she only one's not his kid, but Bluey treats her right, real proper. No different the others.'

John Conrad studied Lena closely. 'Then do it, girl, marry him.'

Marriage was an all-encompassing thought for Lena. 'Ah dunno about that.'

John Conrad was emphatic. 'I mean it, Lena, you should get married. Hargy would want you to. It would make things better for you in the long run. Legally.'

Lena's expression showed she did not comprehend.

'Don't worry about it. I'll talk to Bluey. We might be able to arrange something before I leave next Wednesday.'

Lena's hand went up to her forehead as if the thought of such speed of action was too much to comprehend. Then she shook her head. 'Didn't know ya leavin'. Lena miss ya real bad.'

John Conrad was uncertain how to broach what he had to say next, so he let go her shoulders and paused briefly before he came straight out with it. 'Lena, I'm engaged to a nice girl. Going to marry her. There's a party tonight at the Bellevue Hotel to celebrate it. I . . . wanted you to know about it.' He hesitated. 'I'll come by afterwards and bring some party food . . . It's just that, for Hargy's sake, I badly wish I could have invited you.' He halted.

Lena's eyes half closed and a knowing expression settled on her small face. She lifted her bony hand and took her visitor's arm. 'Don' feel bad. Huh? Lena no good at party. Lena know. Lena know. John Conrad got best heart . . . real good. Hargy loved ya. Woulda done anythin' for John Conrad. Lena smart too. Lena understand lot o' things.' She squeezed his arm. 'White fella party for you first. Then come here. Ya gonna have real nice party.'

Lena recognised the truth and had a patent understanding of the situation. His eyes remained in contact with hers for a few more seconds, then he leaned forward and kissed her forehead.

At the bottom of the rickety stairs he turned back. 'When Bluey comes home today talk to him about the wedding. Please. Then perhaps we can arrange something when I call by tonight. But it'll be after midnight before I'm here.'

'Midnight's good. Kids all sleepin'. Real good time ta talk.'

As he untethered his horse from the front fence she waved her fragile arm. He raised his eyes past her dark thin frame to where Dave peered out of a broken glass window, his big round eyes so reminiscent of Hargy's. John Conrad saluted and Dave laughed with delight.

While John Conrad mounted and rode off Lena stood musing. She liked the thought of marryin' Bluey, she really did. *Mrs Bluey Sands*. Marryin' a white fella! Who woulda thought it?

As Caro entered the back door of the house in Hamilton Heights, Matilda called out, 'Josephine love, Caro and Matthew are here with Katy and Harry.'

Josephine's voice sounded down the hall. 'I'm coming.'

Matilda bent down, opening her big welcoming arms, and the children immersed themselves inside her embrace. 'Oh, it's lovely to see you and to think you're staying all weekend. We'll have a grand time.'

'I brought my doll,' Katy said, proffering it high in the air.

Harry turned round to Matthew. 'Where's my hoop, Daddy?'

Matt's eyebrow rose as he moved across the room on his cedar cane. 'Ask your mother.'

'It's with your case,' Caro answered Harry as Josephine came hurrying in.

'Oh, look who's here. My sweethearts, to have you all here all at once – it's positively delightful.' She bent down to the children, who dutifully kissed her on the cheek.

'Mother dear, do stop twittering like a bird,' Matthew said, settling himself on the windowsill. 'It's not a good example for the children.'

Josephine looked hurt and Caro smiled sympathetically at her mother-in-law, while Katy offered up her doll for inspection.

Matilda turned to the hob. 'I've the kettle just on the boil. So a cup of tea, eh?'

'I'd love one,' Caro replied looking over to her husband. 'But do we have time, Matt?'

'We need to be there about twenty minutes before the opening. Yes, we've plenty of time.'

Harry moved across to his father. 'Come into the garden, Daddy. I want to see if the pretty cockatoo is there today.'

'Yes, yes,' Katy cried in agreement, 'the pretty cockatoo!'

Matthew rose languidly from the windowsill. 'All right, my son. Though your suggestion has little appeal, remaining in here with three women has zero . . . away we go.'

'Do you want me to bring your tea outside?' Caro called as Matt left the room with the children and the raising of his cane above his shoulder appeared to be an affirmative response.

'Have you read the *Courier*?' Josephine asked Caro as the young woman sat down.

'No, we've been up and going since early. I've had no time. Why?'

'Well, listen to this.' Josephine took up the newspaper from the table and as Matilda made the tea, she sat down and read. 'Page three: Mr Matthew Craken's new exhibition of art opens today at the Dorrit Rooms in Adelaide Street at noon. The exhibition entitled "Works from the New Century" is made up of forty new works painted since his last exhibition three years ago, plus a few previously unseen pictures from the nineties.

'The *Brisbane Courier*'s art critic, Mr Neville Robinson, had this to say about his preview of the works: "Matthew Craken is maturing. The forty works hanging in the Dorrit Rooms are startling images all. Some more so than others. In fact his single biblical work is quite confronting and not for the squeamish. Since his last exhibition in these same rooms three years ago, this artist reaches another stage, a place somewhere on his own. He is not Sid Long nor is he Streeton or Roberts. His impressionism is his own. Craken's work is more controversial than any of these painters would know how to be. The influence of his time in the Orient is still present in some of the works and his versatility is apparent in the scope of his themes. My hope is that Queensland does not lose this painter to the Southern States. In Matthew Craken we have our own leading exponent in the world of art." ' Josephine looked up at Matilda. 'I do hope Matthew's paintings won't upset the ladies from our bridge club.'

Matilda ignored this and asked, 'Have you read it all?'

'Oh, there's a little more . . . "The majority of the exhibits are for sale, though some are from Mr Craken's own collection, which are not for sale. The artist's work can usually be found at Coates' Art Gallery in Elizabeth Street."' Josephine smiled, folding the paper. 'That's it.'

'Here's your tea, dear.' Matilda handed the cup to Josephine. 'Well, that's as good a report as you could ever hope for in a newspaper. You know what journalists are like.'

Caro picked up Matt's tea in one hand and the *Courier* in the other. 'I'll just take it out to him so he can see it himself.'

She found Matthew sitting on the garden seat with his eyes closed. He appeared to be meditating. The children were running around shouting and playing. 'Matt, there's a very good article in the *Courier*. Here, read it.'

He did not open his eyes. 'No, you read it to me.'

She sat down beside him, placing the tea on a wicker table and read. When she had finished she said, 'Now isn't that good?'

'Mm.' He opened one eye. 'Old Robinson's getting some bloody sense at last.' Then he opened his other eye and bent forward and picked up his tea. 'You know there are some works hanging that I've not allowed you to see.'

'Yes.' She knew all right. He had locked himself in the studio and been up painting until dawn every night for the past week; then sleeping for a couple of hours and painting again. He would not let her into the studio. Knobby had been at the Dorrit Rooms putting in the exhibition all week and only yesterday morning Matt had taken whatever it was to the Rooms and hung it.

He put down the cup. 'I want you to promise me that no matter what you think when you see them, you'll remain by my side for the opening speeches. After that you can go if you like.'

Caro turned abruptly to him on the seat. 'Matt, what have you done? What have you painted?'

He was looking straight ahead. 'Promise me.'

'No, Matt. I knew something was going on, you locked away all night for seven nights painting goodness knows what . . . something I wasn't supposed to see. But in my stupidity I hoped it might be something pleasant, something I might like . . . but I should have known better. It's obviously something which will upset me badly, isn't it? Good heavens, man, we're meant to leave for the rooms in a few minutes. Why tell me this now?'

He turned full round to her. 'Because I thought better of it. I was going to surprise you and then I realised you might walk out on me. Now I can't have that, old girl. So I'm warning you.' He winked at her. 'So you're prepared.'

Caro stood up. 'Oh, God in heaven, Matt. Why do you do these things?'

Suddenly Katy called out, 'Harry's taken my doll, Mummy. Mummy, Harry's taken my doll.'

Caro rounded on her daughter. 'Oh heavens, Kate. Just let him have it.'

At that, the little girl began to cry and Matt leaned forward and tapped Caro's thigh with his cane. 'Caro, Caro, your predilection in your children is showing.'

Caro gave a high-pitched frustrated sound, walked over to Harry and took the doll from him. 'No, sweetheart, you must ask Katy for it, not take it. If she does not want to give it to you then that's that. It's like your hoop. That belongs to you. When someone is upset you must have compassion . . . understanding, remember?' She returned the doll to Katy, who stopped crying, and then she came striding back to Matthew.

She stood in front of him looking down, a very determined expression on her face. 'Matt, what have you painted? I demand to know. Otherwise I won't come at all.'

At that moment Matilda called, 'Caro, your tea's getting cold.'

Caro moaned and turned her head, then endeavouring to sound bright answered, 'Sorry, darling, I'll be there in a minute.' She returned her gaze to her husband. 'Tell me, damn it.'

'Caro, old girl, I hate it when you loom over me. Either retreat or sit down.'

'Matt, I'm serious.'

'So am I.'

Caro sat down. 'Now tell me.'

'I will when you promise you'll remain by my side for the speeches.'

Caro could feel the tears springing to her eyes. Her voice

was tense and forced. 'Why do you do these things to me?' Her shoulders sagged as if beneath a great weight.

Matthew reached out and touched her arm. She withdrew from his grasp. He reached out again and this time held her tightly. 'I do *not* do anything to you. When will you understand it is never done to you? It is only ever done to *the enemy*. If you must always take personally everything that is aimed at him then really, Caro, it's your own doing. It is *you* who make *you* sad, not me. Let me tell you a truth. I am aware you saw him at the railway station. You're lucky I don't seek the bastard out and kill him.'

Caro knew then that little Harry had told him, just as the child had threatened to do. It was loathesome and horrible to think Harry had informed on her. One tear spilled over her lid.

'Now let me tell you another truth, Caro.'

Before he could go on, Harry ran over and stood at his father's side. 'Daddy, come and see the sparrows drinking from the birdbath.'

He let go Caro's arm and smiled at the child. 'I will in just a minute. Let your parents finish their conversation first. Take your sister and show her, there's a good lad. Then I'll come.'

The child ran off and Matthew continued, 'Caro, the truth is, I wouldn't have exhibited the two pictures that are in question. In fact I had no intention until I knew that you had seen the bastard, that you had talked to the bastard and that subsequently you were crying over the bastard. That was when I painted the one and retouched the other. I would not have otherwise. So tell me not, my dear Caro, that it's my fault, when Caro, Caro, it is yours and yours alone.'

Her voice was thin and tired: 'What have you painted, Matthew?'

'All right, I will tell, in the hope that you will then promise to remain with me. I've painted his head as John the Baptist's on a plate. I've painted you as Salome holding the plate.'

As she sharply drew in her breath he went on. 'Though no one will recognise you old girl, except for us who know your body well and remember the moulding of your breasts . . . for you're veiled, of course. Then the second painting is a nude . . . with your body again, but once more only for the initiated to recognise . . . a certain mole which your clothes hide. It's the date upon the work which is of interest.'

She sat silently and another tear rolled down her cheek.

He tapped with his cane on his boot. 'Now, Caro, my bloody leg's aching and my foot feels numb. I haven't time for your moods. We must leave soon for the city. Will you remain by my side for the speeches?'

Her voice was so low she hardly heard it herself, but he heard it. 'Yes, all right, damn you.'

He stood. 'Thank you. I'll go and see these bloody sparrows that Harry is so damned keen on.' But he did not move, and a few moments later he said, 'Why don't you pop indoors and have that cup of tea before we leave? It'll do you good.' She did not look up and he stood staring at the top of her head, then he reached out and touched her briefly on the curls before he limped away.

She raised her eyes to watch him go down the slope to the children and she heard Matilda call her again. She took a long trembling breath and folded the paper.

It was the name on the back page that jumped out at her: Fleet . . . Blackstone and Fleet. Avidly she read: 'Mrs Gertrude Jerome-Frith and her brother, Colonel Hewitt Harvey, of Madras, India and Mayfield, Sussex, England are pleased and proud to announce the betrothement of the Colonel's ward, Emma Louise Blackstone, to Lieutenant Colonel John Conrad Fleet, eldest son of Barrington Fleet Esquire, owner of Fleet Breweries. Lieutenant Colonel Fleet is home on leave from India where he is a personal aide on Lord Kitchener's personal staff. The engagement will be celebrated tonight, Saturday, 6 June at a gala dinner dance at the Bellevue Hotel in George Street. The lieutenant colonel will depart Brisbane on Wednesday, 10 June on the Steam Ship *Boadicea* to return to duty in Calcutta.'

Caro stood up. Now she was well and truly weeping. She sobbed unrestrainedly as she crossed the lawn back to the house. Instead of going in the kitchen door she moved round the side of the house and rested against the wall. Then she crossed to the gardener's hut and inside to the tap she knew was there. She washed her face and dried it on her petticoat.

In another minute she entered the kitchen.

'Goodness, love, you were so long I've made another pot,' Matilda began then she stopped. 'Oh dear, I think you badly need this tea by the appearance of things.'

Josephine put down her tatting and looked over her glasses at her daughter-in-law. She seemed to waiver in indecision for a second or two before she spoke and when she did her tone was truly sympathetic. 'Come on, dear. Sit down. He'd make a saint cry.' She opened her mouth to say more, but thought better of it and sighing, picked up her tatting again.

It was the first time Caro had ever heard Josephine speak critically of her son, and she attempted a grateful smile.

Matilda reached out and affectionately touched the young woman. 'I made fresh scones early this morning. I insist you have one with your tea even though I know you'll say you don't want one. You must keep your strength up, you know.'

'Oh yes,' agreed Josephine, 'you must keep your strength up.' And as Caro sat she now leant across and patted her hand. 'And don't you worry about the children. We'll take good care of them till Monday . . . Tuesday, if you like. Knobby can always come here and take them to school. Just whatever you say, dear.'

It was five o'clock in the afternoon and the people had all dispersed when Knobby picked up the keys of the Dorrit Rooms and came over to Matthew, Caro and Ian Coates, the owner of the gallery where Matthew normally showed his paintings.

After all, Caro had remained at the exhibition the entire afternoon. On the ride into the city she had begged Matthew to take down the painting depicting John Conrad's head, but to no avail. When she had actually stood in front of it and seen the likeness of which there was no doubt, she had begged him again. But it had remained where it was. It was gruesome in its detail and very real. The oil-on-canvas reality of Matt's horrible wish sustained him: Caro as Salome holding John Conrad's severed head; blood and sinews, gristle and bone. She felt ill and a spasm ran through her limbs. Hurrying out to the ladies' lavatories she splashed cold water on her face.

Later, when she found the nude, in the form of Diana, it was surely her body, not hidden by diaphanous veils this time and showing the small brown mole on her left breast just under the nipple.

Diana lay in the forest with fauns in a ring around her, and her worshippers, shown as midnight revellers, dancing. Diana held a large leaf over her face with only her eyes showing. Caro knew they were her eyes but she doubted the people of Brisbane would realise. Matthew did not need people to know: that he knew, was the point. Both paintings had a little gold sign attached to the frame: 'Not For Sale'.

What had he said about this painting? Something about the date? She glanced to it and it read: '*May 1898*'. What was Matt playing at? She had not even met him until June that year. Then it struck her. It was for John Conrad's benefit. To make him believe Matt was her lover before John Conrad came along! But John Conrad might never even come to the exhibition; never even see this, never know about it. But that mattered not a whit to Matt. She trembled. Its existence was enough for him! How typical of Matthew.

When she turned from the painting she noticed Matthew watching her from the other side of the room. Deliberately she looked away.

Knobby had been the only person in the whole day to comment to her about the nude. He had said, 'My favourite is *Diana and her Worshippers*. For once Matt has painted something truly beautiful.' Caro had met his eyes and uncertain whether he knew or not, took a guess and said, 'Thanks for saying that, Knobby.'

There had been wine and cheese for the assembly and people had come in and out all afternoon. At three o'clock Ian Coates had introduced the Mayor who had duly opened the exhibition with a long boring speech. Then Matthew had taken the floor and given a short, amusing reply. The afternoon had progressed, and now at the end of the day, seven of the available thirty-five paintings had been sold.

Ian Coates was close to ecstatic. 'I never expected it. Let's be honest, Matthew, the prices are pretty high, some might say inflated, but we sold seven. I wasn't expecting to sell any today. It seems people are willing to pay these prices for you.'

Matt pulled his body away, taking a stance where he appeared to look along his nose at the speaker. 'Ian, you startle me at times. Your lack of belief in my ability is somewhat disenchanting. The good people of Brisbane are not all beer and skittles. Some of them have taste.' He put his arm around Caro and drew her into his side. 'At least my wife and my dear Knob believe in me, even if the fellow who gets the ten per cent doesn't.'

Ian protested and Matthew held up his hand to silence him. 'Now we must depart. It's been a grand day after all.'

Ian was ready to agree. 'Yes, it has, though some of the ladies were shocked at *John the Baptist*, you know.'

Knobby smiled ruefully. 'I'll tell you something, Ian. I've noticed the ones who're the most shocked are those who come and fawn over him afterwards.'

'Women are inscrutable,' stated Matt, picking up his cane and slapping Caro gently with it on her behind.

'Give up, Matt,' she snapped without turning round.

When they were all outside and Knobby had locked the doors and Ian had departed, Matt turned to Caro. 'What do you want to do? I'd like a drink.'

Caro rolled her eyes. 'That's a surprise.'

Matthew disregarded this. 'There's the Race Horse Hotel down on the next corner. It's got a decent lounge, hasn't it, Knob?'

Knobby shrugged. 'Don't know, Matt . . . never been in the lounge. How about we walk a bit further to the National Hotel? We know they've got a nice ladies' lounge in there.'

So that's where they went and at seven o'clock after Caro had drunk two gin slings, she turned on the velvet seat to her husband at her side. 'Think I'll go home, Matt.'

'What? I thought you were going to have dinner with me. Make a night of it. Have a few laughs. The kids are away.'

She met his eyes. 'Matt, you've had a most successful day for which I'm happy, and you're enjoying yourself with your best friend, Knobby. Certain things happened today which don't make me the best company for a night of laughs. You know exactly what I mean.' She glanced across at Knobby. 'And I suspect Knobby does too. So I think it's best if you two go on. Eat somewhere and have a good night. I'll catch the tram home and see you there later. I'd really like to wash my hair, soak in the bathtub and just get an early night. It'll be heaven for me just to pamper myself without the kids.' She turned to her husband. 'You know why I continue to be upset, Matt. I need some time alone.'

He leant back against the cushion and, giving her an inscrutable look, shook his index finger at her. 'Promise to be more agreeable tomorrow?'

In frustration she closed her eyes. 'You're impossible, but I suppose so.'

He gave her a crooked smile. 'That's it, old girl. Then we'll see you on to the tram, won't we, Knobby, old son?'

'Of course we will.'

When they stood in the bright lights of Queen Street waiting for the tram, Caro asked, 'Where do you think you two'll have dinner?'

Matthew looked questioningly at his friend and Knobby said, 'Why not here at the National? We like their lamb and old Baines in the dining room is always so pleased to see you, Matthew.'

Matthew smiled assent. 'We might even go down to the Colosseum later for old times. See who's fighting tonight.'

As the tram drew up he pulled Caro's coat more tightly around her and gave her a quick kiss. 'It's getting cold. Sit in the closed-in section of the tram. We won't be late.'

As Caro ascended the vehicle she looked round at her husband. 'You and I have always had a different opinion of what constitutes late, Matt. See you at home.'

When the tram had rattled away the two men waited for a motor car to chug by before they crossed to the footpath. These vehicles were a novelty in Brisbane streets and Knobby pointed to it.

Suddenly Matthew spoke. 'Oh damn it, Knob. We'll have to go down to the Chevron Club! Meant to call in there this morning before the exhibition. Old Lewis was leaving papers there for me to pick up and read tomorrow. There's a board meeting of Lewis and Craken on Monday morning.'

Knobby had no objections. 'No trouble, we'll catch a tram going the other way. Be there in no time. And anyway, it's a good discipline for you, being on the board. I don't know why you accepted it but I think if the truth came out, you actually enjoy it.'

Matthew said nothing, slapping his friend on the arm as they turned round and went back into the street.

On the tram weaving towards the Valley behind them Caro sat thinking. When the vehicle stopped on the corner of Brunswick Street she made a quick decision and got out, crossed the road, and entered an arcade where there was a small bar and restaurant called Ramsay's, the only place hereabouts where a meal was served other than in the hotels.

She sat down and ordered. An hour later she rose, went out into the street and caught a tram returning to Queen Street and the city.

When she descended from the vehicle near Victoria Bridge and walked down George Street towards the Botanical Gardens it was just after nine o'clock.

She stood under a gaslamp and took a long deep breath, then hurried across the road to the Bellevue Hotel, pushed open the patterned glass doors and entered.

A few people were in the foyer and she moved across to the desk.

'In which room is the party for Lieutenant Colonel Fleet?' She was sure her voice was shaky but the clerk took no notice. 'The Victoria Room, on the next floor, madam.' He pointed. 'Take the stairs.'

As Caro crossed to the stairs, above her head, John Conrad and Emma Louise glided to their last steps in 'The Pride Of Erin'. The diamonds sparkled on her hand resting on his arm and she was laughing spiritedly. 'It's just a wonderful party, and everyone looks so lovely.'

'Not as lovely as you,' he said, kissing her nose as he steered her over to her seat near Gertrude. As she sat down he said, 'I'll bring you a drink, darling. What do you want?'

'A small glass of wine like Aunt Gertrude's drinking.'

Gertrude was in deep conversation with Aunt Leigh. They had taken a liking to each other and the Englishwoman was presently explaining the advantages of having servants in India.

As soon as John Conrad left Emma Louise the band started up again and suddenly in front of her stood David. He held out his hand and gave her a charming smile. 'May I have this dance, m'lady?'

She hesitated briefly, looked around, and rose to enter his arms. Around the floor they swirled and when her fiancé returned with the glass of wine he noted good-naturedly that she danced with his youngest brother.

As he turned away to put down the glass of wine he was stopped by Clarence Wiggers, an old friend of his father. 'John Conrad,' he said, 'I saw the strangest thing today.'

John Conrad looked interested, 'What was that?'

'You.'

'What do you mean?'

'Well, it was your head, on a plate.'

'Clarence, I don't know what in heaven's name you're talking about.'

'It was an art exhibit. The latest one by Matthew Craken, your old enemy.'

John Conrad's brows drew together. 'Oh?'

'It's a biblical scene. John the Baptist. His head . . . on a plate. It was a surprise to me, but I can tell you the Baptist's head has your face upon it.'

'And where's this exhibition?'

'In the Dorrit Rooms, in Adelaide Street. My wife, Mary's a one for art so she dragged me in there this afternoon. She wanted to buy a work as well, but I put my foot down there.'

John Conrad had heard enough and moved on by with the words, 'Well, nothing that Craken does really interests me, Clarence. Excuse me, would you?'

Bart leaned up against one of the long windows that opened out on to the verandah; they were closed tonight against the chill breeze. He watched his older brother in conversation with Clarence Wiggers and then his eyes shifted to another part of the room where his younger brother danced with Emma Louise. He attended the dancers closely, biting the side of his lip in thought.

The two people he watched swung round the floor between the other dancers. David held the girl tightly and she edged slightly out of the closeness of his embrace.

'What's wrong?' he asked.

He looked quite wonderful tonight in his best blue suit, and the satin bow at his throat shone in the electric light. Her eyes were on the cleft in his chin as she answered. 'You shouldn't hold me so closely. People might notice.'

'So? I'd hold you a lot closer than this if I could.'

'David, shhh.'

He looked into her eyes. 'You know I'm mad about you. This is all wrong. It's me you should be engaged to, not him.'

'That's a very disloyal thing to say.'

He laughed and pulled her a touch closer. 'Why should I be loyal to anybody when you light a fire in my insides?'

A hot flush rose to her cheeks and she looked away.

'Come on, Em. You like me, I know you do.'

'Stop it or I'll leave the dance floor.'

'All right, all right. I'll stop. But only if you promise me you'll dance with me later again?'

She met his gaze and indecision flickered in her expression. He squeezed her and she answered, 'I might.'

When the dance came to an end Emma Louise beckoned Sophie over and the two women left the room to go to the ladies' room, which was along the hall. As they came out into the corridor a woman standing down at the end reacted to them, turned and hurried away.

Emma Louise's expression was puzzled. 'Now who's that? She looked familiar to me. I'm sure I know her from somewhere.'

'Who?' asked Sophie. 'I didn't see anyone.'

'The woman who went round the corner.'

Caro hurried along the corridor. She saw a glass door in front of her and opened it to find herself on a verandah. A cold wind blew and she shivered. When she looked to left and right she realised she was outside the room where John Conrad's party was taking place. With wide eyes she moved in to peer through the windows at the festivity inside. The first person she saw was the man she loved. He was facing her and talking to someone she then recognised as Bartholomew.

An hour later the wind had risen and there was a fine rain falling on Caro where she remained standing rigid with fascination, watching through the glass to where the lights were warm, people were happy, merriment abounded and the man she loved was with a girl called Emma Louise Blackstone. She was so cold her hands were numb, but her eyes were riveted

to John Conrad Fleet. She imagined being the girl in his arms
as he swirled the one with the radiant hair around the floor.
She remembered the night he had come to her after Hargy's
death, his desperate need for her and the warmth of him. She
was suffocating with sorrow, with the lingering dream of all
that could have been. And as if all the moisture in her body
were tears, she gave up little sobs of misery into the black
wet night.

Caro was oblivious to the tableau of repetition taking place:
ten years before, when John Conrad had stood sentinel in the
street during her wedding breakfast she had been unaware, and
so too on this night, John Conrad was ignorant of Caro's staring
in at his betrothal party.

She came to her senses when she realised the trickle down
her cheeks was rain and not tears. She forced herself to move
across the verandah and inside the hotel where the warmth of
the interior hit her like a physical thing. She moved along to
the ladies' room and inside she tidied her hair, brushed the rain
from her clothes, wiped the water from her face and dabbed
powder on her nose. When she descended the stairs into the
main foyer and crossed to the door she was thankful that it
had stopped raining. She looked through the glass door and
saw two hansom cabs waiting at the kerb.

Matt put down his serviette and peered though the window of
the Chevron Club. 'Well, Knob, my dear, as we've finished
dining and it seems to have stopped raining, why don't we
climb aboard a cab and go down to the Colosseum for a few
fights before wending our way home?'

'Suits me, Matt.'

They paid the bill and left the club.

'There'll be a cabriolet round at the Bellevue Hotel for
sure,' Knobby said as they issued on to the verandah of
the club.

'We should try to be home by twelve,' Matt stated as they
headed towards the Bellevue. 'Sort of promised Caro to be
early, after all.'

Knobby was a bit the worse for wear, and he began to giggle.
'Definite, must keep our promise. Caro's a good kid.'

They were fifty yards from the front door of the hotel when

Knobby stopped walking and pointed. 'Hey Matt, that looks like her.'

His companion halted beside him. 'That *is* her. What in Hades goes on here, Knob, old son?'

They stood watching as Caro crossed the footpath to where the two hansom cab drivers lounged on a seat, smoking and waiting for a fare. She spoke to one, who nodded, stood up and helped her into the first vehicle at the kerbside. He cracked his whip and drove away.

Matthew turned to his friend, 'Knobby, my dear, I fear this is serious. Come.'

As the cabriolet drove off into the night Matthew approached the remaining driver. 'Halloa, friend. Did you hear where the lady asked to be taken. Was it New Farm?'

The driver looked surprised. 'Why yes, matey, that it was.'

Matt's smile was cold. 'So she now goes home, close to four hours later than she led us to believe. What goes on here, Knobby?'

Knobby, who was fast sobering up, shrugged his shoulders.

Matthew moved towards the door of the hotel and as he reached it Knobby spoke. 'Perhaps we should leave it, Matt. Forget it and go home.'

Matthew glanced back across his shoulder. 'That doesn't sound at all like the way I approach matters, old son. Let's go inside.'

In the foyer all was peaceful. Matthew looked round. He could see through to a lounge where a few people sat drinking. Music came from above and he noted the staircase and the front desk to the right of it. As he began to move over to speak to the clerk he halted, for his eye had caught a notice board. Framed in silver it announced:

Mezzanine Floor: Albert Room: 8 p.m. Annual Dinner
County Ladies' Association with Lecture by Dr Donald
Briggs: Life in the Tundra Wastes
Mezzanine Floor: 8 p.m. Victoria Room: Dinner Betrothal
Dance:
Lieut Colonel Fleet & Miss Emma Louise Blackstone.

Matthew stood motionless, staring at the board. Automatically he tapped with his polished gunmetal cane upon his boot. 'Ah!' he exclaimed, turning round to Knobby. 'We've found the object of *my wife's* interest. The enemy's engagement party.' He gave a sinister smile. 'Perhaps we should go up and become acquainted with Fleet's fiancée.'

Knobby spoke quietly. 'I don't think so.'

Matthew was less discreet. His reply was audible to anyone in the vicinity. 'Why not, old son? She might appeal to me. Wouldn't be the first female Fleet had eyes for that I was partial to!'

Knobby shook his head. 'No, Matt. Let's leave it. We don't know what's gone on. Nothing probably. All you know is that Caro was here. That's all.'

'All? All? That's more than enough, Knob, old son. She told us she was going home and she came here. Lied to us, Knob, straight-faced and cool and cute as could be. Why? To see him, that's why. You're right I don't know what's gone on.'

'Matt, you've had a fair bit to drink. Hell, it's obvious the party's still going on. Listen.' He pointed upwards to the sound of the music. 'She probably just came in to see where it was. No harm's done.'

'No harm done? Is that what you think?' There was fury in Matthew's black eyes and he shook his cane restlessly on the side of his leg.

Knobby took his friend's arm, his tone conciliatory. 'Matt. Sure, we can go upstairs and create a fracas. Spoil the man's party and upset his family and friends. We've done such before in our time and I'll follow you and not let you down if this is what's really in your mind tonight. But I tell you as your oldest friend, my heart's not in it. What do we achieve by that? More notoriety for Matthew Craken? And what if the police are called? Not that you'd care, but I would, and your mother would and your wife and children would.'

Matthew lifted his cane and moved out of Knobby's grasp. 'No, Knob, old son, let's tell the truth. My wife would *not* care, so leave her out of your discourse.'

Knobby gave an extended sigh. 'I've known you a long time. You can be bloody heartless, but, damn it, no matter how you protest I know you care more about Caro than anyone.' He paused. 'Matthew, I'm sorry about all this, but breaking in on Fleet's bloody party won't solve a thing. Better you have it out with Caro, ask her what happened. She's the one who knows. You're hurt and you're not thinking clearly. Anyway, I've said my piece now and I'll do whatever you want. But I'd much rather go home and have a nightcap with you . . . smoke a cheroot and go to bed. I'm getting too old for bloody skirmishes.'

Matthew ground his teeth together. 'Pretty speech, Knobby, my dear, even plausible. Much of what you say has validity, but two things I must clarify. One: I *am not* hurt. There isn't a woman born who can do that, Caro or no bloody Caro.'

Knobby locked eyes with Matthew. 'All right, Matt. Have it your way.'

'And two: I will *never* ask her about tonight. Blast her. I'll not demean myself. I'll bide my time until I'm ready. And I want you to promise me you'll not mention it either.'

Knobby closed his eyes and nodded. 'Of course.' He took a step towards the door. 'Matt, please? Can we go?'

They had gained the attention of the night clerk, who watched with concern from behind the desk.

The crystal chandelier above their heads radiated points of light on to Matthew's cane as he lifted it high in the air, twirled it and smiled broadly in the manner of one whose cares have faded completely from his consciousness. 'Yes, my dear, you're right, a nightcap and a cheroot. Brilliant idea, Knob. Let's away.' And if it is possible to swagger with a cane and a limp, Matthew Craken glanced smugly round the foyer and swaggered out the door.

On Monday morning at ten Bartholomew checked the Dorrit Rooms and verified that neither Matthew nor Caro were on the premises. He returned to John Conrad, who waited outside and they went in together. There were only two men in sight and John Conrad stood a few minutes in front of the painting of John the Baptist. There was no doubt what Clarence Wiggers had said was true.

He also decided Salome looked like Caro, but this was not truly clear. She was hidden by the veils.

Then as he and his brother gave a quick glance over the remainder of the paintings he halted in front of the nude Diana with her followers. There was no doubt this was Caro's body. The muscles of his jaw tightened as he looked at the little mole on the undulation of her breast. He stood silently scanning it and he hated the fact that he recognised the talent of the artist. It reminded him of Goya nudes he had seen in Europe, though it was more modern. The date scrawled in large red numbers in the right-hand corner jumped into his eyeline and a small pulse in his temple accelerated. 'May 1898'. He loosened his tie. The disclosure agitated him even after all these years. John Conrad had not taken her out until the middle of June and here she was nude, with Craken painting her a month before.

He remembered how he had felt seeing her again at Roma Street Station. The sad encompassing nostalgia that had filled him when he touched her; the painful joy of it. His hand came up to his temple; his head ached slightly. He was disgusted with himself. Turning to Bart, who stood behind him, he declared, 'I've seen enough,' and he spun on his heel and made for the door.

As they left the building he spoke again to his brother, though his eyes were looking straight ahead. 'Caro Dere is the right wife for Craken. She's no better than a whore.'

They said no more about the exhibition and that afternoon at three John Conrad and Bart witnessed the marriage of Lena to Bluey. His wedding present to them was a second horse for Bluey and a China tea service for Lena; she cried when she opened the parcel. There was a great celebration back at the small house in Spring Hill and half a dozen of Bluey's mates turned up to join in the festivity. At seven o'clock John Conrad said goodbye and Lena cried again and the children all hugged him and called him Uncle. He promised to come back and see them when he came home to be married himself.

As the two brothers descended the rickety steps of the house Dave's voice stopped them. 'Uncle John Conrad?'

'Yes, Dave?'

The boy came down to them. 'I wanted to tell you. I'm going to be a soldier just like you when I grow up. I'll fight with you against the enemy, I will.'

John Conrad put his arm around the child. 'We'll see, Dave. We don't really have an enemy at the moment, but one thing I know. You'll make a fine man whatever you do.'

'But I want to be a soldier.'

His uncle ruffled his black hair affectionately. 'All right,' he laughed. 'But for now, you go to Miss Howard and be conscientious and learn as much as you can.'

As they left the boy on the steps and waved to his small figure back-lit by the wan light from the little house, John Conrad smiled. 'He's a great little kid; has Hargy's eyes and personality, that's for certain.'

The following day the betrothed couple spent together and that night they had an intimate dinner at Brewery House with their close families.

At almost midnight, when everyone had gone to bed except for John Conrad and Emma Louise, they sat talking in the firelight in the front parlour.

The grandfather clock in the hall chimed the hour and Emma, whose head lay on John Conrad's shoulder, turned in to him and brought his face round to where her lips touched his. For a few seconds he seemed almost to resist but then his head moved firmly down to hers and his kiss was long and passionate. When they separated it was only for a few brief moments and then his mouth hovered over hers again and he pulled her closer to feel her body through her silken dress as he kissed her once more. His fingers found the top of her bodice and his hand slipped down inside to knead the warmth of her smooth skin and the pert nipples of her breasts.

The girl was trembling with emotion. 'That feels so good,' she whispered.

Emma Louise's wet tongue caressed his ear lobe. 'You're going away for so long. I don't know how long. Love me . . . properly, give me something to remember before you go.'

His fingers stiffened on her skin and he pulled back from her. He removed his hand from inside her dress. 'No, darling. No. I . . .' He kissed the tip of her nose. 'We must wait.'

Emma Louise felt hot ripples of frustration. She knew what love was about. Hadn't she slipped out at night in Madras and met Hector Flynn under the great frangipani trees near the walls that led to the river? She knew about love, she knew she liked it and she knew she wanted her fiancé to hold her and to do things to her the same way Hector had. But every time she tried to tempt him, he resisted.

339

'I need you,' she whispered in her direct manner, 'I need to remember you close to me . . . with me *properly*.'

Tiny beads of perspiration were forming on John Conrad's temples and a hundred demons chewed at his insides. The last time he had loved a girl this way and then left her to go back to the army all hell had descended into his life. It was not that he didn't want to, he desperately did . . .

John Conrad turned away from his betrothed and rested his elbows on his knees, chin in his hands. The flickering firelight washed his fair hair in burnished gold as he took an extended breath. 'Let me try to explain. You're lovely . . . beautiful . . . and I want you, make no mistake about that. But it's not right. I'm leaving you tomorrow for a long time and it wouldn't be fair if we took this further tonight. There was a girl in my life; here in Brisbane once before. I thought I was going to marry her, and I made love to her before I went away, back to the army. Once I was gone, she married another man . . . Matthew Craken, an enemy of mine. It wasn't a good time in my life. I just don't want to spoil . . . us . . . what we have. The possibility of history repeating itself. You're too important to me. Let's just say I'm superstitious.'

He turned round to her on the seat, took up her hands in his and kissed her fingertips. 'I will love you one day, and how I'll love you, but at the right time, believe me. Say you understand.'

Emma Louise did not understand, but she nodded her head all the same. 'What was her name?' she asked.

'Caro Dere.'

'Where is she now?'

'Still here . . . I think.'

'Did you love her very much?'

He let go her fingers and paused a few seconds while he patted the back of her hand. 'At the time.'

'As much as me?'

He kissed her forehead. 'There's no comparison. That was then and you are now.' He stood and put out his hand to her. 'Come. It's late.'

She peered up at him from under half-closed lids. 'I know about her. Some of the ladies at my birthday party told me . . . about you and her . . . and Matthew Craken.'

He recalled what he had overheard that night. 'Yes, well, you don't need to worry about it.'

'What would you do if I marry someone else?'

She was amazed to see his blue eyes cool and harden. He withdrew his proffered hand and his tone became callous. 'I'd shoot you.'

Adrenaline pumped fear though Emma Louise and her heart began to race. She felt frightened of him and her eyes opened wide with shock. And then he gave a broad smile and laughed out loud. The girl was totally confused, she did not know what to think.

He bent down to her and helped her to her feet. 'No, you're too lovely to die. I'd shoot *him*.'

Emma Louise said no more; for once she was not outspoken and straightforward.

As they reached the hallway, the front door opened and David came in. Slightly drunk, he eyed the engaged couple. He had gone out immediately after dinner and had been drinking brandy over at a friend's house.

John Conrad smiled a welcome to him but he did not reply in kind.

'I'm off to bed then,' Emma Louise spoke as she put her foot on the stair.

'Yes, darling. Good night.'

The eyes of both men followed the swirling movement of the pale blue skirt up the staircase.

'So,' John Conrad asked turning round to his brother, 'did you have a good night with your friends?'

The young man nodded.

'Do you want a nightcap with me?'

'No thanks, had enough. I'll turn in.' And he crossed to the bottom of the staircase.

'David?'

The young man halted and glanced back.

'I'm uncertain when I'll return here. But it's been marvellous to be home . . . with the family. Bart says you're learning the brewery business well. Do you like it?'

'It's all right. Better than university was. If you'll excuse me, I'm tired.'

'Are you coming to see me off at the ship tomorrow?'

341

'Yes, probably. I think so. Good night.' David spoke over his shoulder as he ascended the stairs.

John Conrad had expected no more. It was ever thus with his youngest brother. Over the many weeks of his homecoming he had attempted conversation, but the boy would never extend himself. John Conrad had suggested outings but David always had an excuse. The young man thwarted every attempt at any real communication. John Conrad shook his head as he crossed back into the parlour to put out the fire.

At the top of the staircase David hurried along the hall. He paused silently outside Emma Louise's door as if waiting for something. When he heard John Conrad mounting the stairs he moved quickly on down to his own room, his expression hostile.

It was bloody well wrong for Emma Louise to be engaged to John Conrad. He was too old for her and just a good-looking fop, a fool. His conversation was all of soldering and armies, the South African war, and India. He was a bloody know-all and high and mighty with it. What did she possibly see in him? He might be a stinking officer and a high-ranking one at that, but if all Kitchener's soldiers were like this one, God help Australia and the Empire.

Behind him, the brother he could not have misjudged more entered his own room, mystified at his youngest sibling's rejection of him.

Caro pulled Harry along the wooden planking past the warehouses. 'Come quickly.'

She could see the crowds of people on the dock as she passed the openings between the buildings, and the noises of the departing ship and the sounds of the goodbyes echoed along Hamilton Reach.

She came to the wooden steps she searched for. 'Up here, darling, come.'

'What for?'

'We're seeing a big ship depart for faraway places. It's a nice thing to do. Just the two of us. We've never watched a ship leave before.'

The steps ran up the side of one of the large warehouses that fronted on to the wharves. At the top she halted briefly,

342

breathing heavily. She again pulled her son swiftly along the wooden platform and around the corner to where she could see in the distance the SS *Boadicea*'s main deck at eye level as it edged away from Hamilton wharf out into the Brisbane River. A cool breeze blew clouds upriver to hide the fearless Queensland sun and to lower the temperatures.

'I'm cold,' Harry complained.

'But look! The big ship is leaving.' She bent down to him. 'Don't you like it? Doesn't it look grand?'

Harry showed marginal interest. It was a very big ship and lots of noise and excitement came from the wharf below. He supposed it was fun. 'I think I do,' he responded.

'Now why don't we play a game, just the two of us?'

'What is it?' Harry asked, looking up at his mother.

'Let's pretend Daddy is on this big ship that's leaving and we're seeing him off.'

'All right.'

'Now come on, we'll wave.'

The SS *Boadicea*'s horns blasted and Harry jumped and laughed in surprise.

Caro laughed too. 'That's it. Come on, wave . . . Daddy's leaving.' Caro lifted her hand high and Harry followed suit.

'Goodbye, Daddy,' Caro called as the ship rounded away from the dock.

'Goodbye, Daddy,' Harry shouted beside her, joining the spirit of the game.

Caro's eyes searched each deck in vain, her heart raced as the ship veered away, swinging out into the middle of the river . . . and then she saw him.

John Conrad stood looking down to the receding wharf where Emma Louise and his family waved up at him amongst the multitude and din of those watching the departure.

He blew a kiss to Emma Louise, who did the same in return, and then she blended into the mass of people milling and shouting, calling and hooting. He waved again and as the ship turned out into the river, his eyes lifted across the warehouses at the back of the dock. He started. A woman and a child waved from a platform. He recognised Caro and her son. They were shouting something.

The ship was turning swiftly out into the channel, bringing

its huge bulk around; Caro would be gone from view in a few seconds. He could not help himself. Though later all of him raged against it and he reviled himself for it, he lifted his hand and waved back to Caro. In another moment she and her son were lost from sight.

But Caro had seen the acknowledgement and in the second John Conrad disappeared from view her spirit lifted into glory as her eyes filled with tears and her heart beat wildly in her chest.

He had waved to them, she knew he had! God in heaven, he had waved . . .

In the din rising from the wharves her laugh rose stridently, uncontrollably and she shouted wild-eyed, while her son, innocent of his mother's charade, and infected by the hysteria of the game, laughed and shouted in unison.

Chapter Twenty-three

Twenty months later: 22 December 1909

'They're in Port Darwin!' Aunt Leigh let out a hoot of delight. She came running out of the kitchen on to the verandah, waving the *Courier* high in the air. 'He's home! He's home!'

Barrington, who stood by as brewery labourers lifted casks of ale on to a dray, turned at the shouts, and Bart, with one foot raised on a crate and marking entries into his logbook, halted and called back, 'What's that, Aunt Leigh?'

Barrington listened holding his hand to his ear.

'Our boy and Kitchener of Khartoum are in Darwin!' She came hurrying down the stairs and over to them. 'Here in the *Courier*.' She pointed. 'It says they'll be in Brisbane on New Year's Day.'

Barrington took the newspaper and scanned the article. He smiled widely. 'Aye, they're here all right. It's a tour of Australia by Lord Kitchener to examine our defence forces, after the end of his Indian service and his trip to Japan. Listen to this. "Lord Kitchener said before embarking on HMS *Encounter* in Port Darwin that it is a challenge to examine the defences of such a huge country with its almost three million square miles and yet its small population of just over four million souls of whom only one million two hundred are males of fighting age." And down here it says "He is accompanied by two of his personal aides, Queensland-born, Lieutenant Colonel John Conrad Fleet, and Colonel Oswald Fitzgerald." He beamed with pride as he handed the paper on to Bart.

Aunt Leigh voiced her thoughts. 'I wonder if Emma Louise knows. But how could she? She wouldn't have seen the *Courier* yet, it's not delivered in Southport until the late afternoon.' She sighed. '"Journeys end in lovers meeting, Every wise man's son doth know." Shakespeare.'

David's voice cut across the yard from the brewery office door. 'What's all the fuss about?'

'John Conrad's in Port Darwin,' Bart responded, regarding his young brother speculatively.

'Oh,' David replied, and turned back into the brewery office. Inside he sat down and put his head in his hands. Everybody was always so thrilled to hear news of bloody John Conrad. Aunt Leigh insisted on reading out his letters and acted like it was the second coming whenever the man arrived home.

He blew air from his mouth in a belligerent sound of anger and disgust. And Em – well, she belonged to him now, not to John Conrad, the poor bastard. His *big brother* would soon know. They had gone too far now, no turning back. Em was his . . . in every sense of the word.

He stood and went back to the door. The others were still discussing the impending arrival and he called, 'When does it say he'll be here?'

Aunt Leigh had the newspaper back in her hands and it was she who answered, her voice continuing shrill. 'We don't know, but it says that Lord Kitchener begins his tour here in Brisbane on the first of January. He'll spend Christmas on Thursday Island, it seems.' She glanced to Barrington. 'I wonder if John Conrad will come home to stay with us?'

'Oh, don't put your hopes on that, my dear, he's on duty, you know.'

But as if Aunt Leigh's query had been transmitted straight to the heavens there was the sound of a voice calling from the front gate down past the stables. 'Hallo there, is this where Mr Barrington Fleet lives?'

Bart spun round. 'Indeed it is.'

'Telegram for him then.' And the boy came in the gate as Bart strode forward and took it. He opened it while the others clustered around him, even the labourers, who had ceased work and now joined the family excitement.

Bart looked up and caught David's eye before he read, 'Arrive Brisbane 1 January. Must attend official functions but have permission to remain Qld for rest of month. It's signed, John Conrad.'

Barrington let out a hoot of delight and, lifting his walking stick, spun round to Aunt Leigh. 'What do you think of that? Home for a month . . . happy day.'

There was general speculation and chatter in the brewery yard and the only one to remain aloof was David, who left immediately after Bart's reading of the telegram and took refuge in his office once more.

Half an hour later he had done little work. He toyed with the pen in front of him as the door opened and he lifted his eyes to see his brother enter and close the door behind him. David leant back in his chair, but did not speak.

'I want to talk to you,' Bart began.

David stood up. 'I'm busy.'

Bart moved across in front of him barring his way. 'No. This time we talk.'

David gave a frustrated sound but he retreated a step. 'What do you want?'

'Look, I know you go to Southport a lot and I know why.'

The younger man looked contemptuously at his brother. 'Been spying, eh?'

'No. I didn't have to. I was aware from the beginning that you coveted Emma Louise. It was obvious to me right from the night of the engagement party, but I thought you might get some sense when she returned to Southport and only came up here to visit us occasionally. But no. You began disappearing most weekends. Off with your mates, you said, and for a long time I tried to believe just that, but, David, the fact is that you've been seen by my friends three times with her in Southport. Kenny Neverson saw you a couple of times early in the year and then Bill Matterson and his wife saw you in September. I said you were just visiting her, being her fiancé's brother, but Bill said it was a funny way for a fiancé's brother to act . . . on the beach at dusk, kissing her quite passionately.'

David still said nothing. He remained eyeing his brother belligerently.

Bart went on, 'I've let the months pass because frankly I didn't really know what to do. I supposed I hoped it would fade and die. But it hasn't and now things'll come to a head, David. As we all know, Emma Louise and her aunt arrive here on Friday to spend Christmas with us and no doubt with John

Conrad's appearance here shortly after that Emma will remain. Aunt Leigh and Father have no idea of what's going on, and I'm assuming that Emma's aunt doesn't know either.' He hesitated. 'Last time I saw Emma I asked her if she were writing to John Conrad and she looked at me in surprise and said, "Of course I am, why wouldn't I be, he's my fiancé."' He halted, looking in expectation at his young brother but David said nothing.

Bart inhaled in a whistle between his teeth. 'I thought that bloody odd as I know damn well what she's doing with you. I only hope you both haven't gone too far. John Conrad'll be home in exactly nine days. What the devil's going to happen?'

The younger man turned his back on his brother and moved across to a window where he stood looking out into the yard. It was a brilliant summer day with pristine blue skies and glaring sunlight, and he closed his eyes momentarily against the brightness.

'Well?' Bart asked behind him.

He spoke without turning round. 'We're going to tell him. Anyway, she's too young for him and she's the right age for me.'

'Where's your loyalty? What've you been thinking of all this time? I'm furious with myself for not making an issue of it before. I feel I've let John Conrad down.'

'Oh for God's sake!' David spun round upon his brother. 'You make me sick. You all make me sick. It's as if he's God or something! He's just a bloody soldier, a killer.' His eyes bulged and his smooth face contorted as the blood rushed to his head. 'Bugger it, why should I be loyal him? What's he to me? I don't even know the man.'

He moved to push by his brother but Bart's arm went out across his chest and stayed him, holding him and restraining him. 'Now you listen to me. You've been spoiled all your life, and I've helped, damn it. Letting you get way with so much because you were the youngest and lost your mother as a tiny child, but I'll not listen to this. John Conrad's a good man, decent and principled, a man to be proud of. Don't you tell me the sort of soldier he is. I was in South Africa and I know. Don't you ever call him *killer* to me again, you bloody young fool. He had to be tough, but he was always fair. He's seen things you've no conception of and he's maintained his dignity and his integrity. And you . . . all you've done is run off with his girl behind his back. You've got no morals and you're a bloody washout!' He threw his arm down and released David, who pressed past him and swept to the door.

As his fingers touched the handle he halted, spitting words back over his shoulder. 'I don't care what you say. You're jealous of me because you've no woman of your own. Bloody John Conrad's nothing to me. I hate him. Em's mine, not his.' And he flung the door open and stormed out into the brewery yard.

That night, as a warm breeze blew and a full moon bestowed its shimmering limpid glow on the gums and acacias of the Southern Queensland landscape, Caro moved across the verandah at Cedar Grove and rested against the railing looking down the avenue of tall cedar trees standing like black sentinels leading to the road.

She breathed in the pure bush air with the hint of eucalyptus floating on the breeze. Her fingers tapped restlessly on the wood beneath her hands and when she moved it was with nervous staccato steps. She had been almost irritable with the children at dinner and now that Jane had taken them to bed she was pleased to be alone at last with the night and the clean air. Her whole consciousness had been on John Conrad Fleet ever since she had read the *Brisbane Courier* this evening. He was coming home . . . would be back in Brisbane on New Year's Day!

Jake Simons dropped the newspaper in each weekday on his way home from the sawmill where he worked. He passed the lonely general store where the Brisbane newspapers arrived at three in the afternoon and he picked one up for the Cedar Grove property. This year Queensland had celebrated fifty years of being separated from New South Wales and there had been so many events that Matt and Knobby wished to read about that they had come to an arrangement to pay Jake half a shilling every month for this favour.

When Caro had seen the piece about Kitchener of Khartoum's arrival in Port Darwin her eyes had skipped and scanned the article until she found the mention of John Conrad. She assumed Matthew had read it too. He was in Brisbane with Knobby – had been for about three weeks. Caro trembled at the thought of Matthew's reading the news of John Conrad's imminent arrival.

She had been married to Matthew for over eleven years and he was as much a stranger to her as ever. She shared his bed and she hated herself for the pleasure he could make her feel. She shuddered thinking how he manipulated her body. Her mouth set defiantly . . . But he could not manipulate her mind. Inside her soul she remained true and constant to the love of her life. Matthew could never reach that, contaminate that. She did not feel guilty for she believed that infidelity came naturally to Matt and that he continued after marriage much the same as he had before. He was never indelicate enough to vaunt his conquests and he had the decency to keep his transgression to Brisbane when she was at Cedar Grove. But the occasional piece of feminine clothing that was not hers which innocent Mrs Manning, the daily helper, had placed in her drawers in the past told Caro all.

It had hurt her pride at first, but as time passed she became immune. Matthew was immoderate and excessive and remained an enigma with his cold calculating mind and his irreverence.

He was imperturbable; only Knobby and Harry ever seemed to be able to raise any strong feeling in him or give him any pleasure. Whenever Caro found herself feeling any kind of care or solicitude towards him she had trouble imparting it to him for she felt sure he would give nothing of himself in return, but remain remote and aloof from her as he did from everyone. So Caro would withdraw her feelings and return to exalting in her hidden love, in the verity and constancy of her attachment to John Conrad Fleet.

Naturally Matthew was an enigma to her parents. They were mystified by him. Her mother used to call him a libertine: but in recent years she had to concede that he seemed to be home more often and his paintings were gathering a following, and that he was, at last, not relying solely on his inheritance from the department store.

She would be seeing Matt tomorrow. She and Jane, Knobby's wife – they had been married last June – were meant to travel down in the train to join the men for a large family gathering at her parents' home on Saturday – Christmas Day – just three days away.

And now she knew John Conrad would be home a week later. If only she could see him . . . Thank God they had decided to have Christmas and New Year in Brisbane and not here on the farm like they had last year. Her mind raced with a hundred mad ideas of how to manage to see the man she loved. He had restored her faith in everything the day he had waved to her as he departed on the SS *Boadicea*. He had given her hope. She was not even sure of what, except that it meant he still cared, that there might be a possibility of some meaningful contact with him. For the past twenty months that single memory had sustained her.

She must think of something . . . she must, somehow, some way, she must see John Conrad.

Matthew exhaled a long tube of smoke, put down his glass of rum and stepped back a few feet to scrutinise the painting on the easel in front of him. He had begun it in plein-air a few weeks ago and had brought it back to the studio to complete. There was not enough light to paint well – electricity had not yet reached this part of Brisbane and the gas light was weak – but he was determined to finish. He had promised Ian Coates to have a batch of his work completed by the first week of January. The man had found him an outlet in Sydney and Melbourne where his paintings were selling well and his reputation grew.

On his studio walls hung works he would not sell, amongst them his *Diana and her Worshippers*. He would have hung Salome and the head as well, only Caro had prevailed in that one. She had wanted to burn it but Matt had railed against that, so ignoring his protests she had wrapped it in newspaper and put it out in the stables. Matt smiled when he thought of it; she was a strong bloody woman was Caro, he had to admit that.

But tonight Matt's face was pale, and his right leg ached. He gave a small groan at the thought of Caro's return tomorrow and as he stepped back in to his work to add another stroke the door opened and Knobby entered.

He halted in surprise. 'Heck, Matt, I thought you'd given up opium,' he said, sniffing the air.

'I had.'

351

'Well, it seems not. I thought you said it wasn't doing you any good. You haven't taken any for six months, why in hell have you slipped back now?'

'I knew it would help me to achieve the images I want.'

'Matt, this is silly. You're no longer a young man; you can't do this to yourself. You drink too much and now you're back on opium. You're into middle age, for heaven's sake. It'll kill you.'

Matt inhaled and turned languid, weary eyes on his friend. 'Knob, old son, don't preach. *Middle age* is a dreary modern reference to the beginning of the years of maturity in perception, judgement, discernment and reason. Please rephrase your prognostications.'

Knobby looked skywards in exasperation. 'Matt. Come on, you promised . . . me and Caro. You said to us you wouldn't smoke opium ever again. You were adamant. What's happened?'

Matthew continued to paint and did not look round. 'Knob, don't depress me. Don't bring up my wife. I don't need a lecture, I need to be indulged. I felt sorry for Won Won the Wonder One, hadn't seen him for ages; all that spare opium over there in Wooloongabba. Now you've been out all day, and if you cannot come home and partake with me in a drink, a smoke and a pleasant hour of reminiscence, then my dear . . . bugger off.'

Knobby knew it was useless to argue. He crossed back to the door. 'I'll see you in the morning, Matt. But heed me, please. Quit the opium, have a glass of water and go to bed.' He exited and closed the door behind him.

In the hall he met Mrs Manning in bonnet and with bag in hand. 'Master Matthew's not taken his supper yet. I don't want to miss the nine thirty tram, so I'm going, Mr Knobby. It's keeping warm on the hob. Good night.'

'Good night, Mrs Manning. See you tomorrow.'

As the good woman plodded down the hall she said, 'Exciting, isn't it, about Kitchener of Khartoum visiting us and all? Fancy him in Brisbane. The Empire's hero.'

'What's that?' Knobby asked.

Mrs Manning turned back smiling. 'Haven't you seen today's newspapers?'

Knobby shook his head.

'Oh, there's one out there in the scullery. Kitchener's coming to Brisbane on New Year's Day. The *Courier* and the *Telegraph* are full of it.' And she turned to the front door.

Knobby stood unmoving for a moment while the implication of Mrs Manning's words sank in. He hurried to the scullery where he found and read the newspaper. When he had finished the story he folded the paper and placed it back on the cabinet. He sighed and spoke aloud. 'Well, Matt, you're a bloody good actor, but now I know why you're back on the opium.'

He returned to the studio where Matt remained in front of his painting, dabbing colour upon the figures of bush wood-cutters he was creating.

Knobby moved in to his side. 'Listen, Matt. I've read the *Courier* now, so you're not fooling me. The one thing I didn't realise, and which amazes me, is that you fear the return of Fleet so bloody much that it's influenced you to begin using opium again.'

Matthew paused, his hand in midair. He did not speak but stepped away from the canvas, carefully placed his brush and pallet on a shelf nearby and wiped his cheek with his fingers in a gesture which appeared almost as if he must remind himself of the scar upon his cheek. Then he took one long deep inhalation and puffed upon his pipe before he turned it upside down in a flourish and tapped it on the shelf, emptying its contents on to the floor. He used the foot of his bad leg to stand on the ashes. He cleared his throat, picked up his ebony and silver cane, and limped to the door where he hesitated and half turned his body towards Knobby, yet did not make eye contact. Both men stood without speaking as the seconds dripped by.

Finally Matthew spoke, his tone clipped and businesslike. 'Knobby, my dear, I know you've my best interests at heart. That you're possibly my only true friend. At least you've been my bloody constant companion for the better part of two decades and even I've noticed that. Tonight you're here with me while our wives are up-country. I realise I'm hardly the easiest of companions but you never seem to care. Very rarely have I ever thanked you. Now I come to think of it, I'm bloody sure I never have. Well, Knob, tonight I'm thanking you.' He faced completely round and at last met his friend's eyes. His voice softened slightly. 'I'm not sure I could do without you, old son.' Then he winked. 'But don't expect this to become a habit.' In one move he pivoted on his good heel, pushed open the door with his stick and called, 'I'm off to have my dinner now, Knob. Why don't you join me in a glass of wine? Oh, by the way, if you're looking for that opium to get rid of it, you'll find it in the bottom of the cupboard to the left of the easel, old son.'

Christmas Eve was a glorious Queensland day. The sky was a clear brilliant blue, the flowers and trees glowed with the vivid colours of the southern lands, and even the dull waters of the Brisbane River seemed to sparkle. The spirit of Christmas was abroad in the city and people greeted each other enthusiastically.

Matt and Knobby had gone out early, and Caro, Jane and Mrs Manning spent the morning putting the last touches of decoration on the Christmas tree and wrapping gifts. The children had a marvellous time tying pretty bows and writing on little cards. Lunch was taken on the terrace and when Mrs Manning left early at two o'clock Jane took Harry and Katy out to play in the garden.

Caro picked up a pencil and paper and went through to Matt's studio where a year before a telephone had been installed. She picked up the receiver, held it to her ear and, leaning into the small horn-shaped mouthpiece, wound the lever and spoke to the lady at the central city telephone exchange. 'I would like the phone number for Fleet Breweries in the West End, please?'

'A few moments, please, and I'll switch you through to the telephonist with that information. Is it a new number?'

'No.'

She heard the ringing and the voice that answered gave her the information she required. She replaced the receiver on the hook attached to the side of the brown pedestal-like telephone. She dared not make the telephone call from the house for she knew that when the telephone bill came in it was Knobby who paid it. The listings were all there beside the numbers: who had been called and what date and time.

She went out to Jane and the children, and made an excuse that she must go to town for something she had forgotten, and within half an hour she was passing through the Valley on a tram.

In Queen Street she alighted in front of the post office and once inside she found the long room where public telephone calls could be made. She gave the lady at the front desk the number she wished to be connected to and the party she wished to speak to. She was told: 'Come back here and pay me after you've made the call.' Three minutes later it was her turn and she was taken down a narrow hall and into a cubicle with a single electric light bulb hanging above. Caro picked up the receiver and leaned in to the mouthpiece. 'Hello.'

The telephonist's voice crackled down the line. 'I believe you require Mr Bartholomew Fleet?'

'Yes, that's correct.'

'Wait, please. I'll try the number.'

Caro's heart accelerated.

Some seconds later the telephonist spoke again. 'He's on the line.'

'Oh, er . . . thank you.'

She heard Bart's voice. 'Bart Fleet here.'

'Bart, it's Caro.'

Silence. All she could hear was the crackling of the line. 'Bart, are you there?'

'Yes, Caro, I'm here. You just gave me a surprise, that's all. It's been a long time.'

'I know. And I don't know any other way to say what I have to say other than to come right out with it. So . . . I read in the newspaper a couple of days ago that John Conrad's coming home . . . visiting here with Lord Kitchener. Arriving on January the first.'

'That's right.'

'Bart, I must see him.'

Bart hesitated a moment. 'Caro, with the bad blood between my brother and your husband I don't think that's such a good idea.'

'Bart . . . please.' A tear rolled down her cheek. 'I must . . . I must. I'll go mad if I don't.'

A long sigh quivered down the phone. 'What do you expect me to do?'

Her voice caught in her throat. 'Y-you could arrange it.

Please. I've been thinking.' She sounded breathy and the words tumbled out. 'You know there's a public holiday on Monday the third of January, because of New Year's Day falling on the Saturday? Well, even if John Conrad has official duties all day and night he has to have some time off in the evening, probably around five or six. Are you still there?'

'Yes, Caro, I'm here.'

'Bart, I haven't seen you in years, but we were close once. Acted almost like the same family, you remember?'

'I remember, Caro.'

'Then please, please do this for me. Please bring him to where he used to fish with Hargy. It was down from the brewery about half a mile. It's still deserted. Much the same as it used to be. You remember the single weeping willow there on the bank?'

'Yes.'

'I'll be waiting by it . . . from five in the afternoon until half-past six on Monday the third.'

'Caro, I know this seems important to you but I—'

'Bart, for God's sake, please? It's the most important thing in my life! I'm desperate and there's no one but you to help me.'

The silence hung over the static of the line . . .

She heard him take a long deep breath. 'All right, Caro.'

K, John Conrad and Fitz stood in a row at the bulwark as the ship came to rest at the dockside in the Brisbane River. They were all immaculately attired in their day uniforms, even their leather bandoliers gleaming in the ruthless Queensland summer sun.

'So,' the leader said, glancing to John Conrad, 'this is your home town.'

'It is, and it's nice to be back.'

'A great and magnificent land mass, this Australia. But almost impossible to defend with such a sparse population and twelve thousand two hundred and ten miles of coastline.'

'Is that so?' John Conrad replied. 'I've never been aware of the exact measurement before.' He smiled and caught his leader's eye. 'Trust you to know.'

When they disembarked an hour later, the dock-side was

lined with people and the welcome for the western world's best-known hero became rowdy. People called and shouted, wolf-whistled and waved. The band on the pier struck up 'Land of Hope and Glory' and the Governor and his wife stood at the end of the red carpet waiting.

K, who was not fond of ceremony – even actively attempted to avoid it – looked back to John Conrad as they walked down the covered gangplank to the wharf. 'Let's hurry this through if we can.'

John Conrad nodded. It was not that K did not appreciate the way people reacted to him; he did. When they had left India in September, people in their tens of thousands had walked miles to line the roads to wave him goodbye. This had quite overwhelmed K, and he had been overawed by the wealth of feeling he inspired.

When the formalities were over K made a short speech. John Conrad stood behind him, looking benignly upon the man who had become his mentor and his friend. He was a glamorous figure, tall and prepossessing with his startling eyes now faded to an ice blue by the years of strain in hard sun-drenched lands, and as he came to the end of his speech the people of Brisbane cheered their rousing welcome. John Conrad felt strange. He would soon be leaving K. His pulse accelerated at the thought. He had been with the man for eleven years: a large slice of his life had been spent in K's military formality, his wars and his intrigue. John Conrad was not sure what the devil he would do afterwards: probably transfer to the Australian army or take Emma Louise back to England if he could get a position with one of the regiments there.

He had informed K about his fiancée only after he had been back in India for many months. He remembered the moment well. It was Christmas Eve and they had just taken a drink together alone on the terrace looking out over the Maidan and Calcutta. There was a new moon in the sky and it was a dank heavy humid evening. John Conrad turned to his leader and finally it came out. 'I've something to tell you, K.' And before the older man had an opportunity to reply John Conrad launched forth and related the meeting with Emma Louise on the ship out to Sydney, how she happened to be going to live within fifty miles of his home, how he visited her and how after seven weeks he had asked her to marry him and she had accepted.

When he halted K did not reply. Instead he took a mouthful of his gin and swallowed it. Then he purposefully put his glass down on the edge of the stone wall, and took a seat where he leaned back and eyed his companion. At last he spoke.

'Do you love her as much as you once loved Caro Dere?'

John Conrad was amazed. He had not spoken Caro's name to K since the night all those years before at Wellington monument.

His expression showed how taken aback he was. He hesitated. 'It surprises me you recall her name.'

K nodded. 'I recall many things, Johnny, many things. Now answer me.'

'Now that you ask I . . . am not sure. I think I do. But it's not the same, K, it cannot be. I was young and wilful; I did not think clearly with Caro. I was besotted. With Emma Louise, I find myself happy to be in her company, even enchanted with her, comfortable and looking forward to the future. I feel sure of her and what she means to me.'

K coughed. 'I see. Nevertheless I'd prefer I were losing you to someone whom you loved intensely, whom you were once more absolutely besotted by.'

'Well, perhaps I am. I don't intend to leave you just yet. We don't know exactly what we'll do, come next September and our Indian service ends, do we?'

K shook his grey head. 'No, we don't, but I'm beginning to feel I need a holiday and with your news I'm sure I will. You've become my right hand, you know that.' He looked away. 'I might suggest to the Home Office that I take a tour of the east, Japan perhaps. I'd even mulled over visiting your fair country if they'd like me to.'

'I'm sure they'd jump at the chance.'

There was silence for a time, each man with his own thoughts.

John Conrad broke the silence hesitatingly. 'Perhaps . . . I . . . wouldn't need to leave you. Perhaps whatever we do, Emma Louise could fit into it. Accompany us. I could still aide you, being married shouldn't have to—'

K cut him off. 'Johnny, Johnny. A marriage is a life-time

commitment. And assisting me's a full-time occupation. I know. I'm aware how irascible I am, how much attention I need. How I like to sit and talk late into the night surrounded by my boys. Something a wife would not endure for long. I also know that the men with me will be in the forefront of any war that Great Britain finds herself in. How can I expect one hundred per cent commitment from a married man?'

'But you've got Fitz and the others. I'm only one of a group.'

'And the one I rely upon the most. The one whose attention and opinion I seek first. It wouldn't be fair to your Emma Louise. I would upset her and upset your marriage.' He forced a smile. 'No, Johnny. Marry your girl with my blessing and be happy, but find a good position with one of the settled regiments.' He took a deep breath. 'I'll help you.'

John Conrad forced a smile in return. 'Thank you . . . sir.'

K stood and walked over to where his glass rested. He picked it up and took a mouthful. 'But promise me one thing.'

'Yes, of course I will.'

K's strong brows drew together, and in the lantern light on the terrace, the thick white strands in his hair were noticeable; and there was white in his grand moustache. The early signs of the puffiness of age could be seen under his eyes, though his face remained firm and handsome. John Conrad felt a surge of guilt at the thought of leaving him.

K replaced his glass on the rampart and looked to his companion. 'When I was twenty, between leaving Woolwich in December and taking up my commission in the Royal Engineers and reporting to Chatham in the spring, I decided, with the intemperance of youth, and a young companion called Henry Dawson, to join the French army as a private. We believed we wished to fight the Prussians and gain some experience of war, you understand. My battalion was part of the reserves for General Chanzy's Second Army of the Loire and in a six-day battle near Le Mans I saw my baptism; the massacre of many men and horses. We lost the fight.

'Subsequently I ascended in a balloon wearing no warm clothing and from that caught pneumonia and pleurisy. I was left very ill in less than sanitary conditions, might have died except that my father was in France and he rescued me . . .

took me to England. The whole affair gained me a certain reputation and taught me the necessity of organisation, but had I known the consequences of my impulsive act of joining the French army with sanguine attitude I might have thought twice the day I did. Now why do I tell you this, Johnny? Because the promise I want you to make me, is: to be sure the move you're embarking upon is what you truly want. If you want it, then I want it for you. Just be sure.'

And John Conrad had promised, and the evening had advanced and Christmas had come and gone and the months had passed, until now they found themselves in Brisbane where he would see Emma Louise in a mere handful of hours. The twenty months away from her had made him sure. He would always miss K but he loved Emma Louise, wanted to marry her and settle down.

K and Fitz's trunks were taken to Government House where they were lodging with the Governor, and John Conrad's trunks were delivered to West End and Brewery House.

When the ship docked John Conrad had been given a notice by his batman. It invited him to dinner that night at Government House and informed him that his fiancée and his father had been invited also.

From the ship they transferred to Government House where K and Fitz decided to rest for the few hours prior to their dinner engagement. There were to be drinks at seven on the beautifully presented Government House terrace. The Governor's wife was a true socialite and she had been working for weeks on the table arrangements for the special event.

John Conrad took leave of his leader and his friend, and the Governor's driver motored him across Victoria Bridge to the West End and Brewery House in the Governor's own shining black motor car.

As the vehicle drew up the whole neighbourhood were out in force. They had seen his trunks arrive three hours earlier and had gathered that the arrival of the man himself must be imminent.

'Welcome home, sonny,' called Jake Crane, who had lived across the street all his life.

'Hey, John Conrad, you look spiffy in that uniform!'

'How's Kitchener of Khartoum these days?'

360

The locals gathered around the car, which was almost as much a thing to be admired as John Conrad. He alighted, thanked the driver and returned the greetings.

As the car edged off through the neighbours John Conrad made his way into the Brewery Yard where his family waited. The first person he saw was Emma Louise. He strode to her and clasped her to him. 'How I've missed you.'

She murmured something against his lips as he kissed her, and then he was in Aunt Leigh's arms and Bart's arms and finally his father's.

'My son, my boy, home again to us.'

It was not until they were all inside and the neighbours were crowded upon the wide verandah all jostling each other and talking at once, that John Conrad realised his youngest brother was nowhere to be seen.

'David's not here?'

'He's away in Bundaberg.' It was Bart who replied. 'I've sent him up there for a couple of weeks. We're putting in some new systems come Monday when the men are back after the Christmas break. He's overseeing it.' Bart somehow seemed oddly ill at ease, but as John Conrad's attention was all on Emma Louise he did not concentrate on his brother's behaviour.

It was a fine homecoming and Aunt Leigh's delight was almost tangible. She made tea several times and kept appearing with cakes and biscuits, quoting happily from all manner of poets. John Conrad wished he could get away somewhere alone with Emma Louise but he could see that would not be today; his family wanted him and so did the neighbourhood.

That night the formal dinner was a marvellous success. K watched Emma Louise closely and the girl was at her best: charmingly forthright she captivated the Governor and the other guests. John Conrad was very proud of her, yet he was mildly surprised that she did not catch his waiting eye as often as he would have liked. As they made their goodbyes at eleven o'clock, the Governor took her hand and said, 'Good night, Miss Blackstone. Lieutenant Colonel Fleet must bring you to Government House again.'

K bent over her hand and met her eyes as he straightened. 'Miss Blackstone, I hope you'll allow me to prevail upon you to meet with me on Monday. John Conrad, Major Fitzgerald and I visit barracks and rifle ranges for most of the day, but I'd like you to do me the honour of taking tea with me at five in the afternoon. Would you?'

The girl paused so long that John Conrad prompted her. 'Of course you will, darling, won't you?'

'Yes . . . I . . . yes, of course. Thank you, m'lord.'

'The Governor tells me I can use one of the fine parlours here at Government House. Please present yourself at the main gate as you did tonight.'

When they arrived home Bartholomew and Aunt Leigh rose as one from the seats on the wide verandah where they had awaited the trio. Leigh wanted to know everything, from the colour of the Governor's wife's dress to what they served for dessert. Emma Louise was forthcoming, and they sat round the wicker table on the verandah and the early hours of the morning soon arrived.

When Barrington excused himself – 'It's been a grand night but it's well after my bedtime, I'm off, my dears' – Aunt Leigh stood up as well and to John Conrad's surprise, so did Emma Louise. He had hoped she would remain after the others had gone to bed. He had missed the touch of her and healthy male desires stirred within him. He had made the decision that now he could, and would, marry her, they should wait no longer to consummate their love, just as she had requested him to do, long ago.

Emma Louise bent forward and brushed his forehead with her lips. 'Darling, I'm exhausted. It's been a big emotional day. You must be tired too.' She looked at Bartholomew. 'Perhaps we should *all* retire and take things up in the morning.' But Bart did not move, so she turned and followed Aunt Leigh.

Bart crossed and uncrossed his legs. He looked along the verandah and then back to meet his brother's eyes. 'So it sounds like the dinner went well. Do you have a busy day tomorrow?'

'Yes, we're off to look at the Queensland defence forces – what there are. There'll be plenty of activity, I suppose, until K and Fitz leave Brisbane, then I'll remain home here for January. I'll have to rejoin K at the end of the month because Fitz's going back to England for a short period and he'll need me on the tour of New Zealand. But after that I think I'll be able to come home again.' He grinned.

Bart had hardly heard this reply; he had a lot on his mind; had been thinking of Caro's telephone call and the other more onerous matter he must discuss with his elder brother, so he launched forward into the least distasteful of his tasks. 'If you had the chance to see Caro again, would you?'

John Conrad leaned back and crossed his arms. He remained that way for a few seconds then shook his head. 'No.'

'Are you sure?'

'Yes. I never told you but I ran into her the last time I was home. At Roma Street Station. I have to admit I felt very odd seeing her again. She looked sad . . . and quite lovely. Couldn't help but think about what might have been. It was disturbing, really. But you know, Bart, we can't change things. All water under the bridge. She belongs to Craken, always has, as far as I can judge. I don't hate her any more. I just feel sorry . . . about it all. But to see her again – no, nothing to be accomplished by that. I truly hope to heaven I don't run into her this time.'

'Well, I'd best tell you I've heard from her.'

'You have?'

'Yes, she made a telephone call to me on Christmas Eve, wants to meet you down by the river next Monday. Had read in the newspaper that you were coming home. She said she desperately needs to see you.'

Recollections like winsome longings pursued one another up and down John Conrad's senses until gradually he rejected them and asserted his will. He shrugged. 'There'd be nothing to gain. It'd be opening up a painful past. She's got two little kids, and what is, is. Our lives are divergent now and it's best I don't see her.' He hesitated. 'Could you possibly go in my place and tell her . . . tell her . . . gently?'

Bart shrugged. 'I'd rather not.'

'Please, Bart. I'd hate to think she kept the tryst and neither of us met her.'

His brother weakened. 'I suppose you're right. I'll go.'

John Conrad gave a grateful smile. 'Thanks. Anyway, there's Emma Louise to consider. We need to decide all sorts of things. The date of our marriage is one, because that means I'll have to leave K's service. God, I'll miss him.'

Bartholomew cleared his throat It was an odd, unsettling sound and John Conrad looked uncertainly at him. 'Are you all right?'

Bart found his brother's eyes in the haze of light through the windows of the house. Now he must attack the remaining task of the night. 'No, I'm not.'

'What's wrong?'

'A great deal, I'm afraid.'

John Conrad leant forward and took hold of his brother's knee. 'Oh, I'm sorry, old mate. Can I help you? What is it?'

Bart shook his head. 'It's not me. I'm all right. It's you.'

John Conrad withdrew his hand. 'I'm not following this.'

'I know. It's the worst thing I've ever had to do, but I just have to let you know and without any more delay. It's my duty.'

John Conrad had a very bad feeling. It was rising through him as if it began in the soles of his feet. 'Let me know what?'

'Emma. She didn't want to tell you herself.'

'What the hell are you talking about?'

'Oh damn it, John Conrad. Promise me you'll stay calm.'

'Calm about what? Tell me.'

'Look, it's about Emma and David. You've been away a long time. They're both young, carefree, so much in common. I don't approve, it's bloody awful, but they've been seeing each other virtually since the day you left. That's why I made sure David wasn't here. Emma should be telling you herself but when I tackled her about it, she . . . Well, it seems she's afraid to – something stupid about your going to shoot her or David.'

John Conrad's eyes had frozen. The features of his face stiffened and a tiny throbbing began in his temple. His voice was passionless, which made Bartholomew cold with fear. 'Are you telling me that my brother and my fiancée are lovers?'

He gave a single nod of his head. 'I'm sorry . . . and . . . I'm more sorry because Emma and David must be married right away. The girl's more than two months gone. Father and Aunt Leigh don't know anything about it. I didn't know till Christmas Day when they told me.'

'Jesus Christ!' The blasphemy penetrated the night air like a cannon blast as John Conrad leaped to his feet, the indifference gone from his voice to be replaced with a crude brittle sound. 'How in the name of God can this have happened? The second woman I'm going to marry gets pregnant to another man behind my back. What in Jesus's name did I do to deserve this?' He took three steps to the door and flung it open. 'God damn you, Emma Louise!' he shouted into the house.

Bart followed, grabbing at his arm in an attempt to temper him, holding him back, but he was thrown off so aggressively that he staggered backwards. John Conrad crossed to the staircase and as Bart regained his balance and yelled, 'No, please don't!' his elder brother bounded up the flight of stairs and along the hall.

Bart was shocked to the core. He had expected John Conrad would be hurt and angry but he had not been ready for this. As he ran up the flight of stairs behind his brother he heard him kick open Emma Louise's bedroom door. He heard her scream and by the time he reached the bedroom it was to see John Conrad drag the shrieking girl from her bed and throw her across the room. 'You bloody whore!' he shouted as he stood over her.

'Please, John Conrad, leave her, she's pregnant,' Bart cried.

'What the hell's that to me?' And he bent down and lifted the now sobbing, terrified girl to her knees with his left hand, as his right came forcefully down to back-hand her across her face. She screamed again as Bart grabbed hold of his brother in an attempt to pull him away.

'You faithless, treacherous bitch!' John Conrad's voice filled the room, the house, the neighbourhood.

Aunt Leigh appeared at the door white-faced and behind her came Barrington, his eyes wide with shock.

'What in God's name is going on?' the patriarch shouted. 'John Conrad, have you gone insane?'

And as if his father's voice transmitted reason and order to the madness in his head John Conrad shook his brother off and stepped away from the distraught girl. As Aunt Leigh ran forward to help her, John Conrad swung round to his parent. He was still in dress uniform and he made a startling figure there in the small bedroom in the stretch of moonlight and the faded light throwing a beam from the hall.

'Merely *déjà vu*, Father,' he said, attempting to drop his

voice to a normal tone. He looked round with disdain at the weeping girl. 'And as for shooting you, I wouldn't waste a good bullet on your trivial life.' He turned back to his father and did not look at Emma Louise Blackstone again as Aunt Leigh helped her over to the bed where she fell upon it, moaning.

John Conrad's family watched in alarm and confusion as he spoke again. 'Sorry about this incident. The whore on the bed's having dear little David's child. Amazing, isn't it, how the women I offer to marry become pregnant to all and sundry the minute I turn my back? Such loyal creatures I choose. I'll be leaving now, and I'll return when she's gone. Make sure she does leave, won't you? Or you might never see me again.' He turned round to his brother and his eyes glinted in the insipid light from the moon. 'Thank you for telling me.'

He strode forward to his father and touched him on the shoulder as he passed. 'Do let me know when she's gone.' And with that he proceeded down the hall into his own room where Aunt Leigh had diligently removed his clothes from the trunks and placed them neatly on hangers and away in drawers. He took two clean uniforms, some underclothes, his razor and his boots; ripped the blanket from the bed and wrapped them in it; swung it over his shoulder like a swag; returned down the hall where the sounds of Emma Louise's sobs still filled the house and his family milled in confusion; strode down the stairs and out the front door to the stable where, with decades of expertise, he swiftly saddled a horse, mounted it and rode away.

As he sped through the black early hours of the morning, the wooden houses all like rows of little square boxes in the moon glow, he was reminded of the furious ride of so long ago – sixteen years and more – when he had sought Craken after the death of sweet Emma Louise. How could he have mistaken this one for the other? This one was dead to him now too. A peculiar smile more like a sneer pulled his lips apart. He was always mentally burying women. He spoke aloud to the passing night. 'How the hell did I think you worthy?'

The night clerk at Lennon's Hotel in George Street was surprised to see the soldier in full dress uniform looking like something that had stepped out of a fairy tale come walking into the foyer at 2 a.m. Sunday morning and demand a room.

He dutifully complied, and some time later, John Conrad finally closed his eyes in a fitful sleep.

When he presented himself to K at Government House the following morning his eyes were bloodshot and his face was set in weary lines.

'Good heavens, m'boy, I've never seen you look this way. What's happened?'

John Conrad stood stiffly formal. 'I hope you'll understand, sir, when I say I'd like to remain on your staff . . . permanently.'

K rose from where he sat behind a substantial partner's desk set before the French windows in his room. The morning sunlight shone upon him as he came forward, slowly nodding his head. 'I see. I'm very sorry.'

'Don't be. I'm not, sir.'

'Please don't keep calling me *sir*.'

John Conrad took a long deep breath and gave a weak smile. 'There's something I must go and do.'

'I gather I'll not be taking afternoon tea on Monday with Miss Blackstone.'

'That's right, sir.'

'Do you want to talk about it?'

'Yes, I'd like to tell you everything. But not now, K. I must go first and complete what needs to be done. I'd like your permission for twenty-four hours' leave.'

'Is that all?'

'Yes. If I make good train connections I should be back tomorrow night at the latest. All I need is to borrow a small travelling case. I think Fitz has one.'

K placed his hand sympathetically on John Conrad's shoulder. 'Right, off you go . . . and hurry back, m'boy.'

As the younger man rapidly exited the room K perched on the edge of the desk. This was a most unforeseen event. He was deeply sorry that John Conrad had been hurt, he wished he could have saved him from that, but he knew the boy was strong. Even so, he could not help the spark of happiness that had ignited in his chest knowing that his *good right hand* was remaining with him.

John Conrad just managed to catch the 10.20 a.m. northbound express to Gympie. It arrived in that small country town at 12.50 p.m., where the ticketseller looked over his pince-nez and informed him in the strong Australian accent derived from the cockney, 'The only way ta get ta Bundaberg taday is ta catch the two o'clock slow train ta Maryborough, which stops twice and has connections ta Kilkivan and Degilbo. In Maryborough ya'll have a two-hour wait before ya could connect with the five forty-five p.m. afternoon daily ta the destination ya seek. That'll be ten shillings and four pence, please.'

As John Conrad paid he asked, 'And is there a train back out tonight?'

'What? Outa Bundaberg?'

'Yes, back here? Later tonight?'

'No, don't be daft, this is Queensland, mate, not London. First train out's in the morning. I'll have ta look that one up.' From a shelf above he lifted down a collection of finger-marked pages and, licking his thumb, leafed through them. 'Yeah here it is. First train out on Monday mornin's the six fifteen, next is the eight forty-two.'

'What time does the eight-forty-two arrive in Maryborough?'

He returned his gaze to the pages. 'Ten fifteen.' He eyed the soldier. He had rarely seen a man in uniform, and never one as prepossessing-looking as this. 'Heck! Ya're not stayin' in Bundy long then, are ya?'

'No.'

The monosyllable clearly indicated that convivial conversation was out of the question and the man handed the ticket across without further communication.

When John Conrad arrived in Bundaberg, it was close to eight o'clock on a hot Sunday night and there was no one on duty to take the tickets. Darkness had descended an hour before and the station was lit by a faded light emanating from three gaslamps. In the deserted streets the only light was from the waning moon and the windows of buildings.

It did not take long for him to find the Fleet Brewery on the banks of the Burnett River but there was no light anywhere and not a soul in sight.

He supposed he could go to each hotel and eventually find his brother, but it might take a long time. He was weary, needed a good night's sleep, and could count on the fact that his rage would be just as powerful in the morning.

He traversed a wide thoroughfare, noting the name 'Burbong Street' on a dilapidated sign on the corner outside an hotel. Lamplight through an open window showed him three men and a woman sitting playing cards at a round table. So much for Sunday night! He tapped on the sill and the woman looked up. 'Yeah?'

'Is it possible to speak to the publican? I'd like a room for the night.'

She rested her cards on her voluminous breast and smirked, showing a large gap in a row of long teeth. 'You're lookin' at the publican, love.'

'Oh good. Do you have a room?'

She lifted her cards and placed them carefully face down on the table, rose and came closer to the window. When she saw the uniform she whistled and glanced back to her companions. 'We've got a live one here. Straight from a fancy-dress party.' Then she faced round to John Conrad. 'Come to the side door round the corner, me beauty. I'll let you in.'

And so began John Conrad's brief acquaintace with Ma Tooley, who ran the Empire Hotel. She attempted to inveigle him into the card game but when he gave her a golden guinea for a meal and the night's stay she felt she had already got the better of him and pursued him no further.

He asked to be woken at six o'clock and when he lay down in the clean white sheets in the small but tidy room overlooking a fowl pen, he was soon asleep.

As good as her word, Ma Tooley woke him at six. Cocks crowed in the yard below and another searing January day on the southern Queensland coast emerged from the fiery dawn.

Work at the brewery began at seven, and at eight o'clock Gerard Grant looked up from the mashing machine, through the window in the front shed, and saw a soldier enter the yard. He moved into the open doorway and called, 'Looking for someone?'

The soldier advanced. He was quite breathtaking, tall and impressive in his knee-high shining boots and his khaki uniform with red bandolier. He put down the leather bag he carried and answered, 'I've come to find my brother, David Fleet.'

'Oh goodness,' Gerard began, coming quickly out and across the yard, hand extended. 'Where are my manners? I'm the manager here. Gerard Grant. I've heard all about you. It's a pleasure to meet you.'

John Conrad took the man's big country hand and spoke quietly. 'Forgive my brevity but it's an urgent personal matter I'm here on. Could you tell me where my brother is? I must see him immediately.'

'Why, of course.' He pointed across the yard. 'See that green door? Well, go in there, along the corridor, there're three offices on the left. His is the last.'

'Thank you.'

'Don't you want your bag?' the man called as the soldier walked away.

'I'll pick it up on my way out.'

When John Conrad entered the hallway and proceeded along the dim corridor a young woman came from the opposite end and made for the door he advanced upon.

'Excuse me,' he said. 'Is David Fleet in there?'

'Why, yes, I'm taking this to him.' She carried a cup of tea.

John Conrad placed his hand on the handle of the door. 'I suggest you come back with it later.'

The suggestion was undoubtedly an order and the girl instantly stepped back. 'All right, I will.'

John Conrad opened the door and David, who stood with his back to it, said, 'Is that you, Myrtle?'

In the instant John Conrad replied, he turned the key in the lock of the door. 'No, you little bastard, it's not.'

David spun round and at the moment that he recognised his eldest brother he felt as if the roof had fallen on his face as John Conrad's fist burst into it, instantly breaking his nose and knocking him backwards to sprawl across his desk. David let out a howl of pain but his brother was on top of him, pulling him upright to knock him hard in the face again so that this time he completely lost his balance and fell on the floor.

'Stop, please!' the young man cried in agony, but there was no stopping in John Conrad's soul. David kicked out in defence with his boot and caught John Conrad in the groin but it only served to enrage him more. His hand went out and grabbed David's raised leg to drag him forward, and stepping across him in one quick-silver move, he pulled his young brother up

370

by his shirt as the buttons burst from the rent material. Blood spurted from the young man's nose, mingling with the tears that ran down his face. He attempted to fend John Conrad off and swung at him with his right fist but his brother parried it with a rock-hard forearm. He struck David again and as he did he spoke, his voice impassive as if he had not exerted himself at all.

'Remember this every bloody time you're between her legs. Remember this and I hope you think she's worth it. You deserve each other. You're both trash.' And he hit his brother's bloody face twice more, back and forth, as David whimpered in pain.

There was banging and shouting coming from the hall outside the locked door, and loud cries of 'Are you all right, Mr Fleet?' and 'Open up!'

David was crying openly now. His face swollen, cut and broken as he rolled over and spat blood and a tooth from his mouth.

John Conrad took a handkerchief from his pocket and tied it around his knuckles where the skin had come off. 'You false and treacherous fool.' His tone remained clinical and utterly devoid of concern. 'I've killed men in hand-to-hand combat. And better men than you. It would've been too easy to kill you today.' The words richocheted around the office and for years to come David Fleet would awaken crying from nightmares filled with his eldest brother's fists.

The banging and shouting in the corridor outside continued as John Conrad unlocked the door. Two men almost tumbled into the room and the girl he had seen earlier looked in with wide, fear-stricken eyes.

'What in heaven's name has gone on here?' Gerard Grant demanded.

'A family disagreement,' John Conrad informed him as he passed along the corridor. 'I think he needs a doctor.'

When John Conrad came out into the yard, work had ceased and men were standing about. He said good morning to them, walked across to his bag, which still stood on the ground where he had left it, picked it up and left the brewery and all it entailed behind. He caught the 8.42 train to Maryborough in ample time.

Behind him a telegram had just been delivered to the brewery addressed to Mr David Fleet. It would be that night before the addressee was well enough to read it. It was from Bartholomew: 'John Conrad knows everything. Safest you remain where you are until you next hear from me.'

David would never again think of his eldest brother as a fop or a fool . . . and when John Conrad did come to his mind he would tremble automatically.

When the train left the station John Conrad found an empty compartment. He sat down to the rhythm of the steam engine as it clacked and swung through the cane fields covering the countryside. Long streams of men moved through the tall rows of cane. Not too many years before these fields had been filled with Kanaka labourers brought in from the Pacific Islands, but with the Queensland labour movements vociferous anti-Kanaka stand the last of them had been repatriated and now the fields were manned by white Queenslanders only.

John Conrad watched the men bending forward wielding their great machettes. An hour later the fields had given way to bush and he still stared out the window at the swiftly passing landscape dotted with banksias, spotted gums and iron bark gums.

It was almost a surprise to him quite suddenly to become aware of a stinging sensation in his eyes and, blinking, he realised that tears were falling quite rapidly down his cheeks.

Chapter Twenty-four

Through half-closed lids Matthew watched Caro and Jane playing with the children down on the lawn.

Knobby, who sat at his side sipping a beer, smiled. There was something warm and friendly about the comforting heat of the day. He inclined his head to Matt. 'January the third, eh? How the years fly by.'

'Mm,' was the response.

'Matt?'

'Yes.'

'Are you happy? I mean . . . satisfied with . . . things?'

Matt's right eyebrow rose. 'What's the meaning of waxing philosophical on me, old son? What sort of things?'

'Well, I suppose I mean are you happy having children and all?'

Matt turned his head and eyed his companion. 'Don't tell me?'

Knobby looked a little sheepish and swallowed another mouthful of beer.

'Is your Jane expecting?'

Knobby coughed, and gave an embarrassed grin. 'We're not sure yet. That's why I asked you the question, I suppose. Being an uncle to your two is one thing – I love that – but being a father myself . . . well . . .'

Matt took a swig of his rum. 'Knobby, it happens. One copes. You took long enough to become a husband, so I suppose it balances that you become a father swiftly. Jane, no doubt, will make an excellent mother, as . . . Caro did.' He took a deep breath. 'To my continuing amazement the children are encouragingly normal. That's because of the mother, doesn't matter what we're like. As long as they have a stable mother, they're all right. Now take my two, I like them both. They're good little buggers, especially Harry, though I wouldn't want them around all the time like Caro has them. I've told her she has to let Harry off her apron strings. He can't continue to be trotting up to Cedar Grove and taking lessons from his mother . . . then popping back here to Brisbane and attending a regular school. It's not going to work in the long run. The boy's ten. He's intelligent, reliable, enthusiastic, but needs his energies channelled . . . needs proper discipline. I think he should attend boarding school soon. I know it's a Catholic institution and I'm not exactly close to the cloth or familiar with the Bible, but Nudgee College seems to be the one. They have the best reputation.'

Knobby began to laugh.

'What the devil's so amusing?'

'You. Harry needs his energies channelling? Discipline? You of all people. You never had any!'

Matt screwed up his mouth in thought. 'Knobby, perhaps – mind you, only just perhaps – that's the point.'

'Oh,' uttered his friend.

'Irrespective, if we're discussing a coming introduction to your family, Knob. It'll make a man of you. You'll have to take life more seriously.'

Knobby sniffed loudly. 'Why? You never did.'

Matt angled his head to meet Knobby's eyes. 'Here we go again, reviewing my conduct. You don't actually mean to tell me you could be deranged enough to believe that my actions should be imitated?'

'I might be.'

Matthew burst into laughter.

Knobby, apparently seeing the humour of this, followed suit, leaning back in his chair and venting his amusement. They both howled at the absurdity of the thought.

'I'm an example to all,' Matt spluttered as he roared with laughter.

The two children, down on the lawn, rotated in the direction of the hilarity. 'Daddy's laughing,' shouted Harry, jumping to his feet and running up to Matthew.

He took Matt's hand. 'Daddy what's so funny?'

The mirth began to dissipate and both men slowly regained their composure. 'Ah, my boy,' Matt answered still amused, 'Uncle Knobby has the quaint idea that there are actions of mine that have some worth, that I do some things correctly.'

The child looked askance. His tone was stern and serious. 'But you do, Daddy. You're wonderful. You're the best father in the world, Daddy.'

Matthew sat staring at Harry. He did not speak for many seconds. It was as if the tableau of Matt, Harry and Knobby were distilled into the realm of pure emotional intercourse, the players communing but sitting in total silence. If there had been onlookers less partisan than Knobby and Harry they might have suggested that Matt lost his sang-froid. He leaned forward and took the boy in his arms, smoothed his hair and kissed him. 'There never was a boy like you. You're truly my son.'

'I know that,' Harry answered laughing, 'and you're truly my daddy.'

As Matt held the child to his heart he closed his eyes.

When he opened them, Caro was standing a few yards away, holding Katy's hand and watching them; her face set in tight lines.

Matt lifted his hand towards her. 'Come, old girl, sit and join us awhile.'

She shook her head, 'No thanks, Matt. If Jane and I are taking Katy over to my parents we'd better get a move on. It's after two already. Now, are you sure you and Knobby don't want to come.' She made this statement earnestly as if she truly desired their company, and Matt shrugged and turned to his friend.

Caro's heart sank. She was playing a dangerous game. She had made the arrangement to meet John Conrad; it was merely a pretence of wanting Matt's company. She turned nonchalantly back to Jane, who was picking some flowers. 'Come on, Jane, dear.'

Matt sat up straight. 'What are you going over to your parents for anyway, old girl?'

Her answer was light-hearted as she bent and smoothed her daughter's hair. 'Remember I told you yesterday. Mum just wants to fit Katy for the new frock she's making. You know, for the children's concert next month.'

'Well, we could come, I suppose . . . Do you want to go, Knob?'

'Dunno, Matt, I'll do whatever you want.'

Matthew smiled, and for the first time in ages she noticed the chip on his eyetooth. His teeth were perfect but for that. She waited, her heart thudding, while she prayed that her face remained calm.

'Aren't you taking young Harry?' he asked.

He still held Harry in the arc of his arm and the child turned to his father. 'No, Daddy, if you're staying home then I'd rather stay with you and Uncle Knobby.'

'There you see,' Caro answered, a mite too quickly. She could not afford to take Harry. He would report anything and everything to Matthew. 'He's better off here with you. One child on a tram's enough.'

Matthew smiled, dropped his hand from the boy to his rum, lifted it and swallowed. Caro waited until she could not stand it any longer and kept her voice as indifferent as she could. 'Well, Matt, I'm off.'

'Yes, old girl, we won't come, but thanks for asking. I really should keep on with painting this evening and take advantage of the golden light. We'll wait dinner until you return.'

'All right then, we'll probably be gone for the afternoon. Home around half-past eight . . . in time for dinner with you.' She caught Knobby's eye. 'Make sure Harry eats at six, please, Knobby.'

'Sure.'

Caro swung round and called to Jane. 'I'll just wash Katy and change her dress. Meet you in the front hall in ten minutes.'

'All right,' the woman answered as she came up the lawn to sit by Knobby.

Caro brought Katy forward to Matt's side. 'Kiss Daddy goodbye.'

Katy did so as he said, 'Bye, little one,' and his eyes came up to Caro, who leaned down and brushed his lips with hers. 'Bye then.' She touched him on the shoulder as she moved off.

She was crossing the terrace with Katy when Matt spoke to her back. 'Don't be late, old girl.'

She paused, one foot on the doorstep. 'No, Matt. It's a nusiance really that we have to go at all, but the dress must be fitted.'

Matt's gaze followed her as she passed inside.

As Caro hurried through to her bedroom and washed her

376

daughter's hands and face and changed the child's dress she felt relieved. *Good. Matt suspects nothing. I'm safe.*

After Caro, Jane and Katy had departed, Matt and Knobby remained in the sunshine for a time. Harry was absorbed by a caterpillar that had crawled out of the garden on to the stone of the terrace.

'Knobby, old son?'

'Yes?'

'There's a matter I must attend to. Will you take care of Harry for a couple of hours?'

Knobby brought his gaze around to his companion. 'Oh really?'

Matt nodded.

'Where are you going?'

Matthew gave no reply.

Knobby exhaled loudly. 'Why do I get the feeling that you're off to check on something.' He couched his words to keep the meaning from Harry. 'Don't tell me you have a suspicion about a certain person and that person's whereabouts? We were asked to join that person. That wouldn't have been suggested if there were any mischief going on.'

Matt raised an eyebrow. 'Ah . . . now, Knob, it's all a game, you know that. And with a certain other person back in town I believe I'm much like Othello, "Who dotes yet doubts, suspects yet soundly loves."'

'Oh, Matt . . . Is it worth it to torture yourself this way?'

'No torture, old son. Merely verifying to myself that what I believe to be true, is in fact, true. I'm regarding it as an exercise of sorts: a theorem to prove you know, QED.'

'Don't go. Even if you're right and I reckon you're not, how can it help?'

'It won't help, help's not part of the equation, but I'm an obsessive bugger – have to assure myself of the astuteness of my ongoing perceptions in the matter.'

Knobby looked down and shook his head. 'Why do you do this?' Then he sighed. 'All right, I'm coming with you. Mrs Manning's here until five. I'll ask her to stay a bit longer, look after Harry.'

Harry lifted his head in interest. 'I want to come. Where are we going?'

Knobby put up his hand to the boy. 'No, lad, not this time. We'll play snakes and ladders when we come home, though. You'll like that, won't you?'

Harry was not to be placated. 'Mummy and Aunt Jane took Katy. Why can't you take me?'

Matt tapped his mahogany and silver cane on the stone. 'Give it a rest, son. Uncle Knob will stay with you.' He lifted his finger for emphasis. 'Now, Knobby. First point: Mrs Manning will whinge if you ask her to stay longer. I know the old biddy. Second point: I prefer to go alone this time.' He looked hard at his friend. 'I'll do nothing wild, I assure you. Stay with Harry and don't argue.' He stood up, leaning on his cane. 'While I'm away you two play snakes and ladders.'

'Daddy . . .' Harry ran to him and hugged him.

'I'll be back before you know it.' And Matt kissed the top of the boy's head before making swift progress across the terrace and through to the front hall where he changed his mahogany cane for the red cedar one: the one which contained the blade.

'Are you taking the motorcar?' Knobby called as Matt crossed the garden. He had purchased a vehicle the previous summer, but it was an unreliable machine and had the habit of chugging to a halt at the most inopportune times. Mobility was of the essence today. 'No, Knob, I'll take the grey.'

'Matt? Be careful. I should come with you.'

'You worry too much old son, I'm always careful.'

He was soon mounted and a few minutes later riding through the Valley.

Across the other side of the city the tram on which Caro, Jane and Katy travelled, glided to a halt. They alighted and headed towards the Dere house which stood two streets away. When they arrived, Jack Dere's wide smile welcomed them. He took Katy in his arms and gave her a big bear hug. 'My little darlin', how good it does my old eyes to see you.'

'It's good to see you too, Pa,' the child responded.

Caro's father had recovered completely from the illness he had suffered in 1901 but he could no longer do the heavy work of his younger years, though his smile and his mind were as bright and lucid as ever, and for this his daughter thanked God.

Elizabeth fussed and kissed them all, and they were soon in the big homely kitchen of Caro's youth, drinking a pot of tea.

At Katy's insistence her grandfather took her for a ride on his horse while the ladies went out into the garden. When the riders returned Elizabeth fitted the child's new dress, a blue silk frothy affair that delighted the child.

'You'll be the belle of the concert,' Jane told her and the child frowned.

'What's a belle?'

'A beauty, the centre of attention.'

Two hours after they arrived, while Jack amused his grand-daughter down on the lawn with books and toys, Caro and Jane had retreated into the shade of the verandah. Caro turned to Jane, who sat knitting. Elizabeth was inside sewing Katy's new dress.

'Jane love, I'm going over to the stables to take Ned out for a while. I miss riding.'

Jane frowned. 'Goodness, Caro, how can you miss it? We've only been down from the farm less than two weeks.'

'It still feels like a long time since I was on a horse. I like to ride every day really, you know that.'

'Why didn't you go with your father and Katy earlier?'

'I don't know. I didn't feel like it then.'

Jane put down her knitting. 'Oh, all right, but I really don't feel like it now.'

Caro held up her hand. 'No, love, stay here. You don't need to come. I'm happy to go alone.' And she stood up and moved across the verandah. 'Tell Mum and Dad would you? I'll be back before seven.'

'Good heavens!' Jane shook her head in surprise. 'I should think so, that's over two hours away and it's close to dark by then. Where on earth are you going?'

Jane had asked this question in all innocence, and Caro could have avoided an honest reply but for some reason she did not. She spoke frankly, much to the perturbation of her friend. 'Jane love, it's best you don't know. Let's say I'm just going for a ride.'

Jane put down her knitting and rose. She thought a lot of Caro; they had become close over the years. 'Caro, it seems

379

to me you're going to place yourself at some sort of risk. I'll be worried about you. Please, what's going on?'

'Don't worry, love.' Caro returned to kiss her on the cheek. 'I can't tell you any more. Just tell Mum and Dad I needed to get out in the fresh air. There's a dear, thanks.' And she hurried away down the steps leading from the verandah.

Jane watched her pass the bakery and hurry on until she was hidden in the trees. She was remembering something Knobby had told her a long time ago: that there had been a soldier in Caro's life who was now close to Kitchener of Khartoum and that the same soldier was a deadly enemy of Matthew. And the whole of Australia knew that Kitchener was here in Brisbane right now!

Jane might appear to be a quiet country girl, but she was no fool, and her intelligent hazel eyes closed tightly with the impact of the many disturbing possibilities that were running through her mind.

It did not take long for Caro to reach the river. She was at the weeping willow by five. She slipped off Ned and tied him loosely to a small gum. She was convinced Matt had swallowed her story and she was calm about that; but she was very uncalm about the impending arrival of the man she loved. Folding her arms tightly across her body she waited, from time to time biting the edge of her lip.

He must come to her. He must. She thought of their meeting on the station, the glorious pain of touching him again, and the wonder of the moment on the quayside when he waved to her. The intense sweet agony of loving him so; of seeing his face every night before she went to sleep; of pretending it was he who reached for her in the darkness, who kissed her mouth and entered her body.

God must allow her to tell him, explain to him, that she had always loved him, and no other, that it was fate alone which had bedevilled them so. All manner of wild notions raced through her mind. If she could stop him from marrying the girl Emma Louise, then . . . if he would wait . . . she could divorce Matt. Matt had committed adultery and she could prove it. She would tell John Conrad that Harry was really his son: that would do it. That would prove to him how much she loved him. She had only married Matt to save face for her and her baby. To give the child – John Conrad's child – respectability. Too much time had gone by, over a decade of her life wasted. She knew now what a mistake she had made. Her love for John Conrad was the only thing that held her together. John Conrad would understand, she knew he would: he must.

She stroked the small indentation on her lower lip. The part of her that Matt regarded as marred, the legacy of the last time John Conrad's mouth had touched hers, the part that was not a scar to her, but was now a thing to be cherished.

An hour passed in restless movement and distracted thought. The sun was beginning to tire of the day and it edged towards the horizon, casting long shadows across the water of the river.

Caro's agitation was almost unbearable as her eyes roamed over the long paspalum grass and the shrubs and trees of the straggling growth along the riverside. Once, just after six, her heart leapt as she saw a man coming along on a horse in the distance, but he rode on by without turning towards her. A hundred times she checked the tiny timepiece she carried in her pocket and when half-past six crept ever closer tears floated in her eyes.

And then she saw him! Dear sweet glorious heaven! Riding through the brush in the dying day, coming straight along the river path towards her. She moved out of the long draping fronds of the tree, a look of boundless love in her eyes. She raised her hand in joyous greeting, her mouth open to speak. And then recoiled, stunned.

She stepped back and her hand fell impotently to her side. For some seconds she actually believed her heart had stopped, for there was no beating in her chest. As the horseman rode ever closer a crippled word issued from her suddenly dry mouth. 'You!'

'Yes, old girl,' Matthew said as he brought his horse right up to her. 'Me.' He dismounted, sliding to the ground with his left leg and reaching up to the holder on the cantle to remove his red cedar cane. He waggled it in her face as she remained rooted to the spot.

'The enemy won't be coming. So your deception was a waste of time. You've made a fool of yourself. Not unusual for you, I'm afraid.'

The scar on his cheek glimmered in the waning golden light as he shook his head. 'Ah, Caro, what am I to do with you?' He brought the cane up to touch her under the chin.

She twisted her head to the side, for she knew this was the cane that held a rapier blade within it. She trembled. 'What have you done to him?'

'Nothing.'

'Don't toy with me, Matt.' Her eyes were frantic. 'He was meant to come here. He would have come, I know he would! What in God's name have you done?'

'I've done nothing in God's name, that would be a mite presumptuous.' He turned his back on her and threw his horse's reins over the low branch of an acacia.

Something snapped in Caro's head. 'Damn you!' She leapt forward, striking him on the back and pushing him off balance so that he had to throw out his cane to stop himself from falling. 'What've you done to him?' she screamed. 'Answer me?'

He spun round on his good leg and grabbed her, bringing her body to his and pinning her hands to her sides within his powerful arms so that she felt the breath from his mouth as he spoke into her face.

'Listen to me, Caro, and for once get it through your head. He was *not* coming! He was never coming. I met his brother – it was *his brother* who was on his way to deliver the message to you – only I preferred to deliver it, considering you're my wife.' As he said the last two words he squeezed her even closer so that his mouth was almost touching her face.

Caro tried to pull out of his hold but it was useless. His arms were iron hard, made so by constant use in concession to the lack of strength in his bad leg.

'You followed me, how could you?'

'I could because I had no choice. And while *you* waited here *I* waited down by the river road until the enemy's *dear* brother came along . . . alone . . . do you understand? He was alone! I challenged him and the bastard almost had a heart attack.'

'No, no, let me go, Matt.'

'Bart Fleet was amazed to see me. Bloody embarrassed too.' Matt's voice grew cruel and cold. 'I was deeply disappointed that the enemy did not come. I had brought my special cane to greet him.'

Caro squirmed in his grasp. 'You're mad.'

'No, old girl, not mad, merely confirmed in my view.'

She could not move, so constrained was she within his arms. 'Bart Fleet told me he had come to inform you that the enemy *did not want to see you.*'

'I don't believe it.' Caro's eyes filled with tears and she began to sob. 'I don't believe it.'

Abruptly, viciously, he let go of her and she fell heavily to the ground. She lay where she fell, sobbing uncontrollably, abandoning all restraint.

Matt edged to where the toe of his boot touched her garments. 'You bloody fool of a woman. Get it through your head. *He does not want to see you.*'

As the last rays of daylight illuminated the riverbank Matt remained standing above her, looking down, his dark eyes dimmed with despair. Finally he made a small cheerless sound. 'Caro! I saw you the night you went to the Bellevue Hotel, to his engagement party. The night you were *so* keen to leave me and go home and be *alone*! By bloody accident Knobby and I came upon you. So your subterfuge was all for nothing. I knew then as I know now, that you've deceived me in your heart every moment of our life together.' His hand went up to hold his forehead. 'If just once, just bloody once, you had shown a quarter of this emotion for me.'

She lifted her head. Streaks of tears stained her face and her eyes were brittle. 'Why should I?' she cried. 'Marriage made no difference to you. You've been faithless all these years. You're disgusting.'

Matt took a deep breath. The tone in his voice was no longer cold; it was replete with an infinite weariness. 'You genuinely don't understand, do you? Let me tell you a truth. And attempt to grasp it; just this once apply yourself.' He slowed down his speech so that each word was expelled almost in isolation. 'If . . . only . . . you . . . had . . . been . . . faithful . . . to . . . me, I . . . would . . . have . . . in . . . all . . . conscience . . . kept . . . only . . . unto . . . you.'

In the fast-fading dusk Caro shook her head in disbelief. 'What? Why do you say that? I *have* been faithful to you, damn you, though why I don't know.'

For a moment Matt raised his eyes to the sky, then he kneeled on his good knee and brought his face down to where he stared straight in her eyes. 'Caro, that's not true. Infidelity came naturally to you. I've always known you made love to the enemy. It was never me. It's for ever the enemy lying there between us. Separating you from me eternally. Every time I put my mouth upon yours or caress your body or pull you to me, you imagine him. I know it. Your whispered love words are to him . . . even when you beg me . . . it's never me who enters you and brings you to cry out in pleasure. In the depths of you, in your mind, where you live, in the soul of you, it's *never* me.'

Caro could not continue to meet his gaze and she looked away. He remained kneeling, watching her, until at last he reached out. She flinched as he brought his hand to her face but all he did was touch her tenderly on the tear stains of her cheek. She brought her eyes back to his and they held position, simply staring at each other.

In a sudden move he dropped his hand and held it out to her, and she took it. Then, taking his weight upon his cane with his other hand, he stood up and pulled her to her feet.

They stood toe to toe and she looked fixedly up at him.

'It's time we went home.' He spoke matter-of-factly. 'So let's go back to your parents and collect Jane and the children.'

Her reply was a nod.

As she let go his hand he said, 'Caro?'

She looked round. Night had arrived but she could make out his face; the face she had come to know so well.

'We married each other for our own infernal reasons and I made a pact with myself that day. I decided I could live with the enemy in my bed. I accepted it then and I accept it now. That the status quo continues, is clearly understood. So don't ever lecture me about faithfulness, old girl. You haven't the faintest conception what the bloody hell it is.'

John Conrad returned to his family home in the afternoon of Wednesday, 5 January. A message had been sent to him from his father informing him that Emma Louise and Aunt Leigh had left the night before to travel to Bundaberg on the recommendation received in a telegram from Gerard Grant. It had informed them that David was in hospital and he needed to see them. As John Conrad had the afternoon and night off from any formal duties with K he joined his father and Bart at Brewery House.

He explained to his father and brother what had occurred in Bundaberg. 'David was a bit of a mess when I left him. I think I broke his nose for a start. There was no love for me in his soul before, but now I fear there never can be.'

Barrington shrugged his still broad shoulders. It distressed him to know that his two sons were now estranged but he was a strong and honourable man, and he could not help but side with his eldest son; nevertheless he had his say. 'They've acted like the young fools they are,' he said sagely. 'Now they must reap what they've sown. But you,' and he lifted his finger to his eldest son, 'have too quick a temper. This is the second time, that I know of, when you've badly hurt a man. No doubt you believe there was good reason, but it's a part of you that needs curbing. When you beat Craken you were an impetuous boy. It troubles me to see that side of you unrestrained now that you're a man. I wouldn't be a proper father if I didn't tell you.'

John Conrad did not reply.

Bart was his steady self. 'Look, John Conrad, we all realise now that David and Emma Louise must marry soon, and that's left a bad taste in our mouths, I assure you. We're your family and we don't approve of what they've done. It'll be no happy celebration for us. And one thing Father and I – and Aunt Leigh for that matter – want you to remember is that Brewery House's always your home. Never forget that and don't let anything, or anyone, keep you from us if you have the opportunity to return.'

His big brother appreciated the words. 'Thanks, Bart. I'm sorry to leave under a cloud like this but when K departs Brisbane for the rest of his Australian tour I'll be leaving too. He's here to make recommendations to the Federal Government about Australia's defence policies and so there's a lot of work to be done. We go on to do the same in New Zealand and perhaps to see his sister who lives there. After that we'll return to England, for even though we don't have an appointment at present, we'll go back to see what comes up, so I don't expect to be in Queensland for a long time to come.'

And to show his eldest son he held nothing against him, Barrington took his arm, capturing him until four o'clock when Bart gave himself an early finish to the day and rejoined his father and brother for afternoon tea. The men talked of many things, avoiding mention of David and Emma Louise. After the refreshment the brothers were both acutely aware that years might go by before they communed this way again, and so Bart suggested they head off to the Hare and Hounds in Melbourne Street for a drink before dinner.

Clouds drifted across the sky and hid the late afternoon sun as the brothers started off down the street. A few of the neighbours waved to John Conrad, who lifted his hand in response.

Bart patted his brother's shoulder as they strode side by side. 'I'm sure you've forgotten, and I don't blame you with everything that's gone on, but it was Monday that I went to meet Caro down by the river.'

John Conrad slowed at his brother's side. 'I had forgotten, but tell me, what happened?'

'I went but I didn't see her, because Craken intercepted me.'

'What?'

'He was there on his horse by the roadside. I was amazed. He knew Caro was down by the river waiting for you. He was bloody cool as usual, said he was sorry you weren't there as he had a surprise for you. Told me to tell you that you were smarter than he thought to stay away from his wife and to keep away from her if you wanted to continue living. He's a fair bugger.'

'What happened then?'

'I left. I assume he went on to Caro.'

John Conrad remained silent for a long time, walking at his brother's side and mulling over Bart's words before he gave voice to his thoughts. 'I can't imagine why Caro wanted to see me. She's been married to him over ten years. Perhaps they're having their troubles. He'd be impossible to live with, that's certain.' He uttered a small sound of disgust. 'To think Caro and Emma Louise both cheated on me, and fell pregnant to other men, and I would've married each of them. Bart, you've been more than a brother all these years, you've been my friend, and I tell you, Caro's infidelity shocked me to the core, ate at me for years. And while I'm angry and hurt about Emma Louise . . .

it's extraordinary, because already I'm feeling as if it weren't meant to be, as if somehow I'm supposed to stay with K. I'm still churned up inside because I had given my heart again, but I'm more angry at myself for being so gullible. Believing in her. Women are hopeless,' he finished.

In the waning afternoon sun Bart looked sideways at his brother. 'Yes, they're odd creatures all right. It's as if men were conceived on one island and women on another. You know, I've only ever been serious about one girl. She worked here at the brewery: book-keeper. I took her out a few times.'

'What was her name?'

'Marietta MacLeod.'

'I don't recall her.'

'You wouldn't. It was during the first years you were in India. She was very sweet, very young, fine-boned, fair hair, green eyes. I thought she was so adorable. I suppose I was in love with her.'

'What happened?'

'Her parents moved to Sydney. She went with them.'

John Conrad began to chuckle. At first it was quietly but then the volume increased.

'What's so funny?' asked Bart.

'She went to Sydney with her parents,' John Conrad managed to say. He was laughing with gusto now, releasing the tension of the past days. 'Thank God, you lucky man. She went to Sydney with her parents.' He found this so funny that he bent forward, almost doubling up, and Bart, caught up in the mood, roared with laughter too. They halted in the street holding each other up as tears of mirth rose in their eyes and their peals of amusement echoed along the street. 'She went to Sydney with her parents.' It was the most hilarious thing they had ever heard and the afternoon rang with the sounds of their voices.

'I wish I knew your secret, Bart.' John Conrad pumped out between breaths. 'If only mine had gone to flaming Sydney with their parents. If only!'

This was so humorous the brothers staggered along under the load of their laughter, John Conrad tripping as they crossed the intersection of Victoria Street and Montague Road.

'Hey, steady on,' Bart shouted. 'You haven't had anything to drink yet.'

387

Slowly they calmed down and by the time they had walked down the slope and reached the tramline the brothers had regained their composure and sense of propriety. A vehicle was soon along and it was a short ride to Melbourne Street where they alighted outside the Hare and Hounds.

Inside they ordered two beers and sat at the bar, but it was the height of summer and even with all the windows and doors open the holiday crowd was large and the bar became so stuffy, and the flies so persistent, the brothers gradually gravitated to the garden outside where people sat drinking at tables and talking at the tops of their voices. Someone was playing an out-of-tune piano in the ladies' lounge: melodies from a six-penny songbook drifted through an open window to the drinkers in the garden.

Bart took a swig of his beer and with a forthright expression said, 'So you'll remain with K indefinitely?'

'Yes, little brother, that I will.'

'And that makes you happy?'

John Conrad thought for a few seconds. 'Yes, it does. I suppose it's odd being a soldier in peacetime. Some people would say the whole purpose of a soldier is to fight wars, but there's so much more to it all than that. I'm working with the one man in the whole Empire who makes me proud to be with him. He believes, rightly or wrongly, that it's the duty of every able-bodied man to be able to defend his country if needed. He knows about armies and he knows about defence. He's a soldier and won't play politicians' games. He's left India and South Africa more able to defend themselves than at any time in their histories. His opinion on what to do here and in New Zealand will be invaluable. We live in strange times, brother mine. Fortunately, this country is a long way from Europe where, if trouble comes, it'll probably start.'

'How do you mean?'

'We believe, and have for years, that Germany's the danger. They started in the race too late to colonise legitimately and K's of the opinion, as sadly I am, that one day it'll attempt to widen its sovereignty by force. There's no doubt that if they'd had the sea power at the time they'd have helped Kruger against us in the Boer War. And the Kaiser's a bloody madman, by all accounts. He believes Germany's the super-state and is

388

building up his navy to rival Britain. He's said publicly more than once that Germany deserves its place in the sun, and he might just be working on ways to achieve that; it's a threatening thought, really.'

Bart stroked his chin. 'Mmm, why is man always coveting what his neighbour has?' He took his brother's arm. 'You know you live a life I can only guess at – the glamour of it, the people you rub shoulders with. You've got respect and position but you're the right hand of the Empire's blasted demigod, the magical warrior they'll turn to in time of trouble . . . and that means you, my big brother, will be right in the middle of any damn war that starts.' He squeezed John Conrad's arm. 'I had hoped that . . . oh heck, I think you know what I mean.'

John Conrad emptied his glass. 'I do and that wasn't to be. I'd have remained in the army anyway, even if I'd married Emma Louise. I'm signed up for years yet. You see, lad, I'm a professional soldier, have been since I was twenty years old, and while it was foisted upon me then, now, well, I know nothing else. So I must take what comes.' He smiled. 'Let's change the subject.' Looking around he wrinkled up his nose. 'You know, brother mine, I think I've had enough of the Hare and Hounds. Why don't we head into the city? Go somewhere a little more salubrious. Then perhaps have some dinner later.'

Bart thumped his big brother on the back. 'Should have realised this pub wouldn't be refined enough for you these days.' He laughed. 'You bloody toff.'

'Thanks,' answered John Conrad smiling. 'Nice to be understood.'

As they swallowed the last of their beer and stood up, Bart mentioned that he was a member of the Turf Club. 'We could go there; not a bad place actually. You'll find it more comfortable than this.'

'Right.'

'Or on second thoughts, Dad's a member of the Johnsonian Club, they know me well, we can get in. Now that's more you. Nice premises in Adelaide Street, good bar, bit snobby, big billiard room.'

'Excellent. Let's go there.'

A tram was soon along and within fifteen minutes the

brothers alighted in the city and entered the Johnsonian Club. It had been formed in 1878 by a tiny literary circle who had encouraged 'Bohemian wit and sagacity' and constructive argument on many a subject. In the nineties the essence of the club had become more conservative and now, in the twentieth century, the majority of its members were the professional élite, and the club offered a quite sophisticated environment by Brisbane standards.

The grandfather clock in the foyer chimed six as they signed in; the commercial working day was over and the club began to fill with men.

'How's your father?' asked Pat Flattery, one of the city aldermen, who passed the two brothers as they climbed the stairs to the main bar.

'Well, thanks,' responded Bart, sniffing with distaste the puffs of smoke emanating from the man's large cigar.

'Don't you like cigars?' asked John Conrad as they passed on.

'No, dislike them.'

'Wouldn't do for you to be in my shoes then. All K's aides are smokers other than me.'

'How come you don't then?'

'Prefer to drink,' he answered with a wink. 'Come on,' and he took his brother's arm and ushered him into the club bar where they ordered whisky.

'Evening, Bartholomew,' called a man with a goatee beard and a warm grin. 'Haven't seen you for a time.'

'How are you, Andrew?' replied Bart. 'He's the nephew of Robert Philp, our ex-premier, you remember, of Burns Philp and Company?' Bart explained as the man came round the bar to join them.

As Bart introduced him, Andrew took stock of Bart's brother. 'Oh yes, the soldier, right-hand man of Kitchener of Khartoum. I saw you in the parade this morning. You look a lot different out of uniform.'

'Better or worse?' asked John Conrad.

Andrew smiled. 'Neither, just different.'

John Conrad lifted his glass in the air. 'Very diplomatic,' he laughed.

'Do you play billiards?'

'Definitely,' Bart answered for them.

'Good,' said Andrew. 'Let's have a game then. I'll just call Larry Lennox, he's over there.' Andrew pointed to a well-built man leaning on the bar reading a newspaper. 'He's a good mate of mine and plays well. We'll have teams.'

They were lucky to find one of the tables free. Wednesday evening in the New Year season seemed to be an active time at the Johnsonian Club, and men came and went laughing and talking through the rooms and along the corridors.

Andrew and Larry Lennox proved to be genial companions. They remained so even when the brothers took their money on the first game and again on the second. They would have played a third only they felt obliged to give up the table to others waiting to play.

'Well,' Larry held out his hand, 'I'll be off. My fiancée will be downstairs to meet me by now. We're going to a piano recital at the Exhibition Hall tonight.' In the way of the Edwardian world, women were not allowed up into the club but they could come into the front foyer and wait.

Once Larry had gone Bart suggested a meal.

'It's been nice to meet you,' Andrew said as they left the billiard room and moved out into the corridor. 'When will you be leaving us?'

'In a few days, I think,' John Conrad declared as they passed the smoking room, and the door opened and two men came out. The newcomers halted, both recognising Andrew, and one put out his hand. 'Didn't know you were here this evening, old chap, or I'd have drained a glass with you.'

'How are you, Coates?' Andrew took the proffered hand then nodded at the other man. 'Good evening, Martin.'

Martin in turn shook hands with Andrew, who glanced to his companions. 'Let me introduce Ian Coates and Keith Martin, Bart Fleet and John Conrad Fleet.'

Ian Coates' eyes widened. 'Fleet? John Conrad Fleet? The soldier?'

'My goodness,' John Conrad laughed, 'my reputation does precede me.'

Ian Coates raised his hands, palm upwards in an uneasy gesture. 'Actually the fact is I represent Matthew Craken. I sell his paintings, that's why I know who you are.'

'Oh?' For some unaccountable reason John Conrad's monosyllable echoed uncannily down the corridor.

Keith Martin looked questioningly at Andrew, who turned to Bart, who shrugged, but it was Ian Coates who spoke again, looking at John Conrad. 'I'm afraid I'm aware there's very bad blood between you and Matt.'

John Conrad inclined his head. 'You're right.' He grinned. 'But that doesn't need to spoil our night. I won't hold it against you for representing him.'

'Generous of you,' replied Coates, 'but what you don't realise is that Matt's downstairs.' He pointed along the corridor at the staircase to the lower floor.

Bart winced. 'What?'

'He was here with us in the smoking room until a few minutes ago. He went ahead with Knobby Clark to make some booking or other at the front desk. They'll be waiting for us. Matt's had a few as well.'

Bart looked quickly around. 'John Conrad, we can't go down. We must wait until he's gone.'

Martin pursed his lips and looked over his horn-rimmed glasses, down his substantial nose. 'Wait till he's gone? Discretion's the better part of valour is it?'

Ian Coates replied sharply. 'Keep out of it, Keith. You don't understand.'

But Martin's words had already stung John Conrad. 'I've no intention of waiting until anyone's gone. Craken in particular.'

Bart took his brother's arm. 'Please, John Conrad, ignore this. We don't need it. Let's wait here. They'll be gone in a minute or two.'

But Martin's taunt had inflamed John Conrad and he nodded formally to Ian Coates. 'I appreciate what you attempted to do.' And he started off to the stairs.

'Bloody hell!' exclaimed Bart tensely. 'This is madness.' He hurried after his brother as Keith Martin swiftly followed in anticipation of what was to come and Ian Coates and Andrew brought up the rear.

As John Conrad's footfall sounded on the top step of the polished wooden stair the two men waiting at the desk below looked up, expecting their friends.

'Good God,' blurted out Knobby. 'It's Fleet.'

Matthew's hand tightened automatically on his cane as distaste flashed in his eyes and hatred waxed in his heart.

John Conrad came steadily down the stairs, each footstep deliberate, disdain in his eyes and his palms prickling with tension. 'I can't say it's a pleasure, Craken.'

Affecting listlessness Matt slowly lifted his cane of inlaid beech and black walnut. A succession of expressions swept across his face as he draped his elbows languidly back across the flat surface behind him and rested his body against the counter. 'Now fancy running into you.' He eyed his enemy up and down. 'I thought I was going to see you on Monday, and here you pop up two days late; just like a bad penny.' He wiggled his walking stick in the air.

John Conrad grunted distastefully, pointing to the cane. 'Got a blade in this stick, Craken? It's typical of you. I've noticed you usually need a weapon to defend yourself when we meet.'

A sneer curled Matt's mouth. 'Now, soldier-boy, let's get things in perspective. You have the advantage of unimpaired limbs; on the other hand you have the disadvantage of a violent temper. I have neither of these novelties.'

Bart lifted his hand in a conciliatory gesture. 'We're on our way out, Craken. Come on, John Conrad.' He pulled his brother's sleeve but he did not move.

Ian Coates and the others made a half-circle behind John Conrad, all fascinated by the conflict, and the clerk behind the counter frowned in concern as he put down his pen. This was a respectable club and he did not want trouble. He wondered if he should call the evening manager.

It was Knobby who responded to Bart. 'Yes, we know you're on your way out and that's a good thing. Don't let us keep you; goodbye.' He put his hand on Matthew's arm in a placating action, but Matt brushed it aside.

'Don't intervene, Knob, my dear. I miss hearing Fleet's diatribes against me. Years pass between such treats.' Matt's eyes flashed with the animation of five rums and as many beers. 'He seems to hold all manner of odd things against me: deaths, loss of female companionship, et cetera, et cetera.' He raised his eyebrows enquiringly. 'What other of your misfortunes do you blame me for, soldier-boy?'

393

'I find you and your way of life contemptible.' Intimidatingly John Conrad took a step closer and Matt, moving unnaturally fast, raised himself from his slumping position. They were of similar height and their eyes were locked, yet in the periphery of John Conrad's vision Matt's scar gleamed menacingly.

A few men had come into the foyer and now stood listening as the clerk left the desk to hurry up the stairs to find the manager.

John Conrad focused on the man in front of him again and his tone was full of contempt. 'I suspect you remain the immoral ignoble libertine that I had the misfortune of knowing a long time ago. Sewer rats don't transform.'

Matt flinched but he stepped deliberately closer to John Conrad as Knobby burst out, 'For God's sake, Matt, it's not worth it.'

At that moment the door to the street opened and a child's voice called, 'There he is, there's Daddy!' Harry let go Caro's hand as she entered the doorway and he ran across the carpeted foyer to Matthew.

The moment was neutralised; but the two men suspended in the vale of hostility did not move. The child ran right up to Matt's side. 'Here we are, Daddy. Can we go to Grandma's now?' Harry grabbed at his father's hand and looked up to the face of the man opposite. The child started violently and moved quickly behind his father in fear.

Caro halted, rooted to the spot, holding Katy's hand. Jane hesitated behind her, looking in amazement at the scene.

Matt's hand went out to Harry as he brought the boy forward to his side. 'Don't be afraid, Harry. I see you recognise him and you're right, *my son*, it's the enemy.'

John Conrad shook his head with disgust. 'Don't bring the child into this.' As he said it he looked down at the boy, who returned his gaze with a venomous expression and snuggled into Matthew's side.

A film of uneasiness washed over John Conrad as he took in the blue eyes, the fair hair and the child's face.

'My son feels what I feel,' Matthew replied. 'That's how it is with blood relatives.'

Caro's face was ashen as her daughter pulled on her hand

and asked, 'Who is it?' prompting Jane to step forward and take the child from her mother with a 'Sshh.'

'Come, son,' said Knobby as he edged round Matthew and took hold of Harry's shoulders but Matt did not release the child's hand.

'No, Knob, let him look at the soldier-boy; let him remind himself of the enemy.'

Bart tried to intervene. 'Please, Craken, this isn't right—'

But it was Caro's voice that stunned them all as she forced herself to move across the carpet towards them. All she could see was John Conrad's face. She almost stumbled as she spat the words. 'Stop! This is obscene!'

'Get her out of here.' Matt turned to Knobby but Knobby wavered indecisively between Harry and his mother, and in that moment Caro snatched Harry to her and planted herself in the valley of hate between the two men. 'Oh God, John Conrad! You must know . . . you must see . . .' she shouted, looking pleadingly into the face of the man she loved.

'Caro, I'm sorry, this is not what I would have had happen. I—' John Conrad began but Matthew swung nimbly across the floor to Caro's side, his left hand slid possessively round her shoulder as he drew her sharply to him and brought his face right down into her hair. 'All right, old girl, everything's all right. Calm down. No harm's been done. Now we'll all leave together: our children and you and me.' He glanced to Knobby. 'Let's go.'

Knobby started into action and moved across to Jane and Katy as Matthew began gently to pull Caro away from John Conrad.

Caro's lips were trembling, her eyes were filled with tears as her husband moved her steadily back across the room. She was aware that Knobby took Harry from her grasp but her eyes never left John Conrad's. To her it was as if the imaginary thread which joined her to John Conrad Fleet eased out and lengthened, as if her spirit ebbed from her while Matthew backed her away . . . away . . . across what to her was the chasm of carpet leading to the door.

Her, 'No . . .' hung feebly in the air.

At the door Matt eased her out on to the street where she stood dazed and unfocused. Then in one quick move her husband leaned back in the doorway. 'I'll see you in hell, Fleet!' he called.

'Hell's too good for you, Craken!' came John Conrad's automatic response.

As the door closed Ian Coates and Keith Martin made swift time towards it and the manager appeared at the top of the stairs to witness all quiet in the foyer below.

'Well,' breathed Andrew loudly, 'I'm glad that's over.'

'Me too,' answered Bart with a sigh.

John Conrad did not speak. He stood watching the door, thinking of Caro and the distracted beseeching in her eyes.

'Well, good night then.' Andrew shook hands with Bart and he offered his palm to John Conrad, who took it and shook it absent-mindedly.

After Andrew had gone, Bart held his brother's arm. 'Come, big brother, I think we've had enough for one evening.'

But John Conrad shook his head. 'Don't want to go home. I want to see Lena . . . and the children. Let's go there.'

And so half an hour after the débâcle in the Johnsonian Club, Lena, wearing a happy smile, poured out frothy beers while Jenny, chattering at the top of her voice, put oatcakes in a bowl and Tess giggled with joy as Danny sat on John Conrad's knee and Dave and Bluey and Bart sang 'Auld Lang Syne'.

THE WAR

Chapter Twenty-five

England, over four years later: Bank Holiday, 3 August 1914

The gleaming limousine purred its way along the winding roads of Kent, making steady progress towards Dover where the occupants were to cross to France on the second leg of their return journey to Egypt.

By the car windows, in a parade of chocolate-box pictures, flashed emerald-green Kentish fields, small villages, stone farmhouses, meadows edged with oaks and beeches, hedgerows filled with wild roses, brambles and daisies, dark copses and docile streams. The summer day was fair and the world, taken on the view from this passing vehicle, falsely proclaimed itself both temperate and benign.

The men who rode inside looked thoughtfully out upon *the green and pleasant land*. Fitz, sitting in front, half turned his head to K and John Conrad sitting in the back seat.

'We should be there by half-past twelve at this speed. The channel steamer departs at five to one and the Foreign Office have reserved us a compartment on the two fifty from Calais to Paris.'

'So we sleep on the train from Paris to Marseilles?' John Conrad asked.

'Yes, then by the orders of the First Lord of the Admiralty we've a cruiser to take us from Marseilles across to Alexandria.'

'Nice of Winston,' said John Conrad, smiling.

'I should think so,' murmured K. 'Churchill should take care of us.' He smiled, settling into the corner of the leather seat.

They were all quiet for a time, K leaning back, eyes closed, until Fitz broke the silence. 'K, I suppose it's likely that Germany will march into France next, now that they've declared war on Serbia and Russia. Don't you think it feels like we're on the brink of being in it too?'

'Yes, sadly I do. Though we've no duty whatever to France, no treaty of alliance with her. It's Belgium's neutrality that we've guaranteed, and there *is* a treaty to that effect, signed in the 1830s, I believe.'

John Conrad turned on the seat to his leader. 'So if the Germans enter Belgium, we'll be at war?'

'Yes, we will.'

'But if that happens they'll want you,' Fitz declared. 'And here we are heading off back to Egypt.'

'We've no reason to stay, Fitz.' K spoke thoughtfully, solemnly. 'I think that Mr Asquith and the government still believe it's unlikely the whole of Europe will be forced into war over a local skirmish in the Balkans. Bonar Law of the Tory opposition apparently feels the same and as I've not been party to the moves upon the diplomatic chessboard of Europe, made back and forth over the past weeks, I'm not in a position to really know. But one thing I do know is that the Kaiser, whom we've met more than once, and were not impressed by, you'll recall, has made the assassination of the Austrian archduke his excuse to now move upon his neighbours.'

They were passing through a small village and he looked out the window to where a group of boys played cricket on the village green. He eyed them speculatively and his tone sobered even more. 'I fear the present case in Europe may prove Sophocles' observation that great events appear to spring out of trivialities, but the causes are invariably profound. Modern Germany has come into its premier position by the sword. Their psyche is that of the Teutonic warrior nation; a past where Bismark ruled with blood and iron, where Heine instilled hero worship into them, Nietzsche imbued them with his *superman* culture and Bernhardy with his belief that war was the father of all things. Yes, my boys, Germany has been biding its time for decades since the Franco-Prussian war, and after my lunch with the German ambassador two weeks ago, I was convinced that the time was imminent as sadly, it's turning out to be.'

'Then why on earth are we leaving?' John Conrad asked.

'Because we haven't been requested to stay, Johnny.'

And that was the end of the matter until they arrived at the steamer waiting within the shadow of the castle at Dover. There they were informed that the others of their staff who were to join them for the crossing and then return to Egypt had all been detained in London.

K looked over his great moustache at the captain. 'Make ready to leave. We three will go at any rate.'

It was perhaps five minutes later, as the captain was about to pull up the gangplank, that a man ran up along the wharf to deliver a telegram to Lord Kitchener. K read it with a deep crease of concentration between his eyes. It was brief, a matter of a single line, and afterwards K lifted his gaze to look out across the English Channel. 'As it turns out after all, we return to London. Germany declared war on France today,' he told his boys, standing behind him: John Conrad, Fitz, and Edward Cecil, the other aide with them. 'The Prime Minister requests that I not leave England after all.'

'Oh God, then we must have declared war on them,' John Conrad stated quietly.

K nodded solemnly. 'If not, I'd say we're about to.'

The return journey to London was quiet, each of them with their own thoughts. They were on the outskirts of London and clouds had hidden the afternoon sun, when K interrupted their meditations. 'From memory I believe we have fewer than a 140,000 regulars in the British Isles and about 60,000 overseas whom we could draw back – all thoroughly trained specialists, but such tiny numbers. The territorials, with 14 divisions – about 250,000 odd – are grossly undermanned, and in my opinion, grossly undertrained, in fact, almost useless. We might double the numbers adding Indian and colonial establishments, but if we're to win this war, and any other outcome is inconceivable, I hate to say it but we'll need millions. I don't know how we can get enough men.'

John Conrad was unequivocal. 'If Mr Asquith makes you the Minister for War, and methinks the people will force him to do exactly that, it'll be up to you to recruit them.'

'Oh my God,' was the only response K gave.

When they arrived in London, K learned that Britain had given Germany an ultimatum: not to enter Belgium. The following day Germany marched into the Low Countries, ignoring Britain's ultimatum.

In reply, Great Britain declared war on Germany; becoming the single country to hold that distinction.

One day later, 5 August, *The Times* strongly urged Mr Asquith to surrender the War Office to Kitchener and the people of Britain clamoured for their hero to take the post. On 6 August the Prime Minister appeased the public and acquiesced in their demands: Lord Kitchener, at the age of sixty-four entered the cabinet as the Secretary of State for War, a soldier without politics surrounded by politicians, and the only serving military man to sit in the cabinet since the Duke of Albemarle in 1660.

The tumult of popular approval which greeted K's appointment reverberated around the globe. K did not introduce conscription. Instead, he made his entirely personal appeal to the nation and to the Empire, to those who had responded to his appointment with vigour and delight, to volunteer to fight with him. Personal posters appeared everywhere depicting his recognisable face, his piercing eyes, his awe-inspiring moustache, and his statement, 'Your Country Needs YOU'. In response the British nation, her Empire and her colonies around the world gave up their sons in inordinate numbers never before dreamed of: the Great War; the war to end all wars, had begun.

The first letter John Conrad wrote home after the declaration of war was not long. Eight and a half weeks after he penned it and a world away from the conflict, in the homely kitchen in the West End of Brisbane, while the sun headed to the horizon and an early spring wind blew across the brewery yard, Aunt Leigh, pulling her cardigan more closely around her and putting on her glasses, opened it to read it to Barrington and Bart, sitting with her at the big table.

12 August 1914
London

My Dears in Brisbane,

This is the first moment I've had to put pen to paper. The last week here has been insane. By the time this reaches home, you will be aware of the dreaded conflict which now engulfs Europe, and of K's appointment to the cabinet as Minister for War. With his instinct for things he is the man of the hour, and is working tirelessly, and Fitz, I and the others along with him. Already men are volunteering in their thousands to fight for him.

Today we've declared war on Austria-Hungary, and too we have sent our poor little British Expeditionary Force of a mere 100,000 men to reinforce the French in Northern France. Damn the Germans to hell for starting this. They already have 1,500,000 men in the field! Overpowering numbers, but don't despair, my loves. We know Australia, God bless her, and the other nations of the Empire are standing with us, and we will overcome the aggressor in the end. We must, for the sake of Europe and liberty.

The Government here and the Defence Committee are stating the war will be brief but K is of the opinion they are incorrect and that it will be a long-drawn-out war, and not won on the sea but fought on the ground in Europe. For once I pray he's wrong, but I'm afraid I know he's probably right.

I can tell you no more.

I miss you all and wish that I could see you. Don't worry about me. Always remember, every day, I am trained for this very state of affairs, that my whole adult life has been a preparation for this event, even though it is totally distasteful and repulsive to me.

Your loving son, nephew and brother,

John Conrad

PS For now you can write to me c/o 2 Carlton Gardens, London. Even when I make trips to the battlefield I will return here.

PPS Oh, and I'm now a full colonel and no longer an ADC. I'm one of K's Personal Military Secretaries, the other is Fitz. He needs both of us!!

Aunt Leigh lifted her glasses and wiped a tear from her eye with her apron. 'Ah, so there it is . . . Our lovely boy over there in another war, "The much-vaunted crime of slaughtering whole peoples". Seneca. I don't know if my poor old heart can stand it.'

'You'll be all right, dear,' Barrington patted her considerable arm. 'Even Fisher of the Labour opposition has said we'll stand behind England to the last man; the last shilling. And we must . . . all of us.'

'Pray God it doesn't come to that,' she said as she stood and moved across to the range to put the kettle on. 'Let's have a nice cuppa of Billy Tea.'

Bart sighed and leaned back in his chair. 'Yes, I've been to a war and I know. Though the South African one may prove to be a skirmish in comparison to this one, I reckon. The young men here are just like I was in '99 – all keen and thinking it's some sort of a spree. Can't say I wasn't the same, but there's no bloody glamour in warfare.'

Aunt Leigh rounded on him. 'Bartholomew, cease! There'll be no swearing in my kitchen, war or no war.'

He grinned raising his hands in supplication. 'Sorry, Aunt Leigh.' He looked across at this father. 'Dad, you should have seen the men pouring into the town hall to recruit. They say it's been the same every week since it started. We're backing the mother country, all right. Yesterday, Albert Square was full to the brim. And Kenny Neverson says the army camp in Bell's Paddock out at Enoggera is overflowing; can't fit any more tents in, no space.' He picked up one of his aunt's lamingtons and took a bite. 'They were arguing in the brewery this afternoon that the war'll probably be over before our boys get there. Takes six to eight weeks on a troop ship to France, you know, and the feeling is it'll be over by Christmas. But from what John Conrad says, that's not right.'

'Yes, lad, unfortunately, I'd put my money on John Conrad in this one.'

Aunt Leigh raised her eyes to heaven. 'I pray to heaven he and his K, as he calls him, are both wrong and it is over swiftly. Men dying and women widowed and bereaved – it's all too much. That horrible Kaiser, I hate him.' She took two teacups and saucers from the wall cupboard and moved to place them in front of her menfolk. 'Thank the Lord you're both too old to go.'

Bart took a deep breath and glanced at his father. 'That's not right, Aunt Leigh. I'm not too old, not at thirty-seven.'

The woman's face blanched and one of the cups fell from her hand to smash upon the floor. Bart scurried forward to pick up the pieces.

'No!' She moved quickly to stand in front of him. 'Tell me you won't volunteer. There are tens of thousands of men who should go before you. You've been to one, you've done your bit.' She took hold of his shoulders and brought his face round to hers. 'Promise me you won't.' She looked across to Barrington as the tears rose to her eyes. 'Barrington, please, support me. He's got the breweries to run. Tell him.'

'It's all right, Aunt Leigh,' her nephew kissed her cheek. 'I'm not joining up today. Don't worry.'

'She's right, lad,' his father spoke up. 'You went to fight the Boers, you've no need to go again. Country doesn't expect that.' He pointed to a chair. 'Sit down and drink your tea.'

'I'll pick up the broken cup first,' his son replied, kneeling down.

'Bart?'

He looked up to meet his aunt's eyes.

'It'll kill me if you go too. It's enough for me to pray every night for John Conrad, to live in fear of his life. I couldn't bear it, love, no, not if you went as well.'

Her nephew smiled. 'Don't worry about John Conrad. He's a colonel now, and K's aide. It's unlikely he'll be in the very forefront of battle.'

Barrington sighed gently. 'You never know, son, you never know.'

But Leigh had noticed that no promise had been forthcoming from her nephew. She tapped his shoulder as he knelt picking up the pieces. He raised his head as the angled afternoon sun glinted on the skin of his face. He looked boyishly young for his thirty-seven years. 'Please promise me?' she asked.

'I'll promise you I won't go . . . for now. That's all I can do.'

Exactly two miles away in a straight line across the river from the Fleet kitchen the cricket team and the parents and supporters of the under sixteens from the Mounthaven School for

Young Men cheered wildly as fifteen-year-old Harry Craken reached his eighty with a four straight to the boundary over square leg.

The team of the Brisbane Boys' Grammar hooted in disappointment. The ritual and important match between the two schools, which kicked off the cricket season, was over. Harry had carried his bat and his eighty had come with the last man in at the other end. They had beaten the Grammar School 174 runs to 171.

'Daring, daring, wonderful shot,' Headmaster Raleigh said above the clamour as he smiled broadly and applauded. At his side Mr Reath, the chemistry master and the coach of the team, who was the most understanding teacher to the boys, agreed heartily. 'The winning shot. Craken's saved the day.'

The winners jumped high in the air and shouted and slapped each other on the back. Harry was raised to their shoulders and carried off the field. The passers-by on College Road and Gregory Terrace bordering the ground, stopped to watch and listen as the boys began spontaneously to sing:

> 'Once a jolly swagman camped by a billabong
> Under the shade of a coolibah tree,
> And he sang as he watched and waited
>   till his billy boiled,
> "Who'll come a-waltzing Matilda with me.
>
> "Waltzing Matilda, waltzing Matilda,
> Who'll come a-waltzing Matilda with me."
> And he sang as he watched and waited
>   till his billy boiled,
> "Who'll come a-waltzing Matilda with me."'

Knobby grinned. 'That song's certainly caught on.'

Matthew, sitting between Caro and Knobby, gave a slanted smile. 'Hasn't it? It's somehow redolent of this country, speaks of Australia. Fascinating how a culture takes shape.' He lifted his cane and pointed to the group carrying Harry from the field. 'Little bugger's a good batsman, no doubt about it, but I'm afraid I cannot become enamoured of the game, even with our Harry at the crease.'

'He was great,' Knobby said proudly.

Caro beamed. 'Oh, but wasn't he?'

While it had been a less spectacular affair this year, owing to the beginning of the war, and more restraint had been shown by dropping the gala buffet luncheon for parents, it was still a special day for the boys and they now crowded round the dais just off the field in sight of the parents where the two headmasters and coaches moved to address them.

The headmaster of the Grammar School spoke briefly but graciously, and gave credit to Mounthaven, Mr Reath and, in particular, Harry Craken. Mr Raleigh responded and congratulated the losers on a 'splendid innings'. He too praised the teams and the coaches, and 'young Harry Craken, a sportsman to be reckoned with'. He ended with the words, 'And so begins another cricket season, and the harmony and goodwill between our two schools continues. In these troubled times it is of immense importance to keep our values. While our men join up to support the mother country in her fierce battle against aggression, our boys here today prove that the prescribed order of things, normal life and customs are precious.'

His counterpart then rose again to his feet. 'Thank you all for attending and tea will now be served in the quadrangle.'

Matt rose to his feet as the other parents milled round them. 'Do you want tea, Caro? Personally I'd rather have a rum at this time of the afternoon.'

Caro caught Knobby's eye. 'Fancy that.'

'No cheek from you, old girl. Wouldn't you rather have a rum, Knob? We could slip down the hill to the Chevron. There's a ladies' bar there now.'

'Suits me, but hadn't we better thank the headmaster?'

'I'll do that,' Caro said, standing and picking up her umbrella.

Matt turned his eyes skywards. 'Thank heaven. The old fellow's a bloody bag of wind, if you ask me.'

Just then Harry burst through the throng upon them. 'Dad, did you see my winning four?' His eyes were shining and his face was pink from his hours in the sun.

'I'm not blind, old son, bloody brilliant.' He slapped Harry's shoulder almost enthusiastically as Knobby took the youth in his arms and hugged him. 'Great, kiddo. You won the

407

match for them. Knew you would. Carried your bat too, what an effort.'

The boy beamed proudly. 'Wish we'd annihilated them, not just beaten them by three runs.'

'It doesn't matter. You were wonderful, darling,' Caro finally managed to tell him. 'But remember, have some compassion for them. They tried their best.'

Harry knew *compassion* was his mother's watchword so he smiled tolerantly. 'Thanks, Mum.'

After Caro had made their goodbyes Harry saw them off. He was congratulated by parents and boys alike as they made their way through the crowd to the street.

'Thanks for coming, Mum and Dad, Uncle Knobby.'

'We'll see you on Saturday, darling,' Caro called as they drove away.

Harry waved them along Gregory Terrace and turned back to the Grammar School grounds. He was soon joined by Luke Marland, his best friend and another boarder. Luke's father owned a sheep station out near Charleville in Western Queensland and he remained at school all term. Some weekends he went home with Harry, either to Cedar Grove or staying in town, depending on where Harry's father was. The two boys loved the trips up to Gatton in the train; they smiled and laughed at all manner of things and generally amused themselves the whole way.

'What did you reckon about that?' Harry asked.

'About what?'

'My winning four.'

'You're not still on about that, are you?' his mate laughed, thumping him on the back. 'I could have hit that one given half the chance.'

'Then how come you were out for a duck?'

'Thanks for reminding me.' They laughed again and ran back to join their mates. As they passed under the arch leading into the quadrangle Mr Reath came out of a door to their right. His warm face wrinkled into a smile behind his horn-rimmed glasses. 'There you are, Craken. What a nice innings.'

'Thank you, sir.'

'Pity about the duck, Marland.'

Luke stretched himself up to his full five feet six. 'Ah, sir, that was sheer bad luck. I was pulling that for four; ball just slipped between my bat and my body, that's all, and the next thing, well, hit the stump. Absolutely unlucky was all it was.'

The master kept a straight face. 'Well, Marland, fortunately it's left your ego intact.' He nodded and walked off.

Harry dug his friend in the ribs, 'You'd talk your way out of a paper bag.'

This was the funniest thing they had heard all day and they laughed all the way across the quadrangle to join their team-mates in doing justice to tea and cakes.

Later that night after lights-out, the two friends lay in their beds side by side in the small dormitory for just eight boys in a wing above the assembly hall, where bougainvillaea trailed in over the windowsill and the sweet aroma of jasmine from the plants outside drifted in through the open windows.

Luke whispered to Harry. 'Got a letter from Mum this afternoon. My uncle's joined up.'

'Really?'

'Yes, Uncle Bill, best horseman and shot in the whole Charleville area. He'll give the Germans what for. Wouldn't surprise me if he ends up a general.'

Harry was silent for a few moments, then he replied. 'Would you join up, Luke?'

'Yeah, I would if I were old enough.'

'Reckon I would too. They say Spall's going to join.'

'What, the maths teacher?'

'Yeah. Apparently some of the boys heard him say so.'

'Gosh, never thought of him as a soldier. Reckon I'd make a good one though. I'm a damn good shot too, you know. Uncle Bill taught me. I can hit a tin can on a fence stump at fifty paces, right slap in the middle.'

'I've never seen you do that.'

'Next time we're at Cedar Grove I'll show you. Your Uncle Knobby's got a rifle, hasn't he?'

'Of course.'

'Can't you two shut up?' complained Larry Patterson from the bed opposite. 'Some of us are trying to sleep.'

The two friends began to giggle but soon their mirth subsided and they drifted into sleep. Harry dreamed of shooting at tin

cans with Mr Spall sitting on a fence watching him. Luke
dreamed of his Uncle Bill.

Some hours earlier when Caro, Matthew and Knobby had
driven down into the city and parked the car in William Street
outside the Chevron Club, they had crossed the wide verandah
and entered the open French doors into the ladies' lounge. It
was an attractive room with green and white striped wallpaper
and flowers in polished copper urns on the bar, though in the
last few days beside the flowers had appeared small containers
with signs upon them: 'GIVE YOUR CHANGE TO THE RED
CROSS AND THE WAR EFFORT.'

Matthew had chosen a deep comfortable chair and lazed
back in it, pointing to the one beside it for Caro.

'What'll you have Matt?' asked Knobby. 'A rum?'

'Yes, please, old son.'

'And you, Caro, your usual brandy, lime and soda water?'

Caro hesitated. 'No . . . just a lemonade tonight, Knobby.'

Matthew turned to her. 'What's wrong?'

'Nothing, Matthew. Just got a queasy tummy, I think.'

'Better to have the brandy then. It's good for that sort
of thing.'

'No thanks, just the lemonade.'

Caro did in fact feel queasy. She had for a week or two
on and off, especially in the mornings. She feared the truth.
A woman whose monthly change came regularly to the day,
Caro was now four weeks overdue. She hated the thought that
she might be pregnant again. It was abhorrent to her. She was
always so careful and tried to be away from Matt in the weeks
of the month when she knew she was vulnerable. She was angry
and indignant. The last thing she wanted was to bear another
of Matt's children: one was enough. Not that she didn't love
Katy. She did. As the years had passed Caro had seen the child
for what she was: charitable, warm-hearted and obliging, much
like Caro's father's mother, who had died when Caro was ten,
but she well remembered her placid sweet grandmother. Katy
looked exactly like Matt, but she had her great-grandmother's
disposition. But another child? No, she could not bear it, though
she feared it were true.

Three weeks later she was positive. She thought wild things

like finding someone to terminate it, but just as she had rejected that alternative sixteen years before, so she did again. She accepted her condition; but nothing, nothing, would make her happy about it.

She did not tell Matthew, but finally he guessed. One early evening on the verandah at Cedar Grove, Caro sat, head buried in the atlas looking at Dunkirk, Ostend, Ypres, Mons and Conde, and Matt stroked Rubens who had lost his partner, Hogarth, the previous year. Matt broke the silence. 'So you're having another baby, old girl?'

She looked up. 'I thought you'd work it out eventually.'

'Caro, I've known ever since the night at the Chevron Club when you knocked back the brandy or at least let's say, I suspected then. I was waiting for you to tell me, but I suppose I would have been presented with the little bugger first.'

Caro did not answer. She sat looking at the atlas.

Matt eyed her silently for a time, before he took her hand. 'Come on, old girl, why is it you're so unhappy about this?'

Caro shrugged and, removing her hand, responded without looking up. 'Oh Matt, I'm thirty-five, I've got all the family I want. Two are enough.'

'How unfortunate,' he said slowly, just as Knobby and Jane and their little daughter, Isobel, came out to join them. As they moved to the white wicker sofa, he lifted his glass of wine to them. 'We're going to have another Craken in the family.'

Caro looked up quickly, annoyance on her face. 'Matt . . .'

Jane smiled happily and came over to Caro. 'Darling, you never told me.'

'No, well . . .'

'Hey, that's great,' said Knobby, sitting down beside Matt. 'Wondered why you weren't joining us in a little tipple of late, Caro. Thought you'd become a member of the Band Of Hope.'

Caro managed a small smile. 'I'd love to have a drink, Knobby, it's just that I feel rotten all the time.'

Jane patted her hand. 'That'll pass, love.'

Matt put down his glass, leaned over and touched Caro gently on the shoulder. 'Well, I'm glad, anyway. Well done, old girl.'

'Yeah, congratulations,' said Knobby. 'It'll be good to hear the patter of little feet again.' He lifted his small daughter on to his lap and kissed her. 'Might give us some more incentive, hey, Jane love?'

His wife smiled, embarrassed. 'Oh, Knobby, don't say things like that.'

Matt picked up his glass and drained it, eyeing his wife, who finally put down the atlas.

'Let's talk about something else,' she said.

Chapter Twenty-six

Four months later, the early April sun rode in a wide slanting corridor across the verandah and through the kitchen door at Cedar Grove, where Caro lifted her head to look up as a strand of curly hair fell over her eyes. She tucked it back behind her ear as Matt entered.

He swung round the table as she put down the iron. His hand went out to rest on her extended stomach. 'Is it kicking?'

'Not at the moment.'

'We'd better get back to Brisbane soon where there's proper medical care. It's due in two months, isn't it?'

'Yes, about that, Matt. Anyway, it's Harry's birthday in a couple of weeks so yes, we all should be down there.'

'I think Knobby and I'll go down tomorrow afternoon then. Why don't you and Jane and the girls follow in a week or so at your leisure? That'll be about the right time for Harry's day, won't it?'

Caro could not help it, it was out of her mouth before she knew. 'So I'd be too much trouble to travel with, would I, Matt? Yes, that's right, leave it to Jane to bring the fat cow and Katy and Isobel to Brisbane.'

Matt eyed her speculatively for a few seconds. Two flies, insistent as only country flies can be, buzzed round his face and he swung at them with his hand as he spoke. 'I've three pictures to deliver to Coates the day after tomorrow, that's why I'm going, and Knobby and I are carrying the canvases from here. Actually, I thought it'd be awkward for you to travel with us as I'll be taking the dray to the station, not the most desirable vehicle for a girl in your state, but yes, we can depart together, old girl, I've no objection to that.'

Caro picked up the iron in front of her and began to press a dress.

Matt remained where he was for a moment and then sat

down, putting his cane on the end of the table. 'As for being a *fat cow* I know it wasn't your intention to have another baby, Caro, and you aren't happy about it, that's been obvious from the beginning, but personally, old girl, I think you look quite beautiful.'

This was too much for Caro. A compliment from Matthew was more than she could stand. Her reply was snappish. 'All right, Matt, we all know that's not true, for a start. And yes, it's the wrong time for a baby. I feel so guilty bringing one into this world when thousands of boys are dying. Eight months of war now. Where will it end?' She waved away the same flies, which had turned their attention to her, as she busied herself with the dress.

'Where indeed? All of them killing each other. Dead and maimed for what? The old Kaiser is a mad bugger, by all accounts, can't imagine why anybody would be fighting for him, and Austria-Hungary, all they did for the whole nineteenth century was have rebellions and fight everybody.' Matt's lip curled. 'And as for the Turks – for heaven's sake, descended from the Tartars and the Huns, all blood-thirsty buggers as well. Like a war, that lot do. As for our side, there they were, a few weeks ago when I was in the city, the big-boned brawny soldier-boys, marching down Queen Street row by row to join the ships, cheered on all sides. All neat in their uniforms, neatly marching off to oblivion.'

'Don't say that, Matt. It's horrible. They're good brave men. You just have a thing about soldiers. They're dying for freedom over there. Britain had no choice but to fight Germany; she'd made a pact with Belgium and she's not the kind to renege; and we along with her. All those reports in the *Courier* and the *Telegraph* of our boys coming in to join up from all over, the towns and settlements, the sheep runs and the farms, the furthest parts of the territory, they're enlisting in their tens of thousands already. I'm proud of them.'

Matt laughed. 'Now you know what? You should be in the parliament, old girl, then instead of just berating me, you could tell them a thing or two. Give Fisher and his lot what for.' He wagged his finger at her.

Caro gave an exasperated sound and went back to pressing.

He watched her silently for a time, resting the ankle of his bad leg up on his good knee. Then he took an envelope out of his pocket. It was long, brown and official, and had OHMS in the corner. 'I came in to show you this, actually.'

'What is it?' she asked, not looking up.

'A letter from the Federal Government. Came in the batch Matilda sent from Brisbane. Arrived this morning. Seems there's an idea being put forward in Britain that eventually they might create an official scheme whereby artists will go to the war zone and depict what they see. It's only an embryo of an idea yet, but some bugger has generously given them my name. Don't know who to blame for that yet. As if I'd be mad enough to want to go over there.'

Caro put down the iron. 'You're a fine artist, Matt, there's no doubt of that. Perhaps you should consider it, if it comes to pass. Queensland would be proud of you. No one could depict it better than you. The way you paint can be very telling.'

Matt's eyes widened in horror. 'Goddam it, old girl, while I delight in the verity of your opinion on my work, battles are not my style. I'm a bit old for all that, and just consider it – all the way over there on my own, what would I possibly do without . . .'

Caro looked up quickly and Matt finished the sentence, 'Knobby.'

She actually smiled. 'You're incorrigible.'

'Mmm, I know.' He leaned over and patted her on the bottom.

'Give up, Matt,' she said, lifting the iron towards him menacingly. Then suddenly her face contorted in pain and she dropped the iron back on the table. She drew in her breath sharply and held the lower part of her stomach.

Matt moved surprisingly nimbly round to her. 'What the devil's wrong?' He eased her down into a chair. 'Can't be the baby yet, can it?'

Slowly her face relaxed. 'No. It was nothing. Short pain. I get them sometimes.'

'Doesn't that mean something? How often do you get them?'

'Not often,' she lied, for she had had these odd sharp pains in her lower abdomen now for weeks on and off.

'Come on, stop ironing. I want you to lie down.'

'I'm all right.'

Mary and Jane and little Isobel came in from the hall. Jane had a pile of washed clothes in her arms. 'Everything all right?' she asked.

Matt shook his head, 'No, Caro's not well . . . a pain. I want her to lie down.'

The women were all concern. 'Come on, love.' They helped Matt to lift Caro to her feet.

'I'm all right,' Caro insisted. 'I can walk, you know.'

'Then do so, into the bed: now,' Matt insisted.

When Caro lay propped up by a mass of pillows Jane brought her some water and Mary patted her forehead. 'I was just going to make a cuppa anyway, so I'll do that and bring you one.'

As she left the room Jane and Matt sat on each side of the bed. Jane lifted Isobel into her arms as Matt spoke. 'No heroics now, just the truth, old girl. Are you all right, really?'

'Mmm, these things happen to people in my condition.'

'I suppose so,' he nodded.

She gave a smile. 'Off you go, Matt. If you're to take those paintings to Brisbane tomorrow you'd better get Knobby and pack them now. It's after five already.'

He gave her an odd look, which made her somehow uncomfortable. 'Caro, I won't go to Brisbane if you're not well.'

'What about Coates and the paintings?'

'Bugger Coates and the paintings.'

She sighed. 'I'll be all right. I'm pretty strong you know . . . have to be to put up with you. Off you go.'

He stood and moved to the door where he looked back and pointed to the bed with his cane. 'Make sure she stays there until dinner, Jane. I'll come in here and have a drink around seven.' He grinned at Caro. 'You can watch me.'

'Thanks,' she answered dryly as he closed the door. He would never alter, she was sure of that. She looked up at Jane, who shrugged, saying, 'Matt's a one.'

'Yes, he is.'

'He's right, though, you must rest. There was no need for you to be doing that ironing with Mary and me here. You really should take more care of yourself. Have you had this pain before?'

'No,' she lied again.

'Thank heaven.' Jane lifted her daughter forward. 'Kiss Auntie Caro and we'll leave her to rest.' The child kissed Caro's cheek and Jane departed with her.

Alone in the room Caro looked around. The pale pink lace curtains stirred in the breeze. It was a balmy afternoon, quite pleasant, though in high summer in January and February they had been subject to some bad heat. The movement of the lace in little rhythmic leaps reminded her of a dress she had worn to the concert with John Conrad so many years ago: pink with little lace insets in the skirt. Yes, back in '98, the night dear Hargy died. To think of that made her sad, even after all these years, but it was also that same night that John Conrad had first held her and loved her. She trembled even now at the memory and possibly it was that very night when she and John Conrad had made Harry. One life disappeared off this planet and another was made. Harry, the light of her life.

They would have a lovely party for him for his sixteenth birthday. He seemed to like boarding school now. Matt had wanted to send him to Nudgee and Matt's mother had been ecstatic, being a Catholic, but Caro had prevailed as she often did where Harry was concerned and he had been accepted into the Mounthaven School for Young Men. With his father's eyes and hair, she saw John Conrad every time she looked at him, though she suspected no one else did, for while his colouring was definitely John Conrad's, as he was growing up some of his features were like those of her own father. Trust Matt to be so lucky.

She closed her eyes, thinking of John Conrad as she did habitually every day. She wondered where he was. On the kitchen wall above the sink she had hung a recruiting poster. Matt had objected, saying it was bad art and he didn't want it anywhere in his house, but it was her kitchen and she had insisted. Beside it she had hung a map of Europe and the Middle East, and marked the war zones. She looked at it often and thought of John Conrad and how brave he was. She prayed for his life every night.

Her baby moved slightly and she put her hand on her stomach. What she wouldn't have given for this child to be John Conrad's and not Matthew's; but that was life; and life had a way of kicking you both inside and out. She gave a wan smile at the epigram. Yet her smile faded quickly, for the baby had not really kicked as much as she thought it should in the last few weeks. And coupled with the pain, she was worried now. She decided she would go back to Brisbane with Matt tomorrow afternoon after all. She made herself more comfortable and resolved she would see a doctor as soon as they got there.

But it was not to be, for at midnight while Matt and Knobby sat out on the verandah drinking she had massive shooting pains that racked her whole body and as she clambered out of bed and staggered along the corridor to call for Jane and Mary, the blood came. At four in the morning she was delivered of a baby, a stillborn little boy.

Jane and Mary had consoled her and tended her and at last she had drifted off to sleep only to wake for some reason and to see Matt standing silently beside her, with an expression on his face that surprised her: a look of abysmal mournful sadness. He called her 'darling', and bent down and kissed her forehead, and she fell back to sleep. The next day she believed it must have been a dream.

They named him Roy and put him in the ground at Cedar Grove down the gentle slope that led to the creek in a grove of pale green acacia trees where she had planted deep purple bougainvillaea, and he could feel the tenderness in the breeze as it wafted up the hill at dusk. Knobby ordered a headstone of shining white granite and on it, highlighted in gold they carved the words:

> Roy Craken, who left his life before it
>   began on 7 April 1915
> A tiny star which never was to shine

Caro did a lot of thinking after the ordeal; the loss of the baby affected her more than she could have believed. She would ride off alone sometimes for hours, letting the wind blow in her hair and communing with the rhythm of the bush. It gave her solace for there was a great guilt living in her soul. Part of her believed because she had not wanted the child; thus the child, in the everlasting wisdom of the eternity of the unborn, had rejected her and had not come to her. She always rode home past Roy; stopping and talking to him, telling him of her love for him and apologising to him as the tears flowed in desperate sorrow from her heart to her little boy in the ground.

Katy was being a sweet companion. At thirteen the child realised her mother's sadness and would do all sorts of little jobs for her and hang about her, hugging her. Caro was deeply grateful for her daughter's understanding and companionship.

It was about six weeks after the ordeal that Caro came riding into the stable-yard just on dusk; she had been out in the bush for over an hour and sitting beside Roy's grave for half that time. There, leaning up against the east wall of the stable was Matthew. He had yellow oil paint on his trousers and another little bit in the flash of grey hair at his temples. As she dismounted he came forward. She noticed his scar; it seemed strangely prominent in the dying afternoon sun.

He watched her take the saddle off the horse. As she did Jacob Brady came out of the stable and took it from her. 'Don't worry, I'll put the mare to bed,' he said.

Caro smiled. 'Thanks, Jake.'

Then she turned questioningly to Matthew. 'Why were you waiting for me, Matt?'

He gave a crooked grin. 'Knob and I are going back to Brisbane tomorrow.'

She nodded. 'All right.'

His dark eyes looked oddly sympathetic; it surprised her. 'Thing is . . . I'm thinking you need some bright lights, old girl. I want you . . . and Jane and the girls to come with us. All of us to go down to New Farm. Time you saw your mother and father again anyway.'

She stood looking at him and suddenly she felt as if she were going to cry.

He waved his cane in the air. 'So, we'll leave tomorrow. I'll tell Jake and Mary so they can make ready. Right?'

She held her emotion in and gave a little nod. 'Right.'

'Good,' he said, and pushed himself forward on his cane. As he passed her he halted, putting out his hand and stroking her on the face, before he limped away.

Behind him her eyes filled with tears and broke over her lids.

* * *

The following week Bart sat behind his desk dealing with the ubiquitous paperwork that gathered in the running of a business. They had opened another brewery in Gympie a year before and it was doing well too; beer sales did not seem to be affected by the war. He lifted his gaze to the open window and there on a branch that hung across it was a magpie; so close that his sleek ebony and white wings glistened as if they were waxed. Bart watched as the bird moved in staccato-like steps sideways along the branch to the end, where it swayed under his weight and he flew away.

The magpie made him think of the magic of flight and how he had read in the *Courier* that aeroplanes were being used for reconnaissance in the war zones and that in time they could be used actually to fight battles in the air; once they could equip them with guns. It was astounding to imagine it. The newspapers of late had carried much about the Australian and New Zealand troops in the Dardanelles, though as yet he had not read about aircraft being used there.

He went back to his mountain of paperwork, and a gentle rap sounded on the door. In came one of the secretaries, Miss Burton, a lady of indeterminate age, who had been so for the ten years she had worked at the brewery. She had the quaint habit of threading a lead pencil through her hair behind her ear.

'Someone to see you, Mr Fleet.'

Bart shook his head, 'I'm not expecting anyone.'

'I know, but she says it's very important. Her name's Caro, that's all she said.'

Bart's eyes closed momentarily. 'Send her in.'

When she opened the door Bart remained sitting behind his desk. 'Caro, fancy seeing you here.'

'Yes, I knew you'd be surprised. What is it? Four or five years, I suppose?'

'Mmm, must be. What can I do for you?'

Caro brought her hand up to touch her lip as she answered, 'I'd like a few minutes of your time.'

Bart made no reply but he gestured to a chair, and when Caro sat, she went on, 'Is . . . John Conrad still in the army, that is . . . still with Kitchener of Khartoum?'

'Yes, Caro, that's right.'

'I see. Then now we're at war, he'll be fighting.'

'Well, he'll be in London and their headquarters in the field a lot, I'd imagine, but yes, at times, I suppose, he must be in the actual fighting zones.'

Her hands felt damp and she wiped them on her skirt. She hesitated a moment or two. 'This war has changed things. It alters people.' She was uncertain how to go on, so she paused, then said, 'I've just lost a baby . . . that is, a little while ago. I feel a need to do and say things that perhaps I wouldn't have before. I think it's to do with losing the baby . . . and the war. I want to be honest, that is.'

Bart eyed her speculatively and remained silent. All he knew was that when Caro appeared so did trouble.

'Could you tell me where John Conrad is?'

Bart rested his chin in his hand, elbow on the desk, staring at her. 'Caro, I don't know where John Conrad is.'

'But you receive letters from him, surely?'

'Yes, of course, but he's a colonel in the British army. He's not allowed to give his whereabouts.' He grunted in exasperation. 'Caro, what's this really about?'

She had come to tell him that Harry was John Conrad's son. She had decided this sitting alone one afternoon by Roy's grave. She believed that someone in John Conrad's family must know the truth. Bart was the one. Little lost Roy had made her think about life and death and truth. She wanted to tell Bart the truth so badly it hurt her insides. She actually bent forward and held her middle before straightening up.

'Caro, I haven't got time for this,' Bart's tone was irritated. 'What are you really here for?'

'I . . . I've come to tell you something.'

'Yes? What's that?'

Her eyes had the wild look that Bart had seen in them at the Johnsonian Club and he was worried she might shout and make a scene. But he was wrong. She began to speak very softly. 'I, that is, John Conrad and I . . . when we were together in . . .' Then she halted and suddenly the fire went out of her, and she sank back in the chair, seeming much smaller.

She could not say the words. Perhaps she had held the truth in too long: perhaps her sworn promise to Matthew made her withdraw. When she spoke again her voice quivered out of her, changing her reason for coming, faltering on the brink. 'Would it be possible, could you . . .' she hesitated. Then she took a deep breath. 'Could you please allow me to read his letters? It's not that I want to keep them, just to read them.' She could see he was shaking his head ready to decline and she hurried on, 'I suppose you think I've got no right to ask, as someone else's wife, but, Bart, please . . . try to understand.'

'Caro, Caro, what do you expect? When John Conrad was home last I did as you asked and if he had come to meet you by the river, he would have run into Craken, and God knows what would have occurred then. It was bad enough the night in the Johnsonian Club: that awful confrontation. Don't you realise that your husband has a terrible temper where you're concerned? Why, if he knew you were here now I bet there'd be hell to pay.'

Caro shook her head vehemently. 'That's as may be, but I don't care.'

'Then you *should* care. You're correct in saying I think you've no right to ask for John Conrad's letters. I do. So there's no more to be said.' He stood and moved round the desk, pointing to the door.

Caro stood but she did not move away. 'Please, please, Bart, let me say a little more. Please . . . for what we used to mean to each other.'

Bart's expression was resigned. 'Why do you always say that?'

'Because it's true, we were close once. And I still miss Aunt Leigh and Uncle Barrington . . . and you.'

Bart shook his head. 'It's been over fifteen years, Caro.'

'Seventeen, Bart, and I think of it every day.' She looked down and did not meet his gaze as she found a little of her former determination and, making tight fists of her hands at her sides to give herself strength, she said, 'I loved your brother then, and I love him now. I have never for a minute stopped loving him . . . not when I stood at the altar, not when I was delivered of my children, not for any day in the seventeen years . . .' She looked directly into Bart's eyes, '. . . and not now,' she finished.

'Oh, Caro, how the devil do you expect me to believe that? You've just told me you lost another baby, Craken's baby.'

She nodded. 'Yes, poor, poor little thing. It was a mistake.'

He made a scoffing sound. 'The third mistake . . . that I know of.' He moved to the door.

She took a step forward towards him, lifting one hand with shaking fingers in a pleading motion. 'I've had no other avenue to take in my life, Bart. You mightn't believe it but it's true. Please, please, just let me have a little bit of John Conrad now, now when his life might be in danger. All I ask is to read his letters and only the ones you think fit. That's all I ask. To touch his life ever so remotely once again. Oh God, Bart, can't you have it in your heart to help me? Have compassion. If anything happens to him . . . I—'

'You made your choice, Caro. All those years ago. You could have had John Conrad – he was mad about you – but no, you were off with Craken behind his back. Caro, this is silly. I think it's time you went.' His hand went out to the door and he turned the handle to open it, but suddenly Caro was at his side, holding his arm, staying him. 'All right, Bart, perhaps it was wrong of me to come, to say what I've said, but I've spoken truth today, whether you believe me or not.'

'Then why, Caro? Why the devil did it all go so wrong for you two?'

The only reply she gave was a heaving of her shoulders and a sigh. Then she tried to smile, but she couldn't and her eyes filled with tears. He stood there with his hand on the door knob, peering at her, and the kindness and charity that was ever a force in Bartholomew's character swelled up and overcame.

'All right, Caro. I don't know why I'm doing this, but you can read some of his letters.'

Her lip began to tremble and she tried another smile.

'He's only written a few times since the war began, anyway, and he usually writes to all of us. Aunt Leigh keeps those, but there was one just to me, which I have. In future I'll keep the ones he writes to me here in the office and if I deem them suitable I'll let you read them. But you can't come here again. For heaven's sake, you could have been followed today; your husband seems to be expert at that.'

'No,' she looked into his eyes. 'I swear he doesn't know.'

Bart opened the door and with the words, 'Wait here,' he disappeared to return a few minutes later and hand her an envelope.

She took it as one might take the Holy Grail.

'Now listen, Caro, you made a telephone call to me once before. If you place a call to me when you can, say, every few months or so, then I'll let you know if I have any letters or not. If I do I'll meet you somewhere while you read them. You can't keep them – that'd be too dangerous with the bloke you're married to. So I'm going outside now while you read this one. I'll be back in a couple of minutes.'

'Thank you,' Caro managed to say as he departed.

And so she feasted on John Conrad's words, written just before Christmas. He was in France for meetings with the French High Command; that made her feel such pride. That's all there was about his whereabouts, and much of the letter was taken up with detail about the cold weather and the rain and what they might have for Christmas dinner back in London if they were lucky. There was a mention of the troops being in good spirits, but it was his own handwriting she gloried in and she thrilled to hold the paper he had written upon. She kissed the words, 'Your loving brother, John Conrad', and she memorised the address: 2 Carlton Gardens, London.

When Bart returned she handed him back the letter, shook hands with him and met his eyes. 'I will do as you ask and I thank you from the bottom of my soul for this kindness you have done me today.'

He gave her a hollow smile and she departed.

When she was out in the street heading to the tramline in the glaring brightness of the Queensland sunshine she thought that after all it had been a successful visit. No, she had not told Bart the true reason she had come, but she now had access to him and through him to John Conrad, how ever tenuous the link. That very thought lifted her spirits and she hummed a little tune to herself as she walked along, the dust of the unsealed footpath lifting to stain the hem of her long skirt.

Ten minutes later, Miss Burton was back in Bart's office. 'An army officer, Major Littlefair, here to see you, sir.'

Bart looked surprised. 'My second unscheduled visitor. Send him in.'

The major entered and Bart came round the desk to shake hands. 'What can I do for you, Major Littlefair?'

He was a short, good-looking man, finely built with sun-bleached hair and bright eyes above a freckled nose. 'There's a war on,' he said, rather redundantly to Bart's way of thinking.

'Yes.'

'Well, Mr Fleet, it's come to my superior officer's attention that you were in the South African Campaign. Made captain shortly before demobilisation, I'm told.'

Bart nodded and motioned him to a chair.

He sat and Bart did the same. 'Got any plans to join up?'

'As a matter of fact I'm considering it. Reason I haven't as yet is because there was some talk it'd be over in a few months but that didn't happen so I feel pressure to do my bit for King and country. Are you on a recruiting drive?'

He grinned. 'Sort of. Fact is, we need officers. Trained ones, that is, to train others. We need them here in Queensland. We're desperate for men such as yourself. Files say you left the army in 1903 so it's only coming up twelve years since you were in uniform. You must recall some of it. Also said you were graded A-one in all aspects . . . very impressive; there weren't a lot of you. Doesn't look like conscription'll be coming in, so we've got to convince you to join up. If you do you'll be given your old rank and sent on a short training course to remind you of what's what and to familiarise yourself with modern weapons and strategies. We'd like you to consider it. Would you?'

'If I join up I'll be wanting to go to fight. That's where you need men, isn't it? In the battles?'

'Well yes, of course we do, but at present we need officers to train them more. We're desperate really, as I said before. You could make a hell of a difference.'

Bart sat looking steadily at his visitor.

'Will you think about it?'

Bart nodded and stood up and the major, taking his cue, rose and moved to the door. 'A phone call to Enoggera 891 will get me any time.'

'Thanks,' replied Bart, 'I'll let you know.'

At one o'clock Batholomew crossed the brewery yard, passed through the white gate and under the mango tree, mounted the steps to the wide verandah and entered the kitchen of Brewery House.

'Lunch ready, Aunt Leigh?' he called, as his father entered from the hall and they both sat down where their places were set neatly on a bright floral tablecloth.

'Yes,' came the reply as the woman entered from the scullery, carrying a side of meat on a white platter. As she placed it on the table she said, 'There's a letter from David and Emma Louise. Came this morning.' David and Emma Louise had departed Australia with their baby daughter when Emma's Aunt Gertrude and her Uncle Hewitt had decided to return home to England.

Aunt Leigh looked hard at Bart. 'I know you're not fond of your young brother, but you should at least read it. They've got rationing in England now, the poor souls.' She waved her hand across the meal in front of them. 'And we're in the land of plenty.'

Bart did not reply.

His aunt cut a slice of meat. 'Who was that I saw leaving the office block at half-past nine?'

Barrington looked up. 'Who? What do you mean?'

Bart shook his head. 'I know what she means, Dad.' He eyed his aunt. 'You know exactly who it was.'

'What was *she* doing here?'

'She? Who?' questioned Barrington.

Bart addressed his father. 'It was Caro. She came to visit me.'

There was surprise in Barrington's voice. 'Oh I see.'

'Well, I don't,' said Leigh, peevishly. 'What did she want with this family?'

Bart gave an exasperated look at his aunt. 'I can't tell you. It was personal and private.'

Leigh was cutting the meat with very definite movements. 'Ah, personal and private, is it? A secret. Well, Bartholomew, "Nothing is secret that shall not be made manifest": the Gospel according to St Luke.'

Bart's tone became exasperated. 'I didn't say it was a secret, I said it was private. Look, Aunt Leigh, I think it should be enough for you simply to accept what I say and not pry. Anyway, she won't be coming again.'

His aunt gave a small disgruntled sound. 'Well, that's the only good news you've told us so far.'

Barrington lifted his hand in the air. 'Could we have our lunch now and talk like family instead of foes, please?'

'Certainly,' stated Bart. Then he gave his peace offering. 'Looks like a nice lunch, Aunt Leigh.'

The woman handed him his plate. 'And what did the army officer want?' she asked.

'My goodness, do you look out the window all day long?' her nephew responded.

'No,' the woman sniffed. 'Truth be told I just happened to be putting the clothes on the line when I saw him leave your office building.'

Barrington was curious. 'I didn't know there was an army officer here.'

'No, Dad. Well, he was just interested in our donating to the war effort.'

'We do already,' Barrington answered.

Bart gave a sharp nod of his head. 'I know. He does now too.'

'Thank the good God in heaven that's all it was,' Leigh stated, taking a tomato and slicing it.

Chapter Twenty-seven

York House, St James's Palace, London: October 1915

John Conrad slipped the letter opener into the next envelope on the pile on his desk. It was from Dave, Lena's son. The young man had ever been a favourite of John Conrad's, reminding him so much of Hargy, and Dave had taken it upon himself to be the family correspondent. His writing was laboured but his spelling and grammar were testaments to the years under Miss Howard's teaching skills.

Dear Uncle John Conrad,

We are well. Mum says to tell you she is growing her hair long again and the second-hand business is going well. Dad and I make a living and that's the main thing. Mum thought we might be having another family member about a month ago, but no, it was a false alarm. She's pleased, reckons there are enough of us.

I suppose you are still in the middle of this war. We read about the battles and I wonder if you and K are in them? I hope you stay safe and I pray for that each night.

Reckon I'll join up when I'm eighteen. I'm half British, after all, even though most of the blokes around here call me an Abo. I'm proud of both sides, I suppose.

We miss your visits. It's been so long. Mum won't let us use the tea set you gave her for the wedding. She's says it's for best, though I don't know when that's supposed to be. Probably when you visit us again. Will you come home after the war's over? Gosh, I hope so.

Well, until then, I'm still working hard. I've got Dad to let me keep a book where I write up all our sales and what the original item cost us so I know what profit we made. Dad was impressed.

Miss Howard still takes Tess and Danny three times a week. I'm glad I had schooling, boy, it makes a difference.

Jenny went away out west with a bloke. Mum tried to stop her but she's twenty-one now, so what could Mum do? Jen wouldn't listen. Said she loved him and that was that. His name was Kenny Miller. Mum was so mad. Cried a lot too. She got thinner as well after that. And she's thin enough.

Well, I hope you and K are winning this war. Reckon you will in the end.

Dad sends his best and Mum said she would really like to see you.

Your loving nephew,
Dave

John Conrad folded the letter and placed it in the file behind him where he kept personal papers. He was always interested in the happenings of Lena and Bluey's family. Brisbane was so far away that it was like a different planet and yet there were people there who were of great importance to him. Suddenly he thought of Caro Dere. He had not thought of her in years. And then a picture of her son, Harry, came into his mind. He felt uncomfortable with these recollections and he stood and moved round his desk as the door opened and Mrs Vermont, the housekeeper, came in with a cup of tea.

'I'm off to bed now, sir.'

'Is Lord K still in his study?'

'Yes, just took in his tea.'

John Conrad took the cup from her and walked along the corridor to K's study. He knocked gently and opened the door.

K looked up from his desk and moved his chair back a few inches as John Conrad entered.

At the side of the desk on the deep blue rug lay Caesar and Calpurnia, his two adoring collies. Calpurnia looked up with her perfect almond-shaped dark brown eyes and noted lazily that it was John Conrad who entered.

They had left Carlton Gardens and moved to St James's Palace earlier in the year on King George's insistence. He had lent it to K 'for the duration of the war'.

K gestured to a chair. 'First moment I've had to look at *The Times* today,' he said. 'Did you read about Churchill?'

'No.'

'Seems he might go to the front. He still has his commission in the Queen's Own Oxford Hussars and since he lost the Admiralty to Balfour in the spring, he's been in a metaphorical no man's land. Says here that he's taken up painting.'

Churchill, as First Lord of the Admiralty, had been made the scapegoat for the failed Dardanelles campaign. John Conrad knew that K and Churchill had not seen eye to eye on the Dardanelles. There had been a disagreement early in the offensive about troops. K had seen it in the beginning as a naval campaign only, though later he had altered his mind. Then as time had passed the Allies' position had deteriorated. The campaign in the Dardanelles and Gallipoli had not been waged as Churchill had wanted; perhaps if it had, the result may have been different, and even though the manoeuvres of the campaign had been intricate and involved, and everybody in the cabinet should have taken equal blame, because of his desire for it and his initial strong enthusiasms, the result had been to blame Churchill and this had ended in his removal from the Admiralty.

'Painting? Heavens, never thought of Winston as a painter. Must be another side to his soul.'

In the pale electric lamplight John Conrad thought his leader looked tired, the lines and slight puffiness under his eyes more pronounced than a year before and the sombre expression indicative of the weight of the hundred dilemmas he carried.

He still wore his customary dark blue uniform which he had put on at six that morning and it was now after ten at night. 'Anyway,' K said with a grim smile, 'Churchill's many things but, I do believe, a survivor. Remember him when he was correspondent for the *Morning Post* in South Africa, young, clever, pushy and personable, and so damn sure of himself?'

John Conrad nodded.

'And carrying a commission as well. Somehow he managed to get away with that. Yes, this is a mere setback to Winston.

I've always admired his ability in public speaking; he seems to relish it. Wish I did. His ego'll remain intact and he'll come back bigger and better than ever, mark my words.' He looked grave. 'Though he won't like it in France.'

'No one does.'

K looked up and nodded almost imperceptibly.

'Mrs Vermont's about to retire, she made the tea for you. Herbert's gone for the night as well.' Herbert Creedy was K's private secretary.

'Thanks, Johnny.' K put down his silver fountain pen and motioned to the high-backed chair in front of the desk. He rubbed his hands across his eyes. 'I'm not good in night light, Johnny; find it hard to read. My eyes have never been the same since I made that two-hundred-mile ride in the desert. Glare was so bad couldn't see a lot of the time, and the winds so strong, sharp fragments of scrub blew in our faces. We had coverings up to our eyes but they were exposed, of course.'

While John Conrad knew of the event he had never heard these details before. 'Was that when you fought the Mahdi and the dervishes?'

'No, my boy, well before that.'

K eyed the teacup. 'I'm sorry I promised the King not to touch alcohol until this war's over. I fear it's to be a long time yet.'

John Conrad could not help himself, he retorted, 'Did the King promise you the same?'

K smiled. 'I'm afraid not.'

'Then I think that cancels your obligation.'

'Mmmm, my boy, well that's kind of you, but I don't think the King would see it that way.' He straightened and picked up his tea. 'You know, Johnny, if we'd had the million and a half trained men that Germany had at the beginning of this war, I'm sure they wouldn't have had the guts to begin it.'

'It was the policy of our politicians not to mobilise, wasn't it?'

'It was. I wonder what the devil they thought Germany was mobilising all those years for. Do you know, m'boy, that to put a single fighting man in the field we need eight in support?'

'As many as that?'

'Yes; or so it says here in this report.' He tapped some papers in one of the piles in front of him. 'I don't know what to do about this stalemate in Belgium and Northern France, the way things are bogged down and with the inevitable losses. The current offensive at Loos hasn't gone well. You'll be near there on that assignment for the cabinet, won't you?'

John Conrad nodded. 'I'm packed ready to start early tomorrow, this time covering the entire front.'

'Away what? A month?'

'About that. They've asked me to report on ancillary services in the main. From information this week, we did break their front line at Loos but we don't have the numbers or the munitions to push through their second line.'

'I know. We've moved a bloody mile and a half at one point for God knows what losses. Apparently we've had major communication problems, telephone lines cut by enemy shelling even though laid in triplicate in places . . . back to using runners, all exacerbated by rain and mist.'

'Haven't we authorised the use of carrier pigeons?'

'Yes, in August. We used another lengthy bombardment again before the attack – a tactical success for us on Vimy Ridge – but not this time.' He put his hand on a pile of telegrams at his right hand. 'Seems the enemy's defences are sound and getting stronger all the time. And our supply of ammunition's been inadequate, and our retaliative gas attacks have failed.' He shook his head; he still had a fine full head of hair though it was greying. 'Joffre wanted this offensive and so did General French . . . it's a pity I agreed.'

'K, the way I see it Haig's waiting in the wings for French's position.'

'Yes, inside these walls, he is. The heavy losses we've sustained in our offensives at Neuve Chapelle, Aubers Ridge, Festubert and now Loos, will go against French. He seems more touchy and excitable these days, and I think he was wrong and perhaps vindictive in replacing Smith-Dorrien as commander of the Second Army during the second battle of Ypres.' He sighed. 'But we've all made blunders. This war's nothing like anything that's occurred before in the world's history, Johnny.'

The young man spoke grimly, 'Yes, you're right. By the way, I saw the message from Asquith.'

'Which one?'

'Where he blames you for the shortages of men at the front in and around Ypres. Says the directions given some months ago by the War Committee haven't been carried out.'

K nodded solemnly.

John Conrad bristled. 'I don't know of any directions from the War Committee that haven't been carried out as far as humanly possible. And I would, if there'd been any, as they all cross from your desk to mine to the correct military authorities.'

'Ah, Johnny, I know you're angry on my behalf . . .'

'Too right I am. The people adore you, applaud you in the streets, they recognise your dedication. They tacitly understand you've given your all . . . but not the buggers in the cabinet and parliament. No, not them. They're blaming you for their own failings.'

K stared gravely across the desk. He thought the world of the man opposite, and while he was naturally reticent he needed Johnny as a sounding board these days. 'Johnny, I'm not complaining, but since hostilities began, you know I've had to accept, and try to juggle, the views of John French as commander-in-chief of our forces, of the French Government and the French High Command. They've all been vehemently opposed to diverting British military strength from their desire to free the invaded industrial provinces of France, and I understand. But it's tied my hands more often than I've liked. I see it as one of the reasons Ian Hamilton's failing in the Dardanelles. Good, brave man, Hamilton, but perhaps not the leader I needed there.

'Now Churchill's gone, the cabinet steadily gathers forces against me. Lloyd George is vocal in getting rid of me, I know that.' He patted Calpurnia, who had come over to him. 'I've offered to go out to the Dardanelles, make my own inspection. Asquith has agreed; perhaps next month. I must confer with General Birdwood. He's one of the few good things about the Gallipoli campaign. Birdwood's turned out to be the perfect commander of the Anzacs. Apparently the rank and file affectionately call him *Birdie* just as we do.'

He wiped his hand across his forehead briefly closing his eyes. 'I think now that we should've followed up immediately with landings on the peninsula in February after the warships destroyed the Turks' outer ring of forts. Then perhaps the whole Gallipoli campaign would have succeeded. Sending the troops in at the end of April was too late.' He sounded disgusted with himself. 'How easy it always is after the fact.'

John Conrad agreed. 'Yes it is, but there've been times we've come close to success even though we've been outnumbered and outgunned.'

K nodded soberly. 'Yes, every division there's fought like lions, even the untried Australians and New Zealanders beside their trained British counterparts.' He gave a small smile. 'Should've realised that your countrymen wouldn't give in easily. They're very brave men, wonderful fighters, and little New Zealand's given a formidable account of itself too. Both can hold their heads up as nations now; no doubt about it. Bloody shame they had to be christened this way.' He shook his head. 'I feel very badly about it.'

John Conrad's tone was dismal. 'Yes, we all do. I understand what you say but had it been successful it would've put an end to Germany's ideas for expanding in the Middle East. It was actually a very good tactical plan.'

K shook his head. 'Johnny, my boy, the only *good* tactical plans are the ones that succeed. We hang on now by the skin of our teeth in the Dardanelles. And even though I've been against evacuation . . . well, I'm beginning to feel we must. It's one hell of a decision to make.'

He pursed his lips in thought. 'Remember the four divisions the French High Command offered me for the Dardanelles in early September?'

'I do.'

'And how when they weren't forthcoming we were told we must wait until after the results of the offensive of late September were known before the French could do anything? Well, it's now October, the offensive was this debacle at Loos, and the bloody divisions are in Salonica in Greece. There's been a British defeat at Sulva and Bulgaria's come into the war on Germany's side; so that's the end of our chances at the four divisions. Message came through tonight.' He pointed to the top telegram.

John Conrad shook his head. 'Oh hell.'

K stood up and the dogs went with him across the room to

434

his large map of Europe and the Middle East. It took up fourteen feet of his study wall and was detailed in various colours. He pointed to the Balkans. 'The Bulgarians are launching a flank attack on Serbia. The Austro-German forces will invade from the north, and they're suggesting that we ship Hamilton's army from the Dardanelles to the Balkans.' He stood there shaking his head, the spark and determination of the past missing from his faded blue eyes.

John Conrad hated to see him like this: tired, frustrated . . . and uncertain.

'The truth is that I don't dare to think of corps and brigades and battalions as real living men. I simply can't allow myself to . . .'

He returned to stand behind his chair and took hold of the back of it in his long fingers. 'I'm going to France again. Must confer on this Balkan business with Joffre and Millerand. I don't like any of it.'

John Conrad moved over to him. 'K, if you don't mind my saying so, I think you should go to bed and forget it all for tonight.'

K gave a sharp nod. 'You might be right, my boy. I'm a bit disillusioned at present. Kitchener's Army,' he said despondently. 'Yes, I suppose they're right saying I have difficulty working in a team, but the politicians I daily deal with are totally beyond my understanding. I feel as if I'm from Mars. I was made aware today that Henry Asquith is enamoured of a girl half his age, the Prime Minister mind you! And I've known for some time that John French is having an affair with Winifred Bennet; won't mean anything to you but she's the wife of a diplomat . . . I can't believe it at such a time as this! And Lloyd George? Well I'm afraid he's too much . . .' His eyes went to the ceiling.

John Conrad shook his head. 'We all know about him. Unfortunately the whole of the War Office's aware of his indiscretions. They talk of him behind his back as *Lewd-George*.'

'Do they?' said K gravely, 'I didn't know that. Shame. With a bloody war on; men dying in their droves; Southern Belgium and Northern France sickening blood baths and the Dardanelles littered with dead bodies and new fighting in the Balkans; there are the men I have to deal with carrying on like wanton schoolboys, and as well, they gather forces to finish me.'

John Conrad came round to him. 'The people will never let them get rid of you. You're as popular today as you ever were. But you're human, K, like the rest of us. How in hell can all your decisions be right?'

K gave a wan smile. 'Ah, my boy, if only my average would improve.'

He moved to the window and looked out. 'If it weren't so late I'd walk over and see the King.' Buckingham Palace was only a walk along the Mall.

John Conrad smiled. The King and K seemed really to understand each other. Theirs was a solid friendship and the King had appointed K a Knight of the Garter in the summer. 'Yes, but it *is* too late and as you're off to meet the French High Command in the morning and I'm off to the battle lines I suggest we call it a night.' He pointed to an untouched scone. 'Aren't you going to eat that?'

K shook his head. 'I'll turn in. Good night, Johnny.'

'Good night, K.' He gave a quick token salute and received a wan smile in return, then he bent down and patted Caesar and Calpurnia on their smooth flat skulls.

Later, between the clean white sheets John Conrad lay for a time, eyes wide, thinking. The strain on K was immense. He kept most of his feelings inside and it was unusual to hear him open up like tonight. He was sixty-five and had never played political games, and now he was surrounded by consummate politicians, supreme survivors. K would forge on and on, but it was taking a great toll on him.

John Conrad had been with K so long now that he did not like leaving him at all, but Fitz would look after him for the coming weeks. John Conrad had been to France a number of times since August 1914, mostly with K and Fitz for meetings with General Joffre and the French High Command, usually many miles behind the battle lines.

It was different as a cabinet observer, there to report. It troubled him. He had been at the second battle of Ypres earlier in the year when the bloody Germans had first used gas upon the British: men blinded and burnt by the gas, confusion and shock rife. It had been unnerving studying that disorder and chaos and then a week later to be transported back to London, and to sit writing a report on clean white paper with birds twittering outside the open window, back in civilisation with all the rules of culture and social conduct in play, knowing that just across the channel mayhem reigned.

Tomorrow he would most likely witness the death-throes of the battle raging now around the small mining village called Loos. How many more battles would there be?

. . . And so, young Luke, my lad, think of your Uncle Bill dug in here amongst the blasted old Turks – Abduls, as the boys call them. It's steaming hot and sunny just like Queensland. Not getting to ride any, which I've missed greatly since leaving Charleville. I'd give anything to be on a horse.

I do not think of the danger here, though I've buried some good blokes six feet under. Actually a lot of the time I feel like I'm off on an exciting chase or something. It's a stirring business, all right, some of it brutal, no doubt, but great mateship all around. We play some cards when we can and got in a game of cricket yesterday down behind the hill on a flat spot we call Shell Green.

This saluting each and every officer is a bit of a lark, can't understand how we're going to win the war by getting housemaid's knee in our elbows! But that's the blinking army, I suppose.

With year's end coming up we wonder what sort of a Christmas we'll have. Anyway, work hard so your mother will be proud of you.

I'll be thinking of you,
Uncle Bill

Luke finished reading, his eyes shining and his cheeks flushed. 'So what about that eh?' He lifted his gaze to Harry, sitting on the bed opposite.

'Read it again?' Harry asked excitedly.

He began again. As his youthful, clear voice echoed round the dormitory Alexander 'Naffer' Naughton came in and sat down to listen too. Naffer was Harry and Luke's 'second best friend', a slightly overweight boy who had not grown like his classmates had; all were taller than he and both Harry and Luke had shot up in the last year to around five feet ten.

When Luke completed the letter Naffer put his leg over the iron rail at the bottom of his bed and waved a ruler in the air shouting, 'I'm Uncle Bill fighting the Turks. Get out of my way! Bang! Bang! Bang!' The other two burst into laughter and dragged him down so that they all fell on the bed and then on to the floor, the sounds of their high spirits ringing round the dorm. It turned into a wrestling match with the three of them hooting and laughing and rolling under the beds.

'Stop that!' came a severe voice from the door. 'Get off that floor. What sort of hooligans are you?'

'Oh-oh,' said Harry, lying with one leg over Luke and his head under Naffer. 'It's MacDonald.'

MacDonald was the geography and French teacher and their dormitory master and a more serious-minded intellect was never in the company of buoyant, cheerful boys; he would have been far more suitably employed working with inanimate objects.

The boys unravelled themselves.

MacDonald carried a whipping cane, a thin piece of bamboo which he used indiscriminately, and now waved furiously in the air. 'Detention for you all. Two hundred lines *I will not shout in the dormitory and upset the equilibrium of the school.* Hand those in to me tonight by six o'clock.'

'But, sir,' began Luke. 'It's four o'clock and we're meant to be at football practice in fifteen minutes.'

MacDonald's face reddened and he swept the air with his cane, landing it on Luke's shoulder so heavily the youth winced. 'No football practice. Get into the classroom and write out the lines.'

The three youths dismally trooped out past MacDonald in single file. He followed them to see that they sat and took out paper, pen and ink.

'How do you spell *equilibrium* sir?' asked Harry, disconsolately. MacDonald wrote it on the board, and then, standing stiffly under the wall clock, repeated the sentence they were to write out and left. 'I'll return at six,' were his parting words.

Glumly the trio began the task. 'I'll never write this two hundred times before six o'clock,' moaned Naffer. 'It's taking me almost a minute to write it once with this blasted nib, and my hand's aching already.'

'Keep going old son,' said Harry, 'that's all you can do.' He had picked up the phrase *old son* from Matthew. He liked to use it; it made him feel grown up.

Six o'clock came and so did MacDonald. Harry had managed to write the necessary two hundred lines and so had Luke, though the last fifty did not resemble writing so much as scrawl. It was poor Naffer who had not reached the required amount.

MacDonald pushed Harry and Luke out into the corridor to wait, and poor old Naffer had to drop his trousers and take six cuts.

'I hate MacDonald,' Harry said, listening to Naffer cry out.

'Me too,' agreed Luke.

They consoled Naffer by allowing him to eat half their bread and butter pudding at meal time, and when they all mounted the stairs to the dormitory their spirits were somewhat higher. They read Uncle Bill's letter again before lights out and as they put on their pyjamas Luke looked across to Harry and said softly, 'Wish I were eighteen.'

'Why?'

'I'd join up . . . too right I would. Get away from mad old MacDonald and being told what to do by him every day, see the world and be treated like a man . . . just like Uncle Bill, darn right.'

Harry grinned in ready agreement. 'Reckon I would too.'

As they climbed into bed Harry said, 'Do you think the war will still be on when we're eighteen?'

'Might be,' Luke replied.

'Righto. Good night then, old son.'

'Good night, Harry.'

Under the spring moon Caro walked out onto the verandah at Cedar Grove, her hair trailing over her shoulders in the gentle breeze that drifted through the trees and wafted the clean scents of the bush across to her on the balmy air.

All was quiet. The house was beautifully peaceful and the mellow lantern light engulfed the wide verandah in a warm glow. The friendly shadows of the night gave her a true sense of peace and she sat down upon the rocking chair near the steps.

Matthew and Knobby had arrived up from Brisbane on the afternoon train and for once Matt had seemed tired and had gone to bed early . . . well, early for Matt: around ten thirty; his usual bed-time was closer to one in the morning. She and Jane had remained up knitting socks for the Women's Auxiliary for the War Effort until about half an hour ago they had made tea and then Jane had said good night. Caro had bathed and changed for bed then come out into the night air.

Her father and mother were arriving tomorrow. This was a major event. Jack Dere enjoyed coming up to the property, but Elizabeth had only been a few times over all the years, maintaining steadily to her dislike for the country. They were coming for a few days because it was Jack Dere's seventy-ninth birthday and he was enjoying better health than he had in years. Caro and Joseph would meet them at the railway station at Gatton and bring them home.

Caro loved the bush. She was at her happiest here at Cedar Grove. She even liked the farm work, not that she did the hard heavy tasks but she fed the chickens and groomed the horses and milked the cows. The physical work uplifted her and she felt a wholesome tiredness at the end of the day.

She stretched out her legs and let her bare arms drop down over the sides of the chair. She wore a pure white cotton nightgown with lace bodice and a wide scooped neckline exposing the tops of her still firm breasts. As she sat there in the wan lantern light amongst the shadows of the night her white gown contrasted with the sun-deepened colour of her skin.

A stream of thoughts came and went across her mind and as always in times of stillness and introspection she reflected upon John Conrad Fleet. Strange that she had gone to Bart to tell him the truth and in faltering had latched upon the idea of John Conrad's letters. Now her lifeline to him was through them. She kept a dream inside her – there it lived under all the layers of herself – the dream that one day somehow she and John Conrad would be reunited. Their son reinforced her dream. Of course Harry believed, as all the world did, that Matt was his father, but that did not matter to Caro.

The splendid truth was otherwise and one day it would all be healed.

She lifted herself out of the chair and moved over to the wooden post supporting the verandah roof. She leaned upon it, resting the side of her face against the cool painted wood. The years rolled away – she was with John Conrad. And existing in the memory she moved her head back on the post and emitted a sad, yearning sound.

'So here you are,' the voice sounded behind her in the darkness and Caro started and spun around.

Matthew moved across the verandah, his dark eyes lost in shadow but the scar upon his cheek glistening wickedly in the flickering lantern light. He wore nothing on his upper body, showing the perfection of the muscles of his chest and arms. His dishevelled hair hung in waves to the nape of his neck and the odd streaks of grey at his temples gleamed strangely in the beam from the lantern. Anyone other than Caro would have thought him wildly handsome and desirable.

'Oh, it's you,' she said. 'You frightened me. I thought you were asleep long ago.'

'I woke and found you gone.'

'I haven't been to bed.'

He did not have his cane and he took hold of the railing as he spoke. 'You seemed a long way away, old girl. Got quite a start, didn't you?'

'Yes.'

'What were you thinking about?'

Caro moved away down the verandah. 'It's late, Matt. I really should've come to bed earlier. Come on, I'll put out the lanterns.'

She crossed to the nearest and turned it down, the incandescence fluttering and dying.

He followed her. 'Caro?'

She turned around. 'What? Come on, Matt.' She moved to the second lantern and did the same.

'Come here, old girl.'

She came back the few steps to him. There was frustration in her tone. 'What is it?'

He put out his hands and drew her to him; pressing her close within his arms and resting his lips on her forehead. Her breasts pushed through the lace of her gown to flatten against his torso as he felt her arms slip around his back and the flat of her hands rest on the skin of his waist.

They stood there immobile for a time and somewhere in the night an owl hooted. Matt lifted his head back. He could see her eyes by the faint glimmer from the moon.

'It's no good to live in the past, Caro. Come back here to the present with me.' And he bent his head down and kissed the side of her face and across to her lips. His mouth moved over hers in a sensual assault and the habitual response rose within her. She felt it even though she resisted it: the heat of desire kindling in the pit of her stomach and rising through her.

As he continued to kiss her his hands roamed up and down her spine, feeling her through the light cotton gauze, the roundness of her bottom and the firmness of her hips. Then he stepped away from her and reached out and took her hand. 'Let's go to bed,' he said softly, and drew her along the verandah and in through the wide open door.

Chapter Twenty-eight

John Conrad had begun his observation near the North Sea and travelled along the front straight south to Ypres, Aubers, Loos and Arras to Soissons, then the line turned in a south-easterly direction through Chemin des Dames, Reims, Verdun, and on to Belfort near the Swiss border.

His first night in the field, as he bumped along the potholed road approaching the line, red and white flashes of guns stabbed the blackness ahead of them, and the sounds of the heavy artillery boomed a recurrent refrain. His travelling companion was Captain Chris Bateman from the 8th Division HQ and they were driven by a Scottish sergeant. It took hours to reach the assigned battalion HQ to find nothing, just a smashed ruin. The sergeant found some officers, and a batman explained there was nowhere to sleep except in a dugout the bottom of which was covered in mud and water. As they made a makeshift bed from boxes and groundsheets, the batman brought them some hot sweet tea and bread and ham. They wolfed it down and spent the night as best they could.

As the noises of war discharged themselves in ritual confusion not far away, John Conrad listened and in bizarre comparison imagined the comfortable bedroom in London.

As the days passed and he travelled down the line the devastation he saw was hard to accept, to believe. Green copses and hills and dales, farmhouses villages and streams razed to the ground and turned into great gaping holes of dirt, mud and rocks; blackened and charred sticks for what were once living green trees; a nightmare landscape with humans existing in it in long running trenches in the ground, sharing them with lice and rats and vermin; boys from all walks of life thrown into shock and confusion but showing an astounding resilience and camaraderie.

At Loos, where the battle had run for thirteen days, the Allies had not advanced more than a mile and a half to the German second line. They could not break through.

On a morning in late October he was at a British casualty clearing station a couple of miles back from Arras and not far from the front. It was a fine morning and a mist sat in the valley and floated away, edging across the landscape. The sound of the guns could be heard intermittently in the distance but they were far enough away for the noise simply to hang as a distant threat in the air. A truckload of eight-inch howitzers rattled past on the road leading to the front and men lay moaning all about in stretchers, some horrendously wounded, hard to look at: others – the lucky ones – just badly enough to be evacuated home.

Some soldiers played football for recreation in the distance and nearby horses were tied to a broken rail under the awning of a hastily built shelter. He had seen all sorts of animals used along the line. Behind the line in Ypres they were even using elephants to move the heavy guns.

John Conrad walked through the wounded, and the dead. He spoke to some who were conscious. It was always hard to make conversation.

As he rejoined Captain Bateman, he noticed a solid well-built man with a shock of fair hair sitting on the ground cleaning his rifle, and John Conrad, impressed by his diligence asked, 'Off duty?'

The soldier jumped to his feet and saluted. 'Yes, Colonel, sir. Got collared into bringing up some of the wounded. I'm not an orderly.' His rifle shone. It was perhaps the cleanest weapon John Conrad had seen in his entire visit so far.

'What's your name, Sergeant?'

'Murphy, sir.'

'Well, Murphy, that's a very spick and span rifle you have and a great telescopic sight. Evans, isn't it?'

'Aye, sir.'

'May I see it.'

Murphy handed the weapon over and John Conrad looked through it.

Murphy informed him, 'The part of the line I'm in is badly dominated by Hun sniper fire. Morale is pretty low, sir. Lost two men yesterday. I managed to scrounge the telescopic sight. I've been trying to snipe back. I've made some loopholes in the parapet, but I'm not sure if I'm doing it right.'

John Conrad thought for a moment. 'Well, you're showing initiative, good man. What sort of a shot are you, Murphy?'

'Pretty good, sir. I spent some time in Africa years ago. I can hit a moving target all right. So can Blake-Martens, my corporal. Won't admit it but he was a mighty fine poacher back in Essex before we came out here.'

John Conrad was thoughtful. He was of the opinion that sniping was about as mean an activity as there was but this war was not being fought cleanly. There was nothing fair in gas attacks and airship raids on civilians. Men had to survive in whatever way they could.

Captain Bateman spoke up. 'You know, to be a good sniper you need a partner.'

'Sir?'

'One man observes the enemy line with a periscope, or sometimes if you have a hidden position, a telescope; finds the target and the other man shoots. And always choose a spot where you can see into your own trench. Then if you ever lose it to the enemy you've a ready-made position.'

The soldier saw the value of this immediately. 'Right, but we ain't got any telescopes or periscopes. Think only some of the officers have them, sir. Wouldn't be more'n six or seven in the whole battalion.'

Captain Bateman turned to John Conrad. 'Remember that fellow we met at Divisional Headquarters behind Pas-en-Artois, attached to the Intelligence Department? Wasn't he talking about taking sniping seriously and holding classes for men who were good shots?'

'Yes, I think his name was Hesketh-Prichard.'

Bateman nodded. 'It was.'

John Conrad turned the rifle over in his hands and handed it back to the soldier. 'It's a bloody ugly thing to have to do, Murphy – shoot men who can't see you – but this is one hell of a war and sadly we have to meet fire with fire.'

'Yes, sir. Sometimes I reckon I've died and gone to hell already.'

Captain Bateman eyed the sergeant. 'Perhaps I can organise for you to go to Hesketh-Prichard's classes.'

John Conrad opened the leather pouch at his waist. 'But firstly, Murphy, here, take my telescope, and we've got a periscope in the armoured car – you can have that too. We'll replace them.'

Murphy was suitably impressed. 'Thanks, Colonel.'

Bateman took out his telescope as well, and handed it to the grateful soldier.

'And good luck, Murphy.'

'Thanks, sir.'

A week later, when John Conrad parted from Chris Bateman and he arrived at British Command Headquarters, a telegram awaited him: 'Meet me and Fitz at the British Embassy in Paris tomorrow. K.' It was dated 4 November 1915.

John Conrad hitched a ride with a captain going down in a truck to Paris.

When he arrived at the Embassy K and Fitz were already there in company with Reginald, Lord Esher, a sub-commissioner of the Red Cross. K looked weary as he explained the situation in London. 'It's open hostility now especially from Lloyd George. They say I'm an autocrat and don't delegate, and Northcliffe has attacked me in *The Times*. We leave on the morrow for Turkey and Gallipoli. No doubt Asquith and the others will be quick to move against me while we're gone; but go I must. We'll take in the Dardanelles and make some decisions there and then we'll come back.' His voice strengthened. 'When we return to London we'll see what they do to me face to face.'

'Now I like that,' said John Conrad.

'Me too,' added Fitz.

It was not the disconsolate atmosphere they had expected at dinner that evening; in fact the mood surrounding K was more optimistic than it had been for weeks.

On Gallipoli, John Conrad accompanied K on his inspection of the British and French positions at Helles and Sulva, Mudros and Anzac. K was very pleased to see General Birdwood and the two men greeted each other fondly: there was a liking and mutual respect between them. They met the French commander-in-chief and were accompanied everywhere by various officers, one in particular, Major Trent, being attached to them for the entire visit. He was a rotund, rather jolly type with florid colouring, and on the second evening in the transport's mess, as John Conrad entered he overheard Trent expressing his opinion on K: 'Oh yes, he's a cold one, you know, stiff and formal.' John Conrad passed by without comment.

On the fourth day of their visit they were at one of the field bases when K asked to go up to the front line.

'I don't think you'd want to do that, Lord Kitchener,' replied Major Trent, and Colonel Watson, an Australian, concurred. 'No.'

K eyed them. 'Why is that?'

Trent answered, almost severe with the import of his message. 'It's dangerous. We're only twenty yards from the enemy in our forward trench here, sir.'

K answered quietly. 'I would not ask to go to the front line if I didn't require my wish to be granted, Major.'

Trent was dumbfounded and Colonel Watson shook his head in amazement but arrangements were made and that afternoon K walked the entire maze of trenches, including the length of the one closest to the enemy, only twenty yards from the Turks, up a steep climb known as Walker's Ridge. It was held by Anzacs, and K spoke to many of them.

There was a little intermittent fire as they came round a sharp corner packed with sandbags and they halted as the bullets whizzed by overhead. From behind a wooden parapet a soldier with make-shift crutches and a bandaged leg tried valiantly to rise and salute K. K put his hand on to the metal rising sun attached to the shoulder of the man's uniform and pushed him gently back down to his sitting position.

K knelt on the dirt beside him and pointed to his leg. 'Shouldn't you be back in a hospital ship?'

'Will be shortly, sir. Bit of sharpnel hit me in three places but I'll be all right.'

'What's your name?'

'Pike, sir, Gerry Pike.'

'Where are you from, Pike?'

'Outside Sydney, sir.'

'Yes, where?'

'Windsor, sir, only a small place.'

And K astounded the soldier by answering, 'Know it well:

447

beautiful spot. Had a fine picnic out there on the Hawkesbury River a few years ago. Is that little blue and white corrugated iron shed still there? They used to sell bait.' He thought for a second or two. 'Was it called Bean's Bait Shop?'

The man's eyes shone with incredulous delight. 'Yes, that's it, sir. Do I ever know it; Bruce Bean's a mate of mine. He owns it.'

'Well,' replied K, pointing to John Conrad, 'the colonel here was with me that day. He bought our party some bait and we sat on the river bank and fished. Wonderful afternoon. January 1910.'

John Conrad nodded. 'That's right. We had a marvellous day.'

The soldiers standing nearby all laughed at this anecdote and as K rose and touched the man's shoulder he added, 'You tell Bruce Bean to look out for me down there at Windsor after this war's over.'

And as the soldier answered in the affirmative, his words were drowned by the applause of the Anzacs standing nearby as K strode away along the trench. The applause was taken up as if those ahead somehow knew and approved of what had happened and it travelled with K all the way down the two hundred winding yards in front of him.

John Conrad smiled widely. These were the soldiers, the ordinary troops, the ones who had rallied to his call, those who were giving their lives. He could not help himself and he turned to Major Trent behind him. 'Perhaps you might revise your opinion, *cold, you know, stiff and formal*, when next you describe the field marshal.'

Major Trent's high colour turned even more florid as John Conrad walked on.

During the following days, in between his visits to the front and his trips across the allied positions, K sent a series of telegrams to Asquith detailing the plan he had devised for offsetting an abandonment of Gallipoli by seizing Alexandretta in the Gulf of Eskandroon, which was a short distance from the main line of the Bagdad railway. K was ever thinking of moving hostilities into enemy areas to protect Egypt and this strategy had been in his mind for some time. On 19 November K received his reply. The Prime Minister rejected his proposal

448

and told him to confine his opinions to the evacuation – or not – of the peninsula.

Shortly afterwards K's party sailed home via Athens, where he put the allied position to the King before they travelled on through Brindisi, Rome and the Italian front to Paris.

On arrival in London K told John Conrad and Fitz, 'I've thought about it the entire time we've been away. It's probably best that I resign. I'm going immediately to Downing Street.'

K entered the room lit by four ornate electric lights hanging from above. Cigarette butts sat in full ashtrays and the smell of smoke pervaded the air. The weak afternoon sun filtered through a heavily draped window at one end of the room, helping to illuminate the sombre faces.

Of those around the oval table only Asquith attempted a smile and rose to take his hand. 'So you're back early from the Dardanelles.'

They shook hands and K nodded to Lloyd George, Sir Edward Grey and Arthur Balfour.

'Why?' asked K. 'Didn't you have enough time to decide what to do with me?'

Grey and Balfour glanced at each other and Lloyd George spoke up. 'So, do you have a recommendation about the Peninsula?'

'Yes I do. It's all in here.' He placed a brown folder down on the table.'

Asquith nodded. 'Do you have a short version?'

'Yes. After visiting every front, I now believe we must evacuate. General Birdwood's of the same opinion.'

The Welshman made a derisive sound. 'That's what you say today. What do you say tomorrow?'

K met the speaker's eyes. 'I know I've had varying opinions, Mr Lloyd George, but having seen it for myself now, I'll stand by what I say.'

Grey and Balfour began to talk among themselves and Asquith looked pained; he sighed and spoke. 'Fact is, Lord Kitchener, we've lost our faith in what you say these days. There are serious uncertainties about your handling of many matters. Your opinions have varied mightily in recent times.'

'If that's so, Prime Minister, may I remind you and those here present that perhaps that is because we deal with millions of men's lives. They're real men in the trenches, not toy soldiers.' He looked slowly around them. 'Do any of you realise that the life expectancy of a man in the front line trenches is three weeks? For God's sake . . . three weeks!'

Lloyd George made a disgruntled sound and Asquith looked upset. 'Yes, yes, terrible, terrible.'

Balfour looked over his spectacles. 'We need purposefulness from the Secretary of State, not indecision,' he stated calmly.

'Hear! Hear!'

Asquith held up his hand for silence and then placed it down on the folder K had brought. 'Lord Kitchener, we shall read all this and come to a conclusion.' He coughed. 'While you've been in Gallipoli certain actions have been taken . . . resolutions made.'

K answered tolerantly, 'I suspected nothing less.'

'Fact is that we've created a Council for War, a subcommittee within the cabinet. The men in this room will form the nucleus. Tougher measures must be taken if we're to win this damned war.'

'And I haven't been tough enough?'

Lloyd George could not contain himself. 'No, you know it and so do we. And because of it we're in dire straits in all theatres of war, bogged down, getting nowhere. We've been fighting now for nearly two years . . .'

K locked eyes with him. 'And that you see as entirely my fault? May I remind you that *you* in particular were convinced that this war would be over by Christmas 1914! I said then as I say now, this war's nothing like anything the world has ever seen. It's a damned war of attrition. I believe sadly, there are still years in it yet . . . millions will be dead. It's hard to even contemplate.'

'All right, all right.' Lloyd George's tone was long-suffering. 'The point here today is that the war's going badly. We need better decisions. We still haven't the munitions—'

K's faded eyes flashed. 'So munitions! Let's take munitions then, shall we? We began this war with virtually nothing, against an enemy who had been preparing for decades. I would like to state here today, *for the record*, that almost a year ago I contracted hundreds of shipments of munitions and war materials from America and Japan to bolster Russia. You all know the munitions workers were striking while our boys in the trenches were dying. I went to their factories, met and spoke to them. Did any of you do that?' He looked around them. They remained silent so he went on, 'The strikes halted and the unions even accepted lower pay, and by a miracle I received their agreement to allow female labour to bolster male workers in the factories.

'Shell production in this country daily increases dramatically ... it should be up fifty per cent in six months from now.' His eyes gleamed with the fire of old and he brought his fist down upon the table top. 'And just in case you aren't aware, because of my understanding of the need for munitions I've been careful to double every order which has ever crossed my desk. A year from now, we'll be well ahead of German production.' He paused before adding, 'They, gentlemen, are some of the *poor* decisions I've made.'

Asquith raised both his hands in supplication. 'Yes, yes, we don't deny any of this Lord Kitchener, but—'

'Tell him, Prime Minister,' prompted Lloyd George.

Asquith gave a silencing glance to the Welshman and faced back to K.

K met Asquith's gaze. 'Tell me what?'

Asquith coughed; it was not an entirely comfortable sound. He toyed with the cup at his right hand. 'Lord Kitchener, no doubt what you've just said is so, but you don't delegate, and we certainly feel you don't share with us your thoughts. In the last year, we, your colleagues, the cabinet, parliament, have lost confidence in your handling of strategic matters, hence ... we have appointed Sir William Robertson to the post of Chief of Imperial General Staff. This means he will take over much of what you do, lighten your load ... and work ... ah ... with you. You'll keep the title of Secretary of State and you'll join us on the War Council and remain at the War Office. Recruiting will still be your responsibility.'

K nodded slowly. 'I see.' He looked round the faces and met their gazes. He spoke slowly and distinctly: 'With the talk of conscription that's gaining force each month, recruiting won't be the massive task it's been for me up to now. At this point

I wish to tender my resignation as Secretary of State, Prime Minister.'

Balfour mumbled 'No,' and Asquith shook his head. 'No, no that's not what we want.' He cleared his throat. 'Lord Kitchener, the sombre fact is, *you* are a symbol to the free countries of the world and their will to be victorious. We do not accept your resignation. It is you who stand between the great armies of men and . . . political disruption.'

K gave a slow smile. 'Ah, so I'm still of some use to you all then; if only to present a united front to our countrymen and allies around the world. To fool them that all remains the same.'

Lloyd George groaned quietly and Asquith went on, 'Parliament has put pressure upon us. It would be beneficial if you understood that this is not personal.'

'Not personal? It seems about as personal as it can become to me. Fortunately I'll never understand political machinations, Prime Minister; I remain proud to be simply a soldier.' K looked once more around the men who sat in judgement upon him, met their eyes, then stood. He towered there for a few moments, his presence powerful in the room and all the men there felt it.

'Thank you, Prime Minister. I understand your terms . . . and your position. I will continue to do what I can . . . for Great Britain and her allies . . . and for the boys in the trenches.'

Asquith stood and held out his hand. 'I'm sure you will.'

K shook the Prime Minister's hand. He did not look back at the others and he turned sharply and left the room.

When John Conrad and Fitz heard K's voice in the foyer the two had to contain themselves not to run like schoolboys down the stairs to greet him, but Caesar and Calpurnia did, nuzzling up to him and receiving his caresses in return.

K wore his dark blue uniform with his ribbons over his heart. The buttons shone in the electric light of the foyer as he glanced up at the two who stood in wait on the landing. He handed his braided cap to a valet and his umbrella to his secretary. He looked fatigued but he smiled up at them. They could hardly contain themselves as they followed him and the collies through to the drawing room and closed the door.

'Well?' exclaimed Fitz, unable to wait any longer.

K sat down and looked up at them as the dogs edged their heads into his lap. 'The Prime Minister refused to accept my resignation.'

Sounds of relief ushered from both John Conrad and Fitz at once.

'But Asquith said that my colleagues have lost confidence in my handling of strategic matters, that I don't delegate and that basically they wish me to be replaced; but not in any way that the free world senses for I'll remain in council and at the War Office and all will appear the same to our countrymen and allies around the world.' He gave a pallid smile. 'In essence they still need me for it seems I'm a symbol to the allied world's will to be victorious.'

'Cynical buggers!' exclaimed John Conrad.

'I'll remain Secretary of State but the fact is they leave me merely to control War Office Admin and recruiting.'

John Conrad shook his head. 'Bastards.'

Fitz was open-mouthed. 'Yes, they are.'

'William Robertson becomes the new Chief of Imperial General Staff, virtually do much of what I did.'

John Conrad and Fitz both protested but K held up his hand. 'Now, boys, truly, I can work with General Robertson. He's a good sort and capable. Rose through the ranks, without a title, a celebrated name or money and that says a lot for him. It might be for the best. Even now I believe they're not sure whether or not to evacuate Gallipoli.' He looked disconsolately down. 'And the truth is I've been so uncertain that I cannot blame them. My own opinion differed almost daily; though I've finally decided and recommended that we do.'

John Conrad could not withhold his anger. 'K, they fear you, if the truth's known. You stand head and shoulders over them literally and metaphorically and they'll never forgive you for it.'

The field marshal's grand old eyes clouded over for a moment as he appraised the two younger men, then he stood. 'Ah, Johnny . . . ah, Fitz, the two best friends a man could ever have wished for.' He crossed to the window where he pulled back the drape and looked down to the Mall. He leant his head on the glass as Calpurnia came up and licked his hand.

'Life's mysterious. No man in the public eye is ever truly free of malice from others and I mustn't complain, I've had a pretty good innings up to now.'

The Gallipoli Peninsula was evacuated: Sulva and Anzac without loss on 18 and 19 December 1915 and Helles and the other theatres on 8 January 1916, also entirely without loss. All troops from Gallipoli were shipped to Egypt and some months later to France.

It was two days before Christmas. Dusk was descending even though it was just after half-past three in the afternoon and a very fine rain drifted gently down upon the shoulders of John Conrad's greatcoat. He strode down Stratton Street towards Piccadilly thinking of how early he would need to rise to catch the train down to Broome Park tomorrow to spend Christmas with K and Fitz.

It was a sober Christmas but there were some attempts at cheer here in the streets of the capital, and a few decorations appeared in shop windows and the odd Christmas wreath upon door knockers.

Last Christmas, the first of the war, the troops had called a cease-fire in some parts of the front line and actually fraternised with the Germans, some even playing soccer. That had been looked upon askance by High Command: must keep the hatred in the air; there would be no such confederacy this year.

He crossed Piccadilly near the corner of the Ritz Hotel. The lights twinkled through the windows, reflecting on the damp pavement when a young man in civvies and a girl of about nineteen exited the front door of the hotel about twenty yards in front of him. They were laughing merrily at something and as they hesitated on the footpath a woman who stood watching them from the kerb stepped forward and handed the youth a white feather. The young man avoided taking it and the woman's face reddened in anger.

'You should be in France, you coward, not entertaining your floozy at the Ritz. You're disgusting!' She pointed the feather at him and, looking round to people in the street, went on loudly, 'He won't take it. Look at him! Damn coward, letting others die for him.' And she threw the white feather at the young man's face.

The girl with him turned distraught eyes to the youth. 'Tell her, Jack, tell her,' she said, but the boy shook his head and simply stood watching the irate woman, who now noticed John Conrad and his uniform, and came swiftly forward waving her black umbrella in the air. 'My boy's been dead a year,' her voice was now shrilly heartbroken, 'and the likes of him stands here alive.' She took John Conrad's arm, pointing to the young man with her umbrella.

John Conrad patted the woman's arm and released himself from her grasp. 'Now, now, Mother,' he said calmingly to her. 'You go on home. That's enough for today. Forget about it.'

The woman hesitated but she finally moved off, still talking loudly about 'cowards dining at the Ritz', and John Conrad halted beside the young couple.

The girl was in tears and the youth was consoling her. 'It's not fair, Jack,' she said between sobs on his shoulder, 'you should've told her.'

'Sans faire rien, Millie. It truly doesn't matter,' he said to her, meeting John Conrad's eyes over the tearful girl's shoulder. Suddenly he saluted. John Conrad returned the gesture.

'I'm on leave, sir,' he confided, 'just came home from Flanders yesterday. I'm a bombardier with the Royal Field Artillery, name's Jack Harrison. This is my sister. I took her for tea at the Ritz.'

John Conrad grimaced after the woman disappearing in the distance. 'I'm sorry about all that, soldier.' He pointed to Jack's civilian clothes. 'She assumed you weren't in the army.' He touched the girl gently on the shoulder. 'Miss, would you be gracious enough to accept this from me?' He took five pounds from his pocket. 'Please have some dinner and see a show. There's a good comedy on at Her Majesty's, just up here in the Haymarket.' He pointed. 'Please, I truly would like you to.'

Millie lifted big damp eyes to the sympathetic voice and smiled through her tears. 'We couldn't accept that.'

John Conrad was determined. 'Please, I'd be honoured if you had a pleasant night at my expense.'

She hesitated before she reluctantly took the money.

'How long are you home, Jack?' John Conrad asked.

'Just five days, sir.'

'You enjoy it and forget about this.'

'Thanks, sir,' Jack replied with a smile. 'You on leave too sir?'

'Not exactly.'

John Conrad made his way on along Piccadilly thinking of what had occurred. K said they would bring in conscription in the new year. At least it would stop this handing out of white feathers to men assumed to be cowards not taking their share of the war's burdens.

'Never assume,' he said aloud as he walked along.

Still thinking about Jack and his sister, Millie, he turned down St James's Street, and halted on the corner of Jermyn Street to head on down to St James's Palace. He was about to step off the kerb when he looked sideways and hesitated. There was something familiar about the lady crossing the street with quick determined steps towards him, holding a small umbrella, her dark skirt swaying round her ankles in the fast fading light. It was not until she stepped up on to the footpath just a few yards from him that her eyes met his and she halted, dumbfounded.

Neither of them spoke for some seconds.

'John Conrad!' she exclaimed. 'You! I can't believe it.'

'And nor can I, Emma Louise,' he answered. 'What on earth are you doing in London? In England?'

Beneath her navy-blue bonnet her brilliant hair peeped out over her forehead and in front of her ears; but her eyes were brittle, annoyed. 'Of course,' she responded sarcastically, 'they wouldn't tell you. Why would they? Your family naturally would keep such things from you; knowing how you felt about us.' She took a deep sighing breath.

He was thinking of the last time he saw her, on the floor in his father's house in Brisbane; of her terrified scream and how he had hurtled her out of bed and across the floor.

He was amazed to see her; he did not speak as the sounds of traffic whirled about them and the rain drifted upon them, but she did, though her voice remained high and sharp-edged as if she did not willingly supply the information she gave him. 'We came here four years ago. After his Indian service things did not work out in Australia as Uncle Hewitt had planned so he and Aunt Gertrude decided to come home. Under the circumstances, we,' she hesitated, 'David and I . . . decided we should come to England too.'

John Conrad answered calmly. 'I wasn't told. Do you keep in touch with Aunt Leigh? Bart?'

'Oh yes. I write once in a while and Aunt Leigh replies.' Her voice was still strident with emotion. 'She was always more understanding.'

John Conrad nodded, standing in the gentle drizzling rain, feeling it clean upon his face, thinking about things he had not thought of in years.

'I'd best be off,' she said abruptly, and with that she walked briskly on and called to a passing hansom cab.

John Conrad strode up behind her. 'Emma Louise, where do you live?'

The driver halted his horse and the woman stepped up. As she seated herself she looked down and said, 'Near Canterbury.' Then turning her head up to the driver called, 'Victoria Station, please.'

The hansom pulled away and John Conrad watched it disappear. He stood a long time on the kerb as vehicles and people passed to and fro, multitudes of memories and feelings rolling like endless breaking waves across him. He had finished with Emma Louise and David, hadn't thought of them in years. They had become nothing to him, and yet seeing her again he had felt no anger, no grudge. The war had done that: diffused all sorts of emotions; what had been important before did not seem so all-consuming now. He supposed her reaction to him could have been worse . . .

When at last he stirred himself to walk on, the rain had ceased but the wind had come up. He pulled his greatcoat more snugly around him and hurried on down the hill.

He spent a quiet Christmas at Broome Park. K was in the process of making many alterations and beautifying the entire building, but with the war things had virtually halted; still, some parts of the house were quite habitable and all K's wonderful collection of fine art and antiquities stood in various rooms waiting to be placed in their final resting spots.

The entourage, including Caesar and Calpurnia, were back in London on Boxing Day evening and on New Year's Eve they were invited to a small party at Lady Salisbury's, but K declined: 'I cannot go partying while this war's on and there are men living in mud holes in the ground.'

So the three friends had a quiet dinner together. When K rose from the table he looked from one to the other of his companions. 'What a year 1915's been; dismal and cheerless. German airship raids on London and losses and stalemate for the Allies everywhere. And now there's ideological unrest in Ireland, the land of my birth.' He remained silent for a few seconds and looked skywards. 'I wonder what 1916 will bring us?' he finished softly.

Chapter Twenty-nine

Sleet floated down and the sun hid in the mist-covered landscape of Hertfordshire. It was a chill February morning and the trials, code-named 'Mother' were underway. In the bleak light K's eyes shone, watching the unwieldy grey metal monster rolling awkwardly over the field to cross a five-foot-wide trench and continue on. Earlier trials of this weapon had been code-named 'Little Willie', and it was beginning to find favour at the War Office. John Conrad, at K's right side plunged his gloved hands down into his greatcoat pockets as the Chief Of Imperial Staff stepped up to the Secretary of State.

'What do you think? I'd like to know,' General Robertson asked in his plain-speaking manner.

And K replied, 'It's the future of warfare, Will. I think you should order a hundred immediately.'

'Exactly what I was going to recommend,' Robertson answered, stamping his feet to keep warm.

On the way back from Hatfield to London in the car, K was full of interest in the new weapon and he told John Conrad, 'This armoured car or *tank*, as I heard someone call it, is awkward yet, and clumsy to handle, but it's a prototype. They'll become sleek and efficient over time.'

'I agree. You can see that with a powerful gun mounted on it, it'll be formidable against foot soldiers, especially as it can cross broken ground and trenches and afford protection to those inside it.'

K looked out the window. 'In time it'll be capable of more and more: destroying machine guns, breaking through entanglements and climbing earthworks. Apparently it was a brainchild of Churchill's in the first place, and championed along by that fellow we met in the field this morning, Lieutenant Colonel Swinton.'

'Really? Well, it's becoming a reality. Didn't Swinton say

he thought it'd only be six to nine months before we could use them?'

'Yes.'

John Conrad was thoughtful. 'Mmm, let's hope they turn out to be a great advantage for us. But, K, isn't war altering? What with planes fighting in the air, and blasted airships dropping bombs on civilians . . . and now with these *tanks* . . . Weapons are becoming such sophisticated forms of destruction. I suppose war will be different altogether in the future.'

'Yes, you're right,' replied K gravely, 'but not soon enough for our boys in the trenches. War's hateful, but human beings don't seem to have learned this lesson yet.' He gave a grim smile. 'And sadly in many ways my life's been a testimonial to that.'

They were passing through Chipping Barnet and it had begun to snow when K rubbed his gloved hands together and glanced at John Conrad. 'The Prince of Wales is still hounding me to send him to the front.'

'But you can't do that; he could be killed.'

'I know, but he says with four brothers, if he is killed succession's not an issue. I've told him becoming a prisoner would be and that in any case we'd all prefer him to be the next king. The staff work he's doing in France doesn't satisfy him and they tell me he's forever making excuses to get to the front.'

'There's no lack of courage in him then.'

'Darn right, he'll make a damn good regent.'

John Conrad thought a moment. 'We could send him to Egypt. Someone really should report about the situation in the Sudan. That'd give Prince Edward something to do where he could feel worthwhile.'

K moved on the seat to face his companion. John Conrad recognised the look in K's eyes when Egypt and the Sudan were mentioned; the longing for yesterday, of the great victories of his youth. 'Darn good thought, Johnny. Brilliant, in fact. We'll send him there.'

K leaned back in the corner, stretching his long legs at an angle to the side and up on the carpet-covered shaft. He closed his eyes, still speaking. 'How pleasant it would be to leave England and the troubles I have here. All the hostility now, especially from Lloyd George. I feel there's a time imminent when I might have to explain things – attempt a vindication of my administration at the War Office, to the back benchers . . . and front benchers for that matter. You know how I hate public speaking, but I'll have to do it.'

'Yes, I think you will.'

He smiled, eyes still closed. 'If only we could leave and go to Egypt or the Sudan like the Prince of Wales . . . dreams,' he finished.

John Conrad took a quick glance at the old warhorse beside him and some minutes later, he thought K was asleep, but quite suddenly he spoke. 'You know what? After this war's over we'll go out to Kenya to the property, through Egypt and the Sudan, retrace my steps of old. I'd like that.'

K, John Conrad and Fitz had bought a property called the Songhir Estates in Kenya, along with two others: Alan McMurdo who had been with K in the Sudan, and a friend called Leggett who lived in Kenya and managed it for them. McMurdo had died suddenly in 1914 and they had bought his shares in the Songhir Estates.

K, eyes closed, was deep in thought. 'Remember 1910 when we bought it? Had a marvellous trip out through Egypt and the Sudan that time didn't we? Wasn't my nephew Toby with us?'

'Yes he was.'

K's tone was wistful. 'Yes, we'll journey through all my old stamping grounds again, end up at Songhir. Remember how the ground runs up that long conical hill? Well, I think that's where we should build a house, on the slope, you know, looking out over the plain . . . wide verandah . . . it's a marvellous view . . . watch the sun going down. Weren't the local folk pleased to see us?' He gave a tired smile. 'I'd like to be able to speak to them, learn about them.'

'With your talent for picking up languages, that shouldn't take long.'

'After the war we'll spend a straight six months out there, doing nothing except watching the animals and learning about the Kenyan people . . . oh, and taking Scotch and cocktails at six every evening. What do you say, Johnny?'

'I can't wait,' John Conrad said with marked enthusiasm. 'I truly can't wait.'

Some weeks later, a Thursday in March, John Conrad and Fitz had accompanied K to meet with the American Ambassador at a house in Curzon Street. It was a long-drawn-out meeting starting at nine in the morning and finishing at four in the afternoon. When they had come out a number of passers-by had recognised K and stopped in a group on the footpath and applauded him soundly.

K said privately, though not openly, how he wished the United States of America would come into the war. 'We will ultimately beat Germany,' he would say, 'but there'll be millions and millions of dead. It's ghastly to contemplate. Pity *our cousins* the Americans wouldn't aid us in the proper sense before that fateful day.' But there was still no move of real help from that republic, even though they at least supported the Allies with much-needed supplies and munitions.

K's car waited at the kerb to take him for a consultation with the King, and as he entered it John Conrad reminded him, 'Don't forget we have a dinner meeting tonight at the Russian Embassy.'

K kept a close eye on events in Russia. He had maintained a long correspondence going back years with the Grand Duke Nicholas who had been Russian commander-in-chief until September 1915, when the Tsar dismissed him and took supreme command himself, even though his Council of Ministers opposed it. K was concerned about the infrastructure in Russia beginning to break down and thus that country's lack of ability to continue the fight on the Eastern front.

'I'll remember the meeting at the Russian Embassy,' K answered as the car drew away and K gave an informal salute to the men and women who had acclaimed him.

As Fitz had a meeting back at the War Office, John Conrad decided to walk back to St James's. It was a pleasant afternoon, the wind had dropped and the temperature was in the high fifties. Birds sang on tree limbs, some of which had pushed forth green shoots foretelling the coming spring, and the sun bestowed the lemon light of afternoon upon London's West End as he made his way along through Mayfair to join Piccadilly.

At the corner of St James's Street, he halted, about to turn into it, when he recognised the brisk determined walk of Emma Louise about thirty yards ahead.

He did not turn down into St James's but remained the same distance behind her as she moved on. A few minutes later she left the throng of Piccadilly, entered St James's churchyard and hurried past the vestry to enter the Parish hall. On the heavy walnut door she opened, was hanging a red cross. John Conrad tapped on the vestry window and a small smartly dressed elderly man looked up from a ledger. 'Excuse me, can you tell me what's going on inside?'

The man looked over his spectacles. 'Red Cross meet there every Tuesday and Thursday. Members come in from all over the South East, to pack comforts, write letters, you know: all for the boys at the front. Anything we can do for you, Colonel?'

'No, thanks.' John Conrad left by the rear entrance of the churchyard into Jermyn Street and made his way home.

He thought, perhaps, to come back and see Emma Louise sometime. It was not a formulated decision, but it lived somewhere at the back of his mind.

For the following weeks he was thoroughly involved with K and the ongoing Battle of Verdun. It had begun on 21 February when the Germans launched their attack upon the French citadel with a nine-hour artillery bombardment and gas shells: a Krupp fifteen-inch naval gun beginning the fire at a position close on twenty miles from Verdun. The British army holding the line in Northern France took over the French sectors around Arras and relinquished as many French troops as possible for the Verdun battle. It was during Verdun that the Germans first used the diabolical weapon of flame-throwers; and for ten long months the battle raged taking 348,300 French soldiers' lives and a similar number of German. This battle so drained the French that the British were once more pushed into taking the offensive.

The weeks passed in a haze of activity for John Conrad: reports, meetings and decisions. On Friday 12 May K and

John Conrad lunched at the War Office, as they often did: sandwiches and tea.

Suddenly K put down his food and said abruptly, 'I'd just like to live long enough to be on the British delegation when peace is made.'

And now John Conrad asked intrigued, 'Illuminate me, what would you do or not do when you are at the peace negotiations?'

'Well, my boy, one thing I would *not* do is to take parts of one country and give them to another. I see that as a huge mistake. All it breeds is revenge and a need to retrieve the territories over time.'

John Conrad chewed the side of his lip in thought. 'Yes, I see. That makes a lot of sense. I think it's been your stance for a long time because I remember how generous you were to the Boers.'

There was a rapping on the door and John Conrad called, 'Come in.'

Fitz entered, carrying a very ornate package impressed with the Russian Royal Seal. He handed it to K. 'This just arrived from the Russian Embassy.'

K broke the seal and opened it. He unrolled the heavy parchment and read; then looked up at the inquisitive faces. 'The Tsar's invited me to Russia. Wants me to visit the Russian fronts and advise on military co-operation, supply, troop morale; a number of things.'

'Will you go?' they both asked at once.

'I feel obliged. Especially as I think I might be able to help. We need them to keep up the fight. I've been concerned for a long time. The Tsar's too autocratic in some ways and weak in others. He's finding opposition in the *Duma*, his lower house, and the Tsarina seems to be more and more under the strange control of Grigory Rasputin, a peasant and self-proclaimed holy man who's even influencing foreign policy.'

'Is that the one that Grand Duke Nicholas writes is a madman?'

K nodded. 'The Grand Duke also tells me food shortages are beginning and the Russian casualties on the Eastern Front are truly monstrous. If the Tsar doesn't make real changes, true political reforms, I'm afraid things could go mightily awry . . .

and if I can influence him in any way, I believe I should.' He patted the ornate envelope. 'So this could be a most timely invitation.'

Fitz picked up his pad and pen, ready to make notes. 'When will you go?'

'As soon as I can. The suggestion's to depart England next month on the fifth. Probably embark on a ship from northern Scotland.'

John Conrad bent forward, elbows on knees. 'Oh damn, I'm meant to go to Herne Bay as your representative with General Hankey on that very afternoon, for the latest trials of the tank.'

'How long are you supposed to be there?'

'I think only about two days; but I've said I'll continue on from there to Dover, then Eastbourne, Brighton, Portsmouth and on, right along the south coast to Plymouth to review the repatriation hospitals with Gatley of the Red Cross. I'll be a day apiece in each town.'

K looked disappointed, and turning his eyes to Fitz asked, 'You don't have anything stopping you from accompanying me, do you?'

'No, I don't.'

K calculated, 'The Russia trip will possibly last some weeks. Have you committed to Hankey and Gatley, Johnny?'

'I reckon I could get out of accompanying Hankey easily enough, but we've put Gatley off twice before. The Red Cross are becoming a bit paranoid that we're showing no interest in them. And unfortunately this time it's being organised through the PM's, office which makes it more difficult to alter. But I'll give it a try.'

K held up his palm. 'No, don't. Duty first, as I've always said. I would've liked you both with me, but you can be doing a lot of good here by the sound of it.'

John Conrad grimaced. 'I suppose so.'

A month later, on the other side of the world, in the last hours of a southern autumn day, Caro alighted from the tram outside Musgrave Park in South Brisbane and walked through an avenue of dark green fir trees to the seat not far from the football ground. A wind had come up, but the late afternoon sun still affected heat in its direct rays so she found an area of the seat in the sun and sat down to wait. The park was deserted at this time of the afternoon, close to five on Friday, though in the distance on the football field two children played with a soccer ball.

After a few minutes, down the avenue came a man. At first she thought it was not Bartholomew and then she realised with relief that it was. She stood up as he arrived. 'I didn't recognise you in uniform. When on earth did you join up?'

'About two months ago. They badly need officers to train the men. And what with the debate about conscription hotting up it's made me think. If Archbishop Mannix and his supporters do get a no vote it'll mean we need volunteers even more. It's a hard debate both ways, not really sure myself, but . . . well, for me it's the thing to do.'

Caro fixed him with a stare. 'Yes, I understand but there are a lot who wouldn't have enlisted, especially at your age, and as you fought in the South African campaign.'

'Yes, well, they aren't me. It's broken Aunt Leigh's heart, I'm sorry to say, what with John Conrad in the army and David too we've found out, and now me. But a man has to do what he believes is right. She thinks it's not fair on one family, but I believe there are large families, even some of nine and ten boys, who've all joined up in the Old Dart.'

He moved his head out of the sunlight into the shade of the branches. 'You were lucky to get me on the phone at the brewery yesterday. I was visiting Father and Aunt Leigh. I won't be there in future. There's a new camp out at Redbank. I'm going to be stationed there.'

Caro's eyes clouded with worry. 'You mean I won't be able to read John Conrad's letters any more?'

'I'm afraid not.'

Her face fell. 'But I must. They keep me . . . sane. Bart, I have to know how he is.'

Bartholomew shrugged. 'Look, Caro, I think you have to take account of things; accept what is. I'm in the army now and you won't be able to telephone me any more.'

Caro shook her head as tears sprung to her eyes. A siren sounded somewhere in the distance, heralding the end of the workday in some factory or other. 'No.' She sat down and held her head in her hands. 'No, Bart, I must read his letters somehow. They mean everything to me.' She looked up dismayed.

Bart took a deep breath and sat beside her. He was silent for a few seconds before he came up with an idea. 'All right, listen. Miss Burton is discreet, a good person. She'll know when and if I'm ever home on leave. If you phone her you can find out that way, then sometime possibly, we can meet.'

Caro took hold of his arm. 'Oh, thank you, Bart. It's just keeping the possibility, that's all. You always were a good man.'

'Mmm, I wonder. Good or stupid?'

'No,' she said vehemently, 'good. It doesn't matter if we only meet once a year. I don't want to lose the contact.'

He nodded. 'But if I'm sent overseas that'll be that.'

'We won't consider that now,' she answered.

He took a letter from his pocket and handed it to her. She opened and read it voraciously. When she had completed it she retained it, holding it near her heart. Her eyes met Bart's. 'So he ran into Emma Louise in the London street. That was a coincidence.'

'Yes, wasn't it?'

'Does she ever write to you?'

'No, but she does to Aunt Leigh. David's somewhere in France. He joined a British unit.' Bart held out his hand for the letter but Caro did not return it, she opened it again and looked at it once more. 'He has beautiful handwriting.'

'He does everything well.'

She smiled. 'Yes, yes he does.'

'Well, Caro, I'll be off.'

Reluctantly she handed over the letter and they stood.

Caro held out her hand. 'Thanks, and good luck.'

Bart shook her hand. 'The same to you, Caro.'

After Bart had gone Caro made her way back to the tram. She waited longer than usual for one to come along and by the time it was gliding across Victoria Bridge darkness had descended and she began to be concerned that she would be late arriving at Central Railway Station where she was meeting Matthew, Knobby, Harry and his friend Luke. They were all to travel out to Gatton and Cedar Grove. She alighted in Adelaide Street and began to run up the hill towards Central Station.

An hour before, Harry and Luke had walked with sprightly steps from Wickham Terrace down Edward Street towards the Central Station. They were to meet Matthew and Knobby and Harry's mother on the platform, and travel home to the country with them for the weekend.

Harry was now almost the full height he would grow, being five feet eleven. His eyes were a forthright, clear blue, his hair was wavy and fair, and his features were as they had always been – a mixture of many people, including Jack Dere.

'Pity we've got to read the chapter on the Zulu War,' Luke moaned as they crossed the railway bridge and turned into Ann Street, halting to buy two oranges from a fruitseller's stall. 'It'll mess up the weekend.'

'We'll still have time to do other things, old son.'

Luke picked up an orange and turned it over in his palm. 'It wouldn't have been so bad if old MacDonald hadn't given us the map of Queensland to draw as well.'

'MacDonald can't help himself. Minute he knew we were going home for the weekend he gave it to the whole class. He can't bear the thought of us enjoying any time off: fat old bugger.'

As Luke took the penny from his pocket to pay he eyed his companion. 'Will Katy be there this weekend?'

The two youths had in recent times begun to notice girls. Harry had just turned seventeen and Luke would be eighteen in June.

Harry shrugged. 'I suppose so, she usually is. I think she's up there now with Aunt Jane and little Isobel.'

When they arrived at the station they purchased their tickets and walked by the series of posters depicting faces of Anzacs with their slouch hats, and waving Australian flags and declaring various messages: 'Is Your Conscience Clear? Enlist Today'; 'A Call From The Trenches – Your King & Country Need You. Enlist Now' and 'Make Your Girl Proud, Join Up Today'.

Luke halted in front of 'Is Your Conscience Clear? Enlist

Today'. At the bottom of the poster it had 'God Save The King'.

'I love that Australian flag,' he said.

'Me too. It's a flag to be mighty proud of. The Southern Cross looks beaut with the old Union Jack, doesn't it?'

Luke nodded vehemently. 'It's the best flag in the world. I reckon red, white and blue are my favourite colours.'

'Mine too,' agreed Harry.

'How I'd love to fight for the flag. Enlist right now. I hate the way we're treated like kids, don't you?'

Harry was dedicatedly peeling his orange. 'Mmm, I do.' He took a segment of the fruit and, putting it in his mouth, continued talking at the same time. 'Read that letter again we got from Uncle Bill yesterday. Good orange,' he added.

'What? Read it now?'

'Yes, now. Come on, old son.'

Luke delved into his pockets and, bringing out the letter, stood under the poster stretching high above him on the wall with the smiling Anzac looming benignly over him waving the flag.

Egypt

Dear Nephew Luke,

Here's your Uncle Bill in Egypt now. Hot and sunny just like Queensland. When we arrived in Egypt I was sent to an officers' school. I am enjoying that mightily and getting to ride quite a bit which I've missed greatly since leaving Charleville. But, my heavens, camels are a different kettle of fish to horses. Strange feeling . . . like being on the sea at first, but I'll get used to it, nothing on four legs your uncle can't ride you know.

All the officers and NCOs are ex cavalry and they refer to us as 'gentlemen'. Ha ha . . . regard your uncle as a gentleman now! After Gallipoli this is a breeze. I did not think of the danger when I was on the peninsula, though I've left a lot of good blokes there six feet under.

Don't know if I mentioned it in my last letter but before we were withdrawn from Gallipoli we had a visit from Kitchener of Khartoum. Imagine it! All the blokes cheered like one thing when he came up into the very front line trenches not twenty yards from the enemy at one point.

Anyway, Egypt is an easy life. I could get used to this. We're showing the Gypos a thing or two. There's an awful lot of sand in this country, more than a Queensland beach! I'm bringing Ma home a replica of the Sphinx for the mantelpiece.

Well that's all for now. Work hard.

From your loving Uncle Bill

As Luke carefully folded the treasure to replace it in his pocket Harry slapped him energetically on the shoulder. 'He's a fine one, is Uncle Bill, a real fine one. I love his letters.'

'Afternoon, boys.' A voice sounded along the platform and they turned expectantly to see Matthew coming along on a walnut and pine cane with Knobby at his side.

'Good,' said Knobby shaking hands with them. 'You're early. We've spent the afternoon with Ian Coates; your father has to get busy. More paintings for the Sydney dealer.'

'Guess what, Dad?' Harry asked, eyes full of enthusiasm.

'What, old son?'

'Luke's uncle's in Egypt now. Learning to be an officer.'

Matt attempted a vague interest. 'Well well, has he been to the pyramids?'

'No,' replied Luke, 'but he bought Grandma a replica of the Sphinx.'

Matthew winked. 'Grandma might *be* a replica of the Sphinx.'

Harry burst out laughing, and Luke hesitated momentarily then, deciding it was indeed funny, joined in.

Matt tapped Luke's leg with his cane, 'Thanks for taking it so well, old son. No offence to your grandmother. The Sphinx is an icon and for all I know your gran might be one too.'

'What's an icon?' Luke asked.

'Something highly venerated, especially in the religious context.'

'Gran's religious,' Luke enlightened them.

'Well, there you are then and let's all just assume your grandfather venerated her and we can leave it at that.'

470

Harry leant across and whispered in Luke's ear, 'Don't mind him, Dad can't help himself.'

As they moved off along the platform, Matt turned to Knobby. 'Caro should be here soon so let's take advantage of her absence and have a drink.'

In the station bar Knobby ordered two beers and two shandies – equal mixtures of beer and lemonade. When he handed the youths the shandies their eyes lit up. Harry took his enthusiastically. 'Lucky Mum's not here, she wouldn't approve of this.'

'She will be soon,' responded Matt, 'and this whole trip will turn into a much more sober affair, so drink up and be thankful.'

Luke eyed Matthew with admiration. He loved being with Harry's father. He was such good fun, not like a parent at all. He said and did outrageous things, which appealed greatly to the youths, though Harry regarded him as more normal than Luke did, having grown up with Matt and being used to him.

Ten minutes later Knobby pointed through the window as the dusty grey engine steamed into the station. 'Train's here. Wonder where Caro is?'

Matt swallowed the remains of his second beer. 'She'll turn up.' He waved his cane in the air. 'You two lads toddle off and find an empty compartment. We'll be along in a minute.'

Harry looked knowingly. 'Oh yes, after another beer you mean.'

Matt swung at Harry with his cane but the agile youth ducked away. 'No cheek, you,' Matthew declared.

Five minutes later the stationmaster shouted, 'All aboard the six twenty-three for Ipswich! Change trains there for Gatton and Toowoomba.'

Matthew rose to his feet. 'Best get out on to the platform. The bugger seems insistent that the train's leaving on time for once.'

Knobby looked up and down the platform as they came outside. 'I hope nothing's happened to Caro.'

'Final call. All aboard for Ipswich!'

The two boys were leaning out the windows of the train. 'What do you want us to do, Dad?' shouted Harry. 'Stay in here or get off?'

471

'Oh hell,' retorted Matt. 'Stay there. I wonder where the devil she is.'

Knobby was holding open a carriage door and the stationmaster was walking along slamming doors closed. Knobby's was the last remaining open. 'Close the door please, sir,' he called to Knobby.

'We're expecting a lady. She's not here yet.'

'Can't hold up the train! Close the door. Train's departing.'

Matt looked the stationmaster up and down. 'Can't imagine why you're so bloody eager to keep to the timetable today. Are you new? Haven't your compatriots told you this sort of enterprising attitude won't be tolerated? You'll be black-listed pretty smartly for this sort of discrepancy, old chap.'

The stationmaster was becoming agitated. 'I've got a job to do, sir. Now move away! Train's leaving no matter what.'

Matt lounged on his cane. 'Do you have shares in the railways?'

The train whistle blew and the stationmaster stepped determinedly forward to the door to face Knobby.

'Matt! Knobby!'

They turned to see Caro running down the platform.

'Here she is, thank goodness!' exclaimed Knobby.

'She's lucky then,' pontificated the stationmaster, arms akimbo. 'Train would have gone on time and no mistake.'

Knobby helped Caro up through the heavy door and he and Matt followed as the stationmaster slammed it behind them with gusto, and resolutely waved his flag.

As the train chugged forward Matt followed Caro down the corridor. 'And where the hell were you?'

'I was late back at the George Street office. I was on the delivery truck that took the war supplies down to the transports at the wharves. The truck broke down.'

For six months Caro had been working with a Queensland group called the Women's Auxiliary for the War Effort. She had taken training as a nurse, learned to drive a vehicle, and did general helping at headquarters in George Street. They liaised with the Red Cross and the military forces and did what they could to aid the war effort. What she had said to Matt was not a lie. It had all happened today, but it had occurred some hours earlier.

When they reached the compartment where the youths were Harry eyed her as she sat down. 'How come you were so late, Mum? We almost missed the train.'

His mother returned his gaze. 'I've explained all that already. Compassion, Harry, please. I feel badly enough.'

Harry gave a long-suffering look. It was one of his mother's trite refrains: compassion. She always went on about its being the major difference between humans and animals. He sighed and looked out the window.

An hour later they disembarked in Ipswich to change trains for Gatton, and Matt and Knobby found their way to the bar to wait out the delay.

As they sat on a stool on the platform beside Caro, Harry whispered to Luke, 'No shandies this time, more's the pity.'

Luke shook his head sorrowfully.

In the next train Matt entertained them most of the way, having an opinion on everything the two youths mentioned. When Luke informed them he would like to join up when he turned eighteen, Matt cast a whimsical eye upon him. 'Now Luke, what makes you say this? Is it a fervent loyalty to your King and country?'

'Could be.'

'Mmm, all very commendable. But what if you do eventually join up and you stop a bullet, or a number of bullets or fragments of a shell or worse?'

'But, Mr Craken, that's part of a soldier's lot.'

'True, lad. But I'm of the opinion that if all the boys in the trenches on both sides stood up, dropped their weapons, waved and buggered off home, the irresponsible incompetents in government would have to see sense: sense being to govern their own domains and stop perpetrating violent destruction in others.'

Luke was unconvinced. 'But, sir, that wouldn't ever happen.'

'Decidedly you're right, young Luke, more's the pity.'

Harry resolved to have a say. 'Luke, someone in the Federal Government wrote to Dad, didn't they, Dad? There's some sort of thing going to happen where they'll be wanting painters to go over and be war artists. Isn't that right, Dad?'

Luke's eyes widened with fascination. 'You never told me

473

that before.' He looked with even more respect at Matthew. 'Really, Mr Craken?'

Matt gave a cynical laugh. 'Yes, lad, but if it happens I'm holding out for a personal request from Billy Hughes before I deign to accept.'

'Gosh!'

Knobby piped in. 'He's the best painter in Australia bar none. He's painted me many times and with this head that says it all.'

This brought laughter from the boys and a judgement from Matt as he waved his cane in the air. 'Spoken without prejudice, sentiments unsought, therefore valid.'

Caro sighed and changed the subject. 'It won't be long before we're home. Jacob's bringing the dray so I suppose they'll all come to meet us.'

'If that's the case he'll need to bring two,' said Knobby.

And so he had. When they stepped down from the train at the blue and white painted station house vaguely lit by four sparse electric light bulbs, and they all issued out into the road, there with lanterns illuminating them were two drays, Jacob and Mary in one, and Jane driving the other with Katy and Isobel on either side of her.

Later, in the big house at Cedar Grove in the fertile Lockyer Valley, after the clock in the hall had struck midnight and the house was quiet and the two boys were dreaming, Matthew opened the door of the bedroom he shared with Caro. It was a cool night in the valley and a fire flickered in the grate. Caro had been in bed perhaps half an hour but she was not asleep, and she watched Matthew's shadow loom back and forth across the room as he undressed and moved out into the annex to bathe and return to the bed.

'You awake, Caro?' he whispered as he entered between the sheets.

'Yes.'

He moved over to her and she felt the strength in his muscular arms as he drew her to him. His mouth came down upon hers and the old habitual excitement unfolded inside her as his hands roamed across her body and inside her nightgown. He had always been able to kindle her emotions and arouse her. She supposed she should be grateful for that. There were women she knew who took no pleasure at all in the sex act. As his mouth explored her own and his fingers began to knead her breasts she moved sensually beneath his hands.

He took his lips from hers and whispered against her ear, 'You didn't lie to me today, did you, old girl?'

She tensed slightly. 'What do you mean?'

'About why you were late?'

She gave a small laugh. 'Of course not.'

His head slipped down under the covers of the bed and now his mouth found her nipples, and his hot tongue manipulated them to bring them to harden. He spoke softly against her warm flesh. 'The enemy isn't home on leave or something equally as fanciful, is he?'

Caro took a deep uncomfortable breath. 'No, of course not.'

Abruptly Matt's teeth scraped across her nipple. It did not hurt but it could have. 'Then you'd have some way of knowing, would you?'

Caro pushed him aside and sat up. 'Stop this, Matt. I don't like it. If you're going to talk about him I'm getting up and going to another room.'

Her husband said nothing for a time, but lay watching her sitting in bed in the warm dancing gleam from the grate. She could hear him breathing, then she felt him move and his hands stroked her firm back through her nightgown and then slipped round her waist. He sat up behind her and his breath gave her tingling sensations on the nape of her neck. 'You're right, I shouldn't mention him when I'm in bed with my wife. Bad form.'

He pushed her gown down around her waist and cupped her breasts in his hands before he brought her gently and unresistingly back upon the bed. He bent and kissed her throat all the way up to her lips. Again he spoke softly, his breath against her mouth, but his tone was edged with sarcasm. 'Fact is, if I hadn't brought him up I know for certain that neither of us would be thinking of him.'

'Stop it, Matthew. This isn't fair.' She took hold of his head in her hands and held it firmly to look in his eyes. '*Don't* do this.'

His half-smile edged up the corner of his mouth and he

stroked her tenderly across the faint scar on her lip before he eased himself down upon her.

She felt his long fingers seeking inside her legs, and as his mouth found hers again he whispered against her lips. 'All right, come on, old girl. Let's enjoy this and I'll pretend you're mine.'

Chapter Thirty

May 1916 gave London some glorious sunny days. It was almost hard to believe that just across the channel men lived in filth and mud.

John Conrad had been in Camberwell, at a munitions factory, and returned back across the Thames in the late afternoon. The army truck he travelled in made a stop at Victoria and when he found that it might be half an hour's wait he decided to catch a hackney. 'The Mall, please,' he called to the driver. 'St James's end.'

A breeze caressed his face as they trundled along. The smell of summer was in the air and he closed his eyes in thought. He had much to accomplish in the coming days and K had informed him he wished to make a trip to the French and Belgian battlefronts when he returned from Russia.

Quite suddenly an entirely unconnected idea came to his mind and he shouted to the driver. 'Change of destination. Take me to Piccadilly, St James's Church.'

When he alighted in front of the church he walked quickly down into the yard and over to the door with the red cross upon it. He paused and then pushed it open.

Inside he looked around. It was all activity. A small pinched-faced woman in a green apron asked, 'Can I be of assistance, Colonel?'

He glanced round. 'I'm looking for . . .' then he saw Emma Louise at the end of the hall up on a small stage. She appeared to be counting out socks into boxes. He pointed. 'I'm here to see that lady, the one up there.'

'Off you go then. Don't mind me.'

He came right up to the stage before Emma Louise looked down and saw him. She started. 'Good heavens, what are you doing here?'

'Is it possible to see you . . . after you finish here?

'Why?'

'I'd like to talk to you.'

Hesitating at first, she finally nodded. 'All right. I'll be another fifteen minutes or so.'

'I'll be waiting outside.'

It was about twenty minutes later that Emma Louise appeared, along with a group of others who wished each other good evening and separated. 'I'll see you next week,' Emma Louise said while they eyed John Conrad.

Emma's expression showed her discomfort. 'What do you want?'

'I don't know. I suddenly remembered you came up here on Thursdays.'

'How did you know that?'

'Some months ago, I saw you turn in here.'

'I see.'

'Yes, well . . . what about some tea? There's a small tea shop across the way in Duke Street?'

'Yes, I know it. But I don't think so thanks.' She spoke abruptly.

'Emma Louise, I don't even know why I'm here to see you. It was a sudden compulsion. Perhaps it's an omen to let the past be just that – the past.' He gave a strange smile. 'Are you sure you won't have some tea?'

Her big eyes were filled with uncertainty. She shook her head. 'Perhaps some other time.'

Four women issued out of the hall and passed them, looking back with interest at John Conrad.

'Then at least let's just leave this doorway where we seem to be the cynosure.'

He moved off and she followed him down through the churchyard and the tall iron gate into Jermyn Street. They stood on the footpath unspeaking as the church gate opened behind them and three more women came out, eying them up and down.

'All right,' Emma Louise said, 'let's have some tea.'

They sat at a table beside the tea shop's mullioned window with its blue and white flowered curtains.

Emma Louise fixed him with her clear open gaze. 'I'm not at all sure about this.'

'Frankly, nor am I, but here we are so we can be civilised about it.'

'John Conrad, the last time I saw you, no, the time before, you called me a whore and threw me bodily across a room.'

'Yes.'

'You then attacked the man I had fallen in love with and hurt him very badly.'

John Conrad steadily met her gaze and spoke slowly and clearly. 'You were *supposed* to be in love with me.'

She could not continue meeting his eyes, and she looked away and when she did not answer he went on, 'I thought at the time you both thoroughly deserved everything.'

She still remained silent, though to herself she admitted what he said might be so.

'Would you like to order?' asked a lady in a white apron.

They both ordered tea with milk and sugar.

'We've no sugar, but we've got honey.'

'Yes, honey then, thank you.'

Emma Louise toyed with her gloves. 'The fact is, while I read about Lord Kitchener and sometimes see a photograph of you with him, I never expected to be in your company . . . to talk to you again. This is very hard.'

John Conrad agreed. 'If it'd come to my mind, I would've thought the same. But, Emma Louise, I suppose it has to do with the war. When I met you in the street just before Christmas I . . . well, I suppose it reminded me of all sorts of things. And I think I've realised for a long time now that anger and resentment and grudges are so petty and childishly foolish against the enormity of what is happening . . . this war and all its far-reaching effects. So I suppose that when you came into my mind this afternoon, it seemed right to come and find you.'

He thought of K's wall map in his study, where the dead were marked in blue for tens of thousands and red for hundreds of thousands. There were more red marks all the time. As if he could hold a grudge now, about anything, with anyone. None of it was important any more. The war had altered the way he looked at the world, the way he thought about almost everything.

He raised his eyes to her, as, in her old characteristic

way of moving conversation tangentially she said, 'David's in France.'

'Where?'

'I don't know.'

He shook his head. 'Of course you don't.' He was surprised that David was at the war, though when he analysed it there was no reason he should not be. Millions of men were.

The tea came and the woman poured them each a cup.

Conscription had become law only a few days earlier, so John Conrad realised David had volunteered. 'When did he enlist?'

'Last November.' She altered the subject immediately again. 'Our child is a daughter. We called her May. She's six this year.'

'I see.' He really did not want to talk about the child. 'How's your aunt?'

'She finds the English winters very harsh after so many years in the tropics. She's well but older, of course . . . as we all are. She takes care of May when I'm up here.'

'And your Uncle Hewitt?'

She was beginning to relax slightly and though there was no friendly tone in her voice it was not unfriendly either. 'He actually spends much of the week up here at his club. Comes home to Kent on Thursdays for the weekends. He still has his shares in textile mills. They're very busy with the war on. Uncle Hewitt takes care of us all, very well.'

She drank some of her tea and so did John Conrad.

They were silent for a time as Emma Louise toyed with her gloves again then lifted her eyes to meet her companion's. 'Truth is, since I saw you at Christmas I've thought a lot about the past too.' Then she picked up her cup and finished her tea and took up her handbag. 'I'd best be off; don't want to miss the train. Not that they're always on time these days. Damn war.'

John Conrad put some change on the tablecloth and rose with her.

Outside in the street he said, 'Where exactly do you live?'

An odd expression crossed her face. 'Where exactly do *you* live?'

He gestured. 'Just down there in York House, St James's Palace.'

480

'My my, what an address!'

'Yes, it was lent to K for the duration of the war. So . . . where do you live?'

'We live at Lansdowne Grove, Cosgrove Hill, two miles east of Canterbury on the Wingham Road.'

'I thought your uncle's home was in Sussex.'

She nodded. 'It was, we moved.' She put on her gloves and then held out her hand to him. He shook it.

'Perhaps . . . we'll meet again.'

'Yes,' he said. 'Perhaps we will.'

Harry rolled over and smiled, a long strand of paspalum grass between his teeth. 'Read me the last bit again, the bit with the poem in it.'

'All right,' replied Luke, pulling his knees up and leaning back against the trunk of the tree.

> 'Some of the division moved on last week but our battalion is still here. We'd like to get to the fight and give it to the Huns I can tell you that. Anyway thought that you, young Luke lad, would like this poem that a mate of mine wrote at Gallipoli. He gave it to me not too long before he met a bullet. He was one of the best mates a man could have. He came from Gundagai.
>
> The bugles of England were blowing o'er the sea
> As they had called a thousand years, calling now to me:
> They woke me from dreaming in the dawning of the day,
> The bugles of England – and how could I stay?
>
> Sort of got me, it did. Suppose it was how I felt in a way before I joined up. Like I wanted to help the Mother Country and all. Anyway, hope we'll be in for a real fight of it soon.
>
> Keep working hard and I'll write again soon,
> Your Loving Uncle Bill'

Luke looked up at his friend, his eyes glowing with the fire of youth and the passion of his visions.

'Gosh, that's just a wonderful poem,' Harry said.

'I know.'

Harry chewed his strand of grass and spat some out on the ground. 'It's after five o'clock. We'll have to go in soon or old MacDonald will come looking for us if we don't.'

'Gawd, I hate that bloke.'

'Yeah, me too. Wish he'd have a flaming heart attack.'

This was apparently hilarious for both youths burst into laughter and rolled around on the ground. When they calmed down Luke crossed his legs and waved a piece of grass at his friend. 'I've absolutely decided I'm going to join up.'

'What? When?'

'Soon. Perhaps on Friday.'

Harry was fascinated. 'Really? Friday. But you're only seventeen.'

Luke stood up. 'Yes, but I'm eighteen next month. Don't I look eighteen?'

Harry closed one eye and appraised his friend. 'Yeah, I'd definitely say you do.'

'Stand up.'

Harry stood.

'We're both pretty tall.'

'Do you reckon I could pass for eighteen too?'

Luke sized up his friend. 'I reckon you could.'

'Well, we both shave once a week.'

Luke was clearly excited. 'That's it, we'll both join up . . . you ripper. Fight Fritz together.'

'Hang on, old son. No one's going to give us permission to join up. Gawd, can't you just hear what my mother'll say, let alone my father!'

Luke's eyes narrowed with the adroitness of his thought. 'No one will know.'

'How come?'

'This weekend's home weekend if we want to go.'

Harry pursed his lips. 'We *always* go.'

'Yeah I know. So, we write to your parents and tell them that this weekend we can't come home, that there's a special match or something here at school, but we tell MacDonald that we are. Then when we leave here we go to the recruiting office and join up. No one knows anything until Monday morning and we're soldiers by then.'

Harry's eyes were growing wider by the minute. 'Oh boy, that's a great plan.' He grabbed his friend and started to wrestle with him shouting, 'Soldiers! Soldiers!' Luke leapt to his own defence and tripped Harry, who fell to the ground as Luke came down on top of him and they both rolled across the grass, laughing and shouting. When they finally weakened, Harry said excitedly, 'Come on, let's go back inside and write the letter to Mum.'

They raced each other across the field towards the school building.

Caro opened the envelope with a smile. Any time her son wrote was special to her. He did so about three times a term and he came home once a month at the weekend, usually bringing his friend Luke.

She carried the letter until she found a spot in the sun down by the herb garden across from the milking shed. It was still warm but, being May, the days were closing in and the westerly winds were just beginning.

She read the letter and a look of disappointment crossed her face. She lifted her eyes from the page as in the distance, back towards the house, she saw Matthew and Knobby exit the studio and cross the yard.

'Matt! Knobby!' she called and the two men turned in the direction of the sound.

Matt lifted his mahogany cane in greeting and they came down towards her while she walked forward to meet them. She held up the letter. 'The boys aren't coming home this weekend. There's a special cricket match between the houses and they have to play. I'm so disappointed, what with you two leaving tomorrow for Sydney.' The corners of her mouth drew down. 'Jane and I will be home all alone.'

Matt's eyebrow rose. 'You have an extreme vision of *alone*, Caro, old girl? The truth is you'll be here with Katy, Jacob, Mary and Isobel, yet you insist you and Jane will be all alone?' He turned to Knobby. 'Explain that one to me, can you, Knob, old son?'

Knobby had the good sense to remain silent.

'Oh Matt,' Caro said, frustration in her voice, 'you never understand. I was looking forward to the boys being here while you two were away.'

Matthew's crooked smile crossed his mouth. 'Don't tell me you'll miss me?'

She shook her head. 'Don't be silly. Come on, let's go inside and have lunch.'

Her husband slapped her gently on the bottom with his cane. 'I do believe you don't want me to go to Sydney after all.'

'Cut it out, Matt.' She hit out at him, well missing his arm. 'You must go. It's important that you meet the new agent down there. It could mean a lot to us.' She looked hard at Knobby. 'Just don't let him get caught up with any artists, please. They're profligate, godless, and without restraint of any kind from what I can see.'

Knobby laughed. 'Then Matt'll fit in just right.'

Matt swung up the steps on his cane and turned back to his wife. 'Now look, old girl, Knob and I've been invited by Julian Ashton to spend a few days out on the Hawkesbury River where he used to paint with Nerli and Condor, for heaven's sake. I can't say no to that. There's going to be a fellow there I'd like to talk to. Actually Ashton's mother was the daughter of an Italian count. You'd approve of him, Caro.'

Caro mounted the steps and brushed past her husband. 'No, Matt, I doubt it.'

On Friday afternoon Harry and Luke said goodbye to Naffer. They shook his hand and both gave him a quick hug.

'What's going on?' Naffer asked. 'You've never done that before. You're only going away for the weekend, for heaven's sake . . .' His eyes narrowed suspiciously. 'Well, aren't you?'

They slapped him on the back and left him standing there shaking his head in thought.

'Perhaps we should have told old Naff the truth,' Harry said as they hurried away from the school along Wickham Terrace.

'No. The less he knows the less they can get out of him when we don't turn up on Monday.'

'True.'

'First thing we need to do is go into the lavs at Central

Station and get rid of these blasted uniforms, change into ordinary clothes. That's one thing that'll give us away.'

'Righto, old son.'

They threw their uniforms in a large rubbish bin in the station yard and they stopped at the corner of Ann Street at the shop that sold newspapers and tobacco and bought a packet of Players Navy Cut tobacco and some papers.

'See,' said Luke, as they came out on to the street, 'I reckon that bloke thought we were twenty at least.' They each rolled a cigarette outside the shop, lit up and walked puffing down the hill. The nearest recruiting station was in Albert Square and as they came up to the entrance they halted beside the large poster outside declaring, 'This way; Join up today, Make your girl proud!'

Two corporals stood either side of the door and as the youths arrived one asked, 'Joinin' up, boys?'

'Too right,' Luke replied.

The corporal beamed at them. 'Good lads, this way.' Then swept his hand in a welcoming gesture through the doorway.

Inside there were about a dozen young men standing drinking beer on the far side of the room and three or four others talking to a soldier who lifted his arm and directed them to two desks behind which recruiting sergeants sat with various piles of papers in front of them.

The soldier talking noticed Luke and Harry and halted his conversation. 'Here to join up for King and country, lads?'

'Yes.'

'This way, please.' He turned and shouted, 'Sergeant Kennedy, two more brave lads here.'

Sergeant Kennedy, a large good-looking man with an amiable manner, lifted his head and smiled widely beneath his grand moustache as the corporal walked Harry and Luke across to his desk. There was already a man standing there and the two youths waited behind him. They could overhear all that Sergeant Kennedy said to the volunteer in front.

'So I understand you live in Brisbane?'

'Yes.'

'And your name's Dave Sands.'

'Yes.'

Sergeant Kennedy twirled the end of his moustache in

485

contemplation. 'Look, no offence, Sands, but you're an Abo.'
He turned round in his chair to the sergeant a few feet away.
'Hey, Miller, are Abos allowed to join up?'

'Dunno.'

The Aborigine so spoken about bent over the desk towards
Sergeant Kennedy and winked at him, saying, 'You know what,
Sergeant? I'm half British. So now perhaps you could say that's
the part of me that's enlisting here today.'

Sergeant Kennedy took no umbrage at this, in fact it brought
another smile to his face. He shrugged and flicked through his
papers. 'Sands, there's definitely nothin' here about whether
you can or you can't enlist . . . so . . . I reckon that means you
can, though I ain't seen any others of your sort rushin' us.'

Dave Sands gave a saucy grin. He bent forward again. 'They
probably don't read the *Brisbane Courier*, Sergeant, so my
guess is they don't know there's a war on.'

'Are you trifling with me, Sands?'

'No, sir.'

'Good. Let's get back to the questionnaire, shall we?' And
he tapped his finger on the paper in front of him. 'Are you
eighteen or over?'

'Turned eighteen in February.'

Kennedy ticked a square on the form in front of him.

'Do you have a wife or *de facto*?'

'No.'

Kennedy ticked another square. At this juncture Dave Sands
turned round and looked at Harry. As their eyes met they both
smiled; there was something about Dave Sands that Harry
responded to immediately.

Kennedy spoke again. 'Guess that means you have no
off-spring then.'

'That's right, I haven't.'

'You understand that you'll be paid one shilling a day for
fifty days onboard ship and then five shillings a day after
that plus one shilling deferred pay. In your case, as you've
no dependants, you get the lot yourself.'

'What if I'm on the ship longer than fifty days?'

Kennedy frowned and looked down at the form before he
raised his gaze to Dave Sands. 'Nothin' here about that; let
me give you a piece of advice, Sands. You're a bit of a joker,

and I'm a sergeant with a heart, son, but you're going to meet a lot without one, so be warned. The army doesn't like being asked questions. Understand?'

'I suppose so. It just struck me that's all.' Dave Sands bent forward to Sergeant Kennedy again. 'I'm sorry, Sergeant, but I've got another question, if you don't mind.'

Kennedy looked skywards, then gave the young man a long-suffering look. 'You're incorrigible. Spit it out.'

'Can I give some of my pay to my mum here in Brisbane?'

Kennedy seemed pleased that he could answer this one. 'Yes, I do believe that can be done though I've never had it before. How much?'

'Well, three shillings, once I'm getting that much.'

Kennedy found the right spot on the questionnaire. 'So, three shillings a day . . . to . . . mother.' He wrote something in, ticked another spot and looked up. 'What's her name and address?'

'Mrs Lena Sands, number six, Berry Street, Spring Hill. That's great, Sergeant. I do want Mum to get that – one of the main reasons I joined up really, I heard you could sort of donate some of your pay.'

'Good lad,' Kennedy replied. 'Damn unusual, but good. Now,' his pen hovered over the form again, 'last question . . . religion?'

Dave paused.

The sergeant looked up. 'Well?'

His mouth drew down. 'Ain't got one, though I know a fair bit about the dreaming. Mum taught me that and so did Uncle Wamberro when I was a kid and we used to visit the tribe.'

By now Sergeant Kennedy was wondering what he had come upon in this particular volunteer. He leaned back and appraised Dave for a full ten seconds before he sighed and said, 'Sands, I don't have a square to tick on this form that says anything about dreaming. As far as I know that's what's done in bed asleep. What I have here are legitimate religions: Church of England, Roman Catholic, Presbyterian, Congregational, Methodist or Baptist. Take your choice.'

'Gosh, Sergeant, I don't know.'

'Haven't got an *I don't know* either, lad.' He crossed his

arms and gave a decided nod. 'You're a Roman Catholic like me.' He ticked the relevent box. 'Right?'

Dave took this with equanimity. 'If you say so.'

'I do. Righto, Sands, sign here.' He handed the pen to Dave, who signed on the dotted line at the bottom of the form.

'Oh, and we don't charge you for transport overseas and back.'

'That's real generous,' quipped Dave.

'Welcome to the army. Your number's on here.' Kennedy gave a knowing grin and handed Dave a metal tag, then looked past him to the corporal at the door. 'Take Sands and tell him what will happen on discharge, McIntyre.'

As Dave moved away the sergeant grinned at his back, then motioned to Harry. 'Your turn!'

Harry and Luke stepped up to the desk.

Sergeant Kennedy held up his palm. 'One at a time, lads.'

Luke moved in behind Harry.

Sergeant Kennedy followed the exact routine he had with Dave and when he came to, 'Are you eighteen or over?' Harry took a deep breath. 'Yes, eighteen.'

Kennedy did not even look up. He simply ticked the form and went on. Harry sneaked a quick glance to Luke, who smiled widely.

When Kennedy asked if Harry had a wife or *de facto* Harry blushed and Luke could not help himself from laughing behind Harry's back. Kennedy looked up sharply. 'Your mate doesn't seem to think you're made of the right stuff to get a woman, eh?'

Harry had no answer to this and the sergeant wagged his forefinger at him. 'Lots of fellows without girls get plenty once they're in uniform.' He met Harry's embarrassed gaze. 'So don't despair, lad.'

When the questions were over Harry signed on the dotted line and Sergeant Kennedy handed him his metal tag. 'Welcome to the army. Your number's here.'

Harry was taken away by Corporal McIntyre and told, 'You'll be given your kit out at Camp Hill tomorrow. You have leave tonight to say goodbye to your loved ones but you must be back at camp tomorrow out at Camp Hill by seventeen hundred; that's five p.m. to you. Don't be late: the army isn't tolerant. You'll be given a physical examination then, though I reckon you're all A-one by the look of you – and a haircut. Then you blokes who've enlisted today are the last ones on the train that leaves here Sunday morning at o eight hundred.'

Harry's eyes were afire. 'Where are we going?'

'Sydney, mate, for training, and then on the great adventure. Now when you're discharged – I know it's funny mentioning that as you've only just signed on – but it's the rules. When you're discharged you'll be given free of charge a suit of plain clothes and a cap or twenty shillings in lieu.'

Harry was thrilled. 'I don't mind which,' he answered.

'Good. Now wait here for your mate.'

As Harry spun round to look over to Luke, who was still with Sergeant Kennedy, Dave came up to him and held out his hand. 'I'm Dave Sands.'

'Yes, I heard. Harry Craken, how do you do?'

'All right, thanks.'

'Exciting, isn't it?'

'Yeah. Hope my old man can run our business without me.'

'What do you do?'

'Sell second-hand stuff.'

'Is there anyone else to help him?'

'Mmm . . . got a little brother.'

When Luke had been enlisted they joined the other dozen or so men standing two by two in front of the Australian flag draped across one wall. Sergeant Kennedy came over and faced them. 'We're raising the 3rd Australian Division, boys, our country's answer to those loud voices in the press who've declared that we as a nation would resent the evacuation of Gallipoli and the sacrifices we made there. Shows how little they know of the heart of Australia! Already thousands of troops of the 3rd Division have been sent to England for training. You'll be part of our great tradition.' He spoke proudly. 'There's one more thing to do to make you all soldiers of this great democratic commonwealth of ours,' he smiled, 'and incidentally may it last a thousand years.'

'Hear! hear!'

'Raise your right hands and repeat the oath of allegiance after me.'

This they duly completed and Kennedy saluted them and said, 'Welcome, soldiers of the King, welcome to the Australian Imperial Forces.'

When Harry, Luke and Dave found themselves on the footpath again Harry said, 'So we've got tonight free then.'

'Yeah,' Dave grinned. 'I'm going home to say goodbye to Mum and Dad. I'll see you two at camp tomorrow at five.'

Harry waved off his new friend and Luke's eyes followed Dave as he walked away. 'What did you want to go and make a friend of him for?'

'I like him.'

'How can you? You don't know him.'

An odd expression crossed Harry's face. 'Yes I do.'

'What the hell does that mean?'

'I don't know. I just do, it's hard to explain.'

Luke gave a frustrated groan. 'So now what? We've got twenty-four hours.'

Harry nodded. 'I feel terribly guilty not telling Mum about all this. She'll be pretty upset. I've been thinking. Reckon I ought to go out to Cedar Grove and face her.'

'Well, I can't go out to Charleville, not in twenty-four hours I can't.'

'No. You'll just have to write your mum a letter. Tell you what I think we'd better do.'

'What?'

'I've got to face up to Mum. We're in time to catch the six twenty-three to Ipswich. We'll travel out there and stay the night in a pub. Then in the morning you can write to your mother and we can catch the train to Gatton and go home to Cedar Grove. Dad's gone to Sydney this weekend, thank God. We'll still have plenty of time to catch a train back here and get to camp by five.'

Luke was agreeable. 'Suits me. Have we got enough money for a pub tonight as well as the train fare?'

'I've got two florins.'

'And I've got three and tenpence.'

'Plenty,' smiled Harry. 'We'll get a good meal as well.'

Luke grinned and punched him lightly in the ribs. 'Yeah, the army'll be paying us after this.'

They caught the 6.23 and purchased beds at the Commonwealth Hotel across from the Ipswich Railway Station in Union Street not far from the Bremer River, which ran through the town. Horses stood hitched to the railings along the front of the stone hotel and through the open wooden-shuttered windows they gazed upon the welcome lights in the long public bar.

'Let's have a beer,' said Luke, and rejoicing in his new-found freedom, Harry readily concurred.

'There you are,' whispered Luke proudly, as the barman placed the beers in front of them. 'He thinks we're old enough to drink. Just joined up,' he informed the barman, who replied, 'What both of ya?'

'Yes.'

He grinned at them, showing a missing eyetooth. 'In that case the beers are on the house. No payment required, mateys.'

Luke dug Harry in the ribs with glee.

When they had drained their glasses the barman called, 'Want a refill, boys?'

Harry shook his head. 'No, thanks.' Luke's mouth drew down in disappointment but he went along with his friend and they wandered up the hill of Nicholas Street in the darkness towards the main thoroughfare: Brisbane Street.

It was a cool night and everything seemed to be closed, but they found one café run by an elderly Chinese couple who were just about to close their doors but when requested sold them some fried fish and chips. They crossed the street to find a seat out of the breeze in the dim night glow pervading St Paul's Church of England churchyard.

'This is great!' Harry exclaimed, pushing three chips into his already full mouth, and Luke managed an affirmative grunt.

When they had finished eating Harry peeked in the big open oak door of the church. The metal cross far away down the aisle on the altar gleamed with a pious light. A church had sat upon this spot since the 1850s, and before the colony had separated in 1859 had claimed the distinction of being known as one of the prettiest churches in New South Wales.

'Should we go in and say a prayer?'

'What for?' asked Luke, who mostly tried to avoid religious instruction of any kind.

'Oh I don't know . . . you know, going to the war and everything.'

'You can if you want.'

Harry decided against it and they wandered off along Brisbane Street in a westerly direction, crossed Ellenborough Street and decided to count the hotels.

'When we get to six we'll turn back.'

They began with the hotel on the opposite corner, 'The North Star' and arrived at six just over a quarter of a mile later where a bridge on their right ran over the railway line and the main street wheeled at a ninety-degree angle left, so they turned round for home, and were in bed by eleven in the tiny room with two iron beds and a small table with a lantern.

The following morning Harry rolled over and looked at the streaming sunlight across the unfamiliar room. He waited for MacDonald's voice to shout for them to rise, and when that did not happen he lifted himself up on his elbows and then recalled what had. He fell back on the pillow with an excited exclamation which brought Luke from his dreams.

The hotel did not serve breakfast so they wandered out and found a bakery along the railway line. They caught the 7.35 train to Gatton and Toowoomba and just over an hour later they stood on the Gatton platform.

'It'll take us well over an hour to walk to Cedar Grove unless we can hitch a ride.' Harry looked along the platform to the ticket office in the little blue and white building. 'But firstly better find out the train times back.'

They learned there was an 11.55 express to Brisbane. 'One stop at Ipswich only,' the ticket-seller informed them.

'Can we buy the tickets now?' Luke asked.

'Yes. Two to Brisbane, four shillings, please.'

Harry's face dropped. 'But we've only got three shillings.'

The ticket-seller was not Gatton's most charitable daughter. 'The fares on the express are two shillings apiece. It costs four shillings for two seats, not three shillings.' Her mouth set in a hard line.

'But we should only pay half fares,' Harry protested. 'We're still at school.'

'Prove it,' she said, eyeing the top of the Players Navy cut tobacco packet that sat up out of Luke's top pocket.

Harry gave up in exasperation and they left the platform.

'Hell, now no one will believe our true ages.'

'We'll have to borrow from Mum,' Harry said disconsolately as they headed out into the dirt road behind the station house.

Luke was thinking about the army. 'We've got to catch the express, have to be out at Camp Hill by five o'clock.'

Harry nodded. 'Can't be late.'

They had been striding along the dirt road leading out to Cedar Grove for almost an hour when a dray came by and a sun-burnt individual looked down at them from the driver's seat.

'Harry? Your mother told us you weren't coming home this weekend.'

Harry and Luke looked up into Jacob's face. 'Ah, Jacob, grand to see you. Yes, well, we've . . . something special to tell Mum.'

'Climb aboard,' he said.

They rolled along in the pleasant morning with the crisp Queensland sunshine crystallising on the leaves above their heads and raining dappled links of light down upon them and enhancing the coupled colours of pink and grey in the palette on the trunks of the iron bark gum trees. The dazzling day bestowed a clarity to the rich brown soil on the winding dirt track ahead as Harry looked from right to left, breathing in Queensland, yet focused and aware of the great adventures he would have before he saw these brilliant bush pictures again. He smiled with the joy of youth, daydreaming about how he and Luke and his new friend, Dave Sands, were off into another world beyond this placid Lockyer Valley and all it meant.

Caro and Katy were cleaning the front lounge room when Caro looked through the front door and saw the dray rumbling down the avenue of cedars towards the house. 'Jacob's back,' she called to Mary and Jane, who were washing clothes out in the yard.

'It's not just Jacob, Mummy,' Katy informed her, 'it's Harry and Luke too.'

Caro, delighted, ran laughing out through the door along the verandah and down the steps to meet them. 'Harry! Harry darling, you came home after all.'

The two boys jumped to the ground. Harry called, 'Thanks,

Jacob,' and as his mother took him in her arms, his head turned to Luke. 'Best you go into the kitchen, old son, get a drink or something. I'll come through in a minute.' He brought his eyes round to his mother and moving out of her embrace, gave his sister a quick hug. 'You go with Luke, Katy, give him a drink. Oh, and get a florin for me, will you, please? I'll have to borrow it.'

Katy looked to her mother, who nodded approval, and Luke and Katy moved off together as Harry beckoned his mother to follow him. 'I've got something to tell you, Mum.'

Caro followed him expectantly into the lounge room. She had the oddest feeling as he crossed into the dining room, but she came after him and stood in the doorway, a questioning look on her face. 'What is it, Harry? What's happened?'

He turned round near the dining-room table, looking at her with the strangest, self-assured expression. The strong breeze lifted the curtain behind him to flap high in the air and delineate him in a world of blue, his excited azure eyes peering at her and his shock of fair hair hovering on his forehead. Caro would remember this careless picture of him all her life. He put his hand into his pocket and threw his shilling coin on to the table. It gleamed as it rolled across the polished surface towards her and spun slowly, forebodingly, to a halt.

'What on earth . . . ?'

'Him,' Harry said, 'the King.' He pointed to the coin.

Nonplussed, Caro stood there.

'I'm going to fight for King George.'

Caro shivered and in an automatic movement wrapped her arms across her body. 'What do you mean, Harry?'

'I've volunteered, Mum. Enlisted. Along with Luke. We're going to the war.'

Caro could not speak. She knew what he had said; she was cognisant of the meaning of the words but she felt as if he were speaking a foreign language. She could only manage to shake her head. Her eyes grew large and her mouth opened wide as if she were suffocating. She felt paralysed.

'I had to come home to see you face to face, Mum. I couldn't just go off without telling you.'

Caro remained silent, shaking her head, her mind numb. Suddenly she grabbed the back of the nearest chair.

Harry could see his mother was very disturbed and he moved towards her, speaking in a cajoling tone. 'Please don't take it hard, Mother. It's really important to me. I've got to go. Luke and I joined up yesterday. We have to be back in the barracks tonight.'

Caro's world was swimming around her; she was drowing in disbelief. Harry, her darling boy, the child she adored, the reason for life itself to continue, stood there smiling and telling her a madness she could not face. When she forced speech from the arid place in her chest the words croaked from her throat. 'You're going to the war?'

'Yes, Mother. I've just told you. Now, please don't carry on. I've got to go. I'm a soldier now.'

'A soldier?' The words exploded from her. 'For God's sake, you're a child! You've only just turned seventeen. What are you thinking of? What madness has been put into your head behind my back?'

Harry was affronted. His mother was overreacting badly. He was surprised. He had expected tears, but quiet tears. He drew himself up to his full height. 'Don't talk like that. Please understand I don't ever want to hurt you . . . but it's my decision. And I want to go.' His eyes met hers: John Conrad Fleet's blue eyes.

Caro shook her head, refusing the fact. Her hands flailed the air in distraction. 'A soldier, just like your father . . . oh God in heaven, how can this be happening?'

Harry was now very disturbed. His mother was rambling. His father was a painter. What on earth was she thinking?

'Mother, please?'

Caro threw herself round the end of the table and clutched her son. 'No! I won't let you go. You can't be a soldier too.'

'Stop, Mum! Stop!'

But Caro was beyond stopping and she began to sob, still clinging wildly to Harry. 'No! No! You're a boy, just a boy.'

Katy had heard her mother's raised voice and now knew she was crying. Luke, embarrassed, moved out of the kitchen on to the verandah and Katy ran through to Caro. 'Mummy, what's wrong? What's happening?'

'He can't do this. Not him too.'

'Do what?' her daughter asked. 'Harry? What have you done?'

'I've joined up, Katy, that's all I've done. I'm a soldier.' He looked back to his mother. 'Please understand, Mother, I *want* to do this.'

Caro's cries and sobs filled the house and within half a minute more, Jane and Mary had entered the room.

Harry pushed his mother tenderly away but Caro would not let go. She continued to cling to him crying, 'No! No!'

Katy attempted an explanation. 'Harry's volunteered to fight in the war.'

Jane strode determinedly to Caro. She could see the deranged look in her friend's eyes and the astonishment in her son's. Taking hold of Caro firmly she eased her into a chair. 'Go into the kitchen, Harry. Please leave us alone.'

Harry did as he was asked and Jane cradled Caro's head in her arms while Mary embraced Katy, who had now begun to cry too.

'Caro, darling, please, calm down. Please, darling. Come on, we'll talk about it.'

'He's only seventeen.' Caro's tears dampened Jane's dress. 'He's still a boy.' Jane sat down beside her and stroked her hair and spoke gently to her until gradually Caro calmed and the aberrant look in her eyes died.

Seeing her mother collecting herself helped to quieten Katy, and Mary took her gently from the room. Jane turned Caro's face to hers. 'Now, darling, let's talk sensibly about this. You say Harry's joined up?'

Caro nodded.

'It seems odd they would take him at seventeen.'

'Must have said he was eighteen.'

'I suppose so. And Matt and Knobby gone to Sydney, oh dear. But don't worry, darling, there might be something we can do after all.'

Caro nodded. She could think of nothing. It eased her to have someone else doing the thinking.

At that moment Harry returned with Luke behind him. 'Mum, I'm so sorry about all this but we must be going . . . have to catch the train back to camp.'

Caro said nothing and Jane asked innocently. 'And where's camp?'

Luke opened his mouth to answer, 'It's—' but Harry struck him hard in the side. 'Sorry, Aunt Jane, we can't say.'

With that Harry came over and kissed his mother on the top of her head. 'Goodbye, Mum, I'll write a lot.' He bent and kissed Jane's cheek. 'Aunt Jane, please make Mum understand that this is my choice.'

Caro raised her eyes to his and they filled with tears once more. She watched unspeaking as her son walked out on to the verandah, where he hugged his sister and Mary and Isobel, then went down into the yard to Jacob waiting by the dray.

As Jacob urged his horse and vehicle forward to take Harry and Luke away Caro crossed the verandah and stood trembling against the railing. 'My only son,' she said as the tears rolled down her cheeks.

Katy came to her and hugged her. 'I'm still here, Mummy.' And Caro turned unseeing eyes to her daughter. 'I know, sweetheart, I know.'

Fifteen minutes later Jane came to Caro, who sat head in hands on the rocking chair on the front verandah, looking down the avenue of cedars where Harry had disappeared from her view. Life had dealt her another body blow for which she had been entirely unprepared.

Jane put a cup of tea down on the stand beside her. 'Here, love, drink this.' She smiled encouragingly. 'Surely if we could go to Brisbane, to Harry's commanding officer, we could stop it. He's only seventeen, after all. We could probably have his whole enlistment made null and void.'

Caro shrugged. 'I've been thinking about that but he wouldn't tell us which camp he was in and there are at least five in Brisbane now.' She brought her red eyes up to her friend. 'I know an officer well. He might help. He's at Redbank.' She wrung her hands and looked distractedly about. 'But if I do anything Harry might never forgive me.'

Jane took up her friend's hands. 'If only Matthew were here.'

'What could Matt do?'

'He knows a mighty lot of people, and many in high places. When does he come home?'

'Not for at least a week.'

'I have the name of the hotel they're staying at in Sydney. We could send a telegram.' Jane gave Caro a smile and squeezed her hands. 'That's what we'll do. The post office in town is closed now but I reckon I could get Mrs Stanley, the postmaster's wife, to open up. She's a good stick. We send a telegram this afternoon and it'll be delivered first thing on Monday in Sydney and if Knobby and Matt come back straight away they could be here by Tuesday some time.'

'But . . . what if they've gone out to that Hawkesbury place with the Ashton man?'

'No, no, that was to be later in the week, darling, I'm sure. Tomorrow we'll go and see this officer whom you know. I understand you think Harry might be angry and no doubt at first he will be. But he should never have joined up. It's wrong. Now you drink this tea and Katy and I'll drive into town and send the telegram.'

Caro picked up the cup and took a sip as Jane went on encouragingly: 'And don't worry, the army does nothing in a hurry and Matt and Knobby'll be home before you know it. Now between them and your officer, we'll get Harry back.' She leant over and stroked Caro's hair affectionately. 'Who's the officer you know, by the way?'

Caro looked up and met her eyes. She took a deep breath and then looked away. 'I'd prefer not to say. But yes, I'll go and see him tomorrow.'

Chapter Thirty-one

The iron engine spat steam across the platform in great gushes.

'All right, you lot, into this carriage! At the double. Say goodbye to Brisbane.' The corporal waved his hand through the open carriage door and the group of volunteers, including Harry, Dave and Luke, flowed forward past him and up into the train. 'Find a seat . . . stay out of the first compartment, that's for officers!'

They scrambled along the corridor, by and around dozens of uniformed men. 'In here,' pointed Luke, 'this one's empty.'

They entered and took their seats, removing their packs and generally settling in. Within a few more minutes all the seats were taken.

'When do we get our rifles?' asked Frank Birtenshaw, a new arrival with carrot-coloured hair and a bright smile.

'In Sydney, I suppose,' responded Dave.

'We'll feel like soldiers then, boys.'

'Are you a half-caste?' asked Frank.

Dave nodded. 'Reckon I am.'

'What're you doin' in the army?'

Dave leaned back and brought his black eyes up to his inquisitor's. He lifted his index finger and wagged it. 'Have you got an uncle who's a full colonel in the British army?'

'Hell, no,' replied Frank.

'Well, I have, so get out with your questions.'

Frank's wide mouth opened in disbelief. 'Aw, come on, mate, I don't believe that one.'

Luke made a sound of disbelief between his teeth. 'Ah . . . tell us another one.'

Dave shrugged his broad shoulders and looked from Frank to Luke. 'It doesn't matter in the least whether you blokes believe me or not. The fact remains and that's that.'

Luke gave a loud guffaw of amusement and one of the other soldiers said, 'Sounds like the Abo's dreamin' to me.'

Dave just sat there grinning and now began to whistle. Luke opened his mouth to say more when Harry broke in, 'Look, you lot. Leave him alone. He's in the army for his own reasons, as we all are. And if he says he's got an uncle who's a colonel who are you lot to say he hasn't? Leave it. All right?' He looked hard at Luke, who closed his mouth as Frank spoke up: 'Doesn't matter to me if his uncle's the bloody Duke of Wellington.'

'Good,' stated Harry. 'Then we'll all get along perfectly well.' He glanced across at Dave who winked and gave him a wide smile while Luke raised his eyes to heaven and in disgust settled back into his seat.

A few minutes later the train lurched forward and the soldiers in Harry's compartment began to sing 'Daisy Bell'. Their voices rose and swelled along the train, others taking up the song or beginning anew on another. The singing rebounded around the carriage, and the general uproar and laughter reverberating from compartment to compartment was that of a holiday camp. 'Daisy Bell' was followed by 'I'm Going to Leave the Old Home' and 'Goodbye Girlee'. Finally there was a sort of quiet.

As the train gathered speed Luke turned to Harry. 'There's only one thing I'll miss.'

'What's that old son?'

'Bloody old MacDonald's face when he finds out what we've done!'

Caro stood under the single leafless tree at the entrance to Redbank Army Camp for twenty minutes until the sentry came back. 'Captain Fleet's not here until tomorrow, ma'am.'

'But he has to be. I must speak with him, it's urgent.'

'That's all they said. Not here until Monday morning at O seven hundred.'

Tears of frustration sprang to Caro's eyes but she held them back. 'Do you know where he is?'

'They don't tell sentries that sort of thing, ma'am. Why don't you come back in the morning?'

Caro did exactly that and at eight o'clock on Monday morning she stood under the same leafless tree and asked the same question of another sentry.

He left her as the other one had and entered the cement blockhouse office behind him. He returned with a smile. 'Seems he's here, missus. Came in early this morning. But you'll have to wait until he can be found.'

'I'll wait.'

It was over an hour later before Caro was taken into an office building some two hundred yards from the front gate. She had been asked twice her name and business. She had offered them her name but said the business was private: that it was crucial, a life-and-death situation for her and that she must see Captain Bartholomew Fleet.

She sat waiting in a small annex to the office building where outside the window, through some straggling purple bougainvillaea she watched soldiers drilling and men on horses riding back and forth and drayloads of materials passing by. Occasionally a bugle sounded in the general goings-on and all seemed hustle and bustle.

When she heard the door in the far wall open she spun round to see Bartholomew enter.

'Thank God.'

'Caro, I couldn't believe it when they said you were here. Come this way, we can be private.' He frowned. 'Though I haven't got long.'

He took her through to a small office with a desk and a Remington typewriter and a telephone, and faced round to her expectantly.

'I had no one to go to but you.'

He brushed away a fly. 'About what?'

'My son, Harry, he enlisted on Friday. God, Bart, he's still at school. I can't let him do this . . . it's wrong. Please can you help me?'

Bart sighed. It was always the same with Caro: could he help her? Would he help her? With Caro there was always crisis. 'What do you expect me to do?'

Caro's eyes grew wide. 'Well, you're a captain; you can find out what unit he's with. He only enlisted on Friday, for heaven's sake, in Brisbane. You can have him discharged.'

Bart held up his hand. 'Hold on, Caro. The boy has a right to join up. If all the mothers in this country went around doing what you're attempting we'd have no army and the Kaiser would have his way.'

'You don't understand. He's under age, he's only seventeen.' She took Bart's arm in her frantic fingers. 'He came and told me yesterday. Oh, Bart, I'm at my wits' end.'

Bart extricated himself gently. 'I see. I'm afraid it does happen, Caro. Recruiting sergeants don't ask for birth certificates, you know. We probably have more boys of seventeen than we realise.'

'Not my son, you don't. Please, Bart.'

She thought she saw uncertainty in Bart's eyes; but he was not wavering in indecision, he was actually deciding if there were anything he could do.

Her eyes were big with concern, almost wild like he had seen them at times before.

'Look, Caro, you've got to stay calm. I'm an officer in the Australian Imperial Forces. I really cannot go interfering in another regiment's affairs. I'm afraid you have to accept this as your son's choice.'

A tear broke over her eyelid. 'No, I can't. You must help me. You must.'

'Caro, it's not simple, if the boy's joined up as you say he has, I really don't think I can do much about it, even though he's only seventeen.'

'Bart, please, please, listen to me. He cannot go to the war. His father would not want him to, I know it.'

'Well, naturally . . . no father would, I suppose.'

'I mean his *real* father, for God's sake.'

Bart shook his head in confusion.

Caro's face was pale, taut and strained, her fingers flew to his arm again and grasped him ferociously. 'I'm talking about Harry's real father, for heaven's sake, John Conrad. Your brother! Harry's father.' She shook her head and released him to cover her face in her hands, weeping into her palms. 'Oh Jesus, forgive me, but it's time you at least knew the truth. You're his flesh and blood too.' She lifted her face to him as the tears rolled from her eyes and ran down her cheeks. 'I've lived this farce longer than I can stand.'

Bart did not speak. All he could do was shake his head with the impact of her words.

'I was going to tell you before, last year when I came to see you at Fleet Brewery . . . but I couldn't, but now . . . Oh heaven, Bart, Harry's all I've got of John Conrad. He's my life. He can't be ripped from me like this . . . please, please' she sobbed, and her body shook. 'Please, Bart, help me.'

He took her arm and led her to a chair.

She fell into it, still crying. 'I don't know if I can go on.'

Bart exhaled noisily. 'Caro, I had no idea. This is . . . I don't know what to say . . . Let me think.' He took his handkerchief from his pocket and handed it to her, touching her tenderly on the shoulder in the process. 'Here, use this. Stop crying. Please.' He moved over to the desk and sat on it. 'I need to sit almost as much as you do.' He was quiet while her pain filtered around the room and across his consciousness, filling years of ignorance with the shock of incredible truth.

Caro lifted her face again, and the words tumbled out in extemporaneous explanation. 'I was alone. John Conrad had gone away back to the army. As far as I knew he was off to England, not to return for years. I found that I was having Harry. I was distraught. I loved your brother desperately, but what could I do? I was only nineteen. You don't know what goes through a girl's mind in a situation like that. The only man I knew who would accept such a fiction of a marriage was Matthew. He did it for his own disturbed reasons, I did it for mine. John Conrad came home suddenly and the wedding had already taken place.' Her voice caught in her throat. 'I would *never* have married Matthew Craken if I'd known your brother were coming back.' She looked away at some imaginary horizon and brought her fine fingers up to touch the mark upon her mouth. 'God damn John Conrad for not coming back sooner.'

Her words hung around the room, filling his mind, tingling in the air around his head.

'Ah, Caro, it's a bloody sad revelation . . . and I'm deeply sorry, though it makes no difference I fear.'

She shook her weary head. 'None at all?'

He was silent for a time and she sat there watching him spiritlessly, her shoulders dropped, her hands clasped round her knees.

'Tell me, you say Harry enlisted on Friday. Do you know where – which recruiting office?'

'No, but I'd guess in Albert Square, as he went from school.'

'Do you know what camp he's in?'

'No, he wouldn't tell us.'

'Caro,' he stood and came round close to her, 'the best thing you can do is leave this with me. I'll make some enquiries today. See if there is anything whatever I can do. Where are you going now?'

'I'll go home to our house at New Farm.'

'Do you have a telephone?'

'Yes, Brisbane one seven seven three.'

'Are you alone there?'

'No, my friend Jane, Knobby Clark's wife, is with me.'

'Good. Look, I'm tied up all morning here, and probably part of the afternoon but I'll travel into Brisbane and see what I can find out later. I'll telephone you.'

Caro nodded.

'By the way where's Matthew Craken?'

'In Sydney, though he's been sent a telegram. He could be home tomorrow . . . or Wednesday.' She paused for a moment. 'He will not like what's happened. If he cares for anyone, it's Harry.'

Bart stood thinking, rubbing his chin in contemplation. 'Caro, what if your son doesn't wish your interference?'

Her eyes took on the wild look again. 'It doesn't matter. I'm his mother, I must take the risk.'

'All right.' He held out his hand to her and she took it.

'Thank you, thank you.'

'The weight of the responsibility you've handed me is enormous, Caro.'

Caro met his eyes. 'God, Bart, what else could I do?'

'John Conrad's my brother, and more than that he's my friend.'

Caro closed her eyes and shook her head. 'Keep my secret, Batholomew . . . don't let me down. I've told you for one reason only to help me get Harry back.'

'I'll see what I can do.'

When Caro departed, Bart stood in the small office thinking.

His mouth was set and he shook his head sadly with the memory of the volatile meetings between John Conrad and Matthew Craken. All these years Craken had known the truth. He remembered how Craken called his brother 'the enemy' in front of the little boy, Harry, and how the meetings with Craken were always full of vitriol and bordering on violence. The night in the Johnsonian Club had such significance now. He saw Caro's wild eyes again, and her hands on the boy's shoulders, looking with desperate entreaty into John Conrad's eyes. It was all patently clear to him now.

He sighed. No wonder Craken was so fiercely territorial about Caro and the boy; now it was obvious. And John Conrad had been oblivious all these years . . . it was a lot for a man to take in.

By five o'clock that day he had been into Brisbane and attempted to see the officer in charge of all Queensland regiments. He was told that the colonel was in staff meetings and unavailable, but he kept perservering and finally was granted an interview with Major Seaforth, one of the officers in charge of troop distribution.

When Bart explained that in last Friday's recruitment, there was a volunteer from Brisbane, or even two he suspected, who were both only seventeen he received a cool reception. 'Yes, I suppose there are the occasional volunteers under age, Captain, but we don't ask for proof of age, you know. They'll have to take their chances with the rest.'

'One of the boys' mothers is . . . an old friend. She's distraught that her son's joined up.'

'Mmm, mothers tend to be, no matter what age their sons are.'

'Would it be possible to find the boy, have him discharged?'

The major looked up from under his eyelids. 'Are you serious, Captain Fleet?'

'I suppose so.'

The officer did actually muse on the situation for some seconds. 'I'm sorry but finding him's going to be difficult. I can tell you all volunteers from Friday's Brisbane recruiting offices were sent out to Camp Hill and from there on Sunday morning they were transferred to Sydney on a troop train.' He stood and moved over to a filing cabinet. After leafing through some files he took out a piece of paper and read it. When he returned it to the file he informed his visitor. 'They're on their way to France. It's a federal order. We've already been training divisions in Egypt constituting two army corps, the 1st and 2nd Anzac, which are presently being shipped to France to supply more troops for the Somme; they badly need them. The current recruits will be trained onboard ship between here and France and when they reach Marseilles, my information is, they'll be three months in training before joining one of the divisions from either the 1st or 2nd Anzac and be sent to the front.'

Bart reacted. 'Only three months? Sir, I've got lads at Redbank who've been in camp close on six months already. How is it raw boys have been sent off like this?'

'Fleet, it was an order from Canberra. Immediate mobilisation. This is the army, man, you know that. Fact is, your lot will be going off now too. In today's orders Redbank was mentioned.' He took up a pile of papers and leant forward confidentially. 'As far as the boys you mention are concerned, I've no way of finding a single man. I don't know where they'll be billeted in Sydney. It'd probably take me a week to find out where the battalion is or what ship they're embarking on. And frankly, I've more to do than that.' He moved to the door. 'While I'm not unsympathetic, Captain Fleet, you'll just have to tell his mother the army's the army, not a school band.'

'Yes, sir, well, I'll be a little more diplomatic than that.'

The major nodded. 'You know your way out.'

When Caro picked up the ringing telephone her heart was thumping, and as Bart explained the outcome of his mission it sent a pain right through her mind. Her voice was flat, lifeless. 'So you could do nothing.'

'Caro, I tried, but *no one* can do anything. The Prime Minister would have trouble. They don't know where your son is, except that he's been sent to Sydney and will be embarking for Marseilles in France forthwith.'

'Oh God, he's just a baby.'

'Yes, I realise. Caro, you won't do anything silly, will you?'

'What do you mean?'

'I'm worried about you. I can't come to see you because I must return to camp.'

'I understand. Thanks, Bart. You did what you could.'

'Caro, I know you can't accept what's happened. I wish I could do more.'

'You did what you could.'

There was a brief silence. Bart knew Caro was crying.

'Caro, I'm truly sorry. Let's just pray this whole mess of a war's over soon.'

He could hear her hurried breathing.

'Bart?'

'Yes?'

'You said they were being sent to France . . . did you say Marseilles?'

'That's what the major I saw told me. It seems the boys from Brisbane will be heading there.'

'Thank you, Bart.'

'Caro, I'll stay in touch with you somehow. I'll always let Miss Burton at the brewery know where I am. You can even write to me care of her if you wish. Do you understand?'

'Yes, thank you.' Her voice was breaking with emotion. 'Keep my secret.'

Caro's hand shook as she replaced the receiver on its stand. She turned around to see Jane waiting in the lamplight by the door. Her voice too was strained. 'What's happened?'

'My friend tried but he can do nothing. Seems Harry's on his way to Sydney and then to France.'

'Oh God.'

'Yes. He's gone, out of our range, out of our care.'

'Look, love, Matt might still be able to do something.'

Caro nodded, lifting her hand to wipe a tear from her face. 'He might, but he isn't here yet and Harry's speeding ever away from us.'

Jane came forward and took her friend in her arms, speaking gently in her ear. 'Now listen to me, darling, you're over-wrought and stressed to the point of breaking. I'll make you a nice dinner and we'll go to bed and I'll read some Shelley to you. You'll like that. We'll try to be as peaceful as we can.'

Caro lifted her head back to look at her friend. 'You're wonderful to me, Jane, but I've been thinking. You'll take care of my Katy, won't you?'

'What do you mean, love?'

'Just promise you will.'

Jane nodded. 'You know I will always, but—'

'Good. For there's only one course left to me.'

Jane's hands brushed Caro's hair back lovingly. 'And what's that, darling?'

'I must follow him. I must go to the war.'

Jane tried, almost successfully, to keep her voice level and calm. 'Well, sweetheart, we can talk about that when Matt comes home.'

'I don't know if I can wait that long.' And now a peculiar light flickered in the depths of Caro's mind making its way to the surface in the glint that formed in her eyes. 'I have skills, I can drive vehicles, I can nurse people. I'll be helpful in the war zone. They need people like me. Yes, this way I can be near Harry . . . I can be near Harry and near—' She broke off and gave a bitter smile. 'You see, love, I feel better now that I have a plan.'

Caro turned and left the room, and Jane, with concern all over her face, watched the slender stiff back of her friend as she followed her along the corridor to the kitchen.

As the train rattled in the darkness towards Sydney, Harry made his way along the swinging carriage to Dave, who stood in the corridor smoking. An hour before they had stopped at a small station and had been supplied with a meal of lamb stew and bread. Now many of the boys were sleeping.

Dave drew on his cigarette in the gas light of the narrow corridor and the smooth skin on his cheeks gleamed as he smiled at his new friend.

'Dave?'

'Yes?'

'I don't know how to say this exactly . . . but . . .'

'What?'

'It's about what you said.'

'What?'

'About having an uncle who's a colonel in the British army.'

'Yes, what about it?'

'I think it would have been better if . . . well . . . perhaps if you'd said something else. The boys don't go for that sort of thing.'

Dave drew on his cigarette and blew smoke at the window. It snaked up the glass in little cloudy puffs. 'Now don't say you don't believe me either? You stood up for me and all.'

'Yes, I know I did. I wasn't going to let you down in front of them.'

Dave half closed his eyes, appraising Harry. 'That was real good of you, Harry, but let me tell you something. I was telling the truth. All right, he's not my *blood* uncle, but he's part of my family through and through. Mum thinks the world of him. He was her own brother's dearest friend. I've known him since I was born. He cares about us, paid for our schooling and a whole lot more, and we all *call* him uncle. So to me he's my uncle, right?'

'Oh, it's like that, is it? Righto, I see. Sorry I doubted you, old son.'

Dave took another puff on his cigarette. 'Want a smoke?'

'Yeah, all right, guess I do.'

Dave perched his stub between his lips and took out his tobacco and a paper, rolled a cigarette, handed it to Harry and lit it for him.

They stood side by side in the corridor, blowing smoke at the window; both cross-legged, both entirely comfortable, both silently communing, just as Harry's real father and Dave's uncle used to do.

On Thursday afternoon Matthew and Knobby stepped down on to the station platform in Brisbane. The train had taken twenty-five hours from Sydney, and as they emerged into the street a downpour greeted them.

The telegram which they had received at their Sydney hotel on returning late Monday night after an uproarious dinner with Julian Ashton, had simply informed them: 'Come home. Harry has joined up. Caro distraught. Jane.'

They had immediately decided to return home, but the following morning they had learned that they must wait until Wednesday to catch a northbound train to Brisbane; they only ran three times a week.

There was no other way: the train was the speediest form of transport. All the journey they had conjectured about the telegram. And now, standing in the street outside the station under the wide awning, Matt rubbed his right thigh as Knobby looked for a hansom to take them to New Farm. Matthew's bad leg had been aching on and off throughout the journey and it had worsened in the last hour.

As he watched the tall frame of Knobby in the distance moving through the throng and waving his arms he heard his name called and revolved on his cane to see Jane hurrying towards him.

'Oh, you're here at last,' she said as she came up to him and hugged him, her soft features strained. 'I've been waiting for you. I came here on Tuesday just in case you'd—'

'What the devil's happened, Jane?' Matthew broke in on her. 'And be succinct, please.'

Jane took a deep breath. 'Harry joined up last Friday. Caro couldn't take it. She went to some officer she knows and tried to have Harry discharged but there was no hope. The unit he was in had already gone straight south. I think to Sydney, to be sent overseas.'

'Ah hell.' Matt's tone was grave. 'The poor damn silly kid. How's Caro now?'

Jane hesitated.

'Well?'

'She's not here, Matt.'

'What the devil's that mean?'

'She left yesterday. I tried to stop her. Did what I could. When you didn't arrive on Tuesday she just took it upon herself to follow Harry. Said she could wait no longer. She's got a passage on a ship leaving Sydney Saturday for London.'

The sensations in Matt's leg were discharging pain along his nerves into his back and right up into his neck. He lifted his right leg from the ground. 'Bloody hell, has the woman gone completely mad?'

Jane grasped Matthew's arm and looked up into his face. 'She wasn't in any state to be halted. Said she had to follow him, no matter what. At times she rambled. But she's determined on a plan to join one of the nursing units or ambulance transport units or VADs or something when she gets to London. She said she just had to go even if she never saw Harry again. She had to be in France near him.'

A faraway look came into Matt's eyes. He rested the heel

of his bad leg down on the glistening footpath. 'Did she leave a message for me?'

Jane sighed. 'No. I'm sorry.'

Abruptly Knobby's big frame appeared beside them. 'Jane!' he exclaimed, taking her in his arms and kissing her. Then he looked at Matt and, seeing the expression on his face, said, 'What the hell's happened now?'

'The boy volunteered and Caro's followed him.'

'Never!' exclaimed Knobby. 'It can't be.'

Matt's jaw was clenched. 'It is.'

Later, at New Farm, when they had accustomed themselves to the inevitable state of matters in their lives, Knobby came to Matt sitting in his studio, looking out across the river and the falling rain, his bad leg up on a stool.

Knobby gave a tired smile. 'How's your leg?'

'Bloody awful, old son. Giving me hell.'

'I've brought you some aspirin.' He handed it to his friend. 'Take it now, please.'

Matt groaned an objection but Knobby insisted. 'Come on, Matt.'

'Aspirin's useless. It's now I should be on the bloody opium.'

Knobby sat down beside him. 'But you aren't and won't ever be. Right?'

Matt swallowed the aspirin and raised his eyes. 'I'll go out to Cedar Grove tomorrow, old son. Must see Katy. Fear the child will be in a state, what with her brother in the army and her mother gone.'

Knobby nodded. 'You're right. Though no doubt Mary and Jacob will be taking good care of her. We'll go on the morning train.'

Matt lifted himself up and limped to the window. He stood looking out on the waning evening and then lifted his elegant long fingers and ran them down across the pane. 'Weird existence, this life on the third planet from the sun. There we were in Sydney on Monday night, carefree, arguing with old Ashton about free form, laughing with that fat barmaid with the red hair, oblivious of what awaited us; and here we are a brief time later . . . in bloody disarray. My son's gone . . . my wife's gone . . .' He gave a sharp rueful laugh.

'Though the latter has forever been a possibility these many years.' He forced another laugh. 'It's as if humans must never reach any level of true peace.' He leaned his forehead on the cool glass of the window and rotated his head to where his eyes met Knobby's. 'Bloody disconcerting, actually.'

Slowly returning across the room he picked up a letter that lay on the top of a small pile of correspondence. 'See this. The latest from the Federal Government informing me that in Great Britain they're now bringing in a scheme for war artists, and it's going under consideration here. Three days ago I would have said that if they ever asked me I'd be rejecting any appeal until ceasefire . . . but . . . life has its way of altering the most vehement belief. So . . . I reckon I'll reply to this and say I think it's a brilliant idea and that I'd like to be first in line when they make a decision. And that if there's any possible way I can volunteer for the scheme already underway in Great Britain then I'm their man. So, I'll be off to France to depict scenes of carnage at the behest of any government that'll have me.' He gestured in a mock salute and winked. 'Can't have my son and my wife over there without me.'

Knobby stood silently shaking his head. 'You love her that much, do you, Matt?'

Matthew did not answer. The patter of the rain sounded loudly outside as they stood quietly in the studio with the afternoon dying in shades of grey beyond the window. Finally Matt said, 'Ah, fact is, Knob, I've . . . er . . . grown accustomed to that impossible bloody woman . . . and also to her son.'

Knobby gave a grim smile. 'Your son too.'

A roll of thunder sounded in the distance as Matt momentarily closed his eyes. 'Yes, well, old dear, I don't believe it'll come as a great surprise to you today if I finally admit to you that Harry's not mine. That he's the damned enemy's.' He limped over to a chair, sat down and lifted his bad leg across his good one, rubbing it determinedly. 'Peculiar thing is that, to me, Harry's mine – all mine. The accidental seed which began his existence is nothing to do with Harry, *my son, Harry*. And now he's gone off to the war. Can't think of a worse ending to seventeen fairly palatable years.'

Knobby rested his hand tenderly on his friend's shoulder.

'Yes, reckon I've always known. You up and marryin' Caro out of nowhere. Poor old Caro, eh?'

Matt looked up quickly. 'Now don't start that. She knew what she was bloody well doing.'

Knobby imitated a smile. 'Anyway, what the hell, he's *our* Harry and *your* son. Never be anything else.' Knobby folded his arms in a resigned way. 'So, I'd best tell Jane we're leaving as soon as we're able for the blasted war.'

Matt shook his head and, placing his feet back on the floor, stood, and faced his confidant, taking hold of his shoulders and squarely meeting his eyes. 'Knob, old son, you've been my nursemaid for nigh on a quarter of a century. Don't know what I'd have done most of the years but for you . . . but this time, no, you must take care of your wife and little Isobel and my Katy. They'll need you badly . . . more than I will, for once. You must stay here, and while I'll miss you like bloody hell, will be at a loss without you, this time I must do whatever it is on my own.' Then he sniffed. 'Hell, old son, it'll probably take months to organise. I haven't gone yet.'

The two men stood looking at each other. Knobby's eyes filled with tears, and he quickly stepped in and took Matthew in his arms. They held each other close.

'God damn it, Matt. Just you bloody well come back to me, that's all.'

Matthew swallowed hard. He could not speak for a time and his voice broke when he answered. 'That'd be a sensible and fitting end to this débâcle . . . so wait for me, will you, old son?'

Chapter Thirty-two

Sunday, 4 June 1916

John Conrad stood at the edge of the dense thicket of trees, the morning sun spreading careless streaks of gold through the branches above his head. He shouted, 'K, where are you?'

The only answer was the scolding call of two robins in the branches overhead. He strode twenty yards further into the overhanging trees and called again. This time he heard Calpurnia and Caesar barking and received a response. 'Over here.'

He moved in the direction of the voice calling, 'We must start for London very soon. The car's packed and everyone's waiting. What are you doing?' He circled round the bole of a mighty oak and came to a halt.

There on the bank of the tiny stream which flowed through Broome Park, kneeled K, holding in his hands a tiny bird with brown markings. The dogs wandered around sniffing as K looked up, frowning with concern, his cool eyes serious above his commanding moustache. 'Ah, Johnny, I think it's a baby robin. He's fallen from that nest.' He indicated the branch above with a movement of his head. 'Poor thing. I'd say he's broken his wing.'

John Conrad gave a long-suffering smile. It had been ever thus: he remembered stray dogs in Egypt, sick baby starlings and abandoned baboons in South Africa; motherless baby tigers in India, and now a robin with a broken wing. He came forward to look at the tenderly held object. 'What can we do?'

'I'm sure we can put some sort of splint on it. Look here, Johnny. You can see it's broken.' He pointed to the ruffled feathers on the tiny creature's bent wing. 'Now there might be someone here who'll take it home and care for it. It'll probably

514

be all right in a few weeks. Anyway, someone might like the little fellow for a pet.' He lifted it close to his face and spoke quietly. 'Don't worry, young chap, we'll get you right.'

'Well, whatever we do, K, I suggest we do it quickly or we'll be late for the meeting with the War Council, and there's much to do before you leave for Russia tonight.'

They left only twenty minutes late for London, but the baby robin was taken care of by Mr Greer, the caretaker, who had promised faithfully to keep it safe until it could fly again. This satisfied K.

At 8 p.m. John Conrad accompanied the travellers and Detective McLaughlin of Scotland Yard to King's Cross Station, where they found two more of the party waiting for them: Sir Frederick Donaldson, chief technical advisor to the Ministry of Munitions, and Harold O'Beirne, a slender, mild-mannered man, the Counsellor at the British Embassy in Petrograd.

K was in high spirits. 'Where are the rest of us?'

Sir Frederick's hazel eyes met K's. 'Some of the staff and clerks are already in Thurso, sir, but Brigadier General Ellershaw and Mr Robertson from the Ministry of Munitions should be along shortly. When we arrive in Thurso we'll join the *Oak* in Scrabster Harbour and sail to Scarpa Flow to lunch with Admiral Jellicoe on the *Iron Duke* before we join the *Hampshire* for our voyage to Archangel in the afternoon.'

They all stood on the wide platform under the clock for a few minutes, but as K was beginning to gather attention from passing passengers they moved into the carriage which had been set aside for them. There were still twenty minutes before departure time.

When K sat down John Conrad turned to Harold O'Beirne and smiled. 'So what are your feelings on matters in Russia?'

O'Beirne's brow puckered. 'The Tsar's not an easy man to advise. He doesn't seem to realise that there must be political reform but I'm sure Lord Kitchener will be able to help set his military house in order. The Tsar admires him greatly and will listen to him. Fact is, they say that Kitchener, the soldier-statesman, is known to all ranks in the Russian army. Even those who hang on determinedly to the trenches in the Ukraine know who he is and look up to him. The Russian Ambassador told me so himself.'

John Conrad nodded. 'I'm sure it's true. I wish I were coming along, but as I'm not, look after him for me . . . for all of us.'

Five minutes later they were informed that O'Beirne's assistant had been misdirected to another station so that when the time approached for departure O'Beirne decided to stay behind to wait for the man and catch a later train.

When Ellershaw and Robertson arrived John Conrad shook hands with them, then turned to his leader. 'Farewell. I'll be waiting for your return. I'm sure your advice will be of major help to the Russians.'

K smiled. 'Take care of yourself, Johnny.'

John Conrad made his farewell to Fitz and left the carriage. He stood alone on the platform, eyeing K's carriage. He never liked to be separated from K. He felt suddenly very strange. He loosened his tie and undid his top button.

The guard was walking along slamming doors and John Conrad was expecting the train to move off when the carriage door in front of him opened and K suddenly appeared and jumped down and strode across to him.

'Johnny.' He ran his right hand through his fine head of grey hair as he said, 'I wanted to say goodbye again. Don't know why really.' He blinked, a sombre look on his face. 'Just realised that we're very rarely apart. Look after yourself. You're the best of men.' He turned his head aside. 'The very best there is.' Then he brightened and took hold of the younger man's shoulders. 'You of all men know I don't like to make a fuss, or have any carry-on, but I must tell you, you're the closest friend I ever had. I was always a loner . . . even during my childhood in Southern Ireland I felt apart from others. Lord knows I'm not a sentimental man, Johnny, but, where you're concerned perhaps I must be.' He shook his head proudly. 'You and Fitz, my two marvellous boys. Now you look after yourself while I'm gone . . .'

John Conrad could see K's eyes clouding over, but there was no embarrassment between them. His own voice broke as he answered. 'I'll be waiting at the dockside in Scrabster for you when you return.'

K smiled tenderly and nodded, then dropped his hands to his sides and, just as he took a step away, turned and said, 'You know, I dreamt about Hermione last night.' He shook his head wistfully. 'After all these years. We were all playing croquet, you, me and Hermione.' With that he strode back to the train. He waved once, bending his long figure into the doorway as the whistle blew loudly along the platform and the last carriage doors resoundingly slammed.

The train seemed a long time passing by John Conrad, the wheels clickety clacking as it drew out of the station. He stood feeling very much alone. He knew his eyes were wet and he wiped them, now feeling vaguely foolish. He raised his hand as he watched the dark form of the last carriage of the express disappear out of the station in the distance, taking his mentor up to Edinburgh, and Thurso on his way to Scapa Flow.

That night John Conrad slept fitfully, looking at his bedside clock virtually on the hour. At 5 a.m. he rose and went down to have a cup of tea with the soldier on duty in the hall. He was in his office by six, where he spent the morning writing reports for the Department of Munitions. At two in the afternoon he travelled with General Hankey and two brother officers, Majors England and Campbell from the War Office, east on the Chatham and Eastern Line to Herne Bay. There, in sight of the extensive pier which ran over a thousand yards into the sea, they were met by an army vehicle and transported to the spot four miles to the east past Reculver, where traces of walls of the Roman fortress of Regulbium still stood.

The general had read history at Oxford in his youth and liked to air his knowledge. As they drove on the straight track that led by the two twelfth-century towers and the Roman ruins, he waved his arm at the hill on which they sat, and informed his companions, 'After the Romans, this place used to be the Saxon King Ethelbert's palace, then it became a monastery founded by Egbert. Most Englishmen don't know that, let alone you Australians.' He directed his gaze to John Conrad as he stepped down from the truck. Major England raised his eyebrow and winked at John Conrad.

A few minutes later, on the flat plain below Ramsgate, they drew up by some hastily built army sheds and marched across the green fields to within sight of the sea, and there sat three grey iron monoliths with gun turrets attached to the sides.

'Beautiful, aren't they?' said the general.

Major Campbell did not speak but England coughed and John Conrad replied, 'They look like what they are, sir.'

'And what is that?'

'Destructive machines, sir.'

The senior officer made a noise that sounded like, 'Hrmph' before he added, 'Exactly, yes, as I said, they're beautiful.'

Under the striated clouds which ranged across the sky to bunch in shadows on the horizon they spent two hours in the wind witnessing the manoeuvring and speed of the tanks, which were, in fact, all laboriously slow.

At seven they made their way to the lone white-washed inn which stood not far from the coast and the general invited them all into the bar for a gin.

The two majors accepted but John Conrad preferred to walk out in the evening air. 'If you'll excuse me, sir, I think I'll take a stroll over to the sea.'

The general nodded and as John Conrad left by the oak front door the grandfather clock standing by the staircase chimed the half-hour.

It was a pleasant summer evening, the wind having abated to a mild breeze. He was missing K already and really was pleased just to be alone on the great swathes of land leading to the water. He stood meditating on what was happening just across the Straits of Dover, and for a few minutes he stared at two great blue herons standing motionless on a mound at the edge of the sea. He lifted his gaze to the horizon and momentarily K's face flashed into his mind and he started and looked about as the herons raised their wide wings and lifted off into the sky.

He felt decidedly uneasy and for some reason no longer wanted to be alone. He hastily retraced his steps back across the grass towards the inn as a sharp wind seemed to come up out of nowhere and he felt quite chilled. He found his companions in the small oak-beamed bar.

'You weren't long,' Major England said, moving up to make room for him.

John Conrad gave a sharp nod. 'Yes. It's turned cool out there.'

'Really? It was quite warm earlier,' stated the general.

'Perhaps it's just me.'

They remained in the bar until close to nine, when the proprietor's wife made them omelettes, which they ate in the cosy dining room. As the light faded and the general reminded them they needed to be out in the field for the tank trials at seven in the morning, they retired to their tiny rooms upstairs.

John Conrad lay on his bed and read a report from the French War Office before he finally slept. Again he was restless and awoke with a start in the early hours. He had been in a vivid dream about K. The two of them were sailing out to Africa, to Songhir, the Kenyan property, but the ship was filled with robins with broken wings. K was insisting on taking them all. A gale came up, the seas rose and the two men became separated. John Conrad was searching everywhere for K and awoke in panic.

He lay, eyes wide open, for a time after that looking at the milky moon riding the clouds outside the window and when he went back to sleep he did not wake until the landlady knocked on his door at six in the morning.

At ten o'clock they halted the tank manoeuvres for tea. Two batmen had prepared it and placed it on roughly hewn wooden tables at the edge of the fields. It was during this break that a corporal came running across from the army sheds waving his arms.

'Colonel Fleet?' he called as he came up to them.

'Yes, here.'

'Ah, sir, there's a man come down from London. Says he's a secretary on Lord Kitchener's staff and that he has an urgent message for you.'

John Conrad put down his glass cup and looked across at the general. 'Excuse me, General Hankey,' and he turned and followed the corporal back over the uneven ground to the shed.

Outside on the newly cut path waited Anthony Beatty, one of the secretaries from St James's Palace.

'Anthony, what brings you here?'

The young man smiled. 'Don't know, actually.' He handed John Conrad an official envelope with the significant red stamp of *Military Urgent* upon it. 'This came for you from Number Ten Downing Street at nine this morning so I thought I should come down here with it straight away.'

John Conrad hesitated, then took the proffered envelope. It was from the Prime Minister's personal secretary.

HMS *Hampshire* sank off the coast of the Orkney Islands on Monday, 5 June with very few survivors. Lord Kitchener is unaccounted for.

A special cabinet meeting is called for Wed 7 June at No. 10 Downing Street at 0730. You are requested to attend.

The keen eyes of Anthony Beatty watched him, waiting for a response, but John Conrad could not speak. He crumpled the paper in his hand, turned sharply away, and walked towards the sea.

A breeze plucked at his shirt sleeves and a light rain began to fall but John Conrad was aware of neither. There seemed to be noises and sirens in the air, but he supposed they were all in his head. It was not possible that K was *unaccounted for*. It was not possible that the *Hampshire* had sunk.

Anthony Beatty stood watching him striding away towards the water. It was obvious that something of moment had occurred, Colonel Fleet appeared deeply distressed; he charged away as if he were going to stride over the rise and disappear into the sea. Anthony moved forward after him.

At the top of the mound he halted. Fifty yards away, on the beach of pebbles and mud, at the edge of the lapping water, John Conrad stood in the increasing rain. He faced to the north and did not move.

Anthony waited but the rain intensified until he retreated back to the shelter of the shed, where, as the minutes passed, it turned into a downpour.

Twenty minutes later the rain had finally abated to a drizzle and a corporal wearing a sou'wester arrived from across the field to ask where Colonel Fleet was; that the general was waiting. Anthony said he would inform the colonel.

He mounted the rise once more and saw John Conrad still standing at the water's edge, looking northwards. He moved down towards the rigid figure and as he came close to his stiff back he called quietly, 'Colonel Fleet, the general's waiting. Can I do anything for you, sir?'

John Conrad turned. His boots were covered in mud and water; his uniform was drenched and his hair was soaked. He looked ten years older than the man who had opened the message. He nodded. 'I'll come now.'

As they moved in tandem up over the hillock John Conrad halted. He did not face round to Anthony but said, 'It appears that K is missing. His ship went down off the Orkneys yesterday.'

Behind John Conrad Anthony nodded very slowly, a look of sadness settling on his face. 'I guessed as much, colonel.'

Then John Conrad strode towards the sheds and Anthony came along behind. As they made their way back John Conrad spoke again, throwing the words over his shoulder. 'Do you know when there's a train back to London today? I must meet with the Prime Minister tomorrow.'

'Fact is, colonel, that the direct line from Herne Bay is closed this afternoon, but there's a military truck going into Canterbury; we can get a lift on that. Catch an afternoon train back from there.'

John Conrad did not look at his companion. 'Yes, we'll do that.'

The rain had finally ceased when they reached the shed where General Hankey had been sheltering and was eating a biscuit. 'Good God, man, what happened to you? You look dreadful.'

John Conrad's voice sounded thickly in his own ears. 'General Hankey, I have been requested to attend Number Ten. The *Hampshire*, carrying Lord Kitchener to Russia, sank last night off the Orkneys. There are very few survivors. Lord Kitchener is unaccounted for.'

The senior officer's face blanched. 'No, never. Kitchener . . . I can't believe it.'

John Conrad found it very hard to speak again. He lifted his hand in a type of salute. 'So . . . if . . . you'll excuse me, sir . . .'

'Of course, Fleet, of course.'

General Hankey had lost his appetite and threw away the remains of the biscuit as he watched John Conrad turn on his heel and cross back to Anthony Beatty who waited at the entrance to the shed.

* * *

521

John Conrad and Anthony travelled the eight miles into Canterbury in silence. When they were dropped outside the railway station John Conrad stood by the door while Anthony enquired about the trains.

'Nothing to London until the three o-nine p.m., Colonel.'

John Conrad shook his head. 'Then I'll see you back here in time for the train.'

'Of course.'

John Conrad walked aimlessly along the banks of the Stour. He saw Canterbury's great cathedral in the distance and people were passing back and forth about their business. He found it hard to concentrate. Of course there was a terrible bloody war on and men went missing all the time. *But not K . . . But not K . . . But not K . . .*

He did not know where he went but he found himself in a public garden and when he registered that the sun had come out from behind the clouds he noticed children playing.

He sat on a stone bench and after a time closed his eyes. He remembered K on the station at King's Cross, saw his face and heard him speak, *I don't like to make a fuss, or have any carry-on, but I must tell you, you're the closest friend I ever had . . .*

He opened his eyes. A small girl stood in front of him. She had long copper-coloured plaits hanging on either side of her face. She was about six years old, and eyed him speculatively. She reminded him of someone, though he could not think who.

'Were you asleep?' she asked, her bright round eyes assessing him.

'No.'

She nodded thoughtfully. 'You look tired. Were you thinking?'

'Yes.'

'What do soldiers think about?'

He really did not want this inquisition, and as he uncrossed his legs to stand up a woman appeared behind the child. 'There you are, my dar—' the voice broke off and John Conrad looked up into the face of Emma Louise. 'John Conrad?'

For a moment he just gazed at her, then he stood up. 'What are you doing here?'

522

'I live here, don't you remember I told you? Our house is along the Wingham Road.'

He put his hand up to his glazed eyes. 'Ah, yes . . . of course.'

The child looked up at her mother. 'Who is he, Mummy?'

Emma Louise did not answer but touched her daughter's curls affectionately and faced back to John Conrad. His eyes were on her but he seemed not to be registering anything, as if he looked through her. She could see there was something terribly wrong. 'You look dreadful. Is something the matter?'

He forced himself to focus on her. 'I've had some bad news.'

He did look so distraught that she said to her daughter, 'Darling, pop over there and play with your friends again. Mummy will be along in a minute.'

The child obeyed.

'John Conrad, is there anything I can do? Why are you here in Canterbury?'

'I was on a field expedition north of here. The railway's closed so I came in to catch the train back to London.' Then it came out of him, blurted forth. 'You'll know soon enough. The whole world'll know soon enough. The ship that K . . . Lord Kitchener was sailing on sank last night.'

Emma's mouth formed an O of shock and surprise. 'Oh dear, he wasn't drowned?'

'He's unaccounted for.'

Before Emma Louise realised it she had taken hold of his hand. 'Oh, John Conrad, I'm so very sorry. He meant so much to you.'

'Yes . . . yes . . . he did.'

Emma drew him back to the bench and sat with him. 'Please, I know it's hard . . . I do truly know how you feel. Oh, John Conrad, I'm so sorry.'

He did not reply and they just sat there side by side, her hand holding on to his.

Emma Louise looked sideways at him. It was so strange for her to be sitting here with him. She moved her hand to rest sympathetically upon his arm. She felt almost unnerved by touching him so intimately. She felt so badly for him. He had loved K, as he called him, like a father.

The children ran back and forth across their vision.

Sharply he broke the silence. 'What did you say your little girl's name is?'

She was surprised but pleased. 'Alexandra May, but we call her May.'

'I like that,' he said. Then he added, 'When she stood in front of me she was reminding me of someone. It was you . . . when I first saw you as a child on the train. When you gave me the holy card.' He turned his eyes round to hers.

'Yes . . . and you carried it for years.' She gave a nervous laugh.

'That must be over twenty years ago.'

She gave a quick self-conscious smile. 'Yes, it is.'

He made a long sad sound and she tenderly squeezed his arm, letting go when he stood up.

'I'd better get back to the station.'

He held out his hand to her as the child came running over to them again. 'My daddy's a soldier,' she said, looking up at him with her mother's flaming hair and her mother's big eyes.

'I know that, little one,' he answered softly, as Emma Louise took his outstretched hand.

'Do you know him?' May asked.

John Conrad tried to smile. 'Yes, I do.'

Emma Louise let go his hand. 'Goodbye, John Conrad. If ever you want to come and see us . . . please do. Two miles east, Lansdowne Grove on Cosgrove Hill.'

He nodded and walked away.

'He knows daddy,' May said, looking up at her mother.

'I know, darling. He's your uncle.'

'That soldier?'

'Yes, sweetheart.'

'I'm glad, I like him.'

Emma Louise said no more. She just stood holding her daughter's hand and watching John Conrad walk out of sight.

For John Conrad the following days were filled with torment. He travelled to the Orkney Islands and walked the lonely beaches between Marwick Head and the Brough of Birsay where the *Hampshire* had hit a mine and gone down. With heavy heart he steeled himself and identified the body of his friend Fitz, who had been washed ashore along with sundry others, but there was no trace of K.

Messages of condolences and grief poured in to England, to the Government, to the army, to K's family and to John Conrad. Many people heard the news with disbelief, would not accept that Kitchener of Khartoum had died. Within days of the sinking, rumours circulated that K was still alive: that he was a prisoner of the Germans; that he had been spirited away to a remote cave in the Shetlands and lay in an enchanted sleep like some Norse king waiting to be woken; that it would not be long before he appeared again to lead them to victory.

On the afternoon of Tuesday, 6 June, when the news was made public to the people of England, Scotland, Ireland and Wales, it was as if a hush had fallen across the countries; never had sorrow for the loss of a human being been taken quite so personally. Everywhere, in the streets and homes, offices, factories and schools, people were in shock. They moved silently and kept their children quiet and there were no loud voices in the streets.

The loss reverberated around the globe.

In Birsay, on the wild coast of Orkney, in a makeshift naval hospital in the tiny, ancient church of St Magnus, John Conrad found a survivor who had actually seen K before the sinking. He sat at the man's bedside in the long light of evening on 9 June and listened to what Leading Seaman Rogerson had to say. He was still suffering from exposure and exhaustion, a youthful muscular man with wide-set eyes and a small beard. He kept his eyes closed for much of his tale. 'We were in a gale north of Scapa Flow, our two accompanying destroyers had been sent back to harbour, most of the hatches were battened down, when I heard an explosion and all the lights went out. A great draught of wind blasted through the mess deck and blew all the men's caps off.

'Orders were at once given to abandon ship and as we reached the decks we saw his Lordship come from the captain's cabin and move calmly to the quarterdeck with two of his company. I knew them for they were all wearing khaki as they had when they came aboard. An officer called out, "Make way for Lord Kitchener," and the men with me opened out to let him pass.

'The crew didn't panic and Lord Kitchener didn't seem in the least perturbed. He calmly waited preparations for abandoning ship. The crew did their best to get out the boats but, owing to the rough weather, those that we attempted to lower were smashed up at once. Some men actually got into the boats and sat waiting in hope that when the ship went down they would float away, but the ship sank by the head.' He halted here for a long time and John Conrad sat silently waiting. Then he moaned and his voice quivered as he went on. 'She did a complete somersault forward, you see, carrying down with her all the boats and the men in them.' The seaman opened his eyes and fixed his gaze on his visitor. 'But three rafts did leave, and I was on one. Fifty to seventy men got on to each of those rafts but there were only four or five survivors from each . . . it was so bloody cold and we took on so much water, men just dropped away or died of exposure before our eyes.' A tear rolled down his cheek. 'I'm a lucky man, I am.'

John Conrad leaned forward. 'Yes, you are.' He touched the man's arm. 'And tell me, what of Lord Kitchener?'

'We heard Captain Savill call him to come up to the forebridge and get into a boat. Whether he did or not, sir, I cannot say, for about that time I sprang on to a raft. I won't say that he did not feel the strain of the perilous situation like the rest of us, but he gave no outward sign of nervousness or worry.'

'No, no, he would not,' John Conrad answered, his voice catching in his throat.

'He must have gone down with the ship, standing there on the deck. I feel certain he did.'

John Conrad spoke almost to himself. 'He hated the cold. He would soon have died in the chill waters anyway. What time did it happen?'

The man thought about it. 'I'd say we struck the mine, for that's what it had to be, about nineteen forty-five. Even though she was a good ship, she sank within fifteen minutes, I reckon.'

John Conrad shivered. He knew in his heart the timing of it, of course, but he had made himself ask. He patted the man's arm.

Rogerson's eyes filled with tears again. 'We'd all been

at the Battle of Jutland . . . gave such a good account of ourselves there.'

'Yes, you did.' John Conrad stood up. 'You all did. Thank you, you're a brave man. Good luck.'

He walked out past the nurse on duty into the glow of evening; he passed along the pebbled beaches and the rocky coastline, looking out to the island off the Brough of Birsay where there had been the gale only three nights before, and now the waves rolled gently in from a calming sea.

Even in early summer the evening breeze was cool and hundreds of seagulls squawked boisterously above his head. He spoke aloud. 'So, K, you hit the mine as I walked alone on the Kentish coast. I think I knew right then. I dreamt of you that night, you know . . . We were sailing to Kenya to the property and you were taking dozens of robins with broken wings . . .' He tried to smile, then opened his mouth wide and gulped the air. 'You must know you too were . . . my best friend. From the minute I met you that night near Wellington Monument.'

He slowly lifted his arms high in the breeze, reaching out to touch his friend in infinity. 'K, wherever you are, please know how much . . . I loved you. How much I love you now.' And then finally, with the birds sceeching and wheeling in the golden glow of the summer evening above his head, on the rocky Orkney beach, John Conrad bent forward and broke his heart.

There could be no funeral as there was no body.

The memorial service was held in St Paul's Cathedral where King George and Queen Mary, Prime Minister Asquith, all of the cabinet, and generals and admirals ranged along the nave. Outside thousands of people lined the streets. Even though hell was raging and men were dying everyday in Europe, K's passing had profoundly moved the world.

Before the service, K's only sister, Millie, as they called her, though her real name was Frances, had taken John Conrad's hand and sobbed quietly behind her veil. 'You knew him and understood him,' she said. 'He cannot be dead. I know he isn't. It's the Unseen Hand that has taken him.' The Unseen Hand was believed to be a malevolent and well-organised society that was devoted to the downfall of Britain; it was thought to be run from Germany and had agents working their insidious evil in the British Isles. Millie sighed and dabbed her eyes under her black veil.

John Conrad tried to speak tolerantly. 'Millie, it's hard for all of us to accept that he's gone. But you must.'

Vehemently she shook her head. 'I'll never believe it. You mustn't say that, John Conrad.'

'Millie, I saw Fitz's corpse washed up on the beach . . .'

'But you didn't see Herbert's,' she broke in. 'He's not dead, I know he's not.'

John Conrad sat behind K's immediate family. As the service began and the congregation lifted their voices in the haunting hymn, 'Abide With Me', John Conrad imagined K, dogs at his side, striding through the gardens of Wildflower Hall in the Simla Hills of India. And when the congregation raised their voices for Psalm 130, 'Out of the Deep', he saw K riding his black stallion across the African veldt and as 'The Dead March' echoed through the cathedral, he imagined K talking to children in the markets of the Sudan. And finally when 'The Last Post', the soldiers' requiem, filled the cathedral with its hauntingly beautiful notes he saw K as he had been that last time, in uniform on the platform of King's Cross Station, his wide-set eyes cloudy with emotion and how he had come back to say goodbye a second time.

As the service was conducted in St Paul's, simultaneously at two-mile intervals guns fired a vale to their hero from London to the valley of the Somme and on to Belgium, where troops came out of the trenches to honour his memory.

Memorial services were held in churches around the globe from St Patrick's in Dublin across the world to St Andrew's in Brisbane; in every capital throughout the vast British Empire, and too, in the United States and France, Italy, Brazil, Argentina, Japan, the Middle East and Russia. Never, not even with the death of the Duke of Wellington in the previous century had people mourned in such numbers, and with K's passing there came a universal grief, an emotional current that joined men and women of all nations and creeds, from Egypt and the Sudan, to Palestine and India, South Africa, Australia, New Zealand, America and Japan. They mourned the man they had believed in their hearts would lead them to victory.

On the steps of St Paul's, John Conrad parted from Millie and K's brothers and the rest of the family, and found himself next to David Lloyd George and Sir John French. John Conrad was well aware of how Lloyd George, in particular, had worked against K and perhaps his cool gaze reminded the Welshman of the man they had been remembering for Lloyd George coughed and said, 'He's the only field marshal ever to be killed by the enemy, you know.'

John Conrad was a head taller than the little man and without glancing down he ignored what Lloyd George had said and gazed straight over his head. He spoke scornfully. 'What I know is that Kitchener stood head and shoulders above all of you.'

'Come, David,' French said, and they moved quickly away.

On the evening of that day John Conrad, still in uniform, sat on a bench in Hyde Park. He had not gone home; rather he had wished to be alone with his thoughts and memories. He sat watching, though not seeing, the habitués of the Serpentine: the Canada geese and the many ducks, swans and coots, gliding on the dark water.

A flock of pigeons landed a few yards away and moved reluctantly aside from the path of two men in hospital blue – indicating they were wounded soldiers – as they came walking across the grass. As they drew in line with John Conrad one looked over and halted.

'Excuse me, sir.'

John Conrad looked up. 'Yes?'

'Weren't you the Australian colonel with Lord Kitchener when he came to the Dardanelles?'

John Conrad's ear picked up the man's Australian accent and he paused before replying, 'Yes, I was.'

'Ah, I thought as much.' He turned to his companion. 'It's him, Smithy.' Then he faced back to John Conrad. 'You mightn't remember me but my name's Pike, sir. I was wounded at Gallipoli last year. It was when you and his Lordship were there. He knelt down in the dirt of the trench by me, he did, never worrin' about his uniform. Chatted away to me about Windsor, my home. He'd been there, little place in New South Wales where I come from. Knew it. Said you'd been there with 'im.'

Then John Conrad remembered. 'Of course. I remember you, Pike.' He stood up from the bench. 'Lord Kitchener talked about a shop there, where we'd bought some bait to fish with back in 1910.'

The man's face brightened. 'Yeah, that's right. Bruce Bean's Bait Shop. You all fished the Hawkesbury.'

John Conrad nodded. 'We did.'

'Me leg got worse after that and I've been here nearly six months now, recovering. Goin' home to Australia in a week.' He chewed the side of his lip. 'I remember Lord Kitchener sayin', "You tell Bruce Bean to look out for me down there at Windsor after this war's over."' His mouth stretched into a sad smile. 'Though that won't be happenin' now, sir, will it?'

John Conrad shook his head.

'May I say somethin' else, sir?'

John Conrad nodded.

'Well, the thing we Anzacs all admired about him was he was so approachable. Now he looked the opposite in a way, tall and rangy like he was, but he was no snob. Talked to everyone: rank and file all alike. He looked the part of a leader right enough, but he gave many a wounded man a new lease o' life, me included. We took to him straight off, all of us. Fact is, the workin' man trusted him, I reckon. The ordinary soldier, like me, we *believed* in him. There's no one else at all we feel like that about.'

John Conrad gave a tired smile. 'Yes, yes, Pike, I agree with all you say.'

'Will you be goin' home to Australia after this stunt's over?'

John Conrad lifted his hands in a gesture of uncertainty.

'Well, if you do, sir, you're welcome in Windsor any time.' He saluted.

'I'll remember that, Pike. Thank you.'

Pike's friend saluted and they moved on into the dying evening.

The following morning John Conrad requested, and was granted, a few minutes with Sir William Robertson, the Chief of General Staff.

As he came into the comfortable office William Robertson, called 'Wully' by all and sundry, smiled a welcome, gesturing

530

to a wing-backed leather chair. They knew each other well, and John Conrad sat as the Chief of Staff spoke warmly to him in his plain-speaking Lincolnshire manner. 'I know you're devastated by your loss. You worked side by side with him for many years, didn't you?'

'For eighteen.'

'Mmm, that long, eh? Even before the Boer War where I first met you?'

'Yes, I joined him in '98. He was . . . my best friend. And I was close to Oswald Fitzgerald too.'

'Yes, of course you were. Lord Kitchener's death is a great loss to the Allies, to us all. He was a most outstanding personality. He displayed only good qualities to me. I know there are some who would like to denigrate him but I'm not one of them.' He rubbed his small neat moustache and said, 'So what can I do for you?'

'I'd like to be given a battalion, if that's possible, sir?'

Sir William's kindly face became grave. 'Look, I know how hard you've worked for the war effort. There're many ways we can use you, more important ways than wasting you in the front line. You know the running of things here at the War Office intimately. You can continue to be a big help.'

John Conrad slowly shook his head. 'I'd prefer to go to the front, sir.'

Sir William pursed his lips and folded his arms. 'Are you sure of this? There's definitely a desk job for you till this whole damn mess is over.'

'No thanks, sir. There's no doubt in my mind. I'd prefer to be given a battalion and go to France.'

'If I cannot dissuade you then I must point out you're overqualified for a battalion my boy. Perhaps I shouldn't tell you this but . . . now that K's gone, there's talk of making you a brigadier. That'll come through soon, you know. Then you'll be heading up a brigade. And I'd guess major general won't be long in coming after that if you give a good account of yourself.'

John Conrad shook his head. 'The truth is, sir, for the moment I'd much prefer a battalion. I want to be . . . nearer the . . . nearer things.'

The Chief of Staff gave a rueful smile. 'First time I've come across such as this in a long career, John Conrad. Very few men resist promotion. You're making quite a memorable stand.' He rose and came round the desk. He was a tall man though not quite as tall as John Conrad. 'I'll tell you what? We'll find you what you ask for, give you six months with a battalion. Then we'll make a brigadier out of you and get our real money's worth.' He held out his hand. 'It seems you're as courageous as the man you served under for eighteen years.'

John Conrad took his outstretched hand. 'I'd like to be, sir, I really would.'

Chapter Thirty-three

As dusk fell John Conrad stood holding the railing on Blackfriars Bridge and looking along the Thames and over the embankment; the scene was an oil painting, with liquid soft colours of the coming night already enveloping the river and its environs. It was this time of day that he missed K the most – just as the day waned into night.

He had received a notification from the War Office yesterday: to leave in two days for France. The odd thing was that he would be commanding an Australian battalion lately arrived in the Somme. The lieutenant colonel who had been in charge had caught a fever in Marseilles where the men had been in training for the front, and as his condition worsened, had been relieved of his post.

John Conrad dropped his arms to his sides and strode across the bridge and along the embankment, past the back of the Savoy Hotel to the small building next door to Somerset House. There, standing outside, was his friend and solicitor, Quinton Rafter.

Quinton smiled a welcome from under his moustache and they shook hands and entered the building together.

An hour later they came back down the steps into the darkness of the embankment and John Conrad turned to Quinton.

'Thank you.'

Quinton was ten years senior to John Conrad, a big muscular man with alert coal-black eyes and a smooth dark complexion. His mother was from St Kitts in the British West Indies and he was one of the very few men of mixed race to have studied law at Cambridge. John Conrad had met him in England on leave from Egypt before the war. He responded immediately to Quinton's sharp mind, his analytical style and the detached way he delivered droll ironic comments about the British class system. There was a certain way that Quinton turned his head and gave the hint of a smile that lifted the corner of his mouth slightly askew and reminded John Conrad of Hargy; perhaps that was part of the reason he had been attracted to the older man.

Quinton scrutinised his friend. 'I've been telling you to make a will for a long time, especially in your line of work, so I'm pleased you've done it at last.'

John Conrad shrugged. 'It wouldn't have mattered before, but now it's different. The money K left me along with the part of the estate in Kenya, makes me far richer than I ever expected to be. He treated me so very well.'

'He obviously thought a great deal of you. A damn sight more than he did of most of his family.'

In the gloomy night light John Conrad looked across the Thames. He could make out dim dancing reflections in the water. 'I'd rather have him back.'

Quinton frowned. 'I'm sure.' Then he coughed. 'I was talking to some people the other day, including young Anthony Beatty. I'm told you've volunteered for active service.'

John Conrad did not turn his head, nor did he speak.

'Ah? So it's true? Now I see why you made your will.'

'Would you like a drink?'

'You're changing the subject.'

John Conrad slapped his friend's shoulder. 'Let's head for the Savoy.'

As they moved forward, Quinton said, 'I realise you don't want to talk about it, but people are saying that without K you've become cavalier with your own existence. Please remember there are some of us who'd like to see you remain in this world.'

'Thanks, I appreciate it.'

'I'm only grateful I'm too old to go over there.'

'You know Haig's given Hubert Gough command of the Reserve army.'

'So I read.'

'K would have opposed that appointment, I know; regarded him as too impetuous, said he was a man who wouldn't listen.' He glanced round to his friend in the darkness. 'I feel for many reasons I need to get to the fighting. I see the best of our side's generals falling foul of Supreme High Command.

I've just heard that Edward Stuart Wortley's been dismissed; something to do with how he handled his part in the July campaign in the Somme. You know, I met him during the Boer War, he's a good soldier: think he began his career as a young lieutenant in the Second Afghan War.' He shook his head in thought. 'Do you know of Horace Smith Dorrien?'

The big man nodded. 'Think he was at Mons.'

'You're right. While he was a bit of a disciplinarian he commanded damn well at Mons *and* at Ypres but John French still got rid of him, and Smith Dorrien began his career in the Zulu Wars for heaven's sake . . . Seems ridiculous to cast aside men with all that experience. I know this war's different, but nothing takes the place of accumulated knowledge.'

Quinton gave a short rueful laugh. 'So you think you should be over there so you can run foul of High Command too?'

John Conrad did not answer and they continued strolling along when there was an explosion to the east and they both swung round. A mighty glow lit the sky in the distance.

'Oh hell,' Quinton shouted, 'German dirigibles.'

There was a second then a third explosion and some time later the sound of staccato ground fire.

Quinton pointed. 'They look like they're coming this way. We'd better go back to the cellar in my building, or there's one in Somerset House.'

John Conrad did not move. He stood, eyes narrowed, following the silent passage of the sinister dark cigar forms against the moonlight as the brilliance of another explosion jumped into the air from buildings a mile or so away down the Thames.

Quinton stood shaking his head. 'To think it's come to attacks on innocent civilians.' He grabbed John Conrad's arm to steer him back to the cellar as people shouted and ran by them. But John Conrad moved out of his friend's grasp.

Quinton paused. 'Come on, be sensible. They'll be here soon.'

John Conrad shook his head. 'No, you go. I'm heading to the Savoy for a drink.'

'Don't be bloody silly.'

John Conrad started off towards the hotel.

Quinton called out again as more direct hits thundered downriver, then he laughed out loud and shouted to the departing back of his friend, 'Oh well, if you're so bloody set on drinking I can't let you do it alone!' And with that he followed John Conrad down to the Savoy.

As they came to the back entrance the doorman halted them. 'Wouldn't go inside, gents. You'll be safer down there.' And he pointed to where a number of men and women in evening dress were traipsing down steps to the lower ground floor. 'Goin' down meself soon.'

John Conrad lifted his palm to the man as he passed by. 'Can't drink down there.' He took the stairs two by two, Quinton coming after him in the same fashion.

And so it was that John Conrad Fleet and Quinton Rafter sat at the window in the back bar of the Savoy Hotel, maroon velvet drapes framing the windows in front of them and with the place to themselves, three gins each at hand, and their feet on a low table, watching an air raid on London.

At midnight one of the zeppelins was hit by ground fire, a victim of the new incendiary bullet. It hovered for a second or two blazing away in the distant sky like a red cigar-shaped meteor, then the glowing mass slipped earthwards. This so delighted the two clients of the empty bar that they burst into 'Land of Hope and Glory'.

The following day the door knocker at Lansdowne Grove was given a sharp rap. Aunt Gertrude opened the door and her mouth dropped open. 'John Conrad. My heaven.' She crossed herself. 'What are you doing here?'

He was momentarily taken aback. 'Hasn't Emma Louise mentioned running into me?'

She shook her head.

'I've come to say goodbye before I go to France. I leave tomorrow.'

Gertrude was obviously out of her depth. 'Oh, I see.' She tried to smile. 'It's just that it's so long since I've seen you. I'm a bit surprised, that's all. Do excuse me for being so offhand.' She stood aside. 'Please come in.'

Her visitor entered the mahogany-lined front hall.

She pointed ahead. 'Emma Louise and May are on a walk up to Hartshead Pike. They were thinking of going riding but fortunately they didn't. I'm expecting them back any minute.'

She looked uncertain what to say next so John Conrad helped her out.

'I suppose I could wait.'

'Of course.' She took him through a parlour with chintz sofas and long curtains and out through French windows on to a small terrace with hanging baskets filled with violas. There, crossing a stile in the back fence were Emma Louise and May. Gertrude's relief was obvious as she called to her niece. 'Emma Louise, John Conrad's here.'

As John Conrad walked towards them the child gave a cry of delight, jumped down from the stile and spontaneously ran forward, straight to him with her arms open. Automatically he bent down and lifted her high in the air. Her blue cotton dress brushed his face and the childish clean aroma of her filled his nostrils. He felt decidedly odd as he put her down.

'My uncle! My uncle!' May shouted. Embarrassed, he laughed.

Emma Louise advanced, holding a bunch of late blooming lavender and daisies. 'I told May you were her uncle the day we met you in Canterbury. I hope you don't mind.'

'Mind? Of course not. I am, aren't I?'

She nodded. 'You are. I wondered if you'd come.' In formal fashion she held out her hand.

He took it. 'I hadn't forgotten. But Gertrude was obviously surprised to see me.'

May was looking up at John Conrad with a wide smile as Aunt Gertrude spoke quickly. 'Why didn't you tell me you'd run into John Conrad, dear?'

Emma Louise did not answer. She let go John Conrad's hand, tossed her hair back over her shoulder and gave a half-shrug before she handed her aunt the flowers. 'Will you put these in water?'

Gertrude took the flowers in one hand and the little girl's hand in the other. 'Come, darling, we'll make some tea as well. I suppose you'd like tea?'

'Oh yes, I suppose so,' Emma Louise said and John Conrad smiled agreement.

'I don't like tea,' May said, twirling round so that her blue dress wafted into the air above her ankles. 'But I like horses.'

537

'You shall have lemonade,' Aunt Gertrude informed her. 'Come along,' and they crossed the lawn to the patio and disappeared indoors.

Emma looked after the departing backs of her aunt and daughter and John Conrad felt that perhaps he should not have come, but he broke the silence. 'Thank you for the letter you wrote me . . . about K.'

She met his eyes. 'I know how close you were. It must have been like losing a father.'

'Yes it was like that, but he was my best friend too.'

'I've met so many people who actually cried when they heard he'd drowned. I did that night after you'd told me. I think everybody thought in the end he'd lead us to victory, and now . . . he's gone. It leaves you feeling somehow vulnerable.' She moved towards two white wicker chairs near a table on the lawn. 'This war's horrible,' she said as she sat down.

He sat opposite. He could hear the trill of a wren in the trees above their heads and as they sat in silence a red squirrel sped down the bole of the tree and paused, standing upright on his hind legs, looking around with staccato-like movements of his head.

'May loves those little fellows; she feeds them.'

John Conrad thought about May then. There was a time when he had not been able to abide the thought of her: the child who had been at the heart of Emma Louise's infidelity. But the little girl was just that: a little girl, the innocent in the whole affair. He appeared to watch the squirrel as it turned and ran across in front of them, then he lifted his gaze to hers. 'I've come to tell you I'm going to France. I've been given an Australian battalion . . .' He was about to inform her he thought they would be heading to the Somme but he thought better of it.

Emma Louise looked mildly surprised. 'Did you ask to go on active service?'

He nodded.

'I see. Yes, I suppose it's best. You'll be happy out there.'

He thought that a rather strange remark and he asked, 'What does that mean?'

She toyed with one of her lace cuffs. 'Oh, I don't know really.' Then in that habitual tangential way she had of talking she said, 'I didn't want David to volunteer, but he did.

He was always trying to prove something to me. I don't know why.'

'Relationships are always complicated,' John Conrad ventured.

'Yes, they are.'

He felt decidedly awkward as the seconds passed and Emma Louise frowned as she continued to play with the lace of her sleeve. She was out of her depth with him here. Ever since she had run into him in the West End the year before she had very mixed feelings about him. And then when she had seen him in Canterbury so obviously distraught and broken about K's disappearance, she had felt so sorry for him. Naturally she had asked him to visit them here, though there was a part of her that almost hoped he would not come, so that things would not be complicated for her. And then, when May had mentioned him from time to time she had wondered about him; once she had dreamed about him. And now he was here, sitting opposite her in the big wicker chair with a lost look in his cold blue eyes and an air of loneliness all around him. She could have been his wife, but she was married to his brother and she did love David, she really did . . .

As she watched him in silence he spoke. 'Look, neither of us has mentioned what happened between us. I think it's time we did, then at least we might be able to attempt to forget it.' He looked expectantly at her, waiting for her reaction.

Moments slipped away as she relived the complications of all her jumbled feelings for this man and his brother. 'I suppose you're right . . . but it's hard. I still feel many things about it all – anger and guilt uppermost, I suppose.'

'Yes.'

She closed her eyes. Perhaps she had always known this conversation would one day take place. She moved uncomfortably in her chair as she opened her eyes. 'I was very young when I met you on the ship. You were mature, close to Kitchener, an important soldier, and I was flattered when you paid attention to me.' She looked down at her hands. 'I thought you were the best-looking man I'd ever seen in my life.' Then she tossed her hair back over her shoulder and brought her eyes to his. 'When we became engaged and you went back to K in India and left me behind in Queensland I . . .' Her shoulders raised and dropped as she sighed. 'All I can say is I was too young to know . . . what I . . . about life. David was my age, full of fun, he made me laugh . . . he excited me.' She lifted her hands awkwardly in an odd gesture. 'He's very . . . physical.' She paused and met John Conrad's eyes. 'I'm not making excuses. I realise I treated you badly. I acted shabbily. It was all so awful. But we've made our lives and we must live them out, I suppose.'

A breeze played about them, gently moving her skirt around her ankles and her hair around her shoulders; birds were twittering in the trees above. It crossed his mind how simple it would be to be a bird. 'Just answer me one thing?' he said.

'What is it?'

'Did you ever really love me?'

Her eyes narrowed and her cheeks coloured slightly. 'A time for truth, eh?'

He did not answer.

'Yes . . . I did, very much. I just wasn't strong enough to be left by myself in those days.'

He could not help himself, it was out of his mouth before he knew it. 'Oh, but you are now, I suppose?'

He saw her skin turn crimson in the opening of her dress as a hot flush rose up her throat and met the pink of her cheeks. Her face contorted as if she were going to cry. 'That's cruel,' she answered. 'But then you can be cruel . . . and violent too, can't you?'

He decided that coming here had been a mistake and he rose to his feet. 'Look, I shouldn't have come. There's so much of a past with us that I don't think we can forget it. Please forgive me for intruding.' He turned and began to walk across to the patio.

'John Conrad?'

Slowly he rounded to her as she moved across the lawn towards him. In the sunlight her eyes shone, as did her glorious red hair. 'Even though your question was harsh I *can* answer you and I will. What happened was seven years ago. I'm different now . . . a different person. Yes, I can be left alone.'

They both retreated a step, as if feeling the tension between them. She could see the muscles of his jaw harden as he spoke. 'The night I found out about you and David I exploded. I'd trusted you implicitly and you'd let me down.'

'I know,' she said quietly. 'I wish it had never happened.'

He nodded to himself. 'I think I've altered. Less liable to lose my temper. I keep it in check.'

She did not believe him and she said, 'Perhaps. Time does alter us. But please don't leave yet, come back and sit down. May would be upset if you left. She likes having an uncle.'

'She's a dear little girl.'

'Yes.'

He tried to lighten the mood. 'The minute I saw her in Canterbury she reminded me of you at the same age.'

And she endeavoured to sound agreeable. 'Yes, and the first time you saw me was on the train in Queensland.'

He paused then said, 'I kept that holy card . . . until seven years ago.'

She understood the implication but said nothing. The awkwardness between them hovered all around.

Suddenly May's voice sounded and they turned their heads to see the child running across the lawn, her dress swirling around her, her face glowing with the excitement of the visitor's presence. She placed two tiny green porcelain shoes on John Conrad's knee. 'My daddy gave them to me. He brought them for me. From . . .' She looked to her mother, who supplied the word.

'France, from France, darling.'

'From France,' the child repeated.

Emma Louise looked lovingly at her daughter and explained, 'He brought them for her on his last leave, well, his *only* leave up to now.'

John Conrad lifted one of the little shoes. It had a red velvet ribbon tied in a bow through the lace holes. 'These are very beautiful, May.' It was the first time he had said the chid's name and he was very conscious of it. 'You must keep these always.' He looked straight into her wide candid eyes and was transported back twenty-three years to Queensland and the train swinging along the track and at his side the child with the bright sienna-red hair, freckles and with the unequivocal gaze, who had taken the holy card out of a little blue silk purse and handed it to him. He was looking into May's face now, and except for the missing freckles it was identical. He lifted his eyes to Emma Louise. 'Yes, it's true she's so very like you . . . were.'

May, oblivious of any undercurrents, stood close to his elbow and smiled widely up at him. 'Do you know my daddy?'

John Conrad remained looking at Emma Louise as he answered the child. 'Yes, he's my brother.'

May took this with the inherent equanimity of a six-year-old. 'Good,' she answered, and the curiousness of her reply actually brought a smile to both the adults' faces.

Gertrude, tray in hands, issued on to the terrace. 'Here's the tea.'

May took back the porcelain shoes as her great-aunt crossed to the table and put down the tray. 'I have some scones if you'd like them. I was lucky enough to get some flour this morning at the Co-op, and now my ration book's nearly empty.'

In unison they both answered, 'No, thank you.'

As Gertrude poured the tea Emma Louise said, 'John Conrad's going to France.'

The older woman crossed herself. 'Ah dear, so he said. And what rank are you now?'

'A colonel.'

'A full colonel, is it? Then you shouldn't have to do any hand-to-hand fighting.'

'It depends,' John Conrad uttered slowly.

'Yes, I suppose it does.'

When they had taken tea John Conrad stood. 'I think I must go now.' He put out his hand to her and the older woman grasped it. 'Goodbye.'

As Gertrude tidied up the teacups, Emma Louise moved back across the lawn to the house with John Conrad. 'How will you get back to Canterbury?'

'I'll walk. Must keep fit.'

May insisted on leading John Conrad to the front door, holding his hand all the way. She kept asking when he was coming back and he promised he would one day.

'When?' the child insisted.

'When I'm here in England again.'

The child's round eyes registered thoughtfully. 'Are you going away?'

'For a little while.'

'My daddy's gone away. He's a soldier of the King.' Then she held out her arms to him and he felt constrained to lift her again. When she kissed him on the cheek he managed to smile. 'Thank you,' he said as he returned her to the floor.

'Come back soon, Uncle,' the child shouted as her attention was taken by three blackbirds on the lawn and she ran towards them, impelling them to flight, their wings beating rapidly as they rose.

He turned to Emma Louise. 'She's really a lovely little girl.'

'Yes, she is.'

'Well, goodbye,'

She pushed her hair behind her ear. 'If . . . when . . . you come home on leave, come and see us again.' She looked across to where her daughter sat on the lawn. 'May would like it.' She held out her pale fingers and he took them.

'Emma Louise, I'm glad I came here though we haven't been exactly comfortable with each other. What happened to us is in the past. It's probably best to leave it there if we can.' He managed a weak smile. 'I can hear Aunt Leigh saying, "Things that are done it is needless to speak about. Things that are past it is needless to blame."'

As he let go her hand she nodded. 'Yes, Aunt Leigh's a wise woman.' She gave him a smile, a real smile.

It was a moment of peace between them, and they both recognised it.

'Good luck,' she said, and he turned away and headed to the small white-washed gate. As he closed it behind him he saw coming up the hill a uniformed man on a bicycle. The hairs on his arms prickled as he spun around to look at Emma Louise.

Even at the distance from her he saw the blood drain from her face. He was acutely aware of her there on the pebble-covered path, with her brilliant hair and the green-patterned dress falling in pleats to her ankles; of the way her hands hung in front of her like limpid gloves from beneath the lace of her sleeves.

The man stopped his bicycle and rested it on the fence as John Conrad faced back to him. 'Is this the home of Mrs David Fleet?'

John Conrad stared at the military envelope jutting from the man's top pocket as he forced himself to nod. And when the man pushed open the gate he managed to speak. 'One moment, please. I must take the child inside.'

The man halted. 'Of course.'

John Conrad hurried across to where May sat on the grass picking small white flowers from the lawn. 'Come dear,' he said, and took her hand. Pleased that her uncle had returned she went happily indoors with him.

'Emma Louise,' was all he could say as he passed with the child by her mother and in through the open front door. He called loudly to Gertrude as he hurried the child down the hall.

Gertrude appeared from the kitchen. 'You're back?' Then she saw his face. 'What is it?'

'Take the child. A message has come for Emma Louise.'

Gertrude drew the unwitting little girl into the kitchen as John Conrad returned to the garden where Emma Louise remained rigid in the same spot. The messenger was back on his bicycle, riding away. John Conrad moved softly forward to the woman's side.

She did not move. She held an Army Form B 101 and her eyes were upon it. The envelope was in two pieces at her feet on the path.

John Conrad spoke. 'Is it . . . ?'

She folded the form neatly as if it had been a letter from a friend. She did not look at him as she answered. Her voice was pathetically matter-of-fact. 'Oh yes. He's dead. I knew he was as soon as I saw that man. I'll never see him again. May will never grow up with her father. He's just one more dead soldier . . .' A tiny muscle twitched wildly in her cheek.

'Oh, Emma Louise, I'm so sorry . . .'

'Of course you are.' Her tone sharpened. 'I'm twenty-nine years old, and I'm a widow, like the countless other widows across this land.' She looked around at him. 'Please go now. I've had enough of soldiers and war for today. I'd like to be alone.'

'Emma, just know that I'm truly deeply sorry.' And he was. Another one of Kitchener's army was dead . . . but this one was his brother. 'We could never have been close David and I, but . . .'

And now the tears broke over her lids, her voice cold and strident. 'No, you're not sorry. You're a professional soldier. You glory in wars. You're the ones who don't care or give a damn. You didn't know David and you didn't like him. It's because of you he joined up. I told you he was always trying to prove something to me. Well, it wasn't true . . .' She began to sob and the paper trembled in her hands. 'It was *you* he had to prove it to. He hated you, but he wanted to live up to you, simply because you were so . . . grand, so important . . . a colonel, Kitchener, everything. He was actually intimidated by you. Oh God, go away.' And she stood there, shaking, as her breath came in convulsive gasps.

John Conrad put out his hand to touch her, thought better of it, hesitated, began to speak and stopped himself, then walked away through the gate, looking back at the house as he passed along the road. There at a window he saw May's little face pressed to the glass. She raised her hand to him and with sadness heavy in his chest he waved back to her. 'Goodbye, little one,' he said aloud.

Behind him, Emma Louise's gaze followed John Conrad all the way down the hill.

Back in St James's he made himself write four letters. His first was to the Tate Gallery. He had received a letter the previous week from the Chairman of the new gallery, dedicated to showing and sponsoring British art. The chairman had detailed expansion plans for the future, listed the distinguished board members and donors and the last paragraph had read: 'The Tate Gallery leads the way in British art and would be delighted if you, as the late Lord Kitchener's strong right hand, would honour us by becoming a trustee.'

John Conrad's reply was short. He thanked them and informed them he was on his way to France and that if they were still interested in his services after the war he would accept in Lord Kitchener's memory.

The next letter he wrote was to little May, filling it with happy thoughts and things he thought a child might like, though he really had not much idea of what they might be. That, he followed with one to Emma Louise in which he told her he understood her anger, that he knew the heartache she was experiencing and that if in time she felt she could write to him he would be pleased to receive a note from her. He told her where to write and that he hoped she would still allow him to come and see little May when he came back to England.

The last letter was to Aunt Leigh and Bart and his father. He wrote of his meetings with Emma Louise and the death of David. He tore up the letter twice before he found the right words, for it was hard to write to his father of the death of one son, while telling him the other was going to the front. He finished with, 'Don't worry about me, I shall be all right, and remember, if anything ever does happen to me, that I made my choice. That it was my decision alone.'

The following day he left for France.

Chapter Thirty-four

Harry looked round as his name was called.

From behind the broken walls of a deserted farmhouse the light glinted in Dave's jet-black hair as he sauntered forward, smoking a Wild Woodbine cigarette.

'Well, old son, how are you?'

For reply he pitched his cigarette into the dirt at his feet, dug his hands into his pockets and, bringing out two bright rosy apples, he flipped one in the air towards Harry, who caught it.

'Golly, where'd you get these?'

Dave gave a cheeky grin as he sat down on a rock beside his friend. Over his shoulder in the distance a herd of mules pulled howitzers along a dusty road and two London omnibuses, looking incongruous, trundled by, past a long line of German prisoners and their guards ambling towards the railway. A game of football was being played in the middle distance.

'I got them down where C Company's tents are going up,' he answered, biting into the apple. 'There was a box of Huntley and Palmer biscuits and right beside it were open two boxes of red apples just lying on the ground. I asked what they were for and one of the fellows said to make apple pie for the officers' dinner tonight.' He gave a snort of disgust. 'Well, as I hadn't had a decent apple since leaving Queensland, I waited until their backs were turned and decided we should partake of a couple.'

Harry spoke through his mouthful of apple. 'That's a charge-able offence.'

'Yeah, I know.'

At this, they broke into laughter. They had been five months in the army, and the high-spirited boy soldiers enjoyed cheating authority as often as possible, and as authority was represented here by officers and army rules they were out to exploit all ranks above them. Being mere lowly privates, this left the entire army at their disposal. For a time they sat munching on their apples, complete in their companionship, watching soldiers of the East Surrey Regiment drilling in a field across from them: the equilibrium and calm between them exactly that which their close relatives, John Conrad and Hargy, had experienced some twenty years earlier.

Yesterday, they had arrived at Château Segard, south-west of the town of Albert in the Somme Valley. One of the soldiers had shouted a greeting as they had arrived, 'Welcome to Château Cigar, boys!'

The building was used by the AIF and the British divisions as a resting place before and after being in the front lines, and a small staff of each nation's troops remained here for administration.

They had quickly learnt that their destination was the front north of Albert where, since July first the Allies had been fighting to force the Germans back across the loop of the Ancre River in the north. The German strongholds in this part of the front had not yielded and the death toll on both sides had been horrendous.

Tomorrow they were to move nearer the enemy to what was to be the battalion reserve headquarters. The boom of distant guns was constant here and occasionally they saw bi-planes overhead.

Dave took the last bite of his apple and pitched the core into the rubble a few feet away. Taking a swing at the ever-insistent flies, he complained, 'Blasted flies. I thought Brisbane was bad enough but this is torment.'

'Yes, well, they thrive everywhere here. Bloke I was talking to yesterday said it's all the dead bodies.'

This chilling thought brought them to silence again. They had passed a number of cemeteries on the way in, large mounds of dirt delineated against the sky.

Dave sat, elbows on knees, pressing the tips of his fingers together as he looked through them towards the far-off sound of the guns, and altered the subject. 'Wonder what it would be like to fly? I hear it's a real thrilling experience.'

'Yes, it would be, feeling the air rushing by and seeing the ground down below. I'd love to do that.'

'And the incendiary bullets flying around you.'

Harry laughed. 'Yeah, that'd be the exciting bit, right enough. I must say, this waiting around, cleaning our rifles and doing arms-drill is pretty boring. Rather be up the line fighting Fritz, eh?'

'Yes, sure would.'

A shadow fell across them and they looked up to see Luke and Frank Birtenshaw and beside them Isaac Walker, a teacher from Townsville, who usually carried a book of poetry with him. Bringing up the rear was 'Curly' Moss, whose real name was Arthur, but his nickname prevailed because even with the razor-short army haircut his black curls strived to emerge. He was a stocky muscular young man from Western Queensland who was older than the others and had fought at Helles in the Dardanelles.

Luke bent his knees to squat, directing his conversation to Harry. 'They're playing cricket over in the field beyond the football game: Welsh Fusiliers against the Prince of Wales's Own. They've thrown out a challenge to us tomorrow.'

'Who?'

'The Prince of Wales mob.'

Harry grinned. 'Good. I reckon they're beaten already.'

Frank flopped down in the dirt beside them. 'Do you know what I just heard?'

'No, what?'

'They say the new battalion commander's arriving this evening.'

'Really?'

Curly stretched out against a rock as Frank went on, 'There's to be a battalion parade in the morning according to Bingo.'

Bingo was what they called Company Sergeant Bingham behind his back.

Harry looked at Frank. 'What's the new bloke, a colonel or something?'

'Yeah, guess so. They usually are.'

'No, most often they're *Lieutenant* Colonels,' Luke informed them knowledgeably.

Curly lit a cigarette and blew out smoke as he spoke. 'Well, Bingo says the new bloke's a full colonel, so there.'

Dave grinned. 'We must be bloody special to rate a full colonel then.'

Harry's eyes narrowed in thought. 'Gosh, imagine that, being a colonel.'

Curly shook his head. 'Strewth, I can't. All I can imagine's being a private.'

Dave made a whistling sound between his teeth. 'I've got an uncle who's a colonel.'

'Oh God!' declared Luke. 'Please don't start that again. We don't believe you, Sands!'

Harry met Luke's eyes. 'I do.'

Luke shrugged. 'Yeah, well, you'd believe anything.'

Isaac piped up for the first time. 'What's he mean, he's got an uncle who's a colonel? How can an Aborigine have an uncle who's a colonel?'

Dave turned round menacingly to face Isaac and Luke as Frank decided it was time to chirp in diplomatically and alter the subject. 'Isaac, forget it for now.' He pointed to the apple core Harry was chewing on. 'Anyway, where'd you get that?'

'Bloke from 10th Brigade just came by, handed it to me.'

'You lucky bugger.'

Dave winked at Harry. 'Yes, aren't I?'

Luke eyed Dave suspiciously. 'More like you pinched it.'

Dave ignored this aspersion and, leaning back on a pile of stones, said, 'There's a bloke called Wild Eye who has more souvenirs than anyone in France or Belgium. He was here yesterday. Gone back into the line. They reckon he needs five bully beef crates to move his stuff around.'

Isaac grinned. 'Yes, I heard that too. He reckons he's going to start a museum in Cowra after the war.'

Luke blew air loudly through his lips. 'Cowra? A museum there? Where the hell is Cowra?'

A long-suffering expression crossed Isaac's face. 'It's a town in New South Wales, about seventy miles west of the Blue Mountains.'

'Thanks, professor.'

Dave lifted his finger in the direction of the sound of the guns. 'Word is we're going up the line soon. I suppose now the battalion commander's arrived we will.'

'Does anyone know his name?' Curly asked.

Frank shook his head 'No. But I'll tell you a good one.

There's a captain arrived ahead of him – his aide or something – called Twistleton Menzies Lang.'

The five of them burst out laughing as Frank went on, 'Isn't it a scream? But guess what? He doesn't call himself Men-zies, he calls himself *Ming*. *Twistleton Ming Lang*. Funniest name I ever heard.'

'Never,' Harry said between guffaws. 'Ming? How can M-e-n-z-i-e-s be pronounced *Ming*? That's just ridiculous.'

Frank pursed his lips. 'Sure is, but that's something else I was told by Bingo, so it must be true.'

Dave was still shaking with mirth. 'Gawd, if that's the name of the captain with him, can anyone imagine what the colonel's moniker will be.'

'Willyclogg Witherspoon,' suggested Isaac, and this brought them all near to hysteria again, Luke and Frank falling back on the ground in their amusement.

'You know,' Isaac said, giggling, 'there's a line of poetry that goes, "And last of all an Admiral came, A terrible man with a terrible name."'

Frank, not to be outdone, sat up and, lifting his hands for silence, told them, 'You know the most terrible names I ever heard? They belonged to two girls who lived in the next street to me in Toowoomba, one was Daisy Crapper and the other was her friend Ruby Ring.'

This sent them all into total hysteria again, Luke and Frank rolling on the ground repeating the girls' names until a shout from behind silenced them and they all sat up and swung round. Sergeant Bingham, his carrot-coloured beard bobbing up and down, was upon them. 'All right, you lot, on your feet, over to the parade ground. There's an arms-drill this afternoon at sixteen hundred and you beauties are in it too, you know. No exceptions in this man's army.'

The six got slowly to their feet.

An hour later they were cleaning their Lee Enfield Mark III rifles for the afternoon parade under a cloudy sky as a troop train rattled by to the west. Dave and Harry sat side by side and Luke, Isaac, Curly and Frank across from them in the dirt.

Luke whistled an out-of-tune version of 'It's a long way to Tipperary' and Frank informed them, 'Saw a nice mam'selle in the fields near the far end of the village today. She smiled at me. I might get lucky if I see her again.'

Harry looked up. 'Shows the poor girl had no taste.'

'Do you know what?' Luke's expression held the assuredness of one who knows a secret.

'No, what?'

'I was talking with Tommy Ward, a Royal Engineer with the 179th tunnellers, and he told me he'd smuggled a girl into the trenches last year. Dorothy something? An English girl . . . she lived with the sappers as a man for a while down near Albert.'

Frank whistled. 'Oh, to have been in the trenches with Dorothy. I could have helped her on with her uniform.'

'What a load of crap.' Curly gave a dismissive grunt and scratched his neck. 'Gawd, you lot, you'd believe anything if you believe that.'

'Tommy Ward swore it was true.'

Luke opened his mouth to give a sharp retort when Sergeant Bingham intruded into their lives again. 'I want two volunteers,' he barked at them, pointing his big forefinger. 'You, Sands, and you, Craken, on the double over here.'

The two boys groaned, put down their rifles and trotted unwillingly across to the sergeant. 'Follow me.'

He marched the youths a couple of hundred yards along the dirt road by rows of tents and over a broken-down wall to a line of duckboards. Once across them they passed a large marquee with a long stretch of grass in front; it being the only grass in sight as most of the encampment, trampled by thousands of boots, had become a mud bath. 'Officers' mess, an out-of-bounds area,' Bingo barked, gesturing to the marquee and the row of tents behind it. Sixty yards beyond the marquee was the cook tent for the officers. Bingo pointed at two shovels and some sheets of tin lying near a set of white marks painted on the ground. 'Now, boys, we need some shallow trenches dug here for cook fires. The cooks will be along at sixteen hundred. Start digging.'

Dave frowned. 'Gosh Sarge, we won't have time to do this and get ready for the drill too. Isn't that at seventeen hundred?'

Sergeant Bingham's eyes flashed as he pushed his bearded

chin forward. 'Sands, how many times have I told you *I* ask the questions, not you? Now unless you want your crime sheet to fill up more quickly than it already is, I *suggest* you pick up the shovel.'

Dave shrugged and did as he was told.

'I'll be back in a couple of hours and I want to see these trenches finished.' And he started off between the tents.

Dave called, 'How deep should they be, Sarge?' And Bingo shouted back over his shoulder. 'Deep enough for fires, you loggerhead.'

Harry wiped his hands across his eyes. 'Lucky us, why couldn't he have picked Birtenshaw and Luke? Oh well, let's start.' And he dug his shovel into the dirt.

For close on an hour the twosome worked away, with no one else in sight. Harry was riveting tin sheeting in a finished part of the trench when Dave put down his shovel and wiped the perspiration from his brow. 'Couldn't we half do with a drink?'

A wind came up and swept some bespattered pages of the French newspaper *La Liberté* across the top of the trench as Harry leant on his shovel. 'Yeah, sure could. But we'd better keep working. Old Bingo'll be back.'

Dave pointed to the marquee some forty yards hence. 'There's no one about so I'm going to take a look along there. See if I can find anything to drink.'

Harry raised his eyes skywards. Dave's inquisitive nature and fun-loving ways had kept them in semi-trouble with Bingo since landing in Marseilles. There was the odd entry on their crime sheets, though nothing serious, not that he cared, the escapades were often his own idea and there was never a dull moment. 'Well, don't be long, old son.'

As Harry returned to his digging, watching out for any signs of life, he thought about how different his life was to the one he had left behind in Brisbane. The French country people were so alien to him, with their wayside shrines, and the way they rode about in dog carts and wore wooden sabots. There seemed to be so many pregnant refugees in their road-side shacks, offering eggs and potatoes for sale to the soldiers, and pipe-smoking old men drinking black thick coffee while the young men were all away.

He did not miss the routine of school work, though it had somehow surprised him when he had used his stumbling French on the locals and they had actually understood him: perhaps there was something to be said for learning another language after all. And he did not miss MacDonald or any of the masters, though he missed his mother and father and Uncle Knobby and little Katy. It made him uneasy to think of his mother. He had hated to hurt her, but she simply did not understand him, or his needs. He supposed all mothers were like that, trying to stifle their sons and mould them to their ways. And yet his opinion of his mother had altered slightly. Once he had believed there was a decided lack of adventure in the female spirit but not any more for she had tracked him down; just as he should have suspected she would.

It had been a summer's day in the training camp outside Marseilles. Harry had just returned to his barracks after completing an assault course and grenade throwing, when Bingo had found him. 'Craken, you're wanted by Lieutenant Marchant.'

They had crossed the parade ground and the men drilling to enter the Nissen hut where the lieutenant's office was.

'Craken?'

'Yes, sir?'

'Your mother's here.'

Harry's eyes widened in disbelief.

'She's with the British Voluntary Aid Detachment on her way to a hospital in the north. She's asked to see you.' Marchant was only twenty-four and perhaps he missed his own mother, for he had been sympathetic to Caro's cause. 'I've said I'd allow you the rest of the afternoon off. Just be back here at twenty-one hundred on the dot.' As Harry saluted and turned away, the lieutenant spoke again. 'She's got some bee in her bonnet about your age, Craken. Tell her, will you, that you're in the army now, no matter what bloody age you are?'

Harry had walked in trepidation to the front of the barracks where long before he arrived he saw the raised hand from the woman in the long blue cape who stood by the sentry post.

As he came up to her Caro attempted to fold the boy in her arms and she began to cry.

He moved out of her grasp. 'God, Mum, please not here. Pull yourself together. Someone might see.'

She had followed his instructions and walked as calmly as she could at his side along the road towards the city.

He halted beside a cypress tree and turned to her. 'Mum, what are you doing here?'

'Oh, Harry, darling.' She took his hand in her gloved one. 'Please be kind. I'm your mother. Always remember to have compassion, Harry, compassion—'

He cut her off, 'I know, it's the major difference between humans and animals. All right, Mum. But what are you doing here?' He removed his hand from hers.

She gave a trembling sigh and for the first time in his life he wondered about the tiny faint scar on her bottom lip; wondered how she had received it.

'When I realised you were in the army irrevocably, which you should not be anyway as you're under age, I knew I must come over here. I wanted to be near you even if I couldn't be with you, and I wanted . . . I decided I must help all those other sons of broken-hearted mothers, if I could.'

He did not feel quite so irritated with her, and he was quite pleased to see her really. 'So how long are you staying?'

'For the duration of the war, son. Well, I suppose I'll get back to England as the rules stipulate, every six months or so, but I'm here to work. When I arrived in England my work with the volunteers in Brisbane gave me enough experience to join the Voluntary Aid Detachment. I'm actually going to nurse and perhaps some time drive ambulances at a base hospital in a little town called Montdidier, about fifty miles north of Paris.'

Harry eyed her. 'I think that's not far from the front.'

'Ten miles or so, I'm told.'

Suddenly Harry felt disturbed for her; up to this time in his existence there had never been a need for anxiety where she had been concerned. He felt uneasy that his mother was going to nurse near the front; it might be dangerous. 'Mum, I don't think you should do that.'

'Why?'

'It's dangerous there. I want you to go home to Australia, please. Go back to Queensland.'

Caro actually smiled at his words. 'Oh, my dear, my dear boy, so now you have just the vaguest idea perhaps of how

I feel about *you*. Now possibly you understand why I worry about *you*?'

He saw the argument patently, as if a crack had appeared in his solid universe. It was indisputable. Slowly he nodded his head, 'Yes I do.' He stood there, his blue eyes catching the afternoon light and her heart shifted thinking how like John Conrad he was. 'But you're wrong to be here. It was my choice as an individual. You should be home with Dad. That's where you belong. You're wrong to be running across the world after me. It's my father you should be thinking of. It's my father you should be with.'

'Yes it is.' Her voice was cold, unnatural, and he raised his hands in a hopeless gesture.

'Then why the devil are you here?'

Caro brought her fingers to her throat and shifted her feet and moved away from him. For a moment she had wanted to blurt out the truth to him: tell him she wanted to be with his father, his *real* father, that that was another reason why she was here. But she held herself to her will, looked away and said nothing.

'See, you admit you should be with Dad and yet you're here with me. Mum, can't you see it's wrong? You're stifling me.'

She spoke without looking at him. 'How can I be stifling you? You're in the army, for heaven's sake. And as far as . . . your father's concerned, I've only had one letter from home, from your Aunt Jane. In it she said he was making arrangements with the Government to try to become an official war artist. She said that while he had not spoken about it to her, he had told Knobby that he may as well be over here too.'

Harry had thrown his hands in the air. 'Oh hell, that's just wonderful. Now we can all worry about each other.'

She faced round to him. 'Harry, I'll try to accept what you've done, all right? But please give me the same undertaking.'

He shook his head. 'That's just it, Mum. I don't understand you, and now you tell me Dad's coming over here. He's obviously followed you.'

'Yes I suppose so.' Then she had taken up his hand and looked keenly at him. 'Please, what's done is done. Now I'm here, I'm going to do my damnedest to help. I shall pray for your wellbeing every night, and if your father has decided to come over too, then we shall just have to take that as it comes.'

Harry was confronting many thoughts he had never had before. He stood looking at his mother and thinking that somehow he was seeing her for the first time. A question pushed itself forward into his consciousness and he asked it. 'Do you love my father? Tell me the truth.'

The pink flush on his mother's neck rose to her cheeks and her eyes glazed over and seemed to look through him. 'Yes, I do. I have always loved your father.'

The frustration sounded in Harry's reply. 'Then why the hell are you here? Why aren't you in Australia with him?'

She blinked and lifted her hand to her eyes. 'Please, Harry, in God's name, can't we just be civil? We only have a few hours to spend together. Let's at least be polite and take some comfort in one another.'

Harry sighed, pursed his lips and nodded. 'Yes all right.'

They had gone into the city and visited the Château Borely which housed the museum and then sat in a café in the shadow of Fort St-Jean, drinking coffee and overlooked by the pilgrimage church of Notre-Dame de la Garde way up on the hill with its huge image of the virgin venerated by sailors and fishermen. They had wandered through the busy port, pushing through the throng and rubbing shoulders with troops and sailors. By this time Harry had regained some of his humour and to her delight had bought his mother a bar of lavender soap made in the town.

When the time came for Harry to return to the barracks Caro had written the address of the hospital on a slip of paper. 'Write to me, son, and I must say, Harry, while I can never be happy about your being here . . . at the war, I suppose as I said before, I must accept what is.'

He managed a smile for her and kissed her cheek. 'And I can never be happy about your being here either, but now you know my battalion, Mum, so write to me too.'

They had parted amicably enough.

It was some sort of solace to Harry that these days when he thought of his mother he no longer saw the distraught face on the day he had left her at Cedar Grove. Instead he remembered the small smile she had bestowed upon him on the outskirts of Marseilles in the tender breeze of the summer evening.

The memory of the meeting in Marseilles left his mind as he stopped work and Dave arrived back, grinning from ear to ear. He slid down to sit, feet planted in the shallow trench.

'What's up?' Harry asked.

Dave winked, motioning over his shoulder with his thumb. 'That marquee I went into, well, it's the officers' mess. There's not a soul in sight and at one end there's a table with some bottles of Rhine wine on it. There're a lot of chits signed with initials in a bowl beside it. It seems the officers sign a chit and that entitles them to a glass of wine.' He raised his hand and mock signed in the air. 'So what do I do? I sign the same initials as the last one in the bowl and I take a healthy glass of wine.' His black eyes gleamed. 'It's pretty good. And it's deserted. Off you go.' He pushed his friend on the arm.

Harry looked dubious so Dave encouraged him. 'Go on, have a drink, there's no one about.'

Harry climbed out of the trench and sidled towards the marquee. Inside he saw a row of tables and chairs with utensils and cutlery upon them and on the end table, just as Dave had described, the open bottles of wine, two unopened bottles of whisky, some glasses and the chits. He took up a blank, copied some initials, dropped the chit in the bowl and poured a generous portion of wine into a glass and drank it. The warm feeling of the wine slipping down his throat made him smile with pleasure. Suddenly an idea had just struck him. He took a dozen chits and signed them all, then grabbed an open bottle of wine, pushed the cork back in, reached for an unopened whisky bottle and ducked out of the marquee and back over to his friend.

Dave rubbed his hands together with excitement. 'Gawd, you've brought wine and whisky!'

'Yes. I signed a dozen of the buggers and dropped them in the bowl.'

'Oh, you clever dick you.'

'Now I reckon if we park these bottles here somewhere safe we can come back for them tonight. What do you reckon?'

'I reckon you're a genius.'

'Gosh; thanks, I'm fond of you too, old son.'

'Give us a swig,' and Dave held out his hand for a bottle.

Harry hesitated. 'Ah . . . Reckon we should wait and continue this party after dark,' and he pushed the bottles under spoil from the trench. 'Reckon we could end up in the cooler if we're found drunk on duty.'

Dave saw the sense in this. 'Yeah, true enough. We'll find a proper hiding place and come back for the grog later.'

The sound of a shout made them start, speedily pick up their tools and make themselves busy.

The voice belonged to Lance Corporal Myles Cullen.

'Oh Gawd, it's the lance jack.'

The newcomer stood arms akimbo surveying them. He was a keen young man from Cooktown with five brothers serving in the army, and took his station seriously. 'The sergeant sent me to see how you two are doing.'

Dave grinned. 'Doing well, Corporal. We'll be finished on time. Tell the sergeant he doesn't need to worry about us.'

The lance corporal groaned. 'Oh yeah? Well, that's not what the sergeant thinks. You're supposed to have this done in another hour. Look smart about it.'

More voices were heard in the distance and Cullen swung round to look.

'It's getting positively lively around here now,' Dave said, eyeing the spot where the bottles lay hidden, 'and it's been so *perfectly*, quiet.' He winked at Harry.

The new voices came from a group of officers moving down between the tents towards the marquee. It appeared that they would pass within about twelve yards of the trench diggers. The officer in the lead they recognised as Captain Hardcastle of their own battalion, but the other three did not look familiar.

Lance Corporal Cullen's hazel eyes narrowed as he whistled. 'Hey those fellows behind Hardcastle came with the new colonel. Wonder where the old man is?'

Dave and Harry downed tools and stood up to look as along came the officers, talking to each other.

'See that tall thin bloke, he's the Ming whatsit who came with him . . . with the colonel. Bingo and I saw him this mornin'. Doesn't he look a sight? Look at those teeth!'

Indeed Twistleton Menzies Lang did have quite long front teeth and added to that the disadvantage of an excessively weak chin which all accentuated his eyes to the point that he looked like a rabbit. Within twenty-four hours of his arrival the men had dubbed him Rabbit Face.

'Ugly bugger, isn't he?' decided Lance Corporal Cullen.

'No doubt about it,' agreed Dave, sitting on the side of the trench.

Cullen determined they had rested long enough. 'Right! Get on with it, you two, or Bingo'll have you on a charge for malingering.'

The two returned to their work and an hour later the trenches were finished well enough for the cooks to use.

Mess-up was at nineteen hundred and by twenty-one hundred the sun had set. All was dark except for the restless horizon where the lights from the guns never ceased.

Luke and Frank, Isaac and Curly left for a card game being organised in the woods down to the south of the château and Dave lifted his kit and moved it inside his tent before returning into the light of the fire where he stood and winked at Harry. 'Reckon there are two bottles up yonder that need our attention.'

Harry grinned. 'Too right. Wonder where Bingo and Cullen are?'

'Not on our path, I hope.'

'Come on.'

'It's off-limits up there, you know.'

'I do, my dear.'

They both laughed with the danger of it as they walked down the dusty track. A chill wind blew at their backs and before long, expressing their bravado, they broke into softly whistling 'There's a long long trail awinding to the land of my dreams' as they passed the rows of tents. A sentry's back was towards them and they swiftly ducked across the broken-down wall to the line of duckboards. This led to the officers' area where they were out of bounds. Glancing right and left they moved across towards the cook tents now empty of their occupants.

Dave put his finger to his mouth and Harry pointed towards the tree trunk where that afternoon they had stashed their bottles. After Corporal Cullen had left the trench diggers the cooks had begun arriving to prepare the evening meals and the boys hurriedly hid the bottles as best they could. The nearest and safest hiding place had been in a hole in the fork of a single tree left standing between the cook tents and the officers' marquee.

This meant they now had to cross near the front of the officers' marquee where the shadows of those inside wavered back and forth on the canvas. Snippets of conversation floated to them on the night air. The lights were limited in the whole encampment for they did occasionally have German Fokkers overhead on clear nights.

A figure backlit by the glow inside moved into the opening of the tent flap. Side by side Harry and Dave froze in the shadows of the night. The officer stood holding a glass and appeared to look outside into the darkness. He continued standing there for a few seconds until someone spoke from inside and he turned back to the voice.

The two youths tiptoed across the grass in front of the marquee, remaining out of the light thrown from the opening. They realised there was another sentry on the far side of the great tent but they could not see him. They halted again as they came to the tree trunk where the bottles were. Harry, who was the taller, reached into the opening.

'They're here,' he whispered as he extricated them and handed them one at a time to Dave. They turned to sneak back, aware of the officers' laughter and chatter just beyond the canvas.

Harry was a yard or so ahead of Dave, and in his haste to depart the scene his boot caught under the rope of a tent peg. A sound of surprise broke from his lips as he pitched forward and threw his arms out, trying to save himself. It was useless; he sprawled forward on to the ground and into the strip of light at the opening of the marquee.

'Well, what the devil do we have here?' a voice asked, stepping out of the marquee to tower over the prostrate soldier.

Dave, in the darkness behind, just had time to throw the two bottles as far away as he could on to the softness of the grass beyond before two more officers appeared, both carrying lanterns.

Harry lay looking up into the face of the captain whom Lance Corporal Cullen that very afternoon had described as an ugly bugger and they had dubbed Rabbit Face. From this angle the description remained apt. The ugly bugger now stepped over him and shouted, 'There're more of you, I know. Come on, show yourselves.'

Dave edged forward, his eyes gleaming in the light. 'I'm the only other.'

'Good heavens,' exclaimed Twistleton Menzies Lang, looking into Dave's face, 'I didn't know we had any black fellows in the battalion.'

Dave opened his mouth to reply but Harry, who was now regaining his feet, silenced him with a shake of his head.

'What are your names?' the ugly bugger pointed at Dave.

'Sands, Dave Sands.'

'Sir!' he shouted.

'Sands, sir,' Dave replied.

'And you?'

'Harry Craken . . . sir.'

'So out with it,' the ugly bugger continued. 'What are you two doing here? You know you're out of bounds.'

'We were taking a short cut,' Dave answered.

The three officers now ranged around the two privates. 'Taking a short cut,' said one of the officers, holding a lantern. 'To bloody where, may I ask?'

Dave looked at Harry. 'To our tent,' answered Harry.

The ugly bugger gave a loud guffaw. 'A likely bloody story. After a night in the cooler you might be more prepared to tell the truth.' At that moment the tent flap was pulled back and another officer appeared. He came forward into the lantern light, speaking sharply. 'What the devil's going on out here?'

Dave actually felt Harry stiffen at his side.

'Blimey,' whispered Dave.

Then as one voice, both youths spoke together.

'The enemy!' Harry blurted out, his voice croaking with astonishment.

'Uncle John Conrad,' Dave said in amazement at his side.

At seventeen hundred that afternoon, as the sun came out from behind a dark cloud and the sky began to clear, John Conrad had arrived in Albert on the train from Paris; a slow journey taken in stages. He had alighted with Lieutenant Robert Dunmore, an efficient twenty-five-year-old Scot from Edinburgh; Captain

Renald Twistleton Menzies Lang, had gone on ahead. The first thing John Conrad had asked the captain when he had met him in London was if he would not mind simply being called Lang as Twistleton Menzies Lang was pretty unwieldy.

The captain had consented: 'Well, er, certainly, if that's what you wish, sir.'

'I do.'

'Then of course. But it's tradition,' he went on proudly. 'I'm the fifteenth eldest son to have been christened this way since 1552.'

'Oh dear,' John Conrad responded, and the captain had blinked with astonishment. He was a bespectacled thin-faced man of about thirty who so far had not impressed John Conrad. He could not help it after all the years with K; he kept judging men by what he believed K would have thought.

When John Conrad had arrived at Château Sigard and the battalion tent encampment his batman had taken his boxes and they had hurried him down to the officers' mess, a large marquee set on a stretch of grass amongst neat rows of smaller tents.

There he had met the other battalion officers with whom he would work closely: Major Roberts, his second in command and Captains Hardcastle and Bader, Lieutenants Dearwood, Palmer and Kenny. He looked around them.

Captain Tom Hardcastle smiled as he moved over to the drinks table. He was a Sydney boy. Born in Parramatta, he had joined the New South Wales volunteers in the very first week of the war. With his university education he was immediately given a commission and he had reached captain in the previous winter. He was only twenty-eight but there were strands of grey hair at his temples and he had deep creases in his forehead and round his lively blue eyes. He had been with General Birdwood in the Dardanelles and his younger brother had been killed at Mudros.

'Like a drink, Colonel?' he asked.

John Conrad shook his head. 'Too early for me, Hardcastle. But go ahead if you'd like.'

Tom Hardcastle took the colonel at his word and signed a chit then looked round for a bottle of wine. On the table where there had been three at the end of lunch; there were now only two and the bottle of whisky had disappeared entirely. He eyed the chits in the bowl. There were a lot of signatures for this early evening hour. He knew all his brother officers and most waited until nightfall to drink. He wondered who had been less than abstemious today.

John Conrad sat down and put his briefcase on the table. Raising his eyes he nodded for the others to sit. He had not missed the swiftly taken large measure of wine Hardcastle had poured himself, though he had liked Tommy Hardcastle on sight. There was something open and frank about him, giving the onlooker a feeling he was incapable of hiding anything. He could hear K saying, 'Like that boy's smile, I really do.'

The others had abstained from a drink and they now spread round the table. The lieutenants whom he had only just met were virtually boys, about twenty-one or so.

Tomorrow he would address all ranks at a parade set for 0700. The following day they would move closer to the war zone, up to battalion reserve headquarters about a mile from the front and later in the week they would take over the myriad of trenches which zigzagged towards no-man's-land and the Germans. They were one of thirteen batallions of Australian, New Zealand, Irish and British troops in a mixed division, their particular brigade being under the command of the British Brigadier Claver-Jensen. They were to relieve a Canadian division going on to Flanders.

John Conrad was used to meetings and detail and he continued assessing all his staff as he spoke. 'Gentlemen, I met with Lieutenant General Birdwood and Major General John Russell, the New Zealand commander, on my way here. They have been in discussion with General Haig and we go on to reserve headquarters on Friday and a day or so later we relieve the Canadians in the forward trenches. Because of the bad weather a final offensive for the year has been postponed a number of times but Haig's keen on it still. So, we'll be in it along with seven divisions of the Reserve army, the New Fifth as it's called. We'll be working closely with Colonel Cohen and Lieutenant Colonel Freyberg commanding the *Hood* Battalion of the Royal Naval Division. The aim is to take the German strongholds around the villages of Beaucourt, St Pierre Divion and Beaufort Hamel, and remove the salient. That's our objective.'

'We thought as much,' Roberts said.

'I don't need to tell you all that the armies here in the Somme are exhausted from these many months of battle. We now have some French reinforcements but many of them are battle-weary troops from Verdun. Since July one, we've advanced only mere miles. Thiepval, which we finally took at the end of September, was a *July one* objective! Ours is an untried battalion except for many of you officers and some platoons, which have survived Anzac.' He glanced around them. 'We'll have a staff meeting at o six hundred tomorrow.'

'There's a parade of the entire battalion at o seven hundred, sir. That's if it's not raining again.'

'Right.'

'Dinner has been set here for twenty hundred, if that suits you, sir?' asked Hardcastle.

'That suits me.'

With that John Conrad left his officers and retired to his own tent which lay by a small stream on the north side of the château. He stood for a moment looking at the water, listening to a frog croaking somewhere in the bank below his feet. He shivered. There was a cool wind blowing and he turned and entered his tent where he found his batman had unpacked and laid out a new uniform for him. He lay on his bunk under his blanket and, putting his hands up behind his head, closed his eyes and thought of K. He tried to imagine what K would do in his situation, about the coming advance on the Germans. He had heard of a colonel who led his men over the top in the second battle of Ypres. Should he do that? He fancied K would probably say no, that he had a responsibility to the battalion to remain alive. Well, that was true but he had been contemplating this for weeks.

An hour later he awoke. He looked at his small travelling clock. There were only twenty minutes before he was to rejoin his officers in the marquee. He was annoyed with himself for falling asleep. He had wanted to do some paperwork. Rising quickly he bathed and, putting on the clean uniform, hastened back to the grass sward at the front of the marquee. He entered through the open tent flap right on 2000 hours.

Dinner was remarkably good considering much of it was from cans and they finished with apple pie, freshly made that day from French apples. The port was being passed around when John Conrad rose, the others around him rising in unison. 'I would like to do some paperwork tonight, gentlemen,' he said looking round their faces. 'Please remain, but I shall retire.'

Tommy Hardcastle smiled and raised his glass to John Conrad. Suddenly there was a loud noise from outside and a body fell into view across the tent opening. Captain Lang, who was nearest, turned and strode out immediately to see what was going on. Hardcastle put down his glass and followed along with Lieutenant Peterson from D Company. Both picked up lanterns on their way.

John Conrad saluted to the remaining officers and, taking up the papers at his side, strode down to the exit. As he passed through the opening in the tent Captain Lang gave a loud grating laugh and John Conrad stepped out into the night asking, 'What the devil's going on here?'

There were two privates rigid in the midst of the officers and all the soldiers turned towards their commanding officer. It was then one of the privates exclaimed, 'Uncle John Conrad'. And the other said, 'The enemy'.

John Conrad immediately recognised Dave Sands, and his gaze moved to the other private soldier, registering the fair hair and the blue eyes and the strong round chin; the youthful face full of astonishment and exuding hatred: Matthew Craken's son!

His officers stood waiting, not understanding. Hardcastle gathered himself first. 'Do you know these soldiers, sir?'

John Conrad did not answer the question. 'Captain Hardcastle, take these soldiers to the detention room in the château.'

Twistleton Menzies Lang offered his opinion. 'This area is out of bounds to all but officers, sir. They're putting across a cock and bull story about a short cut.'

'All right, Captain. I'll take it from here.' John Conrad gestured for Lang to retire as he glanced to Tommy Hardcastle. 'I'll meet you in the château.'

Hardcastle took up the order. He arched his thumb. 'Right, you two, follow me.' And he marched Dave and Harry away.

Lang stepped forward to John Conrad. 'This is hardly a matter for you to bother about sir, I'll handle it if you like.'

'You may be right, Captain. Nevertheless I shall finish it.'

By the time John Conrad came to the small room where the two youths were held he had considered many things. Tommy Hardcastle waited outside. The young man pointed to where a guard stood before a closed door. 'They're inside, sir.'

'Thank you, Hardcastle.'

The captain turned and began to walk away. John Conrad halted him. 'Hardcastle, a minute please.' He felt he could trust the captain. He really felt K would have approved of him.

'Yes, sir?'

'These two boys are from the place I was born. Sands is the nephew of the dearest friend of my youth, dead these many years. He regards me as an uncle. The other youth, Craken, oddly enough as fate would have it, is the son of my worst enemy. I had no idea either of them had joined up.'

Tommy Hardcastle's lined forehead creased in ever more furrows of thought. 'Is there anything you would like me to do to help, sir?'

'No. I just wanted you to understand the situation.'

'Thank you, sir.' Hardcastle saluted smartly. 'Shall I wait here for you, sir?'

John Conrad nodded, turned away and passed by the guard, who opened the door for him as the two boys inside jumped to their feet.

John Conrad addressed Dave first. 'I didn't know you had volunteered, Dave. What does your mother have to say?'

'She's not too happy.'

John Conrad nodded gravely. 'I see. Then why didn't you write and let me know you were thinking of joining up?'

Dave looked down to the floor. 'Well, sir,' he answered without lifting his eyes, 'I did write to you some weeks ago from Marseilles to let you know what I'd done.'

'Mmm, well, I haven't received it.' Then he brought his eyes to Caro's son. 'And you, what about your mother? How did she feel about your joining up?'

Harry had no wish to converse with 'the enemy' but he had no alternative, the enemy being the ultimate authority. 'Er . . . I joined up without telling her.'

John Conrad fell silent for some seconds. He walked to the window and looked out into the night sky, his fingers interlocked tightly behind his back. For a fleeting moment he saw himself at twenty, sent away against his wish to join a life he had no conception about; just as these two boys had no conception of what life held. Yes, they were not much more than mere children. He spoke without turning around. 'You're both in the Australian Imperial Forces now, mothers or not. This is the army, not a holiday camp.' He faced round to his listeners, looking from one to the other and meeting their eyes. 'Soldiers are dying at the rate of *five every minute* just a few miles from where we stand. Think about that and endeavour to understand it. You're both here, much to my surprise, but it's here you'll have to stay.'

He paused for the boys to take in what he had just said. 'I don't know what you were doing in the officers' area and I don't care, but there are rules for all of us . . . rules to protect us, to organise us and to be obeyed. If ever either of you is brought to my notice again, you'll wish you'd remained in Brisbane and never volunteered.' There was no mistaking the expression in his eye and perhaps both youths fully realised for the first time the seriousness of where they were, and the lowly position they held in this man's army.

'Write to your mothers. Consider how they must be feeling. Attempt to put yourselves in their places.' He raised his hand to Harry; the boy's face was still full of youthful belligerence. 'You wait outside, soldier,' he said. Then he turned to Dave. 'You remain.'

When Harry had hurriedly saluted and departed John Conrad gave the hint of a smile. 'So tell me, what were you doing outside the officers' marquee?'

Dave observed John Conrad. This man had been his hero all his short life. He was actually part of the reason Dave had joined up. He had not ever thought to be anywhere near him, let alone serve under him. While Dave was so proud of that he was abashed to think the first meeting between them had to be this way. He thought for a moment to lie, then he remembered the two bottles of alcohol he had ditched on the grass. In the morning they would be found and then there'd be hell to pay. 'Well, Uncle, it's like this—'

John Conrad interrupted. 'Son, you can certainly call me *Uncle* when we're alone, but understand this cannot be when there are others present.'

'Yes, sir, sorry.'

'Go on.'

And so Dave told the whole story. The only differing from the truth was that he did not say that Harry had taken the two bottles; he made out they had decided to do that together.

When he had completed his tale John Conrad pursed his lips in thought before he spoke. Dave waited, very aware of his heart beating. 'I'm real sorry,' he said, and he was. While there was part of him that was pleased he had challenged the authority of the army, now he realised that the army was represented by his uncle and he began to feel ashamed.

'Dave, this is the sort of offence that can have grave consequences. Pranks of this kind aren't permissible in the army. Nevertheless I shall view this tolerantly, but be warned that in future others might not. You and your friend should avoid all further run-ins with authority. Do you understand me?'

'Yes, sir.'

This time we'll forget all about this. You can go now, and take your friend with you. But, Dave?'

'Yes, sir?'

'Don't mention this to anyone and be careful, son. I might not be there the next time you run into trouble.'

As Dave moved to the door he saluted smartly, before hurrying from the room to signal to the waiting Harry that they could leave and pass out into the chilly black French night.

When John Conrad left the detention room, the guard saluted and he found Tommy Hardcastle still waiting for him, standing against the far wall near a faded window seat. He motioned for Hardcastle to fall in beside him and as they walked over the wooden floors of the long hall of the château, their footfalls echoing around them, the ancient floor boards squeaking, he spoke. 'Hardcastle, back near the officers' marquee on the sward of grass in the darkness you'll find two bottles of alcohol. I'd like you to go now and return them to the table inside the tent. As you'll have guessed I let both privates off with a caution.' He looked sideways to the captain. 'It wasn't greed or malevolence that motivated them. They're high-spirited boys, not serious offenders.'

'I agree, sir, still children in many ways, should be in school not in the army.'

'I like to think the troops have a degree of liberty in their lives here for there'll be little where we're going. Though we have a duty to make soldiers of them all, Hardcastle. So don't go lightly on those two in future.' He shook his head sadly. 'We must push them and make men of them before their time.' On the steps of the château they halted. The cold air crept in above John Conrad's collar as he gazed up at the milky moon. 'I'd prefer you didn't discuss this with anyone, Hardcastle.'

'Understood, sir.'

Tommy Hardcastle left the colonel standing in the hazy night light and as he walked away he smiled to himself. He felt gratified that the colonel trusted him. Sands and Craken were indeed just mischievous boys . . . out for some fun. He had seen many like them before. It had intrigued him to see how the colonel had handled it. Before he had arrived everyone in the battalion had been so agog to see what Kitchener's right hand was like in the flesh and tonight had proved one thing and that was that *the old man* had a heart. That pleased Tommy; he had seen too many commanding officers without one. He was sure that young Craken was no favourite and the colonel had treated him exactly the same way as Sands. He was certain he had heard the boy call the colonel, *the enemy*, and the colonel had admittted there was bad blood between Craken's father and himself.

He nodded to himself as he passed through the rows of tents. If old Twistleton Menzies Lang had had his way the two youths would be in the cooler by now.

A few minutes later he took a lantern from the mess tent, and discovered the two bottles in the darkness on the edge of the grass as the colonel had described. Re-entering the marquee he moved across and returned them to the right table.

'Where'd you get those?' Lieutenant Dearwood asked, lifting his cigar to his mouth and puffing vigorously upon it.

'Found them, Dearwood. Now would you like a glass of whisky?'

'Certainly would, old chap.'

'Me too,' chirped up Captain Bader, and this elicited the steward to step smartly forward to pour for them.

570

'And a large one for me, Bentley,' Tommy Hardcastle said, easing his body down into a wicker chair. 'It's been an interesting night,' he added as he mused on the curiosity that had Sands regarding the colonel as an uncle.

Roberts leaned across and met Hardcastle's eyes. 'What did the colonel end up doing about the two interlopers?'

'Cautioned them.'

'Not soft, is he?' asked Twistleton Menzies Lang.

Hardcastle shook his head as he replied. 'No, not at all, I'd say. Rather he's fair, Lang, old boy, simply bloody fair.'

In the commanding officer's tent the commanding officer sat upon his bed in the lamplight. He loosened his tie and ran his fingers over his brow in concentration as he half-listened to the sound of the water and the continuing croaking of the frog outside. Far off in the distance he could hear the faded boom of a field gun, reminding him they would soon be in the line. He was slightly disconcerted to have found Dave in his battalion, and a little more than disconcerted to realise that Harry Craken was here too.

He felt responsible for Dave, but knew in his heart he could not be. Dave would have turned eighteen in February, and had the right to enlist. He felt sorry for Lena, but then he felt sorry for all the mothers of these boys. The presence of Harry Craken disturbed him. He knew the youth could not be eighteen yet and had obviously put his age up to join.

The boy's face had been full of hate, full of anger and surprise.

He closed his eyes and out of the deepest cavities of his mind lurched the memory of the night after Caro had tied herself to Craken, under the trees in her garden, in the cold neutral moonlight . . . all those years ago but it was still here living in his head . . . 'Tell me, is it mine? For Christ sake.' And he had pulled her face to within a finger's width of his own and heard her answer shouted into his face. 'It's not yours. It's his! It's his!'

He lay down and put his hands up behind his head. He had not thought of all this in many years. And now the boy, Caro's boy, was here in France. He moved his head on his pillow. If only he had K's good sense to guide him. God, he missed K.

He closed his eyes. It all seemed so futile . . . K was gone . . . and all he had ever received from Caro was the denial. He must remain in the belief that she had told him the truth; that the boy was not his and was indeed Craken's. Anything else would drive him mad. He saw again the hate on the boy's face. Seventeen years with Craken would have begun to rot even the cleanest soul. Poor old Caro.

He opened his eyes in sharp revelation! It was the first time he had ever felt sorry for Caro. Always before he had felt uncertainty, anger and distrust. He shook his head as if to remove the emotion. He never was comfortable thinking of her, and yet the strain of a recollection amplified itself in his mind and he remembered her face – the nineteen-year-old face – full of love and admiration, looking up at him . . . giving herself to him.

The picture of her ebbed and flowed and, as he sank into sleep, in the moment before his conscious mind seeped into the unaware, she became someone else . . . a girl with vibrant red hair flowing around her slender shoulders, and the two of them glided along into his dreams.

Chapter Thirty-five

England: early November 1916

Matthew stepped gingerly down from the train and, carrying a small case in one hand and leaning on his polished ebony cane with brass handle in the other, limped along the platform. His bad leg was stiff and the chill day exacerbated the dull ache he experienced from hip to knee. He had spent the previous night with Tom Roberts, Arthur Streeton and Albert Fullwood, all Australian painters living in London and working at a military hospital in Wandsworth. It had been an agreeable night and they had toasted his honorary commission as major with the AIF, which allowed Matt to travel on the Western Front as an official war artist. He was the first such creation by the AIF and was a sort of experiment. The British had begun their scheme a few months earlier and Matt had actually been assigned by the BEF but to an Australian battalion.

'Wouldn't mind doing that myself,' Streeton had said, looking over his handlebar moustache.

'You're too old,' Matt replied, swallowing a rum.

Streeton had looked peeved. 'What do you mean? You can give me a few years, old boy!'

'Nevertheless you're too old,' Matt had declared to the enjoyment of the others. It would be two more years before Streeton would, in fact become a war artist.

The one thing that Matt found the most disagreeable about being an honorary officer was having to wear the Australian army uniform. Dull serge army issue, officer uniform or not, did not appeal. The single item he did not mind was the cap, and he wore that slightly on an angle which he felt gave him a modicum of style

Matthew paused for a few moments to stand looking at the

573

great rustic wooden clock that hung on beams above in the golden light of afternoon, and the people toing and froing beneath it, their heads illuminated in the same glow that bathed the clock. He took his sketchbook from his inside pocket and, resting his cane, case and bad leg on one of the long wooden seats, made a quick impression of the scene, writing 'golden glow' and 'pure radiance', 'orange-pink' and 'luminous' at various points upon it, so that when he came to paint it he would recall the effects of the sunshine.

A few minutes later he came out of the station and, heading past a wooden sign reading Castle Street he made his way along until he halted at the entrance to a small thoroughfare with a sign showing Wincheap Grove in tired gold letters upon it. He could see across a yard to an open field that looked as if it ran down to the river. He paused for a few moments, wondering if he should go towards the water, then he decided to continue on along Castle Street to find a tavern; he was in dire need of a drink.

In the distance across the roof tops he could make out the cathedral that dominated the small town of Canterbury. The train from London to Dover had halted here for two hours; something to do with attaching extra carriages. The rumour in his compartment had been that they were taking munitions down to Dover to cross the sea lane to France.

Matthew had been in England a few weeks. It had taken time to organise things in Australia and to catch a ship, but now that he was here he was anxious to get to France. He had spent time tracking the movements of his wife and son, and at least he knew which battalion Harry was serving with and he had a fair sense of where Caro was, having learned she was nursing with the VAD, Voluntary Aid Detachment, and had been sent to Montdidier, a small town of some 5,000 before the war, in Northern France.

He had spent time at the War Office and the Australian High Commission. Once in France he was to report to the Headquarters of the AIF where he would be given a driver who would take him to his assigned battalion.

In London, through Tom Roberts, he had met Alfred Leete, a patriotic poster artist who had drawn the famous recruitment picture of Kitchener declaring that he WANTS YOU. Matthew had ambivalent feelings about the late Lord Kitchener; mostly it was the man's judgement that he held suspect. Choosing the bastard as his closest aide was not something Matthew could accept as discerning. Nevertheless it had been of interest to meet Leete who was full of praise for his lordship and had been for a short period out in the Ypres salient.

He had told Matthew some horror stories about the lines of gassed and dying men after battles . . . men decapitated and maimed in the raw landscape where all was dead, not a blade of grass living, and the stench of the dead bodies which pervaded the air. Matthew had listened silently and drunk another rum. He was not afraid to see and experience such things; he had passed through five decades and more upon this earth without ever perceiving war first-hand, and he had now convinced himself it was time for him to know, time for the artist to comprehend such things. His regret was for Harry, that his son in all his innocence, should be heading into such a chasm.

He continued along looking right and left for a tavern. He missed Knobby badly; how he wished he had Knobby's strength at his side to draw upon. He had first realised his reliance on Knob years and years ago, when he had come to accept that Caro would never love him, never truly need or want him. It was then he had been comforted by Knob's presence, Knob's unconditional giving. Never once had Knob judged him in all their years of friendship. Not that Knob was a substitute for Caro, but he had helped him face up to living with the ghost of the enemy always lying between him and his wife. Knob had taught him, without ever saying a word, that an honest platonic friendship was perhaps one of the most worthwhile things on this disconcerting world.

As he moved by, he drew second looks from shopkeepers standing in the open doors of the small neat shops with their carved detailed fronts. When he came upon a small square with a great yew in its centre and cut by a diagonal walk, he paused briefly to look around and get a sense of the place. Coming in on the train he had guessed it must be a town of about twenty-five thousand, for it felt to him about the size of Ipswich – Ipswich Queensland, that was, half a world away and abundant with wooden houses and dirt streets so unlike this pretty town of brick and stone and paved thoroughfares. Yet he longed for the other . . . to be passing through on the train to Gatton and then out to Cedar Grove, knowing the members of his family were in place and Knobby waited at the station for him.

Shaking the thoughts from his head he pressed on until he saw another sign: Beer Cart Lane. Now this had prospects and he turned left into it. Within twenty yards a smile crossed his mouth as he spied a small inn, and passing round a dray and horse, he pushed on the door but it did not move. The driver of the dray called down to enlighten him, 'Closed. They all be closed until seven this evenin'.'

'Where can I get a drink?'

The driver screwed up in thought his already much lined face. 'Well, now, let me think. Closest place would be the Red Cross Tea Shop. Straight down Stour Street, turn right into High Street Parade. It becomes St Peter's Street ye see but before it does ye'll see the aforementioned tea shop: great red cross in the window, denoting the place.' He pointed with his whip. 'Turn right down ahead. But tea or juice is all ye'll be gettin' there, I'm afraid.'

Matthew's mouth twisted in distaste. *Tea . . . Fruit juice . . .* But he supposed liquid of any sort would have to do. 'As long as they don't offer me bloody water,' he said to himself as he moved down the lane.

Some short time later sure enough he saw the red cross in the window and, passing inside the building, found himself in a hall. Coats and hats hung along a series of hooks and, looking round, he discerned three doors: 'Office', 'Tea Shoppe' and 'Stores' in raised lettering upon them. He pushed open the Tea Shoppe door and was greeted by a large woman with three chins, in a white apron with a small red cross on it. 'Afternoon tea, love?' she asked. 'We close soon you know, but there're some things left.'

'Just a drink,' Matt replied.

'Of course, sit at any free table, love.' She eyed his cane and his uniform. 'Haven't seen you around here before. From away, are you?'

'Yes.'

'Oh, and where's that love?'

'A long way off.'

But she was not to be stopped. 'Oh yes, indeed. I guessed

that by your uniform, not from around here, is it? In Canterbury for long?'

Matt gave her a supercilious look. 'I'm in your fair city for as long as it takes to add a couple of carriages to my train.'

'Oh, is that right? Came in on the London train then, did you?'

This was far too much cheerful conversation for Matt. He pushed past the white apron to an empty table covered by a flowered tablecloth.

There were three of the ten or so tables taken and when he had seated himself he took out his sketchbook and made another quick impression. Everything on this journey from Australia to England had been intriguing and his artist's eye had been captured now by an old man at a corner table with the dying afternoon light slanting through the window upon his emerald-green cloth cap. On the wall beside him a large poster stated, 'When you help the Red Cross you help our boys in the trenches'. He put his pencil aside and watched the fat lady drying cups and saucers and beginning another of her inane conversations with a bearded gentleman who had just entered.

The door behind the fat lady opened and he gave a momentary start. Just for a second he had thought he saw Caro; but he swiftly realised the woman was really quite different: she had brilliant red hair and was younger than Caro. It had simply been her similar shape and size that had briefly fooled him. As he watched her, the young woman, as if bidden, walked over to him. She wore the same type of apron as the fat lady and as she paused in front of him clasping her hands he noticed the smooth luminosity of them and the pink ovals of her nails. Her hair was simply wonderful, a bright sienna colour; reminding him of the glowing hair of Titian's women. She was not beautiful in the usual sense of the word but gained his attention with the sum of her qualities: the Titian hair and contrasting pale smooth skin and her uncommonly large eyes framed by dark long lashes.

Her accent was unusual. 'Good afternoon. We have tea or orange juice. Lucky to have the oranges at all really, and there are a few scones or biscuits if you like.'

He decided to be amiable. The girl appealed to him, might even make a good subject for him. 'Your accent, it's hard to place,' he said, leaning back in his chair. 'Not English, are you?'

She eyed him speculatively for a moment as if deciding in these times of war whether she ought to enlighten him or not. 'I grew up in India, and I've lived elsewhere too.'

'Oh where?' He gave one of his crooked smiles. She had never seen anyone quite like him before. Matthew had never looked his age and having lost none of his attractive qualities, the scar still enhanced his looks to the point of fascination.

She answered, 'Australia, where I'm guessing, by your uniform, you come from, Major. I was there for a few years as a small child and then again for a couple of years back before the war.'

He examined her as he sat up straight.

'Why, what part are you from?'

For some unaccountable reason he decided not to tell her the truth. 'Adelaide.'

It perplexed him that she seemed relieved. She gave a small smile. 'But for the uniform I would have thought you were English.'

He lifted his forefinger towards her. 'Look, I hope you take this as it's meant, which is genuine and sincere. I'm an artist, actually off to the war as it turns out, on behalf of the Australian Government. I'm only here while the train takes on extra carriages. I'd like to sketch you,' he winked at her, 'for a painting I'll do later. You could sit for me? I believe the shop closes soon.'

He could see she was disconcerted and he spoke again. 'Understand that I don't mean to intrude, but you must know your hair gives you a most . . . rare presence. If you would sit down after the shop closes it would only take me a few minutes of concentration to attempt to . . . capture you.'

Confusion and indecision followed each other across her face, though he suspected she was flattered at the same time.

A veil of formality came down as she replied, 'I'm not sure. There's a war on, after all. Let me think about it. Anyway, what do you want?'

He winked again. 'You don't have a bottle of medicinal gin out the back, do you?'

'Of course not.' She pretended to be shocked. 'Now please, are you ordering or not?'

'I am, though it's hard for me to form the words. I'll have an *orange juice*, that's all.'

She moved away and he watched her, leaning back once more in his chair, following her footsteps across the wooden floor, a fanciful expression in his eyes. His fingers rapped a medley on the table top as he decided he actually could make something special of a painting of this woman. There was an unusual quality about her and her flaming hair was the mark of her definitive beauty.

When Emma Louise came back Matt gave a practised charming smile as she placed the orange juice down on the tablecloth. 'I'm paying you a most unparalled compliment, you know?'

She looked him squarely in the eyes. 'It's just that I'm not sure. I . . .'

'It'll be just about twenty minutes or so. Now don't be difficult. Why are women always difficult? I know there's a war on, and you're right being careful.' He pointed to his sketchbook and pencil on the table. 'Now you'll go down in the annals of painting history, you lucky girl. So don't refuse.'

She could not help but be intrigued by this strange man and she succumbed. 'Well, all right, but only twenty minutes. Where will you do it?'

'Anywhere. Here if you like.'

Her eyes widened. 'Oh no, Mrs Greaterex wouldn't approve.'

He pointed to the door through which her companion had disappeared. 'Do you mean the fat lady?'

She suppressed a laugh. 'Yes.'

'I passed a square on the way here. There were trees and a seat under a great yew. We could go there.'

She wavered for a few seconds. 'Yes . . . I suppose that's all right.'

He smiled widely. 'Of course it is. Out in the open, nothing to hide. Even the strictest matron in Canterbury couldn't object to that. Even Mrs *Greater than X* would *almost* approve.'

Emma Louise smiled, and fifteen minutes later she and Matt walked out the door of the Red Cross Rooms together watched through the side window by Mrs Greaterex, whose fat neck wobbled as she shook her head in disapproval.

As they passed along side by side, the golden glow of an hour before had disappeared but there was a muted colour in the air and the brick of the buildings radiated with the soothing light of closing evening. It was cool and the scarf round Emma Louise's neck lifted and strayed out behind her. If Matt had thought about it he would have agreed that she did look charming in her short mustard-coloured jacket with embroidery running from neck to waist and a mustard and brown checked pleated skirt.

'So where did you live in Australia?' he asked.

'I lived in Queensland,' she answered.

He turned his head towards her. 'Whereabouts?'

'Most of the time in a little seaside place called Southport.'

Some sense was prickling at the back of Matt's mind. He did not know what but he felt a certain significance in this chance meeting with this girl.

'How did you hurt your leg?' she abruptly enquired.

And again he lied. 'Fell off a horse.'

'I'm sorry,' she said.

'Don't be. Those of us that have to, learn to live with that which is imperfect.'

She looked sideways at him. He certainly was a most unusual man and the cane gave him a true sort of elegance. 'I . . . I don't think you're imperfect,' she replied.

He halted, and she did the same. His languid eyes burned with an odd light as he surveyed her. 'That was a most cordial observation. Thank you.'

She wanted to ask if he received the scar at the same time, but she did not. Instead she met his eyes and smiled as they moved on. 'What time does your train leave?'

He looked at his fob watch. 'In forty minutes.'

As they came to the square a man in a bowler hat stood up from a bench and coming towards them, doffed his hat to Emma Louise. 'Good afternoon, Mrs Fleet,' he said, eyeing Matthew closely as he passed by.

'Good afternoon, Mr Linfort,' she responded. She was loooking at the gentleman so she did not see the expression alter on Matt's face. The name Fleet had brought a look of some surprise followed by a side-long glance of intense interest. She was probably in her late twenties; said she had lived in Southport; it was only a tiny seaside outpost. Not too many people lived there. He cast his mind back to 1908 or 1909, when the enemy had been home: the night he and Knob had seen Caro come out of the Bellevue Hotel where the enemy had been celebrating his engagement to some girl who had lived in India and resided in *Southport*. Matt winced at the memory.

He had never laid eyes on the enemy's fiancée, had no idea what she looked like. He recalled something about a year later, some rumour that Knobby had heard and passed on to him. That the enemy's fiancée had up and married his younger brother. Now that had really assuaged him, given him a warm feeling of satisfaction. Serve the bastard right he had thought at the time. Now was this woman at his side that same wonderful girl who had thrown over the bastard? Her name was Fleet and she had lived in Queensland round the right time. Perhaps it was merely coincidence, but so much added up. And some sixth sense had kept him from telling her the truth about himself. If this were the right girl she would know about him; somewhere along the line anyone engaged to bloody Fleet had to have heard of the bad blood between him and Matthew Craken.

He smiled to himself. Now fancy if this really turned out to be the bastard's old fiancée. How very diverting.

'You haven't told me your name,' she said as he halted and gestured for her to sit under the yew tree.

He opened his case and took out his large sketchbook and charcoal pencil, and eased himself down upon the grass in front of her. 'Ah . . . Tom . . . Tom Roberts.' He smiled as he saw he had a red pencil in his case as well. He would use it for her hair. 'And yours?' he asked, looking up at her.

She was eyeing him, considering him. 'Emma Louise Fleet.'

It was her. He recalled the name now. Emma Louise Black . . . was it? It amazed him. He was as startled as it was possible for Matthew Craken to be, and yet he sat there looking at her with his sleepy gaze as if all she told him were merely polite talk.

A leaf dropped from the tree above and it sailed down on

to Emma Louise's hair. She felt it and put up her hand to brush it off.

'No!' Matt held up his hand. 'Don't. It looks . . . perfect there. Leave it.'

She withdrew her hand and placed it on her lap.

'But put your hand up towards your shoulder as if you just felt the leaf and were going to brush it away.'

'Like this?'

'Yes.'

She turned to look at a woman and children passing by.

'Don't move,' he commanded, then added quickly, 'if you'd be so kind.'

He drew in silence for a time and she observed him.

'I see you're married,' he said, motioning to her wedding ring.

This had the effect of making her bottom lip tremble.

'Have I asked a bad question?'

She sighed and her bosom rose and fell. 'My husband was killed a few months ago. He was in France.'

'I see.' Matthew had not considered this; it chilled him. The youngest of the Fleets dead! Would have been better if the eldest one were.

He was drawing her eyes as he spoke; her limpid soulful eyes, and he surprised himself as he asked a genuine question, 'Would you feel better if you talked about it?'

Emma Louise looked up and met the artist's eyes. 'I haven't been able to talk to anyone about it. In fact today is the first day I've come back to work in the tea shop. I used to do two days a week there for the Red Cross and go up to London every Thursday. I suppose I've needed the time to think, to analyse my feelings; to face the truth of what I feel and who I am. That's not easy, you know.'

Matthew nodded almost earnestly. 'You've got that right.'

'I have a little girl, just six. Seems wrong that May won't grow up knowing her daddy.'

She looked away and Matthew drew the line of her neck as he spoke quietly. 'I extend my sympathy. We're on a mad world. The maker has a decidedly warped view to have created such a planet. I'm left assuming it was the first one he formed as he bungled it so badly.'

And now there was a hard edge to her voice. 'Yes, perhaps you're right. For there's no rhyme or reason to much that goes on, though I have an aunt who would argue that everything is God's will. What sort of a God would allow this war? The way it's ruining thousands, perhaps millions of lives. I hate it and I hate the Germans.'

'Mmm, that's a common sentiment to most of us.' He knew the answer to his next question but still he asked. 'What was your husband's name?'

She looked back at him, 'David,' and shrugged her spare shoulders and shook her head so that her hair moved round her face. The piquancy of her mood was captivating him. He hurried on, attempting to catch it on his paper.

'He was one of three brothers.' She gave a swift sharp cool smile. 'Now this is a peculiar thing, Major Roberts . . .'

He caught her eye. 'You can call me . . . Tom.'

'You as an artist might enjoy the freakishness of this. I was engaged to his eldest brother, another soldier, only a real one, the true thing. He's a colonel now.'

Matthew said nothing and she went on, 'I became engaged to him in Australia in 1908. His name's John Conrad, but he left me alone in Queensland all of the following year. Well, he had to, he was in the army, wasn't he? While he was gone . . . I was attracted by David – by his charm, by his youthful vibrant manner. I admit now that I've always sought after attention, and while John Conrad was away from home David was very attentive. I . . . well, he was handsome, you know. They all are, the Fleets. And then I found I was having May, well that decided it. I married David.'

'Did you face the . . . other one? Tell him?'

Emma Louise nodded. 'He came home Christmas 1910.'

Matt nodded, he recalled it well.

'He has a violent temper . . .'

'Yes,' agreed Matthew, and Emma's head came up sharply, her expression questioning. 'Ah . . . I mean some men do,' Matt swiftly added.

'He took it badly. Actually went and found David, who was hundreds of miles from home, attacked him. Broke his nose, broke his arm . . .' Her voice trailed off.

Matthew was putting the shading under her chin and a

tremor ran through him. The bastard always liked breaking people's bones.

He felt the nagging ache in his leg as he made himself manage an encouraging smile and she disclosed more. 'You see I think David in some strange way looked up to him and when the war came he volunteered, to prove he was the man John Conrad was, that he too could be a soldier. It's all so very complicated, the whole damn business . . . and now he's dead.'

Matt did not speak.

'I was happy with David, yes, I was.' She sounded as if she were convincing herself. 'If he hadn't been killed I think I would still be happy with him. But since his death I have searched my soul. I think that's why I've taken his death so hard – sort of guilt as well as sorrow, I suppose, because inside myself I've finally admitted things.'

His hand moved swiftly over the paper. 'What sort of things?'

'Personal things.'

Matt lifted his eyes and met hers.

Emma Louise was in a mood for confession. She had not spoken to anyone about this. All these weeks she had kept silent. All these years, if the truth were known. The man in front of her was a stranger, off in a few minutes on the train. She would never see him again. 'Well . . . while I'm too guilty about David to ever do anything about it, I've recognised that I'm still attracted to his brother, that perhaps it's possible that I've never really stopped loving John Conrad . . .'

'Oh Jesus.' Matthew shook his head in disgust.

Emma Louise looked at him in amazement. 'Major Rob – Tom, what do you mean?'

He put down his pencil and book and drew his hand across his eyes.

Emma Louise was startled. 'Oh dear, I'm so sorry, berating you with all my soul secrets, but I felt I wanted to – needed to really. With you here, sitting drawing me, looking into my heart and all, I've just rattled on.' She looked searchingly at him. 'They say confession's good for the soul. But I've bored you, haven't I?'

He shook his head. He certainly had been anything but

bored in this most anomalous of situations. He was simply baffled to think that beautiful women seemed to line up to love unremittingly the bloody enemy. What in heaven's name was it about him? The classic bastard!

'Tom?'

Matt cleared his throat. 'No, you didn't bore me at all, definitely not . . . the reverse, and I'm finished.'

'Can I see?' Her big eyes widened in expectation.

He turned the book round for her inspection.

Her mouth opened, he could see the pink of her tongue. Her eyes were replete with surprise, confusion, pride . . . 'It's well . . . it's me.'

'Of course.'

'It's beautiful, she's wonderful, but her eyes, her mood . . . so damned sad. Am I that damned sad?' She sat back and swung the long scarf up over her shoulders.

Matt looked at his drawing. 'The way I see it, I'm afraid you are.'

'I was going to ask you if I could have it, but now I'm not so sure.'

He stood up and closed the sketchbook. 'I wouldn't have given it to you anyway.'

She rose to her feet beside him. 'That's not very gentlemanly, Tom.'

'I'm not a gentleman.'

She regarded him silently for a few seconds. 'I think you make out you're a lot of things, but I wonder if you really are any of them.'

He held up his hand, his expression infinitely pained. 'Please, please, no analysis . . . not after so brief an aquaintance.' Bending down he opened his case and put the drawing inside, then took a step away. 'I must be going. Train leaves in about six minutes, and as you can see I'm not a distance runner.' He impelled himself from her.

'Tom?' she called, and he rotated on his cane. They contemplated each other across the seven yards that separated them and she pulled her coat more tightly round her as the seconds passed. She nodded slowly, a canny expression on her serious face. 'What's your real name? Where are you really from? And what are you really doing here?'

He lifted his cane and pointed straight at her before he came slowly back to stand in front of her. 'Emma Louise, I suspected you were a cut above most women but now you've proved to me just how bright you really are.' He took a deep breath. 'I *am* really an artist and off to the war. I'm here purely by the coincidence of the train taking on more carriages for Dover. I've never seen you before in my life, and I asked to sketch you because, fact is, you intrigued me. Now all that's true. But you're right about my name, it's not Tom, it's Matthew and I'm not from Adelaide, I'm from Brisbane.' He took a step back and smiled. 'Thank you for making my brief sojourn here most stimulating. I actually do, in truth, wish you and your daughter well, but as it turns out that sentiment does not follow on to another in your ken.'

He took one more step away. 'Sometime I'll turn this sketch of you into a bloody good work. Perhaps I shall even paint a replica and send it to you care of the Red Cross here in Canterbury.' He gave her one of his elegant half-smiles. 'And just perhaps, I shall make it *not quite so sad*. I must leave now or otherwise I'll have to remain in Canterbury with you, and that doesn't fit into my plans and I reckon it wouldn't into yours.'

He turned and moved off on his ebony cane, his left foot planting firmly on the ground and his right skimming the surface in what over the years had distilled into the smooth movement that incongruously was his limp. Behind him Emma Louise stood in confusion, watching him go. His slender uniformed figure was soon round the corner and out of sight. Her brain was racing trying to assess all that he had said. She wanted to run after him and stop him . . . but she did not.

The train taking Matt on to Dover had blown its whistle, pulled out from the station and was passing through the green fields of Kent on its way south before Emma Louise left the old yew tree and walked away from the little green square. She was recalling things from her past: things she had heard; things John Conrad had said, in that short life with him back in those good years before the war.

By the time she bathed little May that night and tucked her into bed and stroked her fair curls and saw her slip into the contented sleep of childhood she had remembered the name of John Conrad's mortal enemy. She had remembered that he carried a scar on his cheek and walked with a cane from injuries sustained in a fight with John Conrad, that he was a painter and that he had married Caro Dere, John Conrad's first love.

She moved downstairs and across the flowered carpet to the parlour where Aunt Gertrude offered her a cup of tea, which she declined. 'I'm going to sit by the fire . . . think for a while.'

Aunt Gertrude tutted. 'You've been doing too much of that lately. Life goes on, Emma Louise.'

'I know, dear, I know. But leave me awhile.'

She sat looking into the fire as her aunt left the room. The fluid restless flames leaped and recoiled as she stared into them. She played with a letter on the wooden stand at her right hand. It had arrived only yesterday from Aunt Nevis in Southport, Queensland so far away. She thought of the little seaside outpost and the picnics they used to have, of the night of the wonderful party when she had been the Queen of the night and danced with her glamorous soldier. It was the next day on the beach that he had asked her to marry him. She knew he had always been Aunt Gertrude's choice and that her aunt had never been happy that she had married David instead. Her mind wandered across the six years with David. She pictured his face the afternoon he had told her he was going off to enlist. Should she have stopped him? She spoke quietly into the fire. 'I'm sorry, David.'

And then she leaned back into the soft cushions of the armchair and she saw John Conrad's face. She remained there with the vision of him before her until she came to a decision. She moved across to the writing desk, lit the gaslamp, took out paper, pen and ink and began a letter.

Dear John Conrad,
    You asked me to write and so I am. Wherever you are I hope it is not too dangerous. I think of you often. Little May is well and so are Aunt Gertrude and Uncle Hewitt.
    Today, a true oddity occurred. I met Matthew Craken. Let me tell you how it happened . . .

In the hotel lounge in Dover Matthew swallowed a rum and

took out the drawing of Emma Louise and looked at it. It was truly a startling likeness. He always had the ability to do that, to capture the essence of a person, just as he had with Caro and with Knobby and others, even with his mother who had been bloody hard to capture, having such a pinched birdlike visage. He knew he had the talent to put something else in their expressions, like this one with Emma Louise, this mood of frozen sorrow. His only real failure with portraits had been one he did years ago of Harry; but then children were so hard to depict . . . no lines, no experience in their faces.

He smiled at the drawing in his hands. Yes, it was really very bloody good. He reclined in the armchair and looked across at the rain hitting the window pane. He wondered what she had made of it all after he had gone. She was no fool, that girl; she would soon have worked out who he was. And tomorrow he was off across the channel.

He moved his bad leg to a more comfortable position as he waved to the waiter to bring him another rum. He had been told they could only sell him two as that was the hotel's ration per person now. He had shaken his head at that bad news for he would have elected to indulge this night. He was on his way to a war where he would really prefer not to be; he had a son who was fool enough to join the army and place himself in harm's way and a wife who did not love him. Caro . . . if only she had cared for him; how different he would have been to her. He thought of the first time he had ever seen her; yes, he admitted it, she had done something to his heart right there in that damn exhibition room in Fortitude Valley; what had been on display? Was it the motor car? What a life they would have had together . . . if only she had cared.

If he had not given up opium, tonight would be the time for a blast, but as he had given it up and it would be bloody hard to find here anyway, rum would have to do. He managed a semblance of his crooked smile as the waiter placed the second glass in front of him and taking a five-pound note from his pocket he slipped it unnoticed by others into the man's hand beneath his tray. 'Pretend I'm two customers, will you, cousin?'

The waiter winked and smiled broadly. 'I can see the two of you quite clearly, Major.'

Chapter Thirty-six

Harry sat on the firestep and looked along the trench to where Curly leant against sandbags and was balancing a tin of Pearl Plate Paste brass polish on his lap and attempting to clean his helmet while keeping his feet up out of the foot-deep water lying at the bottom of the trench; his box respirator gas mask, brand-new issue, lay at his side. Across from Curly, and beyond where Dave slept stretched along the firestep under some corrugated iron which gave shelter and ran from parapet to parados, a large rat followed by a smaller version squeezed between a box and a pole of the forward rampart and like tightrope walkers, almost daintily, avoided the water as they scrambled along the strip of drying mud to disappear beneath a sheet of metal.

Harry shook his head. The bloody rats were everywhere, and the lice the same; all sorts of vermin lived here in the ground with them. Some of the men shot the rats but the numbers never seemed to lessen. There were myriad extensions of trenches here which were joined to the front lines and support trenches by communication trenches zigzagging for a good mile or more from back to front, allowing troops to fade to the rear in relative safety. Within forty-eight hours of arrival the lice had found them and it was a constant battle against them, even in the gaining cold of early winter. Harry ran his bayonet down the side of his puttee in what had become, in the short weeks of trench life, an habitual movement to remove the lice. Apparently the pleated kilts the Scots and Irish wore were nothing but breeding grounds for such filth. He wrapped the scarf more tightly round his throat. It was almost freezing already. The only good thing about winter was it might kill the vermin. It had rained heavily on and off for weeks, leaving pools of water everywhere at the bottom of the trenches; the word was that just to the south, water was up to three feet deep and that the men were living in waders all the time. Thank God it was not that bad here.

The battle in the Somme Valley had been raging all around since July the first, more than four months. The talk was that they were to join in a final push for the year. Weeks before, when they had left Château Sigard and come ever closer to the lines, the noise of the bombardment had steadily grown along with the confusion of traffic behind the lines: engines and water carts and tractors pulling howitzers and buses of munitions, soldiers on bicycles carrying mail; companies of men resting in Nissen huts and the dead and wounded being carried to dressing stations in half-blasted-away buildings.

Close to the lines they had halted at an Australian Comforts Fund stall, a cement blockhouse surrounded by dried mud, and they had drunk coffee. The stall was manned by two privates, Gunn and Nield, who welcomed them to the Battle of the Somme. It was there they had watched lines of German prisoners filing back from the front. There too they had seen a contingent of Australian light horse ride up and the whole of the battalion had cheered like mad. Harry had glowed with pride just seeing those boys on their beautiful horses.

The light horse had dismounted and mingled with them and taken coffee from Gunn and Nield and stories had been spun and a mood of comradeship had fallen all around.

Harry had noticed Colonel Fleet talking to the major in charge of the light horse and Isaac told him later that he had overheard the colonel say that one of the things he had missed most over the years in the British army was seeing the slouch hat.

The heavy artillery boomed constantly and the noise became a surreal companion. The older soldiers said the bombadiers and gunners, even with the wax constantly in their ears, lost a majority of their hearing pretty fast.

Harry lifted the periscope at his side and stood to look through it over the trench top. Periscopes were prized. In the early days of the war there was only about one per hundred men; even now it was still only about three or four per hundred. A Lancashire fusilier who had been taken out with both his legs blown off had given his to Harry. He had looked up from his stretcher, his eyes strained in his white face and handed it to Harry who had been standing at the side of the muddy track where he was being repatriated. 'Take this, matey,' he had said.

'I won't be needing it again.' And then he had locked eyes with Harry and pointed feebly behind him. 'And get right with God before you go up there.'

Harry shivered in recollection. He admitted to himself that the front lines had shocked him, and at first some of the things he could see out in no-man's-land had given him the shakes. There were still bodies out there, half buried, that neither side could reach. Myles Cullen, the corporal with C Company had told them that when they were extending one of the forward trenches they had come across arms and legs in the earth of the new ramparts.

Harry turned his head from the periscope and sniffed the air. Amongst all the terrible smells, somebody was cooking something. Probably Frank Birtenshaw; it was amazing how Frank contrived to find extra food other than the rations, as if he conjured them up. Their official daily rations per man were: one pound of meat (often tinned bully beef), one and a quarter pounds of bread or biscuit, four ounces of bacon, three ounces of cheese, half a pound of fresh vegetables or two ounces dried, and some tea, sugar and jam, but Frank managed to find extra bacon and even pieces of ham and bottles of honey. It was magical. No one knew where he got his supplies and he was not telling. He was a regular little commissariat all on his own.

Harry looked through the periscope. He liked to see out over the top of the ridge that was now the perimeter of their lives. Even from this support trench he could make out no-man's-land in the distance, a pulverised, barren void, cleared of all living things and only barbed wire entanglements surviving. They said in the summer flowers still edged their way up out there, making the view weirdly pretty and supernatural but there were none at the moment, too much mud, and it was getting bloody cold. He looked through the periscope often every day. It appealed to him, and Captain Hardcastle, who knew the value of soldiers with periscopes, had told him to inform him if he noticed anything different in enemy territory. Hardcastle had said, 'The smallest change in a parapet or alteration to the ground works could be meaningful, so keep up the scrutiny with your good young eyes, Craken.'

Harry had noticed that a small section of brick wall about eighteen inches high had somehow survived quite well forward in no-man's-land; he thought it might be slightly longer than it was a day or two ago. He would mention that to Captain Hardcastle today. The one thing in his vision that never altered was the mud. The whole bloody Somme Valley seemed to have turned into a disgusting swamp of viscid mud.

Things were relatively quiet today, though the never ending boom of guns and the closer occasional burst of machine-gun fire reminded them of what things could escalate into at any time. When they had heard the rumour that they were to join in the last push for the year, sometime very soon, a slight tremor had run though him; the feeling that people explained as 'someone walking over your grave'. God, he hoped not. There were thousands of people walking over thousands of graves out here.

Dave moved and lifted his head. 'What can I smell? Is that Birtenshaw cooking again?'

Harry nodded. 'I suppose so.'

There was a formality in their dialogue now, since the night of the stolen grog episode. Even though both of them had come to realise what a lucky break Colonel Fleet had given them, it was still incredible to Harry that the man he had hated all his life was the commander of the battalion. It was even more incredible that the new friend he had made, the friend that he had felt closest to in all his life, should honour the man he hated. It had proved pretty confusing for him; and for Dave as well. It had put a wedge between them.

They saw Colonel Fleet about once a week. He came down from his advance headquarters, which were in an old convent, and toured the lines and spoke to the men. He had a good memory, apparently, for he called a lot of them by their names. The private soldiers liked that, it had impressed them, but Harry was not taken in by it. Harry always tried not to meet his eyes when he came by. Even so, the colonel sometimes spoke directly to Harry and then he was obliged to answer, which he did in stiff soldierly manner.

Dave sat up and sniffed. 'At least it gives us a break from the other bloody stinks around here.' He slid down off the ledge. 'I'm off to see what Frank has.' He lifted his gaze to Harry's. 'Coming?'

'No.' He shook his head and returned to his periscope.

'Curly, what about you?'

'Na, busy here.'

Dave made his way along the trench, avoiding the pools of water and from the other direction Luke appeared, picking his way across the mud and water from high spot to high spot. He climbed up on the firestep beside Harry. 'Can I look through your periscope? I feel so bloody confined in here. And it's so bloody cold.'

'Sure.' Harry handed him the instrument and sat down.

'Thank God for the sky,' opined Luke as he knelt up on the ledge beside Harry.

'You know what?' Curly said, looking up from his polishing and pointing to the water below.

'What?'

'There's a rumour going about that we're being relieved soon.'

'Really?' Luke turned to him hopefully.

'Yeah, by the bloody navy!'

Harry laughed. 'Good joke, Curly.'

'Shit, Moss, do you have to make jokes like that?' Luke turned sharply away and put the periscope up to his eye. 'The bloody pumps are on the blink round in Queen Street so the water's not retreating at all. It's just water and stinking mud all the way along to the tommies' Haymarket.'

Queen Street was what their soldiers had dubbed the new communication trench, after the main street of Brisbane. To name the trenches after places at home was the natural thing for troops of each nation to do, and there were Piccadillys, Park Lanes and Haymarkets leading along to Pitt Streets and Flinders Streets and Champs-Elysées up and down the line from Ypres to the Swiss border.

A shout sounded along the trench and they turned to see Bingo coming round the corner with two soldiers carrying a bucket between them. They avoided the water, keeping to the high ground and the duckboards. 'First things first,' Bingo said, signalling to the privates with him. One of them dug into the bucket and brought out three tins of Gordon's Ointment, a grease made of whale oil. 'Here you are, fellas. Now remember to coat your feet, boys, before putting on clean socks.'

'Yeah, we know,' piped up Curly, parrot fashion. 'We

have to fight trench foot, to enable us to continue the fight against Fritz.'

Bingo almost smiled. 'Right, son, you've learnt that. Now on to the next thing: looking for volunteers.' He eyed them above his ginger beard.

Curly leaned back against the tin sheeting on the forward trench wall. 'What for, Sarge?'

'Need two more men to accompany Captain Hardcastle out tonight, I've already got my eighteen others.'

'What? A raid?'

Bingo nodded.

Harry felt Luke move at this side. He looked round as Luke faced away and leaned into the periscope lifting it again to the trench opening.

Bingo sniffed. 'Two of my blokes have come down with something, so I need to replace them, briefing to start immediately.' He gave them a fixed look. 'So?'

Curly raised his hand almost as a student might in a schoolroom. 'Why ask us, Sarge? We've only been here a few weeks, what do we know about raids?'

Bingo's expression hardened, but his voice remained steady and cool as if explaining to a child. 'Son, we're fresh to the lines, you see. The others here are tired, worn from months of fighting, exhausted. That's why. So any takers?'

Harry shook his head and Curly mumbled 'Na, sorry, Sarge,' and slipping his tin of whale oil grease in his voluminous pocket went back to polishing his kit.

'And I take it you're not volunteering, Marland?'

Luke continued looking through the periscope. 'No, Sarge.'

'Gawd, Sarge,' spoke up Curly again, 'Lieutenant Dearwood was just through here not an hour ago asking for volunteers for tunnellers, some poor buggers got blown up down there underneath us this morning and now he wants more simpletons to take their place. Not me, Sarge. I like the safe jobs.'

'It's for King and country, boy. We won't win this little skirmish without volunteers for tough stunts.' He put his hand inside the warm skin waistcoat he wore over his greatcoat and took out a card. 'But perhaps I've got something here more to your liking. This one's a stroll in the moonlight.' He ran his forefinger down the paper. 'I need three more for a carrying party to bring up rations and mail and duckboards from the rear. Now how about that? Going in the opposite direction to the enemy should be more to your liking, eh, Moss?'

'Yeah, it would be, Sarge, only I can't. I'm first gas sentry. I've got an understanding with Sergeant Dobb every night after stand-to.'

'I'll go,' Harry declared.

Luke did not speak.

'Marland?'

The youth brought his eye from the instrument he held. 'Yes, Sarge?'

'What about you?'

'Yes, all right, I'll go too.'

Bingo wrote their names on the card and slipped it back inside his greatcoat pocket. 'Right. Two hours after stand-to, see Sergeant Major Collins. He'll take you through to the end of the support trenches to where the horses and carts'll be waiting. I'm told the road's not too bad all the way back to headquarters.'

Harry looked up. 'Why won't you be giving us our orders, Sarge?'

Bingo thrust his beard forward before he answered. ''Cause I'm going on the raid, laddie, that's why.'

When Bingo had gone Curly spoke up. 'Gawd, bloody raids. A long time ago I decided to volunteer for flamin' nothin' like that; reckon that way it gives me a *small* percentage of a *small* chance of gettin' outa here alive.'

Luke turned round sharply and handed the periscope to Harry. 'Ah, shut up, Moss. Do you have to talk bloody stupid all the time?' And he jumped down from the firestep to land on a dry spot, and made his way back along the trench and disappeared round the corner.

'What's wrong with him?'

Harry shrugged. 'Don't know. Might be the cold. We're not used to the cold.' He moved closer to Curly along the ledge and sat silently for a time watching him.

As a loud rattle of machine-gun fire sounded Harry spoke as nonchalantly as he could. 'Curly? Have you ever been . . . well, you know . . . frightened? I mean, of what's coming?'

Curly lifted his sun-browned Queensland head from his

polishing and shuffled round in his oversized greatcoat to face his companion. 'I don't think about fear, matey. Like I said to old Bingo, I'm volunteerin' for nothin' dangerous. Me old lady – me wife, Gloria – made me promise to be careful before I left Roma. She's a little beauty is Glor, so I fight when I have to; like I did against bloody Saladin in Turkey. What you have to remember here's that the bloody Bosche started it and keep that in mind all the time.' He screwed up his mouth as he studied Harry. 'Why? You're not scared, are ya? Ya don't seem the type.'

'Well, I don't know. It's just that it's nothing like I expected it.'

'What did you expect?'

'I don't know.'

'I'll give you a tip, Craken, just stay calm. Don't expect anythin'; just expect *everythin'*, that way you can't be surprised.' He held his helmet up to the light and smiled with satisfaction. Then he glanced back at Harry. 'It's a bloody war, matey, that's what it is.'

'Yes,' Harry said decidedly, as flakes of snow floated down and settled on his shoulders. 'I reckon that's right.'

John Conrad looked up from the pile of papers on the small table as the door opened and Tommy Hardcastle bent and looked back up the steps before he entered the officers' dugout. As he halted in the lantern light near an upright Hardcastle's shock of hair seemed to have more grey in it today, the silver strands spreading out from his temples to extend back over his ears.

In the short weeks of their relationship a certain relaxation of manner had developed: since the night of the drama with Dave and the Craken boy when John Conrad had confided in Hardcastle, it had been proved that his confidence was well placed and he had come to trust Tommy Hardcastle. He acknowledged that he probably felt towards Hardcastle in a similar way that K had felt towards himself and Fitz and the others of their group.

Hardcastle saluted and grinned at his superior officer 'The others are coming. I just passed Captain Bader in the trench outside.' He plunged his hand into his greatcoat pocket and took out a book. 'When I was told you were down here from advance headquarters, I thought I'd bring this to you.'

John Conrad turned it over in his hands.

'I've read it and so has Bader; thought it might amuse you.'

'*The First Hundred Thousand* by Ian Hay. Ah I see . . . *Accounts from the Men of Kitchener's Army*. Thanks, I was looking for another book to read.'

'Yes, apparently the author was a soldier. Some of it's a bit fiction-cum-fact, but it's a laugh in places.' He sat down on a rickety stool and blew out air in a long noisy breath. 'If any of this can be funny.' He moved his gaze to the map on the wall. 'There's a raid set for tonight.'

'Who organised that?'

'Major Roberts.'

'Why on earth have a raid now when we're trying to surprise them with the attack next Monday?'

'That's his strategy. Roberts says a raid will put them off, make them think we're just settling down for the winter here like they are, making just the occasional raid and expedition into their trenches. That way they won't think we'll be coming over in force on the thirteenth.'

'Well, it's a point of view, I suppose, though I'm not certain I share it. My opinion differs with General Haig's in that I think when the barrage starts on Friday we won't be fooling them after that.'

Tommy Hardcastle shrugged. 'Probably true.'

'Who's taking this raid?'

'I am.'

John Conrad looked up sharply. 'Why?'

'Well, it's really Captain Durst's turn but he's come down with a fever, so I'll do it.' He looked around and espied a bottle of gin on the makeshift shelves against the dirt wall. 'Do you mind, sir?' he asked, gesturing to the bottle.

'No, go ahead, but if you're set on leading the raid just have enough of that lad, not too much.'

'Of course.' He moved across and poured out a measure. The ground shook around them and a small amount of rubble fell from the ceiling to the floorboards as a lonely burst of machine-gun fire radiated in reply somewhere outside.

John Conrad gestured for Hardcastle to sit. 'Who'll you take with you?'

'Sergeant Bingham; he's a bloody good man. And I'll take West; he's the best sniper we have and knows the territory. The others will be volunteers. Best to take volunteers. That way they have opted to be out there with you.' He nodded to himself. 'You can rely on volunteers.'

John Conrad did not like the thought of Hardcastle taking the raid when it was not his turn. He did not like the idea of raids anyway; he thought them too dangerous for what they achieved. He would tell Roberts, but it was too late to stop this one now. 'Well, one good thing, it hasn't rained for a while. That should help though there'll still be mud and water everywhere.'

'Mmm, we're heading along the south-eastern ridge where it'll be at its least soggy. I've studied the most recent photographs of their front line and the ridge runs close to where a single forward Hun trench comes to a salient all on its own. That's the objective.'

The young man eased himself back down on to the stool. Neither of them wished to continue analysing the coming raid and Hardcastle altered the subject. 'By the way, two days in a row we've had sentries wounded in the shoulder by Bosche sniper fire. I couldn't understand how Fritz could have been on the right angle but this afternoon young Craken informed me of something – he's one of the boys with a periscope. He tells me there's a small section of stone wall left standing in no-man's-land that he thinks might have grown slightly larger in the last few days, large enough to hide a man. If that's the case it would be on the right angle for a sniper there to have seen the left side of my sentries. I've taken a compass bearing on the wall and after this meeting I'm going back to get the artillery to fire on it.'

'So how do you think young Craken and Sands are doing?'

'It's hard for me to know about Sands. But because he has a periscope and I actually deal with Craken, I think he's sharp and keen. Though there's one thing I can tell you about Sands which sets him in a certain class. Sergeant Bingham just informed me on my way here that he was down by two men for the raid tonight and that Sands volunteered.'

John Conrad eyed Tommy Hardcastle before he spoke. 'Look, lad, I'm not pleased that you're taking the bloody raid for one thing and now Sands is going on it too.'

Tommy smiled. 'Colonel, you're not responsible for Sands, and you're not responsible for me.'

John Conrad continued studying the younger man for some seconds. 'Yes, I know that.' Then he lifted the papers in front of him. 'Right . . . so to something else. I was speaking to some fellows from London yesterday. It seems that Lloyd George's now undermining the Prime Minister whenever he can. Not that Asquith doesn't deserve it; he's been uninspiring to say the least.

'There'll be no surprises to see the PM go and be replaced by Lloyd George, and, Tommy, my boy, while I have to tell you my experiences have left me with no love for Lloyd George, he's perhaps one of the few in the Government who possess any understanding of war. Any intelligence of what is truly happening in this war is lost on the others in the cabinet.'

'That's pretty negative, sir.'

'Yes, isn't it? But then I know them . . . intimately.'

Hardcastle looked sideways at his colonel. 'One likes to think the men in charge know what's going on, understand. Otherwise . . . all this . . .' He gestured forlornly, then dropped his voice to a confidential tone. 'Surely Kitchener understood?'

'Yes, he did, and it saddened him immeasurably.' John Conrad gave a brief wry smile. 'He could see it would be a long war won only with frightening loss. But even he couldn't have realised what would be the extent of it.' He touched Hardcastle on the shoulder. 'Look, don't mind me, lad; it just bothers me. One of the reasons I asked for a battalion was to get away from politicians.'

The door opened and Roberts, Bader, Dearwood, Palmer and Kenny trailed in.

John Conrad raised his hand to return the salutes. 'Good afternoon, gentlemen. Find a seat if you can.'

The few stools were soon taken and Palmer found a backless chair outside in the entrance to the dugout and brought it in. He looked to John Conrad. 'Lang offers his apologies, sir, he's got stomach cramp.'

John Conrad gave a sharp nod before he pointed to the

map pinned on the wall beside them. 'As you're all well aware, the battle continues raging on and off only miles away. We've at last taken Thiepval and some July one objectives, and Haig's desiring a final push here for the year. He wants the German-held villages – or I should say what remains of them – of Beaucourt, St Pierre Divion, Beaumont Hamel and Serre, if we can take it. Also Y Ravine.' He tapped the map. 'The entire area's catacombed with trenches and there're tunnels on all sides of Y Ravine and, we think, well-provisioned dugouts too. The general's keen to end the year with all these points on our side of the line! We believe the Germans have settled down to pass the winter here and that they've no idea we intend to continue the battle. He's of the opinion that even when we begin the barrage on Friday that the Germans will think it's just a last show before we dig in for the winter.

'Haig's opinion's to stay aggressive while anxieties mount in the minds of the enemy. They have to face the facts of some of the Russian successes on the Eastern Front as well as the gains in the Isonzo offensive, and now the Romanians have entered the war on our side.

'We're here as an addition to General *Gough* and the Reserve Army . . . I should say the New British 5th Army, as it's now called.' He lifted his hand to the map. 'This is where we are . . .' He pointed to their position across and south from the German-held Hawthorn Redoubt, which had been blown up on 1 July. 'The British boys have tunnelled back under the redoubt and are setting thirty thousand pounds of explosives beneath it so we'll detonate it again after the attack begins. On July One it was detonated before the attack and the bloody Germans were alerted. Don't want that again. The explosion should cover the German trenches in enough debris to keep them down! We'll be aiming to help the 51st Highlanders take what was Beaumont Hamel.' He skipped his finger across no-man's-land and the blue and red lines of the two fronts to the cross representing the remains of the village. 'The place is covered in mud and much of the battlefield remains thick sticky slime, like glue, but the rain at the start of this month has now given way to some dry days and we're lucky enough to be where it's not too bad. So we'll fight on the right flank of *Gough's* Army . . .' He had said the last general's name twice in a way that made Tommy Hardcastle decide he did not respect the man.

'Will we have tank support, sir?' asked Major Roberts.

'We're uncertain whether we can get tanks up, and apparently Haig hasn't yet agreed. There's a hell of a lot of mud for them to get stuck in out there.

'Now our battalion's fresh, in a manner of speaking, only you,' he looked at Tommy Hardcastle and Jack Bader, 'and those of the men who've been in the Dardanelles are tried . . . and respected. The Australian 1st and 2nd Divisions have accounted bravely for themselves at Pozières and Mouquet Farm. Along with the Australian 4th Division they've been transferred to Ypres so we're left here to keep up the fine tradition. So if the weather remains dry enough, next Monday the thirteenth at O six hundred, we go in with the British 5th Army on our right flank. There'll be cavalry waiting to follow if we break through, and reserve troops will come up behind us.

'The men are not to be informed until forty-eight hours before, just enough time for them to be briefed and to write home, secrecy in all matters being the first essential to our ultimate success.'

Captain Bader looked doubtful. 'I think the men have guessed there's to be a last push for the year, sir, and when the barrage starts that'll just confirm it in their minds.'

'Nevertheless, don't you confirm it. A detailed briefing for all officers and warrant officers will take place at brigade headquarters tomorrow morning after stand-to and breakfast. It'll be taken by the brigadier at O eight hundred; make sure all are there.' He looked at Tommy. 'As you'll be busy tonight, you'll be relieved of attending that, Hardcastle, and Roberts can fill you in later.'

They all looked at Hardcastle, and John Conrad turned to Major Roberts. 'And you'll inform Lang that he's *not* excused from the briefing, stomach cramps or no stomach cramps.' He crossed back to the table as the door opened and his batman appeared with a tea tray.

The light was fading when Harry watched through his periscope and saw the wall in no-man's-land blown up. One second it was there and the next dirt and rock jumped high in the air and crashed back down in a golden fury. 'It's gone,' he said to Curly and Isaac, who knelt on the firestep with him.

Curly put out his hand for the instrument. 'Let me see.' When he took it and put it to his eye he smiled. 'Yep. It's gone, all right.'

'So, we'll find out if the sentries still get shot,' Isaac declared. 'And if they do, Harry, my boy, your tip will prove incorrect and you'll be Captain Hardcastle's little genius no longer.'

Harry spoke as he moved away along the trench. 'Didn't know I ever was, Isaac. I'll see you at stand-to.' And he vanished round the corner.

Stand-to lasted for an hour before dawn and an hour at dusk each day; hours of vigilance waiting to see if the enemy would attack. The evening stand-to came and went, and Curly left on first gas sentry as rifles were inspected and Harry's platoon moved along their section of the trench doing repairs. It was around 1900 when they had returned to their dugout that Harry signalled to Luke. 'We should be off. Have to meet the sergeant major at nineteen thirty.'

Luke sat up on a makeshift cot and lifted his hand in reply. 'Right, I'll just get my rifle and find my scarf.'

On the far side of the dugout Dave also rose to his feet, 'Well, I'm off too.'

Harry looked round as Isaac glanced up from the poetry he was reading and asked, 'Off where?'

'I'm going with Bingo.'

Harry said nothing but he listened as Isaac shook his head and asked, 'Why'd you do that?'

'Well, I'm young and fit and Bingo needs blokes like me.'

Isaac looked in disbelief at Dave. 'Do you know what you could be in for on a bloody raid?'

As Dave replied, 'I'll find out,' Frank stood up from his makeshift cooking stove. 'Well, I'm off to help Sergeant Dobb sink a new latrine.' He gestured to Isaac. 'You're supposed to help too, Walker.'

Isaac raised his hands in mock horror. 'I'm interested in poetry, not shit!' But he put his poetry away in his knapsack and picked up his coat and balaclava in readiness to follow Frank to the door.

At that moment there was an explosion, the ground shook and dirt fell from the walls.

'Hell, that was close,' Harry declared, lifting his rifle and putting on his gloves.

One of the boys who had been at Gallipoli enlightened them from where he lay on the floor. 'Don't worry. We're doing plenty of shelling ourselves by the sound of it. Starting to soften them up for the flaming push.'

Dave, who was already in his greatcoat, took up his rifle and bayonet and moved to the door with Isaac and Frank.

'You won't be takin' your own rifle,' Frank informed him knowledgeably. 'Bluey told me you'll be given a sawn-off one and a knife and a truncheon, my boy, and you'll leave your helmet behind too. You'll be wearing a woollen cap comforter.'

Dave put his hand on his chin and looked squarely at Frank. 'I know all that. I *was* briefed this afternoon you know.'

Isaac laughed and slapped Dave on the arm as he followed Frank outside. 'Good luck, Sands.'

'What time will you be back?' Harry managed to ask when Frank and Isaac had gone.

Dave paused. 'We're going out about midnight. Bingo just wants us all together early – to brief us and black up and stuff,' he laughed. 'Though that won't be a concern for me. Bingo said we'll be out there about an hour.' He spoke brightly, confidently. 'Should be back here by not long after O one hundred, if it all goes well. Just in time to put on the billy and catch Birtenshaw and Walker coming off latrine duty.'

Luke mumbled something which nobody caught and as Dave said, '*Au revoir*, fellas,' and opened the dugout door, Harry stood quickly and, passing by Luke who was looking for his scarf, followed him outside. 'Wait.'

Dave turned to look at him. 'Yes?'

'Why are you doing this?'

'What? Going on the raid?'

'Yes. Don't you know how bloody dangerous they are?'

Dave's dark eyes assessed Harry. 'Yes I do. And like I said,

I'm young and healthy and Bingo and Hardcastle need blokes like me.'

'You could get killed.'

Dave sighed. 'Look, Harry, if the word's right and we're to go into battle soon, then perhaps in a few days from now we could all be killed. If I'm killed tonight it's merely early.'

'You only speak like that because you're pretending you don't care.'

Dave shook his head. 'Harry, Harry, you might be right. But I'm here and someone has to do these things. If I didn't intend to fight I should've stayed back in Brisbane and not joined up in the merry month of May.'

Harry sniffed and rubbed his nose on his sleeve. 'Yeah, you might be right about that.' They eyed each other in the glow from the ambient flashes made by the shells overhead. 'Anyway, you'd better not get killed –' abruptly Harry held out his hand – 'you mad bugger you.'

Dave grinned and took the extended palm. 'I only volunteered so you'd worry about me and be friends with me again.'

Harry laughed in disbelief. 'Yeah, yeah, tell that to the marines.'

Dave continued to shake Harry's hand. 'I know it was strange for both of us about my uncle . . . the colonel and all. But can we put that aside? Be like we were before?'

Harry nodded. 'I'd really like to. I'm sorry, old son. Guess we'll just have to differ on our opinion of him.'

'Yes, right. I'm sorry too.' Dave released his grasp and stepped away. 'Keep the billy on the boil for me, will you?'

'My oath.'

Dave made his way off into the black mouth of the trench and Harry stood looking up to the streams of light passing overhead: each light a butterfly of death. He sniffed again in the bitter night air. He whispered as his friend disappeared, 'Please God, bring Dave back and if there is a battle keep us all safe.'

Four hours later Harry plodded along in the dark, watching the back of Sergeant Major Collins leading the horse which pulled the cart that Luke drove. Behind them came two more vehicles led in the same way, all full of duckboards and food supplies and big boxes of mail. It had been a glorious release to be out in the dark walking up on the ground where men were meant to be and, in the respite of headquarters back from the lines it had been like a short blissful holiday. There the noise of the guns had been more distant and Harry and Luke had been given hot sweet tea and biscuits, and Luke had seemed to regain some of his old spirit and told them a story of his Uncle Bill buying a relic from the pyramids while on leave in Egypt. Harry had heard it before but he laughed anyway.

They had loaded the duckboards and the food supplies and while they waited for Sergeant Major Collins to reappear, Harry had stood for a while under a shattered portico talking to men from the Black Watch who were in to pick up supplies too. A few minutes later Sergeant Major Collins appeared through the open door to the commissary's office and called to him, 'Craken?'

'Yes, sir?' he trotted over.

'There's a box of mail missing here. There are meant to be five boxes. Take this torch.' He pointed into the darkness. 'Go along to the duty office round the back. Must have been left there. Sergeant Crystal's on duty.'

'Yes, sir.'

'And on the double, Craken.'

Headquarters, the deserted convent, was now surrounded by tents and various makeshift shelters. The dull roar of howitzers and the boom of other field guns in the distance continued like some familiar repeated refrain and in about a minute Harry came to the duty office to find the door closed and on it a note pinned: 'Back in 5 minutes.' He shone his torch through the window and sure enough the fifth mail box sat in a corner on the floor. Back he hurried to the sergeant major. 'Sir, there's a note on the door saying back in five minutes.'

'In that case, Craken, return and wait.'

He did so and stood waiting. After a minute or so to keep warm he stamped his feet and wandered back and forth along the office front. At one point he heard voices and stepped round the corner, thinking it might be Sergeant Crystal returning, but it was not. The voices came from a lantern-lit tent across the way. A sentry stood near the side of the tent. Harry could not make out what was being said, but with his strong young eyes he could see through the wide tent flap that one of the soldiers inside was *the colonel*.

He had wondered all the way here if he would see him. He did not want to and yet he did. He felt mystified and at a loss about it all. Harry had not said it, but it was a confusing ambivalence he had towards the colonel, *the enemy*, a desire to see him and yet not to see him. He hated him. The colonel was a bad man – he knew he was for his father had told him, and yet, when Harry thought about it, his father had never explained why.

Out of the long ago, came a memory of being a small child standing on a railway station somewhere and watching his mother talking to the colonel. She had left him and little Katy in the waiting room with their storybooks but he had gone outside to find her and there, along the platform he had seen his mother talking to the enemy. He recalled berating his mother when she came back and threatening to tell his father. He fancied that it was the first time his mother had ever spoken to him about having compassion, but he could be wrong about that. There were other times he had seen the enemy too. The first time he thought was at night. Was it at the horse races? He had been lost and the enemy had found him. His father had turned up and been angry. Another time he recollected – he would have been about ten or eleven – when he and his mother and Katy had gone to pick up his father at the Johnsonian Club. He had run through the doorway and up to his father, who had been standing with the enemy arguing, and his mother had intervened. He could not remember what had been said but he knew there had been a violent clash between the two men. He did remember that his mother had cried and been withdrawn and pale for a long time afterwards.

He stood watching as the colonel lifted his arms in the air to make a point to the two soldiers with him. One, Harry observed, was Rabbit Face, the ugly bugger; he could not see the other.

He watched as the colonel bent forward. If Harry tried to discount the personal venom he felt towards the man, he would have to admit the colonel was charismatic. But then Harry supposed that men of ill repute were often strong personalities. He continued watching the colonel leaning forward, his fair hair gleaming in the lantern light. Suddenly he had a thought. Could it have been that his mother had been the colonel's girl before she married his father? Was that it? But surely it was not just that. His father would not hate a man for that . . .

'Craken! What the bloody hell's kept you?'

Harry actually jumped in the air and swung round into the Sergeant Major's wrath. 'We were waiting so long for you, boy, and here you are loafing about. What are you bloody well doing?'

'Ah, sir. Sorry, sir, I suppose I was daydreaming.'

'Daydreaming, is it? At night, boy? We don't allow that in this man's army. The duty office is open. Now get back there on the double. Get that mail box and move!'

'Yes, sir. Sorry, sir.' Harry ran back to the duty office, picked up the mail box and had it back at the cart in less than a minute.

On the return journey to the lines a series of explosions lit the sky in front of them almost constantly and there was a big bombardment going on to the south. It was somehow easy just to look at the beauty of it and not realise that each light could kill and maim.

Twice the last cart became stuck in the mud and they had to push and pull it free.

As they approached the unloading point, gas horns were going off and men were shouting alarms and beating on eighteen-pounder shell-cases. They immediately donned their gas masks, making them look like goggle-eyed monsters, and waited in the uncomfortable hot headpiece only to hear a few minutes later as they were unloading, the shout of 'All clear'.

'Bloody false alarms,' Luke said.

'Thank God it was.' Harry sounded relieved, and then suddenly he realised it was after midnight. Dave would be on the raid.

At that precise moment Dave was crawling through no-man's-land towards the German trenches perhaps a hundred yards away, the boots of the man in front six inches from his face. They had been informed that the barbed wire had been cut by a party the night before and bursts of machine-gun fire probably on some previous daytime trajectory rattled overhead. They had been briefed by Hardcastle before coming out, had studied a map and been told they would keep to the north side of a ridge which carried them in a reasonably dry state straight to their objective, a single forward trench. They had been given rum to drink and reminded more than once they would spend only two minutes in the enemy trench and were to collect insignia and documents and anything that could be of help to determine more about their opposing regiments and battalion, and to take a prisoner if possible. They were informed they would go in after Bingo and Corporal West had cleared the trench.

'Cleared it how?' one of the first-timers had asked.

'With Mills bombs,' had been the reply.

Dave stayed close to the boots in front as they crawled across the hundred yards of no-man's-land under the blinking sky, and sure enough the barbed wire had been cut in the places meant, and foot by foot and yard by yard they made their way ever closer to the Germans. He had heard a song sung by some of the boys from the 8th Suffolks who had been at Thiepval in September and it kept repeating in his head as they edged on their backs through the barbed wire entanglements with the hint of gas fumes in the air.

> If you want the old battalion
> We know where they are
> Hanging on the old barbed wire . . .

It kept on and on in his brain until the boots in front halted and the man's hand came back, beckoning him to come forward. Dave relayed the hand signal to the man behind.

His heart skipped a beat when he heard voices . . . speaking in German. God, they were close! They sounded just a few feet away, clear and uncompromising in the cold night air. A man laughed and another gave a guttural wail. He heard the words 'Sie war wunderschön' unmistakably. His heart was pounding. He looked at the glinting eyes of the men around him.

> If you want the old battalion
> We know where they are
> Hanging on the old barbed wire . . .

Abruptly Bingo went from a prone to a kneeling position, for a second his black shape silhouetted against the sky, and in the same instant so did Hardcastle and West; all three heaved their grenades in the German trench and dropped back to the ground. After the trench exploded in front of them Dave leapt to his feet with the others. In five or six bounds they were over the earth of the parapet and jumping down to where a mad confusion reigned. Dave and three others held torches and shone them through the dust and debris in both directions. To the left West took one of the torch carriers and five or six others, doubled over, moving at speed along the trench, the front pair shooting as they went into the smoke and darkness. Dave shone his torch in the other direction where a German was dragging himself up through the smoke to attempt a standing position and Hardcastle shot him through the head. Another soldier staggered towards them, covered in blood, and Bingo standing on what remained of the firestep took him out at blank range with his bayonet. It was hard to see anything in the night and settling dust and rubble, but Dave's torch showed two Germans lying twisted on mounds of dirt and apparently dying of their wounds. Captain Hardcastle scrambled over them, followed by seven or eight others, to continue down the trench enfilade firing all the time.

Bingo was near the dying Germans and he looked up and shouted, 'Here, Sands,' as he bent to the nearest man, and began rifling through his pockets. Dave scrambled over the rubble and broken spars of wood to hold his torch steady for the sergeant.

'And quick, lad, pick up those trench maps and papers.' He pointed with his long knife at a tin which lay smashed open, and Dave grabbed them and stuck them up inside his multiple sweaters.

As Dave turned back, Bingo stood up from the fatally wounded men to move along the trench, and only Dave saw one of the dying Germans in supreme effort draw a handgun from his side and lift it to Bingo's back. Without thinking Dave threw himself across the space and knocked the gun from the dying man's hand. The gun discharged into the air as he landed on top of the German's chest. A rattling grating sound shuddered from the German's lungs and blood ran from his mouth as Dave pulled himself away from the body.

Bingo swung round. His voice was high but he held it calm. 'Thanks, laddie. I'll remember that.'

They ran along the trench as best they could and met Hardcastle coming the other way. Dave's torch showed the men behind the captain pushing a German along in front of them.

'Good,' said Bingo. 'We got one.'

In the torchlight Hardcastle's uniform was spattered in blood and his eyes were overbright with adrenalin. 'Got to get him home yet. On the double, boys, back as fast as we can. Where's West?'

Bingo pointed in the other direction. 'Not back yet.'

Hardcastle yelled into the darkness, 'West? West? Come on!'

At that moment there was a shout in German from around the trench corner. '*Schnell! Kommt hier rüber!*'

Already men were scrambling back up over the earth parapet and out into no-man's-land, heading home. 'Out! Out!' Hardcastle shouted and the men with him thumped the German in the back and he climbed out with them. Dave struggled up over the dirt and rubble and in desperation stumbled and fell. He felt something cut the side of his neck but he was on his feet in less than a second and scrambling forward. Twenty yards behind them, the parapet over which they had just climbed blew up and bits of dirt and rock descended upon them. A German must have thrown a grenade. Machine-gun fire rattled near Dave and in the brightness of the explosion he saw the way ahead and ran forward through the opening in the wire.

> If you want the old battalion
> We know where they are
> Hanging on the old barbed wire . . .

They slid along the side of the ridge, doubled over and running like mad. To stop their own side shooting them out of hand Hardcastle called out the password as they came close to home and they stumbled down into the trench. Captain Hardcastle called the role. They were present except for West and five others. Half an hour later one of West's group came in alone.

Hardcastle determined they had killed probably ten or twelve Germans, and taken one prisoner for the loss of five men.

'It's a pity about West. He was a bloody good shot. I'll miss him.'

Around 0200 Dave, his throat bandaged, came along the trench to where his platoon slept and found Harry waiting for him.

'God! What happened to your neck?'

'Caught on the barbed wire.'

> If you want the old battalion
> We know where they are
> Hanging on the old barbed wire . . .

'Do you want to tell me about it?'

Dave shrugged. 'Yes, but tomorrow.'

'Bloody cold, isn't it?'

'Sure is. Been waiting long?'

'About an hour. Got the billy on the boil in the dugout, old son.'

'Thanks, mate.'

Down past Queen Street, in one of the officers' dugouts, John Conrad had waited. He had insisted on remaining at the front overnight and had asked to be informed the minute the raiding party was back.

When he was told that Hardcastle had returned with most of his force and a prisoner too, he gave no outward sign of relief. 'Good,' he said quietly. But he had to wait until Hardcastle himself came in before he knew Dave was safe.

Tommy Hardcastle spoke loudly. 'The stunt was a success.' Soldiers used *stunt* to describe actions of any kind. Tommy was pumped up, stimulated, looking to John Conrad for approval. 'We took out ten or twelve and got a prisoner into the bargain. He's being questioned right now.'

'Good work. Have a Scotch,' said one of his brother officers, handing him the bottle.

John Conrad stepped forward and slapped Tommy on the shoulder. 'Well done. Good to have you back.'

So they had only lost five; five brave men were almost as nothing in this neverending loss of life . . . John Conrad watched Tommy drinking his Scotch. But still they had been men, with all their needs, hopes and fears, until an hour or so ago. There's no Scotch for them, or the men they killed.

Chapter Thirty-seven

Matthew leant back in the light-weight motor lorry as it rumbled forward along the road from Beauvais to Amiens. He had been assigned to the 6th Mixed Division in the Somme, which included Australian, Irish and British troops under the British Brigadier Henry Claver-Jensen.

At his side Cliff Evans, his driver, spoke as he pointed through the windscreen. 'Goin' to rain again, governor. See.'

'That's all it seems to do in this country.'

The New Zealand corporal laughed. 'Yep, sir, this part of the world's still actin' like part of the ocean. And it's so freezin' cold here now that the rain's often sleet. What'll it be like in January and February? Doesn't bear thinkin' about. Can't imagine why they're all fightin' over any of it. With weather like this I'd give the bugger away.'

Cliff had kept up a running commentary on a variety of matters since they left Paris: ridiculing the army, the handling of the war, the Germans, the French, the English, Welsh, the Irish and every nation that came into the conversation, and now the weather, all of which suited the cynicism of his passenger.

'Indeed,' Matt agreed. 'Tell me some more.'

Cliff glanced round at the aquiline profile, not sure whether his passenger toyed with him or not. 'More of what, sir?'

'Of anything. Tell me anything. You have a definitive stance on all worldly matters, Corporal Evans, and it's a long time since I've met a man who had the courage to be opinionated on *everything*. You invigorate me. Here I was thinking I'd be fatigued, even bored by the sensitivities of a lorry driver but no, your thoughts come unclouded by reserve or analysis. You're the most refreshing company I've been in since I left Queensland. Tell me anything at all.'

This had the effect of bringing Cliff to total silence.

Meanwhile Matt looked out on a countryside that had changed greatly since the busy streets of Paris. He made quick reference sketches as they drove by rail carriages full of men and munitions, regiments of soldiers on foot, ambulance wagons, horse-drawn carts carrying supplies and farmhouses which had been turned into relay stations. He made Cliff halt when a line of tractors pulling howitzers appeared down an avenue of trees and he hurriedly did as much of a detailed drawing as he could.

Earlier that day, as they had stopped while the overheated engine of the lorry cooled, Cliff pointed out that if they listened they could hear the big guns even though they were still close to fifty miles from the front. And true enough they could. About half an hour later they had seen German bi-planes overhead.

Arriving on the outskirts of Amiens in the late afternoon, they spoke to some British officers who looked at their papers supplied by the Australian High Command in Paris and directed them to the 6th Division's headquarters in the city. 'In the railway station, keep going straight, you'll come to it. Once you pass the cathedral, it's not far.'

They soon found the cathedral, which prevailed imperiously over the city, and the streets around it were crowded with soldiers and munition lorries, riders on horseback, ambulance wagons, stretcher bearers and pedestrians. Matt imagined it would have been an elegant city before 1914, with its tree-lined streets and imposing buildings, but all had altered under the pall of war.

By the time they came to the railway station it was dusk and a cold wind met them as they descended from the lorry. Showing their papers to the guards at the front entrance, they were ushered into the station and along the platform, past boxes of pigeons stacked two by two along much of its length, to an overbridge which took them to a building painted a khaki green. Inside they were shown to a room where a youthful sergeant asked them their business.

Matt explained who he was. 'In Paris I was told to see a Lieutenant Colonel Burnett, the chief Administration Officer of this division, and told he would attach me to a battalion and give me clearance to travel freely in the department of the Somme.'

When he finished speaking he received a response he could not have foreseen. The sergeant's eyes shone and he threw what could only be described as a beautiful salute to his visitor. 'Oh, I'm honoured to meet you, Major Craken, sir. I'm a student at Julian Ashton's School of Art in Sydney. I know exactly who you are, sir. We're all so proud of you. I'm a devotee of your work. Your *Doss House Singapore* and *Canecutters* are legend, sir.'

If it were possible for Matthew to give a spontaneously genuine smile, then that is what occurred. 'How encouraging to find someone who has a background in art. Yes, I know old Julian. What's your name?'

'Pat Kelly, sir.'

'How do you do, Pat Kelly? This is my driver, Cliff Evans.'

And so things from this point on happened swiftly for Matthew. Young Kelly left them and went off to pass on knowledge of the visitors' arrival to the right sources, and within half an hour Matt had been seen by Lieutenant Colonel Burnett and been assigned a billet in a nearby house where some of the officers lived; arrangements too had been made for Cliff Evans. Matthew was then given passes to see him along the battlefront and he had been told he would be given a batman-cum-assistant on the morrow.

He spent some time that evening with the lieutenant colonel. Alec Burnett had been born in Scotland but had been in Australia since he was fourteen. There was still the Scottish lilt to his words. 'So you're assigned to us for a year?' he asked, pouring Matthew a Scotch.

Matt reflected for a few moments before he answered, 'Yes. Let's hope the war's over by then.'

'I'll drink to that.'

'But if it's not, I believe I can remain or ask for a transfer to Flanders or another part of the line after six months if I wish.'

'Ah, not sure of that, old fellow. You'd have to apply to GHQ. I know they've appointed you to us, an Australian battalion: thought you'd prefer to be with your compatriots rather than an Irish, Canadian or British battalion. We've got all of them round here.'

Matt shrugged. 'Don't think I care really, but whatever's done is acceptable, I'm sure.'

'You're a bit of an experiment, I hear. First of your kind for us, a *war artist*. You should be able to follow the battalion wherever it goes, that's certain, and I'll send a request with you for billets for you and your driver and assistant at battalion headquarters.' He grinned. 'That probably means a bed in a building of sorts for you and stretchers in camouflage tents for the others.'

'Thanks. There's another matter,' Matthew stated, downing his second Scotch. 'I'm told it takes about three hours to reach Montdidier from here.'

'Yes, that'd be so, it's the opposite direction to Albert. And even though it's only twenty-three miles south-east the roads are hopelessly congested around here. It's the same way all along the front, I'm afraid.'

'Yes, I know, I've just come through a lot of blocked areas. How far back from the line is Montdidier?'

'I'd say ten miles or more. It was taken by the Germans in their first advance in 1914 but it's been on our side of the line since. Why? What's in Montdidier?'

'Not what, it's a who, someone I want to see.'

The lieutenant colonel was a worldly man. He was aware that artists all led strange lives, so he enquired no further. 'Yes, you should be there in three or so hours I'd say. I can arrange for you to go there.'

'Thank you.'

Burnett leafed through some papers. 'Ah yes, here it is, your battalion's the 16th AIF.' He walked to the wall map and pointed. 'It's here in the line north of Albert near Auchonvilliers.'

Matt's languid eyes widened momentarily and his fingers gripped the glass in his hand more firmly as he moved in his chair. 'The 16th you say?'

'Yes.' He tapped the map. 'Though, truth is, I've been told to keep you here until further notice.'

'Oh, why's that?'

The lieutenant colonel did not answer; he eyed Matt over his glass as he swallowed.

Matthew drank the last of his Scotch. The 16th Battalion of

the Australian Imperial Forces was the one Harry was serving with. His mind worked at speed. 'I think what you're *not* telling me is there's going to be a battle or something and they'll be in it.'

Alec Burnett coughed. 'Look, old man, at a time like this you'll probably just be in the way. Once it's over – and it'll probably be short-lived . . . time of the year . . . cold . . . snow and ice coming – you can join them and paint and sketch your heart out all through the winter. All right? Now you want to go to Montdidier. Do that. Stay a few days, make some pictures there and when you return here I'll tell you where exactly your battalion is, and let's hope it's a few miles further into enemy territory than it is now. And you can trundle up and settle in.' He lifted the Scotch bottle. 'Like another?'

'Indeed,' his guest replied; it would do two things: calm him after the news he had just heard and compensate for the racking pain in his leg which had continued all day in the bloody cold weather.

Matt had hoped to see Harry somewhere sometime, but it seemed that fate had intervened. His boy was to be in a battle. When he joined the battalion next week, his son might not be alive. No, that was too much to consider, too much to even think about.

That night Matt eased himself down and sat on the floor of his room in the muted slant of a beam thrown from a radiant moon in the clearest night of the year. It was cold and there was no fire, though he had been given numerous blankets for his bed. He wrapped one of the blankets round his bad leg and, keeping it straight, he pulled the other up by the ankle and placed the sole of his foot on the inside of his thigh. His leg throbbed from ankle to hip. He could hear the noises in the street below and if he listened, planes in the sky and the guns in the distance. He must shut them out and bring back the exercises he had not done for years . . . mind exercises given to him twenty years before by Long Chi in Penang when they had worked every day to ease the torment from the multiple fractures in his leg. Tonight he needed peace from worry and release from pain. He lifted his head and turned his closed eyes to the ceiling, his scar gleaming for only the moonlight to see, while he concentrated.

Long's patient musical voice edged its way down the lanes of his memory, calling him *Matyou* over and over again, and as the moments passed he imagined he felt the Oriental's strong fingers playing the ancient signs on the muscles of his leg. '*Follow me to where Nature's unselfish task is done, give me your self-forgetting soul and I shall take you through the manifestations of the universe higher and higher. Do you feel me Matyou? Forget the trackless desert of life and heal yourself. Move through your thoughts to the time when there is no beginning, no end. The infinite stream of life flows into the ocean of self-perfection, self-realisation. You have the power within you, the self-emanating power of the masters who have gone before. The power will heal all pain . . . in the mind and in the body.*'

Matthew breathed the extended and sustained inhalations and exhalations in the pattern of the mystical teachers and took his healing once again from the memory of Long Chi living in the river of his soul.

Before he slept, Matt said two words that most of his acquaintances would have been surprised to hear him use. 'Thank you' he whispered to the night.

The following morning, he made his way along a wide boulevard down to the Somme River, his cedar cane clicking with each step and walking more easily than he had since arriving in the northern hemisphere. At his side Bert Strutt, his batman-cum-assistant, a thin, freckled-faced boy from Perth, carried his art case in silence and led two horses lent to them. Bert had said, 'How do you do, sir?' when they first met and had carried out his duties in total silence since. It appealed to Matt's sense of humour that in Cliff and Bert he had been saddled with loquacity on one hand and quiescence on the other.

Once at the Somme River, he sketched wounded soldiers convalescing under the trees on the banks and did a fine detailed drawing of a group of river barges which were used to ferry the wounded from the battlefields along the Somme into Amiens.

'Now to the cathedral, Strutt. I wish to make a quick sketch of that.'

They could see it over the buildings and house tops as they rode towards it, and soon they stood looking at the façade, flanked by two square towers and displaying three portals decorated in a profusion of statuary, the central portal featuring a remarkable thirteenth-century statue of Christ. Matt made his sketch and Strutt constructed an entire sentence. 'Are we going inside, sir?'

Matt eyed him speculatively. 'Good heavens no, Strutt. Please don't tell me you're religious, boy?'

Strutt looked abashed. 'Not overly sir.'

'Thank goodness. Churches are only of interest from the outside. As a child, when I had no say, my incompetent mother took me to church, until I rebelled at age ten. Since then I've been inside one, a single time. To be married. That's all churches are good for, son, to be married in, if you're that way inclined. Oh, and to draw, of course, from the exterior.'

They returned to headquarters for lunch and there immediately afterwards the uncommon threesome began their journey to Montdidier. As they rattled through the French countryside Cliff kept up a semi-perpetual discourse on the universal while Matt made his customary sardonic comments and Bert sat silently in the middle.

As the hour approached four, their lorry approached Montdidier, a small town which sat on an eminence on the right-hand bank of the Don River. For the fifteen minutes before their arrival Matthew had closed his eyes and allowed Cliff's persistent unvaried rhetoric to be a vocal background to his meditations. He was imagining Caro, and how she would respond to his arrival. Part of him expressed derision at his need to seek her out. He smiled mockingly to himself. Hell, after eighteen years wasn't it time to give up? To let her chase the enemy and fulfil her all-consuming dream? He wondered why she had remained with him: in her own way the woman was as perverse as he was.

He opened his eyes and glanced right and left as they began to ascend the hill into the little town. 'We look for number seventeen stationary hospital. I'm told it's up in the town.'

Caro stood from the small table where she had been rolling bandages, and crossed to the window. She rubbed her eyes. She was tired. It was not surprising for there had been so many casualties since she came here they were all working

619

two shifts, and now one of the girls, Annie Tarrant, had fallen ill.

She looked out across leafless trees over to the road which led up the hill into the town. The November nights were closing in, and in the encroaching dusk she watched a lorry making its way up past two omnibuses full of soldiers going down. She shivered. She really must cheer up. She would write to Harry. She wondered where he was and how he was. She prayed constantly for him to be kept safe . . . and his father.

She rested her head against the cracked pane of glass and recalled the days when she had been allowed to read John Conrad's letters. Bart had been good about that. They had kept her sane. She wondered where John Conrad was now that Kitchener of Khartoum was gone. She closed her eyes and imagined him. She wondered if she would ever see him again.

Then quite suddenly across her mind came her husband, with his slanted smile and ironic remarks. She felt awkward about leaving Brisbane the way she had. She probably should have waited and seen Matt first, but she had been fearful he would have talked her out of coming and she had been so obsessed with following Harry at the time. Finally she had written to Matt, explaining her actions. She hoped he understood, she really did. She had written four more letters to him in recent weeks: just felt she wanted to, just somehow needed to. No doubt he was being well taken care of with Jane and Mary at Cedar Grove and Mrs Manning in Brisbane: not that he would take any notice of what they said. He really could be so irritating. She just hoped he was being sensible enough to eat properly.

Her thoughts were interrupted by the whimper that had risen and fallen for the last seventy-two hours. It came from an Irish boy who had been hit in the pelvis and in the face with a shell splinter. The whole of his head was bandaged. She had not been on duty when he came in, but she had dressed the wounds since. The first time he had screamed as she had lifted the bandage from his face and her stomach had turned from the smell and the sight of nothing but blood and jelly-like flesh out of which one bloodshot eye gazed at her. She had swallowed hard and prayed silently to God to show no emotion and had looked back at him straight in his single eye and made herself smile at him. She tried to be as gentle as she could but she felt clumsy and inept. To take her mind off his face and to attempt to help him she talked quietly to him about the day and the cool winds and the mixture of birds that even now congregated near the kitchen windows. Afterwards she sat and held his hand until she was called away. She had steeled herself again today and dressed his wounds and talked softly to him, and thankfully he had not screamed though she knew in her heart he was in agony all the time.

It was the first bad face wound she had seen and it had shocked her to the core. Serious wounds on other parts of the body were terrible and it was harrowing to see young men limbless, but the patient still had a face, was a recognisable human being. A missing face was the saddest thing she had ever seen. She had learned his name, Michael Leahy, and each time she passed she bent down and tenderly touched his arm and said, 'It's me, Michael, Caro. I'm not far away.' But he was not eating or drinking and his whimper was breaking her heart.

The wards were full and when an omnibus load of wounded had come in yesterday, they had needed to put stretcher beds in the aisles of the wards. Today, the less serious cases had been taken on to Beauvais where there was a large army hospital; that had helped things a little. All the patients here were privates and non-commissioned officers. The officers had hospitals of their own. It seemed a useless rule but that's the way it was. Caro supposed it was something to do with officers always having to maintain some sort of dignity in front of the rank and file. All a bit futile in her opinion. Wounded men were wounded men no matter what their station.

Every man who came in she prayed for, and some lived and some died. She treated them all as if they were Harry; as if each one were her son. It was very wearing and sometimes she thought she should be more callous, but it was not in her to be that way. Some of the young VADs and nurses laughed about the places the wounds were and some of them could even chaff the boys about their injuries. Perhaps it was her maturity, that she saw the world differently from them, but she could not, for the life of her, make jokes about them.

'Miss Craken?'

She turned from the window to see the stern face of Matron Steele; all the girls called her 'Iron-heart' behind her back. The small rotund woman waved her hand in the direction of the ward. 'Stop gazing out the window. It'll be time to light the lamps soon. Run along.'

Caro moved off in the direction of the stiff-pointed finger. Iron-heart managed to make her feel like a schoolgirl even though she was one of the most mature women in the hospital. Most of the VADs were in their twenties – they could not volunteer until age twenty-three – and only a few of the nurses were her age. The soldiers had their own little jokes, calling them Very Artful Darlings or, less kindly, Victim Always Dies.

She noted the time as she lit the lamps. She was off duty in twenty minutes and longed for sleep. She would look in on Annie Tarrant and see how she was first, then get a bite to eat and go to bed. She was on duty in the morning at seven. There had been a whisper that they were getting another twelve VADs soon, as soon as next week. It was the only thing that had kept them all going the last fortnight.

She moved through the wards, placing the precious lamps, only two per ward, one at each end. They were issued battery-operated torches for night work, but these too were at a premium as the batteries were few so candles were used to supplement, but they too were running low. Matron had told them she had appealed to one of the New 5th Army majors who had been visiting the hospital on Monday and he had promised to send them as many boxes as he could spare.

Caro placed the lamp on a shelf where it reflected a little light over Michael Leahy and she moved across to him. It was a pitiful soft murmuring now, so low she could just hear him, the sounds coming in melancholy waves. She took up his hand and he fell silent. 'Michael, it's me, Caro, I hope you can hear me. Now I've left a lamp not too far away so there's some light here at your end of the ward. Now please, please, try to sleep. We must make you well. I won't be away too many hours. I'll be back on at seven in the morning and I'll come straight here to you first thing. Good night, Michael.' She tenderly squeezed his hand and moved away along the ward, saying good night to all the men.

Some returned her greeting and the 'card' of the ward Arnie Jackson, a twenty-year-old from London who had lost a leg from shrapnel wounds, whistled as she reached the door. He had fought in the blood bath during the taking of Thiepval in September. He would often speak out to the whole ward telling them in his proud cockney, 'I was in the Twelfth Middlesex and fought the bloody Wurttembergers at Thiepval, we put paid to the myth that those buggers were invincible.' The Wurttembergers had been a determined German regiment from Wurttemberg and had hailed themselves as invincible. Now the name of Thiepval along with places like Guillemont, High Wood, Delville-Wood, and Pozieres, was synonymous with horror and death. But Arnie, not demoralised by it all, often sang with bravado the ditty the boys who fought there had set to the melody of Moonlight Bay:

> I was strolling along
> In Guillymong
> With the minnywerfers singing,
> Their old sweet song . . .

Caro couldn't help but admire them, they kept this astounding sangfroid, in the face of all their suffering. Arnie Jackson symbolised to Caro the amazing pretence that all was well.

In the office she signed off and said good night to Jill Cossington, who was just coming on duty, then she took off her apron and hung it on her hook alongside the others drooping there, the large red crosses on each of the bodices making a crooked crimson row along the wall. She looked in the broken mirror that hung near the door to put on her bonnet, and pulled on her warm dark blue cape over her uniform. Waving good night to the other girls on duty, she passed by the wards. In the front foyer she opened the wide carved wooden door and made her way down the stone steps in the fading light and the burgeoning evening breeze. The hospital had been the Montdidier library before the war but when the Germans had been occupying the town in 1914 they had burnt all the books.

Making her way up the hill to the square where the VADs all lived in an old villa, she halted to let a lorry full of barbed wire pass and then noticed a soldier in khaki coming down towards her. As there were soldiers everywhere that was not noteworthy, but this one walked on a cane.

She felt a squeal of adrenalin in her midriff. She stood stock still as he came up to her.

He doffed his cap.

'God, Matt, what are you doing here?'

He gave her a smile, a grim smile. 'Caro, Caro, I haven't seen you for six months and this is your greeting? What am I doing here? Now could it be that I actually desired to see you?'

'Oh, I didn't mean it like that. I'm just surprised . . . that you're here.'

He shook his head. 'And why is it so surprising that a man whose wife up and left him without any goodbyes might follow her to ask just what indeed she's up to? It seems reasonable to me that I'm owed some explanation. Mind you, we have not always agreed on rationale.'

'I wrote you some letters.'

His mouth twisted in amusement. 'Did you really? Well, strange I've never received them. The only letter we had from you before I left Australia came to Jane.'

'Matt, I did write.'

He moved forward and took her arm. 'Where can we go to talk?'

'There's a place up in the square. There're usually a lot of soldiers, though.'

'No, that won't do.'

'Well, there's a French canteen at the railway station. That should be quiet this time of evening.'

He nodded. 'We'll go there.'

They had just taken their first steps up the hill when a loud voice called, 'Miss Craken?' and they turned to see the small round form of the matron charging up to them, her expression as dark as the gathering dusk. 'Rules, Miss Craken, rules. Return to the hospital immediately.'

Matt surveyed the arrival. 'Who the devil are you?'

Caro turned to her husband. 'Oh Matt, it's the matron. We VADs aren't allowed the company of officers.'

Matt continued to hold Caro's arm as Matron Steele arrived. 'You heard me, Miss Craken.' She did not look at Matthew.

'We both heard you, old girl,' Matt replied. 'Couldn't help it. You have the most disagreeably strident voice. Surely it upsets the patients?'

Matron Steele was taken aback. She shot Matthew a vitriolic glance. 'You know the rules too, I assume. This girl's on my VAD staff. VADs are not allowed to walk out with officers.'

Matt inhaled languidly. 'First, let me inform you that this *girl*, whom you call *Miss* Craken, is my wife. Secondly, that I will see her whenever I wish, and thirdly, the rule's not only ridiculous it's impractical. There would need to be manifold versions of you, heaven forbid,' he looked skywards, 'running all over France creating pandemonium night and day to have any hope of upholding the rule.' He doffed his cap. 'Good evening, Matron.' And he swung Caro round and, holding firmly on to her arm, moved off up the hill.

Behind them Iron-heart stood flabbergasted, arms akimbo, shaking her head in anger.

In the station canteen there were a few French soldiers in their faded blue jackets at the bar drinking coffee and smoking cigarettes, which were given away free when the canteen had them. Matt walked over and received a smile from Madame Fleurcourt, who ran the place. Behind her on the wall hung a large worn Tricolour. '*Oui, Major?*'

Matt thought he would at least give it a try for a real drink: he winked. '*S'il vous plaît, madame, un verre du vin?*'

She shook her head. '*Non, nous n'en avons pas.*'

'Ah then, *du café et du thé, s'il vous plaît.*'

He steered Caro into a booth near the glowing embers of a tired fire. As they sat down Caro took off her bonnet and turned a worried face to her husband. 'Now I'll be for it, Matt. I won't be surprised if Iron-heart gets rid of me. She won't take that dressing-down from you calmly, that's certain.'

Matt smiled. 'Iron-heart, yes, that suits the old beggar beautifully. Caro, you worry too much. They need as much help out here as they can get. And if she does make things awkward then you can go home to Brisbane where you belong.'

Caro placed both her hands flat on the table and met her husband's gaze defiantly. 'Don't make trouble for me, Matt. I'm here because I want to be here. Those boys in the hospital need me.'

Matt stared back into her eyes. 'Oh yes, Caro, my little hypocrite, it's for those boys in the hospital that you came to this part of the world, of course, and no doubt you explained all that to me in the single missing letter which you wrote.'

'Matt, I've written at least five letters to you.'

'Have you now?'

Caro opened her mouth to retaliate as Madame Fleurcourt arrived and placed the coffee and tea on the table.

'*Merci, madame.*' Matthew handed her some coins.

'Now look, all right, we know I followed Harry. God, Matt, you of all people know how I love that boy. I had to see him again and I managed it too . . . saw him in Marseilles.' She closed her eyes momentarily. 'I'm so glad I did that. Those few precious hours with him. Heaven knows where he is now. He's with the 16th AIF Battalion of some mixed division. I just pray he's not in danger.'

Matt knew very well that the boy was in imminent danger, but he was not going to worry her about that. 'His battalion's probably been sent somewhere safe, like Ireland.'

Hope sprang to her face. 'Do you think so?'

'It's possible.'

'Oh God, wouldn't that be wonderful?'

Matt swallowed some of the coffee. It was surprisingly good. 'Yes, it would be.' He fell silent. She looked tired, but her spark was still there: she had always damn well appealed to him.

In the silence she lifted her cup and sipped the tea. When she put it down she sat looking at him for a few more moments. 'I have to start at seven in the morning, you know.'

'Oh, Caro, come on, how long do you intend to go on with this charade? You've seen Harry, you say that's what you came for. So now you can go home. Whether you stay here or not cannot make one iota of difference to the boy's wellbeing.'

Caro drank some more before she spoke. She was attempting to stay calm. 'Matthew, I'm here now. I take what I'm doing very seriously. If I can make a difference to any one of them, make them forget the carnage they have seen, speak gently to them for a moment, ease their pain, help them disregard the maelstrom they came from, then that's what I want to do. Harry may have brought me here, but it's for all of them I'm staying. I do so much want you to understand that.'

He gave her one of his supercilious looks. 'In that case, let's state the genuine unadulterated fact about it, Caro, not the half-truth. Indeed Caro Craken came to France for her son, Harry, but too she came for *the enemy*, that is, not the Germans, but the enemy Fleet. In the hopes that some miracle would place them somewhere together. Well, she has seen her son, but it appears she has not yet seen her other heart's desire; so in the light of that, she remains.'

'Matt, for God's sake—'

'Oh, and to be absolutely impartial in the telling, along the way, she has found a calling. She thinks she can make a difference to the wounded and the dying, so now she's in France for three reasons.'

Caro's chest was tightening and a telltale blush crept up her throat. 'This is dreadful, Matthew. You're only making matters worse. Why do you do this?'

He finished his coffee and leant back, lifting his arm along the back of the booth and regarding her. He tapped on the wood under his long fingers while the light from the lanterns flickered across their faces and one of the French soldiers at the bar began to sing.

'Why do I do this? I'll tell you and, unlike yourself, I won't lie about it so please don't interrupt. Over six months ago my wife disappeared while I was on a trip away. She left no note, no message, no explanation of any kind for me. I was informed by Jane that she had followed her foolish young son who had joined up and been sent to France. I, of course, read another consideration into her departure. So I thought, if my son and my wife are in France, I may as well be too. Thus I asked for a posting which I had virtually to foist on the Australian Government, suggesting to them that they might like to use me as an experiment, a prototype for a scheme I knew they were considering, whereby they could avail themselves of me as an official artist of the war, to attempt to create a graphic memorial of what is happening here.

'Before I left Australia, I found out, as I assume you did, what battalion my son was with, and on arrival in England I then managed to find out where my wife was. I knew from a letter she had written to her friend Jane that she had been accepted as a VAD.'

He lifted his hand from the back of the booth and ran it across his scar as he continued, 'So when finally I tracked my wife down to a small French town back from the front, I was greeted with, *God, Matt, what are you doing here?* Not a welcome which warmed my heart. Since then my wife has spoken about hoping not to lose her position at the hospital, about what time she begins work tomorrow, about her son and also how much the wounded boys here need her. Never once has she said she was pleased to see me, or asked how long I'd be here, or how I got here or how I am.' He made a small grim sound in his throat.

He held up his hand to maintain her silence. 'Now I'm used to rejection from my wife, on all emotional levels . . . have become habituated to it, have had to resort to forcing my physical self upon her to receive any acknowledgement from her that I was even on the same planet. Everybody in Caro's world, whether they be relative or friend, mere acquaintance or passing stranger, deserves more attention than her husband. Now that's gone on for bloody year in and year out.

'But do you know what, old girl? I've had six months to consider what up to now I've called a marriage, and this evening has only verified my position. I've come to a final conclusion, a last judgement, you might say. Caro, I married you for a variety of reasons, but one, the most important of all, in all truth, was . . . because I wanted to.'

He stood up. 'And now Caro, eighteen years later, I'm leaving you for exactly the same reason.' He picked up his cane, gave one of his slanted smiles and walked away.

Caro was dumbfounded. Her eyes were riveted to his departing back. She watched him limp by the canteen bar and lift his cap to Madame Fleurcourt, watched him cross to the door and exit into the night. She felt light-headed and queasy in the stomach. She could not believe what she had just heard but the empty seat opposite was verification of the event.

She was still sitting there when Madame Fleurcourt asked if she wished for more tea. This prompted her to stand, and mutter, *'Non, merci,'* before she left the canteen. She looked right and left, half expecting him to be waiting, leaning on his cane in the street, but there was no sign of him.

She walked home in the wind, feeling at a loss to know what

to think. She felt oddly empty and alone. She attempted to pull herself together, saying all manner of things in her head: she had been without him for six months; she had not missed him in that time; she would not miss him now; she had only married him for a name for her son; she did not love him, never had; she had only remained in her imperfect marriage for convenience. He had in fact done her a favour. She should have left him years ago.

When she arrived at the villa she looked in on Annie and made her a cup of tea. The girl was feeling better. 'I'll be back at work tomorrow.'

'Good,' Caro answered absent-mindedly.

'You're quiet tonight,' Annie observed, sipping her tea.

'Oh am I? I had a run-in with Iron-heart.'

Later when she lay under her blankets sleep would not come. She still had the upset feeling in her midriff, the queasy feeling in her chest. Matt was so jealous of her he would not just up and leave like this. He was obsessive about her. She saw his parting smile over and over again; she saw the sprinkling of lamplight on the scar on his cheek and the way he turned his head to the side; she had noticed for the first time that there were grey strands in the hair at his temples and it had somehow surprised her. She remembered how he had lifted his cane and limped across the canteen floor to the door. It was the early hours of the morning before an edgy disturbed sleep came.

The following morning she felt irritable and tired. She hurried down the hill to the hospital and in the door right on seven. Throwing off her cape and bonnet she took down from the hook on the wall her long white apron with the crimson cross. She hurried through into the ward and over to Michael. For a moment she was disoriented. She turned in a circle, looking along the ward and then back at the bed. This was where Michael lay, she knew it.

'Where's Michael? Why is his bed empty?'

'He died in the night, Caro.'

Caro swung round to see Jill Cossington standing in the doorway. 'I think he wanted to, Caro. He didn't want to live . . . not like that.'

A great swell of emotion overcame her and she hurried away

along the ward, eyes filling with tears. Out along the corridor to the back door she half ran, her sight blurred and she opened the door and stood on the steps, breathing great gulps of air. 'Oh Michael, Michael,' she whispered through her tears. She shuddered and sobbed and looked into the grey sky, and then she became aware of one of the nurses behind her. 'You're wanted by matron.'

Caro brought herself under control and wiped her face and smoothed her hair and reported to matron's office, a small back room with only one window which had stored damaged books before the war. Iron-heart was sitting iron-faced behind her table. Caro stood in front.

'Have you been crying, *Mrs* Craken?'

'Oh, it's nothing, Matron.'

'That's not an answer to my question.'

'I . . . I was affected by the death of Michael Leahy in the night. I . . . well, he had become special to me.'

'You know we aren't meant to become attached to any of the patients.'

'Yes.'

Matron took off her glasses and ran her hands across her eyes. 'Though we do, we do. It's only human, I suppose.'

That was the most understanding thing Caro had ever heard Iron-heart say and she nodded in agreement.

The matron replaced her glasses and took stock of Caro. 'You have a most offensive husband.'

'Yes, I know.'

Iron-heart was taken aback. This was a surprising response. 'Oh, so you know. Is he like that to everyone?'

'Yes, often. He did not single you out, I assure you.'

The matron considered this. 'Hmm. I suppose you know I can, perhaps should, report you for what happened last night and if I'm not mistaken it would lead to your removal.'

'Yes, Matron, I'm aware of that and I'm sorry.'

'Where's your husband's posting? Are we to see much of him?'

Caro shook her head and for a moment the matron thought Caro was going to cry again. 'No, he's gone. Won't be coming back.'

'I see.' She regarded Caro silently for a few more seconds

then touching the folder at her right hand said, 'You also have the ability to drive vehicles I see by your file.'

'Yes, I can. I was told I would be needed to drive ambulances some time.'

Iron-heart took a deep breath and her prominent bosom rose and fell. 'Yes, well, in that case you're valuable. Now go and wash your face and have a quick cup of tea and get back to the ward. There's a lot of work to do, you know.'

Caro gave a noisy sigh of relief. 'Oh yes, Matron, absolutely, of course.' And she turned and hurried out of the room.

Chapter Thirty-eight

Seventy-two hours before the push began Bingo came along the trench and found Dave who was reading a dog-eared copy of *Ginger Mick* by the Australian author C. J. Dennis. It had done the rounds of the entire 16th Battalion. He hurriedly put it on the firestep as Bingo spoke.

'Sands, follow me.'

Dave jumped to his feet and followed the sergeant along to the reserve trench and down to Queen Street, the communication trench. Dave, aware that the sergeant thought he asked too many questions, held himself in until they halted near one of the officers' dugouts. 'Where are we going, Sarge?'

'Captain Hardcastle wants to see you. Wait here,' and Bingo disappeared down the steps to the dugout. When he returned Tommy Hardcastle was with him. He thanked Bingo, saying, 'I'll take over from here.' Then he gestured for Dave to follow him and began heading to the rear.

Dave decided it was time to ask again, 'Where are we going, Captain?'

'The commanding officer wishes to see you.'

Dave spoke under his breath. 'Gawd, Uncle John Conrad.'

Across the duckboards and the water they went in tandem, standing upright in parts of the trench where they could walk normally and bending low where enemy fire had blasted; in these places men heaved sandbags and tree trunks, branches, corrugated iron and anything at hand to raise the breastwork and mend the ramparts. They passed by men sleeping, playing cards, writing letters, cleaning weapons and others in the process of delousing themselves.

At one point at the rear of Queen Street a platoon of sappers were reinforcing a concrete observation block and Tom held up his hand to halt Dave while he went inside and inspected it. By the time they came to advance headquarters a bitter wind was blowing and the two men hurried across the dried mud, past a company of horse soldiers, to the front entrance of the convent.

Dave was shown inside to a room where John Conrad sat behind a table piled high with papers. Hessian bags hung over two missing windows and a fire was attempting to remain alight in the small grate in the wall.

As Tommy Hardcastle withdrew John Conrad spoke. 'Good to see you, Dave.'

Dave saluted. 'Er . . . yes, thank you, Uncle . . . sir.'

'Sit down, son.'

Dave sat.

'How are you liking army life?'

He smiled. 'Not as good as home, but it's all right.'

'Yes, we have to make the best of it. Though the Somme's not the place I'd normally choose to camp out during the winter.'

'Yes it's pretty cold.'

'I believe you went on the raid the night before last?'

'Yes.' The youth was wondering where this polite conversation was going but he was soon enlightened.

'Dave, there are men needed at Brigade and Division Headquarters, good men, like you. I know you're a brave and competent soldier; the report on you from the raid proved that. A position has come to my notice at Divisional Headquarters which I think would suit you admirably. It's in the Signal and Communications Corps.' He smiled and fleetingly a tender look crossed his face. 'Actually a little bit of responsibility comes with it. We'll be making you a corporal. I'd like you to take this position, Dave. It'll be interesting work and a challenge for you.' He leafed through some of the material at his right side and handed Dave a sheet of paper. 'This is your transfer. You can pack your kit and leave tonight. Captain Hardcastle will tell you where to be and at what time.'

John Conrad stood and came round the table. 'Son, I know you'll be a success at whatever you do, but this job's the right one for you. I'm pleased it's come up and I'll look forward to seeing you when this stunt's over . . . you can buy me a beer in Brisbane.' He held out his hand.

Dave hesitated, his mind was racing. Divisional Headquarters? Making him a corporal? He looked at the transfer paper in his palm and he stood up in front of his colonel.

He did not take his uncle's extended hand. 'Excuse me, Uncle John Conrad, sir. If I'm understanding this right you're giving me a job at Divisional Headquarters which will always be well back from the front. You appear to be sending me out of the firing line. Now the word's pretty strong that there's to be a final push for the year and that our battalion's in it and it seems you're trying to remove me from danger. I know why you're doing this and I appreciate it but, sir, I can't accept it.' He placed the transfer paper back in his commanding officer's extended palm.

John Conrad shook his head in disappointment. 'Dave, you know your uncle and I were like brothers?'

'I do but—'

'Then for his sake just take this position. It's as honourable a job as any in the army. You'll do it well.'

'But I'll be leaving my friends, my mates in the front line.'

'Son, I can't transfer all of you.'

'I know you can't and I don't expect you to. I'm truly grateful that you care enough for me to try to give me a safe job. But I'm refusing it, sir.'

'You must know you cannot refuse me, that I can transfer you whether you wish it or not.'

Dave's tone entreated him. 'Yes, I do, but I'd prefer active service, so please sir, don't.'

'Are you sure of that?'

'Definitely, sir. If you were in my position I don't think you'd want to take it either.'

John Conrad gave a wry smile. He thought of his interview with Sir William Robertson in London when he had declined the desk job. He withdrew behind the table and sat down. He examined Dave in silence for a time while the wind rattled something on the roof and momentarily blocked out the sound of the big guns. 'Sit down, son.'

Once more Dave sat.

'I deeply desired you to take the post with Signals and Communications, Dave, but I'm trying to understand your position.' He paused for a moment deliberating. 'I don't agree with it but I'll accept it.'

Dave sighed. 'Thank you.'

'But I've decided to tell you we'll be making you a corporal in any case. Three of you who went on the raid the other night are being promoted. You personally will jump lance jack, son, and be promoted straight to corporal.'

Dave thought that was the end of the fun. He was a corporal now whether he liked it or not. This was serious.

'You really don't need to, sir.'

'A bit of responsibility will do you good.' He stood up and came round to sit on the table closer to Dave. 'As you can understand, son, a colonel doesn't usually inform the recipient of promotions of this sort. It's normally the lieutenant in charge of the platoon. Keep quiet on it and when you're told, act surprised, will you? Which will probably be a week or so from now.' He patted Dave's shoulder. 'One more thing; it's about young Craken. He may or may not have explained that his father and I are bitter enemies, I'm afraid. Are you two still friends?'

'Fact is, sir, we were estranged for weeks. I was really mad that he called you *enemy*. But the other night, the night of the raid . . . well, we decided to keep our own opinions but remain friends.' His face screwed up with the gravity of his thought. 'We get on really well, but I can't understand how anyone could possibly hate you, sir.'

John Conrad smiled. 'Thanks, my boy. Sadly we all have enemies in this life. On the national scale we have the Germans and their cohorts and on a personal level we still manage to alienate. Don't attempt to alter your friend's opinion. I don't want anything to do with me to interfere in your mateship.'

Dave could not help it, he answered without thinking, 'But I would *like* to change his mind. I want to. He doesn't know you, he doesn't have any idea of the wonderful things you've done. I wouldn't have had any schooling but for you. Mum and Dad would be up queer street but for you. My brother and my sisters wouldn't have—'

John Conrad held up his hand. 'No, son, leave it. There's an old saying, "A man convinced against his will is of the same opinion still." So don't try and foist your viewpoint on him.

He'll only resent it. Far better to let your friendship grow and perhaps things will alter naturally in time.'

He held out his hand and this time Dave took it. 'As I said about your promotion, keep it to yourself for now.' He squeezed Dave's hand. 'You must realise I feel a responsibility towards you but I don't know when we'll speak again. I can't keep you safe, son, but please be as careful as it's possible to be. And don't try to be a hero . . . just don't.'

Dave did not reply. He saluted smartly and walked to the door.

'And, Dave?'

The young man turned.

'When you write to your mother, send her my love.'

Dave smiled and left the room, and behind him John Conrad took a long deep breath. What he had not told Dave was that they had decided to promote young Craken too. Captain Hardcastle had reported favourably on him after the boy had noticed that a German sniper had extended a section of wall remaining in no-man's-land. They had decided to make Craken a lance corporal. The other thing John Conrad had not told Dave was that they were waiting until after the push to promote them. That was why he had told the boy it would not happen yet. The grisly fact was that they would be promoted if they lived and the reality was that in all probability after the battle the battalion would be short of non-coms.

He had tried to do his best for Dave, but the youth had proved stubborn as youth often was. Dave had the spunk that his Uncle Hargy had displayed all those nights ago at the Colosseum. For a few moments he thought of Hargy, saw his lively coal-black eyes and heard his laugh as they sat on the bank of the Brisbane River fishing. He looked across at the hessian bags moving in the wind and spoke to himself. 'I miss you, old friend. Remember when we were going to travel round Australia together? Remember how people looked at us, disapproving of our friendship? But we didn't give a damn, did we, pal? How well I remember the night you died in my arms.' This conjured up the scene in the street outside the Colosseum and he recalled the arrival of Matthew Craken and the bitter words they had said, and how later he had gone to Caro . . .

It was all water under the bridge. He shook his head as

he stood and listened to their long-range guns. They had intensified this morning and would keep up the barrage each morning until Monday, in an attempt to soften up the enemy, to blast their lines into oblivion before the boys went over the top. Sadly, in the last four months this had not worked as well as they had hoped. The German bunkers were deep and often impenetrable and the Germans just went to ground. But this time they had been assured by their spies and by the observation teams that this part of the line was not as well bunkered as to the south; assured that this strategy here would be more effective.

This morning at dawn he had gone to the heavy artillery range with Tommy Hardcastle at his side. As they drove up in their armoured car Tom had informed him, 'There are three of our batteries and three British batteries here side by side, sir, mostly hows.' *How* was the shortened form of howitzer and most soldiers referred to them this way.

On the range the noise was deafening; even with the wax in their ears the howitzers boomed a steady ear-splitting refrain. It had been cold, and a chill wind had been blowing all the way up the Somme Valley and along the Ancre but it was so hot at the gun sites that many of the gunners were in summer clothing.

As the first fingers of light pierced the day, they passed by the back of a British gun and one of the bombardiers turned from the barrel as it recoiled discharging its shell. Sweat was running down his body, his shirt wet even in the chill day, his face blackened from the continuing blasts, but John Conrad recognised him.

He strode forward to the man as the rest of the gun crew went about their business. The bombardier looked up in surprise at the colonel who singled him out, and in the throbbing noise, John Conrad shouted, 'Jack . . . Piccadilly outside the Ritz!'

There was a moment of confusion and then Jack Harrison broke into a wide smile, showing pure white teeth against his blackened skin. The young man shouted back, 'It was a fine show at Her Majesty's, sir!'

John Conrad smiled and slapped the young man affectionately on the shoulder. 'Good work, Jack! Remember me to your sister when you write. And good luck.' And he and Tom moved on past the other guns as the young man waved.

Later, on the way back to headquarters, he explained to Tommy how he had met Jack in Piccadilly when an old woman had given the boy a white feather.

'If nothing else, conscription's stopped that.'

John Conrad moved back behind his table and sat down. They were brave, these lads, all the Daves and Jacks out there, even with the carnage going on they still believed in their millions that the Germans must be stopped. He just hoped Dave would not try to be too damn brave.

He closed his eyes in thought. He had been to battles here in France before, with and without K, but always in the past he had been an observer. This was different, on Monday he and his men had to take Beaumont Hamel . . . they just must. For the hundreds of thousands of boys whose unmarked graves were out there in bloody no-man's-land and for every one of them who lay rotting now on the wire and in the mud. He must not analyse it. He must not think of the Germans as men. He was a British Australian battalion commander, here to help win the war, and he must lead his men to victory.

He had to do K proud; he had to. He moved back behind the table and took up his pen.

On Sunday evening by candlelight Dave was playing cards with Isaac, Frank and three fellows from C Company who formed a Lewis light machine-gun team, Wells, Lockert and Lloyd. Beside Wells lay his thirty pounds of Lewis gun which he called Jessie and carried with him everywhere. They sat on boxes in a shallow dugout at the back of the trench and their game was interrupted when Harry's voice sounded from around the bend. 'All right, fellas, I'm collecting the letters for home on Sergeant Dobb's behalf.' They had all officially been told on Saturday that there would be a dawn attack on Monday and to write letters home if they were so inclined. That was when Dave knew absolutely that John Conrad had attempted to remove him from the firing line. They had guessed there was to be a final push for the year when all the officers had been to briefings during the entire previous week, and each day they had become more certain. Now they too had been briefed and knew their objective. Tomorrow they were to take the German stronghold in and around what had been the village of Beaumont Hamel.

'Here I am, boys,' Harry called, stooping and coming up to his mates. 'Any letters?'

Wells handed two across. 'Yes.'

'I'll get mine.'

'Here you are.'

Dave put his hand in his pocket to pull out his letter when suddenly the noise ceased and a total lull fell. The envelope made a brittle crinkling sound in the uncanny hush as he drew it out. 'Gosh, that was strange,' he said aloud. Then he turned to his mates. 'Count me out of this round. I'm reading this again,' and he read it to himself one more time.

Dear Mum, Dad, Tess and Danny,

Well the big stunt begins tomorrow. They'll come and collect these letters tonight, so it shouldn't be too long before you have this in Brisbane.

I'm all right. Don't worry about me. I'm a good fighter, I reckon, and with Uncle John Conrad in charge I'm feeling safe enough.

I bet Brisbane's hot. It's hard to imagine heat as it's so cold here. But we have greatcoats and blankets and I can't complain. It's good when a parcel comes. I got the socks Tess knitted, thanks. Have you heard from Jenny?

Well, that's it, I suppose. If anything happens to me, remember I was always, Your loving son,

Dave

PS: Uncle John Conrad told me to give his love to you, Mum. Don't be jealous, Dad.

He folded it and handed it to Harry.

'Any more?' Harry asked, looking around at the members of his platoon. 'Have you written one, Luke?'

Luke sat on the firestep a few yards down beyond the card players, drinking coffee. He shook his head.

Harry came up and knelt down on the duckboard beside him. 'Luke, mate, haven't you even written to your mum?'

'No.'

'Gosh Luke, I think you should have.'

Harry was a bit worried about Luke. Luke was short-tempered and withdrawn; had been ever since they arrived in the trenches. A few days earlier Harry had taken Luke aside after stand-to one morning and asked him what was the matter. Luke had looked at him with bloodshot unhappy eyes. 'Nothing.'

'But, Luke, old son, I'm your friend.'

'No you aren't, you're the Abo's friend,' he had snapped back.

Harry had taken hold of his friend's arm. 'Strewth, Luke, is this what this is all about? Look, I'm your friend too, I always will be. Nothing will alter that.'

'Yeah, you were my friend for a while here again when you weren't speaking to him, but now you've made it up, I'm out in the cold.' Luke's expression hardened. 'And it's bloody cold enough here. Anyway we decided to join this bloody mess together, didn't we?'

'Sure we did. We can all be friends. Come on . . .' He attempted to pull Luke along but he withdrew from Harry's hold. 'No, leave it. I'm all right.'

'Please, Luke.'

But Luke remained adamant. Later Harry had told Dave about it and Dave had gone to Luke himself and tried to put things right, but Luke had been surly and uncooperative, and Dave reported back to Harry that his attempt at reconciliation had been useless. Harry had tried to jolly Luke along and yesterday, when they had been told about the push, he had spent the whole day in his company except for his duty times and only seen Dave in passing, in the hopes Luke would understand they were still friends, but Luke had remained quiet. And now he had not even written a message home.

Harry patted Luke's knee. 'Would you like me to help you write a letter? I don't have to take these to old Dobb for a while yet.'

Momentarily Harry thought he saw a breakthrough, for Luke's eyes brightened, then his face dropped again. 'No. I'd rather not. I can't stand all this bloody noise all the time.' He put his head in his hands and Harry raised himself from the floor and sat beside him.

'Yes, it's loud all right. But, old son, it has to be done. We've got to fight the Huns in the morning and noise is all part of it.'

At that moment there was a retaliatory blast from the German side of the line that hit not less than a hundred yards away and all the card players threw themselves to the floor as dirt and bits of rubble rained down on them.

'Shit, that was close.'

'Jesus, they ain't all dead yet.'

Everyone else had dropped to the duckboards but Luke had not moved. He still sat on the firestep.

'We'd better get along and see if anyone's hurt,' Dave said, regaining his feet and hurrying away along the trench followed by Wells and Lockert.

Luke's eyes followed their departing backs.

'Well, I'm going to have a read and try to get some sleep,' Isaac said, moving away towards the dugout. 'This is our first stunt and I for one wish to be prepared.'

'Yeah, good idea,' and Frank departed, followed by Lloyd.

'Now come on, Luke,' Harry attempted to cajole his friend. 'Let's write that letter to your mum and then I'll take them all to old Dobb.'

Luke lifted his eyes to Harry, shook his head and buried his chin in his greatcoat. 'No, nothing to say.' And he moved hurriedly away after Isaac.

Although Harry was due to take his batch of letters down to the sergeant he quickly wrote another there in the light of the candle.

Dear Mrs Marland,

Luke's got a cut finger on his writing hand. Nothing bad at all, just did it on a piece of tin sheeting yesterday.

He wants me to tell you he's well and that things are going pretty fairly over here. We've been busy cleaning weapons and getting ready for a bit of a skirmish we're supposed to have tomorrow.

Food's not as good as we get back home, but we can't complain.

Well, that's it. Luke just wanted me to let you know he's all right and that he's thinking of you and home.

He sends loving wishes
From your son, Luke

He folded it, addressed the envelope and added it to the mailbag.

He had completed his own messages early that morning after stand-to and breakfast. The ink in his bottle had frozen overnight but he had melted it and had written one to Knobby, Jane, Katy and Isobel, one to his grandparents, one to Grandma Craken and another to his mother. He did not know where to write to his father. His father had informed him some time ago that he was leaving Australia and coming to France and that he would be in touch in time. The wording of Harry's letters deviated slightly but the message was virtually the same: that he did not want them to worry; that while the army was not exactly like being at school, he was fit and well; that he missed home and Sunday roasts and the Brisbane heat. In his mother's he wrote that he had enjoyed seeing her in Marseilles and he hoped she would understand and accept what he had done. He added that if she saw his father to tell him he loved him. He finished all four with exactly the same sentence: 'A friend here told me to always remember that the Bosche started this ruckus. And that's what I'll be remembering in the morning.'

When the mail sergeant arrived at headquarters John Conrad had written letters to his father and Aunt Leigh, Bart, his friend Quinton and Emma Louise.

Forty-eight hours before he had received a letter from Emma Louise. She had written it on 2 November and in it he was astounded to read that she had met Matthew Craken in Canterbury. It seemed he was on his way to France. The bastard was a government artist of some kind.

He came into the tea shop and later sketched me in one of the squares here under a yew tree, and like a fool I did not know who he was. At first he said his name was Tom Roberts and then later on he admitted his name was Matthew. Also at first he said he was from Adelaide and then again later he changed it to Brisbane. When he had finished drawing me he made an oblique reference to 'someone in my ken' he did not wish well. It was afterwards I remembered the name of your mortal enemy and that he carried a scar on his cheek and walked with a cane from injuries sustained in a fight with you, and that he was a painter who had married Caro Dere. That's when I knew for certain I had met Matthew Craken. He wore a major's uniform and, by the way, though he did a wonderful likeness of me I did not like it, for he had made me look so sad.

John Conrad, I feel a fool in some ways about this but really thought you should know. He is an odd one, all right. I hope I did not let you down in allowing him to draw me. I never would have if I'd realised at first who he was.

Emma had written then about her aunt and uncle and that she had returned to work at the Red Cross, finishing with the words,

I am coming to terms with things, David's death and all. By the way, little May was asking about you. Perhaps after all, you will come and visit us when you return home on leave.

    Fondly,
    Emma Louise

PS: I have been thinking recently about the day we spent at the beach in Southport when I cast myself down off the rocks into your arms and you caught me. What a special dreamy day that was.

He hardly read the PS, so taken with the body of the letter was he. So bloody Craken wore an officer's uniform and was coming to France. Well, France was a big country and there were close to five hundred miles of front, that ought to be enough to keep them apart; one more piece of vermin on French soil.

He had reread the letter. Craken was like some insidious disease seeking people out; the latest find being Emma Louise. It amazed John Conrad, though he was pleased Emma had informed him. Perhaps he would go and see her as she suggested. One thing he admitted: he did like receiving her letters.

He looked at the lamp glowing on the desk beside him. Tomorrow he could be dead. Many of the men in the trenches out there in front of him would be dead. It was one of the bizarre certainties in this ungallant war. Well, if he were dead then there would be two Fleet brothers buried in the mud of France. He shivered, he must not think like that. And how dearly he hoped the third brother, Bart, would never be anywhere near here.

He brought his mind back to the moment and returned to finishing his last report before the action on the morrow.

Fifteen minutes later there was a knock on the door. 'Come in,' and he looked up to see Tommy Hardcastle give a quick salute. 'Just to tell you that the cooks say dinner will be early tonight, around nineteen hundred. A few of the officers are here, the others are in the line.'

'I'm not having dinner now, Tom, I'm going into the line too. Tell the cooks I'll eat later when I return, probably about ten.'

Tommy looked surprised. 'Going into the line? May I enquire why?'

John Conrad stood up, took up his greatcoat, put it on and threw his scarf around his neck. He eyed his companion. 'I'm told we have one thousand one hundred and nineteen men in our battalion, that is, as of fifteen hundred today.'

Tom nodded. 'Sounds right.'

'Tomorrow at this time some of those one thousand one hundred and nineteen in the trenches now smoking, reading, trying not to think about tomorrow, will be dead. Now that stand-to's over, I'm going with as little ceremony as possible to move through the line and speak to as many as I can.'

'But you don't need to do that. You do that every week. You're already getting a reputation with the men. They're . . . almost fond of you.' He grinned. 'Well, as fond as they can be of a commanding officer.'

John Conrad smiled. 'Mmm, perhaps.'

Tommy Hardcastle hesitated and a frown lodged between his eyes. 'Can I ask you a question, sir?'

'Certainly, Tom.'

'It's not true what I was told by Major Roberts, is it? That you're going over the top with the men? It's not right, is it?'

'Yes, it is.'

'It's a wonder Brigadier Claver-Jensen has agreed.'

'The brigadier wasn't happy about it, but I prevailed.'

'Please, with deference, it's not necessary. No one expects it. I've only ever heard of such a thing a couple of times. They say that young Lieutenant Colonel Freyberg, the New Zealander commander of *Hood* Battalion with the Royal Naval boys, does it and keeps getting wounded, and then, with respect, there was a demented colonel with the Canadians.'

John Conrad halted at the door. 'Tommy, I know Bernard Freyberg, he's a damn brave fellow.' He came back into the room a step. 'I've studied the battles here in the Somme since July one and it's obvious that with the lack of communication, command becomes pretty limited once an action begins. In wars before now, generals could traverse the entire battlefield and personally control the action. But here, other than the operations that ran into massive resistance, the successful ones have been those where the orders were clear, the objectives were definite, all precisely understood, especially by the leading companies in the attack. Now I . . . we . . . have done as much as we can to ensure each company, each platoon, knows *exactly* what it is to do. The briefings have been long and involved but clarity has been my main object. I want to lead the men over the top to continue with that policy. So that they see I am following through right down to the point of collision with the enemy.'

Tommy Hardcastle did not speak, he just sighed.

'And while I know that they can't relate to me on a personal level, if I can be perceived as one of them just for tomorrow, it might make a difference. You know, Tommy, I think it was a philosopher slave in Ancient Greece who said "Perceptions are truths because people believe them."'

'That may be so, but there's no need for you to be perceived as one of the troops.'

John Conrad thought of K and why he was here, and he shook his head and gave a rueful smile. 'Ah, Tommy, if I believe there is then that's the end of the matter.' He opened the door. 'Now, my time's limited and I'm off to see as many as I can.'

'I'll come with you, sir.'

He put his arm around Tom's shoulder. 'Good, I'd like that.'

Five hours later John Conrad had spoken to some hundreds of the troops. He had moved through the lines, halting briefly with as many of the men as possible, sometimes just patting them on the shoulder or wishing them good luck or telling them to try to get some sleep. It was obvious to Tommy that the men appreciated it, that they thought a great deal of their leader, some he could see even idolised him, it was evident by the way they hung on his words and watched his every move, nodding in agreement as he spoke. He had informed some that he would be with them in the morning.

They were passing back down Queen Street to the accompaniment of the blasts of long-range artillery fire and the screaming whistle of shells followed by the inevitable explosions, when a blast from the German lines shook the ground. They were in a part of the long trench which had no supports or bolstering of any kind and was really only an extended ditch, so fragments of the earth rolled down, splashing in the water at their feet.

'That must have hit not too far away,' Tommy said as they steadied themselves and moved on towards a corner of the zigzagging trench in time to meet a private coming from the opposite direction and carrying a box of grenades. The private saw the two men approaching him, but in their greatcoats and wrappings evidently did not recognise them. 'Make way for Lord Kitchener,' he called jocularly as he went to pass them.

'What the devil did you say, soldier?' John Conrad rounded furiously on the man, who stopped in his tracks, balancing on the duckboards and holding the box on his shoulder.

In the reflected light from all around the man saw who had addressed him. 'Gawd, sir, didn't know it was you.' He attempted to salute.

'I said what the bloody hell did you say?'

As the man stumbled over his words to reply Tommy spoke in John Conrad's ear. 'It's a saying, sir. All the men in the British forces are using it. They mean nothing by it. In fact I think they do it to keep his memory alive. There's no disrespect, of that I'm certain.'

John Conrad inhaled and felt his anger dissipate. He made a

rumbling sound in his throat. 'Oh, I see. Well, I haven't heard it before.' He looked back at the private, who stood in awe of the proceedings. 'All right, lad, move on, I understand. And get some sleep tonight.'

The private speedily complied as the colonel and the captain moved on and were back at headquarters by 2230.

Behind them in the trenches and the dugouts men tried to sleep with the ever-present thought of the morning and what it would bring.

John Conrad had not been to the part of the line where Harry and Dave were, though they heard about his visit.

'The old man was going through tonight,' they were told by Curly when he came in off gas sentry duty. 'He patted me shoulder and wished me luck for tomorrow, said to say the same to the whole platoon, so there, fellas, I've told ya. Direct message from the colonel via me, Curly Moss.'

'Shit,' Harry said softly, 'who cares?'

Dave made no retort, but Frank Birtenshaw spoke up. 'Well, I do. I reckon it's decent of the old bastard to bother.'

Dave smiled and moved across to lie beside Isaac, who closed his poetry book and said as he lit a cigarette, 'Do you blokes know that Henry the Fifth brought his soldiers right through here before Agincourt?'

Harry's voice sounded through the gloom. 'Yes, that'd be right. We learnt it in history. Agincourt's in Northern France somewhere.'

Dave lay down near Isaac. 'Never heard of it. What was Agincourt?'

'A battle, we won, we fought the French.'

'Times change,' Dave stated philosophically.

'Yeah,' declared Curly, 'now we're fightin' hand in hand with 'em to save the Frogs' flamin' country. Anyway, thanks for the history lesson, Walker, but I'm goin' to try to sleep.'

Chapter Thirty-nine

At 0400 on Monday, 13 November 1916 John Conrad rose and washed as best he could in the chilly water in the broken dish supplied by his batman. As he splashed the water on his face he recalled his dream. He had been in India riding alongside his old friend Ashok Mahadevan. They had been laughing at something and K had been chiding them; and strangest of all his mother had been riding on his other flank. She had stretched her hand across to him and touched him gently, before she and K had dropped back leaving him and Ashok alone. He had not dreamed of his mother in a long time and had not even thought of Ashok in years. Why would he dream of them now? He hoped his Indian friend was well away from the war.

He dressed and ate a swift breakfast with Tommy Hardcastle before using the telephone to speak with Brigadier Claver-Jensen. The line crackled wildly but they understood each other.

'You will have the cover of a creeping barrage from our side. Have your men follow it as it moves forward and report to me as soon as you can,' the brigadier had said, 'and are you still intending to be a damn fool and go over the top?'

'Yes, sir.'

There was a silence and then the gruff tones of Claver-Jensen had come through again, 'Good luck.'

John Conrad climbed into an armoured car and by zero hour, 0545 when the barrage ceased briefly and a gloomy silence fell while a number of tanks rolled forward, he was in the front lines with the men of C Company, and Tommy at his side. Some of the boys had looked at him in amazement as he strode through to the front lines and others, who had known he was going up with them, smiled and saluted. A Salvation Army chaplain, the first man of religion John Conrad had seen in the very front lines, attempted to speak to him but John Conrad moved on by. He was not in the mood for religion on this of all mornings, but he was impressed to see the man there.

The smell of rum was overpowering and while the first whimsical moments of light plied through the fog the boys around him lifted their voices spontaneously in 'On the Road to Gundagai', he sang along with them.

> There's a track winding back
> To an old-fashioned shack
> Along the road to Gundagai.
> Where the blue gums are growing
> The Murrumbidgee's flowing
> Beneath those sunny skies . . .

When they ceased they heard voices of the King's Own Royal Lancaster Regiment as if in reply drifting across to them:

> Take me back to dear old Blighty
> Put me on the train for London town,
> Take me over there,
> Drop me anywhere
> Birmingham Leeds or Manchester
> I don't care . . .

Men coughed and murmured to each other, and the man on the left side of John Conrad, a twenty-five-year-old from Cloncurry, looked up with admiration and said, 'I'm proud to stand next to you, sir.'

'Thanks, digger. I feel the same way about *all* of you.'

Then, in confidential tones the man added, 'I've got a three-year-old daughter, sir. Will I ever see her again?'

John Conrad felt a surge of complicated emotions. 'I hope so, son, I truly hope so.'

They put on their helmets, fixed bayonets, counted the number of rounds, checked their gas masks, rations and their water bags.

'Grenadiers check your grenades,' called a lieutenant. 'Now all wire cutters attached? And don't forget your shovels.' By now it had become clear that assault troops had to have tools which allowed for consolidation and repair of trenches, hence the shovels had become part of the ground troops' already heavy, unwieldy loads along with their weapons and 170 rounds of ammunition each.

They heard the signal for the advance. John Conrad gestured to Captain Durst from C Company, who stood a few yards from him and the captain shouted, 'Make for the line directly opposite! Use the shelter of the tanks when you can! Ready!'

There was a moment of expectancy when John Conrad smiled encouragement at Tommy and then lifted his hand and his voice sounded along the trench. Tommy at his side blew his whistle. 'Up, boys! Straight ahead!' And the big guns seemed to take up the command and the creeping barrage making way for them began again with new trajectories on the German lines.

John Conrad leapt up from the firestep, and scrambled over the parapet as all those around him did the same, springing on boxes, up ladders and out. He raised his arm in the mist with Tommy at his side, and shouted again, 'This way! Let's go!' charging along with his men across the mud and waste, bounding over debris, surging through the previously cut wire, running through the morning mist towards the enemy.

Along in section 51, the part of the trenches occupied by Harry and his platoon, they heard the heavy morning barrage of the Germans beginning at 0300, and just prior to 0530 the rum came – in buckets. It had arrived at the front in heavy earthenware jars stamped 'SRD' – Service Rum Department – and then been poured into the buckets for easy distribution. Bingo, with stooping shoulders, wandered through the men his red beard thrust forward as he bellowed, 'Those that want the rum here it comes. Fortify yourselves, boys, and remember the bloody Huns are just across there!' He pointed with his rifle. He was followed by Captain Bader, who shouted that it was not compulsory to take the rum. This rule was left to the battalion commander and John Conrad had seen fit to let the men make their own decision.

The majority took it; in Harry's platoon only Isaac declined.

The sickly sweet smell pervaded the trench and the cold night air. The buckets sat on the duckboards and they dipped in their cups. They had to shout to be heard.

Harry took his and gulped it down.

'Want another son?'

He shook his head.

Dave took a cupful, Frank two, Curly two and Luke the same.

Harry noticed Luke spilling the rum, his hand was shaking so much.

'What's wrong, old son? Nothing to worry about, we'll be all right. Just remember everything we learnt.'

'Right, men, you got all your kit?' Lieutenant Bradshaw's voice sounded along the trench. 'You can't come back if you've forgotten something. The tanks are going in now and as soon as we can see at all, we'll follow.'

Just before the dawn drove its insidious fingers of light through the mist and into the trenches, and while the continual blast of the artillery attempted to close out all thought, Harry crept along to where Dave was. 'Just wanted to see you again. Good luck, old son.'

'You too. You're my best friend, Harry.'

Harry put out his hand and Dave took it. 'And you're mine. We'll be in Beaufort Hamel by tonight. Frank gave me some cheese, Gawd knows where he got it, but we'll share it over there.'

'Too right.' He withdrew his hand and slapped Dave's shoulder. 'Well, I'd better get back to Luke.' He sighed. 'He looks pretty scared.'

Dave nodded. 'Yes sure.' He gave a brave grin, 'I reckon a lot of us are.'

Isaac stood next to Dave. He tucked his small poetry book in a pocket on the inside of his greatcoat and giving a faint smile said,

> 'To be or not to be, Dave: that is the question:
> Whether 'tis nobler in the mind to suffer
> The slings and arrows of outrageous fortune,
> Or to take arms against a sea of troubles,
> And by opposing end them?'

Dave grinned. 'Gosh I like that. Who said that?'

'The great man, the bard, our own William Shakespeare.'

'Would you quote some more of that?'

'Tonight in Beaumont Hamel, tonight,' Isaac laughed.

'Too right,' Dave replied, 'and you can teach me some.'

As Harry passed by Curly, he was gulping down some rum. 'Remember what I told you, Harry boy.'

'I do, old son, it's in the forefront of my mind. The Bosche started it.'

'That's bloody right.'

Harry moved on and tapped Frank on the shoulder as he passed. 'Good luck.'

Frank replied, 'Got your bayonet fixed, Harry?'

'Yeah.'

'Then don't bloody well fall over it!'

This made them all giggle and when Harry slipped in beside Luke he was still laughing.

Luke turned on him. 'For God's sake, what's there to laugh about?'

Harry could feel the tension in Luke and he suggested, 'Have another rum, old son. Might loosen you up a bit.' He bent down and dipped in the bucket. Luke took it and swallowed it as Bingo's steady, cool tones observed, 'Now, lads, it's time to mount the firestep. Up you go and remember that the Hun is ready to kill you, so kill him first. We're heading straight across no-man's-land. The wires have been cut by the barrage so there's no worry on that score. The artillery have done a good job and it's up to you to do the rest.' He coughed and spat on the duckboards. 'The first thing is to take the trench opposite – you all know that. Then we'll keep moving forward steadily. When the fog clears right away you'll see the tanks and if it's possible we'll follow them into the objective but remember to stay with me, Sergeant Dobb, the lieutenant or the captain. All understood?'

The chorus came back over the noise of the shelling, 'Yes, Sarge.'

The sun was thrusting its rays through the gloom and the mist. Harry could see the boys along the trench all leaning on the forward rampart rifles up as if they merely rested there awhile. There was an expectant tension everywhere.

They heard Sergeant Dobb moving up and down behind them. 'Now remember, boys, this is a killing morning. I'll take you out straight over the top. Follow me, we'll give the bloody Huns a day to remember.'

Harry became aware of a dead silence. The barrage had stopped briefly. The silence hung about them like the fog, eerie unreal unearthly.

They began to sing 'Waltzing Matilda': loudly proudly.

> '"Waltzing Matilda, waltzing Matilda,
> Who'll come a-waltzing Matilda with me."
> And he sang as he watched and waited
>   till his billy boiled,
> "Who'll come a-waltzing Matilda with me . . ."'

And as they finished and the words died away the light was filtering through even more. Harry looked round at Luke and his friend's face was ashen; there was panic in his eyes. Harry dropped his gaze and saw the wet stain on Luke's cloth puttees and the pool at his feet upon the duckboards. 'Oh God, Luke, please, it'll be all right. Just stay by me.' It hit Harry now why Luke had been quiet all these weeks. He had assumed his friend was put out because of his mateship with Dave, but no, it was obvious now. And Luke was not frightened, he was terrified.

A perverse memory altered the trembling boy beside him into the posturing Luke of the schoolroom. Was it only just months ago? It seemed like years when Luke had said, *'Wish I were eighteen.'*

'Why?'

'I'd join up . . . too right I would. Get away from mad old MacDonald . . . see the world and be treated like a man . . . just like Uncle Bill, darn right.'

Harry shivered, remembering his ready agreement. *'Reckon I would too.'*

Well, here they were; they were being treated like men, and men had to bloody fight.

'Come on, old son, please, it'll be all right, just stay by me. Don't worry.'

Bingo appeared at Harry's side and his calm loud voice shouted, 'This is it, boys . . . up you go!' A whistle blew. 'Now!'

Harry jumped high in the air. The smell of the rum filled

his world and he clutched his rifle in his hands. Feeling his feet were on the dry mud of the rampart he scrambled up and stood tall in the fog. And all along the allied line men did the same: along the miles of misty front the Australian, English, French, Irish, Scottish, Welsh, and New Zealand troops jumped up out of the trenches and ran in frenzy through the hazy fog across that little muddy handkerchief of land full of death and belonging to no man, towards Gommecourt and Serre, Beaumont Hamel, Beaucourt and St Pierre Divion they charged, men of the 13th Corps' 31st Division, the 3rd Division, the 2nd Division, John Conrad's 6th Mixed Division, the 51st Highland Division, and the 19th Division, the 63rd Royal Naval Division – tens of thousands of men all pumped with the bravado of rum and adrenalin.

The booming of the creeping barrage with their new trajectory washed over them from the front and Harry could see dozens of forms moving to right and left as he bent down and started out across no-man's-land. He felt heady, as if in a dream, running alongside the security of Bingo, who shouted encouragement in the cold morning fog. They bounded over wood and broken things, across flattened wire, through grey chalky mud and sticky waste, listening all the while for the machine guns from the Huns opposite but there was nothing. That was the one thing Harry had feared: while he knew the explosions were deadly he was more afraid of bullets.

But no bullets came, though he heard them spattering in the distance somewhere. Then grenades popped death to his left and bright flames sprung up in the corner of his vision, but still he ran with the form of Bingo at his side.

He arrived at the first German trench with Bingo on one side of him and masses of men on the other.

'Down we go, boys.' And they jumped, scrambled, half fell into the enemy trench: to find nothing.

'Jesus, where are they?'

Bingo hurried along the empty ditch, the light of killing in his eyes.

'Can't see any of the bastards, Sarge!'

'No one down this way either, Sarge!' a yell came from around the corner.

Suddenly it dawned on Bingo. 'The bastards must have

thought it was merely another morning barrage. They're not expecting us. They've gone to ground in the bloody bunkers and dugouts here until they think it's over.' He waved his fist in the air. 'Easy meat for us. Come on, boys . . .'

Along he ran with Harry and the others at his heels. He halted at the first set of neat cement steps running down to a dugout.

'Shit, cement! We don't have anythin' that good.'

Bingo raised his hand. 'Back up, boys. We've got a nice surprise for these little bastards!' and he rolled two Mills bombs down the steps.

'Kill any who resist!' he shouted as the first blast threw pieces of cement and dirt and wood in the air.

Harry felt earth rain down on his helmet. There was a second blast and then further blasts along the trench as others, finding the same situation, did as Bingo had done.

Then Bingo amazed Harry by yelling down what was left of the hole, *'Gebt auf! Verlasst eure Waffen und kommt mit erhobenen Händen heraus!'*

And to Harry's further amazement out came men stumbling up towards them, some covered in blood, all in dirt, but each attempting to do as Bingo had ordered: to leave their weapons behind and come out with their hands up.

Then an almighty blast sounded to the north, as if the hills and valleys for miles exploded. It was the Hawthorn Redoubt being blown apart for the second time in four months, by the 30,000lb charge hurling dirt and cement and wood and men high over the mist of the hills and the fog that still clung in the valleys. The British tunnellers had worked for months to run their underground passages back beneath the old crater.

'Right,' Bingo said, smiling widely, his red beard bobbing fiercely in the percolating dawn. 'Lovely. This is just the way I like a stunt to start!'

Dave had run along near Sergeant Dobb at first. He had kept sight of him as they struggled up over the top and charged forward, yelling and screaming. He knew Harry was somewhere to his right and he hoped he would be safe, but that's all he had time for. The fog was helping them, no doubt about about it. At one point he realised both Frank and Isaac were with him but then he lost them and Dobb disappeared too and he was running forward with men he did not know. Then he recognised the shape of Captain Bader to his left and ran with him for a time until he felt the ground rumble and a blast threw mud and dirt over him but he kept running through the flattened wire and over rubble and sticky broken ground. A man in front of him stumbled and fell and cried out. Dave stopped.

'Are you hurt?'

'No, just stuck.' And he was, in thick glutinous mud.

Dave helped him out of the knee-deep slime.

'Thanks, mate,' and they continued on together.

A minute later Dave could hear the field guns start again and he could see explosions through the rising fog and abruptly a burst of machine-gun fire spattered to his right, and he saw men pitch forward like dolls and his muddy friend went down screaming. He stopped running, waiting for the bullets to hit him but none came, the burst of fire had taken out every single man he could see to his right, and yet like some edict from above, had halted with his muddy friend. He spared a moment to look down at him, a second to wonder at his name, and then Dave moved on.

He ran on with the men on his left, the shovel strapped on his back thudding into his thigh. They were at the Bosche forward trench and figures were climbing up out of it. For a second he thought they were British, then abruptly he recognised Germans as he fell to the ground and shot point-blank at a shape in front of him, who was already aiming a rifle. The bullet lifted the form high in the air and it fell backwards out of sight. Around him the other Australians had fallen to their knees and were blazing away.

He jumped to his feet as a bullet whizzed by his neck, and in the gleaming morning light he saw the face of his enemy: big eyes, wide and bloodshot. The man seemed taken aback, unnerved by the personal contact and in that second Dave took advantage, yelled and charged forward as too late the German swung his rifle up to fire. Remembering the training Bingo had put them through Dave slammed his rifle butt hard on to the German's weapon, knocking it to the side as he leapt to the right and, withdrawing his rifle at speed, followed forward with a rapid penetrating thrust that sank his bayonet down deep into the man. The German's hand opened and his rifle fell from it as he crumpled forward, his blood spurting along Dave's gun barrel. Dave had to push the man back and away to enable him to pull the resisting weapon from his stomach.

He had no time to think as he turned to face the enemy again. Still they came up over the ramparts, firing all the time. Suddenly beside him he saw Wells, from C company, drop to the ground and with Lockert helping him, balance their Lewis light machine gun on Wells's knee and begin to pour bullets into the oncoming Germans. Like clumsy marionettes they fell in ungainly postures to the ground.

Then Isaac was back beside him and in another minute the fog had lifted enough to show the awkward heaps of dying and dead in front of them. Some groaned, most were silent.

A massive explosion to the north told them the Hawthorn Redoubt had blown again and as Captain Bader waved the men of the 16th battalion around him forward into the German trenches, Wells's voice sounded strangely in Isaac and Dave's ears. 'Thank God little Jessie didn't jam.'

Mills bombs exploded to right and left, and in twos and threes they followed Sergeant Dobb and Captain Bader, bounding over the dead bodies and scrambling down into the trench. 'All right, boys,' the captain said, lifting his hand, 'we've got this far!'

And the sergeant added, 'Now come! On we go. We must consolidate.' And they followed the officers over more corpses and along the trench.

Dave turned round to Isaac. 'Have you seen Harry or any of the others?'

'No, I started off with Frank but I lost him.'

They stayed close to Dobb and half an hour later Dave, Isaac, Wells and a dozen others, with their eyes on the tanks rolling along a spur in the distance, were in swampy ground, coming up a gentle rise to cross towards what had been the village of Beaumont Hamel.

The creeping barrage had ended and the shells from the allied big guns were exploding miles in front. The fog was lifting and Dave could see about thirty men a hundred yards or so ahead on top of the rise when the ominous shrill approaching noise of whizzbangs filled the air and the ground all around erupted in fire and fury. Dave and those around him fell to the ground as the thirty men in front disappeared entirely into the explosion.

Dave's hands had gone automatically over his head and he felt a thud on his left hand as he rolled over. He had been hit by a piece of stone hurled up in the blast. It had only scraped his skin. 'Blimey that was close,' he said, turning to Isaac who lay beside him on the ground.

Isaac lay there smiling and for half a second Dave began to smile back. Then he saw Isaac's helmet was split open and suddenly blood discharged from his nose. The men around him were getting to their feet and Sergeant Dobb was moving them on.

Dave's shocked intake of breath was lost in the arc of insane noise engulfing them. He lifted Isaac in his arms. 'Oh Gawd, Isaac, no.' The whole of the back of his friend's head was gone. Just like that. In one explosion Isaac of the poetry, Isaac of the knowledge, Isaac the gifted, was gone for ever: only blood and brains and his broken helmet left. As his stomach turned Dave kept down the bile that swelled up in his throat.

The tears stung his eyes and blurred his vision. 'Oh, Isaac . . . Gawd, Isaac . . .' Dave looked around but there was no one else there; the others were filtering on, dark shapes across the rise. He reached in to the warmth of Isaac's body and took the poetry book from the inside of his coat. 'I'll take this, old mate,' he whispered through his tears, then he laid Isaac gently down and stood up in the madness to follow the captain, the sergeant and the others.

Luke had heard the sergeant's voice shout, 'This is it, boys. Up you go! Now!' and he had thought of his Uncle Bill and tried with all his might to urge himself up after Harry but his legs would not move. The apprehension that had been eating at him for weeks descended over him in a net of paralysing fear. He watched Harry's boots climb the parapet in front of his eyes and disappear from his sight. Rubble fell back around him and he had attempted again to move but he was shackled by his terror, listening to his friends vanishing into the fog howling and screaming. This could not be happening. He began to sob, petrified, there in the empty trench in a sudden strange wave of eerie loneliness.

Out of nowhere like a burst of rifle fire Lieutenant Bradshaw's voice rapped along the trench, 'Marland, you bastard, move! At the double, up you go!'

Luke brought his eyes round to the lieutenant. 'I c-can't!'

'You can and you will or I'll shoot you here and now for bloody cowardice. I mean it. Move!' And he thumped Luke hard in the arm with his handgun.

'Please ... I didn't know it would be like this ... please ...'

'Please be buggered. You're a soldier, you arsehole. Move!'

Luke, wide-eyed with terror, attempted to scramble up from the firestep, but he slipped and fell back, dropping his rifle.

'If the whole bloody army acted like you we'd all be dead German meat. Pick up your rifle ... now! And get out there after your bloody mates or I'll blow your fucking head off!'

Blind with fear Luke's shaking hand picked up his rifle and he forced his jelly-like legs to crawl onto the firestep and up the slant of the trench wall over the parapet.

He was on all fours when a gunshot blasted by his ear. In shock he fell forward and then managed to rise to his feet to stumble on a couple of steps in the dry mud. 'Now get outa here,' he heard the lieutenant's voice behind him again, 'or the next bullet's in your back!' And in terror Luke blundered into the morning haze, blinded by his tears.

He could hear booming of guns ahead of him and behind him as he struggled on, not knowing his direction. Something tore at his trousers and he looked down. It was barbed wire; he was caught; he began to cry loudly like a child. It cut his leg as he pulled himself free and stumbled forward through thick sticky mud. He could hear yelling and shouting from across the waste of no-man's-land and there were leaping flames of fire and blasts to his left. He blundered on, he fell over something hard and then dragged himself up under the weight of his kit and the shovel on his back. He tried to run but he had no idea of direction and he only staggered some yards along a stretch of flattened barbed wire until abruptly he felt the ground give way and he skidded sideways, tumbling down into a wide shell hole with murky dank water at the bottom.

He landed on his back, the wind knocked out of him and he pulled himself into a sitting position and looked around. He started in horror. A head, mouth open, protruded from the mud right beside him. The body was buried in water and mud except for one hand, gaunt and inhuman, half eaten away by rats, but still holding a rifle. Shaking in terror he rose to his feet to move away.

He took a step and a harsh crunching sound came from under his boot as his right foot slid into something and stuck fast. Trembling he looked down and through his tears he saw it. It was another man! Luke was standing on him, his right boot was stuck in the man's ribcage, the dry muddy bones clamped round his foot, like a human manacle, his rotting insides throwing up a hideous stench from below his sightless eyes. A big brown rat, fat from human flesh, leapt out of where the entrails had been and ran across the mud. Luke's terror and horror gave voice to the insane scream that rent his lips apart.

Twelve hours later they found Luke in the foetal position on the far side of the same mud-soaked hole in the ground. Whimpering and with foam coming from his mouth, he sobbed for his mother.

Harry had been amazed to find they did not have to engage the Germans in the first of the trenches and as the steady stream of prisoners began filing back across no-man's-land Bingo had grinned. 'Now, boys, don't think it's going to all be as easy as this. We caught this part of the line napping, they weren't expecting us. It won't have been this simple all the way along.'

They headed off in a northerly direction down the captured trench, using enfilade fire as they ran, though they came to no opposition and within a few minutes of zigzagging, arrived on a rise where their view was clear and they saw a few of their tanks rolling in loose formation along a spur running towards the Ancre, the fog hanging in the low lands on either side.

Harry followed Bingo as they left the trenches to cross the undulating plain at the rear of the tanks in the distance. For the first time Harry looked round for Dave but he could not see his friend. He hoped Dave would be all right and that their little group of Frank, Isaac, Curly and Luke would remain unhurt.

He had no time to worry but he knew when he had gone over the top that Luke had not been beside him.

For a while they crossed towards their objective, remote explosions ahead in their eyeline. 'That's where Beaumont Hamel was, it's taking a pounding.' The captain was looking through his telescope and pointed with his gloved hand. 'From what I can see the tanks that haven't got stuck in the mud are close to the remains of the village now and it looks as if we're cleaning out the trenches around it. And to the south of the village it looks like the Highlanders are battering Y Ravine.'

As he spoke a tank in the middle distance burst open like a balloon of flames, throwing pieces of metal high in the air. 'A direct hit,' Bingo informed them. That seemed to begin a series of explosions right across the ridge but no other tanks blew up, even though some took hits. Onward they rolled inexorably, and the Australians, Irish and British were now mixed in together as they followed the vehicles towards their objective.

The boys followed Bingo in and out of trenches and across muddy fields. Finally they joined up with another company of Australian soldiers including Wells and his Lewis gun team of Lockert and Lloyd, who had become separated from Sergeant Dobb and Dave and were pleased to see Bingo and his men. Bingo led them all to what had been a sylvan dale of emerald-green ash trees and was now an unearthly gaunt collection of blasted shapes. The sergeant held up his hand and pointed beyond the mass of dead wood to a rounded shape on the top of a rise, well camouflaged, but out of which machine-gun fire was sweeping the hillside and holding down hundreds of Highlanders, British assault troops, Royal Dublin Fusiliers and Australians in shell holes and an undulation in the ground.

The sergeant signalled for Harry and Wells, his Lewis gun team, and three others to follow him and he crawled away in an arc through the blasted trees over the dried mud. A slope took them down to the south of the hill and into a shallow ditch that edged round and up the far side of the rise. It was possible that it might run fairly close to the loop holes where the rattling German bullets whizzed out.

Bingo cast his fire-eater's eyes around them, and pulled on

his ginger beard with his thick fingers. 'I'm goin' up there, lads. Craken, Wells, Lockert and Lloyd, you come with me.' He smiled at Wells, showing a broken tooth and pointed to his Lewis gun. 'I need Jessie for cover.' He gestured to the others to keep low. 'And you lot keep drawing the Huns' fire from here if you can.'

Harry could feel his heart thumping madly and his head seemed light and unconnected to his body as on all fours he crawled along the shallow ditch behind Wells and Bingo, the hail of bullets seeming only inches above their heads at times. The ditch was damp and there was some mud in places but being on the hillside it had drained well and was not the soggy quagmire of so much of the lower ground on the battlefield. After five minutes of exertion Bingo halted where stark tree trunks gave some shelter on the side of the cleft in which they lay.

'There are four,' Bingo said as he pointed to the German guns. 'One virtually covering each direction.'

'Gawd, Sarge, it'll be suicide if you go out there.'

'There's a war on, son.'

Wells sighed. 'As if I didn't know!'

The three boys at the bottom of the hill were managing to draw the German fire, for the machine guns were sweeping across to them now as well as to where the hundreds of soldiers lay pinned down on the other side of the emaciated tree stumps. As they watched, about a dozen of the Highlanders made a dash for a better position and all but two were mown down before they had run ten yards, the others hurtled into a small shell hole; it was unclear whether they were alive or dead.

'Shit,' breathed Wells.

'All right, Craken, give me one of your Mills bombs.'

Harry handed the sergeant a grenade.

'Now what I want you two boys to do is this. Craken, you and me, we're goin' on over there.' He pointed to where the ditch went on up about ten yards further and then petered out near a blackened tree standing like a twisted witchlike shape against the sky. Beyond that and nearer to the pillbox lay a thin tree trunk flat on the ground and at its far end it met a single boulder about two feet high. 'I'll leave you at that burnt-out tree, Craken. It looks like there's cover enough there for you to fire from that point.'

He turned to Wells. 'Then if you blokes can get a crack at them throw in a few hundred rounds from here and I might just be able to slide on my stomach along that tree trunk to the rock.'

'Sarge, you'll never do that. The tree's too thin, there's not enough cover.'

'I did a bit of tunnelling north of Gaba Tepe, son, so I know how to flatten my body. Now if I can manage and you all open fire, the Huns will then have four points to cover: the blokes in the ravine, our three on the south side, you here, Wells, and Craken over on the east. The second they're busy with all of you I think I can make it across and lob in a grenade or two.'

'Jesus, Sarge!' exclaimed Wells.

'Yes, well, I hope he's on our side, lad.' And with that Bingo motioned for Harry to follow and he crawled away.

The series of events then moved so fast Harry's memory of them was always unclear. Bingo and Harry reached the witch-like tree; Bingo gestured for Harry to commence firing once he was moving in prone position along the fallen tree trunk. This Harry did and took a shot when he could, even though his trigger finger shook. He watched Bingo flatten himself and edge forward on his elbows. The machine-gunners soon found Harry's position and the bullets flew around him. As they rattled by, for a weird moment he thought of MacDonald at school making them do a hundred lines, yelling at them. He wondered how the old bugger would go here now with the Germans only yards away. Then he gave up thinking about that and concentrated on getting shots in as Bingo continued slithering along the trunk to the boulder, which was only perhaps seven yards from the pillbox. Once there the sergeant moved himself into position and managed to crouch behind the rock.

At the same time, Wells and his team down across the slope opened up a volley from the Lewis gun. All four of the German machine guns went into action and swept the hillside. In the second the bullets left the boulder where the sergeant hid he pulled the pin on two grenades and leapt up and bounded across to the loop hole nearest him. It was as if Harry could see the

German inside falter in amazement – *How could anyone be so close?* – before he rotated the machine gun back round towards the leaping man. In the next half-second Bingo had ditched his two grenades through the loop hole and hurled himself on the ground to the furthest point away from the pillbox.

The wild explosions were contained inside the cement tomb. The machine guns ceased their deadly patter and the soldiers two hundred yards back down the hill stood up and cheered as Bingo lifted himself from the ground and gingerly moved to the back of the mound where a door had been blasted open. He poured in a few rounds from his Mark III rifle to be certain none had survived as Harry arrived at his side.

'Gosh, Sarge, that was nothing short of wonderful.'

Bingo was covered in dirt and mud but his wide grin, showing his broken tooth, was not suppressed. 'Thanks, lad.'

They bivouacked that night not far from the single remaining section of wall standing in what had been Beaumont Hamel: eight feet by six feet of brick and mortar that had been part of the railway station.

Chapter Forty

When John Conrad arrived alongside the Highlanders in the wilderness of shell craters and mounds of mud and dirt, broken rock, busted spars of wood and rubble that before the Battle of the Somme had been the village of Beaumont Hamel, it was mid-afternoon and a fine rain was falling. Another German stronghold taken at last. His own men had joined with the British 2nd Division and Royal Naval Division and overrun the conglomeration of enemy trenches and the main Beaumont trench to link up with the Highlanders on the northern outskirts of the village. He sent a message via the trusty method of pigeon to the Brigadier. 'Y Ravine & Beaumont Hamel taken. Advancing on Beaucourt on the morrow.'

He and Tommy Hardcastle then interviewed Lieutenant Dearwood and Menzies Lang – both of whom spoke fluent German, and who had questioned many of the German prisoners.

An hour later he left Tommy supervising a roll call and picked his way through the devastation to meet with Lieutenant Colonel Freyberg before joining other commanders to discuss the following day's continuing offensive. They had been informed that General Gough himself would be coming down to the meeting by armoured car.

Bernard Cyril Freyberg had been born in England and his parents had immigrated to New Zealand when he was two. He was known as a New Zealander, was only twenty-seven, and had already been wounded three times and awarded the DSO for his bravery at Gallipoli. He was to have a distinguished future and would be the commander-in-chief of the New Zealand Forces, but at this juncture his career was only beginning. His keen eyes lifted to John Conrad as they sat on chairs brought up by mule from the overrun German dugouts. Across from the north side of the ruins floated the sound of the bagpipes and later the voices of the Highlanders singing 'Auld Lang Syne'.

John Conrad knew Freyberg from the briefings at headquarters. 'You know, they think you're mad leading your troops into battle.'

Freyberg smiled. 'Well, now they'll think we both are!'

'I've just received a message that the 39th Division across the Ancre have also taken St Pierre Divion.'

'That's good news.'

John Conrad held his chin in thought. 'The messenger who brought in the news said that there are clusters of dugouts connected by tunnels down there that could house up to a thousand men. One constructed under the shelter of the clay embankment just south of the Ancre River near St Pierre Divion has four main entrances, ventilation shafts, a telephone exchange, pumping equipment and shell-proof accommodation for the headquarters' staff. Seems these systems of tunnels and dugouts run all the way through from north of the Y Ravine down to Mouquet Farm and beyond.'

'God, that must be four or five miles.'

'I know. My staff tell me the prisoners say that some fellow called von Fabeck, nephew of Hindenburg, improved and extended the underground complexes in April, May and June.'

'No wonder it's taken us so long to break through. It's been a regular fortified rabbit warren.'

John Conrad looked down at the map spread on the flat surface between them. 'Yes, but what a hell of a cost for a few miles of ground.'

'Oh yes. Even with the successes of today we can't go on here much longer. It's cold already, and now with the rain and probably snow before long we'll stagnate during winter and the bloody Germans will retrench. It looks as if it'll be a long war yet.'

'I'm afraid so.'

Freyberg gave a tired grin. 'Well, the Scots are having their day. I saw one of them with a pack of Wills' Gold Flake Cigars he'd taken from Y Ravine. Apparently the banks of the ravine were riddled with well-provisioned dugouts, like nothing our boys have ever seen.'

John Conrad agreed. 'Yes, our fellows do it the tough way. The most surprising piece of booty I noticed was a Scot carrying some silk stockings and gold slippers. Said he'd found them next to a piano in a dugout in the ravine.'

'A piano?' Freyberg's voice cracked in amazement.

John Conrad shrugged, 'So they say.'

Freyberg shook his youthful head. 'It's hard to believe, knowing how our fellows have to exist.'

'Yes, you can't blame our boys for taking the stuff. They deserve any booty they find as far as I'm concerned.'

As evening fell they joined Colonel Campbell of the 7th Gordon Highlanders and Colonels Bell and O'Leary of the 36th Irish Division, plus two colonels from advanced headquarters. They met in a tent raised in a shell hole on the outskirts of the former Beaumont Hamel.

While they waited for the arrival of Sir Hubert Gough someone had found a case of Scotch whisky and a bottle or two of this warmed their throats and their souls. Finally a message came that the controversial Irish cavalryman who commanded them was not coming after all. The message said that while they on the right had succeeded in taking their objective, the left of the force had failed and he had gone there.

The plan as now shown to them was to continue on to Beaucourt and to push as far ahead as they could.

After discussing the tactics for the following day they rejoined their own troops in the taken German trenches.

When John Conrad met again with Tommy Hardcastle and his staff he was told the only one of his personal aides who had been injured in the day's fighting was Lieutenant Stephen Palmer. He had been hit in the leg while advancing on Beaumont Trench.

Tommy informed him. 'Palmer's still here. There's a well-preserved cellar over on the east which we're using for an aid post. I'm afraid it's full already.'

John Conrad answered, moving along the trench: 'I'd better get over and see Palmer right away. A well-preserved cellar, eh? The only thing I saw remaining above ground was one section of a wall of the railway station.'

'Yes, the whole village was razed to the ground months ago, I'm told.'

667

'Wonder if the people will ever come back to live here.'

'I doubt it, sir.'

'Did Lang send us that count on the German prisoners taken?'

'Not yet, but I believe there were hundreds. There's a flood of them going to the rear now.' Tommy grinned. 'Needless to say we've had plenty of volunteers to accompany them.'

Past the lines of blinded gassed men, eyes bandaged, each with his right arm outstretched to hold the shoulder of the man in front, all coughing and spitting blood, by the stream of stretcher bearers and their human burdens, Tommy Hardcastle escorted his colonel down into the below-ground regimental aid post. The smell of blood was overwhelming and the medical units worked ceaselessly in the lantern light. John Conrad spoke to Steve Palmer and the young man managed a smile.

'I'm all right, Colonel. I'll be back here with you again by spring.'

'Yes, we'll see. You just get well, m'boy, and forget about the war for awhile.' He spoke to some of the other wounded and as they moved back towards the door, Tommy Hardcastle pointed to a Royal Irish Fusilier who lay with a bloody bandage covering most of his left leg. He whispered to John Conrad. 'That's Danny Burke, sir, a well-known member of the Irish Republican Army.'

John Conrad eyed the young man for a moment and then went across and knelt down beside him. He spoke softly. 'Burke?'

The man turned his head, 'Yes, sir?'

'How's the leg?'

'I'll be all right.'

'I wouldn't have thought you'd have felt this was your war?'

A flash of light sparked in Burke's blue eyes. 'I'm not here fighting for your British Empire, I'm here fighting *against* the bloody Germans, sir.'

John Conrad smiled. 'Well, whatever the reason, son, we're grateful to you. I spent nearly twenty years with a man who was born in Bally Longford in Kerry and loved Ireland, and yet was all English. He was always for a peaceful settlement to the whole unfortunate Irish question.'

Burke sadly shook his proud head. 'What with last Easter's uprising, I'm afraid I doubt that, sir.'

'Well, son, I only hope you're wrong and that the differences in your homeland can be solved without more bloodshed.' He looked around the cellar across the rows of wounded. 'There's been a surfeit of that.'

He patted Burke on the shoulder and moved away.

When he and Tommy came back outside it was dark and cold and was still drizzling rain.

They were getting intermittent fire from the German lines around Beaucourt and the shells lit up the sky.

That night they could hear many songs drifting on the bitter wind. But one melody began with a lone longing voice and soon unified all the boys of the Empire as they joined in and sang along together:

> There's a long, long trail a-winding
> Into the land of my dreams,
> Where the nightingales are singing
> And a white moon beams.
> There's a long long night of waiting
> Until my dreams all come true,
> Till the day when I'll be going
> Down that long long trail with you . . .

When the day's fighting ceased Harry had been put on grave-digging duty. They were all exhausted but Bingo rostered various teams of twenty men to dig for half an hour each until stand-to.

In a rare moment of sensitivity, Bingo had talked sternly but kindly. 'Now lads, I know we're all tired but we have to try to keep up with burying our mates, even though we know it's impossible. There are already too many dead men on both sides without graves in the Somme. Come along,' and he had worked along with them in the first team. 'If you can find them, remove each man's identity disks.'

The heaps of dead were quite overwhelming and every now and then Harry shuddered as he recognised a mate.

The rest of the battalion, covered in chalky mud and dirt, just sat silently looking into space, or eating what little food they had. Captain Hardcastle had told them to recuperate and gather themselves for the morning; orders had been issued that they were to advance on German-held Beaucourt a mile and a half across the ridge.

Later, Harry went in search of Dave. He stood for a minute watching a group of signallers laying a line of telephone wires forward, and looked across the landscape behind them where the ghostly forms of the blasted out trees hanging on the edge of craters looked like another planet. A wind dashed at him and he hurried on where finally he found Dave in a shallow trench to the south of what was left of the village, sharing Dry Pearl biscuits with Curly. They sat on empty bully-beef cases and sheltered from the drizzle under wooden sheeting covered in a large piece of canvas.

Dave beamed. 'Gawd, I'm pleased to see you. I looked around but couldn't find you.'

The two youths embraced.

Harry turned to Curly. 'Good to see you, Moss.'

'Yeah, you too, Craken.'

Harry looked around. 'Anyone seen Birtenshaw?'

'Yes,' replied Dave, 'he's all right. I saw him earlier. He's down with the 22nd Battalion of the Royal Fusiliers, scrounging some food I'd say.'

'What about Isaac? Where's he?'

Dave and Curly did not reply, a look passed between them, then Dave simply shook his head.

Harry groaned as Curly found his voice. 'Poor Isaac. He was so bloody smart, a school teacher and all; a real poet too. It's a bugger all right.'

'Yeah, isn't it?' Dave put his hands inside his greatcoat pockets. 'It was real quick. I . . . kept his poetry book. Thought his mum might like it if . . . we make it home.'

The three eyed each other and no one spoke. Harry sat down in the ensuing silence and after a minute or so Dave asked, 'What about Luke?'

Harry met his friend's gaze. 'I reckon he stayed behind.'

'What?'

'Yes, I do. I don't think he went over the top with the rest of us. He was pretty scared.'

'Gawd!' exclaimed Curly, his face flushed with surprise.

'They'll shoot 'im. That'll be regarded as flamin' cowardice in the face of the enemy. I've never seen that in all my time in the army. Never saw anybody turn tail. I saw them pale with terror but never knew 'em stay put or run or nothin'.'

'Are you sure he didn't go over with us?'

Harry sniffed and rubbed his nose on the arm of his coat. 'I can't be one hundred per cent sure, but I'd lay bets on it. He was standing right beside me.'

The wind raced up the trench and the canvas above flapped loudly as Dave picked up a piece of wood and attempted to clean the mud from his boots. 'He might have followed us even if he didn't start at the same time.'

Harry thought about this. 'He might have, but I saw how he was, and he was . . . well, sort of petrified.'

Curly decided to have his say. 'If he showed cowardice he'll be for it. You can't just renege and not fight. The big boys don't like that.'

They were all contemplating the validity of this theory when Frank appeared and slid down beside them, eating an orange.

Curly's eyes widened. 'Jeez, mate, trust you to find a flamin' orange in the middle of all this. Where the devil did you get it?'

Frank sank his teeth into the fruit as he replied. 'Now as a rule you know I won't reveal my sources but this time I'll make an exception, Curly old boy. Got it off a Jock; he found a case of them in Y Ravine. You should see the booty those fellas have got. It's amazing. I saw a bloke with a fur overcoat and a china teapot.'

'Gosh, wish we'd been at the ravine.'

'I don't know that you do, mate. It was pretty hard fighting, the Jocks reckon, and they're plenty bloody tough. Do you know what they're calling this stunt we're in?'

'No, what?'

'The Battle of the Ancre.' Frank looked around. 'Isaac'll probably be able to tell us who named the bloody river in the first place. By the way, anyone seen him . . . or Luke for that matter?'

This induced the previous bleak conversations to be revisited and afterwards they all sat hushed for a time with the weight of their thoughts and only the staccato noise from the artillery as an adjunct to their musings.

The drizzle stopped and for a few minutes the horizon cleared, allowing the fading sun to hurl streaming yellow rays of light upward to tinge the grey clusters of clouds with rose and gold.

Harry looked up and sighed. He thought how incongruous it was to have beauty like that above them when all around were ruins and gaping holes in the ground and mounds of mud and dead things. He was the first one to mention what was uppermost in their minds. 'It was pretty weird today, wasn't it?'

Everybody knew what he meant and Dave replied, 'Yes, it was. We'd been prepared for it and yet not prepared for it at all.'

'Yeah,' agreed Frank, 'that's how I felt.'

Dave looked around. 'I mean, do you blokes want to talk about it?'

No one answered and they sat for a time watching Dave clean the mud off his boots. The late afternoon sun glinted in his black eyes as abruptly he raised his head and without taking a breath told them, 'I would've been a gonner in the first few minutes if it hadn't been for Wells and his Lewis gun team; the Huns were pouring out of their trench with guns blazing – old Wells and Lockert saved us.'

'Jeez, you were lucky.'

'Yeah, I reckon that's true.'

Frank sighed and edged slightly forward on his box. 'Did . . . did any of you . . . you know, have to fight hand to hand?'

Dave closed his eyes. He saw the German he had bayoneted, the surprised expression, his eyes startled, unnerved. He saw him pitch forward on to his blade and the blood gush out. No . . . he could not talk of that.

Harry answered, 'We were expecting to. Charged up and into the first trench and guess what? No bugger was there. They'd all gone to ground during the barrage. Bingo made short work of them, blew them to bits in their dugouts and we got a few later with enfilade fire down the trench. But I have to tell you being with Bingo was amazing. It's like he's got no fear. He took out a German pillbox where they had some of our blokes pinned down for hours. I was right there sort of covering him with Wells and Lockert further away firing Jessie. He crawled along behind a section of a tree trunk no wider than my thigh, right under their noses, and suddenly he up and crossed to the loop hole and lobbed in two grenades, like he was out for a Sunday stroll. It blasted the whole interior to kingdom come.'

Curly exhaled in a long noisy breath. 'Jesus, he sure practises what he preaches, no doubt about it. By the sound of it he'll get a bloody medal.' Then he puffed on his Woodbine, continuing in his own inimitably laconic style, 'Well, I'm not interested in medals, though, Frank, my lad, in answer to your question, yes, I did do a bit of hand to hand.' He laughed and his nose, blotchy with red marks from lice bites, wrinkled. 'Hard not to with the whole bloody Hun army breathing down ya neck.' He blew out a long puff of smoke. 'So we're goin' to have a try at Beaucourt tomorrow. It's just over there.' He pointed in the direction of the noise of the guns.

In pregnant silence their gazes followed his finger.

Frank shivered and cleared his throat. 'How will we ever be able to explain this to anybody? I mean how'll we tell it to anybody who wasn't here?'

'We won't.' Dave imagined Isaac, the thinker, with the back of his head blown off. He felt the tears spring again to his eyes.

Curly simply shook his head. 'I'd like ta tell me wife, Glor, but reckon she wouldn't have the faintest idea . . .'

Harry looked down at his hands. He knew he was only seventeen but he felt so very much older. He felt as if in this one day he had lived a life time. His voice shook a little as he spoke but it was definite, unequivocal. 'I for one won't want to talk about it,' he said slowly. 'You either were here and know about this . . . or you weren't and you don't.'

That was the consensus. They sighed and looked round into the suddenly infinitely old eyes of their companions, then all began to talk of other things until they heard Sergeant Dobb shouting for a roll call.

In their original platoon of thirty-five there were ten missing. When Isaac's name was called Dave looked down at the ground; he felt again the tears stinging his eyes, and the ridge of sorrow in his chest. When Luke's name was called Harry glanced round at his mates but no one spoke.

Stand-to came after the roll call and an hour later, when they stood down, Harry searched out Bingo. The sergeant sat under a piece of tin sheeting cooking Maconochie in his mess tin over a small open fire and sipping his rum ration from a metal cup.

'Er, Sarge, could I speak with you?'

The red beard shot forward as he lifted his head. He pointed to a wooden box beside him and gratefully Harry sat.

Bingo swirled the food in his pan. 'What do you want to talk about?'

Harry looked round to see who was nearby but there was only a single sentry about ten yards along the trench. He delayed a second or two to find the right words. 'If a bloke didn't go over the top with his mates . . . I mean, if a soldier reneged and didn't fight, if he were too scared to go and he stayed behind, what would happen to him?'

Bingo's beard came down to rest on his formidable chest as he eyed the youth. 'Hmm, now why would such as you be askin' me that?'

'I was just wondering, Sarge.'

'Were you, now, wondering about what we would term *cowardice in the face of the enemy*, eh?'

'Yes, Sarge, I suppose so.'

'And why would that be?'

Harry was evasive. 'I don't know really. I just got to thinking about it and thought you'd be able to enlighten me.'

'Hmm? Well, lad, first of all this man who did such . . . he'd be court-martialled for cowardice from the sounds of what you've told me.'

'What would happen to him, Sarge?'

'Let me explain, boy. I started out life in the army when Australia was six proud colonies. It was 1895, to be exact, before you were born, eh?'

'Yes, Sarge.'

He moved his mess tin from the fire and spooned some of his meat and vegetable stew into his mouth. As he chewed he continued, 'In those days we were a direct part of Great Britain and the law was to shoot deserters, cowards, mutineers and the like. The opinion of British military commanders, lad, is that the death penalty is essential to fighting efficiency. Now in the main I'm no man to argue with that. A soldier shouldn't be able to feel that it's acceptable to let his mates down or to be able to shirk a battle and get away with it. Where would we all be if that were condoned? But since Australia became self-governing in the first year of this new century, 1901, the army applies the death penalty only for mutiny, desertion *to* the enemy and, I believe, some forms of treason like delivering up to the enemy a garrison or a ship, et cetera. Thus, my lad, in the Australian army at present we don't shoot men for cowardice.'

Harry murmured a sound of relief as Bingo swallowed a mouthful of his rum. 'And so the answer to your question, for whatever reason it is you really wish to know, is that if a soldier didn't fight, if he stayed behind in the trench or wherever, my guess is he'd end up serving time, possibly even life, in military prison.'

Harry frowned and rose to his feet. 'Thanks, Sarge.' He turned to walk away.

'Craken?'

Harry spun round to see Bingo looking up with one eye half closed while he scrutinised him through the other. 'So, son, who is it that you suspect of cowardice?'

'God, Sarge, I only asked to be informed about things . . . you know . . . to understand the army.'

Bingo's red beard lifted threateningly and Harry wished he had never asked the question. 'Well, Sarge, it's not that I suspect anyone—'

'Don't mess with me. Spit it out, soldier. Who is it?'

'Sarge it's not anyone I can identify for certain.'

'Sure of that?' He swallowed more rum.

Harry moved awkwardly from one foot to the other. 'Sure, Sarge. There's nobody I can say for certain.'

Bingo gave a swift grin. 'You did good today, boy, covered me well.' He lifted his strong forefinger from his tin cup and pointed it towards Harry. 'Bugger off, Craken.'

Harry smiled widely. 'Thanks, Sarge, yessir.' And he spun on his heel and hurried away.

Later that night after a dinner of bully beef, dry biscuits and cheese, as sleet drifted down on to the trenches, Dave and Harry sat under a lean-to wrapped in their greatcoats with woollen balaclavas over their faces, the bottom half pulled down under their chins to enable them to smoke.

Dave blew a long trail of smoke up into the chill atmosphere.

Harry did the same and half turned to his friend. 'If Luke did . . . stay behind he won't be shot.'

'How do you know?'

'I asked Bingo.' He took a draw on his Woodbine and spoke through the smoke. 'He'll be court-martialled. Might get life in prison. They won't shoot him because we're the only army in the whole Empire that doesn't do that.'

'Shit?'

'Yeah.'

'If he did stay behind I suppose he's lucky then.'

'I suppose so. Though the thought of the next forty or fifty years in a military prison . . . well, that's bloody awful.'

'Yeah, but they might let 'em out when the war's over, you never know.'

Harry shook his head. 'I doubt it.'

They fell silent for a while, smoking their cigarettes, until Harry returned to conversation. 'You know, Dave, if we hadn't joined up, we probably never would have met.'

Dave gave a muffled laugh. 'Reckon you're right there, mate. The circles you were moving in and those of my family's aren't quite the same – might say a flaming world apart. My mum's a full-blooded Aborigine and my dad sells junk; your father's a famous painter and your mother's a lady – not that my mother isn't a lady, I reckon she is, but Brisbane society wouldn't think so.' He gave another laugh. 'Do you know, though, being away from my mother like this has made it easier for me to understand her . . . and my grandmother. You see my grandma was the one that broke away, left the tribe, came to Brisbane with her two kids, my mother and my Uncle Hargy. It seems she believed it was the only way to give her kids a better life. That was pretty brave, you know, doing that around forty years ago, coming into a white man's town and trying to live there. Gosh, you reckon I get insults from some people, imagine what they said to her.'

'I'd say she was bloody amazing.'

Dave half turned to meet his friend's eyes in the moody light thrown through the sleet by the artillery fire. 'Yeah, you're right. The colonel's mum was the only person in the whole of Brisbane who'd give my grandmother a job, that's how my Uncle Hargy and the colonel became friends.'

Harry made a half-interested sound and Dave went on. 'And because of that friendship, the colonel took care of my education and that of my sisters and brother . . . Helped Mum and Dad too, and he treats my mum right. Actually, while we're talking about ladies, he treats her *like a lady*. My mother thinks the world of him.'

Harry gave an exasperated groan. 'Yes, yes, Dave, all right, so this is a pep talk on how good Fleet is.'

His friend shook his head. 'I'm simply telling you the truth.'

'Yes, well, I have my own opinions on him, and if you recall we said we'd agree to differ, old son, so—'

'All right, Harry, I'll say no more. Then tell me about *your* mother.'

This was complicated and he hesitated before he spoke. 'Ah, she's amazing too in her own way. Coming all the way over here from Queensland, joining the VADs. I suppose it was to be where I am, which really doesn't help me any. I reckon she should have stayed with Dad, at home . . . and now he's here too somewhere, because of her, I guess. But she's always been a bit of a free spirit, done funny things. You know, I remember one time she had me playing this game. We went and saw a ship off from Hamilton Wharf, just the two of us. We were yelling at it and pretending my father was on board leaving the country . . . funny woman, I suppose, but then she's my mother, isn't she? So she's the only one I've ever known.'

'Yes, women do odd things, I reckon.'

'Dave?'

'Yes?'

'Have you ever . . . you know? With a girl?'

Dave took a long draw on his cigarette and exhaled up in the air. 'Ah well . . . not really, no. Have you?'

'No . . . don't think I'd like to die without having done it, though. From what Curly and the blokes say there's nothing like it.'

Dave began to giggle.

677

'Well, what's funny?'

He dug Harry in the ribs with his elbow. 'We'll just have to keep on living then, won't we? Can't leave the planet without knowing what it's all about.'

This made them both giggle: and in the moody darkness of a muddy trench north of the Ancre, with sleet drifting over the flimsy corrugated iron and wooden lean-to, shrinking in their greatcoats, with rats edging along the duckboards in the chill night not a yard distant, the two youths puffed on their cigarettes; puffed and laughed and puffed and laughed.

The following day they took Beaucourt in the rain, and the whole Somme and Ancre valleys congealed with mud.

Freyberg and John Conrad led the assault at dawn and the battle was as furious and ghastly as the day before. The Royal Naval Division fought alongside the Australians and by noon, even though there had been much confusion earlier, they were close to taking the area. Much to the chagrin of the senior army officers the naval boys kept to their own traditions, even when fighting in the field.

Harry, Frank and Dave fought side by side. If they had any time to think, the youths faced the truth of their own mortality: they had seen about a quarter of their platoon killed and another quarter wounded in just two days.

At about 1100 hours they were advancing up out of a series of deep trenches and dugouts they had taken on the north side of where the village had stood. The men were amazed, as the Highlanders had been when they overran Y Ravine, to see the quality of the German trenches. There were proper cement dugouts with beds and lanterns, and the Australians laughed saying, 'This'll do us for the winter.'

They had passed virtually through the ruins of Beaucourt when they came up against German soldiers holding the remains of a single burnt-out house while their comrades retreated into a shallow trench under heavy mortar fire from the British naval troops. The Germans had a machine gun and a *Minenwerfer*, and they steadfastly hung on.

As Harry, Frank and Dave advanced through the twisted and broken buildings they saw John Conrad.

'Look, there's the colonel,' Frank said, pointing.

Harry was unimpressed. 'So what?'

'He's here amongst it again.'

'I can see that.'

'Well, it makes you feel good.'

Harry's voice was sharp. 'Does it?'

Dave did not speak.

They watched John Conrad, Captain Hardcastle and Bingo all dive with a few others into a shell hole some seventy yards in front. John Conrad put up his hand and signalled for the men ahead of Harry, Dave and Frank to advance. He pointed to where a Vickers gun team and a trench mortar team were setting up behind a broken section of battered and blasted stone wall closer to the Germans.

Dave, who was now some yards forward of Harry and Frank, left them and ran with the others towards the new position alongside the trench mortar team.

The bullets from the Germans were spitting all around, and as Dave scuttled away Frank moved up quickly into his previous position. Frank had not been there more than thirty seconds when he said, 'Oh hell,' and pitched backwards to fall at Harry's feet.

Harry looked in horror as blood seeped from under Frank to stain the ground around him. 'Frank, Frank, old son?' Harry felt hot and cold at the same time as nausea rose in his throat.

One of the soldiers of his platoon edged across and leant over the body. 'Struth, he took it in the chest.' Meeting Harry's eyes he spoke the sober fact. 'If Sands hadn't moved up with Bingo he'd have got the bullet.'

Harry could not speak. He crawled round Frank and cradled his head in his arms. Isaac dead yesterday, Frank dead today, along with so many others he knew – gone in just two days. The lump in his throat expanded while he tenderly closed Frank's eyes. 'Goodbye, old son.' Then he rolled Frank in close behind the wall and stared at the rain spattering in black blobs on Frank's back: little pearl-like random black blobs that seeped into one another on his friend's back until they flowed like miniature rivers across the khaki serge to blend and blot.

A minute passed while Harry bent over, gaze fixed on Frank, his own stream of tears mingling with the water, until into the periphery of his blurred vision thudded the form of

Sergeant Dobb, doubled over, rifle in hand, along with four or five others.

'Watch the colonel,' Dobb ordered, 'we'll follow him in.'

Harry returned to the conflict around him as a couple of German spherical 'cricket ball' Kugel grenades were lobbed from behind the wall of the ruin to explode near five of the men who were advancing with John Conrad and Bingo. Two men went down wounded, but the others kept progressing from cover to cover.

When the crew lobbed a 'toffee apple' bomb into the building holding the Germans Dobb yelled in delight. 'They've got the trench mortar going!' And he jumped to his feet and ran after the Colonel, Captain Hardcastle and Bingo as they sped towards the explosion, a hundred others bringing up the rear. The direct hit seemed to dismantle the *Minenwerfer* and the Australians quickly spread all over the ruined building.

Harry and the others followed to join the colonel and his men, and the Germans inside, greatly outnumbered, could see the fight was useless. Some fell back, running away through what remained of the streets, and as the British naval boys and the Australians surrounded those inside the shelled building they surrendered.

Many of the Australians continued on down what was left of the streets, firing at the disappearing Germans, and John Conrad led the others on into the shell of the building where they were rounding up those who had surrendered.

Bingo shouted. '*Ihr da! Kommt mit erhobenen Händen hier rüber!*' And the enemy so ordered walked towards him hands up.

Harry was still in shock from the loss of Frank. When he caught up with Dave he told him. Dave covered his face. 'Oh Gawd, no. Hell. Oh hell.'

'It would have been you, old son, if you hadn't moved up to join Bingo. Frank took the exact spot where you'd been kneeling. Hadn't been there half a minute when the bullet hit him.'

If it were possible for Dave's skin to blanch, it did so.

Suddenly there was something new in the way the youths looked at one another, and there was something else unspoken, trickling into their awareness, to lodge and abide in their minds; as if time were precious, and all friendship must end in pain.

They stood looking at one another for a few more seconds then dropped their eyes and moved on to where Captains Lang and Bader and Lieutenants Young, Kenny and Dearwood were gathering the Australian troops together. Across a mound of rubble they saw the colonel talking to Bingo as the prisoners were marched away. Harry and Dave stood silently as their leader proceeded across the rubble towards them. He was followed by Captain Hardcastle, and they halted next to Lieutenant Dearwood.

The colonel lifted his arms. 'The action's over. Beaucourt's been taken. The trenches all around in every direction are in our hands. Well done, all of you.'

The men cheered. The captains and lieutenants began to give orders for the troops to find their own units. John Conrad climbed across the fragments of stone and wood and left the destroyed building, picking his way along what was possibly the remains of a street and talking with Tommy Hardcastle until, a couple of hundred yards on, they halted at the side of a single ruin. After a few minutes they were joined by a major from the Royal Naval Division.

'I'm sorry to have to inform you, sir, that Lieutenant Colonel Freyberg has been seriously wounded.'

John Conrad closed his eyes. 'I must see him. Where is he?'

'He's been taken back to the field dressing station to be transferred with all speed to a hospital in Warloy.'

'Do you know what happened?'

'No, sir, I was just sent to inform you.'

John Conrad looked round at Tommy. 'It's the third or fourth time he's been wounded . . . damned brave man. Fought the whole Gallipoli campaign.' As he struggled to take in the news he saw young Harry Craken passing by.

Harry was in front of Dave Sands and Curly Moss at the head of a group of about forty or so men marching along and heading towards what was left of a stone corridor leading by the single ruin to a series of abandoned trenches. All around were piles of rubble and the only clear way was through the corridor. In fact it was surprisingly free of debris as if it had somehow magically survived the destruction all around.

As Harry stepped to within a few feet of the entrance, John Conrad threw his arms in the air and shouted, 'Craken! Halt! Don't go in there!'

Harry froze. Dave and the men behind him collided solidly into his back, pushing him on a step or so, and Tommy Hardcastle started in surprise. 'What is it, sir?'

John Conrad shook his head. 'I . . . don't know.' Slowly he crossed over to Harry and the men who now all stood alert, attention-like, waiting on the colonel's next order.

'I've got a very bad feeling about this.' John Conrad looked round to Tommy who was right behind him. 'It's something about this clear way where Craken was leading the boys. It's the *only* clear way in this whole blasted area. Doesn't that seem odd? As if it's asking you to walk through it. Back up, men. Let's go back twenty-five yards. Right back.'

'Move as the colonel orders!'

There were mutterings and speculation among the men as all the troops in the vicinity were rounded up and returned to positions well away from the section of corridor.

John Conrad moved back with them. 'I might be wrong but I'm guessing about that corridor . . .' He waved his hand across the men. 'I want a few good throwers to lob some heavy stones or brick pieces into that and then hit the decks . . . and we'll see what happens. Now take cover!'

Harry picked up a brick as did seven or eight others. On an order from Tommy Hardcastle they pitched them into the corridor. There was a moment of hushed expectancy as the bricks sailed through the air, most coming down on their mark. The explosions that ensued blew the corridor and the remains of anything around it high in the air.

'Holy shit!' exclaimed Curly in Harry's ear.

When the fragments hit the ground the men rose to their feet and gave three cheers to the colonel. Harry found his voice and on the final cheer joined in.

John Conrad wiped his hands across his eyes, gave a quick salute and moved off with Tommy at his heels.

'If you don't mind my saying so, that was bloody amazing, sir.'

'No, Tommy, that was luck. It was all *déjà vu*. It reminded me of something that happened near the town of Ponchefstroum during the Boer War. A cluster of farm buildings had been blown up, but there was one section clear, just like here. It almost beckoned you to come through. And when our boys rode into it they were blown to smithereens. We used to call them ground torpedoes down there. If I hadn't had that experience, I would've been fooled too.'

'Well, those men owe you their lives.'

Fifty yards behind John Conrad, Harry stood motionless, watching the colonel walking away. This was a new and confounding complication. It was simple for Dave: his hero had saved him, but for Harry the fact held bewildering consequences. *The enemy* had saved his life.

Bingo was made a warrant officer and awarded the Victoria Cross for his action against the German pillbox. *For conspicuous bravery in the face of the enemy.*

Lieutenant Colonel Bernard C. Freyberg recovered from his wounds and was awarded the Victoria Cross. *For conspicuous bravery and brilliant leadership as a battalion commander.* He would be wounded nine times by war's end.

Colonel John Conrad Fleet was awarded the Distinguished Service Order. *For outstanding leadership as a battalion commander.*

Chapter Forty-one

Luke had been taken to the rear of the Australian trenches and in orthodox Field Punishment No. 1 had been roped to a wagon wheel crucifix style.

They left him there for two hours in the bitter wind and drizzle until Luke saw, through the haze of his confusion while he drifted in and out of consciousness, a torch shine in his face. Unceremonious tones sounded from behind it. 'You're for the clink now, shirker,' and as Luke felt them untie his frozen hands and feet he sank to the ground with relief.

The corporal who had spoken had been wounded in the July assault on Pozieres, and looked upon *shirkers* as scum. He signalled to the privates with him to lift the prisoner and dump him in the back of the lorry which would take him to battalion headquarters. Luke was virtually unconscious and hardly aware of being carried to the lorry, thrown in the back under a canvas cover and driven the distance to the convent. There he was placed in a locked room with straw on the floor.

He lay in a stupor until the following morning when he was aroused and given water, bread and cheese and at 0900 hours taken out of the room and marched around the convent walls to the rear of a lorry where two other privates stood roped together. He was tied to them and the three of them left there.

All around was activity. Luke watched through glazed eyes as supplies moved by on horses and donkeys, men in carrying parties passed with stores on their backs and sergeants shouted for haste.

As an omnibus full of men and Stokes guns trundled by the lorry the man nearest Luke turned and said, 'What'd ya do?'

Luke did not reply.

An hour later they were herded into the back of the lorry and driven five or six miles south over bumpy roads into a small town where they were delivered into the hands of two French soldiers and taken to what seemed like a town gaol. The stone building had lost part of its roof but the cells were intact.

Later that day, as the sun sank and candle lamps were lit in the corridor outside his cell, he was interviewed by a British captain, who asked him a series of questions to which Luke gave no replies in his own defence. After a few minutes the captain shook his head.

'You do realise your behaviour carries with it a cowardice charge? Possibly desertion of duty as well.'

Luke nodded. 'I suppose so.' His eyes filled with tears and he lifted his shaking hands to his head.

'Where were you before the war, boy?'

'How . . . how do you mean sir?'

'What business were you in? What did you do for a living?'

His answer shivered from his throat. 'I was at school.'

'Shit!' The captain shook his head. *A bloody schoolboy.* He stood up and came round the table to perch above Luke and study him for a time.

Luke lifted his swollen eyes and as the tears ran down his face he asked, 'What'll they do to me, sir?'

The captain stood; he had a son still at school, probably not much younger than this boy. 'Damned if I know, son. You're a soldier now and soldiers are meant to fight, not remain behind when the army goes into battle. So I'm afraid you'll be court-martialled, and if you were in a British regiment there'd be a good chance you'd face a firing squad.'

It was the evening of Saturday 18 November when Matthew arrived back from Montdidier, left Cliff and Bert in the sergeants' mess and passed through the railway station to meet with Lieutenant Colonel Alec Burnett.

He sat waiting in Burnett's office, deep in thought. Life seemed more serious than he had ever known it. He pictured Caro in the canteen in Montdidier, the way the lamp light had played across the planes of her face. He thought at least she had been surprised by his statement about leaving her, if nothing else. That gave him the smallest of satisfactions for it took a lot for Caro to notice anything he did. He shook his head and moved his bad leg to a more comfortable position.

'Major Craken?'

'Yes?' He looked up to see a corporal.

'Lieutenant Colonel Burnett has sent a message asking you to join him in the officers' mess.'

Matthew arrived there almost at the same time as Burnett. 'Good to see you, Major Craken. How were things in Montdidier?'

The corner of Matthew's lip lifted in what could have been interpreted as a sneer. 'Satisfactory, thanks, Lieutenant Colonel.'

Burnett, uncertain of how to construe this reply, did not invite the major to enlarge upon it. 'Yes, well . . . the news is that you can go up to your battalion pretty soon, possibly as early as the day after tomorrow.' Burnett opened his briefcase, took out a military pass and handed it across to his visitor. 'This'll get you through the supply lines and up to your battalion. Now even though this is still classified information I can tell you the 16th battalion – the one you're joining – has been in a successful operation. The Battle of the Ancre, they're calling it. Fighting's ceased. The rain and mud have made it impossible for us to go on. It's such a cold snap that the snows are probably already descending.'

He took out an ordnance map from his briefcase. Pointing, he explained, 'While this whole Battle of the Somme's been a disaster, in the last couple of days we've managed to salvage something. We haven't taken Gommecourt or Serre but we've taken Beaumont Hamel, St Pierre Divion and Beaucourt. About bloody time! The front in this part of the line's moved about two miles into German territory. Your 16th under Colonel Fleet is here at present.' His wide forefinger tapped the map.

Matt's sleepy eyes opened slightly and for someone who knew him well, the way he lifted his long fingers and brushed them across his scar would have shown he felt a strong emotion.

'Fleet's battalion and the Irish and the Highlanders and I believe, *Hood* and *Hawke* battalions of the Naval Division, were all successful.' He shook his head. 'Both sides will consolidate now; the fighting for 1916's over. Fleet'll bring the 16th out and will return here, I'm told.' He pointed to a position near Albert. 'They'll bivouac, get some rest and stay

686

in support of the front lines. Perfect time to join them and to do some painting, I'd say.'

Matt cleared his throat. 'Does the commander of the 16th know I'm coming?'

Burnett closed his briefcase and called for the barman, ordering two Scotches. 'I'm not sure.' He laughed. 'As soon as we got word here that you were on your way from England we sent him a message that a war artist would be attached to his command. Though, of course, the man's been in a bloody battle since then; hard to know whether he'd have seen the paper or not. Anyway,' he grinned, 'he'll know when you turn up.' He looked thoughtful. 'But I think we've got a line through to his headquarters so I'll get Captain McAskill's office to telephone him in the morning. Won't matter in any case, you've got your papers, haven't you?'

Matt nodded and his voice remained casual. 'Then probably he doesn't know my name?'

'No, shouldn't think so, old man. We didn't know it until you arrived here.' He smiled. 'Fleet's an interesting character. Was Lord Kitchener's trusty right hand for ages . . . about twenty years in all. A colonel, though wouldn't surprise me if he's a brigadier any minute. He knows the right people. Unmarried.' He laughed. 'Married to the army I'd say. The word is he was devoted to Kitchener, was broken-hearted when he drowned. They say he blames himself for not travelling with the old boy and dying with him. Funny that: there's no understanding what I call *psychotic loyalty*.

'Good-looking bugger too. My wife met him in Sydney in 1910 when he was out there with Kitchener. She still mentions from time to time how bloody handsome he was . . . you know what women are.'

As two Scotches were placed in front of them Alec Burnett went on, 'They say he could have taken a division, but he wouldn't, even though Lord Robertson pressed him. Wanted to be closer to the action. Damned odd really. One view is he doesn't care whether he lives or dies now that his mentor is gone. Well, I'd say in the last few days he's had plenty of action. We usually hear quickly if a commander's wounded or killed, so I'd say he's still in the land of the living.'

His companion made such a peculiar sound that Burnett asked, 'Pardon?'

Matt exhaled. 'Nothing, Lieutenant Colonel, nothing.' He picked up the glass in front of him. 'I've got a query . . . is it unchangeable that I join the 16th? Is there any other battalion around here that I could be allocated to?'

'Why? What's wrong with the 16th?'

Matt trained his eyes on his host and again trailed his long fingers across his scar as he answered. 'It's the battalion my son's serving with; let's say that perhaps I'd prefer not to be in such proximity to him. I might not be as effective as I would like, being aware he's in harm's way right under my nose.'

'Yet, you know, we even have some fathers and sons who joined up and are serving together.'

'I do, and there's no accounting for people's behaviour. There's an infinite variety of acts of madness on this planet.'

Alec Burnett decided not to pursue this point. He did not have any children but he thought he could understand. His forehead creased in a frown. 'Fact is, Craken, I think you'll have to be with the 16th for now, see how you go. If you're not happy we'll apply to GHQ to have you moved on. That could take a while . . . you know how these things run.' He smiled and sipped his Scotch. 'Anyway, the real fighting's over for a few months . . . not too much danger now. Might be nice for you to see your lad.'

Matthew hoped he had a lad to see. 'Mmm.' So it seemed he would have to spend time in the enemy's company no matter what. He wondered if Harry had come across him but thought not. He was a private, after all.

The door to the left swung open and four men trailed in. They halted beside the lieutenant colonel. 'Evening, sir.'

Alec Burnett gestured for them to sit down. As they moved into their chairs he introduced Matthew. 'Major Craken has an honorary commission. He's an artist here, as a vanguard for others, I'm thinking. Some scheme for recording the war in pictures that the Commonwealth Government's going to set up like the British one that's just begun. Is that right, Craken?'

'That's close enough,' Matt responded. 'I'm here to record in paint, anyway.'

'Meet Major Jones, Captain McAskill and Lieutenants Gedge and Hunter, all on the staff with me.'

They all shook hands.

As he shook hands with Matthew the major asked, 'Where're you from?'

'Brisbane.'

Captain McAskill laughed. 'Didn't know there were any *real* painters in Brisbane. What sort of painter are you? Do you belong to a movement?' He gave another short laugh. 'That is what to ask, isn't it?'

There was amusement in Matt's eyes as he answered, 'Yes, that's what to ask. And as I haven't been influenced by Nietzsche, I'm not a futurist or a vorticist, neither thank heaven, am I a Pre-Raphaelite though I do believe Holman Hunt, sentimental as he is, has his place. I'm partially devoted to Velázquez and an old friend of mine called Gauguin, odd twosome though they are, and as I like to rid myself of the trammels of artistic tradition I've dabbled in cubism and impressionism. I admire Cézanne though I don't ape his style. So, to answer your question, I don't think I fall into any movement.' He gave a charming smile. 'Perhaps I'm a Crakenite.'

McAskill shook his head. 'I'm sorry I asked.'

Major Jones laughed. 'A Crakenite, I like it. It'll be a fascinating new movement, I'm sure.'

Matt winked. 'No doubt.'

'Well, it'll be winter landscapes for you now. There was sleet in Albert this morning when I was up there.' Jones glanced to Burnett. 'By the way, I've been asked to preside over a court martial there tomorrow, sir. They need an Australian court – well, the president at least, as there's an Australian prisoner to be tried. They'd been looking around for an officer to do it and when I turned up they grabbed me. So I'm it.'

The lieutenant colonel gestured to the sergeant barman for more drinks as he replied, 'Do you have the time?'

'Yes. They tell me it'll be over in one day.'

'Do you need to take anyone else?'

Jones pointed to the lieutenant beside him. 'Hunter says he can come.'

Lieutenant Hunter nodded. 'I was on a court martial a few

months ago over in Corbie, and I have the time to accompany the major tomorrow. The fellow we tried was caught miles away from his battalion, in a brothel. He'd been AWL for weeks.'

'The worst I ever heard of,' the senior officer cleared his throat, 'was a mutiny in 1915, November, the French Third battalion of the Sixty-third infantry regiment refused to go over the top at Vimy. The whole battalion was court-martialled, nine hundred and forty-nine men, and one man from every company was shot.'

Major Jones cleared his throat. 'I've never heard of that sir.'

'Well it happened.'

Lieutenant Gedge looked across at Major Jones. 'Will there be a CMO tomorrow, sir?'

'Don't know.'

'What's a CMO?' Matt asked.

Major Jones enlightened him. 'A *courts martial officer*; it's a relatively new introduction. He's an additional member of the court and always a bona fide member of the legal profession, so he's there to give advice on proper legal procedure and points of law. But he votes in the ordinary way on guilt or innocence. They've only been around a little time, haven't they?' He looked at Captain McAskill, who kept records and statistics.

'Yes, sir, only about two months. Before that most courts martial had no one with any legal capacity involved. We had to rely on army discipline and rules as our yardstick. Made it hard on the average officer.'

Burnett nodded. 'As I believe there are only about forty-three of them on the whole western front at present they'll be busy I'm afraid. Sadly, we Australians don't exactly have a good record with desertions. I was looking at a file of statistics from you, McAskill, yesterday and in the last six months out of five hundred convictions for desertion in the entire British Empire Forces our few Australian divisions account for more than twenty-five per cent of all of them. It's intolerable, of course . . . such a large margin.'

Matt's tone was dry. 'I assume you put that down to the fact that the deserters know they won't get the death sentence.'

'Exactly. You know about that do you?'

Jones decided to express a view. 'I know that General Haig wishes for a change to the Australian law but Billy Hughes is unconvinced and as he's the Prime Minister, he's the one with the say. Actually I think most of us in the service would welcome the death penalty for desertion and cowardice. It's not at all bloody fair to the majority.'

The senior officer was less forthright. 'It's a difficult moral issue, Jones, when we have an entirely volunteer force. I know General Birdwood's of the opinion that if we ever do bring in conscription then that is also the time to bring in the death penalty for such as desertion and cowardice.'

Major Jones turned to Matthew. 'You see, a prisoner knows that even if the death sentence is pronounced, it'll be commuted. And a lot believe they'll be released when hostilities cease at the end of the war.'

'And is that the case?' asked Matt.

The major shrugged.

'I don't believe it will be,' Burnett opined, sipping his drink. 'It'll depend on the charge and the circumstances of the charge. And military prison's no place to spend a long time, I can assure you.'

Jones nodded. 'Yes, sir, but you might say that those without a sense of honour and who believe they'll be released at war's end, could prefer to spend the entire war in a military prison than at the front line.'

'Yes, you're right there,' conceded the senior officer. 'But then a good Australian soldier has no equal. It's a conundrum, for in the main we're as brave as any. And also remember that in any case the men who go before a court martial remain an infinitesimally small proportion of the men in the armies of the world. There are hundreds of thousands, perhaps millions, fighting on every front right now, who whilst they might be miserable and ill and afraid and even terrified, overcome their personal devils, support their comrades and endure hardship, uphold the rules, maintain their spirits and carry on.'

Lieutenant Gedge nodded vigorously. 'How true. The majority of our fellows live in hell and make the best of it. It's really only a few who malinger.'

Matt could not help but have the last say. The lamplight

reflected in the sheen of his dark hair as he bent forward to pick up his drink. 'In the Dantesque landscape and environment of the front line, where I would assume that the constant companion of hovering death, the screeching falsetto of the artillery and an extended loss of sleep bring nightmarish mirages even to the steadiest mind, there, men might be forgiven for being pushed beyond forbearance, and for pursuing actions that run the entire gamut of human behaviour.'

The soldiers were silent and in seeming acquiescence took up and swallowed their drinks.

The following day Luke stood in front of the four officers who sat behind a marked and pitted sixteenth-century oak table in the back room of the Maison Sarabane, the only café still operating in the war-torn town of Albert, centre of activity for the Somme Valley. There were a small number of *estaminets* where soldiers could find companionship and drink, and one or two shops still traded, but the town was virtually closed down.

Faded russet drapes falling in weary folds to the floor almost covered the long windows behind the officers, and dust particles could be seen floating in the jaded beam of wintery light that forced itself through the break in the curtains.

From where Luke stood he had the strangest vision through the cracked and dirty window. Above the rooftops he saw the ruin of the town basilica and its tower, which partly shattered as it was, remained crowned by the five-yard-high Golden Madonna holding the baby Jesus aloft and coated in gold leaf; except that now instead of being vertical it balanced at a hazardous angle below the horizontal, as if diving into the street and appearing to be ready to drop the baby Jesus at any moment. This was due to having been hit by German shelling in January 1915. There was rumour that some of the French and British forces believed that the war would end on the day the statue actually fell, but as precarious as it looked it had not yet fallen.

Luke appeared to concentrate on this particular vision as the officers of the court put down their files and papers and took up their pens. The day before he had been introduced to Lieutenant Trimmingham who was to defend him and who was known as 'the prisoner's friend'. The lieutenant now sat near him.

Major Jones, who had arrived in Albert an hour before, presided, and on his right sat Lieutenant Hunter who had come with him from Amiens. Beside Hunter was another officer, Lieutenant Laidlaw Dempsy, and on the president's left was Captain Benjamin Wright, who was a courts martial officer.

Luke was asked his name and number, regiment and battalion. He answered in a low voice and was told to speak up.

Before the court proceeded Lieutenant Trimmingham stood. 'May I request a chair for the accused.'

'Denied.' Major Jones lifted his pen. 'Has the prisoner been seen by a medical officer?'

'Yes.'

'And the conclusion?'

'The prisoner was seen and examined by Captain Hughes of the RAMC and is reported as being both mentally and physically normal, rational and in charge of his faculties.' The report was handed to the president, who tabled it on top of his other papers.

The major pointed his pen at Luke. 'Do you understand the charges?'

Luke's voice sounded thin as it squeezed through the constricted passage in his throat. 'I think so, sir.'

'Read out the conviction.'

'The conviction from the provost marshal is recorded as Refusal to go into attack: i.e. Disobedience and Cowardice in face of the enemy, and Desertion from the scene of battle.'

'And how is the prisoner pleading?'

'Guilty.'

Major Jones and the other members of the court looked at each other. In a tone of surprise the president repeated, 'Guilty on all counts?'

'Yes, sir.'

This was almost unprecedented and the court looked with new eyes upon the thin-faced glazed-eyed prisoner. Major Jones glanced at Captain Wright, the CMO, who concluded, 'We'll go ahead and read the conditions of the charge.'

The president pointed his pen. 'In that case what are the conditions of the charge?'

'On Monday, 13 November 1916 at approximately eighteen hundred hours the prisoner, Luke Raymond Marland was found hiding in a shell hole. This was twelve hours after the commencement of battle. He had sustained no injuries. Prior to this the prisoner had been discovered remaining in the trenches when his battalion went over the top into battle.

'Lieutenant Colin Bradshaw, an officer of the BEF 2nd Brigade support troops, has written a report which is tabled now to the court, in which he gives evidence that he came across the accused in section 51, addressed him and ordered him to join his battalion. The prisoner refused and Lieutenant Bradshaw forced him at gunpoint to follow his battalion into the battle.'

The report was handed to the court and for some time all the officers looked at it.

The president, in what now had proved an habitual movement, lifted his pen and pointed it at Luke. 'Then you admit you deliberately remained behind when your regiment went into battle?'

'I . . . I suppose so.'

The president looked at the CMO and Captain Wright said, 'We need a yes or a no.'

Luke nodded, 'Yes.'

Jones pointed to the records sergeant. 'Record a yes.' He regarded Luke for some seconds then asked, 'And you admit that you refused to join your comrades but hid in a shell hole and avoided hostilities?'

'I . . . I fell into the shell hole, sir. I was trying to go forward . . . I was running, the ground gave way. When I fell there was a man, dead . . .' Luke began to tremble with the memory. He continued shivering until his whole body shook. 'And . . . then . . . I stood . . . I . . . stood on a man . . . the crunching . . . Oh God.' He was trembling so violently he appeared to be about to fall again.

'Give the prisoner a chair.'

Lieutenant Trimmingham jumped forward and slid a chair into Luke's knees as he crumpled into it.

Major Jones extended his pen in Luke's direction once more. 'Go on, young man.'

It was then Luke began to cry.

The officers of the court looked at each other. Lieutenant Hunter shrugged and took a drink of water and Lieutenant Dempsy wrote something down on his pad.

The prisoner's friend spoke. 'Marland seems to be suffering from some type of *shell shock*.'

The president went into a huddle with his court officers and after a few minutes of discussion he lifted his head, pointed his pen and said, 'It's the opinion of the court that the prisoner's been deemed A-one by a medical officer and thus we'll continue. Is there a defence?'

Lieutenant Trimmingham stood and spoke for Luke. He pointed out that Luke had been in the schoolroom until just over six months earlier, was plainly unaware of what he was volunteering to do and that he was obviously unsuited to army life.

The president nodded and asked, 'But he was trained for active service, was he not?'

'Yes, his record shows apparently on the troop ship from Australia and for three months and seven days in Marseilles, and then training continued while his battalion was in reserve at Château Segard south of the Somme River and before his battalion moved into the line.'

'Had he seen any action before?'

'No, sir.'

'So this was to be his very first action.' The president, with pen raised, addressed Luke. 'Do you understand that in pleading guilty, you admit openly to the charges in what appears to be a prima facie case against you?'

Luke's eyes left the Golden Madonna and he dropped his chin to his chest. 'Yes.' The word shuddered out.

Lieutenant Trimmingham put his hand on Luke's shoulder. 'Major Jones, I've explained at length to Private Marland what it means but he does not wish to alter his plea.'

Major Jones once more waved his pen in Luke's direction. 'The prisoner has here today admitted to the charges against him. Are the officers who found the prisoner first in the trenches and then in the shell hole here in the court?'

Lieutenant Bradshaw and two other soldiers, a sergeant and a private, stood.

For some time, the president, and Lieutenants Dempsy and

Hunter put a series of questions to all three, finishing with a question from the president to Lieutenant Bradshaw. 'So in your opinion when you urged the accused at gunpoint over the top of the trench in section 51 of the front line, would he have remained in the trench and avoided the battle if he could have?'

'Yes, sir, definitely. He was not going anywhere without real intimidation.'

At this juncture the president shook his head in thought. 'Does the prisoner wish to give evidence on oath or to make an unsworn statement of any kind?'

Luke managed to stand, holding on to the back of the chair. He looked at Major Jones and the officers with him. 'I'm sorry, sir . . . I wish I could have been brave . . . like the others.' Tears rolled down his cheeks. He bent his head. 'I just never thought it would be like this . . .'

Major Jones sighed audibly. 'Hand me the prisoner's B22 and his pay book. The court will recess for a decision.'

The conduct sheet and the pay book were passed across.

Everyone including Luke, who was supported under the elbows by Lieutenant Trimmingham, stood as the officers of the court martial left the dank back room in the café and went into the bar.

Luke was given a drink of water and in the minutes the officers were out of the room the Golden Madonna disappeared as the daylight through the broken window faded and the lamps were lit.

When the officers returned Luke was strong enough to stand and Lieutenant Trimmingham approached the table, his boyish forehead creased in lines of concern. 'Sir, may I suggest leniency in this case? The accused is basically still a schoolboy. He's obviously out of his depth in the army. He was clearly terrified on the day of the battle.'

Major Jones spoke. He kept it brief. He said the court understood that Private Luke Marland might have been terrified as many a soldier at times had been, but that he had volunteered to fight for the Australian Imperial Forces and as a soldier of that army was subject to its discipline. It was his and the court's opinion that Marland was not suffering from the new sickness known as *shell shock*, as had been asserted, because Private

Marland had not been on any active service before the said event, and shell shock resulted from being under fire: and that in any event Marland had been passed as fit by an officer of the RAMC.

Following court procedure the president asked if there were any evidence in regard to the prisoner's character and Lieutenant Trimmingham presented what he had. It was passed from the president to Hunter and Wright and Dempsy. All officers looked at it and then the president asked for Luke to move forward in front of the table.

'Private Luke Raymond Marland of the 16th Battalion of the 12th Mixed Division of the AIF and BEF, under the jurisdiction granted to the officers of this court you are informed that all officers concur with the finding. You have pleaded guilty on all counts and are found guilty on all counts. A sentence of death has been imposed and forthwith commuted to imprisonment with hard labour. You will be informed of the length and details of your sentence after you are returned to your battalion and the normal review procedure has taken place.'

Luke gave no indication that he had heard. He stood in the wan lamplight with his chin on his chest and his eyes trained on the wooden floor until Lieutenant Trimmingham urged him from the room.

On the evening of Monday 20 November, as dusk swiftly fell, Matt stood across from the Carlton-Belfort Hotel on the far side of the Rue de Noyon and made a quick sketch of the front of the hotel and the painted sign on the wall to the right of the main entrance: 'No Lorries Through Town'. Then when the light faded and a chill rain began to fall he crossed the street and passed into the hotel.

He sat for a time in a tattered velvet wing-backed chair, watching the decay in the ornate cornice at the top of the foyer and musing on the matters of his life. He had decided to leave Amiens on Wednesday and head out to join the 16th where he hoped to find Harry alive and well. The enemy he would handle as best he could. He refrained from thinking of Caro, but he did think of Knobby and as he rubbed the knee of his bad right leg he imagined how appealing it would be to have his friend walk through the door of the hotel. His habitual crooked smile edged his mouth up at the thought.

When a group of marines came in and moved noisily over to sit on benches near one of the long windows he again took out his sketchbook and drew them. Some time later a mam'selle in a stained apron came over and asked if he would be dining with them, to which he replied in the negative and headed across to the front door. As he reached it he ran into Major Jones and Lieutenant Hunter. They halted and Jones asked, 'How's the artist?'

Matt rested on his ivory cane. 'Well enough. How did your sojourn on the court martial go yesterday?'

'Oh hell, a bloody kid up on cowardice, desertion and disobedience charges. First court martial I've ever done and the last, I hope. He pleaded guilty, was guilty, and needless to say we had to find him guilty. Now it's up to the officers of his regiment and battalion to review his file and sign it and then his divisional commanding officer, Brigadier Claver-Jensen will pass sentence. He'll get twenty years at least, I'd say; might get life.'

'Are you leaving?' Hunter asked Matthew.

'I was.'

'Care to join us for a drink?' the major offered.

Matthew tapped his cane on the floor. 'Sure.'

As the trio turned and walked across the foyer to the corridor that led down to the bar Major Jones asked, 'You're from Brisbane, aren't you, Craken?'

'Yes.'

'So was the kid who was court-martialled. Went to school there.'

Matt looked round, an expression of mild interest on his face. 'What was his name?'

'Marland, Luke Marland.'

Matt halted in the corridor. 'I know that boy.' In a very uncharacteristic moment he had almost added: *He joined up with my son*, but he had restrained himself. He sounded completely calm as he enquired, 'Was he the only one you court-martialled?'

'Yes. He was with the 16th Battalion, reneged on going into battle, hid in a shell hole. How do you know him?'

698

Matt shook his head. 'It doesn't matter. Just sorry to hear about him, that's all.'

'Yes,' the major went on, 'almost felt sorry for him myself, sensitive kid, he made a pathetic little speech, said he was *sorry* he couldn't be like the others, that he didn't think the army would be like it is.' He shook his head in recollection. 'Poor devil.'

Lieutenant Hunter was less compassionate. 'If you'll excuse me, sir, what did he think the bloody army was going to be like? War's war and he's a soldier, after all. He's not on holiday. If all members of the AIF acted in the same manner as bloody Marland we'd all have been massacred by the enemy years ago. If you're a soldier you have a duty not to let your comrades down. Marland's a coward, shirked his duty and deserves what he gets.'

Matt raised his eyebrows to the youthful lieutenant. 'An obdurate point of view, Lieutenant, and no doubt you're right about needing more brave men than cowards to win wars and that certainly seems to be the aim here.'

Hunter spoke positively. 'Yes it is.'

Matt lifted his cane, and for emphasis, tapped it on the side of his boot. 'I too have no love for the nefarious Kaiser and his cohorts and how they have rattled their sabres across Europe for decades, so I shall leave aside the debatable question of whether in fact we should have rallied to Belgium's aid and simply point out to you, Hunter, old chap, that all men are not of identical ilk. And when a kid thinks he's going off on an adventure and it turns out to be the hell of the Somme Valley, it shouldn't seem particularly odd that he cracks. Whether he's dealt with harshly or leniently is another matter; but unfortunately, Hunter, in your thesis of duty all men would have to be born with identical strengths allowing them to act in precisely the same manner. It seems to me that in the discussion of *duty* it's *your duty* as an officer in charge of men to realise they're not all out of the same mould.'

Matt glanced to the major and back to the lieutenant. 'And therefore as the years ahead pile on your shoulders, old son, you should attempt to understand the possibility that a youth *might* be driven to act in what you term a *cowardly manner*, or you may find to your regret that you beget such a creature, and where would you stand then?'

'Hell, Major Craken, that's all very well and a pretty speech, but if I had a son who turned out to be a coward, I'd disown him.'

Matthew gave one of his slanted smiles. 'Now that's an amusing stance, Hunter. We definitely must stay in touch, old son.'

The lieutenant was at a loss to reply and as they moved on Matt asked the major, 'Where's Marland now?'

'Still in the town gaol in Albert, I'd think,' he answered, as he pushed open the door to the bar where the noise was such that all normal conversation ceased. They found a few stools and drank a couple of glasses of red wine.

When Matthew left the hubbub of the Carlton-Belfort and crossed the square to headquarters he wore a serious expression. He did not sleep well and presented himself to Lieutenant Colonel Burnett's office straight after an early breakfast. Captain McAskill was there and informed him that Burnett was in a meeting in the commissariat and would be along shortly.

'I'll wait.'

An hour later Burnett came in huffing and puffing. 'So bloody cold out there and I can't get any sense out of those people and there are thousands of bloody troops to feed.' He saw Matt. 'Ah, Craken, what are you doing here? Thought you'd be on your way to join your battalion.'

'I'm off first thing tomorrow, but I have a query if you have a moment?'

The senior officer nodded and gestured for Matt to come into his office. He moved round his desk and sat down, blowing on his fingers and rubbing his hands together. 'So what is it?'

'You'll recall that Major Jones presided over a court martial the day before yesterday.'

'I do.'

'The soldier he court-martialled joined up last May with my son. They went to school together.' Matt tapped his cane on the floor. 'While I've no reason to fear for my son, knowing his friend has been court-martialled disturbs me to a certain extent. Regrettably having such an acquaintance breeds the unpleasantness of some responsibility and as I'm going up to the battalion tomorrow where no doubt I'll hear news of my boy, what I want to know is, could I get permission to see Marland on the way? I believe he's still in the town gaol in Albert.'

Alec Burnett rested his heavy chin in his hand. 'Hmm, I understand. I think I can arrange for you to see him. I'll speak with the provost marshal. Was this young man found guilty?'

'Yes, apparently he pleaded that way.'

'That's surprising. What's his name again?'

'Private Luke Marland.'

He wrote the name down. 'Come back around eighteen hundred. I won't be here but I'll leave the pass with McAskill's sergeant. If I have difficulty in arranging your request there'll be a message as to what you should do next.' He stood up and Matt did the same. Matt gave a semblance of a salute, which brought a wide grin to Burnett's face. 'You'll have to work on that, Major.'

'Yes, I suppose I will.'

'And let me know if you're serious about requesting a different battalion posting in the new year.'

'Indeed.'

The lieutenant colonel held out his hand, 'Good luck.'

'Thanks.'

As Matthew made his way from the lieutenant colonel's office and fought through the wind whipping along the station in Amiens, to the south in Montdidier, Caro was called in to Matron Steele.

The older woman sat wrapped in a blanket and gave the semblance of a smile.

'Yes, Matron? You asked for me?'

'Sit down, Mrs Craken.'

Caro squeezed into the chair which was wedged between the desk and the door of the cramped office.

'You'll recall our conversation of a week or so ago where I mentioned your ability to drive vehicles?'

Caro nodded.

'Well, you're needed north of here. There's been another battle in the last week near the Ancre River. They're asking for anyone I can spare who can drive. And as you can nurse as well, you can be most useful. You're being sent up north to a little place called Aveluy where they've set up casualty clearing stations, CCSs as they're called. There are a few in that area. I've just spoken with Jill Cossington and she's going too as she also drives. They need help to get the wounded from the railways to the CCSs and then on to the base hospitals in Domart, Doullens and Amiens.' She handed Caro two passes. 'I'm told to inform you to pack immediately and leave today. You'll report to Captain Cadee of the RAMC, who apparently is working in the village church hall in Villers Bretonneux all today. You'll travel from there to Aveluy with him.' She tapped a paper at her right hand. 'There're Nissen huts there, and one is set aside for female quarters I'm told.'

'Is this a permanent move, Matron?'

'I'm uncertain. The VADs are *lending* you is my understanding of the matter.'

Caro nodded and stood up. 'I'll do my best.'

Iron-heart stood and proffered her hand from under the blanket across the desk. Caro took it. The matron closed her eyes and when she opened them Caro was amazed to see tears brimming there. The matron spoke almost in a whisper. 'The name of the Somme will bring tears to my eyes for the rest of my life. All we can do is to try to lessen their pain a little.'

'I know,' Caro said and she squeezed the matron's hand and covered it with her other. 'I know, and thank you.'

Chapter Forty-two

The light was fading and sleet was drifting when Caro and Jill arrived in Villers Bretonneux. They had travelled north with Roland Mountfort, a corporal in the service unit of the Royal Berkshire Regiment. They rode in a munitions train into Amiens, where after a long wait they caught a ride with a convoy of lorries carrying food supplies to the front. The road travel was much slower than the rail as the roads were blocked with all sorts of traffic. They had not moved at all for long periods and at other times had limped along at a walking pace in the effort to get through the ubiquitious mud.

On arrival in the village of Villers Bretonneux it did not take long to discover the church hall and they were relieved to find Captain Cadee and two assistants there. Percy Cadee was a round-faced, congenial man with kindly eyes and ready with a quip and a joke even in the dire circumstances of war. He welcomed the two women.

'Good to see you, but I was told I'd be receiving at least five of you. Nevertheless you're as pretty as five, I'm sure.' He grinned and slapped the top of the table. 'Ah well, I'll remain positive and expect more later.' He took them round the corner to an *estaminet* where he had beds organised in the upstairs room for them for the night.

Throughout the war zone, there were thousands of *estaminets*, civilian bar-cum-cafés usually run by females whose males were away at the war: this one fell into the normal catogory and was run by Madame Haricourt and her daughter. The older woman was affectionately known by the British soldiers who frequented her establishment as 'Beanie'. When she was a young woman her husband had fought in the Franco-Prussian War and if ever she was heard to bemoan 'the war' it was not the current one but the previous one of forty-six years before.

Caro and Jill ate the sparse meal provided by Beanie's

daughter and, fatigued from their journey, retired early and drifted quickly off to sleep even though substantial noise filtered through the thin flooring from the one-roomed bar below.

The following day at first light Captain Cadee brought his omnibus-ambulance to the front of the establishment and as the women climbed aboard, he affectionately patted the metal of the door. 'This jalopy was commandeered in Paris in 1914 and I've never let it out of my sight since. Call it Daisy, and with a bit of luck she'll have us in Aveluy in no time.'

The two women shook their heads. 'You'll need a lot of luck all right if our road journey yesterday is anything to judge by.'

Beanie, leaning on a crooked tree branch walking stick, waved them off. '*Au revoir, à bientôt.*' And Daisy bumped along out of the town.

Matthew, his driver, Cliff, and batman-assistant, Bert, had been delayed in Amiens. Their lorry had failed to start and it had taken Cliff most of the morning to find new spark plugs. When finally they set off they had a passenger in the back, Timothy Lewis, a bombardier from the 1st Battalion of the East Surrey Regiment returning to his unit after a short leave.

Matt had leaned back with eyes closed in expectation of Cliff's constant discourse and appraisal of all things, which as usual, swiftly came to pass.

After five hours of travel the sky was darkening and they were still not in Albert. 'It'll be tough goin' in the flamin' dark,' Cliff informed them. 'That's the trouble with the bloody mud. What if we get stuck? Goin' dark at this hour, that's the real problem with winter, these early nights. I don't think we can travel in the dark. Suppose we could all sleep in the back if we have to.'

At this particular point, after many hold-ups, the road was blissfully free of movement and Matthew turned his head sideways to speak in Cliff's ear. Earlier, amongst a myriad subjects and opinions, Cliff had been informing them of how his wife's mother was a disagreeable old biddy whom he detested, that she never had a decent word to say for anybody, and that the only good thing about the war was that it removed her from his vicinity.

'Look, old son,' Matthew said, 'keep your foot hard down on the blasted accelerator, give yourself some real inspiration by pretending it's your mother-in-law's face, and before you know it we'll be in Albert.'

Cliff gave a guffaw of amusement and accord, and with that thought in mind kept his foot firmly in place and within twenty minutes they trundled into Albert in the dark.

The town's streets offered only ruins but through some of the windows glowed weak candlelight, and after a time of knocking and searching they came to the gaol. There Matt was informed in broken English that under no circumstances could he see the prisoner Marland. At first, the best Matthew could make out with his limited French and the gaoler's limited English was that it appeared the refusal was owing to the irrelevancy that Marland was an Australian detainee, and that he, the man in charge, was a French gaoler. After some more confusing conversation it seemed to Matthew that if he presented himself to the same place in the morning after ten o'clock he would be allowed to see 'Le prisonnier Marland'. He thought the Frenchman was telling him that tomorrow there were Australian Military Police coming to remove the prisoner and return him to his battalion. If this were correct, Matt assumed it was for final sentencing.

Matt then asked if there were anywhere they could sleep and the man laughed, showing tobacco-stained teeth. 'Ah oui,' he pointed with his thick finger out the door. 'Vous pouvez dormir là bas.'

Matthew's lip turned up; he did not fancy sleeping in the street. 'How very gracious of you, cousin.'

They left the lorry where it stood and after a surprisingly brief search found what passed for an *estaminet*. There some francs from Matt's pocket to an elderly woman endowed them with a warm meal, scant though it was, some passable wine and three mattresses in a back room. The last comment of Cliff's audible to Matthew was, 'It's bloody rainin' again, sir, what a country, at least we're in here and out of it. What I wouldn't give to be back in Paraparaumu.' With that quaint remark ringing in his ears Matthew sank into sleep.

The following morning Matt presented himself once more to the gaol. This time the greeting was more welcoming. There were three French soldiers on duty and one spoke impeccable English: 'I worked in London before the war.'

Matthew handed over the form, which gave him permission from the provost marshal at the Division Headquarters in Amiens, to visit the prisoner Luke Raymond Marland.

The English-speaking soldier retired behind a desk where a pistol and two Berthier rifles with angled bolt handles lay on a shelf behind. He stamped the form, handed it back, took the handgun and beckoned for Matt to follow him. They passed through a second office and out along a covered stone walkway.

'The prisoner you speak of is in a cell alone. He was not happy in with others, he would scream and cry that he wanted to be alone, so we removed him. He asked me for a pencil and paper this morning. I think he wants to write to someone. They have all had breakfast, so soon we will take them for a walk around the yard.' He pointed out to the right where over a low broken-down wall Matt could see an open space about thirty yards square where some grass grew and a few large pots stood. In the distance was a second higher wall with barbed wire running across the top and boards and wire blocking a gap in the middle obviously made by a shell.

They passed by a number of cells, all with men inside. 'You seem to have quite a few inmates.'

The soldier laughed. 'Always. Crime does not cease during wartime.'

He halted outside a mottled wooden door with a rusty grille about five feet from the floor. Hanging on the wall to the right of the door was a large polished brass key. Matt thought how incongruous it was to have a shiny key in these surroundings; yet it pleased him to see someone had enough pride to bother to clean it.

The French soldier opened the door, 'Private Marland you have a— *Mon Dieu! Comment ça?*'

Beyond the soldier Matthew saw Luke sitting against the wall. His body lay at a distorted angle like a discarded marionette and the straw beneath him was soaked in blood. His eyes stared into infinity and his blood-covered clothing could not hide the fact that he had gouges in his wrists and his neck and at his inner thigh. A knife lay to the side of his body.

Matt dropped his cane and rushed across the intervening space to the youth's side, shouting to the soldier, 'Quickly, man, get some bandages, cloth, anything, *vite, vite*.' Matt took out his handkerchief and wrapped it round the boy's neck in an effort to stop the blood from draining away.

The French soldier disappeared from the room and Matt picked up the blanket that lay on a bench nearby and folded it round the boy's wrists.

Matt put his hand near Luke's mouth. He was uncertain whether the boy was breathing or not; if he were it was very faintly.

There was a shout along the corridor and in another minute the soldier reappeared carrying an apron, which he tore into pieces. Behind him, come to see the spectacle, arrived his two comrades, talking loudly. Matt removed the blanket and with the makeshift apron bandages wrapped Luke's wrists and his leg.

'Where the hell would he get a knife?'

'*Je ne sais pas*. We don't give them knives.'

He looked up to the soldiers. Is there a hospital? *Est-ce que un hôpital ici?*'

'No . . . no hospital.'

'Blast.'

The soldier who spoke English pointed in the direction of the yard. 'There are a number of your British casualty clearing stations north of here.'

'*Je pense qu'il est mort*,' decided one of the soldiers who bent over Luke.

Matt looked at the English-speaking soldier. 'Help me get the kid outside. I have a vehicle. I'll take him.'

But the soldiers did not move.

'Come on . . . hurry.'

The English-speaking soldier shook his head. 'Major, you cannot remove the prisoner. I cannot release him to you. Not without the right form.'

Matt took a deep breath. 'I don't know whether the boy's alive or dead. But surely you see we have to try and save him. Come with me, then you won't have released him, you'll still

707

be with him. Look, man, be reasonable. If we can we've got to give the boy a chance.'

This apparently made sense to the soldier. 'All right. But he was to have been handed over to the Military Police today. What will we tell them?'

'I'll take responsibility. Major Matthew Craken, AIF, 16th Battalion, 6th Mixed Division.'

The soldiers lifted Luke and carried him out. Matt moved to follow and noticed a paper and lead pencil lying near the door. He picked up the paper. It was a note from Luke:

> I just couldn't face my friends. What I've done is bad enough. Please don't tell my mother or my Uncle Bill. I beg of you to let them think I died in battle.
>   Luke

Matthew folded the paper, put it in his pocket and hurried from the room. Out in the street where Cliff and Bert waited in the lorry Matt called for their attention and they sprang into action, leaping down to help the soldiers place Luke in the back of the vehicle.

Matt explained. 'I think the kid's still breathing. We must get some help.' He turned to the English-speaking soldier. 'Which is the nearest medical centre?'

'There's one not far along the Bapume Road.' He pointed out the direction and gestured for one of his comrades to go along in the lorry. 'I must remain here. I am in charge but my comrade will go with you.'

Cliff said, 'What about Timothy? He's gone off somewhere.'

Matt shook his head. 'We can't wait. Let's go.'

As Cliff moved round the engine to climb up into the cabin he halted. 'Look what's coming!' and pointed excitedly down the street at the vehicle which lumbered towards them past the ruined basilica of the diving Golden Madonna. It was an old grey omnibus but there was no mistaking the red cross in the white circle on the front.

Matt walked out into the middle of the street, waving his cane for the vehicle to stop. As it braked in front of him a man in RAMC uniform leaned out of the cabin. 'What's up, old chap?'

708

'I've got a boy here with slashed wrists and neck . . . tried to commit suicide. Can you help?'

The man opened the door and jumped down from the bus followed by another two men and two women. The second woman's voice rang in the cold November wind. 'Matt, you here? What in heaven's name's going on?'

Matt restrained himself from surprise or greeting. 'Caro, you've told me how devoted you are to nursing strangers. So now you can tend a boy you know.'

Caro's face blanched. 'Oh God, Matt, no, not—'

'No, Caro, not Harry, but Luke Marland.'

When Captain Cadee saw Luke he just said, 'He's still breathing faintly. Needs a blood transfusion. I'll drive as fast as I can. It's just over a mile to our CCS.' He looked at Caro. 'Travel with him and bandage his wounds. We won't move him.' He jumped down and ran to his ambulance, found bandages and threw them across to Caro, then signalled to Matthew, 'Follow me,' and drove off.

As the two vehicles started up Timothy Lewis came round the corner whistling.

'Hurry up, mate,' Cliff shouted through the window, and Tim ran and jumped up on the dashboard and climbed over the back as they trundled out of Albert.

The English-speaking soldier watched them drive away and turned to his comrade. 'What is all the fuss over a suicide when hundreds of thousands of young men have died without help of any kind just over there.' He lifted his thumb and indicated east in the direction of the front line and with a grunt of disgust spat on the footpath and strode back to the gaol.

In the direct rays manifested by the climbing sun in a surprisingly clear sky outside the convent window John Conrad's pale silhouette swelled up the stone wall behind him as he stood and looked up at the ceiling where paint peeled above his head. He was back in the battalion headquarters at the convent. His men had proved themselves in the Battle of the Ancre and they had taken hundreds of German prisoners. He spoke aloud like a boy to his father, 'Wherever you are, K, I hope you're proud of me.' He gave a wan smile, and brought his eyes down at the sound of a knock on the door. 'Come in.'

709

Tommy Hardcastle entered and saluted, 'You asked for me?'

'Yes. Amongst everything else I've got a blasted file here on a court martial that took place when we were up the line.' He lifted it. 'One of ours, a private called Marland. Do you know anything about it?'

Tommy shook his head.

'Then you'd better ask the others and get me Bingham. The fellow was in his platoon. It seems this Marland didn't go over the top with the rest of the lads on the thirteenth. He's been found guilty on desertion and cowardice charges. All happened in Albert a few days ago. He's in gaol there. It seems he's to be sent back here for sentencing and I think from what I read that two military police will have gone down already to bring him back.'

Tommy's brow creased in thought. 'Marland . . . no, don't know him. We've got a bloody good record in this battalion. All we've had have been a few drunkenness charges and a couple of petty thefts; the odd AWL in Marseilles but nothing since. If he's under Bingham then his company officer was either Kenny or Young. Captain Bader would have known him too.'

'I'll need to speak to them.'

'I should get Kenny or Young for you then, sir.'

John Conrad held up his hand. 'No, get me Bingham first. I'll speak to the others afterwards.'

Tommy moved to the door. 'Right, I'll get Bingham and check if anyone here knows any more about it.'

'Oh, and, Tommy?' The young man turned. 'I've got to go and see the old man in Amiens on Friday. Accompany me, will you?'

Tommy smiled. 'Yes, sir, absolutely. After the mud of the Ancre, Amiens will be a real treat.'

An hour later, a small fire had been lit in the grate and the wood in the windows, replacing the hessian bags of yore, rattled in the gusts of wind as Bingo was brought into John Conrad.

'Ah, Sergeant Major. I've got a file here on one of your privates, fellow called Marland. He didn't go into battle on the thirteenth, was discovered in the trenches and later hiding in a shell hole. He's been court-martialled. And as you're aware, I'm required to supply my remarks and signature before I hand it over to the brigadier for his final decision on length of sentence.'

Bingo nodded his fiery head and pulled on his beard. 'Ah, so that's what happened to Marland. Nervous sort of kid, never seemed happy. So by what you say, sir, he's been found guilty?'

'*Pleaded* guilty, actually.' He handed the file across the desk. 'There isn't a lot here so I'd like you to go into the next room and read it. Then come back to me.'

Bingo left with the file under his arm and twenty minutes later he returned.

John Conrad motioned for him to sit. 'What's your opinion?'

'Well, sir, yes, by this he's guilty, poor devil. I can only report my dealings with him. He was not one who took well to army life, I'd say. Never volunteered for much unless it was a *safe duty*, but having said that he wasn't a *bad* soldier. He never gave me any trouble and his conduct sheet is pretty clean, as you'll have seen. Good at drill, smart enough with his weapons. Played around a bit in Marseilles but most of them did. I didn't see any of this coming on, sir, or I might have been able to talk to the boy. Seems like the shit was scared out of him.'

'Indeed. Who were his friends?'

'I think he was close to a few of the blokes: Isaac Walker, who was killed on the first day of the battle, and Frank Birtenshaw, who was killed on the second, and also an old Anzac, Curly Moss, but his closest mate's a kid by the name of Craken. The one we've just made a lance jack.'

John Conrad nodded. 'Yes, I know him. Well, thanks, Sergeant Major. You've been a great help.'

Later John Conrad interviewed Jack Bader and Lieutenants Kenny and Young but none of them could enlighten John Conrad with anything more.

At lunch John Conrad shared a drink with Tommy Hardcastle. Tommy swallowed his straight down and his senior officer pointed at the empty glass. 'Too fast, Tommy. You must not drink so fast.' He paused for effect, and added slowly, 'Nor so much.'

The younger man met John Conrad's steady gaze. 'Thank you.'

'What for?'

An expression of gratitude dwelt in Tommy's grey eyes. 'For caring, sir.'

John Conrad's tone became gruff. 'Yes, right, well, I've got enough worries without concerning myself about your welfare so try and bloody well take a grip on your drinking.'

Tommy gave a small smile. 'I'll try.'

'Don't try. Do it.'

'And what else are you worrying about, sir, if I can be so bold as to ask?'

'About the bloody court-martialled boy.'

Tommy bent towards the dying fire and rubbed his hands together. 'From what you've said it's cut and dried. He's lucky he's not in another army or he'd be going before a firing squad.'

'True enough. But I have to think carefully what I write. It'll have a bearing on Claver-Jensen's decision on the length of sentence.'

'I'm sure you'll decide what's right.'

John Conrad rubbed his chin in thought. 'I'm thinking of all the dead boys still lying out there buried and unburied in the Somme mud, many of them who were terrified but forced themselves on, and there's a part of me that's furious with anyone who didn't do his duty. But at the same time there's another part of me that says no one should have to experience this. So now I have to try to reach into myself and attempt to understand the action of a sensitive and terrified boy.'

Tommy Hardcastle eyed his superior and thought how lucky he was to serve under him.

After lunch John Conrad wrote his note on Luke's file. 'Good conduct sheet. Never made trouble. Obviously not soldier material, should never have volunteered. Suggest leniency.'

Beneath the overhanging branches of a tall oak tree, Cliff bumped the lorry to a halt behind the omnibus ambulance. Beyond the tree were pitched three large tents with red crosses on them and behind them stood a farmhouse and three Nissen huts. In the distance was a munitions depot. Matt climbed down out of the cabin. He looked back at Cliff and Bert. 'Wait until I see what's what.'

He strode round to the back of the lorry at the same time as Captain Cadee arrived.

They both looked up to where Caro nursed Luke's head in her arms. The tears were rolling down her cheeks and dripping from her chin. She looked much younger than her years, almost girlish in her grief.

Jill shook her head. 'It's too late. He's dead.'

The two men with the captain ascended and prised Luke from Caro's grasp. She remained in the back of the lorry. Only her eyes moved as she watched them take him away.

As Jill comforted her, Matt turned to Captain Cadee. 'I don't think we've introduced ourselves. I'm Matthew Craken.' He motioned to Caro. 'That lady's husband. Would it be acceptable to you if my wife did not begin her duties today? I'm actually on my way to the headquarters of the 16th Battalion north of here up near Auchonvillers. But I can join them tonight or tomorrow.'

The RAMC officer sighed. 'I wish I could say yes. But there'll be a load of wounded coming in later today and I'll need her to drive an ambulance. They come in each evening to the station nearby, then we take them to the base hospitals. You see, Major, I was expecting five drivers and they supplied me with two.'

Matt nodded. 'I understand. Then could she be excused for an hour or two?'

'Yes, that'd be all right. Fact is, I can do without her until about fifteen hundred.' He looked at his watch. 'So you've got over four hours.'

'Thank you, I'll have her back. What will happen to the boy now?'

'I'll need to be in touch with his battalion commander. We can bury him here. There's a cemetery just along there.' He pointed beyond the Nissen hut.

'Thank you. I knew him and I know his parents.'

Matt left the captain to tell Cliff and Bert what was going on. 'So wait here. Get yourselves a drink and some food and have a few hours off. We'll travel on at fifteen hundred. I'm taking the lorry for a few hours. How's the petrol, Cliff?'

'I've got another two-gallon tin in the back. We'll get to Auchonvillers as long as you don't take it too far now.'

'Right.'

Tim was leaning on the engine for warmth and Matt called to him. 'See if you can find a ride onwards. If not, you can travel on with us later.'

'Thanks, Major.'

Matt returned to the back of the lorry where Captain Cadee was helping the women down. Jill was obviously aware who Matthew was for she was quick to say, 'Don't worry, I'll look after your wife, Major.'

Matt stepped forward and took the unprotesting Caro from her grasp. 'No, *I'll* look after my wife, thanks. Just be congenial enough to take care of her possessions, would you?'

Caro looked up at her husband. 'Matt, I'm all right. I've come to terms with death. I've seen a lot of it, you know. It's just that I got a shock when it was Luke. He's stayed so often with us at Cedar Grove. He was . . . one of the family.'

'I know that, old girl, but I'm taking you away for a few hours. It'll do you good.'

Caro glanced to Captain Cadee, who smiled approval. 'Your husband says he'll have you back on time.'

Matthew nodded to the captain, who extended him a quick salute, and he moved Caro across to the lorry. North on the bumpy potholed road he drove for about half a mile, past all manner of supply and munition vehicles and troops on the march. When he saw a checkpoint ahead he turned left off into a narrow side road that led down to a grove of trees.

Caro had been silent on the ride.

He braked in front of a yew tree. It was cold but for once it was a clear day and the sun glinted on the window as he moved round to help Caro down from the cabin. She stood beside the lorry, eyeing Matt, then pulling her overcoat more tightly around her drifted to the front of the engine to stand in the sun.

The trees and the vehicle formed a compact windbreak and helped make a small suntrap on the grass. Matthew moved to the back of the lorry and out of his knapsack took a waterproof sheet which he spread in the sun at Caro's feet.

'There, sit on this.'

Caro sat and Matthew eased himself down beside her. She moved her body round to face him, lifted her eyes from her

714

hands to meet his and sat there looking at him. For minutes they remained motionless, their eyes trained on each other's face as if in such scrutiny they might see something they had not noticed in all the years before. They were so still a robin landed near the blanket and walked close to the edge of it where it pecked something in the grass before it fluttered away. Caro sighed and drew up her legs to rest her chin on her knees. 'I was surprised to see you, Matt.'

'And I also to see you.'

'I'll be driving ambulances now for a while.'

Matt leaned back on his elbow and pulled a blade of grass. 'Yes, I know.'

'Why did Luke do what he did?'

'Ah, Caro, are you sure you want to know?'

'Yes, I do.'

'He'd been court-martialled for desertion and cowardice. Seems he reneged on going into battle.'

Caro's mouth opened with shock. 'Oh my God! What about Harry? Is he all right?' Her tone was strident, fearful.

'Now now, old girl, calm down. There's no evidence to point to anything but that Luke acted on his own. Poor devil, seems he was terrified. Just couldn't *go over the top*, as they say. I met the fellows who court-martialled him. The boy pleaded guilty so there wasn't much they could do.'

Caro shook her head and wiped another tear from her eye. 'Oh dear, poor Mrs Marland.'

'Yes. The kid left a pathetic note asking that she be told he was killed in battle.'

Caro sighed. 'God rest his soul. God rest all their souls.'

Matt looked skywards. 'That which is nonexistent can never come into being and that which is, can never cease to be.'

Caro looked round. 'What did you say?'

Matt gave one of his wry smiles. 'Nothing, old girl. It's just something I learnt a long time ago.'

'That's you, always enigmatic.' She shook her head dismissively and lifted her skirt and coat to get the sun on her legs. 'You know, in Montdidier, when you said Harry might be somewhere safe like Ireland . . .'

'Yes.'

'Well, he's not. He's here in France.' She put her hand in

715

her pocket. 'Please God he's still alive. I received this letter from him the day before yesterday.' She handed it to Matthew. 'He says he didn't know where to write to you. He wrote it the night before a battle. Must have been the same one where Luke—' She broke off.

Matthew took the letter and read it.

When he folded it and handed it back she stated, 'He must be near here somewhere if Luke was.'

Matt observed her quietly for some moments before he made a decision. 'It's just possible I might see him.'

'What? Where?'

'I think he might be with the battalion I'm going to join.'

Caro's eyes were alight. 'You're joining the 16th? How did that happen?'

Matt shook his head. He would have liked the answer to that one himself.

She moved towards him on the blanket and the sun gambolled in the curls of her fair hair. Her voice was high with entreaty. 'Oh, Matt, please let me know if he's all right. You will, won't you? Promise me?'

He held up his palm. 'Of course. Yes.'

'Exactly where is it you're going?'

'I don't think I'm supposed to tell you, old girl. Let's just leave it that I'll write to you and let you know how he is. What number's your casualty clearing station?'

'I think it's eighty-two, but we can check when we go back.' She moved away again and looked round. 'Oh please God in heaven let him be all right.'

Matt winced. 'Caro, will you stop beseeching your particular form of the Almighty for this and that. What is *is*, and Harry will either be safe or he won't. All your prayers and pleading won't alter a damn thing.'

'I'm his mother, damn it, Matt. I worry about him.'

'And I'm his father, Caro. Worrying is not your exclusive domain.'

Caro had opened her mouth with the obvious retort but she checked herself. She gave a sharp laugh. 'I didn't know you ever worried about anything.'

Matt did not answer. He lay back on the blanket and closed his eyes. Caro watched him for a time; he seemed so in control

. . . that was Matt. The sheen of the sun sat on his face creating a lustre on the mark across his cheek. She noticed the way his dark lashes were thicker than she recalled; and there were wider streaks of grey now darting back through his hair than she remembered. In an automatic action she put out her hand to touch his hair but as he appeared to be asleep she paused and withdrew her fingers. She recognised there was a part of her that felt calmer having seen him and eventually she too lay down. After a few minutes of the sun kissing her face, the repercussions of war were blocked out and in time the only sound in the little French glade was the steady noise of their breathing.

Caro woke with a start. She was covered with a blanket. For a few seconds she was uncertain where she was, then solidly in her vision appeared Matthew, peeling an apple. She remembered everything and sat up. The sun had gone and there were clouds overhead. She shivered. 'What time is it?'

'Round fourteen fifteen. We'll need to leave soon. You've been asleep for about two hours. Here.' He handed her the apple. 'I have more in my kit.'

Caro took a bite. 'Why did you do this?'

'What?'

'This. Bringing me here. Being with me? I thought I'd never see you again . . . well, anyway for a long time.'

'Is that so? Well, I can assure you I thought the same.' He stood and moved around the vehicle, returning peeling another apple. 'Let's just say that when you were miraculously repositioned once more into my ken, I felt responsible for you and decided to give you a few hours' respite after the shock of having Luke die in your arms.'

She was chewing the apple and eyeing him. 'Thanks.'

He ate his fruit in silence.

When she had finished Caro threw the core off into the grass.

He handed her a water bottle and she drank. 'I have nothing else to offer.'

'That's all right. I don't want anything else.' She stood up. 'Well, we'd better go.'

He pushed himself up on his ebony cane and they lifted the ground sheet together. As they folded it her hand touched his.

Momentarily they both paused. She was aware of his gaze upon her; of the nearness of him. She did not meet his eyes, then avoiding looking up, completed the task.

On the short drive back they rode in silence.

Caro finally spoke as they entered the yard at the clearing station. 'It is number eighty-two. See, on the sign there.'

They climbed down into a buzz of hustle and bustle: men with five-gallon drums were filling the petrol tanks of nine ambulances, and orderlies were stacking stretchers in rows. Cliff and Bert appeared along a path and Jill Cossington waved from one of the tents.

Caro looked up at Matt, comfortable again in the bosom of activity. 'Thank you, Matthew, I feel normal again. So . . .' she spoke lightheartedly, '. . . to the tasks ahead. Don't forget to let me know how Harry is.'

He regarded her. 'You'll make a good ambulance driver, Caro.'

She hesitated. 'Now what on earth does that imply?'

He doffed his cap and left her standing there.

She watched him wave Cliff and Bert over, and remained watching them all climb up into the cabin, Cliff in the driver's seat, Bert in the middle and Matt on the far side. Caro lifted her hand as the lorry jerked forward and rumbled out into the road, where it turned northwards. She remained with her hand high, hoping he would wave, and was somehow disappointed that Matthew did not even look back. Shortly the lorry disappeared from view.

'Well, we've got a busy evening ahead.' Jill's voice sounded behind her and she turned to see her friend dressed in dark blue skirt with a matching jacket and her usual navy-blue cape round her shoulders. 'Yes, new uniform,' Jill smiled, 'well, sort of new; they've all been worn before.' She sniffed. 'They assure me they've been washed. Yours is over in the Nissen hut. We wear our nursing uniform when we're on day duty and this in the evenings when we're on the ambulances.'

'When do we sleep?'

Jill gave a rueful smile. 'We're off duty when we return at night and depending what time that is, we either start day duty at eight hundred or twelve hundred.' She screwed up her face. 'Still get a half day off each week and one Wednesday a month, though socialising seems to be almost out of the question, but guess what. I've seen a couple of doctors here that'd make you swoon.'

Caro sighed. Jill was twenty-five and her priorities deviated from Caro's. 'I'd better get changed then.'

'Yes, you'd better.' As Jill followed her along the path to the Nissen hut she said, 'Gosh, your old man's a looker for his age, and that scar! Well it's so . . . so . . . well, dashing like a pirate.'

Caro managed an expression of amusement. 'I must tell him that.'

John Conrad was coming down the corridor from his office. What had begun as a clear sunny day had turned cold and over-cast and he was wrapped in his greatcoat and carried a scarf.

As he reached the outer door he was called from behind, 'Sir, Colonel Fleet?'

He turned to see Menzies Lang approaching. 'Yes, Lang, what is it?'

'Two things, sir. The military police who went down to Albert to pick up the court-martialled prisoner, have found he's not there. I've just had a telephone call.'

John Conrad shook his head. 'What do you mean, *not there*?'

'The telephone call was a bit hard to understand, sir, but it seems Private Marland . . . well, it sounds like he cut his wrists and he's been carted off to a casualty clearing station.'

For some seconds the commanding officer seemed to be cal-culating this information. 'Hell, Lang. How the devil could that happen? Then find out where he is. Where are the MPs now?'

'Said they would try to find him, sir.'

'Let me know as soon as you hear anything.' John Conrad strode on.

'Sir?'

He rounded back. 'What now?'

'There were *two* things, sir . . .'

'Yes, all right. Get on with it then.'

'We seem to have inherited an artist.'

The superior officer looked nonplussed. 'What the hell does that mean?'

Lang's receding chin appeared to recede even further with the look of guilt that crossed his face. 'Well, I'm sorry, sir. I did take a phone call about it from GHQ last evening but I thought he wasn't coming until tomorrow, so I didn't see the haste to inform you. And apparently there was another message sent weeks ago which I don't believe we received. But anyway, he's here.'

'For heaven's sake, Captain, explain yourself. Who's here?'

'Apparently an artist, sir. An honorary major. He's waiting out in the long room.' He sighed with concern. 'He's got a batman and a driver and I've got to find somewhere for them to sleep. The artist's been attached to us, you see, to remain with the 16th for a year, his form says. We have to make a report after three months and so does he. It seems if he goes all right attached to us the Australian Government will begin a fully fledged war artists scheme, like the one the BEF have instigated.'

'Just what we need, a bloody artist.'

'May I suggest, I think you should see him, sir? Even if it's brief. His papers are meant to be signed by you on his arrival.'

John Conrad grunted. 'Damn it, if it's not one thing it's another. I'm already late for a meeting with Ordnance. All right, where is he?'

'This way sir.' And Lang careered off down the corridor ahead of him. As John Conrad followed Lang he felt an unaccountably weird sensation like a premonition of some troubling event.

Around two corners and along another hallway the commanding officer, his brows drawn together in thought, followed the captain. He was recalling the letter he had received from Emma Louise before the Battle of the Ancre, telling him that she had seen Matthew Craken and that he was on his way to France as an official artist. And even as Lang halted at the door and his hand moved to open it, John Conrad shouted, 'Lang, is the painter in there alone?'

Lang swung round to his superior. 'Yes, sir. His driver and batman are waiting outside with his vehicle.'

'Then leave me. I shall see him by myself.'

'But I was going to introduce you, sir.'

'Didn't you hear me?' He pointed firmly along the hall and Lang, with an expression of amazement, backed away.

John Conrad stepped to the door. He hoped with all his might that he was wrong as his hand closed over the handle and he swung it open. But no, whatever dark force had given him the premonition, it now proffered the reality of his omen as Matthew turned from the window and advanced giving what could only be described as a desultory salute.

'*Colonel Fleet*, they tell me I'm assigned to your battalion.'

John Conrad returned the salute in the same haphazard fashion. 'How very bloody cosy that'll be.'

Matt took his left hand from behind his back and handed John Conrad a sheet of paper.

As John Conrad took it, recognising the likeness of Emma Louise, Matt's voice grated on the air between them. 'Thought you would like to have this, Colonel, for old times' sake. I must say, all your women are intriguing, though it's amazing, isn't it, how you just can't seem to hold on to any of them? And yet they seem to turn up around me?'

John Conrad stood without speaking. Craken had no idea John Conrad knew all about his meeting with Emma Louise in Canterbury. In this case forewarned was forearmed. For once he was a step ahead of Matthew Craken. Finally John Conrad smiled as he rolled up the drawing. 'Thanks, Craken. I believe you liked Canterbury. Emma Louise *is* intriguing, I agree with you.'

And, he turned away, lifting the rolled drawing high in the air. 'I'll send Captain Lang back to take care of you. Sorry I can't say I'm happy to see you, after such a pleasant gift.'

As John Conrad departed Matthew gave a disdainful look at the closing door and spoke aloud to himself. 'Hmm, seems that surprise fell on arid ground, Matt old son.'

721

Chapter Forty-three

Christmas Eve 1916

In the Australian Imperial Forces' rest camp near Acheux, north-west of Albert and Aveluy, snow was falling and sliding down the curved sides of the Nissen huts to pile on the ground.

Matthew was drinking coffee and waiting for the snowfall to cease. At his elbow lay a week-old copy of the London *Daily Telegraph*.

Matthew had toiled for the past month, especially on the few good days that he had encountered, sketching all manner of outdoor military activity. The rest of the time he had worked inside and had already completed one painting. He had claimed an area as his studio at one end of a Nissen hut where there was the glory of two windows and thus some natural light flow, insipid as it often was. As the huts were half-circle shapes of corrugated iron, the only place for doors and windows in these particular specimens was at each end.

He often had soldiers coming in and viewing him at work. At first he had been inclined to tell them to move on, that he preferred his own company, but he had decided that after what they had been through he should at least be sociable enough to allow them to watch; though he drew the line at conversation and would not allow speech. He painted a sign and had it on the wall above him: 'If you want to converse, reverse.' He could imagine Caro saying, 'That's right, Matt, promote a disagreeable impression. Don't spoil your image.'

He had written to her, as she had requested, to inform her that Harry was alive and well which he had learnt shortly after his arrival to the battalion. It had been a brief letter, to the point:

Dear Caro,

Our son is alive and I'm informed also well. I spoke with a Captain Hardcastle here who tells me the boy accounted bravely for himself in the Battle of the Ancre and that they are promoting him to lance corporal. That's as lowly an appointment as it's possible to have. But he'll be pleased, no doubt.

If you wish to write to him just address it as usual to the 16th Battalion AIF 6th Mixed Division.

Matthew.

He was intending to write to her again tonight as he knew he soon would be seeing his son for the first time. Half the battalion was already here in this semi-haven of the war zone away from the front line where they were resting from active service, the other half was arriving any time soon.

Through the window he could see men laying duckboards across the snow-covered ground even in the still-drifting snowflakes. Then he saw Bert coming towards the door and he stood as it opened.

'Sir, Major Craken?'

'Yes, Bert.'

'Captain Lang says the colonel wishes to see you, sir. It's important. He asks for you to come to his office forthwith.'

This was a long statement for the laconic Bert. Matthew moved slowly over to his cane, 'Forthwith, eh? Thanks, Bert. Just remain around in case this blasted snow clears. I wouldn't mind going down into the valley past the ruined church and doing a quick sketch of the camp from that angle.'

'I'll be around, sir.'

When Matt passed the sentry in the tent outside John Conrad's Nissen hut Tommy Hardcastle was coming out the door. Matt hardly recognised him wrapped as he was in his greatcoat and sheepskin jerkin and a woollen cap on his head. 'Ah, Major Craken, are you joining us this evening for the Christmas Eve concert?'

Matt halted and pursed his lips. 'Didn't know there was one.'

'Yes, it's been hustled up pretty quickly. They're rehearsing now down in hut number four. It's beginning at twenty-one hundred after dinner.' He pointed across to the lone church that stood at the edge of the valley. It had lost two of its walls and was unusable but the stone church hall at the back was intact. 'We're having it over there. The chaplain wants it over by twenty-three thirty in time for his church service.'

'Captive audience, eh?'

Tommy grinned. 'Something like that. So will I put you down for a seat?'

Matt nodded. 'Yes.'

Tommy Hardcastle passed by and Matthew entered the Nissen hut to be greeted by Lieutenant Dunmore and Captain Lang. As Matt made his way towards the makeshift wall beyond which John Conrad's office lay, Lang enlightened him. 'He's not in there Major. He asked if you would go over to number seventeen.'

Hut number seventeen was the officers' mess.

Matthew almost said, 'What game's the bastard playing?' but he suppressed it and nodded, turning on his heel and proceeding outside. He was surprised and pleased to see the snow had stopped falling.

Across the duckboards he made his way under the clearing sky. A blast of wind lifted his greatcoat and it flapped around his knees. The signs of a bitter winter had been tormenting them in November but now the promise was a reality and it was bone-achingly cold.

The mess was at least warm. A brick fireplace and chimney built into both ends helped, and possibly even the four tiny Primus stoves boiling vaporised paraffin oil helped to improve the temperature. Two cooks were warming soup on the stoves but there was no one else in the building except for a steward behind the bar, and John Conrad, who rose from a chair at the far end when he saw Matt enter.

The two men were often in the mess at the same time of an evening but each had done well at avoiding the other's group, hence they had not spoken since the day of Matt's arrival a month previously.

Matthew's cane thudded dully on the flooring: duckboards covered in groundsheets. John Conrad pointed to a chair as Matt lifted his hand in a quick salute and sat down. 'You asked to see me?'

'Yes. I decided it was better to have the meeting here than in my office. Less chance of being overheard here at this time of day.'

'So?'

The steward came over. 'Anything I can get you, sir?'

Matt shook his head.

As the steward departed, John Conrad picked up a cup of tea at his right hand and drank before he answered, 'So . . . it's Christmas Eve and the rest of the battalion will be arriving by mid-afternoon. Along with that comes your son. Now that's not so unusual: there are a number of fathers and sons, brothers, cousins and so forth in some units. But in your case it's different, isn't it?'

'How so?'

'Look, Craken . . .' He took another mouthful of tea, swallowed it. 'There's only one way to say it. I can't have the situation where you cause trouble, in other words exacerbate any feeling that might already exist.'

Matthew almost smiled. He reclined in his chair, 'And what feeling might that be?'

John Conrad inhaled deeply. 'Craken, don't play games. We're too old and have come too far for that. For once let's just say it as it is. Your son already has no love for me, and that doesn't matter. Battalion commanders aren't here to be loved. But his prejudices come from you, his father. When he finds you're here and is once again under your influence he might talk more openly to his friends and pass on your opinions. I don't know how you feel about this . . . or anything, for that matter, but I wouldn't like to think that your and my differences were aired by others. That it became common knowledge in the battalion that we're . . . enemies.'

Matt shook his head. 'It seems to me you're taking your position a mite too seriously.'

John Conrad expressed a small sound of frustration and he clenched his fist but he kept his voice steady and quiet. 'I feared that sort of response from you. That has nothing to do with it. What I'm saying is that how we feel about each other is a private matter. I'd like it to stay that way. Your son's a good soldier, a brave young man, but he's very young and might talk more loosely with you here to fuel his thoughts and opinions.'

Matt remained in his lounging position and John Conrad took another sip of tea.

'I won't *fuel* Harry's thoughts and opinions. I agree that how we feel towards one another is no one's business in this godforsaken world except yours and mine . . . and perhaps one other. But Harry's a good kid, as you've noticed, and if I tell him to keep mum he will. So you can be sure the men won't realise about us, or what there is between us.'

John Conrad gave a grim smile. 'That would suit me very well.'

'Fleet, these are the most words we've said to each other since 1893.' John Conrad had long forgotten the year, but it had always loomed large in Matt's mind and he could see the man opposite him calculate the passage of time.

'God, is it that long? Yes, I suppose it is. In our more recent meetings we would have been at each other's throat long before this.'

'Indeed.'

And then John Conrad said something that almost amused the two enemies. 'We must be growing up.'

A glimmer of a smile played at the edge of Matt's mouth. 'I doubt that, Fleet. I think it's due to wearing the same uniform.' His tone was droll. 'Sadly, it somehow suppresses us.'

John Conrad gave a fleeting expression of amusement as he shook his head and stood up.

Matt put his weight on his good leg and rose along with him.

In the dead silence between them, for the first time ever in his life John Conrad saw Matthew Craken – saw his dark enigmatic eyes, saw the scar, saw the cane that he leant upon, and comprehended the injuries that he had inflicted so long ago. He thought for the first time for years of his sweet sister, Emma, the shock of her loss and the reason for the fearful enmity which had manifested and developed to massive proportions between them. He remembered the passion that he had felt for Caro Dere and the devastation brought upon him by her marriage to this man. He thought of the intervening years that had altered him entirely, and this war which had revealed to him that all grudges were insignificant.

He did not offer his hand but he offered the kindest words

he had ever said to the man opposite him. 'Yes, it's best if our business remains our business. Merry Christmas.' And he turned on his heel and walked away. There had been no sarcasm in his tone, nothing veiled or unspoken.

Matthew was as close to astounded as it was possible for him to be. 'Thanks,' he replied quietly to John Conrad's departing back.

Matt's reunion with Harry was a wonderful thing. Harry was amazed and delighted to see his father. They laughed and hugged each other and both talked at once. Harry introduced him to Dave and Curly, but when they were alone Matt had to bring up the fact of Luke's suicide. Harry sat with grim face as he listened and when Matt had finished the boy groaned.

'I've wondered every day what happened to him. And when I spoke to our sergeant and he told me that he wouldn't be shot, well, I thought at least he might get out at war's end. We heard on the grapevine that he'd been court-martialled.'

'Apparently he was to be brought back to the battalion for sentencing. He just couldn't face it.'

'At least he died in Mum's arms.'

'Yes, at least.' Matt put his arm round Harry's shoulder. 'He left a note. I passed it on to Fleet the day after I arrived here. It asked for his mother and uncle to be told he died in battle. Poor devil.'

'Will they do that, Dad?'

'I don't know.'

They went to the concert together and the old church hall rang with the laughter of what was left of the boys of the 16th. They had fared better than most: out of 1,119 men there were now 801, whereas some of the battalions that had been fighting in the Somme had gone in with a thousand men and been decimated to such an extent they had virtually disappeared altogether. On the first day of the Battle of the Somme, 1 July, six months previously, the total casualties in the British Expeditionary Force had reached the unprecedented proportions of 57,000 men from one single dawn to one single dusk!

But on Christmas Eve 1916 the boys of the 16th forgot for a few hours that they were only in respite and that come 1917 they would return once more to hell. In the hall warmed by the body heat of the hundreds of men they sat in all manner of warm clothing: greatcoats, knitted cardigans, woollen vests, sheepskin coats and jerkins, thick socks, boots, gloves and Balaclavas and caps. They shouted and laughed and when a comedy turn lifted up their voices the whole battalion sang with them:

> I will have a night tonight,
> The missus is out of sight,
> The woman who lives next door to me,
> Her old man has gone out to tea,
> She has invited me in, you see,
> I will have a night tonight.

As the evening drew to a close the host, who was a smart young sergeant major from Liverpool, called for the commanding officer to appear beside him. The call was taken up by the entire battalion and John Conrad was forced to leave his seat in the front row and climb on to the stage.

As he began to speak, Harry looked round to Matthew to see his reaction, but instead of seeing his father's expected glower at the man on the stage, Matt sat expressionless.

Standing in the flickering candle and lamplight facing his men John Conrad looked every inch the commander he was: and his clear, well-modulated voice rang down the hall.

'I wasn't expecting this, but I'm glad to have the opportunity to speak on this eve of Christmas. The war hasn't been kind to the Allies in the Battle of the Somme, but we've finished the year with a few gains against the Germans and some of those gains are due to you – the fighting men of the 16th! This time last year I had no idea that I would command a battalion in the Somme Valley, and take that battalion into battle. I'm a mighty proud man to have been given the privilege. We don't know what 1917 will bring; we all hope the end of the war . . .' There were calls of 'Hear, hear!' around the hall, '. . . but for now, rest and attempt to find some peace and calm away from the line. And to every one of you, thanks, mates, you're the best there are in this world, and Happy Christmas.'

This was followed by three cheers for the colonel, which no

matter what, Matthew could not bring himself to join, though he heard at his side Harry's half-hearted shouts.

The final act was a singalong, a mixture of a few Christmas hymns and evergreens, and the very last song every man in the hall sang, even Matthew lifted his voice.

> Pack up your troubles in your old kitbag
> And smile, smile, smile,
> While you've a lucifer to light your fag,
> Smile, boys, that's the style.
> What's the use of worrying?
> It never was worthwhile, so,
> Pack up your troubles in your old kitbag
> And smile, smile, smile.

If there had been rafters in the hall they would have rung with the sound which echoed across the snow-covered valley.

The night ended with 'God Save the King', the National Anthem.

In January the temperatures fell below zero and remained there. Snow and ice covered the battlefields, lay along the trenches, covered the dugouts. There had never been such a winter in living memory and certainly not since records had been kept. The channel ports were fogbound for weeks at a time, hence rations became tight and comforts were none. Ice filled the shell holes, and coal was hard to find. Even in the hospitals they had to do without, for the miners in Britain were on strike, and for the troops who lived with only thin coverings of wood or flapping canvas and corrugated iron it was a chill cold frozen hell. 'The bastards' was the way the troops referred to the miners across the sea. 'We're fighting for the bastards and this is how they repay us.' Men who had never thought about politics began to hate the unions and what they stood for.

The 16th Battalion was relatively lucky. Free from the rigours of the front line, in the rest camp life was a comparative haven, and for those weeks Matthew and Harry saw each other every day.

Twice Harry had broached the subject of John Conrad but each time Matthew had said, 'He's the colonel of this battalion, we must live with that, and that means unfortunately we must suffer the predicament of respecting his position. So, old son, I won't enter into a discussion about him. All right?'

It was a day in early February when the snow was piled high between the huts that Harry came to tell Matt that he had a weekend pass for leave in Amiens. Matt was alone in his Nissen hut studio, wrapped in a greatcoat, wearing gloves with the fingers cut from the one on his right hand so that he could feel the paintbrush. Harry entered and picked up a blanket, wrapped it round his shoulders and opened a copy of *The Bystander* magazine to a Bairnsfather cartoon. The never-say-die wit of Bruce Bairnsfather who had been at the front since 1914 and was a regular contributor of 'war comment' cartoons to the British press, appealed to Harry as they did to many a soldier; there was something inherently British about being able to laugh at yourself under the most appalling of conditions. He grinned and lifted it up to show his father. Matt perused it with a cynical eye. 'Partly amusing,' was his dry comment.

Harry affected a long-suffering expression as he sat on an empty biscuit box, closed the magazine and told Matthew about the leave pass. 'So Dave and Curly and I are off within the hour. We'll catch a ride into Albert and with a bit of luck we'll get on a train into Amiens.'

Matthew had told Harry on Christmas Day that his mother was just miles away near Aveluy but while Harry had written to her two or three times he still had not been down to see her. Matt lifted his paintbrush and jabbed the air. 'You'll have to pass right by where your mother is to get into Albert.'

Harry sighed. 'All right, Dad, I'll see her either going down or coming back.'

'Make sure you do.' Matt moved back to his canvas.

'Dad?'

'Yes?'

'There's word going round the camp that we're being sent back in the line soon.'

'Is there now? Then, old son, I suggest you enjoy your weekend in Amiens and forget the war.'

'I reckon you're right.'

Matt painted silently for a time.

'Dad?'

'Yes?'

'I know you don't want to discuss the colonel but—'

'You're right, I don't. In fact I've said before that I won't so let's leave it there.'

'He saved my life.'

Matt was facing away, his hand flinched and he smudged the paint on the canvas in front of him, but his voice held steady as he answered. 'And how did that happen?'

Harry told him the story. 'So you see, Dad, it's hard for me to sort of keep on hating him. I had another argument with Dave because he said I was wrong to have enmity towards a man who saved my life. And I retorted that the colonel never would have bothered to yell out and stop us from walking on the mines if Dave hadn't been right behind me. But I never really meant that. I didn't believe it. I just said it.'

Matthew exhaled in a long breath. 'So . . . you've spoken to Dave about your . . . *our* feelings towards Fleet, have you? Who else have you told?'

'No one, only Dave. And we agree to disagree, if you know what I mean. See, Dad, most of the lads admire the colonel. Some of them sort of worship him. And to me, well, he doesn't seem to be a bad man . . . like I thought he was. I feel a bit strange about it all.'

Matthew continued to paint, but he lifted his left hand and ran his fingers across his scar. 'Well, don't. I suppose it's time to say *feel how you like*, and leave it at that.'

'Dad, why are you enemies? Does . . . does it have something to do with Mum?'

Matthew put down his paintbrush and turning round, clasped his hands together, drawing them up to his chin as he met Harry's eyes. 'Now, old son, what would make you ask that?'

'Well, I got to thinking about it and you aren't the sort of bloke to hate someone for nothing. Fact is, I don't believe you hate anyone but him.' He gave a weak smile. 'You never seem to expend too much energy on anything, Dad, and it takes energy to hate.'

Matt limped over to the window and stood looking at the ice collecting on the pane. He put his hands out and braced himself upon the cheap woodblock of the sill.

Harry was still talking. 'So I sort of worked out that perhaps Mum had been his girlfriend, like before she married you, and that's what caused you to hate each other. Something like that. Was it?'

For the very first time in his life Matthew felt out of his depth, but he rallied as all clever minds do. 'Harry,' he turned to look into the youthful blue eyes behind him, 'this isn't something which you should concern yourself about. And in a way you're right, your mother was close to Fleet before she married me and the enmity did begin in those times. But it's an ancient resentment which doesn't necessarily have a place in your life today. Now to you . . . you've been a marvellous son – you *are* a marvellous son – and who's to say whether I was right or wrong to influence your thoughts on the man. He's been my enemy for so long that I sought to make him yours also.' His slanted smile aspired to his mouth. 'We're all indoctrinated one way and another by our parents and the adults in our lives.'

Harry laughed and stood up, dropping the blanket to the floor. 'Except for you and Grandma Craken. You never agree with her.'

Matt was delighted with the subject change. 'Ah, don't bring my feeble-minded mother into it, please. It's a constant cause of wonder to me that I survived babyhood in the arms of that woman.'

Harry laughed again as Matt stepped forward and drew the youth into his embrace. 'Now you just think as you please. Take this bloody old colonel on his merits as you see them, just don't end up too loyal to him and break your father's heart.' He said it light-heartedly and the boy hugged him close, laughing as he did so. 'Of course I won't. You're the only one I'll ever be loyal to, Dad.'

Matt's eyes closed as he held his boy close. When he let him go he said, 'And as well as seeing your mother, write to your sister and to Knobby. Understood, old son?'

'Yes, yes, I will as soon as I get back.' And giving his father an exaggeratedly flourishing salute he opened the door and exited into the snow.

Matthew limped across to the window to watch him, rubbing his thigh where his bad leg had begun to ache. He spoke aloud.

'So Fleet, not only do you have my wife's affections but now you steal those of my son.'

As Harry left Matthew he hurried across the duckboards to his Nissen hut. Within ten minutes more he, Dave and Curly were out at the front of the camp where Dave had convinced the corporal driving a supply lorry into Albert to give them a lift. They were waiting by the lorry and stamping their feet to keep warm when Major Hardcastle, who had been promoted from captain in the new year, came by.

'Going somewhere, boys?'

Curly grinned. 'Amiens, sir. Got a weekend pass.'

'Been there before?'

'No, sir.'

He wore a sleeveless woollen wrap over his greatcoat and he lifted it to search in his pockets for a lead pencil and paper. Finding them he wrote down a few names and handed the paper to Curly. 'These are all good cafés with music and dancing.'

The youth's eyes gleamed with the thought. 'Gosh, thanks, Captain.'

'Major,' corrected Harry.

Hardcastle waved away the slip. 'Forget it. I've been wearing these pips so long I still feel like a captain.'

'When will you get the crown sir?'

Tommy shrugged. 'Who knows? A major might have to die first.'

Dave tapped his corporal's insignia. 'That's how I got my stripes – off a dead corporal's uniform.'

This sort of thing happened all the time so it did not even draw a comment.

Tommy pointed to the lorry driver striding towards them across the snow. 'So, catching a ride with Gregory, are you?'

The youths replied in unison, 'Yes, sir.'

'Well, enjoy yourselves but if you do visit a *maison de tolérance* use safeguards and be careful.'

Maisons de tolérance were brothels. Harry and Dave gave embarrassed laughs and Curly replied, 'I'm a married man, sir, to a true blue little beauty, and the only woman I'll let these two get caught up with is Harry's mum. She's down at casualty clearing station eighty-two.'

Tommy looked interested. 'Is that right, Craken?'

'Yes, sir, she's driving ambulances.'

'You're quite a family, I must say.'

He watched as the three young men climbed up into the lorry before he moved on.

He dined that night with John Conrad, Jack Bader and Robert Dunmore. He was trying to drink less and did not indulge at all during the day, limiting himself to one Scotch before dinner and one during, plus a port or sherry afterwards. This received the approval of his superior and as the steward offered them the rare treat of an apple pie and all accepted, Tommy noticed Matthew leave the table at the end of the hut where he had dined. He took up his cane, which lay below an Australian flag hanging on the wall, and limped to the door.

Tommy waited until Bader and Dunmore began a conversation of their own and he turned to John Conrad, speaking quietly. 'Do you know what I learnt about our artist friend today?'

John Conrad shook his head.

'His wife's in France too. Now they're a surprising family, aren't they?'

John Conrad met Tommy's gaze. 'In France?'

'Yes, quite near here, actually, South-west about eight miles or so. The British casualty clearing station at Aveluy. She drives ambulances.'

'How do you know?'

'Saw young Craken and two mates off to Amiens on a weekend pass. They told me.'

John Conrad leaned aside to allow the steward to put down the pie. 'Then it must be right.'

Tommy Hardcastle was not a curious man by nature but knowing about the hostility between Craken and his colonel he could not help but ask, 'Do you know her?'

John Conrad picked up his spoon as he answered. 'Yes. I used to know her well, but that was a long time ago.'

Tommy Hardcastle diplomatically left it there.

The following morning John Conrad took a telephone call after which he sent for Tommy.

When the young man joined him John Conrad was alone

in his office hut. He sat with a thoughtful expression. 'Well, lad, I've been called to London by the War Office. Robertson wants to see me along with some of the British High Command like General Birdwood. Apparently Generals Monash and McKay and some of the other Australian military hierarchy are there too.'

'A summit meeting?'

'Sort of, I suppose, but why do they want me?'

'Probably going to make you a brigadier and give you a brigade.'

John Conrad picked up his pen and rolled it between his fingers. 'I hate to think so, but I'm afraid you could be right. Robertson promised me I could remain here at least six months.'

'Yes, but that's up soon.'

'Another thing.' John Conrad tapped his pen on the pitted wood of the table. 'The battalion's going back into the line. It's been decided. North towards the border.'

Tommy shook his head in wonder. 'Well, I have to give it to the 16th's grapevine, that's the rumour we've been hearing for weeks.'

'We leave next weekend. There's talk as well about Flanders but I don't know how realistic that is. Now I'll need to get to London on Tuesday. Speak to Lang and have him make arrangements. They want me at the War Office on Thursday.'

'Right.' Tommy rose to his feet. 'I think there are vessels from Boulogne.'

'And, Tom?'

'Yes.'

'I'd like you to come with me.'

'I believe Menzies Lang thinks it's his turn to accompany you, sir. His nose will be out of joint.'

John Conrad grinned. 'I don't like to be personal but it's not his nose, it's his chin that's out of joint.'

This amused the two men and Tommy laughed as he replied, 'Delighted to accompany you to London, sir.'

The three friends reached Albert and in waiting for onward transport found themselves buying drinks in an *estaminet* run by three French women: a grandmother, her daughter and granddaughter. Before the war Albert had boasted 7,343 people, now there were less than 150. But those who had remained were made of sturdy stuff and eked out a living somehow. One of the most popular ways was the civilian bar-cum-café trading for the soldiers.

When they entered the establishment run by the three women, Curly had simply stood at the door and whistled at the females and shaken his head. 'Gawd, lovely, I'd forgotten what they looked like. Wonderful, aren't they?'

'Well, I'm not so sure about the old girl,' Harry had responded.

This particular little establishment in the front room of the family house had a bar against one wall and four tables and sixteen rickety chairs. By 4 p.m. the room was full, and soon the wan light behind the chintz curtains began to fade as the soldiers drank and talked.

Harry had caught the eye of the youngest female, a girl with doe-brown eyes and pale skin, who appeared to be around his own age. She smiled at him so much from behind the bar where she poured drinks into small glasses that he beckoned to her.

When she approached him he had enough French to carry on a stilted conversation and he began by asking her name.

'Madeleine . . . and yoo?'

'Harry.'

She smiled and repeated his name, ''Arry. Where . . . ah . . .' She reverted to French. '*Vous êtes d'où?*'

'*Australie.*'

She laughed. '*C'est très loin.*'

'*Répétez-vous s'il vous plaît.*'

She repeated her words slowly and he understood this time. '*Oui*, yes, it is a long way away.'

'Too right,' said Curly. 'And not far enough away from this snow. If I'm never in the bloody snow again I won't care.'

Dave sat quietly and as he lifted his drink, Madeleine touched his hand to feel his dark skin. She said, '*Très noir.*'

'What's that?' Dave asked Harry.

'She said *very dark*. Don't think she's seen many of your type around here, old son.'

736

Dave smiled at her. 'Yes, I'm very dark Dave Sands from Brisbane, and you're very white Madeleine from Albert.'

Madeleine laughed. She did not know why she just felt happy with these young men.

Madeleine's mother called to her and the girl turned her head and answered but did not move. It was Curly who stood up. 'Reckon that train'll be by pretty soon. Come on, fellas, or we won't get to Amiens tonight.'

Harry and Dave stood and Madeleine's face dropped. '*Pourquoi* you go?'

Dave explained as best he could they were on leave and going into Amiens.

'*Pourquoi?* Why you no stay *ici*?'

Harry looked as if he could well succumb to this suggestion and Curly took hold of his arm. 'Now come on, none of this. We're not stayin' in this dump. Let's go.' And he threw two francs on the table. He eyed Harry almost contemptuously. 'You don't think for one minute you're special, do ya, Craken? Bet she carries on like this with every soldier that comes by?'

Harry did not wish to hear this and he moved out of Curly's grasp. 'All right, all right, I'm coming. Go on outside. I'll follow you straight away.'

In the fading evening light the young girl looked sad and pretty and fragile. She reminded Harry of a china shepherdess his mother had on a shelf above the settee at Cedar Grove, and as Curly and Dave moved to the door, he shrugged. 'I must go. *Je pars.* I'm sorry.'

'Please . . . *Reviens me voir s'il vous plaît?*'

He looked nonplussed and in her best English she attempted it again. 'Please coming back yes? To me?'

And he decided on the spot. 'Yes, I will, on Sunday. Er . . . *oui.*'

She laughed with delight. '*Bon. Quand?*'

'On Sunday in the evening . . . *Dimanche soir.*'

She gave him what he thought was the closest thing he had ever seen to an angel's smile, and he shook her hand rather vigorously and hurried out into the street.

As they ran along in the wind towards the railway station Curly's voice was as austere as the weather. 'All right, she was pretty, but Gawd, a girl like that. Ya can't go fallin' for every bloody mademoiselle we meet.'

'I'm not,' replied Harry grimly, running at his side.

Two hours later they were in Amiens. By midnight they had tried two of Tommy Hardcastle's cafés and in the early hours of the morning, singing and laughing, they found a pension that was at least dry if not warm.

On the following day they met up with three other Australian soldiers and fell in with them. It was a bitterly cold day but the sky was clear and in the afternoon they sat for a time joking and talking in a sheltered spot in an arm of the Somme River.

While they were all joking and laughing Dave noticed his friend was not completely joining in. 'You're a bit quiet, Harry.'

'Sorry, old son, I'm thinking I suppose.'

Dave winked at him 'What? About that girl?'

One of the newcomers, Malcolm, a loud sort of boy from Melbourne, overheard. 'What girl? Has young Harry got a girl?'

Harry shook his head in embarrassment. 'Get out, Malcolm. I haven't got a girl. It's just someone I met.'

Malcolm gave a burst of laughter. 'That's how it starts, Harry lad, that's how it starts. Where is she?'

Harry stood up. 'I'm going.' And he moved off on his own.

Dave stood and, looking at Curly, said, 'I'm going too, are you coming?'

This had the effect of moving them all on; Malcolm and his two mates, Colin and Shorty, following as well.

Dave eyed Malcolm. 'Well, if you're coming, all right. But leave him alone. He doesn't want to talk about it.'

'All right, Abo lad, we've got the message.'

'And I'm not *Abo lad*, I'm Dave.'

Malcolm looked around the others. 'Gawd, we've fallen in with a touchy lot here.'

But nevertheless they remained together and by midnight were wandering down one of the narrow streets in the old quarter near the canal in the north of the city. They were all a little worse for wear, having consumed large amounts of alcohol in a number of back-room establishments, and

Malcolm pointed up as they passed a door with a blue light and wandered on further down the street where he halted in front of a door with a red light. The red glow illuminated his face as he looked at it. 'This'll do me, boys. Blue for officers and red for us, come on.' He gestured for them all to follow.

Dave looked at Harry. 'Do you want to go in there? It's a brothel.'

Harry shook his head. 'I'd prefer another drink.'

'We'll get another drink in here,' Malcolm urged them. 'Come on, fellas. I for one need the arms of a woman around me, no matter what they're like. Even if they're French.' He turned back to Harry. 'I'm guessin' ya've never done it, sonny. Well, it's about time ya did. It'll do ya good.'

Harry's reply was surly. 'I only want a drink.'

Curly hesitated. 'I'm a married man.'

'So am I,' Colin giggled. 'But what does that matter? We're a long way from home, boy, and who knows, if we don't do it now, we might never do it again.'

Curly sighed.

Malcolm put his arm round Harry's shoulder and his warm alcoholic breath lingered in Harry's nostrils. 'Listen, kid, ya can get a drink in here. Come on, just a drink then, see how you feel after that.'

Harry looked round into the glowing red face beside him. 'You're a creep, do you know that, Malcolm?'

For a minute Harry thought that Malcolm was going to land a fist on his chin, but abruptly Malcolm gaffawed loudly and, pushing Harry towards the door, said, 'Yeah, so they say, kid, so they say.'

Colin had already opened the door and they trailed inside one behind the other.

'At least it's a bit warmer in here,' Curly stated, moving past a curtain that hung from the low ceiling to the floor.

Beyond the curtain a fat elderly woman in a red satin cape emerged. A used and tired smile drew back her painted lips. 'Gentlemens, gentlemens, com in pleeze.'

As they passed through another doorway and another curtain they pushed by two soldiers coming out. One of them, in Canadian uniform, lifted up his hand and placing his forefinger on his thumb to make a circle, clicked his tongue and told them, 'The best place in Amiens!'

They found themselves in a small room where a lantern illuminated six women in various stages of undress all huddled in front of a weak flame emanating from a grate in the wall. They ranged in years from what Harry thought must be about fifty down to a girl similar to his own age.

Malcolm had soon chosen a woman, an ugly girl but with big breasts pouting over the top of her green brassiere, and Harry watched him feeling her bottom when they disappeared along the hallway together. It wasn't long before Colin followed with another of the women.

The fat lady then began to propel the other women across to the four remaining soldiers. 'Com along, gentlemens . . . nize girls.'

'No,' Shorty said, holding up his hands, 'we just want a drink.'

'Yeah,' agreed Curly, shaking his head, 'we only want a drink.'

Harry and Dave vehemently concurred.

The fat lady looked disappointed but she moved away and returned with an opened bottle of what looked and smelt like rum. She poured a measure into four dinted tin cups and handed them to the soldiers.

'All the comforts of home,' Curly laughed.

They sat at a round table on chairs without backs, the shadows of the room hurling grotesque arabesques about them. After they had taken one drink each, the remaining women crowded round. In the moody darkness the young girl turned the handle of a gramophone on a shelf near the curtain, and as the music began she moved across and placed her thin arm around Harry's shoulders and kissed his ear.

He pulled his head away. 'Don't do that.' He thought of Madeleine, the girl in Albert, and a cold shiver ran through him. He looked across at Dave, who had a woman of about forty draped over him.

'I'm going, old son.'

Dave nodded. 'I'm coming with you.' He glanced at Curly, who was kissing one of the women on the mouth.

'Curl, we're off, you coming?'

Curly drew his lips away reluctantly. 'Ah strewth . . . fellas . . .'

Shorty looked up as Harry and Dave rose. 'Don't go. Nothin' wrong with this – a drink and a kiss. You can't get VD from this.'

Dave dropped two francs on the table as Harry pushed the curtain aside to leave. 'We just don't go for this sort of thing. You coming, Curly?'

As Curly somewhat unwillingly stood, the fat lady began protesting and demanding more money, so Dave threw down another two francs and proceeded after Harry into the street. A blast of freezing cold air hit them as they emerged.

At their heels came Curly. 'Well,' he said, rubbing his mouth, 'that old woman's as bad as Ned Kelly. Four francs for a few bloody drinks. Anyway, I'm glad I did nothin' wrong. Thanks for savin' me. Wouldn't want that on me conscience when I go home to my Gloria. She's a mighty fine girl, faithful as the day is long.'

The following day Harry told Dave and Curly he was going back to Albert.

'Why?' Curly asked. 'We don't have to be back in camp until fourteen hundred tomorrow.' Then it dawned on him. 'Of course, Mademoiselle Madeleine. Now, lad, how do ya know she isn't makin' money on the side just like them girls last night?'

Harry swung his fist at Curly's head and Dave jumped between them. 'Come on, don't fight. That's just silly. We're all good mates.' He pushed Harry away a few steps. 'You go to Albert. We understand and we'll see you back in camp tomorrow. Right?'

Harry gave a sullen nod and Dave rounded on Curly. 'And you leave him alone or we'll start making jokes about the faithful Gloria.'

Curly gave him a fierce look. 'Ya better not. She's true blue, she is.'

'All right, so let's all just be civil, shall we?'

Harry left them at lunchtime and, catching a munitions train full of 18-pounder field guns and French auto cannons bound for the front through Albert, arrived at the little *estaminet* soon after fifteen hundred.

Madeleine had been watching through the front window on and off since noon in the expectation of his arrival. Her face lit up and she ran to the door when she saw him coming along the road towards her.

The establishment was empty and they sat and talked, chaperoned by the girl's grandmother, who never left, and sat mending near the bar.

Harry's French was better than Madeleine's English and silently he thanked old MacDonald for being so strict with their pronunciation in French class. He learnt that Madeleine's father was away at the war, that he had survived the horror of the Battle of Verdun and that they did not know where he was at present.

She asked him what he did in Amiens and when he replied, '*Tu m'as manqué*,' she smiled in delight to think he had actually spoken aloud that he had missed her.

As the early winter night wrapped Albert in its blanket of bitter cold the girl rose and lit two candles. Harry watched her, thinking she was the loveliest thing he had ever encountered. Soon the room filled with Irish soldiers and the body heat and cigarettes added a semblance of warmth to those within.

Madeleine and her mother served drinks and the Irish boys sang 'Galway Bay' and 'Danny Boy' in hearty voices to the accompaniment of one of their group on a mouth organ.

By an hour to midnight the little *estaminet* was empty and Madeleine had asked her grandmother if Harry could sleep in the spare room at the back. The grandmother replied yes, if he paid like any other, and while the girl looked askance at the suggestion Harry happily handed over payment for the privilege.

The following day after breakfast he helped Madeleine clean the tables and chairs and wash the floor in the bar. She wore a small gold cross on a chain around her neck and it dangled down as she rested on her knees. When they had completed the task their hands were so cold they had turned bright pink, but they were so happy in one another's company that they were unaware.

They ate some bread and cheese and then Harry stated he must leave. 'I have to be back at camp at fourteen hundred.'

She walked out with him into the street and they stood under

742

the naked branches of an oak tree that had lost part of its trunk in the German shelling of January 1915, and yet had miraculously survived.

She wore a long coat to her ankles and a warm scarf tied around her head and knotted under her chin. She had been so happy in his company and had never felt so close to a male before, except for her father.

She lifted up her pale hand and touched his face, '*Ecris moi s'il te plaît.*'

'What's that? *Ecris moi?*'

She mimed writing in the air.

He understood. 'Oh write to you, I see. Yes I will . . . ah . . . *Je le ferai.*'

She smiled. '*Reviens me voir?*'

He nodded 'Yes, I'll come back.' And he tried to explain that he would come before they went back into the line if he possibly could. He wrote his battalion address on a slip of paper and tucked it in her hand and he repeated what she had said to him, '*Ecris moi.*'

'*Oui.*'

They were standing facing one another and he stepped in closer to where he was only inches from her. He leant in and, closing his eyes, tenderly rested his lips on hers. It was a strange and awkward action but the intimate touch of her mouth was blissful to him. She lifted her gloved hand and rested it on his arm. '*Au revoir, 'Arry,*' she whispered against his lips.

Then he was running at speed down the street, running and calling goodbye to her as she stood at the side of the oak tree and waved her hand. As he turned the corner in the distance a tear broke out from under her lid and fell across her cheek.

He caught a ride on a tractor convoy carrying howitzers and heading north, and he left them at Aveluy where he approached the casualty clearing station anxiously. He hoped his mother would not make a scene.

He made his way across the duckboards and found her drinking tea in the ambulance drivers' long room, the kitchen of the old farmhouse that stood behind the medical tents and Nissen huts.

She was overwhelmed to see him and clung to him for a long time, until he extricated himself from her embrace, but he was pleased to see she did not cry. He knew she had been holding Luke when he died; his father had related to him the horribly sad story of his friend and he told her now he was glad that Luke had been in her arms for his final minutes. 'He would have felt comfort, Mum, knowing you were holding him.'

She sighed and nodded. 'Yes I truly like to believe so.'

They talked quietly about many things and for the first time ever he was surprised to notice that she spoke to him like an adult: surprised and pleased.

And when it came time for him to leave and for her to go back to work, she said, 'Well, darling. I'm just so happy to have seen you. Thank you for the letters you've written. Please continue. And come to see me again, if you can. It seems I could be stationed here for a long time.'

Harry looked doubtful. 'I will if I can, Mum, but there's word that we'll be going back into the line pretty soon.'

Caro pushed a stray curl back behind her ear. She spoke as calmly as she could. 'I didn't want you to come here, son, and I'd change that if I could. But I'm glad *I* came – if only to hold Luke in his last minutes, and . . .' She pointed to the Nissen huts where the wounded were.

He nodded. 'Yes, Mum, I know. I've been in a battle now. I've seen men dead . . . and worse than dead . . .'

And for the first time her lip trembled and she took on that frightened expression which warned Harry that perhaps there was motherly hysteria to come. 'You shouldn't be here, Harry, you're only a boy. It's wrong . . .'

He held up his hand. 'Don't spoil it, Mum, please. I've been glad to see you. Don't spoil it.'

And Caro, with a great effort of will, controlled herself.

He kissed her and she put on her overcoat and they walked out into the snow together.

She accomplished a cheerful smile and as he went to walk off he hesitated momentarily. She knew her son through and through, no matter what he thought, and seeing his uncertainty she asked, 'What's wrong? Is it something about Matt?'

He shook his head.

'What then? Tell me.'

'Well, I haven't told you in any of my letters because . . .'

'Haven't told me what?'

'My battalion commander.'

'What about him?'

'He's Colonel Fleet.'

For a full ten seconds Caro's face was frozen. To her son she appeared to have turned into stone before his eyes, her face totally expressionless, her body as if petrified.

'Mum, are you all right?'

At last her eyes moved across his face to look into the infinity of the snow beyond. When she spoke, her voice strained from her throat, imparting the words separately in the labour to push them out. 'John Conrad is your battalion commander . . . and Matthew is there too?'

He nodded. And now he sounded like the child that part of him still was. 'That's right. I've done the correct thing by telling you, haven't I, Mum?'

She wrapped him in her arms. 'Yes, yes, of course you have, my darling.' She stroked his face like a child and, embarrassed, he moved from her embrace. 'Don't, Mum.'

A weird unsettled look came into her face. 'Harry, you've been with . . . John Conrad – that is, the colonel – all these months?'

'Well, no, not *with* him, Mum. He's the battalion commander, after all. But I've seen him a few times, yes. He's not such a bad bloke after all.'

There was celestial music playing in Caro's head. She bestowed a beatific smile upon her son . . . John Conrad's son. 'Oh, darling, that's . . . wonderful. You mean you *like* him?'

'I wouldn't say *like* but I owe him something. He saved my life. Dave and me – you know, my friend I wrote about? – well, we would have walked on a mined area, been blown apart but for him. He picked it somehow and stopped us. Yeah, he saved us, right enough. He's all right.'

'Mrs Craken! Mrs Craken!' It was Captain Cadee calling.

But Caro did not turn. A part of Caro's heart had left her body and was up flying with the angels.

Harry tapped his mother's arm. 'Mum, that RAMC bloke's calling you.'

When Caro turned her eyes and Captain Cadee saw her glazed expression he asked, 'Are you all right?'

'Oh yes, yes.' And she placed her arm round Harry's

shoulders, 'My son, he's with the 16th Battalion AIF. He's just leaving.'

Harry saluted.

'Nice to meet you.' Percy Cadee smiled and returned the salute, then looking at Caro motioned back to the farmhouse. 'I need to speak with you before you go back into the casualty ward.'

A fine rain began to fall and Caro pulled her cap down a little on her face. 'Of course, Captain Cadee. I'll come immediately.' She gave her son a glorious smile. 'Write to me, and come and see me if you can.'

As she followed the captain, thinking of the heavenly wonder that Harry no longer hated his real father, her son called, 'Any message for Dad?'

Caro hesitated and threw the words over her shoulder. 'Tell him . . . tell him . . . I'm all right.'

Chapter Forty-four

Harry was back in camp at thirteen thirty and he was immediately called by Bingo to see Lieutenant Young, his platoon officer in Nissen hut 15.

Anthony Young was a good-looking, suntanned fellow from Ipswich in Queensland. He had fought in Gallipoli and had risen up through the ranks. He motioned for Harry to sit on a rickety chair that creaked under the youth's weight as he pushed aside the pile of letters he had been censoring before they were sent on to their destinations.

'Craken, I've been ordered to send you and your B22 up to Major Hardcastle. Do you have any idea why that might be?'

'No, sir, none.'

'Right, well, I've given Warrant Officer Bingham your conduct sheet so off you go.'

Harry looked surprised but stood and saluted. He followed Bingo out into the snow. 'What's going on, Sarge? Sorry, I mean, *sir*, it's hard to remember with all these promotions.'

'Yes, even yours, Lance Jack. And as to what's going on? I don't know.'

They crunched across the snow, and in the wettest places over duckboards, to the hut used as an office by the officers. It was warmer, having a fireplace fitted at one end. Bingo saluted to the lieutenant on duty, handed over Harry's B22 and explained their visit.

Within five minutes Bingo had gone and Harry stood in front of the major.

Tommy Hardcastle liked young Craken. He thought the boy's father was a bit crusty and enigmatic but the son was likeable.

'Did you have a good leave in Amiens?'

'Yes, sir, bonzer, thanks, sir.'

'Right.' He pointed to a chair and Harry sat. 'Now, Craken,

there are some matters that need to be attended to. You're probably aware we're trying to wage an air war as well as a land war.'

Harry nodded.

'You will be aware of the Royal Flying Corps and the Royal Naval Air Service?'

'Yes, sir.'

'Well, we're vastly underdone for pilots. There's been a joint British Australian decision to train squadrons in England for active duty here in France. And while it's not usual to recruit from the army, on occasions we do so. Especially when we see a young man with extremely good eyesight and reflexes. I've been requested to submit two names from this battalion and you're one of them. You'll be relocated to England to a training school where you'll be taught how to fly an aeroplane. I believe you'll have the aptitude. After that it'll be an intensive training course and you'll be back here waving down to us in the months to come.'

Harry was flabbergasted. 'What, sir? I'm afraid I don't quite understand.'

'You're being transferred, Lance Corporal, to join a squadron within the British Royal Flying Corps, nothing drastic.' He smiled.

'Can they do that, sir?'

Tommy smiled. 'Yes, lad, *they* can . . . and have. These are the transferrals.' He tapped a couple of papers on his desk. 'The other fellow going with you is Private Charles McIntosh. You'll leave here when the battalion goes back into the line. That'll be either next Sunday or Monday. Your platoon officer and Warrant Officer Bingham will keep you informed.'

Tom could see Harry was nonplussed. 'Look, Craken, here's a chance to become a pilot, an exciting and wonderful opportunity not offered to many, I can assure you. I know how good your eyes are from the way you handle your periscope in the line, and I know you've excellent reflexes. Bingham and Lieutenant Young vouchsafed for that. You're smart, educated enough, and capable, ideal type for a pilot.' He pointed to the papers. 'Now sign here.' He tapped a dotted line. 'I'm off to England with the colonel in the morning, won't be back before Saturday, but if there's anything else to know, Lieutenant Young and Warrant Officer Bingham will alert you.'

Harry was being rolled along. He felt his feet were not on the floor. He signed beside the major's finger and stood up.

'Good luck, lad.'

'Thanks, sir.'

He walked away, his mind whirling, and as he reached the door of the Nissen hut it opened and the colonel stepped in. He saw Harry and halted.

'Craken, isn't it?'

Harry came to attention and saluted. 'Yes, sir.'

John Conrad looked straight into the blue eyes on the same level as his own. The boy stood at virtually identical height to himself, holding his slouch hat under his arm, his fair hair falling slightly down on his forehead. John Conrad surveyed him for a few seconds then he took his gaze from the fair-headed young man's and cast it beyond him to Tom Hardcastle.

Tommy rose from his desk and came over. 'Craken's off to be a pilot, sir.'

John Conrad paused and gave a strange smile. 'Really? Well, I wish you luck, m'boy. That should be a great adventure.'

Harry tried to be withdrawn, to nod sullenly, but somehow he couldn't. Almost as a spectator he heard himself telling the colonel the truth of how he really felt. 'I'm in a bit of shock, sir. I'd never expected such a thing. I want to do my duty, all right . . . but I'll miss my friends in the battalion. I guess I don't know if I really want to go.'

Tommy went to speak and John Conrad held up his hand for silence as he turned his full attention back to the boy. 'You're right to feel that way, Craken. It's perfectly normal. I remember a long time ago I was sent off to an army I neither wished to join nor understood. And I was confused and wondered why. But you know, lad? I've had a lot of experiences since then that make me look back on that event quite differently. Just because you tread another path doesn't mean you lose those you care about. Your mates here in the battalion will always be your mates. Nothing will alter that. And I know what you mean about not really wanting to go away. A new road in life is often daunting. As dangerous as it is here in the battalion there's a comfort zone with your friends and officers, right?'

Harry nodded his head. The colonel was exactly correct.

'You'll find that just the same where you're going. Now we're trying to win this war any darn way we can, and if it means that you must be a pilot to help us do it then try to go with a positive heart, lad.' John Conrad put out his hand and touched the youth's arm: it was a warm, almost fatherly gesture. 'Be a pilot, be the damned best one you can possibly be; get what you can out of it and make Major Hardcastle proud that he chose you . . . make us all proud.'

Harry lifted his eyes to the colonel's once more. He had an uncanny feeling, standing here with this man who was until recently his enemy, and now seemed more like his friend. 'I'll really try, sir.'

John Conrad gave a small nod of approval. 'Good on you.' He remained staring deeply into the boy's blue eyes. 'That's the spirit and the best of luck, m'boy.'

As Harry left the hut and closed the door Tommy Hardcastle shook his head admiringly. 'Wish I'd said that.'

The colonel watched the door close and though Tommy heard him speak, he was talking to himself. 'I meant every word of it.'

The next morning, just after first light, as the driver of the armoured car went to turn north on the road to Boulogne John Conrad leant forward. 'No, not that way yet. I want you to go first to the CCS in Aveluy. Station Eighty-two.'

Tommy, who sat beside him, turned sharply round but John Conrad did not look in the younger man's direction.

They drove by troops on the march, couriers on bicycles, trucks, lorries, and various other forms of transport and arrived at the casualty clearing station as the sun found a breach in the mass of clouds and strove to hurl a semblance of warmth upon the freezing ground.

As the armoured car halted in the ice and snow of the muddy yard, Tommy asked, 'Do you want me along, sir?'

John Conrad shook his head as he climbed out. 'No thanks, Tommy. I won't be long.'

Tom watched him cross the duckboards to the first of the

Nissen huts with a red cross on the side. Within half a minute he came out beside a nurse who pointed to another hut further away in the field.

Inside the hut, Caro and Jill Cossington were lifting two boxes of dirty bandages from where they stood on the floor.

Caro made a tutting sound. 'Yes, we'll have to take these to the incinerator. They just can't be used again.'

'Right.'

'Open the door would you, please, Pat?' Caro called to the tall attractive VAD who sat writing her report at the small table at the end of the ward. Patricia rose and, wrapping a blanket round her shoulders, moved over to the door rubbing her hands together and blowing on them for warmth. As she pushed the door ajar a colonel stood outside.

Pat started in surprise: colonels were not regular visitors. 'Oh my goodness. Are we expecting you, sir?'

Standing behind Pat, Caro could only see the insignia on the shoulder of the officer's greatcoat, his head was hidden by Pat's statuesque figure. Then she heard his voice.

'No, I'm not expected. Could I speak to Mrs Caro Craken for a few minutes, please?'

Caro stood stock-still. For some seconds she did not move, then slowly, with her eyes upon the colonel she bent down and placed the box on the floor. Jill and Pat looked at her for an explanation. If they had remained looking until war's end they would not have received what they sought. Caro glanced to Jill and pointed to the box. 'Be kind enough to take care of mine too, love. Excuse me, I'll be gone a little while.' And passing out the door to where John Conrad stood, she motioned for him to follow her.

Feeling light-headed being near him again she took him across to the ambulance long room, which was empty at this time of the morning. When she had closed the door on the snow outside, the insipid winter sunshine revealed the face of the man she had dreamt about for what seemed all her life.

For a few seconds they did not speak while the winter wind outside made a dash at the building and the window rattled near them.

'I can't believe you're here.'

'I'm on my way to England.'

Her hand strayed to the neck of her coat. 'But how did you know I was here?'

'I found out accidentally. Your son's in my battalion.'

'I know. He told me.' If only she could tell him the truth: explain the misunderstanding of all these years and yet she had given her solemn word. She heard Matt speaking in her head, his words shuddering out of the past, *I want you to swear to me here on this bright Brisbane day that you will die with the truth never passing your lips.* And . . . she had sworn. Her hand had been forced when the truth was revealed to Bart. That was enough.

She blinked to keep back the tears that threatened. It seemed she had waited for this day for eternity. Her mind strayed to the halcyon days of her girlhood and to a night at a concert when she had been as light-hearted as a blossom trailing on a summer breeze.

'Caro, no doubt you know Matthew Craken's attached to my battalion.'

She nodded.

'That's been character-building for both of us. Staying away from one another's throats.'

She gave the impression of a smile. 'Yes, I can understand that.'

'He would probably be furious if he knew I'd come here. He's nothing if not possessive of you.'

'Well, not any more.' Even as she said the words she saw Matthew as he had been the night in the canteen in Montdidier, picking up his cane, giving her one of his wry, slanted smiles and limping away by the bar to exit into the night.

'What does that mean?'

She thought of Matt's recent letters, clipped and to the point, telling her about Harry and how he was. And the day of Luke's death when he had driven away without even looking back. She trembled and pulled her coat more tightly around her.

'It means I think he's left me.'

John Conrad shook his head. 'No, never.'

'I haven't been exactly a wonderful wife.'

He looked at her and wondered what sort of a wife she had been. In her eyes were a myriad expressions and for the first time in years across his mind surged the night of Hargy's death and how she had held him and loved him for the first time.

'There was a time I was deeply in love with you, Caro.'

Her heart felt as if it would break. 'And I with you.'

'But time alters things, doesn't it? When you married Craken I hated you, carried my hurt and anger for a long time.' He lifted his hands in a gesture of futility. 'But the world we lived in then was not this one and I see things differently now.' He felt awkward, and the guilt was almost unbearable. He thought of how he had dismissed her as a whore and how he had railed against her for betraying him. And now he knew she never had! Yesterday, when the drums of truth had pounded in his head, he had finally realised. When the beautiful blue-eyed youth had locked eyes with him and stood opposite him, in those moments he had actually examined Harry Craken for the first time. Then he had truly known . . . After all the years of *not* knowing . . . of having the possibility drift at the edge of his awareness; of pushing it away and never allowing the contingency to gain any truth, yesterday he had realised that Caro had always lied to him and finally he had admitted the truth.

She saw the extraordinary look in his eyes but she was still overcome by the fact that he was here and, filled with her own needs, she took a step closer to him. 'John Conrad, I've spent much of my life wishing for this day, standing here with you like this. Every time there seemed to be a possibility of that, Matt intervened and stopped it. And now the day's come.' She half smiled. 'No wonder I froze!'

He gave the hint of a small understanding laugh.

'And, I have always wanted you to know . . .' she lifted her hand unconsciously to the tiny scar on her lip, 'that I never meant to hurt you. Never.' She shook her head with the desperation of the memory.

'Caro, I know that now. That's why I'm here.'

The words slammed into Caro's mind. It took her a moment before she calculated the full meaning of what he said. 'You know? How do you know? What do you know?'

'I see so much more than I ever saw before, Caro. Perhaps it's being in this godless war, perhaps the truth edges its way out because of that. But I know he's our son.'

The wind rattled the window again and the sun had gone and

sleet drifted by but Caro noticed none of it. She felt as if all the wonders of the world were exposed in abundance before her. *I know he's our son.* John Conrad had said the words; he knew the truth.

John Conrad broke the silence. 'He's a fine, fine boy.'

And as the tears she could no longer suppress forced themselves from her eyes, he stepped forward and took her in his arms. And as he held her he said, 'Forgive me.'

She was where she had dreamed of being, every day for eighteen years and yet at this moment of exuberance, an empty sad space welled up inside her for she thought of Matthew.

For a long time they stood there holding one another in the chilly ambulance long room and when they stepped apart he said, 'Yesterday for the first time I really looked at Harry, took him in, observed him. And I knew . . . it was just like that. I knew. No one needed to tell me.' He smiled sadly. 'Caro, I know the apology's a lifetime too late, but I'm making it. How clearly I see now there was nothing else you could do.'

She exhaled audibly. 'That's true, there was nothing else I could do. I thought you'd gone away to England for I didn't know how long . . . perhaps for ever, you see. And when I found I was having Harry, Matthew offered to marry me. I swore to Matt I'd never tell you and I've kept my promise all these years.' She lifted her hands in a feeble movement. 'Remember that day on the platform, at Roma Street, when Harry was just little . . . when you were meeting your fiancée?'

He nodded.

'I wanted so much to tell you . . . but I could not.' A tear drifted down her cheek. 'I had promised not to, and it all would have been . . . such a mess.'

He lifted his hand and tenderly stroked her cheek. His voice broke with the immeasurable sadness of it all. 'Ah, Caro . . . how sorry I am.'

'And, you see, Matt so loves the boy. He's Matt's pride and joy. I think he loves him more than I thought it possible for Matt to love anyone.'

John Conrad shook his head. 'No.'

'What do you mean "*No*"?'

'Craken loves *you* more than anyone; much, much more.'
He gave a grim smile. 'He's been prepared to kill me often
enough to prove it.'

She shook her head. It was mystifying and the intricate
emotions were bewildering her but she could see Matthew
in her mind, and in seeing him she wanted to cry again. She
wiped her hand across her eyes in an attempt to focus on the
present. John Conrad was here.

He took up Caro's right hand. 'Caro, there's something I
should tell you. Harry's been chosen to be trained as an
aeroplane pilot to join a squadron in the Royal Flying Corps.
He's being sent to England.'

She looked startled.

'Please don't worry. Frankly, he's probably better off. We
go back into the line soon. His training will take many months.
He'll pick it up easily. He's a smart, bright boy.'

Caro's eyes glowed with the release of that which she had
hidden for too long. 'Yes, yes, he is.' And now she needed to
be guided again. 'What do we do now?'

There was a tapping on the door and they both turned towards
it as Jill Cossington entered.

'I've just come to tell you we need you.'

'Yes, of course,' Caro said. 'I'm sorry, I'm coming.'

Jill took a long interested look at John Conrad and he
motioned sharply to the door she had just come through. 'Mrs
Craken and I are trying to finish our business. I'm sure you'll
be kind enough to let us do just that.'

Jill's face dropped and, deflated, she exited and closed
the door.

John Conrad's brow creased in thought and he spoke slowly.
'You must know there's a part of me that wants to shout this
from the rooftops. But that would be selfish and, if anything,
this war's taught me to guard against that. Let what's passed
between us today remain with us. There's nothing whatever to
gain in exposing Harry to the truth.'

And again Caro thought of Matthew and an expression of
fear crossed her face. 'You won't tell Matthew, will you?'

John Conrad shook his head. 'No. What's there to gain for
any of us in that? Except more pain, and there's been a plethora
of that.'

'It's the only thing I think would break Matt's heart . . . to lose Harry.'

John Conrad gave a wan smile. 'Sometimes I think he might have a heart after all.'

She spoke softly, with a faraway expression. 'With Matt you can never be sure.'

He took her hand again. 'I'm glad I came. We can never be the two people we were all those years ago, and time and this war have altered us for ever, but at least now we can talk . . . we can be friends.'

Her voice broke as she answered. 'I have *always* been your friend.'

And he placed his other hand over hers and lifted her fingers to his mouth and kissed them. 'Yes,' he almost whispered. 'I do believe you always have.'

Their eyes met again and they were filled with the thoughts of all that had been said; of all the years that had passed; of all that might have been.

He gently let go her fingers and opened the door for them to pass out into the chill of the moody day. They walked side by side back to the Nissen Hut, her long coat brushing the piled snow as they moved along.

He hesitated near his vehicle and faced her. He had recalled something. 'Caro, the day I left Brisbane for India on the ship, you brought Harry. You were up on a verandah of a warehouse.'

How well she remembered. 'I wanted him to . . . see you off, even though he didn't realise. I felt he should. You did see us and wave to us, didn't you?'

'Yes, I did.' His eyes clouded with emotion. 'I'm so glad you did that.'

She nodded tenderly. 'Me too.' Then she put out her hand and he held it once more, and lifted it again and pressed his lips upon it. As he released it she met his eyes. 'Stay safe, John Conrad.'

'And you too, dear, dear Caro.'

He gave her a smile out of the long ago; parting his lips just slightly as his eyes seemed to haze over for a second.

She murmured to herself in poignant counterpoint as she watched him climb into his armoured vehicle and she lifted her hand to his at the car window as he drove away. Where minutes before she had felt drained, now she was aware of the relief that washed over her.

After all the years John Conrad had come to her. No, she was not the Caro of her youth and nor was he the boy of his, and she recognised the world was not the one she had harboured her troubled dreams in for all those years. Life had altered them, but they had made a fine wonderful young man in Harry and they had survived to this day to recognise the fact together.

Later that night Caro wrote to her father and to Bart. She found comfort in writing to her father; even now in her maturity he was still a rock for her heart to latch upon. While she did not enlighten him of the reason she told him she had seen John Conrad, that it had been a good meeting and she felt so much better for it. To Bart she wrote a positive letter and she wrote it confidently, informing him that John Conrad now knew that Harry was his. She mentioned that they had had a brief meeting but that it had consoled her and helped her and it had released her heart from the shackles she had worn since 1898. She told him she had always appreciated Bart's help and his understanding in the times when she needed him. She thought it best that if ever John Conrad mentioned it to him that he should admit he had known and had kept faith with her by his silence. Finally she told him she and John Conrad had decided for a multiplicity of reasons, to keep the truth from Harry. She wrote that she hoped he was happy and well and that this hellish war would soon be over. After she had signed it she added a postscript: 'Matthew will remain unaware that John Conrad knows the truth.'

As the day had passed and she went about and tended the wounded and drove the ambulance to the base hospital in Doullens, she felt many emotions; they wafted across her consciousness and brought her to sighing a hundred times. But as the winter night descended and wore on and at last she climbed into bed she finally acknowledged that it was not John Conrad who filled her mind, but the man she had lived with for all the years of her adult life: Matthew of the dark ironic eyes and scarred face and slanted smile.

*   *   *

The first person John Conrad ran into in London was Winston Churchill; he had not seen him since K's death.

While Tommy waited for him in the outer offices of the Ministry for War, John Conrad passed along one of the many long corridors heading to his meeting room, when he saw Winston coming the other way. They halted and shook hands.

'So, John Conrad, why aren't you a general?'

John Conrad smiled, 'And why aren't you Prime Minister?'

'Touché.' And Churchill gave a wide smile. 'I intend to be one day. For the time being I'm in the wilderness. I'm minister of nothing.'

John Conrad smiled. 'Poor Winston, you'll survive, you always do. They'll give you a ministry soon, they're just making you pay.'

A grim laugh rumbled in Churchill's throat. 'I was talking to "Wully" Robertson the other day and he said he couldn't believe that a man like Lloyd George could continue as Prime Minister for long. His words were, "Surely some honesty and truth are required."'

John Conrad concurred. 'Well, you know that's my opinion and the same goes for most of the cabinet.'

'Yes, they didn't exactly play fair with your mentor.'

'Indeed.'

'Why are you here? I heard you'd done what I did . . . went up to the front.'

'Yes, I've still got a battalion in the Somme.'

'Makes you realise how much we owe them, doesn't it? I mean, never in the field of human conflict have men suffered so much.' His eyes were aggrieved. 'Vale Valhalla.'

'How right you are. Yet each one of them deserves Valhalla.' John Conrad held out his hand. 'I'm actually on my way now to see Robertson, Birdwood and some others.'

Winston shook it. 'Well, don't know when we'll meet again. Good luck.'

'And you, Winston.'

When John Conrad entered the meeting-room the Chief of Staff was already there with the Generals Birdwood and McKay and the New Zealander, General Sir Alexander Godley. General Monash was missing.

John Conrad saluted and the others responded in kind.

William 'Wully' Robertson pointed to an empty wooden armchair and John Conrad eased himself down into it as tea was called for and for a few minutes the men talked pleasantries. Then the Chief of General Staff looked at John Conrad, 'Congratulations on your DSO.'

The three generals added their compliments.

'Thank you.'

Robertson looked at William Birdwood, who rose and moved across to the wall map. There he pointed to the battle lines on the Western Front and explained where they hoped to commit the next major pushes during the coming months.

After that McKay spoke about the 6th Mixed Division and how well it had performed at the Ancre.

When silence again fell the Chief of Staff crossed his legs in his velvet wing-backed chair and rubbed his round clean-shaven chin and smiled. 'So, John Conrad, the reason for all this preamble is to inform you of your promotion.' He took some papers from a file, pushed them across the desk and in his plain-speaking manner continued, 'More congratulations are in order, for this lot informs that as of yesterday you're a brigadier. You've had an interesting career, Fleet, and now we want you to take over two of the four brigades in the Mixed Division as we need Claythorne to go to Palestine. You'll take over Claythorne's brigade and another . . .' He searched in his papers. 'Yes, here it is. The 21st Brigade; commander's gone down with some blasted disease. Your command will still be mainly made up of Dominion troops – Australian, New Zealand and Canadian in the main – though Smuts is offering us some South African battalions and you might keep your Irish boys. You'll work independently in your own brigade group.'

'What if I don't want the promotion? You might recall our conversation of last September when I refused it? Well, I feel the same. I'd like to remain as battalion commander of the 16th.'

The generals all shook their heads.

John Conrad ran his eyes across their faces. 'The fact is, I don't agree with much of how the campaign's being run. While I understand I'm simplifying it I've just spent five months in the Somme and it seems to me that the strategy was often to pour more and more men into battles where the Germans were ready for us, saw us coming, went to ground during our barrages and then when we moved forward mowed us down. I know General Haig was under stress to initiate attacks and relieve the pressure on the French forces and that his options were few, but the *attack at all costs* mentality that's been operating in the Somme Valley to gain mere yards are not measures I can agree with. I think you're better to leave me as a battalion commander where I have to follow orders and do as I'm told, gentlemen. I could be difficult if you give me these brigades, especially if, as I suspect, you'll want me to work with General Gough.'

McKay and Godley mumbled something to one another and Birdwood said, 'John Conrad, we all have similar feelings to those you express. And we could sit here and argue all day about the tactics employed, but the fact is that you proved your ability at Beaumont Hamel and Beaucourt and we *need* you.' He looked across at Robertson. 'Isn't that so, Chief?'

'That's so. Keep going like this and we'll be offering you a division.'

John Conrad looked skywards and did not reply.

'General Haig will see you in Paris on your way back to the line. We're told General Gough and General Plummer will be with him. I believe they have plans for you in Northern France and Southern Belgium.' Robertson rose and moved round to the wall map, picked up a pointer and tapped the map around Arras. 'From what we can learn the Germans are retreating to the Hindenburg line, here.' He moved the pointer over the map, 'where no doubt they'll re-form.' He placed the pointer on the desk. 'There'll be a senior staff meeting in Amiens at the end of March for briefing on the spring campaigns.'

Robertson moved towards John Conrad, who stood from his chair. 'So, my boy, that's that. You might be a major-general with your own division at the rate you're going, before this is all over. Now I want you and William, here,' he glanced to Birdwood, 'to go away and go through your responsibilities.' He shot out his hand and John Conrad took it.

John Conrad actually smiled inwardly. These generals had just done to him what Tommy Hardcastle had done to Harry Craken. There was an American expression 'to railroad' and he suspected he had just been *railroaded*. He looked into 'Wully' Robertson's genial eyes and grinned, 'Guess I'll see you in Amiens.'

'Yes, Brigadier, I think you will.'

He left the War Office late and that night John Conrad introduced Tommy to his friend Quinton Rafter and the three men wandered down from Quinton's office on the Embankment to their favourite, the Savoy Hotel. Quinton halted them under the great oak tree, now bereft of its leaves, and pointed into the night sky. 'Tom, this was where we were last September when the zeppelins caught us, and what did John Conrad want to do but go and drink in the Savoy and *watch them* when the rest of London was scuttling for safety.' He laughed. 'So that's exactly what we did.'

John Conrad slapped his friend on the shoulder and laughed too. 'After the front, Q.R., I have to tell you the zeppelin pales into insignificance.'

A serious expression crossed the big man's face. 'No doubt, my brother, no doubt.'

They had a marvellous night, even with the alcohol rationed to two measures each, and as they sat and drank coffee and talked of many things, John Conrad at last divulged to Quinton. 'They've made me a bloody brigadier.'

Quinton beamed. 'But that's wonderful. Congratulations.'

John Conrad pursed his lips. 'Mmm, maybe it is and maybe it isn't. As Tom's aware I don't want too much real authority, or I might tell the hierarchy things they don't want to hear. Anyway, as I'm only a brigadier the strategy will be decided by Haig and the big boys still.'

Quinton laughed and glanced to Tommy. 'Listen to him: *only a brigadier*. The way he's going he'll end up a blasted field marshal.'

Tom grinned. 'Wouldn't surprise me.'

'So you're getting a brigade . . . what's that in battalions?'

'As it turns out, I'm getting two. So it means in all about six or seven battalions.'

Quinton whistled. 'A lot of lives.'

John Conrad nodded soberly.

'Where are they sending you?'

'Why, thinking of coming out to see us?'

His friend grinned. 'I might.'

John Conrad looked at Tom and back to Quinton. 'I wish I could tell, Q.R. but the War Office seems to be sensitive about that sort of thing.'

Harry managed to talk Lieutenant Young into a half-day leave pass.

He caught a ride on a troop bus down to Albert and as he hurried by the ruins in the streets and up to the little *estaminet* his heart accelerated. He knocked on the door. Madeleine's mother answered.

'*Bon après-midi, madame. Est-ce que Madeleine est . . . ici?*'

She shook her head and he gulped. Then she pointed to the basilica.

'Ah, thank you . . . *merci*.' And he turned and ran with the wind.

As he came to the ruined church he looked up at the diving golden Virgin, little knowing that it was one of the last images Luke had in his mind. Much of the centre part of the church, along the nave, was still intact but great piles of rubble lay all around where walls had been. The main arched front door with smaller arched entrances on either side were boarded up but, climbing over piles of dirt, Harry moved round to the side and entered through a shell hole about ten feet high. Gingerly he picked his way along, looking to right and left, and then he saw her. In a small intact chapel with mosaics on the walls all alone and sweeping the floor.

'Madeleine!'

In a moment of shock and recognition she almost threw down the broom and it clattered to the tiled floor as she turned to him. Her face glowed with the delight of seeing him again. ''Arry!'

In the natural prevailing mood of youth their joy ignored the destruction all around, and they ran to one another as if they passed over green grass in an emerald copse under a summer sun. He hugged her close. When she stepped away she asked how it was he had come again so soon, and the answer dismissed the gleam of happiness from her face.

'Oh no. *Tu pars déjà?*'

In halting French he explained that he was being sent to England to learn how to fly aeroplanes.

Her eyes were filled with sorrow and she took his hand and led him to a spot near the chapel where the weak winter sunshine found two smooth stones. They sat on them and she turned her face up to the meagre beams. They had not been there more than a minute when they heard her mother's voice. 'Madeleine! Madeleine.'

'*Elle nous cherche* . . . She is . . . look . . . for us,' the girl explained, and she took his hand again and, holding her finger to her lips, she led him away down a corridor over piles of dirt and across rubble out into a street behind the church: through another destroyed building they went, and along a broken-down lane into a ruined house where again she halted in a suntrap between a wall and a pile of rubble.

She looked at him and her eyes twinkled. He laughed. 'Well, we gave your mother the slip.'

She laughed too. 'The sleep?'

'No, the *slip*.'

They talked and later she told him she was eighteen in April and he smiled. '*Moi aussi*.' They were intrigued when they realised their birthdays were only a week apart. 'I shall send you a postcard for that day,' he said, and attempting to translate it he mimed the act of writing.

She gave a small tinkling laugh and he thought her the most beautiful thing he had ever seen.

When he told her he must leave, her eyes turned sad and she took the little gold cross and chain from around her neck and clipped it around his. 'To keep you . . . *sain et sauf*.'

'Safe?' he asked.

She smiled. '*Pour te protéger*.'

'Thank you.' And he kissed her lips. This time she put her hands around the back of his neck and held him gently; slowly he slipped his round her waist. It was sweet and comfortable; she made him feel as if he floated in feathers and as if one day the world would be kind again.

They walked hand in hand back through the lane to the street and rumbling through was a convoy of lorries.

She waited with him until he caught a lift with an ambulance and the last he saw of her was her fine figure, small even in her brown overcoat, holding her hand high in the air in the fading light of the bitter February day.

This is the picture Harry took of her to England.

It was raining on Friday morning when John Conrad and Tommy caught the train at Victoria Station bound for Dover.

As they settled into the comfortable leather seats John Conrad thought, as he had done so often in these last two days in England, of his boys wrapped in their greatcoats and scarves, lips cracked, cold hands frozen, trying to warm themselves in corrugated iron Nissen huts with a single fireplace at one end for twenty men. A week from now they would be in the reserve lines or even at the front where the conditions would be appalling. A part of his heart hurt for them, his boys. How could a soldier ever explain anything to civilians? They had no bloody idea.

When Canterbury slid by outside the windows, he was reminded of the girl with the flaming hair and her daughter, May. He would have liked to have made time to visit them but that had been impossible. He decided to post a card to them both from Dover.

He and Tommy were back in France by afternoon and he met Haig, the commander-in-chief, in Paris the following morning.

John Conrad recalled K telling him that Haig had married a maid of honour to the King's mother, Alexandra, and grandmother Victoria, and that was how he had gained entry to court circles. On his many previous meetings with Haig, when John Conrad had been at K's side and Haig had been Commander of 1 Corps, he had never found him cold or aloof, which some people charged him with being. But when John Conrad sang the praises of the machine gun and the tank, his opinion that the commander-in-chief was not imaginative or receptive to new ideas was vindicated by the lukewarm reception he received.

Later, Haig told John Conrad that the army must 'hold at all costs', and, 'We must relieve the pressure on the French troops. We'll advance on Arras in early spring.'

John Conrad shook his head and looked into the commander's distant pale eyes. 'But if the Germans have retreated to the Hindenburg line and are re-entrenching there as we are led to believe, what good will a frontal attack on Arras do?'

At Douglas Haig's side stood Hubert Gough and he answered in what John Conrad thought of as typical of his cavalier style. 'The commander-in-chief means we must support an offensive by General Nivelle.' Nivelle was the new French commander-in-chief. 'We cannot do otherwise.'

General Herbert Plumer, who stood on the other side of Haig, gave an encouraging look to John Conrad, who had always respected him. Plumer had succeeded Smith-Dorrien's command early in the war and had held the Ypres front now for almost two years and when Plumer said, 'We'll plan with care, Fleet. Your brigades are to support the divisions of my army in Belgium. We'll work together,' John Conrad was relieved.

On his way north in the armoured car John Conrad confided to Tom that he thought Haig, who had begun his career in the cavalry, still lived in a past where a cavalry charge would save the day. 'It's a bloody shame our commander's not the great leader we need at this time, but I doubt there's anyone else in the whole of the allied armies who would be much better.'

Tommy closed his eyes with that unhappy thought. 'That's not too comforting, sir.'

'You're right lad, it's not. Perhaps I've ruffled his feathers enough for the commander-in-chief to already be wondering why he agreed to my promotion.'

By Sunday afternoon at fifteen hundred he was back in Acheux with the battalion. The new battalion commander was to arrive within twenty-four hours and take the men back into the line.

There was mail for John Conrad sitting on his desk, a bundle tied with string: two letters from Bart and three from Aunt Leigh, and two from Lena, written by her daughter Tess. At the bottom of the pile was one from Emma Louise and one from May. Later that night, when all was quiet, he read them. It was good to have the news from home and Bart was still training men in the camp at Redbank. One part of the letter got John Conrad's full attention:

Do you recall I told you years ago about a girl called Marietta MacLeod who moved to Sydney to live? Well, she's returned to Brisbane and we've picked up our relationship again. We're thinking of marrying. I would like to have you as best man, so perhaps we will wait until this blasted war is over.

John Conrad smiled to himself. He felt honoured. It was just the sort of thing his steady level-headed brother would do; to wait for everything to be right. He missed him greatly.

He left Emma Louise's letter until last. He was surprised at its length. It ran to five pages and told him much of what was going on in her daily life. She mentioned Gertrude and Hewitt, and wrote that May had learnt some new songs. She told about conditions in England and how she thought the strikers were despicable . . . 'With men dying for them in battle now they strike and the supplies can't get to France. Well, I regard them as the lowest of the low.' This coincided absolutely with his own view, and when she told him she was still working with the Red Cross and how she went up to London to the hall at St James's each week he was a little surprised to read her further thoughts.

'I am considering joining a nursing guild or the VADs, for while I don't want to leave May at least I could work in a hospital for the wounded here in England and I'd feel like I was doing more for the war effort. What do you think?'

The last paragraph was the most thought-provoking. He had noticed how often it was that people left their most significant message to the end of a conversation or letter.

I have been wanting to tell you how badly I feel about the past, about letting you down. For being weak and everything. Not that I won't always hold David's memory dear, but I see it all so much more clearly now. My experiences have altered me. I'm not a child any more. I'm sorry for it all and I even understand your reaction, violent as it was. I do understand it now. That day you came to visit in Sept. 1916, before you went to France – the day I heard of David's death – I tried to clear things up with you, but I did not say I was sorry. I am. And I hope you can find it in your heart to forgive me for what I did.

Please don't forget to come and see us if ever you can.

Affectionately, Emma Louise

Dave and Matthew helped Harry pack for England. Well, Dave packed and Matt told him what to do.

At first Matt had been ambivalent when he heard of Harry's transfer. Even in this freezing winter he had enjoyed the weeks since Christmas having his boy close to him. But when he considered it his intelligence told him this could not last and that as a footslogger Harry would be back in the line soon and thus the angel of death would hover above him. So while he was not happy to lose the company of his boy he saw it as an opportunity for Harry to be back in civilisation for many months, perhaps even a year or more, while he trained in comfort to be an airman. He wrote to Caro and told her, little knowing she already was aware.

So don't worry about Harry. He's better off really being in England away from the fighting. I suppose you think airmen live dangerously and they do, but I nurse the hope that the war might end while our boy is still in training.

As usual he simply signed it '*Matthew*'.

Matt and Dave got along surprisingly well. Dave knew not to mention the unmentionable, which was John Conrad Fleet, and in other discussions they were affable enough. In fact Dave was fascinated with the art of painting and would sit under the sign 'If you want to converse, reverse' and watch by the hour . . . in silence.

Harry's last evening he spent with his father and Dave and when it came time for the boys to leave him Matt took Harry aside in the sergeants' mess where they had been. Though Matt, as an honorary officer, had drawn many strange looks the first time he had come in to the mess with his son, over the weeks the non-commissioned officers had become used to the fact he liked to join his son there, and he was accepted.

Matt put his hands on Harry's shoulders and met his eyes. 'I'll miss you, old son. Write when you can . . . especially to your mother. You know how she is about you?'

Harry rolled his eyes. 'Yes, unfortunately.'

'Don't react like that. She loves you.'

'I know, Dad, but I wish she were more like you.'

Matt smiled, 'What? Walked with a cane?'

This made them both laugh and Matt slapped Harry affectionately on the shoulder. 'I'm not comfortable with goodbyes, son, so look after yourself and we'll have some fine times when this stunt's over.'

Harry gave Matt a hug. 'I haven't told you, but most of your work – what you've done here – is just marvellous. I've lived with painting my whole life and you've taught me a hell of a lot, and I know my mates don't know much about art, but they all admire you and Cleaver Richards studied it at university – he's a lieutenant with B Company – and he reckons you're a master.'

A gleam came into Matthew's eyes. 'Heck, old son, it's almost worth losing you to hear you cough that up.'

After Harry and Dave hurried across the duckboards on the snow-covered ground and entered their hut Harry took Dave in his arms and hugged him close. 'We'll celebrate back in Brisbane one of these days, old son.'

Dave grinned. 'I reckon. We'll get as drunk as we like and there'll be no Bingo or Dobb to put us on a charge.'

This appealed to them and they both laughed so loudly that the others in the hut shouted for them to 'Shuddup, Craken!' and to 'Pull your head in, Sands.'

Then as they undressed Harry whispered, 'You know Madeleine . . . in Albert.'

'Yes.'

'Well, I'm going to marry that girl one day.'

Dave laughed. 'How do you reckon she'll take to Brisbane?'

'No trouble. You and I'll look after her, and I reckon my mum'll teach her all she needs to know.'

Dave was convinced. 'Yeah, we'll make a Queenslander of her. She's a good kid.'

Harry went to sleep imagining Madeleine holding his hand and running with him up the avenue of tall green trees and across into the fields out at Cedar Grove.

John Conrad saw Harry once more before the boy left for

England. It was on battalion parade when he handed over to the new commander, Lieutenant Colonel Peter Crundall. He made a brief speech and told them he was not leaving them, that he would see them all from time to time and would be watching them closely always. 'I'm proud to have this battalion included in my brigades. My heart will always be here with all of you in the 16th.'

This earned him rebounding cheers.

Then he inspected the troops. As he passed along their ranks he paused now and then and spoke briefly to a man. He stopped in front of Corporal Sands. 'Corporal, congratulations on your promotion. From what I hear you're a damn good soldier.'

'Thank you, sir.'

As he moved on along the row, he could not help it, he indulged himself by halting in front of Harry and meeting the boy's eyes. 'I'm told you're off to England in the morning?'

'Yes, sir.'

'I meant all of what I said to you the other day; every word. And you'll make a first-class pilot. You'll make the 16th proud, I know it. Look after yourself, think of us sometimes, and good luck . . . son.'

Harry smiled. It was a warm smile; completely gone were the surly looks of the past. 'I'll really do my best for you, sir.'

John Conrad swallowed hard. He wanted to remain: to continue to look in the face of his son; to talk and laugh with him; perhaps just once to hold him close. But he knew none of that could ever be. 'I know you will,' he said, and as a fine rain began to fall he hesitated before slowly he moved on.

In late February 1917 Mary Marland of Craigleah Station outside Charleville, Queensland, Australia, received an official letter from the Australian Infantry Record Office.

It was a form letter but the pertinent information had been written in by hand. It informed her that on the 22nd day of November 1916 her son, Luke Raymond Marland of the 16th Battalion, 2nd Queensland Infantry Regiment had:

Died of Wounds sustained

The handwriting was the same as the signature: John Conrad Fleet, Battalion Commander.

Chapter Forty-five

At Lansdowne Grove, Emma Louise took a last look out at the moon before she pulled the curtains across in the window seat and moved into the parlour. She was home for a week from nursing in the Red Cross Hospital at Folkestone. At work she wore her hair tied back in a bun under her veil, but now it was released and spread luxuriantly around her shoulders. She had felt she was not doing enough for the war effort and had decided to join the nursing service provided she could stay near Canterbury. Because she had worked as a volunteer for the Red Cross since outbreak of war she was permitted to work in Folkestone and come home at weekends.

She had put May to bed, tucked her in and read two stories of Brer Rabbit and the Ice Maiden, then listened to her prayer. The child always finished with, 'And God bless Mummy, and my daddy in heaven, Uncle Hewitt and Aunt Gertrude and my uncle away at the war.'

Emma Louise always sighed when her daughter finished her prayer. She had not suggested that her daughter include John Conrad, the child had just done so. She wrote to him every Saturday and while he did not reply with the steady regularity of her own letters, he *did* write and she kept all his cards and his letters in a tapestry box by her bed, often reading them before she went to sleep. Lately she had taken the bold step of signing her letters 'With Love' and her pulse had quickened when she had read on his most recent message his signature with two crosses beside it and then the words, 'Give May my love'.

She thought of that day so long ago in the train in Queensland when she had first seen him and given him the holy card. Even as a child she had been drawn to him.

Now she sat in front of the fire with John Conrad's latest letter in her hand and she read it over again. As she put it down, Gertrude in unison set down her rosary beads and asked, 'You're becoming really fond of him again, aren't you?'

Emma Louise played with the lace on the neck of her dress as she peered into the fire. 'If you're talking of John Conrad, I don't believe I was ever *unfond* of him.'

Gertrude moved uncomfortably on the sofa. 'I know I championed your attachment to John Conrad in the first place, my dear, and I've always thought him a wonderful catch, but you've only been in widow's weeds for just over a year. Do you think it's fair to David?'

'Aunt Gertrude, please. I've never been in *widow's weeds*. David wouldn't have wanted it and I was a good wife to him and I made the best of my marriage and would have gone on doing so if he had lived. But he *is* gone.' She eyed her aunt determinedly. 'I treated John Conrad badly, I betrayed him and I'm deeply sorry for it. It torments me that I acted that way. I was really still a child when I first met him. Now . . . well, now at last I've grown up. If he's good enough to have forgiven me and kind enough to bother to write me a letter now and then, which I must say makes me very pleased, well, that's all there is to it.'

Gertrude peered at her niece disbelievingly. 'Oh really? Is that all?'

The young woman pushed her gleaming hair back over her shoulder. 'I don't really dare to hope for anything else.' She gave a nervous laugh. 'I haven't seen the man in over a year, though I think about him all the time. And for heaven's sake, there's a war on. I just hope he lives through it. Who knows what will happen?'

Gertrude wore an expression that implied she had a lot more to say but at that moment Hewitt sauntered in with *The Times* under his arm and said, 'If anyone's making tea I'll have a cup.'

The older woman cleared her throat in a decided fashion as she rose and left the room.

The following morning above Canterbury and the emerald downs of Kent, Flight Sub-Lieutenant Harry Craken soared in and out of the clouds in his Sopwith Camel. He was on a routine flight exercise.

On first arriving in England he had attended lectures and practical training in aircraft rigging and understanding engines. He had been assigned to a physical fitness course, which he enjoyed, and after two weeks had made his first instructional flight with Warrant Officer Allan Lodge in a Curtiss JN4, a biplane nicknamed the 'Jenny'. Twelve instructional flights later Lodge allowed him to take the controls alone. From the day he had gone solo up above the Cotswolds he knew that this was what he had been placed on earth to do – fly aeroplanes.

He had been sent on a bombing and machine-gun course in Dover, and received first-class results in both. Recently he had graduated to flying various machines: a Bristol Scout fitted with a Lewis gun, a two-seater BE2c built by Daimler, and a Nieuport two-seater, but of them all he loved best the Sopwith Camel with its 150 horsepower Bentley engine. It was marginally larger than a Bristol Scout with a faster cruising speed and he had taken it up from the RNAS Station at Guston Road near Dover (where he was currently learning to handle the Sopwiths) to Biggin Hill, where the wireless testing park for ground-to-air and air-to-air wireless contact had been set up on 2 December 1916.

Now as he descended into Biggin he flattened out until he was just skimming the surface of the ground before he felt the wheels touch in what he knew was a technically near-perfect landing.

He rolled to a halt, jumped down from the cockpit and bent along the wing to the ground. He had filled out and though he was not nineteen for six more months he moved like a man, there was confidence in his walk and a certain fluidity. He glanced back to the aircraft and smiled. He just liked looking at the miracle machine; it felt like an extension of his own body when he was up there in the blue.

He strode across to the north-west side of the airfield where a tented camp had been erected. He had a laugh with a few of the pilots of D Flight 39 Squadron, who were in from Hornchurch, took a cup of tea and a scone and flew at 7500 feet back to Dover. He thought about meeting his friends in the Sea Lion Hotel and how they would have a little dinner later at Mason's Café on the waterfront.

On his return he was told to report to Captain Pinne, the commanding officer at the airfield, and when he did he was informed he had been posted to France on active service.

'Pack your kit, Craken, you're to leave on Monday at 0 one hundred on HM Destroyer *Falcon*, which will be alongside the promenade pier. It'll take you to Dunkirk.'

Across the Straits of Dover, south of Messines, near the border of Belgium and France, with the distant refrain of the artillery fire a backdrop to his thoughts, Matthew climbed down from the lorry outside the eighteenth-century Château Clare and told Bert and Cliff to meet him back at the same point in an hour. He crossed the swathe of grass to the wide front door carrying the letter from the War Office, and deftly swung himself into the Battalion Headquarters.

He had dreamt the previous night of Knobby, and the illusion had remained with him all morning. They had been at the Chevron Club celebrating something, and he and Knobby had been singing with his old mates Jack Renton, Grahame Magnus, David Webster and Walter Pine. He smiled dryly and hoped that the dream would become a reality before too much time elapsed: he missed Knobby more than anyone; well, more than anyone other than Caro. Funny how that woman had intrigued him from the very first day he had ever seen her.

And while his wife had continued to fascinate him she had remained a distant mystery during all the years, allowing him no access to her heart or her soul. And the other women he had seen in the early years of their marriage had been more to console him for the lack of her love than anything else, though Caro would never believe that. Yet indeed it was true. And he had given up on that sort of thing a long time ago.

And now it was time he gave up on Caroline Dere. He had received a letter from her a few months ago but it had not fooled him. She had written that she wished to talk to him 'about everything', whatever that meant: probably about how they were going to organise living their totally separate lives. He had not replied to her and he had heard nothing more, though he knew she was still in Aveluy at the casualty clearing station.

He decided to dismiss the memory of his wife as he knocked on the ornate gilt and painted door of Lieutenant Colonel Crundall's office. 'Inform the commander I'm here, would you?'

The lieutenant stood from an eighteenth-century mahogany and gold leaf desk and entered an inner room, returning with a nod of his head. 'The lieutenant colonel will see you now, sir.'

Crundall had become used to his artist adjunct, his bitter wit and his frequent requests: to go into the front lines to sketch; to have a pass to travel to Dunkirk and draw the ships; to go with his sketchbook into Hellfire Corner on the Menin road – the most notorious spot in the entire salient, blasted continuously by German shellfire, the *Hottest Spot on Earth*. He almost looked forward to what Craken would want today.

'Yes, Major?' He lifted his gaze from his papers, which lay in the light of the single lamp on his desk and motioned to a chair. Behind him the long dust-filled tapestry drapes that had been hanging since decades back into the previous century blocked out the waning light and attempted to keep some heat in the room, a difficult task with its fourteen-foot-high ceiling.

As Matthew leant on his ebony cane and eased himself down, he spoke. 'You're probably aware that next month I'll have been with the 16th for almost a year.'

'Yes.'

Matt raised the official envelope. 'I've just received a letter enquiring if I'm to return to London and thence to Australia or if I wish to avail myself of a six-month extension. If I do request the extra six months it must be authorised by you and the commander of the brigade.'

Crundall put down the pipe he had been puffing. 'What do you wish to do?'

Matt's mouth shaped a cynical smile. 'Surely you know how fond I am of the war? I wish to remain, of course.'

Over the past ten months Crundall had heard whispers about Craken: that his wife was here and even though they were estranged that he stayed in France to be near her. Not that the major had ever revealed anything about his private life, but Crundall could not understand a man remaining unless something such were the case.

Crundall picked up his pipe again. 'Well, we're used to having you so it's a mere formality for me to sign, which I assume it will be for the brigadier.'

'We'll see.'

Crundall puffed and eyed his visitor. 'Fact is, he's coming here tomorrow. I just now received a telephone call. You can have him sign it then. I was about to send a message to all the companies. He wants to go into the line and revisit the lads. Our boys are due to come out Thursday, the day after tomorrow, and to go into rest. He's requested whatever officers are available to have a drink here with him at seventeen hundred, Thursday. So while you're a bit of an add-on, old man, I'm sure you're included.'

The lieutenant colonel did not know whether the major joked or not when he stood and replied, 'Wouldn't miss seeing the brigadier for the world. I'll be there.'

A spatter of machine-gun fire skipped across the top of the trench as a voice called, 'They must be getting bored over there by the sound of it and have decided to take it out on us.'

Dave looked up from Harry's letter. They heard from Harry pretty regularly and it sounded like Harry had been sent to heaven with his beers at the Sea Lion Hotel in Dover and the Black Horse Inn in Biggin Hill and the comfortable quarters and the flight lieutenants enjoying themselves in the officers' mess. He folded the papers and put them down near Curly on the firestep.

'Here's Harry's latest.'

Curly raised his gaze from the page he was reading and his usual ruddy face was white, even the blotches on his neck from the lice bites had turned pallid.

'Gawd, mate, what's wrong?'

'Nothin'.'

'You've gone white, for heaven's sake. Something must be wrong.'

Curly shook his head. 'Na, I'm all right.'

A more mature man might have taken the hint but Dave, in his youthful unsophistication, carried on, 'Curl, mate, don't give me that. What's wrong?'

Curly's voice was irritated. 'Nothin', I said.'

Dave raised his eyebrows. 'Look, Curl, I know there's something badly wrong. I'm your mate, come on, let me help you.'

His friend put his head in his hands. 'She's left me.'

'What?'

'Gloria, the bitch . . . she's left me.'

'Never, not Gloria. You've always told me how true she is.'

Curl's head came up, his eyes gleaming though no tears fell. 'I thought she was. Jesus. To do this to me, and me here in this lot. How could I have trusted the bitch?' He ran his bayonet down his putee to remove the lice as he spoke and then plunged it into the dirt beside him.

Dave, who had no experience of women at all except for his mother and sisters was at a complete loss. 'Gawd, Curl, are you sure?'

'Sure?' Curl's gruff voice, which had become a comfort to Dave these days, skipped up an octave. 'Yes, I'm bloody sure. Ah hell, you may as well read the bloody thing.' He handed the paper across to Dave.

'Aw, Curl, I don't like to.'

Curl waved it in his face. 'You pestered me, so damn well read it!'

Dave took it. It was true. She wrote that she had met a bloke a year before and that she could not hide the fact any longer that she was in love with him. She wanted to be honest with Curl and hoped he would understand that when he came back she would not be there for him.

Dave was amazed and hurt for his friend. He passed the page back. 'Gawd, Curl, don't take it too hard. Please.'

Curl's tone was broken and bitter. 'She wants me to *understand*. Why did she have to tell me, for Christ's sake? I'm over here. She wants to be *honest with me*. Bloody hell, why?' He hid his head in his hands. 'Oh Gawd, and me the blasted fool . . . believin' in her. The bloody flamin' bitch.'

Dave looked up at the fading light. He was a sergeant now. After the battalion had lost five NCOs at Messines Ridge in June, Dobb had been promoted to sergeant major like Bingo, and they had pushed Dave up. 'Listen, mate, you're on sentry duty soon. Do you want me to get somebody to fill in for you?'

Curly shook his head. 'Na, I'll go.'

'You sure?'

Curly tucked the letter in his jerkin pocket and stood up. 'Yeah, I'm sure.' He picked up his bayonet and his short magazine Lee Enfield rifle and stooped to wander off down the trench.

Dave called out to his departing back, 'I'll get out the Primus stove and have the billy on the boil when you get back.'

He sighed as he watched his mate disappear round the corner. He and Curly were the last two of their original band: Isaac, Frank and Luke were dead, and Harry was in England. There were just the two of them left. Even Wells, Lockert and Lloyd who had been the extended members of their little family group, had been killed at Messines Ridge. While the battle had been an overall success the Anzac troops had incurred big losses. The Mixed Division under Uncle John Conrad had attacked in combination with General Godley's Anzacs.

Thinking of Messines brought back the early hours of the morning on 7 June. In the seeping mist of dawn an ominous silence had hung over them. Then he had fancied he heard nightingales singing; it was a sound he had come to recognise since being in Europe, and it was one of the very few memories he might take away that held a semblance of beauty.

Curly had been leaning on the parapet next to him, waiting. He remembered that he nodded his craggy head and grinned. 'Here we go again.' He had made what they were about to do sound normal, commonplace.

Suddenly beneath their feet the trench vibrated and rumbled and the sound of the most massive explosion ever to be made by mortal man to that day thundered across Rossignol Wood and the Messines Ridge. Sounds of hell on earth escaped to reverberate in shock waves that carried the North Sea and the Strait of Dover to be felt as far away as London, Canterbury and Southern England.

As nineteen of the twenty-four mines tunnelled at depths of fifty to one hundred feet blew apart, Dave looked skywards to see great columns of light appear out of the ground and ascend through the mist to the sky while orange, red, yellow, blue and green flames leapt out to burst and swell in great shapes and lurching masses. The roar of the blast was so enormous that a sharp pain stabbed through Dave's ears and he looked across at Curly in amazement even though they had been expecting it, for all ranks had been warned about the four hundred tons of explosives that had been installed in the ridge under the enemy lines, some of the tunnelling beginning as early as two years previously.

The falling rubble, debris, earth and rock rained down on everything for minutes on end.

Then another noise from hell began as the creeping artillery barrage started and Dobb shouted to urge his boys once more over the top.

'Here we go! Up and over, boys!'

And again Dave and Curly bounded high out of their crooked jagged prisons in the ground with the odour of rum sailing on the air, to scale the parapet and head out across no-man's-land. Over the wilderness of shell holes with the inevitably blasted and broken wire towards the German lines they bounded in company all along the front with other men of Anzac and Plumer's 2nd army of twelve divisions.

The Australians and New Zealanders in the south had met strong resistance from pillboxes and that had been when Wells and his Lewis gun boys had got it.

Nevertheless the army had reached their first objective within thirty-five minutes and by 0900 the British occupied the whole of the ridge. Later in the day Dave had seen Uncle John Conrad and General Plumer on the ridge. They had been brought forward in a tank. The small rotund Plumer, with his large white moustache, looked more like a character from one of Bairnsfather's cartoons than a general, but everyone said he was made of tougher stuff than his looks suggested.

The result was an undoubted victory for Plumer and his right hand, Fleet, and by 12 June they had pushed the Germans from most of what was known as the Oosttaverne line and by the 14th the enemy had retired even further to the Warneton line and all objectives for the British forces had been accomplished.

The success at Messines Ridge had been a small beam of light in the murky sea of darkness in the stagnating war on the Western Front.

They had returned just south of the border to Northern France after that: in great long convoys of buses and lorries and trucks.

It was after that they had heard rumours of the mutinies in the French army and that more would fall on the soldiers of the British Empire.

When they were told that the Americans had at last declared war on Germany and were coming to France and Belgium, there were mixed reactions. Many of the boys had been resentful.

'Christ, they're a bit bloody late, aren't they?'

'Tardy buggers, they'll wander in three years late and try and take all the glory.'

Curly's reaction made Dave smile. 'I've never met a Yankee in me whole life, but I'm ready to welcome 'em with open arms and give 'em a nice big present, I am. Yep, as far as I'm concerned I'm donatin' the entire bloody Western Front to 'em . . .'

'Sergeant!'

Dave left his reverie to turn and see Bingo coming towards him.

'Yes, Sergeant Major?'

'Things are warming up a bit in Section Forty-Two down by Piccadilly, a lot of machine-gun fire. Fritz is cranky. I want some more bags of shingle and sand on the parapet. Get down there, will you, and oversee it for me?'

'Right.' Dave jumped to his feet and hurried along the trench.

After he had attended to the parapet he was moving back to his own section when he heard stretcher bearers coming along behind him. 'Make way for Lord Kitchener!' They still used the phrase; it had become a regular refrain amongst the allied armies. He halted to let them by, recognising them as men from his own platoon, and as they came closer one of them called out, 'We've got to get him down to the aid post. He's bleeding badly, Sarge.'

Dave pushed himself against the dirt to let them by. It was then he saw the wounded man. 'Oh no.'

Blood streamed from Curly's neck and shoulder; his eyes were rolled back and he did not appear conscious.

'Hurry, hurry!' Dave exclaimed as the men moved on and, following them along, stooping behind them, he shouted, 'What happened?'

'He was hit by machine-gun fire on sentry. Don't know how.

He didn't seem himself when he went to the forward post, sort of dreamy and far away, they said.'

'Must have put his bloody head up. Doesn't make sense otherwise,' the other stretcher bearer called.

Dave felt sick. *Bloody Gloria*. She was a bitch, all right. Dave hoped she rotted in hell.

He followed them all the way to the aid post, calling to a corporal to tell Bingo where he had gone. The RAMC officer at the post took Curly's pulse and cleaned up the wounds as best he could and as he moved away to get a bandage Dave knelt down and whispered in Curly's ear, 'Please don't do this to me, mate. I couldn't bear it if you go west too. Gawd, matey, we've got to get together back in the good old Commonwealth of Australia after this stunt's over.' The hurt welled up and overcame him. 'Please, Curl, don't die on me, please.'

Dave remained at the regimental aid post waiting beside Curly, who still had not regained consciousness even when stretcher bearers came to transfer him to the advanced dressing station.

'I'll take over,' he told one of the men, and took a front position on the stretcher. It took four men to carry one wounded man and they conveyed him along a sunken road where at one end the Germans regularly shelled. They waited between blasts and then transported their load as fast as possible by the craters and rubble up a rise to a second road and on by reinforced positions until stooping was no longer an absolute requirement for survival, and the noise of artillery and machine-gun fire became a little more distant.

On they went, until finally arriving at the advanced dressing station they had to wait. The other stretcher bearers left and while they waited Dave sat down beside Curly and talked to him. He imagined even though his eyes were closed that Curly could hear him and it would give him heart. He spoke quietly, leaning forward close to his friend's ear and covered all manner of things. He got to reminiscing about their many days in the line together. He patted his pal's hand. 'Remember when we took that Hun trench three times and they pushed us back three times and you left Fritz a pair of clean boots up on the firestep as we retreated and when we took it over again, lo and behold, there right where you'd left yours was a pair of bright shining German ones? Remember how we laughed and called you *Wolfgang* for ages after that?'

'What are you hanging around for, Sergeant?'

Dave looked quickly up into the tired face of an overworked surgeon. 'He's my friend, sir. I'd like to know how he's going to be before I head back into the line.'

The man unravelled the bandages and the blood began to ooze again as he probed around and examined the wounds. 'A bullet's gone straight through the side of his neck so that's fortunately pretty simple, but there's one lodged in his shoulder. It's smashed his collarbone. We'll have to take that out, but that won't be done until he's transferred to the main dressing station.'

'And?'

'And what?'

'Well, is he going to be all right?'

'I'd say so, Sergeant. Provided it doesn't turn septic, he'll live, though you won't see him back here. He's got his ticket out, lucky bugger.'

Dave sighed and picked up Curly's limp hand, and as if Curly knew it was Dave and it was time to show some life he opened his eyes.

'Gosh Curl, you gave me a fright, mate. You're back at the advanced dressing station now.' He smiled encouragingly. 'You'll soon be going away through nice normal places where there are blacksmiths' shops and horse lines and supply depots and even trees and orchards and green grass again. Yes, mate, you'll be as good as new.'

Curly attempted to speak but only a gurgling sound came out.

'Don't worry about talking. Just get better for me, Curl. Look, I know this isn't much of a time for saying this, but I reckon now's all I've got, so.' He took a deep breath. 'I don't know much about women – fact is, I know nothing – but forget about Gloria. She sure wasn't worth a button and certainly not your life, mate. That's one thing I know for sure.'

Curly attempted a nod of his head.

'And just be waiting for me when I get home to Brisbane.' He swallowed hard. 'We'll celebrate.'

Dave went back to the line with a smile of relief on his

face. As he ran along the sunken road he shouted to the sounds of war, 'At least you've made it out of this bloody asylum, Curl.'

The next day Dave was sent for by John Conrad after he had visited the men in the front line.

Dave made his way back to the château headquarters where he was led through some long draughty corridors with massively high ceilings, and finally came before his uncle, the brigadier. He saluted in style.

'How's my nephew?'

'I'm all right, Uncle John Conrad, sir.'

'Dave, we had a meeting like this over a year ago when I offered you a position in communications.'

'Yes, sir, I remember.'

'This time I'm not offering you a job, Dave,' he smiled. 'I'm ordering you to take one. I was told by Sergeant Major Bingham that when you were in training in Marseilles you learned to drive lorries.'

'Yes, sir.'

'Well, driving a lorry and driving an armoured car or truck are pretty much the same. My driver broke his leg on Monday. So you're the replacement.'

Dave opened his mouth but John Conrad went straight on. 'This is not just a cushy job, Dave. Yes, it's away from the front line, but it's hard work and it would help me greatly to know I've got a man I can trust completely at the wheel and by my side. You've done your duty as a footslogger. Bingham and Young say you're one of the best soldiers they've ever had. They've both recommended I take you on.'

There was silence in the room for a few seconds. Dave thought of the last time he had been before his uncle like this: then he had Harry waiting back in the line for him, and Isaac and Frank and Curly and even Luke. Now his last mate Curly was gone and Harry was far away and never coming back to the infantry.

'I'm on the go a lot, Dave. My driver has to be ready and willing any time of the day or night.'

'Won't they think it's strange that a black fella drives you around?'

John Conrad stood up and came round the desk. 'You know

782

something, Dave? I never did notice what colour your skin was.' He cuffed the young man affectionately across the side of his head. 'Black, is it? Well, I suppose we'll just have to take on anybody who objects to you the same way we've taken on the Germans.'

Dave gave in. 'All right, sir, I'm your man.'

'Thanks, Sergeant.'

Dave saluted with a grin, and as he left the room John Conrad looked skywards. 'I still miss you, Hargy matey,' he whispered, 'even after all these years, and Dave's the closest thing to you I'll ever find in this world.'

When Matthew approached John Conrad he did not receive a smile, but nor was the expression hostile. 'Major Craken, we meet again.'

'I need your signature on my request to remain with the 16th for another six months.'

'So you like the army that much?'

'No I don't, but I have a good reason to remain. While two reasons brought me here, one keeps me.'

John Conrad remembered Caro telling her that Craken had left her. So he assumed it was Harry who kept Craken here. He gave no sign he understood and he bent forward and signed.

Caro sat in the Nissen hut canteen drinking tea. She seemed to live on tea these days. She put down the copy of the *Daily Telegraph* that she had been reading. From what she could gather affairs in Russia were in a state of revolution. She finished her tea and sighed.

She had heard nothing from Matt since he had written to her earlier in the year to tell her of Harry's transfer to the Royal Flying Corps. She assumed he was still with the 16th Battalion.

After she had seen John Conrad in February, Caro had considered her life and her marriage for months. Finally in July she had written to Matthew. It had not been a lengthy missive and she had come straight to the point.

Dear Matt,
    Time passes. The last letter I had from you was the

brief note in February to tell me of Harry's transfer to the Royal Flying Corps. I have waited months for another note but have heard nothing from you. I write to my parents and your mother and they say you are not a good correspondent. Perhaps it would be kind if you could drop them a line. I'll bet you write to Knobby.

I have thought about us, you and me, many times since the night in the canteen in Montdidier when you said you were leaving me.

Matt, I really would like to talk to you about everything. I cannot come to you. Would you come to me? I have some leave due. If you could take some too, which I'm sure in your honorary capacity you can, then we might be able to go to Paris together or even England. It will do us good just to be alone and to be able to talk.

Your wife,
Caro

For the first two months after she had written to him she had watched for the mail every day. She received letters from her parents and Mother Craken, from her daughter, Katy, and from Jane and Knobby and Mary and Jacob up at Cedar Grove, and even the odd letter from Harry, but never had a reply come from Matthew.

She now believed he had meant what he said that night in Montdidier and the more she analysed what he had said, the more she thought it was probably true. She had lived all the years of her marriage with the ghost of John Conrad pervading all her waking moments and many of her sleeping ones; she admitted that now. Everything had related to him and nothing to her husband. Matt had been right when he said that John Conrad had lain between them . . . even when he loved her. And yet when she recalled the touch of loving now, it was Matt's lips and his body she remembered, not the phantom of John Conrad in her mind.

She remembered the night of their marriage when she had been surprised by the bowls of white roses that Mattt had placed in the room. Had that been Matt's very first effort to show her how he truly felt?

And now, in the months that she had had to consider the years of her marriage, she saw many times when he had attempted in his oblique fashion to make an overture to her but she had always deflected him. She recalled again the night she had lost the baby, Roy, and she had dreamed she had seen Matt standing silently beside her, with an expression of mournful sadness on his face. He had bent down and kissed her forehead and at the time she had believed it must have been a dream. Now she knew it had been real.

She had loved the fantasy of John Conrad Fleet for so long, she knew she would carry that illusion with her to the grave, but it was only recently she had acknowledged that perhaps, all along without realising, she had loved the reality of Matthew Craken too.

She wiped a tear from her face and stood up to go back into the ward. Suddenly she heard Patricia calling her and she hurried out into the yard.

Pat's face was distorted with concern; with her stood Carmen, June and Sue, three new VADs. 'Truckloads of gassed are coming in. We've got nowhere to put them but the ambulance long room. Captain Cadee is down there now with some orderlies and Jill preparing makeshift beds from groundsheets. He's asking for us.'

They hurried through the autumn wind: the French summers seemed so short and the rain a constant no matter what month of the year.

As they moved across the yard the first of the ambulance trucks arrived with the soldiers.

The tailboard was lowered and out they came, all suffering from the effects of mustard gas: ethylene in a solution of sodium chloride to the chemist; they were all blinded; their eyes bandaged and their hands and faces and exposed areas blistered with the burns. Some bled from the mouth and others coughed up blood.

They stood in a line, each man with his left hand up on the shoulder of the man in front and then as Captain Cadee led them forward across the yard they edged along: a stumbling sightless khaki centipede.

Caro had seen men gassed before but never this many. Some groaned and others dropped to the ground and vomited; all were gasping for breath. She bent to one boy who lay whimpering on the ground. She took his arm and said, 'Come with me,' and as she lifted him he whispered, 'Mother.' It broke her heart to hear that word, for how often she heard it these days, always on the lips of the dying, the words 'Mother' and 'Mum' were like a litany, repeated over and over. They said it in their sleep, they cried it in their pain, they said it as they slipped from this world into the next.

And so the following days passed for Caro and Pat and Jill and the others with very little sleep, tending the blind eyes all clogged and stuck together and the massive suppurating blisters, their voices cracked and all gasping for breath. The worst cases they covered in tents of propped-up sheets for they could not bear to be bandaged or touched. One boy's face was entirely eaten away and all that Caro and the others could do was pour oil on the wounds. He cried out in agony to let him die. They injected him with morphine but within forty-eight hours he had caught pneumonia and in three days he was dead.

Caro left the ward and went out into the field nearby and, leaning on a trunk of a poplar, cried for him. She had seen many die now, and had become hardened to death, but there were always some that hurt worse than others. Part of her was pleased he had gone, for who would want to live without a face? He had reminded her of Michael Leahy, the boy she had become close to the previous year in Montdidier, and she sobbed once more for Michael's soul; and then she wept for the souls of all of them.

She thought how often she had told Harry to keep compassion in his heart, how it was the difference between animals and humans. As she moved through the wards in the huts, tending the gassed soldiers coughing and suffocating for breath with the agonising burns all over their bodies, she wondered where God's compassion had gone.

The weeks passed and most of the gassed were moved on to base hospitals. Many of them by then could see as the blindness was temporary and lasted between four and eight weeks, but the weakness in their lungs would remain with them all the days of their lives.

A few days after the last of the gassed left, the wind was blowing off the North Sea on a cold afternoon heralding the winter when Caro came out of the ambulance long room and crossed over to her vehicle.

'Mail's just arrived,' Patricia hailed her as she passed with June, both loaded down with fresh bedding. Caro hurried to the hut where the mail came in. Greedily she found hers: one from Mother Craken, one from her father and her brother, Paul, two from Jane and Knobby, one from Harry, even one from Lucy. That was all. Nothing else. She walked woodenly to the door.

Chapter Forty-six

St-Pol Airfield, Northern France: Sunday, 28 July 1918

Harry ran across the grass of the airfield past the Sopwith Camels and Dolphins, Baby Nieuports, Bristol Fighters and Armstrong-Whitworths to his Sopwith Dolphin and climbed up into the cockpit, waving to his friend, Flight Lieutenant Charles McIntosh, who entered his Bristol Fighter at the same time.

They were now members of the Royal Air Force. Since 1 April the Royal Naval Air Service and the Royal Flying Corps had been amalgamated under the new name. There had been bitter air fighting during the very first week of the Royal Air Force's existence and Harry had shot down two enemy aircraft in that time. Nevertheless he was a long way behind such noteworthy aces as MacLaren and Little, McElroy, Woollett and Kinkead, who were all heroes and worshipped as such by Harry and his mates.

Harry had heard that he might be transferred to an Australian squadron soon; a few had been formed within the Royal Air Force. He would like that, but he was pretty happy with the way things were anyhow, and he had some great mates, like Charles, and Paul Quinn, who had shot down sixteen enemy aircraft, the highest score in their squadron.

Not that anyone could ever replace Dave in Harry's affections, and he wrote regularly to him. He knew Dave had been driving his uncle the brigadier, for many months now. They were planning a leave together in Paris in a couple of months' time and the thought of that made Harry grin.

On his Sopwith Dolphin, forward of the circular insignia of the Royal Air Force, Harry had painted the name *Cedar Grove*. He had written to his father and to Uncle Knobby and Aunt Jane to tell them and his uncle had replied that it was the best name in the world for an aeroplane and how proud everyone was of it.

'Greaser' Bruckshaw, Harry's mechanic, helped him start the propeller and the 200 horsepower Hispano engine soon fired up, and minutes later the aircraft gathered speed and lifted off into the balmy summer day to rise through the scattered clouds. Harry looked right and left with elation as he sped through the air behind his friend Charles in his Bristol Fighter. He felt truly alive, living on every nerve end up in the sky, with the purr of the engine beneath him and the wind rushing by his face.

They patrolled the line from Béthune to Ypres at heights of between 10,000 and 12,000 feet; saw nothing in the sky but were fired upon from the ground a couple of times.

When they reached Ypres they turned and headed south again and a minute or so later Charles wiggled his wings, indicating he had seen enemy aircraft. As Harry looked around, seemingly out of nowhere appeared five Albatros Scouts. Harry banked to follow one and it dived vertically away so he opened fire but his tracer bullets went wide. Then to his left he saw one of the others closing in. Bullets whizzed by him and he felt a few thuds in *Cedar Grove* but he dived away, allowing the attacker to speed across the top of him. By the time Harry turned his aircraft Charles was at close range with another and firing.

Before Harry had time to think he caught sight of the remaining two enemy, and banking and turning *Cedar Grove*, he sped straight at one, firing constantly and not pulling out of the head-on course. He knew his bullets had hit the Albatros for as he closed in, it dived away beneath him with smoke trailing behind. He thought it went straight down but he was busy looking around for Charles. Then he saw the glint of the sun on metal and caught sight of his friend a long way in the distance chasing an Albatros, but with the fifth enemy aircraft on his tail. They flew in tandem for a minute or so and suddenly Charles was trailing smoke and he dived away as the Germans passed on and disappeared into cloud ahead.

Harry looked around for more enemy but could see none, so he banked and followed Charles. The Bristol Fighter was obviously in trouble as Charles battled to keep it level.

A piece of Charles's tail was missing and the smoke trail

emanating from the body of his Bristol Fighter seemed to be widening. Harry thought the nearest aerodromes were probably Aire or Freizennes but he was pretty sure Charles would not make either. He pursued Charles down until they were only about a hundred feet from the tree tops. Closer and closer they came to the ground, and as Harry held at a hundred feet Charles touched down in a field and Harry sped past. He banked and turned and came back to see Charles safely out of his aircraft and waving.

Harry thought he would take a quick look back along the front line again and some minutes later he noticed to the south a German kite balloon. The balloons were attached by cables to the ground and Harry closed in and fired about fifty rounds into it from two hundred yards. It sagged badly and then crumpled and went down in flames as Harry hooted with glee. One observer leaped out of the balloon, opened his parachute and drifted down to safety.

Sailing on, *Cedar Grove*'s engine began to misfire. Some of the bullets he had felt in the dogfight might have hit the fuselage after all. Harry put his hand out and patted the side of the machine, 'Come on, *Cedar Grove*,' he shouted, as the air rushed by his face, 'don't let me down.' The engine spluttered as if it were going to cut out, but suddenly for no apparent reason it came back to life and began humming. 'Good girl, *Cedar*,' he shouted to the sky as he sailed on.

He was aware he was getting low on fuel and turned immediately for St-Pol. He sighted no other aircraft and when he saw the airfield in the distance, *Cedar Grove* commenced to misfire again. It spluttered and coughed as he came down but he landed without incident and when Greaser came running over and Harry clambered out and slid across the wing they found a bullet hole in the tail, but to Harry's surprise and delight none in the fuselage.

'It's a bloody good plane,' was Greaser's only comment.

Harry alerted the Depot about Charles, his mishap and his whereabouts, and as he strode back to his hut, there coming in the opposite direction was Paul Quinn, attired in whites with cricket pads under his arm. He raised the bat he carried in greeting. 'Come on, Harry. We've got just about enough lads to make a game of it.'

Three hours later, in the last over of the cricket match in a muted green field surrounded by red poppies, Charles, hands in pockets, came sauntering over to join them.

Harry carried his bat and was top score with forty-four, and as his team-mates congratulated him, he was reminded of the matches he had played at school. Briefly he thought of Mr Reath behind his horn-rimmed glasses, coaching the cricket eleven as he used to do on the playing field at Mounthaven. How his life had altered and he would not change anything; not a thing; not for all the tea in China. Well, that was not exactly right for he would change some things if he could: the losses of Luke and Isaac and Frank; and all the others, but that was war, and the war had matured him. He would always be a product of this war, he knew that, just as they all would be, all the boys who had come over here so confident and sure, altered for ever by what they had seen and suffered. But if he had not volunteered he would never have flown, and flying was what he was born to do. And he would not have met Madeleine or Dave. Once the war was over he intended to stay in the air force; it really was his life, he knew it was.

That night in the mess they told the usual round of stories about the day's exploits. Charles recounted how he had sat in the field for two hours waiting for the vehicle from the Depot to come and pick him up and chatting to a pretty mademoiselle who offered him some fresh eggs.

'Is that all she offered you?'

Charles rolled his eyes and grinned. 'Wouldn't tell you lot in any case, but let it be said I'm going back down there as soon as I can.'

His friends whistled and hooted.

Charles also confirmed that the enemy Albatros Harry had hit had gone down, which brought his score of 'victories', as they called them, to ten.

'Good on you,' Paul Quinn said with his arm around Harry's shoulders. 'I'll have to work hard to keep you at bay.'

Harry gave a modest smile. 'Reckon you're too far in front, old son.'

Paul laughed smugly. 'Yeah, on second thoughts reckon I am.'

The day before Paul had been notified he had been awarded

the DSC and they had all celebrated. Now Harry quipped back, 'Your DSC's going to your head.'

Paul laughed and threw a punch at Harry's shoulder; to which Harry replied by grabbing him in a wrestling hold. The two young men grappled and staggered sideways into a table and the pile of metal trays upon it clattered to the floor. This started the whole mess off and men jumped to their feet as it turned into a free-for-all. Chairs were pitched and cups and glasses crashed to the floor. The flowering plant which lived beside the front door was hurled sideways and the soil spilled out all over the place. The stewards ran to save anything they could from annihilation as yelling and shouting erupted from the billiard table to the bar. Even the 'old man' of the mess, Henry Booker, a thirty-year-old New Zealander, plunged into the fray. Legs and arms, caps and even boots were flung up in the air as the young men dived on top of the mêlée and right in the thick of it were Harry, Paul and Charles.

The turbulent outburst lasted a good five minutes and finally, as all breakable things had either been saved by the stewards or lay smashed on the floor, the scene calmed and the airmen quietened down until they were all sitting on the floor panting and laughing. Then someone began singing 'Mademoiselle From Armentieres' and the Nissen hut mess rang and shook with the hearty sounds of the sheer exuberance of youth.

> Mademoiselle from Armentieres parlez vous,
> Mademoiselle from Armentieres parlez vous,
> Mademoiselle from Armentieres
> Hasn't been kissed for forty years
> Inky Pinky parlez vous.

The long-suffering stewards, who witnessed this behaviour occasionally, shook their heads good-naturedly, for when all was considered these boys could be dead tomorrow. Such outbreaks they accepted.

It was not ten minutes after the free-for-all when an air-raid siren sounded and the lights were doused. Through the windows a couple of German Gothas were shown up by searchlights as they buzzed across the aerodrome, but no bombs were dropped.

As those in the mess gave various opinions on what should have been done and how quickly they could have got up into the air to confront them, Harry turned to Charles and Paul. 'That's it for me for tonight. Got to write some letters.'

Back in his Nissen hut he sat down to write to Madeleine. About a week earlier he had finally told his father about her. He had written:

I haven't told you before but I met a girl last year called Madeleine Baudet. We met in Albert when I passed through there with Dave and Curly on a weekend leave. Dad, I reckon I'm in love with her. She gave me a gold cross on a chain and I wear it all the time. I know when you meet her you'll think she is a little ripper, just like I do. I can hear you saying I'm a bit young for this sort of thing, and when we studied *Romeo and Juliet* at school I thought he was a bit of a gawk, but now I know how he felt. Madeleine is my Juliet. She's like a tender breeze wafting acoss my mind all the time. Don't tell Mum yet. I'll break it to her gently.

Harry knew his father would understand and he believed in time, his mother would come round. Especially when she met Madeleine.

Harry took out his pen and ink and began his letter: *Ma Chérie Madeleine*. She had moved to Amiens and lived with her aunt now. She, her mother and grandmother had been evacuated from Albert when the Germans took the town in their offensive of the spring.

When he completed this letter he wrote to Dave and recounted his day's adventures. As he did so, at his small writing desk beside his bunk, forty miles to the south beyond Amiens at Brigade Headquarters near the village of Boves, Dave himself was going over the following morning's plans with Tommy Hardcastle.

For the previous thirty-six hours the two men had accompanied John Conrad into the front line. As ever John Conrad felt the need to let his men know he was conscious of their situation and the positive response he received heartened him and maintained his point of view.

'So,' Tommy rested back on the bonnet of the armoured car, 'I've just received news that we're to be at tomorrow's meeting by O nine hundred. What time should we leave here?'

The destination was five miles north of Amiens, where, since the end of May, the Australian High Commander, General John Monash, had sited the headquarters of the Australian Army Corps, an incorporation of all five Australian Divisions.

Dave calculated his reply to Tommy's question. 'Well, sir, it depends on the congestion of the roads but I think we should leave at O six hundred, just in case.'

'Right, we'll see you then,' and Tommy swung his body off the car and walked away. Two minutes later he was knocking on his commander's door.

John Conrad lifted his gaze from his papers. By the strong evening light he sat preparing for a summit meeting with General Monash and his Chief of Staff, General Blaimey along with other high command. He thought General Haig would also be there for, while it was yet a secret, they were planning a massive offensive to be mounted on Thursday, 8 August, which the allies were hoping would bring about the end of the war.

After the revolution in Russia and the downfall of the Tsar, Bolshevik Russia had made peace with Germany at Brest-Litovsk in the previous December. Since that time the Germans had thrown all their weight at the British, French and Dominion forces on the Western Front, but the Allies, even with a diminished number of divisions – because of the demands of the Italian Front – had held. Nevertheless the cost had been horrendous with the loss of half a million lives on each side since March when the huge German spring offensive had begun.

Added to the expensive battles of the previous year, like the muddy hell of Passchendaele, in Third Ypres, the morale of the British and Dominion troops had suffered and that was why John Conrad visited all his companies so the men could see him in person, speak to him and relate to him. There had been outright mutinies in the French army, and privately John Conrad held the view that it was a miracle the mutinies had not spread to their own forces.

As Tommy entered John Conrad dismissed his thoughts and

cast his gaze to his senior staff officer. 'Yes m'boy?' As he said it he smiled to himself for it was the exact way K used to address him, and as the time passed he knew he held a similar attitude to Tommy Hardcastle that K had to himself.

Tom, who was his aide-de-camp and staff officer, placed a paper down on the desk. 'Telephone message from General Monash's ADC. The meeting tomorrow is put forward to O nine hundred; seems Haig is coming and needs a little more time to get there.'

'Right.' John Conrad pointed out the window at a biplane De Havilland two-seater aeroplane flying by. 'You know, Tom, in years to come I think we'll be going to meetings in those things instead of by land and sea.'

Tommy nodded. 'I'd say that's right. They're here to stay.'

When Tom left, John Conrad finished compiling his papers for the following day and then took out a letter he had received the day before. It was from Aunt Leigh in Brisbane. He could visualise Aunt Leigh with her pen and ink, sitting in the big homely kitchen, a 'cuppa' at her side. The letter was filled with her homilies and ended with:

Bart came home on leave last week. 'To see him was ever a delight.' He still trains recruits but he says there are fewer and fewer volunteering all the time. His fiancée, Marietta, comes to visit me almost every day. Your father sends his love, and says to tell you the breweries are doing very well. I think of you all over there and I pray each day for the Kaiser's downfall.

Keep faith in your heart, dear nephew, and ever remember the line from *Measure for Measure*: Virtue is bold and Goodness never Fearful.

Your loving Aunt Leigh

He did not wish to argue with the Bard but the last sentence had irritated him. How easy for his aunt to quote such a damn silly thing! It probably sounded appropriate enough to her, thirteen thousand miles from the reality of the war, but he was incensed. Had his aunt but spent a minute in no-man's-land or heard a single explosion which blocked the senses and numbed the brain, or seen one overladen horse disappearing as it suffocated in the viscid mud, or witnessed one rotting dead body, or a gassed man coughing up the mucous membranes of his lungs, then she would know that Virtue and Goodness did not come into the question at all. And if they ever had, Virtue would be timid and Goodness abjectly bloody terrified.

He stood and moved to the window where a convoy of horses pulling 15-pounder field guns crossed his vision. He knew it was impossible for his aunt to have any idea of how things were, and he supposed, after all, he was glad she did not have to realise the truth, or to experience any of it.

The following morning as the golden haze of light revealed another day on the Western Front, they left early for Corps HQ. Dave made good time at the wheel of the armoured car and when John Conrad arrived early he was led into the fifty-foot long ballroom where the conference of the High Command would take place.

An hour later Haig sat in their midst. 'Gentlemen, we are here to discuss the Allied Advance on the eighth of August.'

While the generals were in deep discussion Harry was sent on a special mission. Squadron Commander Shaw told him, 'There's been an enemy Aviatik seen a long way in on our side of the lines. Find it if you can, Craken, and bring it down.'

Greaser started the propeller on *Cedar Grove* and then jumped aside and waved as Harry sped along the airfield. It was a warm summer day of sunshine and rolling cloud, and Harry set off and climbed quickly to 10,000 feet. He headed north, thrilling to the mighty speed of 114 miles an hour but he saw nothing so turned east and as he came thundering out of a cloud he noted the gleam of an aircraft in the distance. He chased it in and out of clouds but did not gain on it and eventually lost it so he turned south, and suddenly he heard a spatter of bullets. Looking back, he saw, not the Aviatik, but a German Fokker D V11 on his tail. He thought he might have been hit on the right wing and banked steeply and entered a cloud. When he reappeared the German was in front of him so this time he let off a few rounds of his own at the Fokker.

They both entered cloud again and on breaking out into the blue Harry looked all round but there was no sign of the Fokker. He continued his search, soaring south but saw nothing else. He knew he was getting low on fuel and would not make it back to St-Pol so he descended to 1,000 feet, looking for a suitable field in which to land. He was aware he was well on the allied side of the line, which was his main concern. As his eyes roved the ground, in the distance, over trees and hedges, he saw a farm and a château and not far from it an aerodrome. He headed for the airfield and at about two hundred feet from the ground the engine gave out. Handling it deftly, he took *Cedar Grove* into a glide and, keeping it steady, coasted down to land.

'Where am I?' he asked the man who came running across from a Nissen hut surrounded by a tent camp.

'Bertangles.' He pointed to a stately château. 'That's AIF HQ.'

'I ran out of juice,' Harry explained as he clambered out. 'Can you fill her up, then I can get back to St-Pol?'

'Reckon I can arrange a requisition, but it'll take a while, you know.'

'That's all right. I'll go for a walk over to the château. Ah, have you got a field telephone so I can call my base?'

The man pointed to the Nissen hut.

'And check my right wing, will you? I think I might have taken a hit.'

After Harry had advised St-Pol that he was alive and merely delayed, he strode across the airfield. Some of the cloud had disappeared, dispersed by a warm wind. The crisp air smelt of summer and not of war, and as Harry passed along a lane bordered by flowered hedgerows he picked a dog rose and in youthful excess of enthusiasm threw it high in the air and ran forward and caught it. He passed a small cemetery and glanced towards it; little did he know that three months earlier the German air ace von Richthofen had been buried there. Perhaps if he had he would have paused, for most pilots knew him well, though Harry's hero was Lieutenant MacLaren of 46 Squadron, who had forty-eight victories to his count. Everybody said MacLaren *was* his aircraft.

He passed the farm buildings he had seen from the air and was halted twice by sentries, and on both occasions by showing his papers and explaining himself he was given permission to pass. But he was not allowed through the two tall pillars on either side of the large open ornamental gate at the front of the château proper. In the forecourt of the grand building soldiers moved about between trucks and lorries, horses and carts. Along under a row of trees stood a line of a dozen or so captured German guns.

Harry was peering in through the gates when he recognised the driver of an armoured car parked some yards inside the forecourt. 'Dave! Dave!' he shouted waving his arms.

Two seconds later Dave was out of the vehicle, and charging through the open gates folded Harry in his arms.

'Gawd, mate. It's you, it's really you.'

'Too right, old son.'

'What are you doing here?'

'Ran out of juice chasing a Hun. They're refuelling me over at the airfield. What are you doing here?'

'Waiting for Uncle John Conrad, he's inside with General Monash. This is the AIF Army Corps Headquarters. He'll be out soon, I reckon, been in there eight hours already.'

They found a spot under a cluster of yew trees outside the huge ornate main gate with the car in their view, and they talked and laughed and forgot briefly about the war.

Harry picked a straw of grass and lay back and chewed on it as Dave did the same. If the eye could have transported them in time and place they were a perfect double for the real father of one and the uncle of the other on the bank of the Brisbane River a generation before.

Harry wagged his finger in the air. 'You remember Madeleine?'

Dave gave him a long-suffering look. 'How can I forget her? Your letters are full of the girl.'

Harry grinned sheepishly. 'Yes, suppose they are. Well, she's living in Amiens now.'

'Really?'

'Moved when the Germans advanced. Do you get into Amiens much?'

Dave shrugged. 'Now and then. Was there all the time a few months back, because our headquarters were there, but we're just south now near Boves, in another château.' He gestured through the gates. 'Not quite as spectacular as this one . . . but we call it home.'

They both laughed and Harry held his stem of grass between

his teeth as he took a pen and paper out of his leather jerkin pocket. 'This is Madeleine's address. If you get to Amiens again go and see her. She often asks about you. I've been to see her six times in the nine months I've been back in France.' His eyes brightened. 'With a bit of luck I think I might get to visit her again next week. Can't wait. Gosh, I'm in love with that girl.'

As he took the paper Dave slapped Harry across the shoulder. 'Yes. I know.' He rolled over and lay on his back. 'How's your mother?'

'Mum's in Doullens now at the base hospital. They evacuated them in March in the German advance. How's yours?'

'Good. She's so proud of Tess because she's helping Miss Howard, the lady who used to teach us. Tess's getting a salary and all, working three days a week. That's pretty good, you know?'

'That's better than good, that's great.'

'Apparently Jenny married that bloke she ran off with, so Mum's resigned to that now, but she's really pleased Tess's *making something of herself*. At least that's how Mum puts it.'

'So are you.'

'You reckon? Well, I've got a bit of catching up on you to do, *Flight Lieutenant*. I noticed in your last letter you've dropped the *Sub* part.'

'True. Fact is, old son, I think they've promoted me because I've shot down ten enemy aircraft, all verified *victories*, as we call them. They probably find me useful.'

Dave's eyes widened. 'Wow. That's been one a month. That must be a high average.'

'Yes, I suppose. But a bloke called Paul Quinn's got the highest score in our squadron.' He looked out towards the green fields in the distance. 'You know, when you're up in the sky, you can't think of the enemy as men. The minute you do that they reckon you lose your nerve.'

This thought brought a brief silence until Harry shrugged and turned to his friend. 'Gosh I love flying, old son. I've decided I'll stay in the air force after the war.'

Dave eyed him. 'You must really be crazy about it to think like that.'

'I am.' Then he wagged his finger at his friend. 'Do you reckon you'll still get that leave we're supposed to spend together?'

Dave looked uncertain. 'I don't know but I sure do hope so.'

'Hey, we might be able to get Madeleine to come along.'

Dave screwed up his face. 'Oh Gawd, that means you'll be mooning and cow-eyed over her all the time.'

Harry mock-punched him. 'You're jealous.'

'Oh yeah? Never . . . Girls aren't for me. I'm too sensible.'

This made Harry laugh and when he settled and they lay back looking at the sky, Dave became serious. 'You know, when I left the battalion to drive for my uncle, it was funny saying goodbye to Bingo and Dobb – well, Bingo most of all, I suppose. I'd been with him since we were shipped out of Sydney. He just stood there looking at me with his red beard thrust forward, puffing on his pipe, and the last thing he said was, "I've been in the army twenty-seven years, lad. I've seen good soldiers and bad, and good men and bad." Then he winked at me and added, "Your category's good on both counts."' Dave turned round and his eyes were watery. 'You know, Harry, that meant a hell of a lot to me.'

Harry cuffed his friend affectionately on the shoulder. 'Yeah, Bingo's no fool.' He made a reflective sound. 'Do you ever think of Isaac and Frank . . . and Luke?'

'Yeah, I miss them all; especially Isaac. You know he was going to teach me some Shakespeare. And I miss Curly, though I'm glad he's out of it . . . lucky bugger!'

'Yes.'

About fifteen minutes later Harry stood up. 'Better get back to the airfield. They'll have filled my tank by now.'

Dave eyed Harry. 'And I miss you too, mate.'

'And I miss you, old son. When this bloody stunt's over we'll have some mighty good times together.'

'Too right.' Dave held out his hand and Harry shook it. 'I'm looking forward to that.'

As the youths separated and Harry moved off, Dave noticed John Conrad and Major Hardcastle arrive on the steps of the château with General John Monash. The lieutenant general in command of the Australian Corps was a slender man with pleasant features and a determined expression under a dark moustache and a fortnight later he was to be knighted by King George V in exactly the same spot he now stood farewelling John Conrad.

Dave moved smartly across to wait beside the armoured car as the corps commander and the brigadier separated and Monash turned and moved back into the château.

When John Conrad arrived at the armoured car he pointed to the distant figure who had now halted and lifted his hand to them. 'Who was that?'

'My friend, Harry Craken.'

A look of disappointment passed across John Conrad's face. It was so fleeting that Dave and Tommy wondered if in truth they had seen it.

'What was he doing here?'

'He ran out of fuel chasing a Hun. Saw the airfield and landed. They're filling up his tank.'

'How long has he been back in France?'

'About nine or ten months.'

'Where's he stationed?'

'In St-Pol.'

John Conrad partially raised his hand in a strange gesture as if to wave at the boy in the distance. 'It would have been good to see him.' He turned quickly to Tom. 'Especially for you . . . as you recommended him for the transfer.'

Tommy smiled. 'Yes, I like that kid a lot.'

And in a statement that took both listeners slightly aback John Conrad said quietly, 'Yes, so do I.'

Harry had seen the brigadier halt on the steps and then descend and cross to Dave and he had surprised himself by waiting and waving as much to the commander, as to his mate. Then he had turned and trotted back down the lane to the airfield, wondering why he had done such a thing.

In fifteen minutes he was up in the air. He flew with a grace that many of his comrades secretly admired and he felt powerful and sublime up there, unfettered high above the world with the unlimited wind of the universe on his face.

He thought about Dave working for the brigadier. Yes, after all, the brigadier was all right. He owed him his life and there was something about him that Harry could not help but like, *really* like, something in his eyes and his smile, almost confidential, though he would never admit it to his father.

He looked around, back and front, but he was alone with the wind and the sky, sailing along at 115 miles an hour.

His mind turned to Madeleine. How dearly he loved her. The last time he had seen her in Amiens, his arrival had been unannounced and she had been home in the house in the Rue D'Or all alone. *The Street of Gold* . . . how appropriate that name was. Without the curbing influence of her mother or grandmother their feelings had overcome them and their sweet kisses had turned to passion. She had called him 'My *Australien*,' and taken him from the parlour with the lace on the windows and the velvet on the sofa and led him by the hand up the carpeted stairs to her room.

She had turned the key in the lock and faced round to him.

They lay on the flowered counterpane in the afternoon breeze as it lifted the net curtain at the wide windows, and for the first time they explored the exquisite emotion of loving. They could hear the sounds of the guns in the distance, for the Germans were again threatening the city. Their inexpert fingers had fumbled with her buttons and ties on her dress. She had laughed with a tender grace and he had removed his own clothes and sat wide-eyed, looking at the beauty of her. She had smiled with delight to see the cross hanging round his neck and she had taken it tenderly in her hands and brushed it with her lips.

She was slender like a reed and he had watched the gentle flush on her neck rise into her pale cheeks as he stroked them. He untied the ribbon and her waves of brown hair had tumbled over her bare shoulders down to her pert round breasts as he cupped them in his hands. Shyly she had leaned in and kissed his eyes and his face and stroked his body until he filled with pleasure. He sat gazing at her and touched the fair skin of her body and slid his fingers along her buttocks and had been in awe of the beauty and gentle lines of her.

She had edged across the counterpane and he moved into her embrace and kissed her mouth. He had felt unsure, for it was his first time and he had not wanted to appear unskilful, but he knew she too was uncertain, and yet she whispered her love for him and drew him down upon her until he moved more surely between her small firm thighs. She did not cry out but merely moaned and smiled as she gave herself to him. Her lips trailed across his face and down the skin of his neck to rest upon his shoulder and he had trembled with the delight of loving her.

'*Mon cher, mon cher.*' She had brought her lips back to touch upon his eyes and told him, '*Je t'aime* . . . forever . . . 'Arry.'

Her imaginary kisses were on his lips now and in the heady excitement and glee of the moment he opened his mouth to burst into song when abruptly he felt a violent thrust from behind and he shot forward as if he had been slammed in the back with an axe. In that moment the engine stalled and he heard the spit of the bullets that thudded into the plane all around him. Looking down he saw petrol pouring out across the cockpit floor and as the Albatros D that had hit him shot by on his right, followed by two more, he attempted to gain control of his aircraft and effect a slow glide to take himself down to the ground.

Blood was gushing from somewhere and covering the front of his clothes and soaking his pants, and he thought he was going to faint. He must not give in and he pushed his head out of the cockpit to try to revive himself in the onslaught of the wind. Drifting in and out of consciousness he tried with all his might to hold the aircraft steady as it attempted to go into a dive. He fought for control as he came closer and closer to the tree tops and the ground rushed by. In the last second the tree tops gave way to a field right in front of him and as his wheels touched the undulating ground he realised there were flames to his right somewhere. The aeroplane jumped and skidded to a halt beneath him and as he battled back from drifting down into the tunnel of black that menaced him he heard voices speaking in French and realised there were hands upon him and that they lifted and carried him from the aircraft.

He felt cold, chilled to the bone and looked up into a sea of faces. What was his mother doing here, bending down and kissing him? And where had Jane and Knobby and his sister Katy and Luke come from? Why were Madeleine and Dave leaning in towards him? He tried to lift his hand to them but they faded away, and to his amazement they were replaced by the brigadier and his father hovering above him. Side by side they came closer and closer, their faces filling his vision as they bent down to him together. He felt their strong hands upon him and they took him up tenderly in their arms.

Harry was so pleased to see them. The cold had gone and now, instead, he felt cosy and secure. He was comfortable and warm in the arms of the two men, the brigadier and his father, so comfortable and warm that he smiled at them as the black pit that had threatened, opened up and consumed him.

Chapter Forty-seven

Matthew pushed himself deftly on his gunmetal cane up the steps and into the château near Boves, being careful where he placed his feet as it was raining heavily. He passed the sentry at the door and took off his oilskin coat and hung it over a hook on the wall.

He had arrived at the château at 1900 after a day sketching out in the field with Cliff and Bert. When the downpour began it had been too far to go back to his battalion HQ near the Somme River, so they had come to Brigade Headquarters.

The quartermaster had informed him their billets tonight would have to be in tents, that's all that could be found. It would be a bit awkward because of the rain, but he did not mind for it was the height of summer, hence his leg was at its best. The only matter to be attended to was his avoidance of the brigadier.

He knew that Fleet had been away the previous day and was in residence tonight. He had been given the information by Lieutenant Colonel Cox, whom he had run into leaving the quartermaster. Matt knew that as a rule Fleet did not go to the mess to eat, but took his meal in his quarters with his staff officer, Tom Hardcastle, and only turned up in the mess for one drink before bedtime. The word was that Hardcastle, who had been a heavy drinker in previous times, regulated himself these days. Thus Matt decided if he went and ate in the mess and was out before 2300, chances were he would not run into either of them.

His belief was shattered as he made his way along the corridor to the mess: Tommy Hardcastle was coming the other way.

They met eyes. 'Afternoon, Major.'

'Afternoon, Major.'

As Matt moved by he was actually pleased he had come

across Hardcastle for the man was sure to tell Fleet and that way they would both be attempting to avoid each other.

Matt wandered into the mess and up to the bar.

Tommy passed Matthew and headed to the Signals, Wireless and Communications room. He would alert the brigadier that Craken was in the château.

Tom had been aware of the bad blood between the two men since that evening nearly two years ago in the Somme Valley when young Harry Craken in company with Dave Sands had fallen over the tent posts. And when Major Craken had been assigned to the 16th Battalion it was obvious they avoided each other. They had seen less of Craken since the brigadier had been promoted, but he did come by from time-to-time with his lorry full of his painting materials and set up with them for a day or two.

The brigadier made mention of Craken once or twice, just enough for Tom to know that long ago Craken had been involved in the death of John Conrad Fleet's sister and the hatred had begun there. Then one night during the Battle of Messines Ridge the brigadier spoke of Craken's wife as being at one time *so special I would have married her*, and since then Tommy saw that the relationship between the two men was much more convoluted than he could have suspected.

He entered the Communications room where the three signallers on duty, Sergeant 'Sparks' Higgins, a corporal and a private, sat surrounded by signal wires, field telephones, wireless and morse code equipment. Tommy squeezed into a chair to go through the messages he wished to send out when the bell on one of the field telephones rang.

Higgins answered it. 'Yes, this is HQ . . . Yes, St-Pol, I can hear you. Wanting who? Say that again. No, he isn't here. Not that I know of. Just a minute.' He stood and crossed to a list attached to the wall. Ran his finger down and returned to the telephone. 'Yes he's one of ours. He's attached to the AIF's 16th Battalion . . . Roger. Going off line.' Higgins hung up the receiver and wrote something down.

Tom turned to him. 'What did St-Pol want? That's an aerodrome, isn't it, Sparks?'

Higgins nodded. 'It was the squadron commander. Wanted

to speak to some Major Craken. I've never heard of 'im.' He pointed to the list on the wall. 'But he's with the 16th.'

Tom nodded. 'That's right, but fact is he's here. I just saw him on his way to the mess, I think.'

Higgins turned to the signalman. 'Up you go, Barnes, bring the major down.'

'Righto, Sarge.'

When Matt had entered the mess he crossed straight over to the bar.

'What'll it be, Major? I've got whisky, rum or gin. And we've even come across a few bottles of champagne down in the château cellar.'

Matt took a moment to decide. 'I'll start with a gin.'

The steward handed him the glass and he wandered by a few officers and found a table near a window. He sat looking out through the rain to the fields behind the château where lightning was visible on the horizon.

A couple of tables away sat two captains. One was Menzies Lang and the other was a fellow called Preston. Matt could hear their conversation quite clearly. They were discussing the possibility of a huge allied offensive.

'It's practically official now,' Lang said, 'the brigadier and Hardcastle went to Bertangles yesterday. Whisper was that Haig was there.'

Preston shook his head. 'I don't know. We haven't been brought into it yet.'

'We will be. And my guess is tomorrow.'

Matthew coughed and they both looked round. And with a condescending smile verging on a sneer Matt pointed with his cane to the sign above their heads and remarked *sotto voce*, 'Not that it's of any great consequence to me, who's merely a painter expressing what he sees, but you gentlemen must believe that message is for others and excludes yourselves.'

They both looked up at the sign above them: 'Loose talk can reach the Ears of the Enemy, Even from this Mess.'

Lang turned red and Preston mumbled something about 'honorary officers' but they altered the topic fast enough and Matt returned to his musings. If there were to be another offensive he certainly hoped it would bring about the end of the war. They would have to stop the bloody fighting soon or both sides would run out of men to kill.

He had just finished his gin and was about to call for another when he saw a private enter and speak to the steward. The steward nodded and came over to Matt.

'Major Craken. Could you go with the signalman please? Seems there's a telephone call of some kind for you from St-Pol.'

An officer near the door saluted as Matt rose and followed the private down the stairs. He wondered what the devil St-Pol wanted. He had painted a series of pictures, *Aerodromes of the Western Front*, and the Squadron Commander of St-Pol had been been mad keen to have his portrait done. But surely he would not use up a field telephone call on such a thing. There was a war on.

As he entered the communications room Tom looked up from his papers. 'St-Pol called for you. Sparks is getting them back.'

'Right.'

Sparks had raised St-Pol again and he handed the receiver to Matthew.

'Major Craken speaking.'

Tommy attempted not to listen but it was impossible.

Matt's voice altered altogether. He spoke in a monotone devoid of emotion. 'Yes. I see. How? . . . Where is he? . . . I would appreciate that . . . Yes, I'll be there. O ten hundred hours unless something unforeseen . . . Yes, I have that. Goodbye . . .' He handed the receiver to Sparks who took it silently.

Matthew's face was rigid. He did not speak to anyone in the room. He looked through Tommy, turned sharply on his cane and moved to the door.

Outside he passed along the corridor, the gunmetal cane clicking ominously beside him with each step, until he reached the foyer at the bottom of the staircase. But he did not go up; he could not return to the mess. He saw through the tall windows that it was still raining heavily and he moved across to one and stood looking out on the lorries and vehicles with the rain splashing upon them.

He was my pride and my joy.

His bad leg began aching and he lifted his foot on to a rail that ran across the bottom of the glass. He stood there leaning on his cane for a long time as soldiers passed back and forth behind him. Someone lit a lantern on a table nearby as finally the light faded into the night. Then he heard a voice behind him.

'Craken?'

He turned his head to see John Conrad standing beside him. The man looked as if he had seen Banquo's ghost. A flicker of the old spark rose in Matt as he said, 'You look odd. Am I still affecting you that badly?'

'I know about Harry.'

'Do you?'

'Major Hardcastle told me what he had overheard, so I telephoned Commander Briggs of 22 Squadron. He informed me.'

Matthew exhaled loudly. 'They're burying him on Thursday. Cemetery near the aerodrome.'

'Yes. Would you mind if I came along?'

Matthew found John Conrad's eyes in the lantern light.

'Why would you want to be there?'

John Conrad did not answer but there was that in his face that told Matt many things.

Matt drew his fingers across his scar but his eyes did not leave his old enemy's. 'You know, don't you?'

'Yes, I know.'

A flicker of anger rose in Matthew. 'Caro . . .'

'It was not Caro.'

'Who then?'

'No one. For heaven's sake, man, he was one of my soldiers. There was a day when I simply looked at Harry; met his eyes and saw him clearly, saw who he truly was. Just like that. I knew.'

Matt's shoulders sank.

Four soldiers passed by and saluted. John Conrad replied in a detached way and noticed more men coming along. He glanced back to Matt. 'He's a great loss . . . to both of us. Perhaps you would come to my rooms.' He gestured up the stairs.

Matt shook his head. 'I'm in no mood to socialise.'

'Not to socialise. Not to do anything. Come on.' John Conrad moved off and Matthew hung back, watching until he saw him begin to mount the stairs. Matt hesitated, shrugged despondently and followed.

In John Conrad's rooms Matthew moved across and stood by the window as the batman lit two candles and a lamp. 'Can I bring you anything, sir?'

'Bring two whiskys.' And as the soldier exited John Conrad called, 'Bring the bottle.'

There was silence until the batman had come and gone.

John Conrad strode across to the side of his old foe and stood looking out the window with him. The rain was still beating on the glass and in the insipid light cast from the lamp and the candles they could see their images mirrored side by side.

John Conrad handed across a whisky and Matthew took it and swallowed a mouthful. They remained quiet for minutes, both conscious of the fretful atmosphere between them.

Finally Matthew caught John Conrad's eyes reflected in the glass. There was another long pause before he said, 'It's possible to say I robbed you of him. And at the time I gloried in just that . . . to have your seed believing he was mine. For nineteen years I've found pleasure in that perverse predicament. And now? I'm tired of it at last. Not that it does you any good. I can hear Caro saying how typical of me it is to grow weary of the game after it's over.'

John Conrad swallowed a mouthful of his whisky.

'He gave me joy as no other has.' Matt endeavoured to smile. 'Apart from Knobby, he was my only *true* admirer. And I'm not sorry, Fleet, for in robbing you I had Harry for nineteen years.'

John Conrad's voice carried an acrid edge. 'Had I known all those years ago you wouldn't have had the chance. And yes, you robbed me, of my son and of the woman I would have made my wife. But I no longer live with regrets. And in my more rational moments I concede that you gave my son a name and the woman I loved a refuge. For whatever your disturbed bloody reasons were.'

A grating half-laughing sound escaped Matt's lips. 'Then perhaps it's time for honesty.' He paused and they remained standing at the window listening to the rain. 'I married Caro because I wanted to. *Love* is not a word I bandy about. Fact is, it's not a word I use at all. I think it should be sacred and yet it's indiscreetly hurled around the globe. But here tonight I'll face it. I married Caro because I *loved* her, that she carried your son was the ultimate prize. And that the boy turned into the sunniest and the best was the glorious, glorious bonus.'

John Conrad did not speak. He held himself in check as he took another mouthful of his whisky and stared at the water running down the outside of the window.

Matt's eyes roved across the glass of the pane until abruptly he swung round on his cane and up out of the discordant patterns of the past he hurled the words, 'And I did not kill your sister.'

There was a threat in John Conrad's blue eyes as he turned to Matt and his voice rose in rekindled anger. 'Don't open that old wound.'

But Matthew was incautious now. 'With Harry gone, it's time to open it. It's time you faced what's real. I would have married Em.'

John Conrad shook his head in disgust and moved a step away lest he did something he might be sorry for.

'You still may prefer your illusion but it's the unadulterated truth.'

'What in hell do you mean? Explain yourself or I'll not be responsible.'

Matthew leaned on his cane and with his other hand lifted his glass to his temple as if the memory hurt. 'It's true. I would have married your sister. I gave her an ultimatum. I told her to prove to me she carried my child, to grow big before my eyes, and only then would I marry her. I'd been deceived the year before, become engaged to a girl who said she was pregnant to me, and as the months passed she was still as slender as the day I met her. So with that in mind, I disbelieved Em, and in giving her the ultimatum . . . I forced her hand. And here tonight I'll say this just once: that was a profound mistake. I was *not happy* to hear of her death. Em was not a plaything, she had importance in my life. But you, Fleet, were in no mind for bloody explanations.'

The rain lashed the window and Matthew's leg throbbed and the scar on his cheek felt tight as John Conrad studied him a long time before he nodded almost imperceptibly in acceptance. 'Your words give me much to reflect upon. I knew your reputation. I was livid and acted impulsively. I thought you immoral and dissolute. And you're right, I wasn't going to listen to anything you had to say. And that, it would appear, was indeed my mistake.'

There was no sound but the water hitting the window and both men were reminded of the unbridled storm that night a quarter of a century before. John Conrad remembered his ride in the howling wind and the rain.

Matt swallowed the last of his whisky and as John Conrad lifted the bottle to pour more it clinked loudly on the edge of his old foe's glass.

Silence fell between them as both men considered all that had been said. Finally Matt spoke. 'I see you could have told Harry the truth. Why didn't you?'

'What? And have confused him and fermented more passion and bewilderment amongst us all?'

Matt cast his gaze down to his glass. 'Yes, that's undoubtedly so.' And now he spoke quietly, 'I think I felt from the day he volunteered that this was coming. I've had no time for this bloody futile war. It's an obscene blot on the history of the world, in my opinion. Harry was a mere boy attracted by the chimera that was a soldier's glory . . . a delusion. Yes, the Germans were spoiling for a fight, but this . . . God!'

'I'm a professional soldier, Craken, and I do my duty. But what you say's all true. It's been a bloody butcher's yard.' John Conrad's voice cracked with emotion as he added, 'It was a hell of a shame Harry was ever anywhere near it.'

Matt lifted his gaze. 'Yes it was. And not that I wanted to know it or hear it, but I'm aware that Harry . . . He liked you.'

John Conrad shook his head and cleared his throat. 'I saw him just before he died, it seems. In the distance at Bertangles.' His voice broke as he added, 'He waved . . . and I . . . sort of waved back.'

Neither said anything for a time and then John Conrad took another mouthful of his whisky. 'Dave Sands should be told. He's Harry's best friend.' He lifted his eyes to meet Matt's. 'Exactly like I was with Dave's uncle.' There had been the faintest hint of a challenge in his words.

Ever so slowly Matthew answered. 'Yes . . . indeed. I do remember.'

'Perhaps it's best you tell him.'

'I'll do it first thing in the morning.'

And as if they were co-ordinated, moving at the exact same moment, they turned away from each other to face again to the window where their images stood mirrored in the pane.

Matt rotated his eyes to the reflection of the man beside him. 'Fact is, Fleet. I think you should be there on Thursday when we bury him.'

John Conrad gave a thoughtful nod of his head.

They remained standing side by side, looking out into the wet inky blackness with the phantom of smiling blue-eyed Harry floating in the air.

Caro drove by the horse lines into the base hospital yard and pulled up under the portico. Across the fence beyond the animals she could see June, Carmen, Sue and Jill all hanging bedding out on the line. There had been a bad storm and it had rained heavily during the night but the sun had shone this morning and things were drying out. As the orderlies came down from the hospital verandah Caro opened the doors of the ambulance and spoke to the four soldiers she had picked up from the casualty clearing station at Bellevue. Three had shrapnel wounds and the fourth had been hit in the cheek with a bullet.

'Here we are, boys, at last. We'll soon have you taken care of.'

'Caro!'

She spun round to see Patricia beckoning her from the verandah.

Caro moved across the yard and mounted the steps. 'There's a major waiting for you. Jill said he's your husband.' Patricia pointed past the patients sitting out on the verandah in the sun. 'He's waiting down in the meadow beyond the incinerators.'

Caro's heartbeat accelerated. 'Thanks, Pat.'

She hurried along the path that led by the verandah and the brick incinerators round the small copse of sycamore trees to the meadow. There, sure enough, leaning on the bole of an oak and looking out across the green fields was her husband.

'Matt!'

He turned and rested on his cane as she ran towards him. He

studied her as she came . . . her navy-blue skirt swinging round her ankles in the long green grass and her fair hair flowing back over her shoulders under the dark cap she wore. Strange to see Caro running towards him. He did not believe he had ever seen her appear eager in the twenty years of their marriage.

When she arrived she took off the cap. Her face was glowing. 'Matthew, you've come at last.' Then she saw the set of his features and felt the tension in him. 'What's wrong?'

'Caro old girl, I'm here to tell you Harry's been shot down.'

Caro froze. She felt unsteady on her feet. 'Shot down? He's not . . . ?'

'Yes, he's dead.'

Caro's whole body sagged. Her face crumpled and she began to stammer. 'No . . . n-not . . . not my Harry. It can't be. Matt, tell me it isn't true?'

He shook his head.

'When?'

'The day before yesterday.'

'Oh God in Heaven.' Her eyes were wild and distracted like he had seen them before when she had spoken of Fleet. She brought her hands to her mouth and looked around searchingly as though she were lost. The misery in her eyes caught at his heart.

'I'm sorry, Caro.'

She thought of all the boys she had nursed, how she had tended each one as if he were Harry. And now her beautiful boy was one of them: one of the dead. She lifted her eyes to Matthew's. 'Oh God, Matt, hold me, please.'

Matthew stepped forward and took her in his arms and now she broke her heart, sobbing uncontrollably as tears flooded from her eyes and she mumbled, 'No, no,' upon his shoulder. He felt her sink in his arms as if to faint.

'Oh, Caro, Caro, I'm so sorry. My love, I'm so sorry.'

He held her as the minutes passed and as he stroked her hair and whispered to pacify her, tears broke at last from his own eyes and slipped down into her curls.

It was a long time before she calmed and when she did she still shuddered with the aftermath of such emotion, but she did not leave his arms.

Finally he moved her back and gazed in her face. 'They're burying him tomorrow in a cemetery near St-Pol. We'll drive up in my lorry. Who do I need to see to arrange your time away from here?'

'Captain Cadee.'

He tucked her hand inside his arm and gently moved forward with her. 'We'll go to him now together.'

She let him lead her across the emerald meadow along the path and back to the hospital. Somewhere she could hear a lark singing. Why did it sing?

His cane tapped on the wide stone steps as they mounted to the verandah where she paused. 'I feel numb.'

'Lean on me,' he said, and she did.

Inside they moved down a dim corridor until Caro pointed to the RAMC officer's room and Matthew knocked upon the door. There was no one inside but the door was unlatched so Matt took her in and sat her down. He touched her on the shoulder. 'Wait here. I shall get you some water, then I'll find Cadee.'

As he closed the door he saw her hunch forward and hold herself tightly. She was still sitting that way when he returned. She drank the water.

'Now I'll find Cadee. Stay here.'

The first person he saw when he closed the door was Jill. She came up to him expectantly. 'Major Craken, can I help you?'

Matt eyed her. 'Yes, you can find Captain Cadee for me.'

'Oh, he's down talking to the orderlies in Ward 4.' She pointed through an archway. 'On the left through there.' Then she looked past him. 'Where's Caro?'

Matthew held up his hand. 'I suggest, strongly, that you leave my wife alone. She's in Captain Cadee's office where she will stay until I return. I hope you understand?'

Jill looked taken aback. 'Oh, all right. Certainly,' and she spun round and walked away.

Matthew had soon located the captain and explained the situation. The jovial man's brows drew together in concern. 'I'm deeply sorry, Major. Of course your wife can go. Take her away. We'll miss her for she's a wonderful woman. Does the work of three.' He held out his hand. 'And please accept my deepest condolences.'

Matthew shook the extended hand. 'Thank you. The funeral's tomorrow.'

He returned and opened the officer's door. Caro looked up. She had been crying again. 'I just can't help it, Matt. I'll try and buck up now.'

Matt shook his head, came forward and knelt down beside her. 'You don't have to, old girl. Just do as you please.' Then he took hold of her hand. 'Cadee's a good sort. He's given you as much time off as you like.'

She looked in his eyes as he knelt in front of her. 'You're being very kind, for I know your heart is aching too.'

'Never thought of myself as *kind*, Caro. But if you say so.'

She endeavoured a weary smile. 'What do we do now?'

He lifted her to her feet as he answered, 'We go for a walk through this French town and we ignore the soldiers and the amunition trucks and the movement of artillery and all the signs of war. We drink coffee in some café and we walk on down a lane to the fields and pick flowers and we talk, and we grieve together for our boy. For you're right, Caro. My heart too is broken.'

She lifted her hand and touched him on the cheek, moving her fingers across his scar. 'Oh, Matthew, I know how he adored you. I see everything so much more clearly these days. How sad it is that it takes us so long to interpret truth.'

Once more he tucked her hand in his arm and took her out along the dim corridor to the yard and into the street.

They did just as he had foreseen, and two hours later in a flowered lane he picked poppies for her and talked about the summer light as it danced in sunbeams through the dappled trees.

'You always notice the light, don't you, Matt? It's the painter's eye, isn't it?'

He nodded. 'I suppose so.' And he took her hand and led her over a stile and they sat on the massive roots of a great elm and Caro insisted on talking about Harry, and she sobbed and Matt held her hand and listened.

'I remember his first teeth, little white pegs. You know, Matt, when I was carrying him I used to talk to my stomach every day – fact is I did that with both of them – but with Harry it was all so new. Remember when I used to walk every morning up at Cedar Grove while you, the night owl, were still sleeping. Well, I would sing to him all the songs I knew, all the way; all through the walk.'

Matt smiled sadly. 'I never knew.'

'You were always asleep.'

'And remember his third birthday? When you and Knobby brought him home a saddle and I was shocked at such a gift for a tiny tot.'

'He learned to ride beautifully, though, didn't he?'

And she closed her eyes with the memory and admitted that he did. And then she could not help it, she began to sob again and when she quietened she said, 'I know his is only one death amongst millions, but the millions were not in my heart.'

And Matt patted her on the back and whispered, 'He was your son, you have the right to mourn.' He looked up at the blue sky and thought of Harry's eyes. 'I think I had that kid sitting on every bar in Brisbane, laughing at Knob and me. You know he never once admonished me for a damn thing. Fancy any kid thinking I was perfect. Amazing.'

'He adored you.' She said it without rancour, when once she would have been jealous of the fact. 'All I ever did was upset him, the way I smothered him with love.'

Matt shook his head. 'No, Caro, don't say that. You were the best of mothers.'

She looked straight in his eyes. 'And it appears, that you, Matthew, were the best of fathers – that is, taking Harry's point of view, and that's the only one that mattered.'

He felt uncomfortable with this approval from Caro. He did not reply.

And she held her head in her hands and thought of all those others who loved him. 'Matthew, we have so many people to tell: Knobby and Jane and my parents and your mother and Matilda. And how will little Katy take it, losing her big brother?'

Matt leant forward, his hands on her knees, and looked her straight in the eye. 'Caro, perhaps it's time to think of going home to your daughter. I'm not denying you've done your bit – even Cadee said you were worth three – but there's naught to keep you in France now. Surely?'

She gave him an odd look and sighed. 'Perhaps you're right.'

They heard an aeroplane overhead and, looking up, saw two Nieuports sweeping across the sky. Caro's eyes filled with tears again and she sniffed as she spoke. 'Every time I heard an aeroplane I thought of him. Don't see how I'll ever be able to see one again without crying.'

When they left the field and returned to the little town, they bought a meal in a canteen filled with soldiers. They sat in a cramped wooden booth with blue paint peeling off the wall above their heads. Caro just picked at her food and Matt gently chided and forced her to eat a little.

The proprietor brought a single candle in an earthenware holder, for it was getting late and the light was going. Matt looked in the flame of the candle and it was then he told her of Madeleine.

'It seems Harry met a girl called Madeleine, a girl he was more than fond of.'

Caro was surprised. 'How do you know?'

'I received a letter from him. It arrived this morning before I left to come here.'

Caro's face blanched. 'Oh, Matt, and he died the day before yesterday.'

'Yes. Strange. The girl lives in Amiens. I spoke to Dave Sands, Harry's best friend, about it this morning.'

In Matt's mind he saw Dave. He had gone to Dave's quarters at 0600 before he left to drive north to Doullens. Dave had taken the news badly. He had wrung his hands and shuffled his feet and looked up to the sky. 'Gawd, that means I was with him just before he died. We laughed and talked and – Oh hell, no. Not Harry too.' His dark eyes filled with tears. 'He was my best friend. We had something . . . I can't explain it, sir. I've never felt close to a bloke like I did to him. Comfortable, sort of right. I really thought we'd both get through this stunt. I really did.' He looked away. 'I've lost so many blokes I cared about and now I've lost him too.' Then Dave had wiped his eyes and held out his hand and said, 'Major Craken, forgive me for thinking of myself. I'm so sorry. I know you must be taking it real hard.'

And Matthew had done something entirely out of character.

He had stepped forward and hugged Dave quite fiercely. 'Don't be a stranger, Dave, once we're home in Australia and this whole bloody mess is over.'

And Dave had blinked through his tears. 'I won't, sir, I promise.'

'I believe there's a girl who lives in Amiens. A girl called Madeleine.'

Dave had sighed. 'Yes, sir. Harry was really keen on her. Said he was in love and I reckon he was. She gave him a gold cross. He wore it all the time around his neck on a chain.'

'Do you know exactly where she lives?'

And Dave had given him the address.

Now Matt took his eyes from the candle flame as Caro asked, 'Is Dave the Aboriginal boy?'

'Yes.'

'Harry wrote to me about him; they were very close. What did he say about the girl?'

'That Harry was in love with her.'

Caro shook her head. 'But he was just a boy.'

'Caro, Caro . . . he was old enough.'

She hesitated and looked at the palms of her hands. 'Perhaps.'

They walked back through the darkened streets together with the sounds of war in the distance. They were both silent, both with their thoughts. Caro's hand rested on his arm. They came into the hospital yard and halted near the steps where he removed her hand from his arm and she let it fall impotently to her side.

There was filtered light coming from the hospital, enough to see each other by; and there was moonlight. Caro looked up into his face. 'Where are you staying?'

'I found a little hotel in a back street in the town. It's clean. My driver and my assistant will be there now.'

In the limited light he could see her eyes were filled with tears again.

'We can't bring him back, Caro. In our own ways we did the best we could by him. Why, you even followed him here and because of that we've had time with him that otherwise we never would have had. So we must remember that. I'll pick you up early, seven o'clock or so.' Then he looked past her and spoke in a matter-of-fact way. 'Fleet's coming too. He'll be there for the funeral.'

Caro's eyes widened. 'What?'

'Yes, I asked him. I'm not sure whether you'll be pleased or not to hear this, but last night, after I heard of Harry's death, we spent some hours together. It led to a lot of catharsis.' He gave his slanted smile. 'I'd say the world's now just about big enough to hold us both. And there's something else I should tell you. He knows Harry was his son.'

Caro thought she was going to fall to the ground, but forced herself to rally, planting her feet and standing fast.

Matt brought his gaze back to hers. 'Did you know that? That Fleet knew?'

Caro began to shiver, even though it was the height of summer.

'Did you?'

She could not speak.

To her complete amazement he shook his head. 'It doesn't matter. I don't need to know. Harry's gone. It doesn't matter at all.' He turned from her. 'I'll see you in the morning.'

He pushed himself off on his cane. She watched the unique motion of his walk, the way he fractionally leant on his stick and then skimmed the ground with his bad leg to propel forward. She had spent her entire adult life with this man; had lived her happy days and her sad ones all within his ambit. For twenty years she had been his wife; not John Conrad's wife, not anyone else's, but this man's: this strange, eccentric, baffling man called Matthew Craken who had brought her son up as if he were his own and given her a beautiful daughter and tried over the ages in his oblique way to let her know he cared.

Out of nowhere she remembered the words he had whispered into her hair when she had been weeping for Harry. *Oh Caro, Caro, I'm so sorry. My love, I'm so sorry.*

He reached the stone wall that surrounded the hospital and was passing through the gate.

'Matthew!' It broke from her along with a sob.

He paused and half turned. 'Yes, Caro?'

She knew she was weeping, that the tears were again flowing from her eyes; the world was blurred. 'Don't leave me!'

He swung right round on his cane. A dark figure delineated against the black night.

She moved a few steps towards him. The words came between the sobs. 'Don't leave me. I couldn't bear it if you do . . . I'll die . . . I know you say I'm strong, but not that strong. I can't live without you and Harry too. I've spent my life with you, not with John Conrad, with you, and I see it all now. I know you're difficult and outrageous and bossy and contradictory and . . . *I don't mind.* I'm used to all that, and I know that you are who you are and I can let you be . . . because I don't want anyone else. It's you, only you, I want to be with.'

He did not move and her heart sank.

She still edged towards him. 'Matt . . . oh, Matt, you called me *love* today. Did you mean it? I've never heard you say that before. Please don't leave me.' She halted a few steps from him. 'You see I know a lot of things now, and I know I'm your wife and no one else's. I wish with all my heart I'd shared things – really shared them – with you, all these years. I never let myself see you before for I was always consumed by the idea of John Conrad. But I don't want John Conrad. I've known for months now that it's you I want. And now with my Harry gone, I couldn't bear it if you go too. Oh, Matthew, can't you see? *Please* see – it's you I love.'

She saw his face in the night glow, the dark patch that was the scar upon his cheek. She saw him lift his hands in the air, the cane glinting in the moonlight and as his arms opened wide she flew into them. She felt his kisses on her hair, on her forehead and her cheeks and her eyes.

She clung fiercely to him as he tasted her tears and he whispered. 'I've always loved you, Caro Dere . . . always.'

And for the first time in Caro's life she held Matthew Craken and there was no one else in the embrace.

Chapter Forty-eight

Thursday, 1 August 1918

A breeze wafted across the meadow, moving the long grass in gentle undulations as the parents of the dead pilot proceeded in company with the air force chaplain towards the graveside in the tiny cemetery near St-Pol aerodrome: only eleven graves; eleven sun-bleached wooden crosses sticking up out of the ground in haphazard pattern of death. The mourners halted to stand in silence beside the coffin draped in the Union Jack and the Australian flag, and the woman removed the black veil that until now had covered her face.

Opposite ranged Harry's friends and comrades in a guard of honour, and beyond them at attention waited an AIF firing party.

At 9.57 a.m. a murmur ran through the ranks as an armoured car pulled up beyond the hedgerow and a Brigadier stepped out into the sunshine to whispered speculation about what relationship the senior officer bore to the family.

The brigadier strode across the turf to the parents as his aide remained by the car and his driver followed him. In low tones he greeted first the mother and then the father of the dead pilot, while the driver, a dark young man with fiery black eyes moved over to stand with Harry Craken's other close friends, Charles McIntosh and Paul Quinn.

The Anglican chaplain lifted his hands. *'Man that is born of woman has but a short time to live, and is full of misery. He cometh up, and is cut down, like a flower; he fleeth as it were a shadow, and never continueth in one stay. In the midst of life we are in death . . .'*

The chaplain read the burial service in a clear voice. He had buried many in these last four years. Some in coffins like today; most without. Many in mass graves. He was sorry for the parents of this boy, as he was for all the parents of all the boys. He looked kindly at Caro, for he was a kindly priest and every mother's sadness he felt as his own. He directed his next words to her:

'*Blessed are they that mourn: for they shall be comforted.*'

He had been surprised, as he thought all gathered had been when the brigadier arrived. He was obviously related to the family for he stood beside the parents. The chaplain lifted his hands and spoke to the congregation.

'We are gathered here to bid farewell to a young man, a hero who fought both in the army and the air force. He rallied to his country's call. He will join the soil of this foreign land and enrich this earth as will so many who are buried here. So many men, hundreds of thousands without any coffins, hundreds of thousands of hearts in the ground of Belgium and France.

'Harry Craken was too young to die, as have been so many I have interred these past four years. He hailed from Queensland, Australia from a property in the fertile Lockyer Valley called Cedar Grove. His family are here today, an unusual occurence in this cruel time of conflict, and to me they represent all the parents of the men I've buried. Harry was one of tens of thousands of loyal, spirited and honourable young men who came across the oceans to fight a war against aggression and oppression, to help the underdog.

'The war continues and inevitably more will die, and each loss is a heartbreak to those who love the ones departed . . .'

As the chaplain's voice continued it was drowned out in Caro's head by her own thoughts, by her own visions. She stood between John Conrad and Matthew, and she looked up at one and then the other: the two men who had dominated her entire adult life. It was a mystical hallucinatory experience to have them on either side of her and to realise that the coming together of these men was through the death of their collective son. She viewed the world through a haze and those others around her appeared indistinct. She knew what occurred but she felt one step removed from the reality of it. Caro was aware that the sun shone: it seemed wrong that the sun would shine, with Harry gone from the light of the world.

As they lowered the coffin into the ground Caro's mind filled with her son. She saw him as he had been that ominous day in the dining room at Cedar Grove, with his head thrown to the side, wearing his strange self-assured expression. Behind him the curtain had flapped high in the breeze and held him there in a world of blue with his excited azure eyes staring at her and his shock of fair hair hovering on his forehead. She saw the careless movement of his hand as he put it into his pocket and drew out the gleaming shilling coin to throw it on to the table. She saw him point to the coin and heard his voice. 'I'm going to fight for King George.'

A tremor ran through her and a sob broke from her lips as she forced herself to look down into the gaping earth at the wooden box that contained him. She was grateful to feel Matthew's arm go round her body in support.

Matthew slipped his arm around Caro and held her as she leaned forward to look her last on Harry's coffin.

To think it had come to this: the day they buried Harry. Matthew glanced up to the sky and there, living in his head, was the boy who had been his son in every way. Each time he had looked into Harry's eyes he had been proud. The boy had been more than he could have hoped for in all things. The last time he had seen him had been a few months ago when he was working on his series *Aerodromes of the Western Front*. They had spent a cheerful afternoon together, just the two of them, and had driven into the little town of Hesdin and eaten bread and ham and drunk beer and talked about what they would do up at Cedar Grove after the war. Harry had said he would like to stay in the air force and Matt had laughed and said they could clear the field by the creek and make a landing strip.

Matt gave a shake of his head as he remembered the day Mounthaven had beaten Grammar in the big cricket match of 1914. Harry had been the hero of the day. He saw the boy lift his bat and hit the last four to the boundary; saw the other boys rush in and raise him in the air on their shoulders.

He imagined the small Harry laughing and climbing ahead of Knobby up the rickety wooden steps to Won Won's dark and fascinating Chinese abode above the cooper's shop in Wooloongabba. He saw the old Chinese man reach out with his veined leathery hand to touch Harry's golden head and he heard Harry's voice trail out of the sadness in his mind. 'You're the best father in the world, Daddy.'

As the voice of the chaplain continued, he turned his gaze across his wife to John Conrad. He could see the scar on the man's neck above his collar, the wound he had inflicted the night of the coming-home party for the Boer War soldiers. He studied his old foe as John Conrad bent his head and stepped forward to watch Dave Sands throw in the first sod of earth on Harry.

John Conrad took a step to the side of the grave and as Dave threw in the first handful of earth he thought of the boy he had known so superficially and so fleetingly.

He could have known him intimately, lived with him, brought him up and cared for him. He considered what might have been. To have been married to the woman at his side; to have Harry know him as a father; to have enjoyed family life. Instead he had experienced just moments with the boy to whom he had given life.

He had loved Caro Dere ardently and impetuously, and in doing so had brought into the world the boy who was no more. He bent down and picked up a handful of earth and as everyone watched he let it dribble through his fingers on to the coffin. 'Goodbye Harry, vale Harry,' he whispered. And as he stepped back he glanced round at Caro and their eyes met. The look between them sent countless messages of promises made and broken, of recollections of tender nights in the long ago, of sweet farewells, of glorious passion, of laughter and poignant sorrow, perhaps of truth at last.

A volley of shots pierced the air as the firing party pointed their rifles to the sun.

As the soldiers returned to attention Caro stepped forward. She had not realised she was going to do this until the very moment.

Her feet were just inches from the open grave as she looked skywards. Then she began to sing: the song of Australia which had become the unofficial anthem, the country words set to the mellifluous music, first sung in Winton Queensland in 1895; the song Harry had sung at school. Her voice rose quietly at first until John Conrad and Matthew both joined in and the Australian firing party lifted their voices to combine and rise in a high and haunting echo resounding in the sunshine across the green fields and the scarlet poppies in Northern France:

> 'Once a jolly swagman camped by a billabong
> Under the shade of a coolibah tree,
> And he sang as he watched and waited
>   till his billy boiled,
> "Who'll come a-waltzing Matilda with me.
>
> "Waltzing Matilda, waltzing Matilda,
> Who'll come a-waltzing Matilda with me."
> And he sang as he watched and waited
>   till his billy boiled,
> "Who'll come a-waltzing Matilda with me."'

As the singing ended Caro turned from the graveside and as she did she took Matthew's palm in her right hand and, holding it tightly, looked up at him, then she raised her left hand and watched it as it moved across the space between herself and John Conrad to pick up his right hand and hold it firmly. Slowly she moved forward and took the two men along with her.

And so all three walked away, across the gleaming grass where minute white flowers grew beneath their shadows, the two men in the khaki uniform of the Australian Imperial Forces, the woman in black: Matthew Craken, Caroline Dere and John Conrad Fleet, hand in hand in the dazzling summer sunshine with blue-eyed Harry caressing their minds and a truce of sadness floating in the air around them.

The chaplain and the others remained at a discreet distance from the two men and the woman, aware that these moments were cherished and not to be interfered with. They watched as the three passed through the opening in the hedgerow and came to a halt a few yards from John Conrad's armoured car.

Somewhere a nightingale sang and its call filtered across the meadow to them as Caro released their hands and they all turned to each other. She gazed at them both, turning from Matthew with his moody eyes and the brand he carried on his face, to John Conrad, who was still good-looking enough to make her catch her breath, but she observed him now with a placid acceptance of the past; it was a revelation to her.

John Conrad strove to smile at Caro. He was not successful and it faded away. 'Goodbye, thank you. I needed to be here today. I wish we could have kept him in this world, but it was not to be . . .'

Caro looked from one to the other again. 'I'm devastated to lose him, but I realise his death isn't useless. It's bridged the gulf of hatred between you. It's through his loss that you both revealed your truths to one another. I do believe that.'

Matthew rested on his cane. 'I'm not certain of much in this inconstant world, but perhaps you're right, Caro. Harry was one hell of a man. He's proved that.' He regarded John Conrad. 'Goodbye, Fleet. I know there're big things happening soon. I hope it means the end of the war.'

John Conrad nodded. 'Goodbye, Craken. Yes. The Germans show the strain of four years of fighting. We might have it over by Christmas.'

He leant forward and kissed Caro on the cheek. 'Goodbye, Caro. I hope we meet again.'

She lifted her hand to touch his face. 'We will.'

John Conrad turned away and took a pace towards his car when Matt's voice sounded. 'Fleet?'

He faced round. 'Yes?'

'I think just this once we should shake hands . . . for Harry's sake.'

They stepped back to each other and as they proffered and grasped hands, John Conrad repeated. 'Yes, for Harry's sake.'

Overwhelmed, Caro watched them, tears again floating in her eyes.

She saw Dave Sands hurry over to the car and open the door for John Conrad to enter. Dave closed the door and turned to Matthew. 'Goodbye, sir.'

'Remember what I said. Make sure you come and see us.'

Dave saluted. 'Yes, I will. Goodbye, Mrs Craken.'

Caro moved in to him and hugged him. 'You must do as my husband says. And I want you to know your Uncle Hargy was my friend too.'

He smiled sadly at her. 'Just like I was Harry's.'

As the armoured car drove away Caro lifted her hand and waved and then suddenly she and Matt were surrounded by the others and her attention was taken by a young man with olive skin and dark hair and a zealous gleam in his eyes. 'My name's Paul Quinn. I just wanted to say what a great fellow Harry was. We shall miss him badly. None of us know what's round the corner.' He looked up at the sky. 'It could be my turn today.'

Caro reached across and firmly took his arm. 'Oh no, don't let it be,' she answered forcefully. 'You must not let it be.'

An hour later as the armoured car slowed to lumber by a battalion of American marines, John Conrad unfolded his arms and, turning slightly in the seat, spoke to Tommy, who sat beside him, and Dave, who drove.

'I know you two are wondering why in the hell I would choose to attend Harry Craken's funeral, and I know you both think too much of me to ask. I also am aware you know full well that I trust you both completely and that if ever there were two men in this world I'm fond of, it's you two. So I'll say this just once and ask you to forget it. You've probably guessed some of this anyway. Caro Craken was a love of mine many years ago; circumstances prevailed where she married Matthew Craken instead of me. Her husband and I have been the worst of enemies since that time, but now for many reasons, we've called a truce. Harry was instrumental in bringing that truce about. I *needed* to stand by Harry's mother on this of all days. It was important that I was beside her. That's why I was there.'

Tommy held up his hands. 'I've already forgotten it.'

Dave's voice sounded from the driver's seat. 'Me too.'

And John Conrad gave a sad smile and patted both men with great affection upon their shoulders.

Caro and Matthew departed from the squadron mess after they had been given Harry's belongings and taken refreshment with Commander Briggs and Harry's friends.

Caro had clung to the chaplain's hand and said, 'Thank you. The words you said were so compassionate. I used to tell Harry to have compassion.' Tears welled in her eyes. 'It must be hard, even for you, to continue believing, seeing what you've seen. I know it's been hard for me.'

The chaplain sighed and patted her hand. 'Mrs Craken, it's

hard for all of us. There have been times in the past four years when I too have doubted God. But I remain of the belief that there must be a reason.'

Matthew's eyebrow raised and he looked skywards, but with an effort he managed to keep silent and not express his differing opinion. He nodded to the clergyman as he helped Caro up into the lorry. He had driven north himself, leaving Bert and Cliff to spend the day in Doullens.

As they drove away from the aerodrome they passed the cemetery and Caro leant her head out the window and looked back with her hair flying in the breeze until the cemetery disappeared from view behind the trees.

They rode in silence for a time and then Matt took the lorry off the road into a grassy patch between a stance of trees where he brought it to a standstill and, turning off the engine, rested his hand on the gear lever and faced Caro.

'Caro, there's one thing I must do. That's to go and see Madeleine. I must do that for Harry. I noticed the Squadron Commander give you Harry's wings and the gold chain and cross he was wearing when they found him. I'd like you to give me the cross to return to Madeleine.'

Caro dug into her purse. She handed him the cross and chain. 'Do you . . . think she would like his wings too? I suppose . . . I could do without them. After all, we have all his other things to keep.'

'Yes I do. Good on you, old girl.'

She handed him the wings. 'When will you go to Amiens?'

'Soon. Perhaps even tomorrow. She deserves to know.'

Caro nodded gently in agreement. 'Matthew?'

'Yes.'

'I've been thinking. If what John Conrad says is true then the war might be in its last stages. I know I agreed yesterday that perhaps it's time I went home to Katy and all that Australia means and, Matt, believe me when I say I do want to go home: I need to be at Cedar Grove and just watch you paint and for us to walk in the fields and ride in the valley with Knobby and Jane. But I hope you understand that I feel I don't want to let Captain Cadee and the girls down now. It's to do with loyalty and also to do with Harry. Not letting him down either . . . Matt, could we stay here? Say just until the end of the year?

It's August now, and if the war's not over by December, I'll go home anyway. But I feel I owe them all a little more.'

Matt managed a half-smile. 'Ah, Caro, while I'm sick of this bloody war, I hear what you say. I've already extended my stay here twice. They'll think I'm a trifle overfond of the bloody army at this rate, but, yes, I'm sure I'll have no trouble in protracting my stay too.'

'Thanks, Matt.'

He opened the door and eased himself to the ground. 'I'll have to crank this engine to start it now. Stay there.'

But she did not. She jumped to the ground and came round to him. She took his hand.

'Caro? What the devil?'

She led him to the side of the lorry under the dipping green boughs of the summer trees and slipped her arms up around his neck. She swayed gently from side to side.

'Caro, what are you doing?'

'I'm thinking of Harry, our wonderful boy.'

She kissed the scar on his cheek and began to hum. It was a tune from out of their long ago and he knew it from somewhere. She took his cane and threw it away into the grass and looked up and smiled tenderly.

'Ah Caro,' he whispered into her hair as they moved slowly in the first steps of the dance.

And as they swayed across the grass she continued humming and he recalled the melody. It was the tune he had hummed to her on that night of twenty years before under the willow trees in the park on the bank of the river. The night they had agreed to marry: the night he had gloated over the fact she carried Fleet's child. The pregnancy that had turned into Harry, *his* Harry.

Matthew could not remember the last time he had danced; perhaps it was that fateful night. Miraculously he felt no pain in his leg as he moved across the undulations of the ground, just as he had felt no pain on that night all those years ago. He recalled his unbounded exhilaration and how they had swirled and gambolled round and round until they found themselves tangled in the draping fronds of the weeping willows.

There were no willows and no exhilaration for him this time as they made their moderate passage under the trees in the French meadow, holding each other in the dappled summer sunshine and stepping to the rhythm of the war sounds in the distance.

But there was union this time: a tender accord that had been missing in the long ago, and as Caro lifted her face up to his and rested upon his chin they moved in the harmony of their mutual embrace. Gentle thoughts of Harry wafted in the breeze, combining their loss of the boy they had loved so fervidly and so dearly, in their flowing placid waltz across the grass.

And as if the haze of summer enveloped them in a dream, round and round they swirled, over the grass and into the meadow as Caro hummed her tune, gliding along in a stream of peace that calmed the anger and grief inside them, a gradual tranquillity that brought consolation and unity to Caro and Matthew at last.

It was another warm sunny day with a mild breeze filtering through the streets of Amiens, when, to the distant sounds of artillery, Matt lifted the brass knocker and rapped on the door of the house in the Rue d'Or.

A woman in her early fifties answered, eyeing this stranger who leant on a cane and wore an Australian uniform. She stood feet planted in the doorway.

'*Bonjour, madame. Je suis le père de Harry Craken.*'

Madeleine's mother smiled. Though she had not wanted her daughter to become involved with a serviceman, nevertheless she liked Harry. He brought some cheer into their lives and laughter to her daughter's lips: that was enough for him to have wended his way into her own affections. Madeleine had confided to her a little time ago that Harry wanted to marry her when the war was over. Madame Baudet thought they were very young, but she had to admit she had only been nineteen when she had married and she knew her daughter well. The girl was steady and reliable and deeply in love. But it was a surprise to see Harry's father, so she asked why he was here.

Matt shook his head. 'I would like . . . ah . . . *Je voudrais venir . . . Madeleine s'il vous plaît.*'

She nodded and stood back from the entry. '*Entrez.*'

He entered and followed her to the parlour with the lace on the windows and the maroon velvet on the sofa. As they walked in she called through the doorway and up the stairs, 'Madeleine!'

It was warm and the woman motioned for Matt to remove his jacket. He shook his head. He would not be staying long.

The woman gestured for him to sit, but again he shook his head, '*Non, merci.*'

She watched him closely and suddenly understood. With a knowing sorrowful expression on her face she said, '*'Arry est mort. Oui?*'

'Yes,' Matt answered, and the woman covered her face with her hands.

A girl of Harry's age entered at a run. She was a fine graceful build and wore a flowered print dress with a blue ribbon in her hair. She carried the untroubled smile of youth and her eager pale eyes latched on to his own as she said, '*Oui?*'

Then she noticed her mother standing holding her hands to her face.

'*Qu'est-ce qu'il y a?* What is it? What's wrong?'

Her mother gestured to Matthew. '*Je te présente le père d'Arry.*'

And now Madeleine's smile died on her mouth and she asked, 'He is all right?'

Matt shook his head. 'No. Non.'

The girl's pale skin turned ashen. '*Mais est-ce qu'il est en vie?* He lives? Yes?'

Matt again shook his head. 'No. His aeroplane was hit. *Il est mort lundi. C'est la première chance que* . . . ah . . . that I have had to tell you.'

He saw the life-light go from the girl's eyes as if a circuit had been snapped. Her mouth twisted in torment and she lifted her hands towards him and then dropped them feebly back to her sides.

Matt stepped forward to her. 'I am so sorry.'

She brought her hands up again and wrapped them around herself as Caro had done in Captain Cadee's office at the hospital.

Matthew took her in his arms and held her and now the girl sobbed into his shoulder, her slender body shaking with the torment in her heart. He looked across her to her mother, who could do nothing.

All Madeleine knew was that her life would never be the same. She would carry her love for her *Australien* to the grave and no man would ever take his place. She cried for a long time before she looked up into the face of his father: a strange classical face with a scar running across his cheek. Her own cheeks were smeared with tears and her eyes were red and puffy. 'I love him very much . . . 'Arry my *Australien*.' And she began to cry again.

Her mother removed Madeleine from Matt's hold and gently led her to the sofa.

Matthew took out the gold cross and chain and handed them to the girl. She received them and lifted them to her lips. Then he handed her the wings from Harry's uniform. 'Harry's mother wants you to have these. *De la mère d'Harry.*'

And these too she pressed to her lips.

Matt took a piece of paper from his inside pocket and handed it to the girl's mother. 'Please write to us. *Lorsque la guerre est fini s'il vous plaît écrivez-moi . . .* if you would like. This is our address in Australia.'

'*Merci, Monsieur.*'

Matthew took his leave of the two women and made his way along the dim corridor to the front of the house. As he opened the door and stepped into the sunshine he heard Madeleine's voice behind him and he turned round.

The tears still glinted in her eyes and her face had turned pink with the heat of her emotion. She lifted her hand to the door jamb and he noticed the white half-moons at the base of her nails. He encapsulated this moment in his artist's mind and years later painted a masterpiece of Madeleine just as she was when she delivered this statement to him. 'I never love anybody else. Never love another. He made me . . . more . . . than I am. *Votre fils était le seul pour moi.*'

He tried to nod gently and turned away.

As Matt negotiated the stone steps to the street his leg ached. And as he crossed the road he felt the girl's gaze still upon him. At the corner he turned and lifted his cane to her and she waved her pale hand.

He was still just sceptical enough to think Madeleine was sufficiently young for time to alter her, that she would forget Harry and marry another. She was pretty; surely there would be one left in the French male population eager enough to capture her.

It would only be in time that Matthew would come to know – when the letters arrived every year for Harry's birthday and at Christmas, year after year long into the future – that Madeleine Baudet would love only once in her life and that she meant every word she said to Matthew on this warm August day in the doorway of the house in Amiens in 1918.

Chapter Forty-nine

In Flanders Fields

In Flanders fields the poppies blow
Between the crosses row on row
That mark our place; and in the sky
The larks, still bravely singing, fly
Scarce heard amid the guns below.

We are the dead, short days ago
We lived, felt dawn, saw sunset glow,
Loved and were loved, and now we lie
In Flanders fields

Take up our quarrel with the foe:
To you from failing hands we throw
The torch; be yours to hold it high.
If ye break faith with us who die
We shall not sleep, though poppies grow
In Flanders fields.

John McRae
(Died Base Hospital 1918)

On Thursday, 8 August 1918 the massive allied advance on the Western Front began.

Although the German army outnumbered the Allies on the Somme by 42 Divisions to 32, the British and Dominion troops, the French and the American troops felt a sense of resolve, a purpose and the means to bring about the end.

Each day the Germans fell back. One by one all the areas of allied carnage and the worst fighting of 1916 were taken and overrun. By the end of the month the Germans were retreating from Flanders.

The Australians captured Péronne on 31 August, forcing the

enemy out of their fortifications on Mont St-Quentin and, with Tommy and Dave at his side, John Conrad strode among the victorious troops, hailing them on every side. Eight Victoria Crosses were won that day.

By September there was talk of defeat among German and Austrian soldiers home on leave. On 8 September the German General Ludendorff brought his troops out in retreat from the St-Mihiel Salient only days prior to what would have been a massive allied attack on the area.

On 11 September in Essen in Germany the Kaiser spoke to the munitions workers at the Krupp's factories. He was trying to rally some spirit for the continuance of the war. He stated to them that anybody who circulated anti-war material or spoke of defeat should be hanged but his words were greeted with no enthusiasm. All he met was silence.

During September the allied generals prepared for final attacks and in Russia the Bolsheviks began their reign of Red Terror.

During October in all theatres of war the armies of the enemy began to falter and as October turned into November the writing was on the wall. Various attempts at truces and armistices were made by the Central Powers.

As if the globe had not seen enough slaughter, an influenza so deadly that no country was immune scoured the world. Had it been the Middle Ages, men would have believed, that coupled with the war, it was the beginning of the end of the world.

But the world survived.

In France Matthew went about painting and following the men of the 16th as they pushed on through the Hindenburg line.

John Conrad remained with his troops with Tommy and Dave at his side, and as well as confidence in the allied ranks, there was a sense of impending victory now: that they were living out the final acts of the conflict.

Caro stayed at the base hospital at Doullens and continued to do 'the work of three', driving her ambulance and caring for the wounded.

On 9 November Kaiser Wilhelm abdicated and went into exile in Holland where he remained in sanctuary for the rest of his life.

On the eleventh day of the eleventh month of 1918, at the eleventh hour, hostilities ceased throughout the war zones. The Armistice had been signed at 5.10 that morning in the forest of Compiegne.

In the last minutes before the hour of eleven John Conrad stood between Tommy and Dave with his other officers behind him and looked at his watch. There was a burst of machine-gun fire from the enemy, a retaliatory rattle from the 16th and then as the minute hand climbed to the hour, an expectant hush, as if all the men of all the armies held their breath.

At the moment of eleven, the silence hung like a visible thing and then a burst of cheering exploded, which to the boys of the 16th seemed to extend around the entire globe. Men laid down their arms, shook hands, cried and laughed, hugged and yelled in exuberance. From London to Brisbane volleys of gunfire sounded and a collective sigh issued forth across the world as millions of people began to celebrate.

John Conrad threw off the shackles of being a commanding officer and hugged Tom and Dave and every soldier within yards, and at the height of the shouting and exultation, a soldier asked him, 'Is it real, sir? Is it really over?'

He patted the man on his shoulder. 'Yes, lad, it's really over.'

His mind filled with the last four years: of the miseries and the suffering, of the courage and the hardship, the comradeship and the pride in his men, the loss of K and the loss of his son. All of it had altered him for ever.

Caro, Sue, June and Patricia were standing on the base hospital verandah as the church bells of Doullens began to ring. A shout came from inside the hospital. 'The war's over!' The girls hugged each other and cried and laughed and Captain Cadee, Carmen, Jill and some nurses appeared at the door with bottles of whisky and wine held high above their heads. Soon all the orderlies and the nurses, the VADs, the doctors, the ambulance drivers and many of the wounded were celebrating. The staff rostered themselves to look after those who needed constant care, but they did not feel tired now and each person went about the wards with a renewed vigour.

Caro left the celebrations and wandered down to the meadow

where Matt had told her of Harry's death. She leant on the bole of a tree and looked up at the overcast sky. A chill wind moved her skirt as she whispered, 'I'll be leaving France soon, darling. The war's ended. I will always carry you in my mind. Adieu, my lovely son.'

Matthew was sitting on the engine of the lorry with Cliff and Bert. They were at the side of the Bapaume Road in the middle of two battalions of Americans and Canadians waiting for the road to clear so they could move on and catch up with the 16th. Cliff was giving a discourse on what governments should do for soldiers, and in particular his opinion of how all soldiers should be granted a life pension. Bert was eating an apple and listening silently when a cry was taken up and passed swiftly through the troops. 'The war's over! The war's over!'

At first they were incredulous and then as the words gained credence and the Americans and Canadians began singing and shouting, throwing their helmets in the air and dancing along the road, Cliff stopped speaking and Matthew said, 'Seems like the war's over, chaps.' He slipped down off the engine and turned round to them. 'It would be too strong a statement to say I'll miss you both, so let's just say I'll expect a letter now and then.'

Bert hooted as he slung his apple high in the air and Cliff pulled him down into the road where they hugged each other and yelled with glee. They turned to Matt, and as he protested they took him in their arms and they spun around clinging to one another along the dusty road to Cliff's joyous shout, 'The bloody war's over!'

Chapter Fifty

February 1919

It was cold on the deck but the seas were amazingly calm as the HMAS *Victory* edged down the Solent and headed out by the Isle of Wight into the English Channel.

Caro, wrapped in a long coat to her ankles, and a woollen scarf around her hair, turned to Matthew, who stood by her side.

'Will we ever come back?'

Her husband bent and kissed her forehead. 'I don't know.'

'One day I would like to. To go once more and stand by Harry's grave. I think I must do that again . . . yes, one day.'

Matthew nodded. 'I know, and we'll do it. But for now, old girl, I have to say all I want to see is Knobby's bloody marvellous face on the quayside as we sail into Hamilton Reach.'

Caro dug him in the ribs. 'And what about our daughter . . . and your mother and Matilda?'

Matt groaned. 'All right, I'll admit I want to see Katy, but my mother . . .'

'Matt, she's a good woman.'

'She's one of the reasons I followed you to France.'

'You don't mean that. You're incorrigible.'

He laughed. 'No, I'm not. I'm positively mellowing. I must be getting bloody old.'

She turned round to him as her scarf danced in the air between them. She put her hand up and touched his scar. 'Not old, you'll never be old, and yes I believe, thank heaven, you are mellowing.'

He shook his head energetically. 'That's enough. I can't have you thinking that. I'm leaving.'

She laughed. 'Where are you going?'

'Down to the hold. I'll see you back in the cabin.' He patted her on the bottom and she looked sharply round in pseudo offence. 'Matthew!'

His paintings were stored in the hold and he had been twice to check on them already. She gave an amused nod of her head. 'You know, Matt, your work's a wonderful bequest to the Australian nation.'

He called over his shoulder as he moved across the deck. 'Hardly a *bequest*, old girl. The buggers think they've got a right to it just because they commissioned me. That's the Government for you!'

She shook her head tolerantly, watching him leaning on his silver cane as he passed by a companionway to enter the interior. No, Matt had not really changed and she supposed if she thought about it, she would not want him to; he was Matthew and that was that. She accepted and understood him at last and was content to be by his side; no, *happy* to be by his side. The war, with all its insanity, had done that for her: allowed her to sort through what was significant and what was not.

She turned back and looked across the dark waters to the shoreline. 'Goodbye, England,' she said, before she smiled tenderly and lifted her gloved hand as she thought of the man who had dominated her mind for twenty years. 'Goodbye, John Conrad. All the turmoil is calm at last, and may you find such peace as I have finally found, my other dear, dear one.'

A chill wind blew and a feeble rain was falling as John Conrad crossed the footpath and entered the Ritz Hotel, taking off his greatcoat, which now bore the insignia of the crossed swords and pip of a Major General. He made his way to the front bar to find Tommy waiting for him. The young man ordered him a beer and they moved to sit at a small marble-topped table.

John Conrad pointed to Tom's glass. 'And how many have you had while you've been waiting?'

Tom shook his head and smiled. 'I've been sitting on this for twenty minutes. You don't need to worry. My heavy drinking days are over. Permanently.'

'Yes, I know they are. Good.' As the waitress placed a

beer in front of him he put down the *Evening Standard*. 'The newspapers are full of the Kaiser remaining in sanctuary in Holland. For the only time in my life I actually agree with Lloyd George. He wants to hang him for the war criminal he is.'

'Too damn right. I'd do it myself. Do you think they'll give him up?'

'It sounds pretty doubtful from what I read.'

'Damned Dutch. Seems wrong, doesn't it?'

'Considering the misery he caused, it's a travesty.' He took a mouthful of his beer and looked into space. 'So tell me, m'boy, have you decided what you'll do when you're demobbed?'

'Go home to Sydney, I expect, back to architecture. I'd only just qualified when the war started. What about you?'

John Conrad sipped his beer. 'General Monash has asked me to stay on. Says the Government wants to revitalise the army. He says the essential components for that are qualified leadership, adequate equipment and trained soldiery.' He put down his beer, loosened his tie and grinned. 'For some reason he thinks I fall into the first category.'

Tommy sighed. 'But I thought you said you'd had enough of war.'

'I did and I have. Once in that butcher's yard is enough for all eternity. We'll all remain aggrieved about it for ever. But having experienced army life in both war and peace, I know a peacetime army's a very different matter. In the last few days I've been thinking. What does a man like me do with the rest of his life? I've been in the army my entire adulthood.'

'Well, you could go home and run the breweries with your brother.'

John Conrad pursed his lips in thought. 'Mmm, that's exactly what Bart says in his latest letter. He's waiting for me to be best man at his wedding.' He swallowed another mouthful of his beer. 'One thing I know: whatever I do I've got young Dave with me for life. He's adamant he wants to stay with me wherever I go. And that'll work splendidly if I remain in the army.' He blinked. 'Hell, it'll work, anyway. He can drive me *and* have a good job at the brewery. He's smart, will pick it all up in no time.'

Tommy peered over his glass and his eyes narrowed in thought. 'You know, I imagine you're right about a peacetime army being different. But it's still the army and you could make a mighty big difference.'

'What do you mean by that?'

'Well, with your experience, having been with Kitchener all those years, understanding how the British army works and the ways of places like Egypt and India and South Africa, and having fought this damn war and won most of your battles, think what you would hand down to young recruits. Did Monash say what he wanted you to do?'

John Conrad bent forward, elbows on knees. 'I think he'd like me to work with him. Restructure the entire Australian army. Said I could even work from Brisbane; anything I wanted.'

A thoughtful silence fell and they remained quiet for a time until Tommy tapped his glass on his front teeth and smiled. 'If you took the appointment, as well as a driver would you need an aide-de-camp?'

John Conrad's eyes gleamed in the lamplight as he raised his beer in salute. 'I certainly would!' He clinked his glass on Tommy's. 'In that case . . . to restructuring the army.' He lifted his finger. 'As long as we can have our headquarters in Brisbane!'

Tommy's face broke into a broad grin. 'To hell with architecture. Here's to Brisbane . . . sir.'

Two hours later, after a quiet and comfortable dinner, John Conrad left Tom on the footpath outside the Ritz. It had stopped raining but there were very few pedestrians braving the fierce January night. He turned up the collar of his greatcoat as he pulled it more tightly around him and, planting his hands in his pockets, turned his footsteps down Piccadilly past Green Park. He walked spiritedly until he came up the slope to Hyde Park Corner where he paused to look across at Apsley House before moving on towards Wellington Monument.

A tramcar passed along in the distance, but he appeared to be alone as he looked around for the park bench. He saw it, in the same spot of twenty-odd years before, just a few feet from the edge of the footpath, illuminated now by an electric streetlamp.

London seemed quiet as he studied the spot and imagined the man sitting there with his face vaguely lit, just enough to show his strong wide jaw and the sun-kissed brown appearance of his skin.

John Conrad stepped closer to the imaginary figure. The truth of the vision living in his mind. 'I'm staying in the army, K.' He spoke softly, confidentially. 'The world's different now, altered for ever, and so am I. But you made a soldier of me, just like you were, a good honest soldier with a soldier's heart and proud to be just that. And you made so very much more of me too. Gave me so much. Thank you.'

He saw the image of K look up at him, call him *Johnny* and smile in agreement before it faded from his head.

Slowly, with precise footfalls, he walked over and sat down, looking around at the stillness of the winter city. He remained for a time thinking of all that had happened and brought him to this night, until at last he felt the cold seeping through his heavy greatcoat.

When he stood he spoke again to the wind. 'There's one more thing I must do before I leave this land.' And he pictured the place he must go and the people he must see . . . to the house on Cosgrove Hill in Kent and the small girl who called him Uncle and the woman with brilliant Titian hair, who tenderly crossed his mind these days. She had asked him to forgive her; and long ago he had. He imagined May running down the hill to meet him and the way he would lift her high in his arms and look up to see Emma Louise smiling and waiting for them at the gate. That thought alone somehow warmed the bleakness of the winter night as he passed by the monument to one of the great soldiers of the realm and walked on.

When John Conrad Fleet returned to Australia he and Tommy Hardcastle were instrumental along with the Returned Sailors' and Soldiers' Imperial League of Australia, in having Anzac Day, 25 April – the day the Anzacs landed at Gallipoli in 1915 – instituted as a statutory public holiday throughout the land, to commemorate the memory of the fallen. By the mid 1920s war memorials had risen around the country and on Anzac Day the returned 'Diggers' marched through the streets in honour of themselves and their fallen comrades, to perpetuate remembrance.

Each year Tommy Hardcastle, Dave Sands and Curly Moss

marched proudly through the streets of Brisbane with what remained of the glorious 16th Battalion, their banner held high.

And each year to the amazement and utter joy of Caro, Matthew Craken and John Conrad Fleet met in the back bar of the Chevron Club overlooking the river, and discussed life.

On Anzac Day 1928, before Matthew left to meet John Conrad, he and Knobby took the painting of *Salome and John the Baptist* out of the stable where it had been stored by Caro, and burnt it.

As the weeks passed into months and years, and the conspicuous joy the cessation of hostilities brought, was transformed into sorrowful memories of human suffering never before seen in the history of the world, people of each nation who had been affected by the great torment lived out their lives. And their legacy remains for there are still those of us who remember a father or a grandfather who fought in that conflict, while the torment it caused has passed into the psyche of those who abide among the white headstones in Belgium and Northern France.

Ultimately the world faced the appalling cost of what had occurred in the Great War. Statistics vary, but it is certain that the casualties of the principal warring nations were no less than:

Australia	58,500 dead	152,170 wounded
Austria-Hungary	1,777,200 dead	3,600,000 wounded
Belgium	102,000 dead	450,000 wounded
Britain	1,100,000 dead	2,100,000 wounded
Bulgaria	75,000 dead	100,000 wounded
Canada	56,500 dead	150,000 wounded
France	1,720,650 dead	4,200,000 wounded
Greece	5,000 dead	9,000 wounded
Germany	1,703,000 dead	4,065,000 wounded
India	49,000 dead	65,175 wounded
Italy	465,560 dead	950,100 wounded
New Zealand	16,500 dead	40,800 wounded
Portugal	7,000 dead	10,000 wounded
Romania	250,000 dead	120,000 wounded
Russia	1,700,000 dead	5,000,000 wounded
Serbia	45,000 dead	100,000 wounded
South Africa	9,300 dead	14,000 wounded
Turkey	250,000 dead	400,000 wounded
USA	56,600 dead	189,000 wounded

This means approximately 10 million dead and 22 million wounded. A total of 32 million military casualties in just four years of war.

As well as military there were the millions of civilian casualties which have never been calculated.

It has been estimated that for the whole of the year of 1916, the bloodiest of the war, a serviceman of either Britain or the Empire was killed every 35 seconds.

These statistics remain incomprehensible when compared with the small populations at the time.

Appendix

My father, to whom, along with so many others, this book is dedicated, fought for the British Expeditionary Force in France during the First World War. By the time I was born to him in his middle age, he had fought again, this time in the Second World War as an officer of the Australian Imperial Forces and against the Japanese.

While I was growing up during the 1950s and 60s he told many war stories and I and my school friends would listen with fascination to him; he was without equal as a speaker and raconteur. But always his anecdotes were from the Second War. I never heard him speak about his days in the trenches in the First War. I now realise the memories were not ones he could possibly relate to a child.

For more than twenty-five years after his death I could not steel myself to read his papers. It is only in recent times during the writing of this book that I have managed to do that. And here below I share with you a passage I found from those days of his extreme youth when he was a boy soldier in France.

GATHERING FLOWERS

When I was a child I lived in a little English village, mellow and placid, where everyone appeared to be kind to children. We, my brother, Jack, my sisters and other young children, used to go in the spring and summertime and gather flowers, wild flowers: bluebells, buttercups and daisies and the wild roses that grew along the hedgerows where mayflower decked the hawthorn. We would wander down Bluebell Clough and along by the path to the River Medlock over the Old Ash Bridge, that used to swing under our weight as we walked across. It was the trunk of a single ash tree some thirty yards long, straight as a die, smoothed on the upper side for a decking. Having crossed the bridge we would meander upstream, past shady nooks and bowers of the vale towards a copse of tall dark sycamore trees under which more flowers grew in great profusion.

We would make the blooms into garlands and wear them round our necks and run across the meadows and over the bridge as they streamed behind us in the wind. We would bring armfuls home in triumph to our mothers to be placed in vases in the living rooms.

I was fourteen when the Great War began with Germany and Austria. 1914 was a milestone in the march of civilised man, but not one that marked his progress. It was a superficial advancement, a retrograding in the fundamentals, a loss of the facets of human dignity and decency with the first use of such puissant weapons as tanks, gas, long-range artillery and planes. I had no idea of what war meant, no idea that there is no romance. I tried to enlist thirteen times and was invariably turned away from the recruiting offices. One recruiting sergeant at the barracks informed me they wouldn't want drummer boys until the war was won. 'Whenever that'll be,' he said.

'Can I join as one?' I asked and he stood from his desk and chased me into the street.

However, eventually, when I looked a little older, I did convince a recruiting sergeant that I was eighteen, and I joined the army. In due course, I passed from England to Wales to Ireland then to France where by the 8th of August 1918 at the beginning of the allied offensive I found myself a rifle grenadier (that is, an infantryman, a bomb thrower), with the 16th Lancashire Fusiliers of the 32nd Division, in the front line trenches in the Valley of the Somme, where life was very cheap, where mercy was at a premium and where pity was a rare commodity.

It was high summer and flowers had begun to spring up through the waste in the fields around our trenches. One night we took over the front line and I went in as gas sentry for a few hours. I was always first gas sentry; Sergeant Dobb had that standing arrangement with me. Whilst I did the first posting he had time to organise the rest of his platoon.

Around midnight a party of us were sent out to crawl through our barbed wire towards the German trenches, perhaps one hundred yards away. We were two parties, in fact, one a covering party which lay close to us with their rifles at the ready whilst our boys started to dig a trench. We had hardly begun before the German machine-gunners opened up, but they were firing five or six feet over our heads and I, digging as the minutes went by, realised that the lower we got (we were digging furiously), the lower the German gunners fired. A few bullets by them at datum level when they first commenced, or into our low parapet when we began digging, and we would have been mown down like grass before a scythe.

However, periodically the bullets whistled over our heads and bodies as we crouched and dug, always seeming to be a few feet above us. When we got down 2′ 6″ or so and had packed earth thrown up in front of us, then and only then did the enemy gunners fire point-blank, ripping into the ground close to our heads, but we could, by that time, continue to dig on our knees or in a crouching position in comparative safety. I came to believe then that the Germans had seen us all along and decided not to kill us. This I never verified, of course.

When we were well dug in Corporal Poole informed me that the covering party had been called in and our platoon was to remain, to continue to man the trench in future and to deepen it.

'But,' said he, 'tomorrow from the German lines the new earth will show like a scar. There are no trees on our front but there are poppies and other wild flowers growing in great masses in the field around us. I want you to go out and pick them and stick them in the new earth of the parapet. Continue covering the parapet with flowers until dawn stand-to. It'll be effective camouflage and with luck the Germans won't realise we've a new trench here in this position.'

Out I crawled into no-man's-land where a little wire had been laid by our boys, to the roar of howitzers and the staccato boom of field guns and the sometimes close crunch of rifles and the spitting of machine guns, and the quiet pop of an occasional gas shell and the sickly whiff in my nostrils of its trailing fumes.

There, with a battle on all around: seemingly north, south, east and west, reaching from the North Sea to Switzerland, I went stepping lightly and brushing past that which I cannot speak of but what one finds in no-man's-land – plucking flowers just as I had done when a child. Gathering them in bunches, in bouquets and armfuls and then moving back swiftly to the parapet, whispering to the sentries whose rifles were pointing straight at me – placing the flowers over as wide an area as possible – pressing them in to look natural – before moving stealthily off again to gather more blooms in that French meadow of no-man's-land in the middle of the night.

I felt light-headed, I felt unreal, I felt like a child again gathering flowers in Medlock Vale and trailing them behind me across the Old Ash Bridge; but this was not a dream. I knew I must carry on and camouflage the parapet of the new trench before the night passed. So I continued back and forth, coming and going, plucking flowers and planting them, on and on, until the sound of the pre-arranged signal called me back, and so I crept through the wire, what little we had, and slithered down into the trench where I joined the stand-to, ready for an attack.

That morning the German planes flew over, shooting down our observation balloons, engaging our fighters overhead and bombing what they thought were strategic points and thereby entertaining us infantrymen. And also, we guessed, photographing our front line so their artillery could line up the range to perfection when desired.

Then early one morning, out of the blue, they opened up . . . apparently every calibre of gun was brought into the bombardment. Their intention quite plain, to blast us into oblivion. The long-range artillery began, its trajectory on our front-line trenches and then the creeping barrage moved its death back to our support lines; and repeated the dose hour by hour. There would come a time near Mont St Quentin when I would be caught in a creeping barrage and survive, but this time the Germans had started shelling on our *old* front line and we, of our platoon, were snug and safe 60 yards in front of that holocaust in the new trench I had covered with flowers.

We had deceived the German observers.

Gathering wild flowers in a French field on a hot sultry midsummer night had paid dividends for our small crowd of the *no-man's-land trench*. We were only the first platoon of a single company of the 16th Lancashire Fusiliers but when the 2nd Manchesters came up and relieved us in our forward positions and we came out on rest, the fact was, we seemed to constitute the entire battalion.

by Alan Chambers

Bibliography

Adam-Smith, Patsy; *The Anzacs*; Penguin Books Australia Ltd, 1991

Aitken, Alexander; *Gallipoli to the Somme (Recollections of a New Zealand Infantryman)*; Oxford University Press, London, 1963

Arthur, Sir George; *Life of Lord Kitchener, Vols I, II & III*; Macmillan and Co Ltd, London, 1920

Babington, Anthony; *For the Sake of Example (Capital Courts Martial 1914–20, The Truth)*; Leo Cooper in association with Secker & Warburg Ltd, London, 1983

Baggett, Blaine & Jay Winter; *1914–18, The Great War and the Shaping of the 20th Century*; BBC Books, London, 1996

Begbie, Harold; *Kitchener*; Houghton Mifflin Company, Boston, 1915

Benns, F. Lee; *Europe Since 1914 (In Its World Setting)*; F. S. Crofts & Co., New York, 1947

Brown, Malcolm; *Tommy Goes to War*; J. M. Dent & Sons Ltd, London, 1978

Bruckshaw, Private Horace; *The Diaries of Royal Marine Light Infantry 1915–1916*; edited and introduced by Martin Middlebrook, Archon Books, Connecticut, 1979

Coombs, Rose E. B., MBE; *Before Endeavours Fade (A Guide to the Battlefields of the First World War)*; Battle of Britain Prints International Ltd, London, 1994

Crundall, E. D., DFC, AFC; *Fighter Pilot on the Western Front*; William Kimber & Co Ltd, London, 1975

Ellis, John; *Eye Deep in Hell*; Johns Hopkins University Press, Maryland, 1989

Esher, Viscount Reginald; *The Tragedy of Lord Kitchener*; John Murray, London, 1921

Evans, Martin Marix; *The Battles of the Somme*; Weidenfeld & Nicolson Ltd, Orion Publishing Group, London, 1996

Field, Laurie; *The Forgotten War (Australia and the Boer War)*; Melbourne University Press, Australia, 1979

Fitzgerald, Ross; *A History of Queensland (From the Dreaming to 1915)*; University of Queensland Press, Australia, 1986

Franks, Norman, Russell Guest & Frank Bailey; *Bloody April . . . Black September*; Grub Street, London, 1995

Fussell, Paul; *The Great War and Modern Memory*; Oxford University Press, London, 1977

Gammage, Bill; *The Broken Years (Australian Soldiers in the Great War)*; Penguin Books Australia Ltd, 1975

Gilbert, Martin; *Atlas of the First World War (The Complete History)*; Oxford University Press, New York, 1994

Gilbert, Martin; *First World War*; Weidenfeld & Nicolson, Orion Publishing Group, London, 1994

Giles, John; *The Western Front, Then and Now (From Mons to the Marne and Back)*; Plaistow Press Ltd, London, 1992

Goodland, David & Alan Vaughan; *Anzacs over England (The Australian Flying Corps in Gloucestershire 1918–1919)*; Alan Sutton Publishing Ltd, UK, 1992

Grew, E.S., MA; *Field Marshal Lord Kitchener, Vols I, II & III, (His Life and Work for the Empire)*; Gresham Publishing Co. London, 1916

Grey, Jeffrey; *A Military History of Australia*; Cambridge University Press, England, 1990

Griffith, Paddy; *Battle Tactics of the Western Front (The British Army's Art of Attack 1916–18)*; Yale University Press, London, 1994

Haldane, Viscount; *Before the War*; Cassell and Company Ltd, London, 1920

Haythornthwaite, Philip J; *The World War One Source Book*; Arms & Armour Press, London, 1996

Hesketh-Prichard, Major H., DSO, MC; *Sniping in France (How the British Army Won the Sniping War in the Trenches)*; Lancer Militaria and R & R Books, USA, 1993

Hogg, Ian V.; *The Guns 1914–18 (Illustrated History of the First World War, Book No. 5)*; Pan/Ballantine, London 1973

Holmes, Richard; *Army Battlefield Guide (Belgium and Northern France)*; HMSO, London, 1995

Holt, Tonie & Major and Mrs Valmai; *Battlefield Guide to the Somme*; Leo Cooper/Pen & Sword Books Ltd, London, 1996

Johnson, J. H.; *Stalemate! (The Great Trench Warfare Battles 1915–1917)*; Arms & Armour Press, London, 1995

Keegan, John; *The First World War*; Hutchinson/Random House, London 1998

Kipling, Rudyard; *His Forgotten Masterpiece – The Irish Guards in the Great War, the First Battalion*; Sarpedon, New York, 1997

Kreckler, John F.; *The Story of Victoria Barracks*; The Army Museum Society, Australia, 1993

Laffin, John & Mike Chappell; *The Australian Army at War 1899–1975*; Reed International Books Ltd, London, 1982

Laffin, John; *Guide to the Australian Battlefields of the Western Front 1916–1918*; Kangaroo Press Pty Ltd, Australia, 1992

Laffin, John; *A Western Front Companion 1914–1918*; Alan Sutton Publishing Ltd, England, 1994

Lawson, Ronald; *Brisbane in the 1890s*; University of Queensland Press, Australia, 1973

Le Bas, Sir Hedley; *The Lord Kitchener Memorial Book*; Hodder & Stoughton, London, 1916

Macdonald, Lyn; *The Roses of No Man's Land*; Penguin Group, London, 1993

Macdonald, Lyn; *1915, The Death of Innocence*; Henry Holt & Co Inc., New York, 1995

Magnus, Philip; *Kitchener (Portrait of an Imperialist)*; John Murray, London, 1958

Manchester, William; *The Last Lion, Winston Spencer Churchill (Visions of Glory 1874–1932)*; Abacus, London, 1993

Millar, T. B.; *Australia in Peace and War*; Australian National University Press, Canberra, Australia, 1978

Monash, General Sir John, KCB; *The Australian Victories in France in 1918*; The Imperial War Museum, Dept of Printed Books and The Battery Press, London, 1973

Ogley, Bob; *Biggin On The Bump (the Most Famous Fighter Station in the World)*; Froglets Publications, England, May 1996

Parkes, Sir Henry, GCMG; *Fifty Years in the Making of Australian History, Vols I & II*; Longmans, Green & Co, London, 1892

Putkowski, Julian & Julian Sykes; *Shot at Dawn (Executions in World War One by The Authority of the British Army Act)*; Lee Cooper, England, 1998

Rogers, Horatio; *World War 1 Through my Sights*; Presidio Press, California, USA, 1976

Stedman, Michael; *Thiepval (Somme)*; Leo Cooper, London, 1997

Sykes, Claud W., ('Vigilant'); *German War Birds*; Greenhill Books, London, 1994

Thomson, Alistair; *Anzac Memories (Living with the Legend)*; Oxford University Press, Australia, 1994

Toland, John; *No Man's Land (1918 – the Last Year of the Great War)*; Konecky & Konecky, New York, 1980

Warner, Philip; *Kitchener (The Man Behind the Legend)*; Hamish Hamilton Ltd, London, 1985

Westlake, Ray; *British Battalions on the Somme 1916*; Leo Cooper, London, 1994

Winter, Denis; *Death's Men (Soldiers of the Great War)*; Allen Lane, Penguin Books Ltd, London, 1978

Official Communiques 1918, Royal Air Force; Edited by Christopher Cole; Tom Donovan Publishing Ltd, London, 1969

Official Communiques 1915–1916, Royal Flying Corps; Edited by Christopher Cole; Tom Donovan Publishing Ltd, London, 1969

Official History of Australia In the War of 1914–1918; Photographic Record of the War (Reproductions of Pictures taken by the Australian Official Photographers); Annotated by C. E. W. Bean and H. S. Gullett; Angus & Robertson Ltd, 1923

People at War 1914–1918 (Their Own Account of the Conflict in the Trenches, in the Air and at Sea); Edited by Michael Moynihan; David & Charles, England, 1973

War Poets 1914–1918 (Up the Line to Death); An Anthology selected by Brian Gardner; Eyre Methuen Ltd, London, 1976